THE WEAPON TAKERS SAGA

BOOKS 1-3

JAMIE EDMUNDSON

Rarn
Publishing

BY JAMIE EDMUNDSON

The Weapon Takers Saga

Toric's Dagger

Bolivar's Sword

The Jalakh Bow

The Giants' Spear

Me Three

Og-Grim-Dog: The Three-Headed Ogre

Og-Grim-Dog and The Dark Lord

Og-Grim-Dog and The War of the Dead

Og-Grim-Dog: Ogre's End Game

THE WEAPON TAKERS SAGA BOOKS 1-3

Copyright © 2019 by Jamie Edmundson.
All rights reserved.
First Edition: 2019

Rarn Publishing

Author website jamieedmundson.com

Cover: Streetlight Graphics

No part of this book may be reproduced in any form or by any electronic or mechanical means, including information storage and retrieval systems, without written permission from the author, except for the use of brief quotations in a book review.
Thank you for respecting the hard work of this author.

DRAMATIS PERSONAE

South Magnians

Soren, a wizard
Belwynn, Soren's sister
Herin, a mercenary
Clarin, Herin's brother
Farred, a nobleman of Middian descent
Gyrmund, Farred's friend, an explorer

Edgar, Prince of South Magnia
Leofwin, Edgar's bodyguard
Brictwin, Edgar's bodyguard
Ulf, an apprentice smith
Bareva, Ulf's wife
Wulfgar, high-priest of Toric
Otha of Rystham, magnate, Wulfgar's brother
Ealdnoth, Edgar's court wizard
Wilchard, Edgar's chief steward
Oslac, Mayor of Halsham
Harbyrt the Fat, Marshal of the North
Kenward, a sheriff
Aescmar, a magnate
Burstan, a captain in the army

Anulf, a soldier
Morlin, a soldier
Hallaf, an outlaw
Ragulf, a standard bearer

North Magnians
Elana, a priestess of Madria

Cerdda, Prince of North Magnia
Ashere, Cerdda's younger brother
Mette, Cerdda's mother
Elfled, Cerdda's sister
Irmgard, Cerdda's wife
Sherlin, an earl

Middians
Brock, a tribal chief
Frayne, a tribal chief

Cordentines
Vincente the Fox, a merchant
Loris, a reeve in Vincente's town
Fulvio, a guard in the employ of Vincente
Glanna, King of Cordence
Rosmont, a Cordentine ambassador

Barissians
Dirk, a priest of Toric

Emeric, Duke of Barissia
Gervase Salvinus, a mercenary leader
Orlin, Emeric's chamberlain
Urval, Orlin's servant
Curtis, a soldier
Dom, a soldier
Bernard Hat, an innkeeper
Werner, a steward in Coldeberg
Heike, a steward in Coldeberg

Kellish
Moneva, a mercenary

Baldwin, Duke of Kelland, Emperor of Brasingia
Hannelore, Empress of Brasingia
Walter, Baldwin's younger brother, Marshal of the Empire
Rainer, Baldwin's chamberlain
Decker, Archbishop of Kelland
Gustav the Hawk, Archmage of the Empire
Inge, Gustav's apprentice
Ancel, a priest
Lord Kass, a nobleman

Rotelegen
Ellard, Duke of Rotelegen
Adalheid, Duchess of Rotelegen
Jeremias, their son
Rudy, a prisoner in Samir Durg
Jurgen, a prisoner in Samir Durg
Veit, a scout

Other Brasingians
Arne, Duke of Luderia
Tobias, his son
Godfrey, Archbishop of Gotbeck
Coen, Duke of Thesse
Theodoric, a linen merchant from Thesse
Lord Emmett, a Thessian nobleman
Trevor, a Luderian woodsman

Guivergnais
Nicolas, King of Guivergne
Bastien, Duke of Morbaine
Russell, Bastien's man

Kalinthians
Theron, Count of Erisina, Knight of Kalinth
Evander, Theron's squire
Sebastian, Count of Melion, Knight of Kalinth

Alpin, Sebastian's squire
Galenos, Grand Master of the Knights of Kalinth
Tycho, Knight of Kalinth, Theron's friend
Remigius, Knight of Kalinth, Sebastian's friend
Euthymius, Knight of Kalinth
Philon, Knight of Kalinth
Leontios, Knight of Kalinth
Coronos, Knight of Kalinth
Proteus, Knight of Kalinth
Nestor, a smith
Jonas, King of Kalinth
Irina, Queen of Kalinth
Straton, eldest son of Jonas
Dorian, second son of Jonas
Diodorus, Count of Korenandi
Bemus, a disciple of Elana
Lyssa, a girl from Korkis

Haskans
Shira, Queen of Haskany
Koren, Shira's uncle
Rimmon, a mage

Jalakhs
Bolormaa, elder of the Oligud tribe
Gansukh, warrior, Bolormaa's son
Qadan, warrior

Persaleians
Pentas, a wizard
Mark, King of Persala
Cyprian, a prisoner in Samir Durg
Zared, a prisoner in Samir Durg
Duilio, soldier
Aulus, flamen of Ludovis
Ennius, flamen of Ludovis

Krykkers
Kaved, a mercenary

Rabigar, an exile

Torinac, chieftain of the Dramsen
Maragin, chieftain of the Grendals
Guremar, chieftain of the Plengas
Hakonin, chieftain of the Swarten
Jodivig, chieftain of the Dramsen
Crombec, chieftain of the Pecineg
Wracken, chieftain of the Binideq
Stenk, a young warrior
Porimin, an historian

Caladri
Tibor, King of the Blood Caladri
Lorant, Prince of the Blood Caladri
Hajna, Princess of the Blood Caladri
Szabolcs, a wise man
Gyuri, a carriage driver
Marika, a carriage attendant
Dora, a carriage attendant
Emese, a carriage attendant
Vida, a carriage attendant
Joska, a carriage attendant
Elek, a carriage attendant

Odon, elder of the Grand Caladri
Agoston, elder of the Grand Caladri
Dorottya, elder of the Grand Caladri
Kelemen, a regional governor
Ignac, a wizard

Dorjan, King of the Shadow Caladri

Sebo, a Sea Caladri captain
Darda, a Sea Caladri soldier

Isharites
Erkindrix, Lord of Ishari
Arioc, King of Haskany

Siavash, High Priest of Ishari
Nexodore, a wizard with a death mask
Ardashir, a member of the Council of Seven
Tirano, a wizard, serving Emeric of Barissia
Roshanak, a wizard, lieutenant of Shira
Mehrab, a wizard, lieutenant of Shira
Babak, Arioc's servant
Harith, servant of Diis
Peroz, servant of Diis

Other
Vamak, a Dog-man
Tamir, a Barbarian chieftain
Sevald, a Vismarian leader
Gunnhild, a Vismarian
Kull, a Drobax

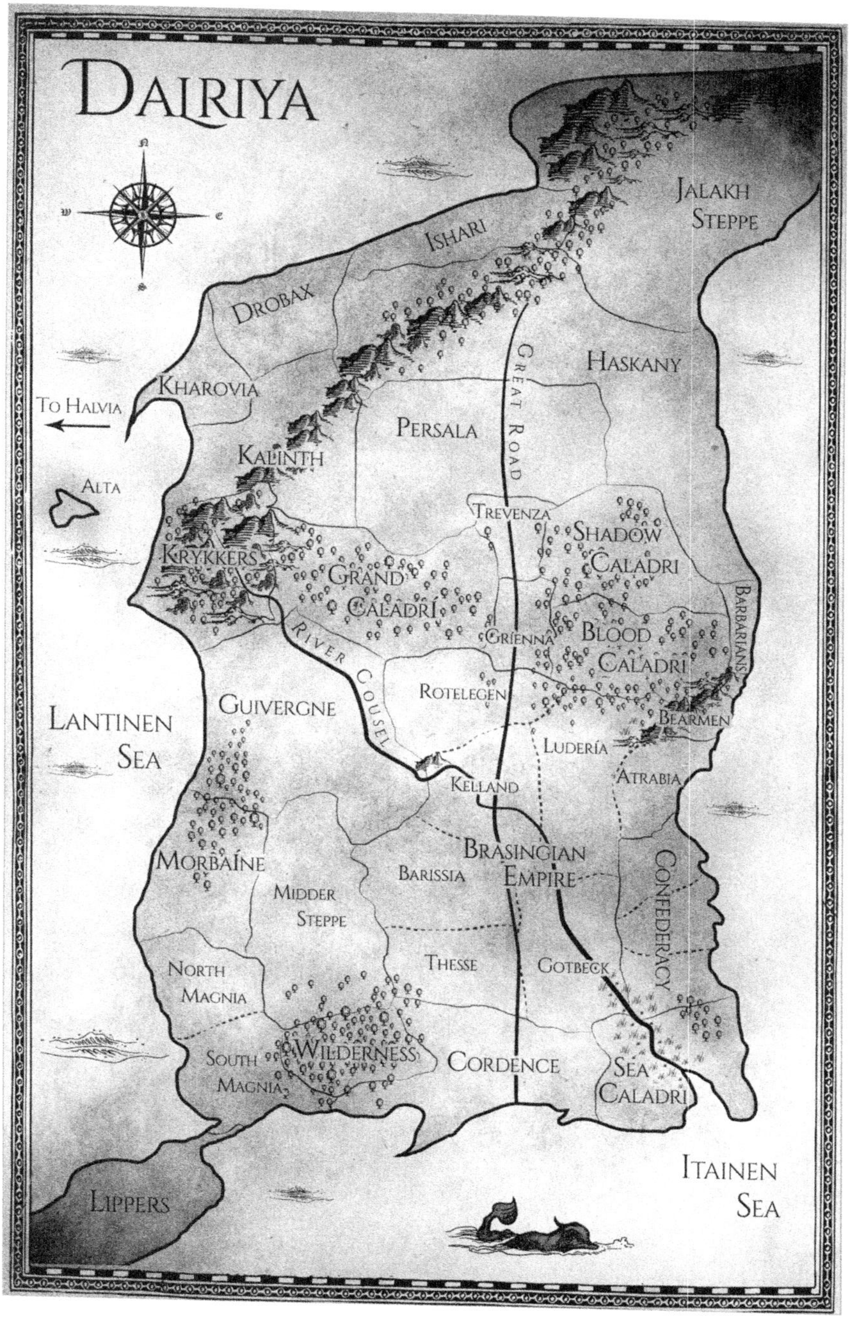
DALRIYA
N
W
E
S
ISHARI
JALAKH STEPPE
DROBAX
HASKANY
GREAT ROAD
KHAROVIA
TO HALVIA
PERSALA
KALINTH
ALTA
TREVENZA
SHADOW CALADRI
KRYKKERS
GRAND CALADRI
BARBARIANS
GRIENNA
BLOOD CALADRI
RIVER COUSEL
ROTELEGEN
GUIVERGNE
BEARMEN
LANTINEN SEA
LUDERÍA
ATRABIA
KELLAND
BRASINGIAN EMPIRE
MORBAÍNE
BARISSIA
CONFEDERACY
MIDDER STEPPE
THESSE
GOTBECK
NORTH MAGNIA
SOUTH MAGNIA
WILDERNESS
CORDENCE
SEA CALADRI
ITAINEN SEA
LIPPERS

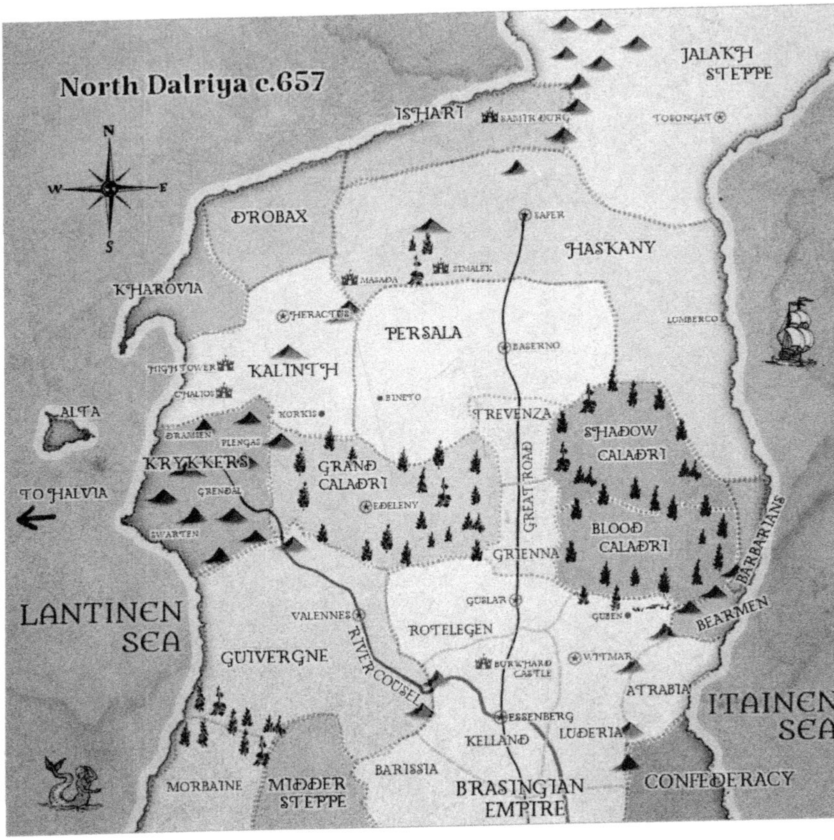
North Dalriya c.657
N
W
E
S
ISHARI
TOBONGAT
JALAKH
STEPPE
DROBAX
SAFER
HASKANY
SIMALEK
MASADA
KHAROVIA
HERACTUS
PERSALA
BASERNO
LUMBERCO
HIGH TOWER
KALINTH
CHALTOS
BINETO
ALTA
KORKIS
TREVENZA
SHADOW
CALADRI
DRAMIEN
PLENGAS
KRYKKERS
GRAND
CALADRI
TO HALVIA
GRENDAL
EDELENY
GREAT ROAD
BLOOD
CALADRI
SWARTEN
GRIENNA
BARBARIANS
GUSLAR
GUBEN
LANTINEN
SEA
VALENNES
ROTELEGEN
BEARMEN
GUIVERGNE
RIVER COUSEL
BURKHARD
CASTLE
WITTMAR
ATRABIA
ITAINEN
SEA
ESSENBERG
KELLAND
LUDERIA
BARISSIA
MORBAINE
MIDDER
STEPPE
BRASINGIAN
EMPIRE
CONFEDERACY

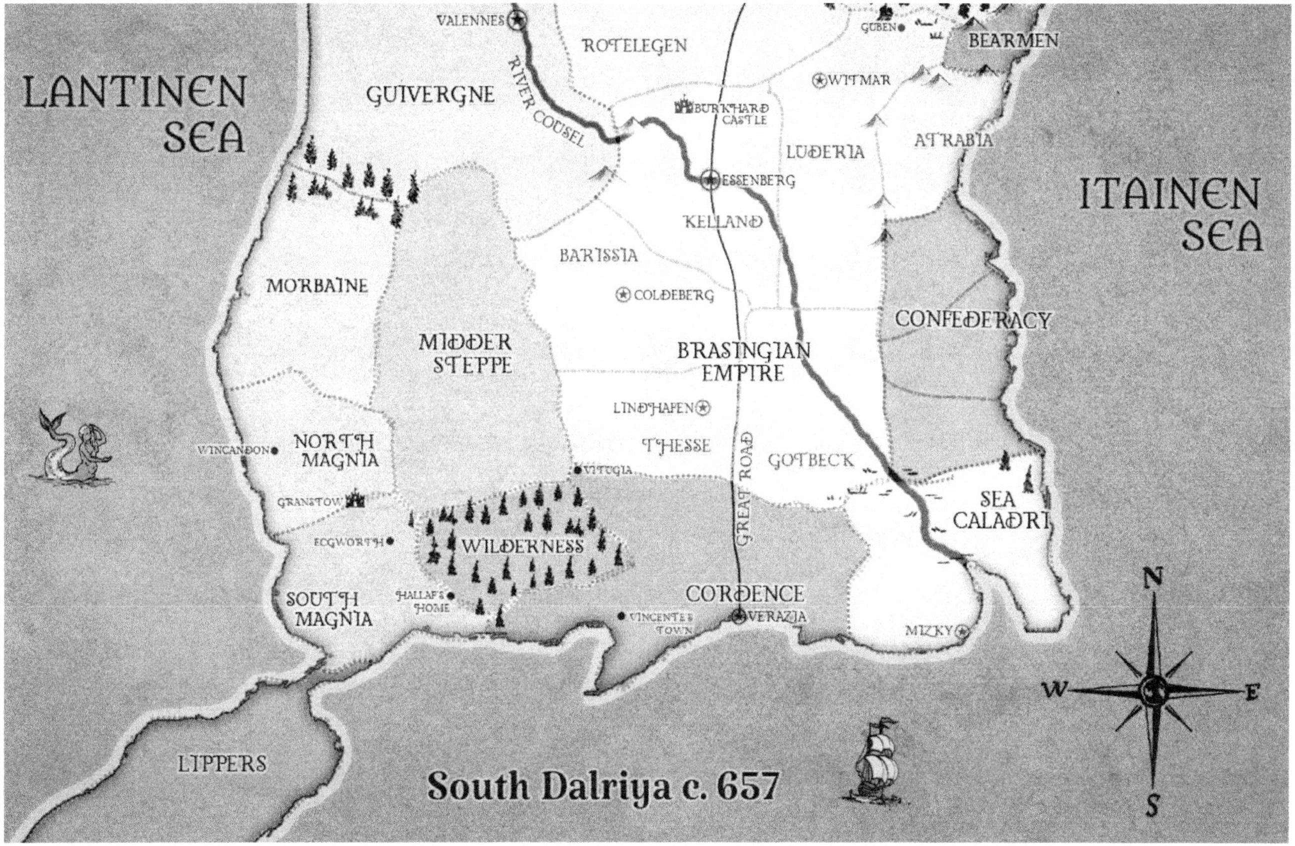

South Dalriya c. 657

TORIC'S DAGGER

BOOK ONE OF THE WEAPON TAKERS SAGA

THREE CORPSES

I

T*ypical, Belwynn said,* looking up as the sun disappeared behind thick clouds and the temperature dropped. *Why did we have to do the walking through the heat of the afternoon?*

Soren didn't turn to look at Belwynn. The twins always spoke in their heads when they were alone. It had become second nature to them ever since childhood. Instead, he squinted up at the sky.

It's going to rain soon. You wouldn't have wanted to walk through that.

Belwynn came close to making an irritable retort, but controlled herself. Was that a spot of rain? They walked on a bit. A drop landed on her cheek.

That was the trouble with her brother. He was always right.

As they approached the outskirts of the town, the spots of rain turned into a steady drizzle.

For all the wealth that's supposedly here, commented Belwynn, *I see a lot of poverty.*

Small wooden huts with sunken floors were scattered about in an irregular pattern. They looked soaked through already, as if they hadn't dried out from the last shower. Pitiful wisps of smoke could be seen emerging from the thatched roofs. They all had their doors open, and Belwynn peered in as she walked past. Babies crying. Women sewing. One woman was brewing beer, the pungent smell of hops emanating from the house. There were no men around — they presumably worked in town. Most of the houses had animals and small garden plots outside, as if the owners couldn't decide between living like peasants or townsfolk. Some kids played outside in the rain, splashing through the mud. They got an earful from a tough-looking matron for running through her garden. But, in truth, it was impossible to tell where the mud ended and the garden began.

They continued into the centre of Vincente's town, where the homes were more substantial. The people they passed looked them up and down suspiciously. They were strangers, so it was to be expected. The resemblance was unmistakeable, too. Both tall and slim, they shared the same soft features, the same blonde hair typical of the Magnians. But Belwynn sensed more tension here than was normal. People who were out seemed keen to get on with their business and get in. Not just because of the rain. There was no chatting or laughter, like back home in Magnia.

Arriving in the market square, Soren looked around, squinting up at the shop signs.

Is that it? asked Belwynn, pointing over to an inn on the opposite side of the square. *The Three Tuns,* she added, reading the faded lettering on the sign; it bore a picture of three wooden casks, the kind that held wine. The front of the inn wasn't much to look at: old planks of wood that would soon need replacing, no windows, a narrow entrance.

Yes, that's it, agreed Soren, and led them over.

Belwynn had never mentioned it, but she was sure her brother's eyesight was deteriorating. Too many late nights reading old manuscripts had taken their toll.

It didn't look much on the outside, but inside, the *Three Tuns* was a substantial building, with a large open plan hall downstairs and rooms for guests on the top floor. It wasn't busy, though. A few groups of travellers had arranged themselves near the fire, and the smell of roasted meat set Belwynn's stomach rumbling. Soren was peering in that direction, but Belwynn was already looking into the shadowy, mostly empty recesses of the hall.

Sure enough, a figure emerged from a secluded table and headed towards them. He was tall and muscular, with dark hair and eyes above a sneering mouth.

'Took you long enough to get here,' Herin spat out.

He led them away from the inviting fire to his isolated table.

He sat down, fingers drumming on the table top. Belwynn and Soren joined him, shrugging off their packs.

'I've already ordered food,' he said in an accusatory tone.

Belwynn knew him well enough by now to ignore his rudeness.

'Clarin's here?' she asked.

'In the privy,' Herin replied. 'I swear, all he does is eat and shit.'

'Why don't you go over the plan?' asked Soren, in the tight voice he used when he was annoyed.

'There is a treasure room in the upstairs part of the building,' Herin began, keeping his voice down and looking around the inn for eavesdroppers. 'It holds chests full of coin and other valuables. There is a lock on the door that requires keys held by three different people, including one by Vincente himself. But we've got Soren to bypass that. So the major problem is neutralising the guards outside the room without drawing attention, then getting out quickly, and without being seen.'

'And we have help with that?' asked Soren.

'Hey!' came a booming voice from across the hall.

Striding over came Clarin, Herin's younger brother. Younger, but bigger. He was only slightly taller than Herin, but he had a massive chest, tree-trunk legs, and bulging arms. He had a mop of sandy hair and an altogether friendlier expression on his face.

'Good to see you both!' he exclaimed as he arrived at the table.

Belwynn and Soren both stood up to each receive a massive bear hug.

'Keep the noise down, you great idiot!' demanded Herin in a hissed whisper.

But it was water off a duck's back to Clarin, who took a seat with a beaming smile on his face.

'Journey reasonable, was it?' he asked them.

'Yes, no complaints,' replied Belwynn.

Soren raised an eyebrow at that.

'I was asking about the help we'll get inside Vincente's house,' said her brother, attempting to return to business.

'Two sellswords in there will help us,' explained Herin. 'We each get a one-sixth share.'

'How trustworthy are they?'

Herin shrugged. 'How trustworthy is anyone?'

'Without the philosophy?' requested Soren testily.

'They want their share of the money, of course; that makes them motivated. If something went wrong, would they turn on us to save their skins? Most definitely.'

'Wonderful,' said Belwynn drily. 'Who are they? What do they look like?'

'That doesn't matter. I've agreed to keep their identities secret; in case anything goes wrong.'

'Secret!?' fumed Belwynn, her voice threatening to climb louder than a conspiratorial whisper. 'So we don't know who's on our side in there? Do you know?' she demanded, turning to Clarin.

'Sure, I've known them—'

Clarin stopped speaking, too late, when he saw his brother staring at him.

'Do you?' Belwynn demanded of Soren.

'No, I don't. Belwynn,' he began, in his *let's be reasonable* voice.

'*Belwynn* what? Why does no-one think—' she continued, only to be stopped by the arrival of a barmaid at the table with the food.

They sat in stony silence as their food and cutlery were laid out. A huge bowl of stew wafted its flavours temptingly while they waited.

'Look.' Herin restarted the conversation when they were alone again. 'That's the demand that's been made, and I'm going to stick to it. Belwynn, your job is to keep everyone's attention downstairs. Clarin will be near you at all times. Soren and I will go upstairs as soon as we get the chance. Keep in contact with each other through your—' He waved a hand, unable to find the word.

Evil touch? Belwynn suggested, privately, to Soren.

It was Herin's most ambitious plan yet, relying on several individuals to carry out a very dangerous but apparently lucrative robbery.

'Who is this guy, anyway?' she asked, changing the subject. 'Why are we stealing his money?'

'Vincente the Fox, he's known as,' Herin explained, pausing as his brother began serving the stew, spooning it into the four bowls provided. 'Trader, smuggler, racketeer, pirate, robber—the list goes on. He controls this little town, but he has an entire network up and down Dalriya. A powerful man, above the law in Cordence. He and a few men like him are the ones running the show in this land.'

Herin looked straight at Belwynn. 'Don't feel sorry for this guy. He's intimidated and murdered his way to that gold over there.'

'And slaved,' said Clarin, dipping a huge hunk of bread into his stew. 'I've heard he's done that, too.'

'Alright, I get the picture. When do we go?'

'We eat,' said Herin. 'We make our preparations, then we go. Time to put your dress on. You did bring one, right?'

'Yes,' she replied, nodding at her pack.

Herin looked at her critically. 'Did you bring some cosmetics? You look half-drowned.'

'Oh, charming! You can shove this little adventure up your arse if you like, Herin.'

Herin and Belwynn stared across the table at each other. Belwynn turned to her brother, who seemed to find something so interesting about his food that he couldn't look up.

'This stew is great,' said Clarin, wiping the last bits in the bowl up with another chunk of bread. 'Anyone mind if I have seconds?'

Belwynn followed the others as they exited the Three Tuns and made their way through Vincente's town.

The sun had almost conceded defeat for another day, and the fading light gave the streets a more menacing feel to them, empty of people and eerily quiet.

Herin led them at a fast pace, flitting from one street to the next, keen not to be seen. Belwynn soon lost track of their whereabouts and resigned herself to just keeping up with the others.

Herin led them to a dark, narrow alleyway, the kind of place you would think twice about walking down, even in the middle of the day. At the end of the alley, Herin crouched down, and they joined him in the same position.

Belwynn took care to keep the hem of her dress from trailing on the ground.

The rain was getting heavier now, and Herin brushed a hand through his wet hair in an irritated gesture, though Belwynn knew him well enough to know that he loved all this cloak and dagger stuff. He pointed ahead and slightly to the left. The end of their alley intersected at a right angle with a much broader thoroughfare. Herin was gesturing at a big townhouse which dominated the area.

The front of the house was stone built with giant wooden doors. It was tall, with a flat roof and crenellations facing the street. The left-hand side of the house had a second storey built on it. Half a dozen armed men stood outside, mostly trying to shelter from the rain in the lee provided by the house wall.

'Always five or six at the front, at all times of day and night. At the back there are grounds that descend to a stream. Inside, more paid men and various retainers, friends and family, probably averaging thirty armed men at any one time altogether. Only other exit is the window that's on the top floor. That's how we're getting out.'

Herin was really speaking to Soren. Belwynn and Clarin were the ones who got told what to do. Herin and Soren were the planners.

'There's no other buildings nearby or in town where he has people based?' asked Soren.

'No.'

'Very well. Let's do it.'

Belwynn's insides churned as they approached the house. She had faith in Herin and Clarin, and most of all in Soren; but still she knew that what they were doing was very dangerous and could go horribly wrong.

The guards outside the house were huddled around a game of dice, but quickly stood when they saw them approaching. Both Herin and Clarin wore armour and carried long swords, sheathed in scabbards at their belts. The guards outnumbered them, but the two men were an intimidating sight, and Belwynn could see them touching their own weapons, checking they were near to hand should the need arise. Emboldened, they moved forward as a group, meeting them a few yards from the door of the house.

'What business have you here?' one of them demanded—a heavy-set man with an unruly beard that dominated his face so much that Belwynn couldn't tell his age.

'Evening,' said Herin calmly, resting his dark eyes on the bearded guard. 'We've come to Vincente's town to introduce him to Lady Melyta, a singer from Magnia,' he said, gesturing at Belwynn.

Belwynn did a small curtsy, while looking into the distance, as if making eye contact with men such as these was beneath her.

'Hmm. It's late for that, isn't it? They've already had their dinner inside.'

'We are late, yes. We have travelled from Magnia, our homeland, where Lady Melyta is known as the best minstrel in the land. She plays for all the lords there, and she is currently on her way to sing at King Glanna's court, at his request. I think your lord would not want to turn her away,' said Herin.

The guard with the beard looked them over suspiciously. He turned to one of his comrades, who shrugged.

'Fulvio,' he said, turning to one of the men, 'go ask for Loris, will you?'

Fulvio nodded and walked back over to the door. He banged three times on the door with his fist.

The remaining guards stood with Belwynn and the others, staring at them in silence.

'What are you, then?' asked the guard with the beard. 'Bodyguards or something?'

One of the doors to the house opened, and Fulvio began speaking to someone in the doorway.

'That's right,' said Herin. 'It can be dangerous making long journeys these days.'

'Indeed it can. Just the two of you?'

'Only needs two of us,' interjected Clarin flatly, and Belwynn could see the hint of fear in the men's eyes at his sheer physical presence.

The bearded guard nodded. 'No horses? Walk all the way from Magnia, did you?'

'I'll ask the questions now!' came a voice from the doorway. 'Over here!'

The guards reluctantly gave way, allowing Belwynn and the others to approach the door. A balding man with sharp features peered out at them, screwing his face up at the rain that threatened to wet him.

'I'm Loris, the reeve of this town. A bard, I understand?' he said, quickly and directly, addressing Belwynn.

'The best in the business,' she replied haughtily.

'With two bodyguards,' added Loris. He looked Herin and Clarin up and down, nodding to himself. 'Your transport?'

'We have taken accommodation at the Three Tuns,' said Herin. 'Our coach is there.'

'And who's this?' Loris nodded in Soren's direction.

'This is Edward, the Lady Melyta's brother. I'm sure you see the resemblance?' replied Herin. 'Unfortunately, the gods decided to take away his sense when he was a small child. But the lady still meets her family obligations and takes him everywhere with her.'

Soren grinned and bobbed his head a few times.

Oh, very convincing, Belwynn said to him.

Soren ignored her.

'I see,' said Loris, 'yes, very unfortunate.'

He made little effort to sound sympathetic. He looked them over one last time.

Belwynn could see his brain ticking over. As a group they were young, wealthy looking; unlikely to be difficult. Two soldiers, a woman, and her dependent brother didn't amount to much of a threat, either. If Vincente could afford to have guards posted outside his house, he doubtless had many more armed men inside.

'All right,' he said, 'come in.'

Loris backed away from the door and gestured them in.

They had made it into the house.

The door was closed and locked behind them; Belwynn just caught a glimpse of the guards still standing outside, looking rather sorry for themselves.

They found themselves inside a porch area, all stone-built, where one guard was stationed on door duty. It seemed to Belwynn like a nicer job than being outside; he even had his own chair tucked away in the corner. Ahead, she could hear the noise of what sounded like a busy hall.

'I will take you to meet Vincente,' said Loris, leading them on through the porch door. They entered a passageway with four doors leading off it, two on each side, and a spiral stone staircase at the end which led upstairs. Belwynn tried to get her bearings. She could smell the kitchens from behind the first door on the left. Loris took them in the opposite direction; through the first door on the right, into the main hall.

It was busier than the inn where they had dined. A large fire burned in the centre of the room. Around it, in a rough square shape, were tables and benches, which may have been organised more neatly before the dinner but were now arranged in a disorderly fashion all over the place. Dinner was over, but drinking wasn't, and the room smelt strongly of alcohol. Some guests were holding mugs of ale; others were drinking wine, with barrels liberally spread among the tables. There must have been at least fifty people in the room, several of whom were armed men, but women and children were also present, as well as a few busy-looking servants. It was noisy, too, with men shouting at each other across the table or over to someone on the other end of the hall. If this was an ordinary night at Vincente's house, thought Belwynn, he must be a wealthy man, ranking alongside the most powerful barons back in Magnia.

Once a few people had noticed their arrival, the hall quietened somewhat. Vincente's guests studied Belwynn and the others.

'Is that your new wife, Loris?' a woman shouted out from one of the tables, to much amusement. Belwynn got a brief glimpse of her: jet black hair with leather clothing and a short sword attached to her belt. Belwynn gave a little smile at the joke, while studying her potential audience. The faces were more interested than anything else, and certainly not hostile.

Loris scowled at the perpetrator, but carried on with his route, around the tables towards the dais at the far end of the hall. He held out a hand for them to wait and approached the dais alone.

There was only one table on the dais where seven men had been talking amongst themselves. Loris was talking to the one in the middle, presumably Vincente. He stood out in purple hose and a long purple jacket. He had grey hair, but a youthful face, and he was tall and lithe-looking.

His henchmen came in all shapes and sizes. At one end of the table was an absolute giant of a man, bigger even than Clarin, with oversized everything: head, hands, feet. At the other was a Krykker, the mountain race who had toughened, armour-like skin on their torsos. They rarely visited human lands, and it surprised Belwynn to see one in this place. The only Krykker she knew, back home in Magnia, was Rabigar, the bladesmith. She knew him to be an exile and wondered whether the same was true of this man. On Vincente's right was an older man with wrinkled, yellow skin, smoking a pipe, while between him and the giant was a small, wiry young man with a thin wispy moustache who looked to Belwynn like he was not yet out of his teens.

What an odd bunch, she commented to Soren.

Maybe Vincente promotes on merit, rather than looks, he observed.

Vincente looked over to Belwynn and beckoned her over with a slight hand gesture. She approached the dais. Some of the men grinned at her, perhaps hoping that she would find the situation intimidating; but she wasn't some country bumpkin to be impressed by a short dais with a merchant sitting on it, however wealthy he was.

'I am told you are on your way to the court of my dear friend, Glanna,' Vincente began, as if he were on first-name terms with the king of Cordence. Maybe he was. His voice was controlled and precise, but bore an unmistakeable Cordentine accent, stressing each and every vowel.

'I am due there tomorrow, Lord Vincente,' lied Belwynn easily. 'I was advised that this was the most important stop on the way. Your house is beautiful,' she added.

So easy, thought Belwynn, as Vincente visibly puffed up with self-importance, a smile playing on his face. He was no lord. But merchants are the same the world over, she thought: aspiring to be accepted into the ruling class. The idea that a royal guest should visit him first was enough to win him over and remove any doubts or uncomfortable questions from his mind; even if some of his colleagues, like the young man with the moustache, still looked suspicious.

'Well, we would be delighted if you would sing for us, Lady—?'

'Melyta.'

'Of course. Such a beautiful name.'

The Krykker smirked at that comment behind Vincente's back.

'You would want to sing up here, as your stage?'

'Indeed.'

'Then we will finish our business here and leave it for you. Loris will ensure you have anything else you need. And I insist you stay the night here at my house, not at the inn. The accommodation there is reasonable, but isn't to a high enough standard. Loris, you will make the arrangements?'

The Krykker's smirk got even bigger. Meanwhile, Loris was nodding in agreement at his instructions.

Belwynn turned to the reeve. 'I would like a drink for my throat,' she said demurely, coughing a little as the smoke from the pipe-smoker blew in her direction.

'Antonio, you oaf!' Vincente scolded the old man, slapping him on the arm several times. 'You have no manners!'

'A thousand apologies, Vincente.'

'Why are you apologising to *me*?' he demanded, raising his voice for the entire hall to hear.

'I beg your pardon, my lady,' said the old man, sounding quite contrite, his face drooping in apparent sorrow.

Everything alright? asked Soren, from his place to the side of the dais.

Yes. It's going well, replied Belwynn.

* * *

SOREN HAD SEEN IT BEFORE, of course; many times. But it still filled him with pride.

When his sister sang, the world stood still.

Standing on the dais, alone, she commanded the attention of everyone in the hall. Soren looked around at the transfixed faces which, moments ago, had been chatting and arguing, shouting and bragging; now they were deathly silent. Strong men, with their bulging muscles and weapons at their belts, now looked wide eyed and childlike. Their women had tears in their eyes. Their children, who had been driving them crazy moments ago with their constant foolery, sat cross-legged and angelic.

The plan was working. Soren turned to Herin, who was standing next to him.

'Time to go?' he asked.

Herin was pulled out of his own reverie and locked eyes with Soren.

'Yes,' he whispered. 'Follow me.'

Soren turned to go.

'Wait,' hissed Herin from the side of his mouth, looking at the stage again.

'What is it?' murmured Soren, after a few nervous seconds.

'Nothing. I thought I saw one of Vincente's thugs—looking straight at us. But he's watching Belwynn now. Come on.'

They shuffled off, backing out to the door from which they had entered the hall earlier. The people around them barely noticed them passing as they focused on Belwynn's performance. One or two moved out of the way for them, but didn't divert their attention to notice who was leaving and where they were going.

We're going, he said to Belwynn, in case she hadn't noticed.

He gave her one last look, noting Clarin's reassuring presence by the side of the dais, before exiting into the passageway.

It was empty, but they knew that there was a guard in the porch area, and they moved quickly and quietly towards the spiral staircase at the other end of the passage. Soren followed Herin up the stairs to the top floor of Vincente's house, where the treasure room was located.

Herin paused at the top to look around before emerging onto an upstairs passage, which ran directly above the downstairs one. When Soren joined him, he had a quick look for himself. The upper storey of the house was much smaller than the lower. Just one corridor, with three doors leading off to the right.

'This way,' whispered Herin, and they began creeping down the hall. 'Vincente's private quarters,' he added, indicating the first door on the right.

They moved on to the second door.

'Let's hope our friends have done their work,' Herin said before slowly turning the handle.

Gingerly, Herin pulled the door open. It was dark inside, with no light source. But slowly, Soren's eyes adjusted, and he could make out a small antechamber. There was another door to the left. Placed at intervals along the far wall were three chairs—each with a corpse sitting in it.

'Come on,' said Herin, ushering Soren into the room.

Soren looked at the nearest body, that of a guard, slumped backwards in the chair. His throat had been cut, and black congealed blood had collected in a pool on the floor. He forced himself to look at the other two victims—two more guards with similar injuries. It was a disturbing sight, made worse by the silence and darkness of the room.

'Did they have to kill them?'

Herin shrugged. 'Probably.' Soren waited while he located an empty sconce on the wall. 'Shit. No-one mentioned how dark it was in here. We're not gonna be able to see anything.'

Soren took a length of candle from his inside pocket and cupped both hands around it. He found they were shaking. He concentrated, gained focus, calling on heat to materialise from his hands onto the wick of the candle. The wick caught flame, and he moved over to the sconce, placing the candle inside.

The small light from the candle created eerie shadows on the walls. Soren had to force himself to ignore the three corpses who shared their confined space, illuminated by the flickering flame. He wasn't a religious man, but it was hard not to imagine that the spirits of the murdered men were in there with them.

He turned his attention to the door to the treasure room. As described, it had three separate locks on it, each with its own keyhole. He grabbed the handle and gave the door a yank, just in case. Locked. Kneeling, Soren flattened his hands against the wood, concentrating, trying to search for the metal mechanism inside.

'Well?' said Herin. 'Can you do it?'

'I think so. I'll need a bit of time. Guard the door while I give it my attention.'

'Fine,' said Herin. He moved to draw his sword, and then, thinking better of it, pulled out a seax which he'd strapped horizontally to his belt.

'No room to swing a sword in here,' he said by way of explanation, handling the weapon; in size, it was somewhere between a knife and a sword, with a wickedly sharp edge. Picking his spot, he went down on one knee facing the door. If anyone did bumble into the room, they were going to get a nasty surprise.

Returning to his work, Soren located the highest lock and formed a connection between the metal mechanism and his hands through the wood of the door. Wriggling his hands up and down, he could raise the internal pins while also pulling the bolt to the right. He opened the lock, resulting in a loud click. Herin looked over.

'One down,' said Soren.

The next two worked along the same principles, and Soren was able to pull the bolt after a bit of trial and error. Standing up, he pushed open the door. Herin joined him with the candle he had retrieved from the sconce, and they peered in.

They had done it. Three large chests sat along the opposite wall, while various artefacts made of gold, silver, crystal and other precious materials lay scattered on the floor. It was an obscenely rich man's treasure hoard.

Herin and Soren looked at each other, smiling in jubilation at their success.

Herin rushed in and lifted the lid of the nearest chest, and Soren peered over his shoulder. It was full, mainly with coins: Cordentine florins, the distinctive wide, thin discs of gold; but also plenty of Imperial thalers, silver Persaleian denarii, and lots more, from all over Dalriya.

'I knew it,' said Herin, dipping a hand into the coins. 'I knew we could do it. This is a massive haul.'

'I know,' said Soren, 'but we're not done yet. We need to move.'

'Right,' agreed Herin, 'we prioritise. First, we get this chest into Vincente's room. Then the next two. Anything else really valuable we take, but otherwise we leave it.'

Herin and Soren grabbed one end of the chest each and carried it out of the treasure room and back into the adjoining chamber, where its three corpse guards still sat in silence. It weighed a tonne, and Soren was glad when Herin signalled to put it down.

Herin peered round the door into the passageway.

'Clear.'

Hefting it up again, they manhandled it out of the room into the passageway, Herin walking backwards towards the stairs, Soren facing forwards.

There were footsteps on the stairs. Quick footsteps.

Before he could react, Soren saw a face come into view. It was a young man's face, thin, with a wispy moustache, making his features rat like. Soren recognised him as one of the henchmen who had been sitting on the dais when Belwynn had been introduced to Vincente. They were in trouble. Unless—was he one of Herin's sellswords?

'Herin,' he murmured, dropping his end of the chest and nodding towards the stairs.

The man had stopped. 'What are you doing?' he demanded in a loud voice.

Obviously not.

Herin turned around. Lightning fast, he pulled the seax from his belt and threw it at his target.

But the man was too quick, diving back down the stairs as the weapon clattered harmlessly against the stonework.

'Shit,' said Herin.

Soren could hear the man shouting as he descended back down the stairs. *Belwynn,* he spoke to his sister, sending his thoughts down to the hall where she was still performing. *Belwynn, get out of there! Now!*

THE SMELL OF FAILURE

II

B*elwynn, get out of there! Now!*

Belwynn stopped singing immediately. She took a few steps backwards on the dais. What am I going to do? She gestured to Clarin for help.

Her audience in the hall murmured, as if slowly awakening from a dream. She could hear shouting outside the hall. Things had stopped going well.

Belwynn looked around, desperately trying to work out where to go. She had no idea. This wasn't supposed to happen. Clarin was heading towards her, but he was being so slow!

Behind him, a woman marched onto the dais, dressed all in black, with black hair pulled back from her face. She walked directly towards Belwynn, who recognised her as the woman who had shouted out when they had entered the hall.

'I think we need to get out of here,' said the woman.

The door of the hall crashed open, and one of Vincente's followers, the teenager with the moustache, tumbled in.

'They're stealing the treasure!' he shouted.

A few moments ago, one could have heard a pin drop. Now, the hall erupted in noise. Men shouted orders at each other. Some rushed out of the hall towards the stairs. Others turned to the dais, pointing fingers at Belwynn and Clarin.

'Yes, Moneva! Get us out of here,' Clarin said to the woman.

The woman Clarin had called Moneva ran past Belwynn, towards the back of the dais, where a small set of stairs took her upwards. Clarin gave Belwynn a gentle push to follow on. She must be one of the sellswords Herin had said was working with them, Belwynn surmised. She hadn't been expecting a woman.

Looking behind her, Belwynn gasped as a group of men approached the dais. Clarin drew his sword, causing them to pause, before he again pushed her towards the back of the dais.

Moneva's escape route took them up the stairs into a large, dimly lit, and musty smelling room. It was a storeroom, with a stack of timber in one corner, a harness for a cart and horse lying in another. Large fabric sacks were lined up against all the walls.

An exit way to the room lay ahead and to the right, which was where the little light in the room was coming from. As Belwynn looked in that direction, an armed man emerged, perhaps a guard to an alternative exit to the house.

'What's going on, Moneva?' he asked, walking towards them.

'Someone's tried to break into the treasure room.'

The guard's eyes widened in surprise.

'Who are they?' he asked, indicating Clarin and Belwynn.

With no warning, Moneva launched a kick in between the man's legs. It connected home with a crunch and the guard doubled over in agony. Clarin was quickly on to him, bringing his knee up and smashing it under the man's chin. Belwynn heard an unpleasant crack from the man's jawbone. Clarin loomed over him, fist raised.

'Clarin, enough!' demanded Belwynn.

Clarin looked up and headed towards the exit to the room, but Moneva reached out and grabbed him.

'No, we'll get trapped that way. Follow me.'

Moneva led them instead in the opposite direction, deeper into the storeroom. Taking a right, she took them into a smaller chamber.

The latrines. A foul smell. And a dead end.

'What—' began Belwynn.

'Hush,' said Moneva.

Voices. A group of men had now followed them up the steps from the dais and into the storeroom. They must have found the injured guard on the floor.

Moneva pointed at the wooden bench of latrines.

'When I say so,' she whispered, 'help me pull off the wooden board. Underneath are holes which go outside. We can lower ourselves down.'

'Into a dung-heap!' hissed Belwynn.

Moneva looked at her. 'You got a better option, princess?'

Belwynn knew the woman was right. If they didn't get out of here quickly, they would be in big trouble. She held her hands up. 'Fine.'

They positioned themselves along the bench. When Moneva gave the word, they pulled up the whole plank of wood, lowering it to the floor, exposing a stone slab with four holes in it. Just big enough to fit through.

'Who's there?' came a voice from the storeroom.

Belwynn looked from Moneva to Clarin. They had seconds to act before they were discovered.

Clarin sheathed his sword, unbuckled his scabbard from his belt, and threw it down one of the holes. He placed each hand on either side of the hole and hoisted himself inside. It was a tight fit for him. He let go, shoving his arms in the air because they wouldn't fit by his sides, and half-slid, half-fell down the hole. Belwynn was convinced she heard an unpleasant squelch as he landed at the bottom.

'Get in,' hissed Moneva.

Belwynn sat on the stone shelf and dangled her feet down the hole. She looked down, and a wave of stench hit her, making her heave.

'I can't,' she began, but she didn't have a chance to finish the sentence—Moneva grabbed her waist and forced her over the hole before shoving her down.

Belwynn slid down the rough stone work and then into empty space—before she landed in a sea of excrement.

The momentum of the drop pushed her onto her knees, and she tilted forwards, arms outstretched, into the muck. It splattered up her chest and onto her face. Big hands grabbed at her, and she was unceremoniously hauled out of the pit and onto wet grass. Clarin stood next to her, equally caked in filth.

A few seconds later and there was a huge squelch as Moneva landed in the dirt. As Belwynn got to her feet, Clarin helped the other woman out.

They stood there a little while, eyeing each other up and down and wrinkling their noses.

'We haven't been introduced,' said Belwynn, holding out a hand. 'Belwynn.'

Moneva looked at the proffered hand, caked as it was in other people's excrement, then looked at her own hand, which wasn't much better.

'Moneva,' she said, clasping hands. 'Pleased to meet you.'

* * *

Soren winced at the sound of Herin dragging the chest towards the door of the first room they had passed on the corridor. Herin had described it as Vincente's private chamber. Soren bent down and grabbed the other side of the chest. They carried it into the room before letting it fall to the floor.

It did not surprise Soren to see that Vincente's room was richly furnished: decorative rugs lay on the floor and ornate tapestries lined the walls. In the centre of the room was a large bed with a canopy over it. There was an adjoining bathroom where he and his family could wash and make their toilet in private.

Soren *was* surprised, however, to see people in the room.

In the bathroom's doorway sat a woman: her hands tied behind her back and a cloth gag over her mouth. Vincente's wife, perhaps, or maybe a servant who had been in the wrong place at the wrong time. At the far end of the room was an open window. By the window was a Krykker man, pulling at a length of sheet he had dangled out of the window. The other end had been tied to one leg of the bed.

Soren recognised him as one of Vincente's henchmen, who had a place on the top table down in the hall.

'What's happening?' said the Krykker by way of greeting, giving his roll of sheets another yank. 'It'll hold my weight, so it should hold yours too.'

'Soren, this is Kaved,' said Herin.

Soren nodded at Kaved in greeting.

'They're onto us,' continued Herin. 'We've got to get out of here now.'

'What!?' said Kaved, disappointed. 'With only one chest?'

'Better one chest and our lives than all three and dead,' said Soren. 'Is there anything we can use to hold this door shut? The bed's being used to hold the rope.'

Soren and Herin both heard a noise and turned to each other. It was the sound of many men roaring as they ran up the stairs of the house.

'Quick! They're here!' shouted Herin, the unusual sound of panic in his voice.

'I'll hold the door for as long as I can,' said Soren.

He backed away from the door and concentrated on building a barrier around it.

The defence spell was the first one he had ever been taught. His first teacher, Ealdnoth, had made him practise it hour after hour. 'The first thing a wizard needs to learn,' Ealdnoth had told him, 'is to defend himself against the many people who want him dead.' Soren had learned how to block a punch, then a sword strike. When he had mastered that, Ealdnoth would test his defences against a magical attack. He would probe and attack until Soren didn't have the energy to hold him off any longer. Eventually, he became so proficient that it was Ealdnoth who had to give up.

While he built his barrier, Herin shoved his weight against the door. Kaved joined them and grabbed the chest.

Soren could hear a crowd out in the passageway. There were lots of them.

'You go, Kaved,' shouted Herin.

Just then the door gave a lurch as someone tried to barge their way in. Herin forced it closed.

'How am I supposed to get down carrying this?' demanded the Krykker.

An axe head chopped through the door, narrowly missing Herin's head. He sprang back into the room.

'Just chuck it out!' he screamed at Kaved.

The axe was pulled back, and a chunk of the door came with it. Faces peered through the door at them.

'Kaved!'

It was Vincente's voice, screaming through the door.

'You treacherous dog! I will gut you for this! What have you done with my wife?'

Soren continued to focus on the doorway, constructing a barrier that was strong enough to hold off Vincente and his men. He heard a grunt from behind him, and then a crash, as Kaved hurled the chest out of the window.

The door swung open, revealing a mass of angry-looking men struggling to get in. Vincente's giant henchman waved an axe in Soren's direction.

'Soren?' asked Herin, brandishing his sword.

'I've got it. You go.'

Herin rushed to the window and began climbing out, following Kaved.

The men at the door tried to barge into the room, but Soren held them out, an invisible but powerful force blocking the entire door frame. They shoved and pushed at it, hitting it with weapons.

'A wizard!' one of them shouted, pointing at Soren. 'There's a wizard in there!'

'Soren!' shouted Herin from outside the window. 'Come on!'

Soren turned around and made for the window.

Suddenly he went sprawling forwards. Vincente's wife had stuck out a leg and tripped him as he went past. His concentration on the door was completely broken, and he heard shouts as the group of men tumbled through it.

Not daring to look back, Soren picked himself up and sprinted for the window as he sensed someone behind him.

He hurled himself out.

He felt a hand grab at the back of his cloak, but his pursuer couldn't hold on. Instead, Soren was falling head first out of the window. In desperation, he stuck his hands forward and tried to create an upward force that would cushion his fall.

He landed on the ground, and everything went black.

* * *

MONEVA LED them around the back of Vincente's house to the side. According to Herin's plan, this was where the others were supposed to have left the building, with the treasure, via the upstairs window.

It was now completely dark outside and still raining. Belwynn couldn't see where they were going and felt sure they were going to get caught any second.

Soren? Soren!

No response.

'He's not replying!' she whispered to Clarin for the third time. The warrior held out his hands in a helpless expression.

Moneva gave a shout, drawing a dagger from her belt. Belwynn made out the form of one of Vincente's men ahead: the Krykker with the smirk.

'Gods, Kaved! I nearly cut your throat!' Moneva hissed.

Kaved snorted. 'You nearly tried.'

So, the Krykker was the second of Herin's insiders.

'Where's my brother?' she demanded of him.

Kaved looked her over and jabbed a thumb back over his shoulder. Looking, Belwynn could see Herin coming their way, her brother's body slumped over his shoulder.

'What happened?'

'He fell out the window,' Herin said, lifting Soren off and passing him on to Clarin to carry. 'He's well enough. I think. But we haven't got time now; they'll be following us.'

'The treasure?' asked Moneva.

'Disaster,' said Kaved, heading away from the house into the grounds at the back and indicating that they should follow him. 'We picked up a few coins from one of the chests that I had to throw out of the window. That's it.'

Belwynn saw Moneva roll her eyes and start to say something, but she controlled herself, biting her tongue.

'Over here!' A shout came from behind them.

'Get on with it,' said Kaved, picking up the pace as the grounds sloped gently downhill.

Belwynn could hear the jingle of metal armour and weapons coming from behind them, seemingly on the trail of Herin and the others. 'Where are we going?' she asked.

Kaved didn't reply, instead sprinting forwards towards a gentle stream that flowed by and appeared to mark the boundary of Vincente's house.

Pulling out a small hand-axe, he hacked at the moorings of a large raft that was half hidden behind a tree.

'Don't worry, Kaved's part of the plan will still work,' said the Krykker in a sarcastic voice. 'Get on.'

Kaved and Herin held the raft steady as Clarin walked on gingerly, gently lowering Soren onto its deck. Belwynn and Moneva followed on, trying to spread their weight so that it didn't tip. From somewhere, Kaved now had a long pole, which he used to push them away from the bank.

'Shit,' said Herin.

A group of about a dozen armed men were running down the slope towards them.

'Faster!' said Moneva.

'I can't go faster!' responded Kaved angrily. 'We're on a raft, not a racehorse!'

He shoved the pole down onto the bed of the stream and pushed them away a little farther.

When the men reached the bank, Kaved had succeeded in nudging them out into the middle of the stream, too far out to be reached by a sword or spear. Some tentatively put their feet into the stream, seeing if they could follow on foot.

Others arrived and crowded around the bank, shouting insults. One of them held a bow and reached for an arrow, ready to nock it and shoot. If he did, he could aim at virtually point-blank range.

'Archer!' shouted Belwynn.

As she did so, there was a movement on the other side of the raft, and a knife left Moneva's outstretched hand, burying itself in the archer's neck.

Those men in the water froze, suddenly wary of their exposed position.

Meanwhile, Vincente had pushed himself to the bank.

'Get them!' he yelled at his men, gesturing angrily. 'You've given yourselves a death sentence for this!' he yelled towards the raft as it picked up a bit of speed in the middle of the stream and floated away. 'You've made one hell of a mistake tonight!'

'Oh, fuck off!' Kaved shouted back at him. 'We didn't get hardly any of your money, anyway!'

Vincente's men were being herded into the stream, some making more of an effort than others. The eager ones were crossing the stream and threatened to reach the opposite bank before the raft did. Kaved pushed them closer to the bank, and Clarin was able to grab hold of an overhanging tree branch, pulling the raft in and then holding it steady as the others clambered out. Herin grabbed Soren under the arms and dragged him onto the bank. Clarin got himself off and picked up the wizard.

Soren murmured something unintelligible.

'Looks like he might be waking up,' the big man commented.

'I hope so,' said Belwynn, peering at her brother. There seemed to be a bit more colour in his face. 'What happened to him, Herin?'

'He held the door closed while we escaped. Then he jumped out of the window for some reason. But he cast a spell that cushioned his fall. It didn't look like he hurt anything.'

'Hit the ground in slow motion, sort of,' added Kaved, sounding slightly in awe of what he had seen.

'He probably used too much magic, too quickly,' explained Belwynn. 'It's happened before. It knocks him out for a while.'

'Well, we better keep moving,' said Kaved. 'Just a little way up here.'

They marched up the riverbank, away from Vincente's town, for a few hundred metres. It was pitch black now, and no-one had a light, but Kaved seemed to know where he was going.

Before Belwynn realised it was there, they had stopped by a cart, complete with two horses attached to it.

'Wow,' said Moneva drily, 'someone's been busy.'

'Yes,' said Kaved, climbing into the driver's seat, 'complete with provisions and enough space to hold three chests full of gold. Looks like all we're taking away is the six of us.'

'We got some of it,' said Herin moodily, helping his brother to lift Soren into the back of the cart. 'It'll cover our expenses.'

'Will it cover the loss of my lucrative wages?' asked Moneva.

Herin turned towards her. 'Just get in, will—' He stopped speaking and wrinkled his nose. He looked at Moneva as if seeing her for the first time, then across at Clarin and Belwynn. He put a hand over his nose. 'What the fuck happened to you?'

INTRUDERS

III

The sun set the world alight: brilliant orange shafts touching the sky, spreading along the horizon and driving down to the land.

My land, thought Farred, as he let his mount walk along for a while at its own pace, content to survey the world around him.

To his left, Gyrmund also seemed content to ride in companionable silence. The early morning was surely the best part of the day: everything to look forward to, and it was when the land here looked the most beautiful. Rolling grassland stretched on for miles in every direction, seemingly unending. The mist of the previous night still hung over the grass, as if the gods had sprinkled Dalriya with fairy dust.

'Do you miss it?' he asked Gyrmund.

'What?'

'Walsted. The land here. The place where you grew up. I would find it hard to leave for as long as you have.'

'It's beautiful,' agreed Gyrmund, looking around. 'But so are other places. Just in different ways.'

Farred nodded. He would like to see other parts of the world too. But he also appreciated what he had here.

'Don't you ever get bored?' asked Gyrmund.

'Bored with what?'

'I don't know. I know you've got responsibilities here. Bored of the same routine. Doing the same things, at the same time...'

'Maybe. Though in some ways I've appreciated having some structure over the last few years, since father died. But I know what you mean. I think I'm ready for a new challenge now.'

They rode on in silence again. It got Farred to thinking.

They had been inseparable as youths, raised as brothers after the death of Gyrmund's family. Farred had thought it would stay that way forever. It hadn't crossed his mind that it wouldn't. Now he could see the differences between them. Farred's parents had owned the estate here at Walsted. His family had done so for generations, since the Middians of these parts had agreed to bend the knee to the Kings of Magnia and their tribal lands were divided up. Gyrmund's parents, on the other hand, had rented their land and worked for Farred's family. That difference hadn't meant anything to Farred when he was a boy, but maybe it had to Gyrmund. And the two of them had wanted different things from the friendship at one point. It seemed strange that Farred was now the only one who called this place home. To Gyrmund, Walsted was still a refuge, a place he could stay if he needed to rest up or get some free lodging and dinners. But it was no longer his home.

'Time to stretch these boys' legs a bit?' asked Gyrmund.

'Come on then, Gamhard,' Farred called out to his mount, nudging him into a trot.

They were heading west, away from the sunrise, to where the plains of Farred's estate ended and became a wood of hills and hollow. Much of Plunder Wood was also owned by Farred, used for hunting game and to fetch timber. Beyond the woods was South Magnia proper, where the soil was deep and they farmed crops rather than animals.

After a while, Gyrmund pushed his mount into a gallop and Farred let Gamhard join in. They raced along the open land, troubled neither by lake nor stream, the ground dry from days of sunshine.

The woods became visible ahead. They headed for a wooden hunting lodge that Farred's father had built when they were youngsters. Here they could see to their horses and sort out which supplies they wanted to take into the woods by foot. Deer were the quarry today, and both men carried long hunting bows. Gyrmund had always been the better marksman, taking the skill more seriously. Farred preferred spear and sword.

Once ready, they followed a well-worn track which took them deep into the trees. Midges buzzed around them, and Farred had to wave them away from his face. He was happy to let Gyrmund take the lead, and eventually they moved off the track and into the heart of the woods, where the going was tougher.

'We'll try up here,' said Gyrmund, pointing up a heavily wooded hill, his breathing heavy. 'We're more likely to find a buck and less likely to run into does.'

It was the birthing season, when does were avoided. They would either be ready to give birth or already have young fawns with them. Killing the mother would mean the fawns would die, too, and that was wasteful.

They settled in place under a tree, which afforded a good view of the surrounding terrain.

After a horse ride and a woodland trek, Farred was hungry. He opened his sack and laid out the food they had brought. Bread, cheese and cold chicken had been wrapped up for them by the cook. They had also picked some blackberries on the way up. Gyrmund produced two flasks of ale from his sack, passing one over to Farred.

'Cheers,' they said, clinking their flasks together.

'You look after me well, Farred,' said Gyrmund, slicing the cheese with a knife and placing a slab on his bread. 'Thank you.'

'It does me good to get out like this. If you weren't here, I'd be working all day.' Farred leaned back against the trunk of the tree and relaxed. 'I honestly don't mind if we don't see a single deer today.'

'You work hard, Farred. Your estate is in good order. Where do your ambitions lie next, though?'

'Ambitions? Well, I wanted to establish myself as a landowner after Father died. I think I've done that, now. If I want more, I'll need to make links with the crown.'

'Prince Edgar? Met him yet?'

'Yes, twice. He actually passed through Walsted last year, first time he's come to these parts.'

'And? What did you make of him?'

'We got on well. He's our age. Seems like a good man.'

'A good man? He won't last, then.'

'Maybe. But I hear that Cerdda of North Magnia has a similar character. Could be an outbreak of common sense amongst our rulers.'

'First time in a few generations if there is, but I suppose Magnia is due. No good for you, though, Farred. If you want to get in with the Prince, you'll need a war to fight in.'

'What about you?' asked Farred. 'No doubt you've got some ideas about where you're going to explore next. You've done virtually all of northern Dalriya now, haven't you?'

Gyrmund's eyes narrowed, and he held up a hand for silence. 'I hear something.'

He moved onto his front and crawled off to the edge of their hill, peering down. He flattened himself down and turned back to Farred. 'You're going to need to see this. Just be careful.'

Farred did as suggested and slid over to Gyrmund's location, staying low and using his elbows to pull himself along.

Gyrmund pointed down the hill. Farred had been expecting an animal. Instead, a troop of mounted figures was passing through the woods. *His* woods.

They were moving through difficult terrain and went slowly, so it was easy to take a good look at them. There were no real distinguishing items, but they were all well armed. Some wore armour, and others didn't, though it looked like the latter group were carrying it on their mounts instead, which was understandable on a day like this. They were moving east to west and passed their location on the hill, no more than about two hundred yards away. Farred counted them.

'Twenty-one?'

'Yes.'

'Well armed. Lightly provisioned. Anything else?'

'Pretty sure they're from the Empire.'

'The Empire? So they've journeyed across the Steppe? And now through my lands, unannounced and on into Magnia? Who are they?'

'Don't know,' said Gyrmund, sitting up as the force moved out of sight. 'But that's our hunting trip over, I guess.'

'Yes. I'll have to follow them. I don't like it.'

'I know. I'm trying to think of a harmless explanation for it, but I can't.'

'Should I go back and raise a force?'

Gyrmund smiled. 'No way. An hour's ride back to Walsted, an hour at the least to gather people up and kit them out, another hour to get back here. They'll be long gone. We go back for our horses and follow them. Just you and me.'

'You're coming?'

Gyrmund looked offended. 'Of course!'

Farred smiled, relieved to have Gyrmund with him. He was the best tracker in these lands, and Farred knew he wouldn't lose his quarry.

'Come on,' said Gyrmund, eager to get going.

They packed their things into their sacks, slung them over their shoulders, and set off down the hill, moving with far more urgency than they had on the way up.

'Tell you one thing though, Farred. This might turn out to be the perfect way to impress your Prince Edgar.'

TORIC'S DAGGER

IV

The midday sun beat down as the three riders entered the settlement of Ecgworth. Edgar, riding slightly ahead of his two companions, lifted his hand to shield his eyes as he peered ahead. He could make out the walls of the temple in the distance.

He had been riding for over an hour now, in chain mail. The summer sun had made the journey uncomfortable, and he had long since broken into a sweat.

He travelled along a dirt track, passing neat and orderly fields to his left and right. The wheat and barley already stood tall, shifting gently when a breeze tugged at them. Insects flew in and out, some filling the air with a buzzing or clicking noise. It had been a good summer so far, warm, but with enough rain as well. Ecgworth was a well-run estate, and it looked like the monks would be well supplied for the winter.

The peasants were busy at work in the meadow, hacking down the grass with sickles to make hay. It was a family affair; the children tasked with spreading out the grass so that it could bake dry in the sun. A few of them looked up as Edgar rode past, but they soon returned to their work. Visitors to the temple were not rare. If any of them recognised their prince, they showed no sign of it.

The track arrived from the west and joined on to the main road, heading north, which took Edgar into the centre of Ecgworth. He now rode past the homes of its inhabitants, simple wooden houses, but well-maintained.

The temple complex dominated the rest of the settlement. It was a large rectangular site with a central location.

As he approached, Edgar could see the modest earthworks, on top of which the walls, made from thick planks of wood, had been driven in and tied together. In time of war, the walls could be manned, and the inhabitants of Ecgworth, and most of their livestock, sheltered behind them.

Edgar had visited the temple several times. It was an adequate defence, but could do little to stop a serious force from gaining entry. Edgar had asked for improvements to be made, and it annoyed him to see that nothing had been done.

The road took Edgar to the southern gate of the walls. Ecgworth was situated on a flat plain, and the site of the temple gave little benefit in natural height. The priests had tried to compensate for this by digging a ditch around the site and using the excavated earth to create a raised surface on which to build. Nonetheless, when the prince stood in his stirrups, he could almost peer over the top of the wall.

Edgar's two bodyguards joined him at the gate. Leofwin had served Edgar for the last four years and had served his father before him. Brictwin was a few years younger than Edgar, and was learning the job from his uncle. Wordlessly, Leofwin drew his sword from its scabbard and banged on the gate three times with the pommel.

Edgar could hear movement on the other side of the gate, but there was no reply. Leofwin rolled his eyes at the delay and began banging again. After another few seconds, he was rewarded with a voice.

'Who is there?'

'Prince Edgar demands entry,' boomed Leofwin with authority.

'Oh,' came the voice, before a head popped up above the wall. The guard was a young man who looked a little nervous at having to talk to Edgar directly. 'Please wait a moment, Your Highness. I will fetch Lord Wulfgar right away.'

Edgar nodded, and then the head disappeared again. He heard the noise of the gatekeeper jumping down from the wall and scurrying off in the opposite direction.

Wulfgar was High-Priest of the Temple of Toric. Edgar's father had given him the position, though not entirely out of choice. As well as being the leader of one of the richest religious communities in the kingdom, he came from a powerful family: his older brother, Otha of Rystham, was one of the wealthiest landholders of South Magnia. Edgar knew both men well, and did not particularly like either of them. They were both arrogant and greedy, but their position of power meant that they had to be tolerated.

It was not long before Wulfgar came marching over to greet them.

'Get the gates open,' he demanded in a voice used to authority.

The gate was slowly swung open, revealing Wulfgar, standing with his hands on his hips. To one side of him stood a small group of priests, simple brown robes belted at the waist. Although slightly red and out of breath, Wulfgar did not betray any other signs that Edgar's unannounced visit might unsettle him. He was a self-confident man, roughly the same age as Edgar's father would have been. He was broad-shouldered and, despite being the high priest, dressed himself in the fine tunic and hose of a nobleman.

'How was your journey, Your Highness?' he asked Edgar as the prince and his bodyguards dismounted.

'It was fine. A little warm,' replied Edgar.

'Good, good,' said Wulfgar, walking over and clasping hands. 'Dirk, see to the horses, will you? If you'll follow me, my Prince?'

Wulfgar led them over to his hall, built on the eastern side of the temple site. It was a typical single-storey nobleman's hall, similar to the one that Edgar had left that morning.

On their way, they passed the temple itself. Beyond its entrance chamber, the main building was circular, with a domed roof. It was originally built some time ago, but its wooden exterior must have been replaced many times since then. It was decorated in a pleasing style. A large carving of Toric's sign of the sun faced them on the curving main chamber. Elsewhere were the buildings necessary for a settlement of this size to function: a stable, a smithy, a granary to store the food.

Edgar followed Wulfgar into the hall. A fire, located against one wall, created a welcoming, smoky environment. Two long tables with benches stretched along the centre of the hall, demonstrating Wulfgar's ability to feed a sizeable number of followers. Wulfgar could also afford to decorate his hall well. Tapestries covered all the walls. The largest showed the rays of Toric's sun hitting the earth and giving life to the land, producing cereal crops, fruits and vegetables, animals and men.

Wulfgar gestured over to the top table. Edgar nodded to Leofwin. It was to be a private conversation. While Leofwin and Brictwin gravitated towards the fire, Edgar and Wulfgar sat down together.

'There was an attack on your temple,' began Edgar.

Until now, the prince had given his host no clues as to the purpose of his visit. For his part, Wulfgar had not shown the least bit of surprise or curiosity at Edgar's arrival. Now, however, with the cards seemingly about to be laid on the table, he could not help leaning forward and stroking his beard in a much more animated manner. He seemed to weigh his response.

'You may have received a somewhat exaggerated report, Your Highness. The night before last, a rabble appeared outside the main gates. They demanded entry, but in all honesty seemed confused about their reasons. We dispersed them easily enough.' Wulfgar sat back in his chair. 'There was no bloodshed,' he added in a reassuring manner.

Edgar suppressed a smile. It was common, in his experience, for priests to exaggerate threats, to extract more funds. It was much rarer to hear one dismissing a threat.

'I have also heard that you have taken a prisoner?'

Wulfgar looked a little uncomfortable. 'Yes, Your Highness—a woman, possessed by some evil spirit, somehow made it past our gates and tried to steal Toric's Dagger from us. She was caught inside the temple itself! This group from the other night were her supporters—amongst other demands, they wanted her released.'

Edgar nodded, thinking over Wulfgar's words. The high priest had tried to hide the fact that he had the prisoner, but he was probably not lying outright.

'Look,' continued Wulfgar, 'maybe you've had a complaint from some of these madmen, and perhaps you feel it's necessary to come here and find things out for yourself. But I can assure you that I have dealt with the matter. She has already been judged according to the laws of our community and is condemned to death. I'm sure I do not need to remind you that, in all matters relating to Toric's Temple, the crown has ceded jurisdiction to me.'

Edgar didn't like the way the conversation was going. Wulfgar was trying to pre-empt any interference from Edgar in the woman's case, but the prince was not to be brushed aside so easily.

'I am aware of your rights, Wulfgar, and I fully support your decision. I would, however, like to see the woman before the sentence is carried out.'

For a moment, the priest allowed a flash of anger to show on his face.

'The funny thing is, Your Highness, the woman says that she has already met you once before. She has, in fact, been demanding to speak to you, although I have explained to her that it is not in your power to overturn the decision.'

Elana was her name. She had come to Edgar's court about two weeks before, and he had spoken to her briefly.

Before then, rumours had already reached the prince of a priestess with unique powers who had been healing people across his kingdom. However, she had not come to court to heal, but to persuade people of some great threat to Dalriya.

Edgar remembered she claimed the Dagger of Toric was vital in averting this threat. She was certainly persuasive in her own way, and although she spoke passionately, she also spoke calmly, and was not, in his opinion, completely mad.

But she had no real evidence to support her claims, and Edgar had explained that, in such circumstances, he was not about to entrust the most holy relic in Magnia into her keeping. When her followers brought her case to him yesterday, it was easy for Edgar to put two and two together and work out that she had taken matters into her own hands.

Wulfgar was right: the law said that Elana was his to try—and to punish. So Edgar avoided that subject and pursued his request.

'I would like to speak with her again. Where is she being held?'

Wulfgar did not answer the question immediately. He glanced over at the two bodyguards who had taken up residence by his fire. Edgar followed his eyes, and could barely believe that Wulfgar was considering resisting his request. He tried to control his anger. He had calculated that he could get what he wanted today with a casual personal visit and without creating a fuss.

If he wanted to, Wulfgar could refuse his prince's request or even have him ejected. Edgar would then ensure that he faced the consequences, but by that stage, people would begin to ask troublesome questions about his interest in the matter.

To his relief, Wulfgar relented and ordered one of the priests in the hall to fetch Elana.

After what seemed an unduly long amount of time, in which the prince and priest sat in uncomfortable silence, Elana was brought into the hall.

Edgar found her to be just as striking as the first time they had met. He had seen women who were more beautiful. But she had strong features and an intensity which drew attention to her. Her pale skin and blonde, almost white, hair gave her an ethereal look.

As she was led to the table where Edgar awaited her, he noticed red marks around her wrists, which Wulfgar must have had tied. Still, that was likely the full extent of her injuries. Female prisoners could suffer much worse elsewhere.

Elana's eyes connected with Edgar's, and she nodded towards him, as if she had been expecting his presence. Considering her situation, she looked remarkably calm.

Wulfgar gestured to where she should sit and she did so, still without speaking.

'Elana,' began the prince, 'you are aware of the sentence passed on you?'

'Yes, my lord.'

'*Your Highness,*' corrected Wulfgar.

'Well...what is your defence?'

Elana looked at him quizzically, as if she were trying to work out the meaning of the question.

'She has already been tried in the relevant court, Your Highness,' interjected Wulfgar.

'I am aware of that,' responded Edgar roughly. He returned his attention to Elana, who was beginning to annoy him just as much as the priest. Despite the fact that he had travelled all this way to intervene in her case, the condemned woman was acting as if the idea of making an appeal to him was somehow unnecessary. Edgar suspected that Elana was one of those pious people who expected their god to save them from trouble without doing anything much about it themselves—and in his experience, such people rarely lasted very long.

To his relief, she spoke up.

'My defence is that this kingdom, and every other in Dariya, is under threat from Ishari, and that to fight this threat I need the dagger of the Lippers. This man—' Elana gestured to Wulfgar '—doesn't want me to have it, because he thinks he owns it. Meanwhile, Ishari's power grows stronger, while I stay locked up in his dungeon. The weapon isn't even Magnia's to give. It was stolen from the Lippers, who were chosen as its guardians, and who would have relinquished it to me.'

Although Elana was now putting forward her case, the bizarre nature of the argument did not help. Wulfgar put a forefinger to the side of his head and twisted it. Edgar tried to continue.

'It is true that Toric's Dagger was won from the Lippers by King Osbert of Magnia some generations ago, but it has been well preserved and honoured ever since, and as its guardians, neither Wulfgar nor I are prepared to hand it over to just anyone who claims it.'

Wulfgar nodded in solemn agreement, but Elana disagreed.

'The powers which have been granted to me by Madria, the true Goddess of Dalriya, are a sign from her that what I say is true and that the weapon should be entrusted into my keeping.'

'Blasphemy!' fumed Wulfgar. 'You would take Toric's holy weapon and use it for the evil designs of your false god!'

Edgar heard raised voices from outside the hall. It sounded like they were about to be interrupted, and he was eager to steer this matter his way.

'Some of what you say may be true,' he began, holding up a hand for silence as Wulfgar started to object.

'I have heard that you possess healing powers, and it is possible that they derive from your goddess. That is why I have decided that your claims should be investigated. If my kingdom is under threat, then I am duty bound to defend it. Meanwhile, the Dagger remains here.'

At Edgar's last sentence, Wulfgar swung round to confront him as it slowly dawned on him what the prince was saying.

'This woman is not leaving my temple. She has been condemned to death and I will not withdraw my sentence.'

'The sentence stands. I have already told you I support your decision. However, this woman may well be aware of a threat to my kingdom. In these circumstances, the sentence will have to be postponed. As soon as I am satisfied that there is no threat, I will personally return her to you.'

The high-priest did not have a ready response to this, and Edgar felt a little self-satisfied with his argument. Of course, Wulfgar knew that if he allowed Elana to slip out of his control, the chances of her being returned were slim, but he could hardly accuse his prince of bad faith.

'Prince Edgar, I recognise that you are acting to protect our kingdom—your motives, I can only commend—but I fear this witch has somehow used her magic on you and is leading you astray. She has broken into one of our kingdom's temples in an attempt to steal our most precious treasure. She is devious and dangerous and I fear I cannot in good conscience allow her to escape when Toric himself has instructed that she should be killed as soon as possible.'

Before Edgar had time to respond, the doors of the hall were thrown open, and the noise outside, of which he had been vaguely aware, burst into the room.

Several of Wulfgar's priests, weapons drawn, burst into the hall and towards the table where he was sitting. Leofwin and Brictwin moved over to the same area, but the priests had come to find the hall's owner.

As he drew closer, the man in the lead began shouting at Wulfgar. 'My lord, intruders have broken through the main gate, and now they're in the temple. At first, we thought they were the prince's men, but—'

'How many?' cut in Wulfgar harshly. He didn't wait for a response, but grabbed an axe from someone and led the priests back towards the doors. Everyone in the hall followed the high-priest's cue, arming themselves and streaming out of the hall.

Edgar and his two bodyguards followed them out.

The prince quickly surveyed the scene in the courtyard. Several bodies lay by the eastern gate, where the defenders must have put up some kind of resistance. The conflict had then moved to the temple, where they could now hear shouting. The speed of the initial attack seemed to have taken the defenders by surprise.

'There are about a score of them, all on horseback,' a priest was informing Wulfgar.

'Follow me,' ordered the High-Priest. 'We'll trap them in the temple.'

Leofwin grabbed Edgar's wrist. 'Your Highness, I don't think you should put yourself in danger here.'

Edgar stopped and looked at Wulfgar's followers, who were earnestly listening to his barked instructions. There were barely a dozen of them, and though they might find reinforcements at the temple, they were in a weak position.

No-one seemed to know who the enemy was, but the fact that they were all on horseback indicated that they were probably well-trained and well-armed warriors, as did the ease with which they had breached Wulfgar's defences.

The Prince turned back to his bodyguard. 'They need our help.'

Leofwin looked at Edgar for a moment, then simply nodded, though his disapproval was clear. 'Look to the Prince at all times,' he instructed his nephew, as the three men jogged over to catch up with Wulfgar's band.

The High-Priest turned around to look at his Prince, but said nothing.

'Is this all the fighters you have?' Edgar hissed at him, gesturing at the armed priests with him.

Wulfgar seemed taken aback by the question. 'Yes—there are others in the Temple, but we've lost those men at the gates,' he said, indicating the men who had already fallen.

Twenty fighters. That was all Wulfgar had to protect the Temple. He had spent too much on tapestries and feasting, and not enough on soldiers. But now was not the time to get into that argument.

They had barely walked a few more yards when Wulfgar's plan to catch the enemy in the Temple fell through. At first a handful, then all the raiders emerged. Upon seeing Wulfgar's force, they quickly mounted their horses. All of them wore armour and carried weapons.

The High-Priest's march came to a halt as his men realized they were faced by an enemy that was superior in every way.

The horsemen slowly trotted forwards. Edgar exchanged glances with

Leofwin: Wulfgar's priests looked nervous and were liable to run if the enemy charged them. If they ran, they would be cut down and dispersed by the horsemen with ease.

The Prince pushed his way to the front. 'Form a semicircle behind me,' he ordered.

The priests looked to their leader, who looked relieved that someone else was taking charge of a situation that was getting more desperate by the second.

'Do as your prince commands,' Wulfgar growled, and took a position by Edgar's left side. Leofwin and Brictwin stood on Edgar's right side, while the priests took up position behind and to the flanks. They seemed a little more confident now that their prince had arranged them into a formation and that they were no longer at the front. Some of the more belligerent ones even shouted insults and curses at the approaching cavalry.

One attacker rode some yards ahead of the others, and Edgar assumed that this was the leader. He didn't wear any identifying symbols to betray who he was or where he was from. As he gradually drew closer, the prince could make out a moustache, and he could tell that he rode his horse naturally. The animal was powerful and expensive-looking.

He stopped some fifty yards from the defenders, and Edgar could see that he was being examined by his opponent in the same way that he was analysing him. He held the man's stare and hoped that he was at least making his foe think twice about attacking. In truth, the numbers and manoeuvrability of the enemy made Edgar's position pretty hopeless.

At first, the Prince had almost subconsciously assumed that these invaders were from North Magnia, the breakaway kingdom to the north with which his own kingdom had been at war for over a generation. Although there had been an official peace for some years now, small raids were not unheard of.

But as the rest of the riders drew up next to their leader and listened to his instructions, Edgar began to doubt this origin. For a start, he had lieutenants on the northern border who should have intercepted a force like this before it had travelled so far south. The location suggested that these attackers came from the east, and this seemed to be confirmed by an examination of the enemy. Many wore moustaches with a shaved chin, a fashion in the Empire. Magnians tended either to be clean-shaven, like Edgar himself, or full-bearded, like Wulfgar.

Edgar's thoughts were interrupted by decisive action from the enemy. The horsemen trotted towards them and gradually picked up speed until they were charging at them, weapons drawn and ready.

'Brace yourselves,' ordered the Prince as his subjects prepared to face the onslaught.

The horsemen were advancing at a rapid rate, and it looked as if they were planning to smash into Edgar's line without stopping. He felt sure that the horses would refuse to do so, but they kept coming. Then, in a perfectly executed manoeuvre, just as the Prince prepared for contact, the horsemen at the front peeled away to the sides and continued harmlessly past the Magnians. The rest of the horsemen followed, swerving either to the left or the right in the same way as their comrades.

Just as the last of the riders galloped past, Brictwin ran out from his position next to Leofwin to challenge the enemy. Acting with great speed, he took a swing at the last of the riders passing by.

This warrior did not look as experienced a rider as some of the others; he seemed to panic at Brictwin's approach and made a wild swing at Edgar's bodyguard, which failed to connect and left him off balance. Brictwin, meanwhile, landed a blow on the rider's leg. For a moment it looked as if the rider might regain his balance, but the speed at which he was travelling was too fast, and he tumbled off his mount onto the ground, while the horse galloped on.

Edgar did not join his bodyguard but turned around, fearing that the horsemen would themselves swing around and come at his position from the rear. He was surprised to see them keep the same course towards the eastern gate. Some of the horsemen closest to the fallen rider did stop once they noticed he was missing, and spied Brictwin, who was standing apart from the rest of the Magnians in a vulnerable position.

'Ho!' went the shout, and those at the front of the cavalry force, already out of the gate, stopped and turned around. They made space for the leader to trot back to the front. It looked like they were readying to attack, to either avenge or to rescue their fallen comrade.

There was a bit of time to act as the enemy pulled their horses around, trying to get back into formation.

'Into the temple?' asked Edgar, thinking they might be better able to hold off a cavalry force there.

'Aye,' said Leofwin, sounding unhappy with the idea, but he had no alternative.

'Wait!' said the bodyguard, pointing to the north side of the complex.

Two men, each armed with bows, had taken up position on the inside of the northern complex wall and had already loosed an arrow each. The dark skin and long black hair of the archers indicated they were Middians.

Pulling back their strings, they aimed a second time at the mounted attackers. One arrow missed its target, but the other hit home, tearing into the flesh of one of the horses. The horse bucked up in pain, dislodging its rider, who twisted away and to the side as he fell, with a great thump, onto the ground.

Edgar studied their leader again; two hostile groups, Edgar's force and the two archers, now flanked him. And the two archers were busy nocking a second arrow to their bows.

The downed rider picked himself up, and, linking arms with one of his comrades, clambered onto his horse.

'We go!' Edgar clearly heard the leader shout as he wheeled his horse back towards the gates and moved off at pace.

The accent confirmed Edgar's suspicions: he was from the Empire.

The two archers tracked the departing riders with their bows but loosed no more arrows.

When they were sure that they had gone, they unstrung their weapons and walked over. As they approached, Edgar thought he recognised one of them.

'It's...Farred, isn't it?' he asked, frowning at the man. He knew him as a nobleman from the plains to the east of the kingdom, but he couldn't understand what he was doing here.

'That's right, Your Highness,' said the man, going to one knee.

'Up, up,' Edgar insisted, and gave the man a hug. 'You have my thanks.'

'They came here through my lands,' explained Farred. 'We happened to be out hunting and saw them cutting through Plunder Wood. We followed them here.'

'I'm grateful that you did,' said Edgar, looking at the second man, who he didn't recognise.

'This is my friend, Gyrmund,' said Farred. 'He's the one who hit the horse.'

This one didn't bend the knee, but offered his hand instead. Edgar was happy to take it.

'That was a fine shot.'

They all stood around for a while, letting their heart rates get back to something like normal.

'I guess they're gone,' said Edgar.

'They've got what they came for,' muttered Wulfgar darkly.

Relief flooded over Edgar as the immediate threat disappeared. He felt like he hadn't taken a breath since he'd first seen the enemy. The priests, too, were feeling the euphoria of surviving a battle, shouting out praise to Toric.

Leofwin, meanwhile, was marching over to his nephew. He was not happy.

He looked down at the body of the fallen rider over whom Brictwin was standing. Leofwin felt for a pulse.

'Alive, but unconscious,' he called over to Edgar. He stood and glared at the young bodyguard.

'You've let me down today, Brictwin. You deserted your prince, whom you are sworn to protect. I even told you to look to the Prince before the fight. Even these priests held their position,' he said, waving his sword at Wulfgar's followers dismissively. He spat on the floor. 'You nearly brought the enemy back upon us.'

Edgar had heard enough of the conversation and walked over to join Wulfgar, who was making his way to the Temple. Farred and Gyrmund came with them. He felt sorry for Brictwin, who had shown bravery and skill in his first real armed encounter; but, ultimately, Leofwin was right. Edgar needed his bodyguards to stay close at all times. Brictwin's youthful rush of blood to the head might have got them all killed.

By the time that Edgar and Wulfgar had reached the Temple, the two bodyguards had re-joined their prince. The six men entered the building.

Unlike the priests at the main gates of the temple complex, the priests inside the temple itself seemed to have failed to put up a united resistance against the intruders. A few bodies lay in random places, neither moving nor making a sound, while their blood leaked onto the floor of their holy temple.

The sight was a gruesome one: the floor and walls were red and sticky in places, and it seemed as if every piece of furniture in the sparsely decorated entrance chamber had been smashed or shoved over. Edgar told Brictwin to go back outside and prevent any of the other priests from entering the temple for now. Wulfgar and Leofwin checked the bodies of Toric's priests for life signs, but all of them had passed away within their god's temple.

Wulfgar, looking sombre, led them into the circular central chamber, the most sacred area. Toric's Dagger was always kept in a chest on a table near the far wall, only removed for religious ceremonies.

Wulfgar and Edgar shared the same expression. They dreaded what they would find, and at the same time knew that their fears would be realised.

As they got closer, they saw a body slumped against the table.

'Anrik!' called Wulfgar, as he recognised the priest. He knelt beside the body.

Leofwin walked over and studied the body, feeling for the pulse.

'He's dead,' said Edgar's bodyguard. He held up an arm by the wrist. The hand was a bloody mess of flesh. The fingers and thumb had been chopped off in a clumsy fashion, leaving stubs of differing lengths.

Wulfgar gasped in horror.

'They tortured him,' said Leofwin, 'then ran him through with a sword.'

'Why would they torture him?' asked Gyrmund.

'I don't know,' said Wulfgar, looking up, distress on his face. 'The dagger is always kept in the chest. It isn't hard to find.'

Edgar marched over to the chest. The lid was up, the dagger gone.

'Maybe they killed him in case he could identify them?'

Wulfgar shrugged, but said nothing. It was a tired, hopeless movement.

The six men left the devastation of the Temple and returned to the main courtyard, where the priests and other inhabitants had congregated in the aftermath of the attack. They all talked for a short while, making guesses about the origins of the perpetrators.

Eventually Wulfgar ordered one of his men to begin the grisly clean-up operation in the Temple.

Edgar noticed Elana kneeling on the ground, separate from everyone else. She was tending to an injured priest, who had presumably been stationed at the gate. She was cleaning his wound and talking in a reassuring voice.

It seemed like an age had passed since they had been arguing with Wulfgar in the High-Priest's hall, but it must have been no more than half an hour ago. It occurred to Edgar that, in the confusion, it would have been quite easy for Elana to have escaped from her captors—but, as before, she seemed oblivious to any danger.

'Are you alright?' asked Edgar. It was a stupid question, but the adrenaline still racing around his body made him speak before thinking.

Elana turned and smiled in his direction. She pressed down on the forearm of the priest she was attending to with both hands. Was Edgar witnessing a healing miracle? It was difficult to say, since the arm was already bandaged. Elana wiped her hands on a scrap of cloth and stood up.

'I think we should leave, Your Highness,' interjected Leofwin.

Edgar nodded, recognising that they were all still in immediate danger. He marched over to Wulfgar. The high priest was surrounded by his followers, all asking him for direction in the wake of this disaster. Edgar noted he was not quite so full of himself any more.

'Wulfgar,' he began, putting as much authority into his voice as possible. 'I need to return to my household now in order to deal with this invasion. I no longer have the time to argue with you. Both you and Elana will accompany me.'

Wulfgar stared blankly at his prince for a moment and then nodded his head in acceptance.

LEAVING

V

Belwynn was now itching to get moving. For every extra minute they wasted in discussion, the Brasingians were getting farther and farther away.

It wasn't Edgar's fault. He had responsibilities to keep everyone happy, and Belwynn felt lucky that she was not tied down in such a way. Still, the Prince had not been without luck himself today.

The rider had arrived at Edgar's estate of Bidcote about midday, informing his household that a small band of soldiers from the Empire had entered Magnia. Everyone who could use a weapon had set out for Ecgworth, fearing that Edgar had been killed or captured. But they had met the Prince and his small entourage about halfway to the Temple of Toric and accompanied him back to the relative safety of Bidcote. He was fortunate that the raiders at the Temple had not recognised him, or they would doubtless have taken the time to capture him as well as the damned relic, earning themselves a prince's ransom.

When he got back, Edgar immediately sent out messengers to raise troops as quickly as possible. There were never more than about forty men in the royal household at any one time, and, with news from the east still patchy, it was possible that the raid on the Temple was a precursor to a large-scale invasion.

In these circumstances, the prince's priority was to raise an army to defend his kingdom. At the same time, he was making plans to retrieve the dagger, and it was here that Edgar was encountering problems.

He had been fortunate that Belwynn and Soren had arrived back in Magnia since they, along with Herin and Clarin, were the obvious choice for this kind of operation.

She and Soren were cousins of Edgar's on his mother's side, and, while they were welcome at his court, their presence was a rare occurrence these days. They had experience of the Empire; they had no duties that required them to stay with Edgar and the army; and they had a couple of acquaintances who could prove very useful. Most importantly from Edgar's point of view, they were family, and could be trusted.

The same could not be said for most other people in the room.

The Prince held the meeting in his bedroom at the back of his hall to lend some privacy to the discussion. It was packed. Loyal officers like Wilchard were here, but so were half a dozen noblemen plus other court hangers-on, all of whom expected to have a say. Some were perched on the bed with the Prince; others had been found chairs; still others stood.

Belwynn looked over to Clarin, who was slouched against the wall, no longer attempting to feign his boredom at the interminable proceedings. As soon as it had become clear that their group of four would form the backbone of the party sent to retrieve the dagger, Herin had ridden off to recruit his friends Kaved and Moneva and to pick up any vital provisions from the town. The question was, who else would be dumped on them?

Belwynn forced herself to turn back to the conversation. Wulfgar, the High-Priest, seemed to have brought all of his brethren who had not been slaughtered at the temple with him. The man's colossal arrogance may have been dented on his arrival, but when he realized that his brother, Otha of Rystham, was in attendance as well, it had made a full recovery. The two men were trying to muscle in on the mission by turning it into some kind of religious pilgrimage. Edgar was dead set against their involvement. Yet he seemed to be supportive of another priest—the mystic named Elana—who insisted that she come along.

Amongst the others present who were trying to get a word in edgeways was a nobleman named Farred. Belwynn had never met him before; he had apparently only recently inherited his father's estate, which lay on the border with the Midder Steppe. It was through these estates that the robbers had passed on their way to the Temple. He and his friend Gyrmund had made a crucial intervention in the confrontation at the Temple. They seemed to be sure that the robbers would be heading south east, giving them the option of slipping back into the Empire via Cordence or the Wilderness.

Farred had suggested that his peers on the border would have been alerted by now and raised their forces, whereas news of the invasion was unlikely to have reached the south. It was a longer route back to the Empire, but probably the safest for the Brasingians.

Otha of Rystham, meanwhile, seemed oblivious to such concerns, but very intent on pressing his brother's claims for religious leadership on the issue.

'What I do not understand, Your Highness, is why you seem to give so much credence to what this heretic says—' Otha waved a hand in Elana's direction—'yet you would deny the Church of Toric any say in your plans to restore His Holy Dagger.'

Otha was living dangerously, almost accusing his prince of heresy. Belwynn could tell that Edgar was reaching the end of his tether, but he had to tread carefully; he could not be seen to support a convicted criminal over the Church of Toric. Otha was experienced in high politics, and he usually got what he wanted. He had almost caught the young Prince in his trap—so the interruption of the conversation by the arrival of Soren and Ealdnoth was an obvious disappointment.

Belwynn's brother and Edgar's court wizard had been interrogating the Brasingian prisoner who had been knocked from his horse by Brictwin. Many in the hall greeted their return with clumsily concealed distaste. Most people connected to Edgar's household had, by now, come to terms with his patronage of wizards, but they still had difficulty with certain innovations they had ushered in. One of these was the use of their powers in questioning prisoners. Otha and his like favoured the traditional methods, which usually involved an assortment of sharp instruments and clamps, perhaps the use of fire, but always a lot of screaming and mess. The fact that Ealdnoth and Soren could get better results in less time, and with less unpleasantness, left them feeling dissatisfied, and even a little cheated.

'Well?' asked Edgar.

'We have a name,' answered Ealdnoth. 'Their leader is called Gervase Salvinus.'

Ealdnoth was interrupted by a whistle from Clarin.

'You know this man, Clarin?' enquired the Prince.

'Know him? Sure. Not real personal, you understand, but Herin and me fought under him a few years back now, and he was making a name for himself even then.'

'Making himself a name as what?'

'As a mercenary leader.'

Clarin regaled the room with one of his war stories. It amused Belwynn to watch. No-one really wanted to hear it, but Clarin was such an intimidating figure that most people nodded along enthusiastically whenever his eyes met theirs.

Has anything been decided? asked Soren.

Not really. Wulfgar and Otha are still arguing with Edgar. It looks like we're going to be bringing some bloody priests with us. Are you alright after dealing with that prisoner?

Soren looked back to full health after the damage he had sustained from his fall from the window of Vincente's house. He had recovered consciousness on the journey back to Magnia in the back of Kaved's cart, though had remained groggy and weak the whole time. Belwynn hadn't wanted him to use his magic again so soon afterwards. There had been many times when Soren had pushed the use of his powers too far and blacked out. Most of the time it had fallen to Belwynn to look after him until he recovered. But it hadn't happened for a long time now, not since he had improved his mastery of his powers and understood his limits.

I'm fine, he said, *no lasting effects. Ealdnoth did most of it, anyway.*

Ealdnoth had been Soren's first tutor in wizard-craft, and they still had something of a father-son relationship. Belwynn could well imagine Ealdnoth taking charge, even though her brother had now surpassed him in power.

Soren turned his attention back to the Prince as the conversation in the centre of the hall came back to the matter in hand.

'So, who do you think he could be working for?' Edgar was asking Clarin.

Clarin shrugged his shoulders. 'It could be anyone—anyone with enough money, that is. Salvinus's services won't come cheap.'

'Did the prisoner know who was paying?' the Prince asked Ealdnoth.

The wizard shook his head. 'He's a new recruit; doesn't know anything about the operation. He seemed pretty sure that they were going to head back to the Empire, though.'

'Right. I think we have wasted enough time already,' said Edgar, rising from his seat on the bed to emphasise the point. 'I've decided that Soren will lead the attempt to recover the dagger. Belwynn and Clarin are going with him, and hopefully Clarin's brother Herin will join up with them later with some extra help.'

Edgar paused and then turned to face Wulfgar and Otha.

'I have also decided that a representative from Toric's community should accompany them, so that He may bless the enterprise. Wulfgar, I give you the choice as to whom.'

Wulfgar screwed up his face as he thought about Edgar's offer. Belwynn doubted whether the High-Priest really wanted many of his brethren to go on this expedition; he had already lost a good number of his priests today, and there was every chance that whoever accompanied them would not come back.

Eventually, he nodded his consent. 'I have a volunteer, Your Highness, an initiate named Dirk who recently came to us from the Empire. He is healthy and strong. He may be of help to your cousins.'

Wulfgar pointed to the priest he had nominated. Belwynn looked him over: he was unremarkable, thin and shorter than average height.

I can't see him being much help, she informed her brother.

Soren grinned at the comment. *Who knows?*

The prince was speaking again. 'I have come to an agreement with Elana. I feel that her powers will be of help to you, Soren, and she is as desperate as anyone here to recover the dagger from the Brasingians. I have therefore agreed that she will accompany you, on the condition that, when the mission is over, whether it be a success or a failure, she returns to the custody of the Church of Toric in order that her sentence be carried out.'

Otha and Wulfgar cried out in protest, but Edgar was in no mood for further debate.

'I want you to leave right now,' he told the twins.

ONCE THE DECISIONS had been taken, things moved quickly, and it was only minutes later that they found themselves in the courtyard of Edgar's hall, horses saddled and provisions prepared.

'If you recover the dagger, there will be handsome individual rewards for everyone who took part,' Edgar announced. 'In the meantime, I am giving Soren enough money to cover any expenses which may occur.'

Edgar led Belwynn and Soren over to one side and handed over a bag of money.

'There's Imperial thalers there as well. Use it all if you must. It is the dagger that is important. Losing the dagger will not help my situation here in Magnia, and I have had to cross Rystham today. There may even be an army headed this way, though I doubt it. It looks like this Gervase Salvinus had a specific mission here.'

'Your Highness, I am sorry to intrude.'

It was Farred, who had company.

'What is it, Farred?' asked Edgar.

'You will recall my friend, Gyrmund. He is well travelled around Dalriya and would like to offer his skills to help your cousins. I can vouch for his honesty.'

'Well,' said Edgar, 'that's very good of you, Gyrmund. I thank you. Soren, what do you think?'

'What can you do?' Belwynn asked the man bluntly.

'I know my way through the Wilderness, which is where I would guess the Brasingians are heading. I tracked them here, and I can pick up their trail again with no difficulty. I am an expert with the longbow,' he said, patting the weapon which was slung across his back, 'and I can fight.'

Well? Belwynn asked her brother.

I don't see why not, he replied.

'It sounds like you might be useful,' Belwynn told the man. 'We could do with your help.' She turned back to Edgar. 'We should make a move now.'

The Prince nodded and pulled Farred aside to speak with Ealdnoth.

Gyrmund and the twins mounted their horses and trotted over to where the other members of the party waited. Clarin was having a conversation with the monk, Dirk, though Toric only knew about what. Elana waited to one side in silence.

As Soren and Clarin led the party of six out of the courtyard, Gyrmund said a quick farewell to Farred.

Belwynn drew up with the two priests.

'I want you two to know,' she told them, 'if you fall behind, we leave you. I will not let either of you put the rest of us in danger.'

* * *

HORSESHOES. Hammer and nails. Pokers. Plough blades. Locks and keys. Cartwheels. Files and chisels. All very good. All very well and good, and Ulf could do a wonderful job of making all of those. But armour? Spears and war-axes? No. Swords? Really fine swords, works of art that could be passed down the generations? No-one was ordering those anymore, and Rabigar had waited long enough.

Peace had come to Magnia at last. It was an idea that was disputed, of course. He still heard dire warnings about the North Magnians. Prince Cerdda and his brother were plotting this or that attack. People needed an enemy to talk about, to scare each other about. But blade-smiths were always the first to know when peace had come. People stopped buying weapons.

Bang. Bang. Bang. Ulf was working hard as usual, powerful shoulders hammering away at the anvil.

'How's it going?' Rabigar shouted.

Ulf stopped. 'What?'

'Do you need a hand? Quite a few orders in, I see.'

'Nah, nothing that would interest you, master. You have a rest.'

'Oh. Right then.'

Bang. Bang. Bang.

He was a good boy, Ulf. Or young man now. Hard worker. Respectful. Grateful. But by the gods, did he piss Rabigar off when he treated him like a hoary relic. He headed for the exit from the forge.

'Master Rabigar?'

Bareva, Ulf's wife. She came waddling into the forge, her pregnant belly now much more of a hindrance than it had been a few weeks ago. She was a big woman, not that much smaller than Ulf, and it had taken a while for the baby in her belly to show.

'There you are. Customer asking for you.'

'Right you are. Thank you, Bareva. You can tell 'em to come in.'

Asking for me, thought Rabigar. *Dare I hope?*

A tall, powerfully built man strode into the forge as if he owned the place.

'Herin? Good to see you.'

'Rabigar,' said Herin, clasping hands and shouting over the noise of Ulf's hammering. 'It's been a while, hasn't it? Boy, she's looking big now, isn't she?' he asked, nodding toward Bareva, who had left the forge.

'Aye. Parents like that, baby's gonna be a monster, isn't it? Well, I'm hoping you've got a job for me.'

'Business slow?'

'Nah. *Business* isn't slow. Our lad,' he said, indicating Ulf over at the anvil, 'is very busy. Just nothing in the way of blade-work.'

'Good. Well, I had a very special favour to ask, and sounds like you might be willing to help me out.'

'Go on.'

'You won't have heard what's gone on at Toric's Temple?'

'Nope.'

'Attacked this morning by twenty-odd soldiers, from the Empire. Broke in and took Toric's Dagger. Worst part about it, I guess, is that Edgar was there when it happened. He's alright, though.'

Rabigar whistled at the news. 'Wait a minute. You're not asking me to make a new Dagger, are you? I mean, I know I'm good, but...'

Herin laughed. 'No. I'm leading the rescue mission for it, though. I need to set off as soon as possible and we need some emergency supplies.'

'Weapons?'

'Yes; only two. One, for a friend—a knife with a sharp point. She likes to throw it.'

'Does she now? Got a nice balanced one she can have.'

'Thought you might. Second, for me. I lost my seax.'

'Careless.'

'Well, let's just say a little adventure down in Cordence went a bit wrong. Thing is, I really need a replacement by the end of the day. Can you do it?'

'I can do it, Herin. But it will be a day-crafted seax, not a week crafted one like the last.'

'A day-crafted one by you is still as good as a week-crafted one from anyone else. I can pay you double. Our little adventure in Cordence wasn't entirely a loss, though we ended up with far less than I thought we might.'

'You can pay me normal rates. I'll enjoy doing it. Might well be the last one I make here.'

'Last one? Are you serious?'

'Yeah, I think so. Time for me to move on. When I first came to Magnia, Prince Edric recruited me personally. The South was pretty desperate at that point, and they needed me to ensure that the army was at least properly armed. He turned things around and the North and South fought themselves to a draw and a sort of peace. I've got nothing against Edgar, but he'll never appreciate me in the same way as his father. For him, I've always been here; he's known no different. Anyway, I'm a weapons-maker, Herin, and there's no great call for it here anymore. But there's plenty of demand for it elsewhere. I've had offers.'

'I'm not surprised you've had offers to go elsewhere. And I'm sure you'd get paid a lot more, too.'

'That's right, and money's important. It's important to everyone, of course. But when you're a Krykker living with humans you really need it. No proper family, no real ties. Someone decides they don't like you around anymore, you have to leave everything behind, fast. I know, it's happened to me more than once.'

Rabigar looked around at his forge. 'Plus, the boy, Ulf. Young man, I should say. He's more than ready to take this place over now. He's starting a family, needs the money. The timing's right.'

Herin looked thoughtful. 'Where will you go? Empire?'

'I've had offers. The agents of Duke Emeric have come calling.'

'I bet they have. Plenty of soldiers to arm in Barissia.'

'I don't know, though. Sentimental, you might think. But I like to think I'm arming the good men.'

Herin shrugged. 'The good men. In my experience, the good men are the ones asking for their plough to be fixed, not the ones asking for a hundred spears. But I'm not pretending to be the best person to judge. I'm just thinking, Rabigar. You're handy with a weapon yourself. I can tell.'

'Of course. When I was younger, I was as fearsome as they come.'

'Then come with us. Edgar is offering a reward to all who take part. Looks like we're heading towards the Empire. You could stay there, or move on somewhere else if it doesn't feel right.'

Rabigar puffed his cheeks out. Tomorrow? After all the years working in this forge, just to up and leave it all behind? That would be a hasty decision. But why did it sound so tempting?

'I don't know, Herin. You haven't given me much warning.'

'I know, I haven't. Not for the blades, either. Tell you what, Rabigar. Make me one last weapon. And while you're making it, think it over. Sleep on it, if I've left you any time for sleep. When I come to collect it first thing in the morning, you can leave with me, or not. How does that sound?'

Rabigar nodded, pursing his lips as he thought through the offer. 'I'll think on it, Herin. Thanks for the offer. I'll think on it and let you know tomorrow.'

A MIRACLE

VI

So far, so good, considered Belwynn.

As Gyrmund claimed, it hadn't taken long to pick up the trail again, and he had the party travelling at a pace that ate up the miles without exhausting the horses. These were roads familiar not only to Gyrmund, but to Belwynn, Soren and Clarin also, and they felt confident they would make ground on the Brasingians, who would be far less familiar with the territory.

This part of Magnia was prime arable farming land, and they passed through one well-organised village after another, well-tended fields that promised a good harvest. All the farming folk of Magnia followed the same seasonal routine. Belwynn knew it well. Their father had owned several estates, and Soren still had one of them, a village called Beckford. Belwynn had lived there by herself for a year and, with little else to do, had got involved in the day-to-day running of the estate: organising the labour, maintaining and upgrading the equipment, trying to improve yields. This time of year, early summer, was hay-making season, a big job which would require the entire village.

When they passed anyone, on the roads or in a village, one of them would offer a quick greeting and ask what they knew of the Brasingians who had passed through. Many had seen them, and the collective opinion of South Magnia appeared to be that they were about five hours ahead.

As for the two priests, they didn't say a word, to each other or to anyone else. Belwynn was used to riding, but she noticed that Elana, in particular, was already showing signs of being saddle-sore. The priestess did not complain, however, and seemed eager to keep up the pace of the pursuit.

As they progressed, they came upon the first patches of woodland which would thicken and become the Wilderness.

The group stopped only once during the day to rest, but as the daylight faded, Soren called a halt to the chase.

'We have to give Herin a chance to catch up to us and there is little point in risking the horses in this light. It will give us a bit of time to make a decent camp-site.'

'Very well,' said Gyrmund, 'let me pick out a suitable spot, then.'

As everyone made camp a few metres from the road, Belwynn walked over to speak to Gyrmund, who was building a shelter for the night while the others fetched firewood and other materials.

'How far away do you think we are?'

'About five hours still. They're travelling just as fast as we are; they're not stupid. As soon as they've left Magnia, they'll begin to feel safe.'

'Do you think we can catch them up?'

'That depends,' he said with a grunt, shoving a log up against the tree trunk he had picked out for the camp. 'They're not making their route obvious; they could be heading to Cordence or the Wilderness. We'll find that out in the morning. I think Salvinus will choose the Wilderness. A large force wouldn't be able to follow them there without stirring up the vossi. He could be relying on that to avoid an army coming after them.'

'The vossi. I've never seen one. Don't wish to, either.'

'I've had a few encounters,' said Gyrmund, now stacking branches against one side of the log to make a walled shelter. 'They're strange. Not what you might expect. Usually, they don't attack unless they feel threatened. But if they do, it's an all-out attack that doesn't stop. With a group our size, they're likely to just leave us alone.'

'That makes me feel a bit better. I was trying to think from their perspective. Whoever planned this, that is. If they choose to go to Cordence, there's always the possibility that the Cordentines will interfere on the side of Edgar somehow. If they get through the Wilderness, they're home.'

'True. I hope you're right.'

'Why? We don't want to go into the Wilderness, do we?'

'Yes, we do. If they choose Cordence, we're still five hours behind them. If they choose the Wilderness, I can catch them up.'

'You're pretty sure of yourself.'

Gyrmund shrugged, a hint of a smile on his face. 'I've been through the

Wilderness a number of times. Few others have. If one of those Brasingians knows the place too, fair enough. But it's not likely.'

'If no-one else would want to go in there, why have you?'

'To test myself,' he said, his half-smile turning into a grin.

'To test yourself,' she repeated sarcastically. 'What kind of a crazy person would do that?'

He laughed, holding out his hand.

'Gyrmund. Pleased to meet you.'

Belwynn shook hands, shaking her head as she did.

Elana and Dirk came back to the camp with an armful of sticks each, which they dropped by the proposed site of the fire. Following behind came Soren, who had collected some stones for the fire pit.

'Gyrmund reckons that we're about five hours behind,' Belwynn explained to the others. 'If we enter the Wilderness tomorrow morning Herin won't be able to catch us up.'

'He'll catch up,' answered Clarin, barging into camp with a clump of green branches he had chopped off. When ready, he would add them to Gyrmund's structure to create a bit of waterproofing and insulation. The fact that Clarin never seemed to experience anxiety of any kind annoyed Belwynn, who often found herself worrying twice as hard about things to make up for it.

'Well, he's *your* brother,' she said.

Clarin just chuckled. As he and Gyrmund finished the shelter, the others gathered round to get the fire ready.

'So—Dirk. Wulfgar said that you were from the Empire—whereabouts, exactly?' asked Belwynn, trying to start a conversation.

'I'm from Barissia. A town called Magen, near Coldeberg.'

'What made you come to Magnia and join the Temple of Toric?' probed Belwynn.

'Serving Toric is the highest honour one can have,' Dirk replied, jutting his chin out somewhat.

Belwynn noticed Elana frowning at that comment, but the priestess said nothing.

'I am under His direction,' Dirk continued. 'He has chosen me to return the Dagger to its rightful place.'

It wasn't really a satisfactory explanation, as far as Belwynn was concerned, and she sensed Dirk wasn't too comfortable with the questioning. Whether he had something to hide or whether he was a private person, it wasn't easy to say. She supposed that being a Brasingian may not have made him popular back at the Temple, and he was perhaps nervous on that score.

'How about you, Elana? Where are you from?'

'Kirtsea. It's a fishing village, just north of the Magnian border.'

Belwynn nodded. 'I've heard of it, never been there. Nice place?'

'It's beautiful.'

'Do you have family there?'

'Yes. I've had to give up a lot to serve Madria. I hope that one day I can go back.'

Another cryptic response, thought Belwynn. *Maybe that's just priests.*

'Where is your home?' asked Elana.

Belwynn thought about it. *Our home?*

'Soren owns an estate called Beckford, right in the middle of South Magnia.'

'We both own it,' said Soren.

'By Magnian law, *he* owns it,' she said to Elana. 'Still, I've certainly spent more time there than him. Our father was a nobleman with lands all over Magnia. But Beckford is all that's left of them.'

'What happened?' asked the priestess.

Belwynn sighed. She looked at Soren, who shrugged his acceptance. 'Our mother was killed when we were ten. A raid from North Magnia on one of our houses. My father was away, fighting in the war.'

Belwynn's voice faltered a little. She still got emotional telling the story. 'They had already raided the village once, and my mother went back to help the people. She'd brought them seeds, animals, and equipment so they could start up again and feed themselves. But the raiders came back. They killed everyone, took everything, and left. They could have got a ransom for my mother. My father would have paid anything, but they just killed her. He never recovered. When the war ended, he just drank. He got into debt and sold off half his lands and kept on drinking. He died five years after our mother. We sold off the rest of his lands to pay off his debts, but he had more debts than he did property by then. Prince Edric had to help us. He was our uncle, you see. He let us keep Beckford. So, anyway, that's our home now, I guess. I lived there for a year. Soren's never been back. Not much of a home, really.'

'I'm sorry,' said Elana. 'It must have been difficult for you to lose your parents like that.'

'It was, I guess. But we weren't alone. We've always had each other.'

Gyrmund and Clarin came to join them.

'Well,' Belwynn said, deciding to change the subject, 'things are likely to heat up tomorrow, especially if we're heading for the Wilderness. Gyrmund, I don't imagine that everyone here is entirely familiar with it. Perhaps you should tell us what we're letting ourselves in for?'

'The Wilderness is dense. If that is where the Brasingians have gone, we'll have to leave our horses behind at some point. There are tracks, but unless you know what you're looking for, it's easy to get lost. Then you've got the inhabitants. There are the vossi, primitive but potentially very aggressive. If they think we're a threat to their territory, they will come after us and they won't give up until we're all dead. There are humans living there as well, but not in big numbers and unlikely to take us on, especially if your friends arrive. Outlaws make a life for themselves on the edges of the forest. If you want to survive in there, you've got to be fit, quick, and silent.'

'What do the vossi look like?' asked Elana.

'About five feet tall. Their skin is brown and hard, tough like leather. They're fast and persistent. Hopefully we won't meet any of them at all, but...' Gyrmund let his sentence hang there, emphasising that, once they entered the Wilderness, the course of events would be out of their control.

'Sounds fun,' suggested Clarin.

It didn't look like anyone agreed with the big warrior, but equally no-one looked like they wanted to argue the point.

'Well,' said Soren, 'we'd better try to get some rest. Might be the last night we get a peaceful sleep for some time.'

'I'll take first watch tonight,' added Clarin. 'Always pays to play safe. Now, come on, Gyrmund, are you gonna get this fire lit? I'm starving.'

IT HAD BEEN a mild summer's night, and Belwynn hadn't been asked to keep watch, but she still felt as though she hadn't slept. Gyrmund got them all up at a ridiculously early hour and got them moving again at the crack of dawn, despite Belwynn's complaints that they had to wait for Herin and the others anyway. Soren left a written message for Herin under a rock at the camp site, explaining the route they were likely to take. Clarin shook his head at the scrawly lines he left on the paper, as if the purpose of reading and writing was beyond him, which perhaps it was.

Clarin's alternative form of communication was to cut a slash into the bark of the tree they had slept under. To Belwynn, this could have meant anything or nothing, but the big man nodded to himself with satisfaction, as if he had solved some weighty problem.

They rode all morning, eating while on the move, stopping once only for a toilet break. The roads of Magnia became tracks on which they had to ride single file. The Magnian villages which they had passed so regularly yesterday became less frequent as the rich farmland increasingly gave way to woodland. Settlements became smaller, isolated hamlets which had been cut out of the forest, or the odd wooden shack that blended into the trees from which it had been built. The people here were warier, alarmed at a second group of riders passing through so soon after the Brasingian soldiers. But they were communicative enough to say in which direction they had gone, and that was all that mattered.

Belwynn's excitement from yesterday had not reappeared today, and she slumped in her saddle, trying to keep her eyes open. No-one else seemed to be in the mood for talking either; Gyrmund was focused on the terrain ahead, and the two priests were trailing behind, their thoughts concealed.

In the end, just to help her stay awake, she asked Clarin to recount one of his war stories. It did little good, since Clarin tended to dwell on marches and formations and long, involved anecdotes about people she'd never met, his voice becoming a background drone which threatened to send her to sleep at least as much as complete silence would have done.

By mid-afternoon they were in the no-man's-land between the state of Magnia and the lawless Wilderness. Officials could draw lines on maps, subdividing the world into neat parcels, but there was no neat border here. This was territory over which Prince Edgar couldn't offer his protection, and was therefore a land of bandits and outlaws.

Gyrmund had stopped to gather them together.

'I've detoured a bit from the route they took. In the next clearing is effectively the last outpost of civilisation around here: Hallaf's Home. Hallaf and his extended family are all outlaws, but he can be reasoned with if he can see a profit to be made. This is the last place we can leave the horses in safety, other than just abandoning them in the Wilderness, which is presumably what Salvinus has done.'

Belwynn patted her horse.

'Well, there's no way we're doing that. But won't that give them an edge in terms of speed?'

'Not really. Either way, we're walking from here on in. The Wilderness is rocky and treacherous; a horse will break a leg before too long in there, and that causes unwanted attention.'

'Let me handle the negotiations,' said Soren. 'Clarin, just look scary and don't speak.'

'Righto, boss.'

They guided their horses downhill through the trees until they saw the roofs of Hallaf's Home below them.

As they got closer, Belwynn got a clearer look at the settlement. She had never seen anything quite like it. Each building was constructed from a variety of the timber materials that surrounded them. They had their choice of tree around here: tall, thin birch grew alongside sprawling ash; mighty oaks shared the land with squat maples. In addition, each building had a completely unique design. There was a sunken hut with four wings, laid out in the shape of a cross. There was a U-shaped construction with a garden in the open courtyard. A tall, thin building, which from the outside looked as if it must have had at least four storeys, had a spiral staircase on the outside leading to the roof. At the far end was a vast building which most closely resembled a warehouse and was the size of all the others put together. There were a dozen of these oddities in all. It looked to Belwynn like everyone had taken part in a building competition. And that they had all got steaming drunk beforehand.

There was no central courtyard or anywhere to head to, so Gyrmund stopped outside the U-shaped house and dismounted. The others followed suit. Belwynn could see how stiffly Elana moved as she tried to dismount, and she gave her a hand down.

'Sore legs?' asked Belwynn.

'I've never ridden so much in my life,' said Elana.

The priestess rubbed at her hamstrings and her lower back. She eased up and stretched, visibly looser.

'Magical powers?' asked Belwynn.

'Healing powers.'

Belwynn wasn't about to be converted by watching someone stretch their back out.

'Mmm. Excuse me if I'm sceptical.'

She looked around her. Slowly, and silently, the residents of Hallaf's Home emerged. Some from their homes, some from the surrounding forest. Adult males for the most part, teenagers through to older men. Many clutched axes, no doubt ready to use them as weapons if necessary, but not threateningly. Not yet, anyway.

A few children came out as well, followed by one older woman with straggly, matted grey hair and eyes that wandered about independently of one another.

The men all had the same look to them, so it was easy to believe they were all related in some way. They had big, powerful shoulders, slightly hunched forwards; prominent brows and foreheads, with big bushy beards covering the rest of their faces. No-one in Hallaf's Home seemed to worry too much about their appearance, with worn and mismatched clothing the norm, where there was any. Most of the men went bare chested; their body hair was apparently all they needed to keep them warm.

Hold me back, Belwynn said to Soren, unable to resist. *I think I've finally found a flock of suitors.*

The people of Hallaf's Home gathered around the house, not too close, saying nothing, neither to Belwynn's group nor to each other. *Perhaps they're mute,* thought Belwynn.

Then the door of the U- shaped house opened, and an elderly man appeared and slowly walked towards them. He was grey and balding on top, with a straggly grey beard. As he approached them, Belwynn saw that he had a patch of raw, red, mottled skin on his face, centred around the left side of his forehead and spreading outwards in an irregular pattern, down to his cheek and the top of his nose. It was an infection, eating into the man's face, stopping the wounds from healing over. And whatever little creatures were doing it, they were really messy eaters.

'Hallaf,' said Gyrmund, nodding in greeting. 'I am Gyrmund. I have visited with you before, you may remember.'

'Yeffin, reckon y'hav,' said the old man. His dialect, if that was the issue, made his words virtually unintelligible.

'This is Soren,' Gyrmund explained.

'Greetings, Hallaf,' Soren began. 'We are heading into the Wilderness and have come to sell you our six horses. As you can see, they are all healthy and strong.'

Hallaf shuffled over and made a show of inspecting each one, though it was clear as day that they were all fine horses in excellent condition.

'Yeffin,' he muttered, presumably in confirmation.

Belwynn raised her eyebrows at Clarin. He just shrugged back, equally bemused.

'Here is my offer,' continued Soren. 'You will pay us only sixty crowns for the horses—'

'Yeffin!' screeched the old woman, shooting one arm up into the air in apparent celebration.

'But,' continued Soren, giving the woman a stern look, which made her lower her arm again, 'you will keep them in as good a condition as you have received them, for half a year. Should we return at any time in that period, we are entitled to buy them back from you, at a total cost of one hundred and eighty crowns. If we do not return before half a year has passed, they are yours to do with as you please. Do you understand my terms?'

'Aye, yeffin I do,' said old Hallaf, and he spat onto his palm before holding it out to Soren.

Belwynn could see Soren look from the wet palm to the sticky red face.

'That won't be necessary,' he informed Hallaf. 'One more thing that you all should know—' Soren addressed the entire community formally, raising his voice. 'I am a spell-caster, and I wreak dire vengeance on anyone who doesn't uphold their side of a bargain.'

Soren held out one hand, concentrating. Hallaf's people watched.

Then, his hand burst into flame, orange and yellow light flickering. With a twist of his wrist, the flame went out. His hand was unharmed.

The old woman let out a blood-curdling scream, while the men who had gathered around took a step or two back, suitably intimidated, it seemed. All except one child, who politely clapped.

Gyrmund turned and looked up the hill they had come down.

'Anyone hear that?'

Belwynn listened. She couldn't hear anything, and neither could anyone else.

'Riders,' he said, sounding sure.

That was enough for Clarin, who drew his sword and moved to face the threat. Gyrmund strung his bow. Hallaf's people followed suit, handling axes and clubs and looking in that direction.

Then Belwynn heard it—horses coming their way at quite a pace. Then they burst into view atop the hill, slowing as their mounts picked their way down through the trees.

'Herin!' called Clarin, waving up at his brother.

The old woman gave another blood-curdling scream, for no apparent reason.

There were three other riders with him: Kaved and Moneva, their new recruits from Vincente's town, and a second Krykker. At first, Belwynn assumed it was a friend of Kaved's—then she recognised him.

'Is that Rabigar? The smith from Bidcote?' she asked Soren out loud.

Soren peered up. His eyesight wasn't as sharp as hers after his years squinting at books in bad light.

'Yes, it is,' he agreed as they approached. 'Looks like he's brought half his merchandise with him, as well.'

Indeed, Belwynn could see various weapons poking out of their saddle-bags. She knew Herin had a silver tongue, but she was surprised to see he'd persuaded Rabigar to come. Still, she had little doubt that he was a resourceful man to have along.

The arrivals immediately brought a new energy and volume to Hallaf's Home.

'More women!' exclaimed Kaved as he approached, leering unpleasantly at Belwynn and Elana.

'I've been trying to understand why he thinks anyone would be interested in an ugly, lecherous, foul-smelling Krykker for over a day now, but I'm still none the wiser,' Moneva said, smoothly sliding from her mount to the ground. 'No offence, Rabigar.'

Rabigar rolled his eyes, as if he had endured enough already. 'I must be mad to have agreed to this,' he said, with little humour in his voice.

Unlike Moneva, he struggled to dismount, dropping to the ground with a clank.

Herin was already down, clasping arms with his brother.

'Did you get my directions?' Clarin asked.

'Yes, and each time I saw one, I thought to myself, 'more pissing about'. I thought you lot would have made better time than this!'

'Did you get my note?' asked Soren, looking a bit put out.

'Erm, yes. I had a read of it while we were following Clarin's directions.'

Clarin gave a self-satisfied smile.

'At least we treated our horses well. Look at these poor creatures!' said Belwynn.

Each of the four horses was in a lather and blowing hard.

'We're in a rush, aren't we?' demanded Herin. 'What's the story here?'

'I've just sold our horses to Hallaf, here,' explained Soren, gesturing to the old man who was looking on with interest.

'Ours, too!' Herin said, barging over to Hallaf. 'How much are we getting?'

'We want you to buy these at the same price,' explained Soren. 'That makes it one hundred crowns for the ten horses.'

'Nah, nuffin doin' on that,' replied Hallaf. 'Sixty for the ten, it be.'

'Nuffin!' shouted the old woman in support.

'We're offering ten prime horses for a hundred crowns, and he's saying no?' demanded Herin. 'Fine, we'll leave and take the lot with us.'

Herin made a play of walking off with his horse, which soon changed Hallaf's mind. The old man was getting a bargain, and everyone knew it.

'Eh, eh, not too fast,' he got out, panicking that he might lose the whole deal. 'Money's coming. Hallaf's good as his word.'

Hallaf went back in to his house and, after some time, re-emerged with a bag of money. When Gyrmund checked it, he was some crowns short of the hundred, and he was sent back in to get the right amount.

'What in hell are we doing messing about with these inbreds?' demanded Herin, chafing to get moving. They had all unloaded their packs from the horses and were standing about, ready to go. 'We're losing time here!'

'Shh!' hissed Belwynn. She really didn't want to get into a fight with Hallaf's sons, who were still standing around, weapons in hand.

Eventually, the old man re-emerged and handed over the money.

'Right, let's get moving,' said Herin.

'One more thing, before we go,' said Elana.

She approached Hallaf.

'You have helped us today, Hallaf. The Goddess Madria would bestow a blessing on you, to ease your suffering.'

The priestess reached out to the old man. He took a step back at first but, looking at her curiously, allowed her to place both hands on his face. Belwynn cringed at the thought of touching those weeping injuries.

Elana held her hands in position for some time, and then withdrew them.

There was an obvious visible difference. The redness was gone, as if the infection had been drawn out. The damage to the skin was still visible, but it looked like an old wound that would scar over and heal.

Elana stepped away.

Hallaf blinked with wide eyes, touching his hands to his face as if he couldn't believe what had happened. The men of the settlement, presumably many of whom were his sons, walked over to him, equally astounded, peering and prodding at the old man. The old woman tottered over, squinting up at him. She drew in a breath, and Belwynn thought she was going to let out another scream, but instead a tight breath escaped from her throat and that was it.

'Thanking you, lady. Thanking you,' said Hallaf, his voice wavering and tears in his eyes.

It was a moving sight. Toric only knew how much irritation and suffering the man had endured. His family gathered around him, clearly happy for the father of their community.

Elana held up her hands.

'Please. Thank Madria; *she* healed you. I am just her channel.'

She turned around and returned to the group.

'Still sceptical, Belwynn?' she asked.

Elana had a funny expression on her face, like a young girl's *I told you so*. It made Belwynn smile.

'That was really impressive, Elana,' said Soren.

'Yep, you don't see that every day,' added Moneva.

'Well,' said Elana, 'as I said, Madria has given me these powers.'

'Good for Madria,' snapped Herin. 'But are we going to leave now?'

'Yeffin,' said Belwynn.

'What?' demanded Herin, as everyone left Hallaf's Home, Gyrmund in the lead. 'What the hell does that mean?'

Clarin slapped his brother on the back, chuckling. 'Herin, you had to be there.'

CREATURES THAT COME OUT AT NIGHT

VII

They travelled on foot in a south-easterly direction to reconnect them to the route taken by the Brasingians, and it didn't take long to find it. The trail they had left was now so obvious that Belwynn could have followed it by herself. Twenty horsemen in single file had thrashed through the forest floor, churning the ground and ripping plants, not to mention horse dung here and there. After a while there were footprints as well as hoof prints, meaning they had stopped riding and were walking their mounts. This was hardly surprising; they had entered difficult terrain.

The trees closed in on them and blocked the sunlight, making it much cooler. Thorns, sprouting from the forest floor, scratched them and got stuck in clothing. The ground underfoot was uneven and sloped up and down, tiring out Belwynn's thigh muscles as she pushed up and straining her ankles as she manoeuvred down. She was fearful of turning an ankle, but Gyrmund kept up a severe pace as he tried to make up time on his quarry. He knew which direction they were going in, and would take them on a shorter or easier route when possible to make up time, always keeping in touch with the trail they had left. As he went he gave warnings about this or that hazard, and they got passed down the line. Other than that, there was no talking—just the sound of breathing from the exertion.

It didn't help that, thanks to Rabigar, they had become a walking weapons arsenal. Belwynn presumed that he and Herin had organised the weapons for everyone, and she had no doubt they might be needed. But in this environment, they made the going even tougher.

Belwynn had a light sword that allowed her to swing and thrust without losing balance. She was no fighter, but she had sparred plenty of times with Clarin and Herin, who had taught her the basics. Herin's sword was much bigger; he used it two-handed and liked to fight with speed. He also carried a seax in his belt and had a bow, coloured black with charcoal. His brother Clarin preferred to use sword and shield. His size and power, however, meant that he could use a sword that was almost the same weight as Herin's with only one arm. Rabigar was the other member of the group who favoured fighting with a sword and shield. Kaved had a sword and hand axe. Both Krykkers wore metal armour on their arms and legs, complementing the hard scales that grew on their torsos. Moneva wore a short sword on each hip. Gyrmund carried sword and bow. Dirk carried a mace, a favourite weapon of the Order of Toric. Soren and Elana carried no visible weapons and were not expected to fight.

They looked the part, and there were some very experienced fighters in the group. But they had never fought as a unit, and Belwynn knew they would struggle to face up to Salvinus and his twenty veterans. In that situation, they'd have to hope that Soren could tip the odds in their favour.

Gyrmund called a halt, and Belwynn peered forwards from her position in the line. It looked like they had come to a clearing. Gyrmund looked around, perhaps fearful of an ambush. Signalling for them to stay where they were, he moved into the clearing, studying the ground, walking a circuit around it. He walked off into the trees on the other side for a small distance, then came back again, gesturing for everyone to enter the clearing.

'We'll have a brief rest here,' he said.

'Thank the gods,' said Moneva, dumping her pack on the ground. 'I hate this place. Why did you bring me here?' she asked Herin accusingly.

'It'll do you good to get some fresh air,' he suggested. 'How are we doing then, Gyrmund?'

Their guide made a face. 'I don't like it. This is where our friends said goodbye to their horses. Vossi tracks come from that direction, to the east. They came here and took the horses, but they were handed over to them.'

'Handed over?' asked Soren.

'I mean both groups were here at the same time. The vossi didn't arrive later. It can't have been an accident; it all looks pre-arranged. Which is worrying.'

'Why?' demanded Herin.

'If Salvinus has an arrangement with a vossi tribe, they could be hostile towards us.'

'What would the vossi do with the horses?' asked Belwynn.

Gyrmund shrugged. 'Eat them, probably. Or sacrifice them.'

'Sacrifice, then eat them,' said Soren.

'Better than riding on the fucking things,' said Kaved.

'Could they have a vossi guide?' asked Rabigar.

Gyrmund shrugged. 'It's possible. I've never heard of vossi doing that before.'

'Any good news?' asked Moneva petulantly.

'Well, they spent some time here, maybe waiting for the rendezvous. We've made up a bit of time on them now. We're three to four hours behind, I would say. They set off in that direction, to the north-east; as we would expect, they're heading for the Empire. They'll be spending the night in the Wilderness. We need to move on a bit more and then find somewhere to make camp ourselves.'

Gyrmund kept them going in the half-light, keen to use his knowledge of the terrain to keep moving after the Brasingians had most likely stopped for the day.

By the time he called a halt, Belwynn was exhausted. All she wanted to do was go straight to sleep, and most of the others seemed set on the same idea. However, as she got ready, she realised how hungry she was, and she lay there, exhausted, watching Gyrmund and the others get a fire going and then put some pans on it. Eventually, he handed out bowls of stew, and she sat up, spooning the hot food into her mouth with her fingers as quickly as she could.

'Now this is good stuff!' Clarin congratulated Gyrmund. Even Dirk mumbled an appreciation.

'So, Elana. That was some impressive magic you used earlier,' said Soren. 'How long have you been able to do that?'

'For a few months now. I wouldn't call it magic, though.'

'A few months?' he repeated.

Belwynn understood what her brother was thinking. He had studied and practised for years, to the point of obsession, to develop his powers. And she had learned to do that in a few months?

'Not magic?' asked Belwynn, intrigued.

'I'm not a wizard, like your brother. I am a vessel; my powers were given to me by Madria. I think it is very different.'

Belwynn nodded. She was still finding it difficult to get her head round the idea of the goddess in all of that.

'And Rabigar. What made you leave Bidcote and your smithy for this?' asked Soren.

The Krykker thought about the question. 'For this?' he said, gesturing at the surrounding Wilderness with a wry smile, 'I have no idea. But I have been an exile from my homeland for many years now, Soren. When you are told that you cannot have something, it makes you want it all the more, am I right?'

'Oh, yes,' said Kaved, grinning. 'When a girl says no, for instance?'

Rabigar looked at Kaved with distaste. Belwynn had been too preoccupied to notice before, but even though they were both Krykkers, their relationship seemed strained.

'I've travelled around the lands of Dalriya for many years now, and when I find a place which lets me live in peace, I settle down. After a while, however, I realise how unhappy I am, and that I do not truly have a home. So I pack up and move on again. The smithy is in good hands; my apprentice Ulf has taken it over. Prince Edgar has been very kind to me, but I do not think I shall return to Magnia.'

'Perhaps you felt moved to leave because you have been chosen, Rabigar,' said Elana in a soft voice. 'Perhaps we have all been chosen, in our own ways, and given a purpose.'

'We Krykker are a practical people, lady. We do not think in such mysterious ways.'

'That is not to say they are not true,' answered the priestess.

'Ha,' barked Kaved. 'Good luck converting Rabigar Din to your religion, sweetheart.'

'What does Din mean?' asked Belwynn. She had only ever heard Rabigar addressed by his first name.

Kaved looked at Rabigar, who didn't look happy.

'You better tell 'em now you've said it,' said the Krykker bladesmith darkly.

'It's not a bad name,' answered Kaved. 'Krykkers have their hierarchies to maintain, and the number of letters in your name denotes your status. Din is a peasant's name. When Rabigar was exiled, he was also stripped of his status—his old name gone, and when speaking of him we are supposed to use the name 'Din'. Those of us with some sympathy call him Rabigar Din.'

Rabigar had been a familiar figure to Belwynn while growing up. Everyone knew about the Krykker bladesmith. They knew he was an exile.

And they knew never to ask him why. Kaved was getting very close to the subject, and Belwynn felt uncomfortable and intrigued at the same time.

'I don't suppose you've told anyone about the reasons for your exile?' Kaved asked Rabigar, grinning.

'No,' said Rabigar.

He wasn't smiling, and the atmosphere was becoming strained. Kaved, however, seemed unconcerned. 'Well, don't worry. Your secret's safe with me.'

'You have the advantage over me,' said Rabigar slowly. 'I don't know what you've done.'

'I do, don't I?' replied Kaved, a smirk still playing on his face.

'What about you, Kaved?' asked Belwynn, trying to turn the conversation around. 'Were you given a peasant's name?'

'Oh, no such excitement for me. I'm from simple warrior stock. No, my reasons for leaving weren't so special. You could say I have a problem with authority. I prefer to make my own decisions.'

'I'll drink to that,' said Herin.

The tension around the fire eased somewhat, and people began bedding down for the night after an exhausting day. Belwynn knew she would sleep immediately.

'We'll have to keep a watch, tonight,' said Gyrmund. 'It's vital. I'll go first.'

Belwynn cringed at the idea of staying awake alone during the night in this place. She closed her eyes and hoped that the men would do it, feeling guilty as she did.

'No, you've worked hard today and we'll need you to be alert tomorrow,' said Rabigar. 'You sleep through. I'll take first watch.'

'Wake me next,' offered Clarin. 'I'll wake up the loudest snorer.'

Not me, thought Belwynn, relaxing a little.

'Are there creatures in here, that come out at night?' asked Moneva after a pause.

'Most of the creatures in the Wilderness are nocturnal,' said Gyrmund. 'You've got all your usual rodents—'

'Wait,' interrupted Moneva. 'Please, forget I asked. I don't want to know. I really don't want to know.'

BELWYNN WAS WOKEN by Soren crouching over her.

We've got visitors, he explained.

Belwynn immediately got up and picked up her possessions. She didn't need to be told that these 'visitors' would not be friendly. *Where are they?* she asked her brother.

Herin says there is a group heading straight this way from the north—he doesn't know how many, but they're close.

Everyone was up and ready to leave. Gyrmund silently beckoned them to follow him in an easterly direction, while Herin and Clarin brought up the rear. The group was kept to a slow pace by the darkness and the need for silence. Soon, however, they heard screams coming from the direction of their night's camp.

'Vossi!' warned Gyrmund. 'We'll have to run for it!'

More and more screams came from behind them, and Belwynn felt sick as she realised what the numbers of vossi on their trail must be.

There's got to be an entire tribe of them out there! she said to Soren as they tried to keep up with Gyrmund.

Before her brother could reply, however, Belwynn tripped over a snag in the forest floor and hurtled face-first into the ground. Soren stopped to pick her up. But by the time the twins were on the move again, Herin and Clarin had caught up with them and urged them on faster.

Belwynn looked behind her and immediately wished she hadn't.

The vossi were plainly visible in the distance. The trees seemed to crawl with them in every direction as they gave chase, screaming at each other, or maybe at their quarry. They all had the same brown, bark-like skin and were running at full pelt towards them. She could make out small weapons glinting in the dark, spears and daggers, weapons that didn't slow down their pursuit, unlike the swords and shields that her companions carried. Belwynn's quick glance was enough to tell her that the vossi were gaining on them. She smiled bitterly as she realised the tables had been turned—the hunters were now the hunted. Gyrmund was taking them in the opposite direction to Salvinus. In an instant, their plans had disappeared.

The pace of the chase began to take its toll on the Magnians as they became tired and ragged. Elana was finding it difficult to keep up and was being helped along by Rabigar. Belwynn's lungs felt like they were going to burst, but fear kept her moving. She heard whistling sounds from behind them and turned to see vossi missiles hurtling towards them. Thankfully, they were falling short of their target, for now.

After heading in a north-easterly direction for some time, Gyrmund tried to change tack and take them north-west. There were vossi there, however, and a shower of missiles forced him to return to his original course.

Herin ran up to speak to Gyrmund. 'We've got to do something! We're going to end up trapped or walk straight into an ambush!'

'I know. I'm working on it.'

'Well, hurry! We don't have much longer. I'm going to buy you some time,' Herin said, returning to his position at the back with his brother.

Belwynn watched as Herin shouted in Clarin's ear. The two brothers stopped running and took shelter behind a large tree.

As Clarin hefted his shield off his back, Herin grabbed his longbow and took an arrow from his quiver. Drawing the string back to his chest, he released the bolt at the nearest vossi. It managed to dive out of the way, but Herin was already releasing his second arrow at another of the vossi, and this one struck its target full in the chest. The brothers' move succeeded in temporarily halting the chasing pack, who stopped to fire their own missiles. Clarin, however, was ready for this, and used his shield to protect both himself and his brother from the long-range attacks. Herin released a few more shots at the enemy, but their position became increasingly precarious as more vossi came into view every second.

Meanwhile, the others had stopped once they had gained a safe distance, and Belwynn watched with increasing foreboding. Kaved must have been doing the same; he now ran back toward the brothers. Belwynn turned to look at Soren, but he was in deep conversation with Gyrmund and Rabigar, while the others were, like her, desperately trying to catch their breath.

The number of missiles raining down on the brothers was now unmanageable, and Clarin was slowly retreating, holding the shield in front of him to stop the darts, spears, knives and other weapons hitting flesh, moving from one clump of trees to the next. At the same time, the vossi had become bolder, and a small group charged at the brothers, both of whom drew their swords. The longer reach of the brothers allowed them to swing their weapons and connect with the vossi enemy. Herin leapt back out of reach of the retaliatory blows, while Clarin used his shield to further effect and stopped any of the vossi breaching his defence.

Kaved had now reached the conflict after running at full speed towards them. 'Run!' he shouted at the brothers as he let his charge carry him into the vossi, sword and axe both twirling about him.

'Move it!' shouted Gyrmund, seeing Herin's stand fall apart. Belwynn forced herself to turn away from what was happening behind them and followed Gyrmund's lead. He was taking them in the same north-easterly direction as before. Her left ankle sent jolts of pain around her body every time she put her weight on it, and she realised she must have damaged it in her earlier fall. The adrenaline of the chase had masked the pain until now, but she was determined not to slow everyone else down and pressed on. Their brief rest had allowed several vossi who had been running parallel to the group to catch up with them, forcing them to head due east as more vossi missiles clattered into the surrounding trees.

Belwynn looked behind her and was relieved to see the figures of Herin, Clarin, and Kaved all sprinting in her direction, followed by the vossi, who now looked even more terrifying as they screamed out their challenges, intent on taking revenge for their fallen tribesmen.

Ahead of her, Gyrmund looked around frantically as he led the group on, trying to find a landmark amidst the endless backdrop of forest. He must have spotted what he was looking for, as he whirled round to speak to the rest of the group.

'Soren is going to cast a spell of protection over us so that the vossi can't reach us. He can only keep it going for a short while, so follow me closely and don't stop for anything. We're heading for a bridge.'

Belwynn let out a whimper as she forced herself to run again. Clarin must have overheard, as he gripped her under the arm and ran next to her, taking some of the weight off her ankle. 'I'm in the wars too,' he confided, and nodded down at his right leg, where a vossi dart was protruding from his thigh.

Belwynn would have asked after his injury, but she no longer had the breath for speech. Gyrmund's route was now leading them into the chasing vossi, who were already dispatching their missiles at him. Soren's magic was working, however, as the missiles which came into contact with his invisible barrier bounced away. Belwynn knew how much concentration and effort was required to keep the barrier effective and was relieved to see that Moneva had guessed as much: the mercenary was leading her brother through the maze of trees and other obstacles.

Gyrmund reached the waiting vossi. He and Rabigar began slicing into the creatures. The vossi couldn't break through the barrier, but they seemed quite able to send their weapons the other way. When Kaved moved up and joined in with the free hacking, the uneven nature of the contest forced the vossi to retreat out of the way, and Gyrmund led them on.

Belwynn sighed with relief as they began moving again. The vossi now surrounded them on every side, pressing in on them, trying to find a weakness in Soren's defences. She could see their faces clearly, painted with red dye, all scarred brown skin and dark eyes staring at her. They were sending killing blows straight for her, and only Soren's magic was stopping them from connecting. She felt panic rise within her and looked over at her brother, knowing that soon his powers would fade and they would be doomed; chopped to pieces here in the middle of this horrible forest. She wanted to communicate with him and ask how long he could carry on, but knew that it would just be a distraction for him.

When would they get to this damned bridge? The only thing keeping Belwynn sane was Clarin's tight grip on her, guiding her along and lending her his strength and confidence.

Then, suddenly, they were upon the bridge. It was a rickety looking thing, made of rope and wood, and Belwynn seriously wondered whether it was safe to cross. She did not for a moment, however, think of not attempting it—such was her desperation to leave their pursuers behind. Some vossi tried to prevent their passage, but Herin moved forward to attack along with the two Krykkers, and they were soon dispersed. The vossi were now totally disorganised—their quarry had turned back in on them and they had lost their shape, along with many warriors. They continued to scream at each other, but none of them seemed able to take charge of the situation.

Meanwhile, Gyrmund led the party across the river.

Elana balked at stepping onto the bridge and stared down at the fast-moving current of the river below. Dirk, however, grabbed her by the wrists with a look of wild panic on his face and dragged her onto the structure.

Clarin shoved Belwynn forward behind the priestess as he and his brother brought up the rear.

By the time Belwynn reached the other side of the bridge, Kaved and Rabigar were already cutting the rope and chopping the planks of wood which kept the bridge secured to their side of the riverbank. She leapt off the end of the bridge without looking back and ran to where the others had taken cover behind a copse of trees a few yards away.

The vossi were still shooting at them across the river, and Soren maintained his spell, the strain evident on his face. Belwynn peeked through the trees to see the two brothers and the two Krykkers sprinting away from the riverside in their direction. The bridge which had saved their lives was now floating on top of the water. On the other side of the river, the vossi screamed in frustration as those who had tried to follow the group across the bridge pulled themselves out.

Letting out a sigh of relief, Belwynn leaned over to speak to her twin. 'You can stop now, Soren. We're safe.'

THE STAND

VIII

As the group stopped to catch their breath and their bearings, Elana tended to the injured parties. She slid the dart out from Clarin's thigh and inspected the wound.

'It's poisoned,' she informed the warrior matter-of-factly.

Clarin frowned, the closest he came to showing any signs of concern. 'Will it be alright?' he asked.

'Yes,' replied the priestess confidently, and forced a finger into the hole made by the dart, wiggling it around inside. She then held her hand over the wound for some time, letting her healing powers flow into Clarin's leg.

'I wish I'd been hit by a dart,' leered Herin, leaning over to inspect Elana's handiwork.

'And not in the leg, either,' joined in Kaved.

Belwynn couldn't appreciate their banter so soon after their near-death experience. Her body was still shaking uncontrollably, and she just hoped that no-one else would notice.

Elana left Herin to bandage up his brother's thigh and walked over to where Belwynn was sitting next to Soren.

She distrusted the priestess. Soren was tired after his exertions, but he would recover, and Belwynn knew best how to look after him. After all, she had been looking after him since before she could remember. It wouldn't hurt to have Elana look at her own ankle, however, and she could examine the priestess's claims of healing powers at the same time.

'Soren is fine,' Belwynn informed her, 'he just needs to rest.'

Elana nodded in acceptance. 'Shall I look at your ankle, then? I noticed you hobbling.'

'Yes, please, Elana.'

The priestess knelt in front of Belwynn and took hold of her left foot, resting it in her lap. The ankle was throbbing. Belwynn doubted whether she could walk on it for some time and feared holding back the rest of the group.

Elana massaged the ankle. At first, Belwynn had to grit her teeth in pain, but gradually she felt her muscles relaxing and the ankle becoming more flexible. As Elana's hands pressed into the ankle, she could feel a sensation of warmth entering ligament and muscle, restoring the damaged tissue. When she was satisfied that her work was done, Elana bandaged up the ankle, giving it support without putting too much pressure on the injury.

Belwynn had to admit, to herself, that the priestess had done a good job.

'Are you able to walk?' asked Gyrmund, putting the question to Soren and Belwynn.

'They need to rest,' Elana answered for them.

'We've got to move,' he replied. 'Those vossi are of the red-face tribe. It wouldn't surprise me if they have made a deal with Salvinus—and even if they haven't, they'll still be after us, and they know exactly where we are. We've got to put some distance in now or it will be too late.'

Belwynn was well aware of the situation they were in. 'I can walk,' she said. She looked over at her brother, who gave her a nod, apparently too tired to speak. 'Soren can, too, but he'll need some help.'

Help was forthcoming, as Clarin and Herin put Soren's arms over their shoulders and grabbed him around the waist. He barely had to carry any of his own weight—just concentrate on putting one foot in front of the other. Gyrmund and Rabigar led the party off, while Kaved guarded the rear. Belwynn stayed close to her brother, anxious for him, yet relieved that he could keep up with the hard pace that was being set.

Gyrmund tried to put as much distance between the group and the broken bridge as possible, but it wasn't long before the vossi reappeared. They were moving in small clusters of two or three, spreading out across the Wilderness, renewing their hunt. One call would soon bring the red-face tribe back on their trail. Whenever Gyrmund heard them approaching—for it always seemed to be Gyrmund who heard them first—he directed everyone to the nearest hiding place to the side of the track. He would then slither off to investigate and return when the vossi had moved on.

As time went by, the vossi came more and more regularly, halting the group's progress. Gyrmund began to leave the others in a secure place for a few minutes at a time while he scouted the area up ahead.

On one such occasion, while Belwynn was making Soren and herself eat something, Herin spotted a group of three vossi heading their way. A whispered warning spread through the group. Swords and knives were drawn in anticipation of conflict. The three vossi were threading their way through the thick foliage of the forest, apparently talking to each other in their high-pitched language. It looked like they had found their tracks.

The vossi continued to move towards them. Herin and the others were confident enough of dealing with them should the group be spotted, but the real danger was that the calls of these three scouts would bring the whole red-face tribe down on them again. Herin began swearing at the absent Gyrmund, but he was not going to save them from this situation.

Moneva interrupted the warrior's list of hissed expletives. 'We're going to have to deal with them before they spot us.'

Herin seemed to muse over their options, but eventually nodded his agreement.

'The rest of you stay here for the time being. Moneva, you swing round to their right and I'll take the left.'

Herin drew his seax and began crawling off in the vossi's direction. Moneva reached down to her right calf where she had a knife of her own attached to her leather trousers. As she unsheathed it, Belwynn noticed it was an unusually thin weapon which ended in an extremely sharp point.

Herin and Moneva soon slid out of sight. As Belwynn concentrated on their movements, she noted that neither was as quiet or mobile as Gyrmund in these conditions.

As the seconds went by, Belwynn and the others strained their eyes and ears, trying to fathom out where the two of them were. The three vossi continued to make their way towards them in a roundabout direction, and Belwynn almost felt sorry for the enemy that had almost scared her witless earlier in the day, knowing that they were totally oblivious to the fact that two trained killers were at this very minute stalking them in the undergrowth.

It happened so suddenly that Belwynn almost shouted out loud with shock.

As the vossi continued to make their search of the area, two black blurs of movement erupted upwards from the undergrowth on either side and darted towards them.

Moneva attacked a split second before Herin did. From Belwynn's point of view, it looked as if she didn't even make contact with her first victim. Before the corpse tumbled to the floor, she reversed the swing of her first strike and drove the sharp point of the blade into the throat of the second vossi, who had not been able to react to the speed of the attack.

Herin, meanwhile, had approached from the opposite angle and grabbed the mouth of the third vossi from behind, ensuring that no noises escaped from his victim as he deliberately and carefully slit its throat. As the bodies of the vossi fell to the ground, so too did those of the killers. Within a matter of seconds, it was over, and the forest returned to peace, as if the deadly spectacle had never happened, but had been some figment of Belwynn's imagination.

It was some time before Gyrmund returned, and his extended absences always worried Belwynn, knowing as she did that it would be much easier for him to slip away alone than with nine other people. Thoughts of escape seemed to be far from his mind, however. 'I've found the trail,' he whispered, perhaps by way of explaining his long absence.

Belwynn had pushed Salvinus to the back of her mind since the flight from the vossi, almost giving up on them rediscovering the trail.

Gyrmund, on the other hand, had obviously kept his mind firmly on his quarry, leading them all not only away from the chasing vossi but back towards the Brasingians. Belwynn noted that surprise registered across the faces of many of the others, an involuntary admission that, like her, they had little idea of which part of the Wilderness they were in now, and were reliant on his expertise.

Herin was not about to admit such a weakness. 'How far behind are we now?', he demanded.

If Gyrmund detected any hostility in Herin's voice, he ignored it. 'We're about four hours behind.' He paused for a moment. 'If we want to follow them, we're going to lay ourselves open to the vossi again. I'm sure that they know that we're after Salvinus and they're taking special care to look in this area.'

Although spoken as a statement, Gyrmund was really asking them a question: were they prepared to risk the vossi again in order to catch up with the Brasingians?

Belwynn wasn't sure if she *was* prepared to risk the vossi again and turned to look at her brother.

Soren stared straight ahead. 'Take us to the trail, Gyrmund.'

As Gyrmund once again led the group through the forest, their spirits rose. Belwynn was no exception and was sure that, like her, the others felt glad to have regained a measure of control over the situation they were in. They were no longer simply running away from the vossi but were taking steps to recover the ground they had lost.

The person they had to thank was a rather enigmatic man. He had joined the group almost as an afterthought, but was now one of its most important members. The challenge of catching up with Salvinus seemed to have evolved into something of a personal test of Gyrmund's abilities, and he accepted the addition of the vossi into the melting pot with grim fortitude.

Belwynn moved up to the front of the line, where Gyrmund was keeping the group some feet away from the main track in an effort to hide them from the vossi scouts. 'How are we doing?' she enquired.

Belwynn studied Gyrmund's face as his eyes glanced towards her to acknowledge the question and then quickly returned to the forest scene, looking to the side, up in the trees and then ahead as he tried to make out forms in the shadows of a rocky outcrop. The man was in a constant state of vigilance, but it wasn't a strained or worried state; it seemed to be his natural way of doing things.

His eyes returned to Belwynn's. 'Not too bad.' He smiled grimly. 'It appears I underestimated this Salvinus. He's kept his group the same distance ahead of me since we left Bidcote.'

Bidcote, thought Belwynn. It seemed like an age since they had parted company with Edgar, but it had only been two days. 'Why did you decide to come with us, Gyrmund? Did Farred ask you to?'

'No. I make my own decisions. Farred is just a friend of mine.'

'How did you meet him?'

'We grew up together.'

'So, why did you decide to go on *this* expedition?' Belwynn persisted.

'Toric's balls, you like your questions, don't you?' Gyrmund admonished with a frown. He shrugged. 'I'm the best tracker around. I was the best person for the job, and the way things turned out, you wouldn't have had a chance without me.'

Belwynn let his arrogance pass, given that what he had said seemed to be the truth. 'But you knew more than everyone how dangerous it would be. It's hardly worth the risk of a bit of coinage or favour from Edgar to you.'

Gyrmund looked at her, as if it was for the first time. 'I'm not interested in Edgar's favour. As for the risk—look, you may be a cousin of Edgar's, but that doesn't mean that you, a woman, have to go charging into the Wilderness after twenty-odd soldiers, does it? The risk is why most of us are here, and why we kept up the chase with the Brasingians. To test ourselves. If we just cared about the money, I'm sure there are easier and safer ways to earn it.'

There was something in Gyrmund's words that disappointed her, though they were perhaps true enough. As they waited to get moving again, Belwynn thought about it, looking around at her companions. The risk, the challenge, the adventure. This was why Gyrmund was here, why Herin was here, even why Clarin and no doubt most of the others were, too. There were far easier and less life-threatening ways to earn money for people with their skill set than this chase through the Wilderness, that was for sure. Herin and Clarin could be highly rewarded by any number of ambitious noblemen or wealthy merchants for doing very little from one week to the next, but drink their host's wine. Instead, they put themselves in danger, to test themselves and hone their skills.

For Soren and herself, though, the danger had never been the attraction. It was the chance to put things right in a world where most things seemed to be wrong. Toric's Dagger didn't mean that much to her personally. But it was a symbol to their people—an ancient relic, plundered by a bunch of mercenaries. It hadn't been stolen on a whim, either; it had been a carefully conceived operation. The whole business felt threatening; even sinister.

Maybe she was just naïve. Maybe right and wrong didn't come into it that much. And then there had been the attempted robbery of Vincente a few days ago. Sure, he probably wasn't a very nice man. Yes, they needed the money. Badly. But since when had her brother use his powers simply to rob people? It seemed like, without her noticing, they had got lost; aimless. Belwynn was beginning to think she'd had enough of putting herself in these situations.

Gyrmund made a flapping motion with his hand, trying to get everyone to crouch down in the undergrowth, but it was already too late.

To their left, on the other side of the track they were following, he had spotted a couple of vossi. Unfortunately, the vossi had spotted them as well.

Hardly surprising, thought Belwynn, with all ten of them trudging through the forest.

At first the two vossi looked shocked and a little afraid at coming upon the enemy, but soon began screaming their find so that the noise carried through the Wilderness.

Gyrmund swore under his breath. He replaced his bow over his left shoulder, which he had presumably unfastened to silence their discoverers. Sure enough, the calls of the two vossi were being answered by the others of their tribe, and the forest around them erupted into high-pitched noise, which seemed to Belwynn to come from all directions.

'We're gonna have to move!' shouted Gyrmund, not waiting to see if people followed but running on ahead.

He took them down a bank and onto a new track, perhaps one made by the vossi or the animals of the Wilderness. Gyrmund's jog seemed as natural to him as walking, as if he could keep it up for hours without losing breath. For Belwynn to go at the same speed, however, sapped her energy and burnt her lungs. The two vossi made no attempt to interfere with their getaway, apparently content to wait for reinforcements. This didn't stop Herin from firing an arrow in their direction, which crashed harmlessly into the trunk of a tree. This aggression brought renewed screaming from the vossi, which only put Herin in a fouler mood than before.

They continued to run along the winding forest track as the red-face vossi behind them organised their chase. Before long they ran into vossi searching parties of two or three, but these did not tackle them alone, preferring to wait for reinforcements. They had obviously learned to fear Herin, Clarin, and the others as a result of the confrontation before the bridge—not prepared to risk joining the other vossi who had fallen under the Magnians' blades.

Soon, however, Belwynn could look behind them and see a large chasing pack of vossi, screaming and letting off the odd dart or stone in her direction.

Elana fell behind, and Belwynn could hear her fighting for breath as her body tried to pump enough air into her lungs to keep her moving.

Ahead, the stronger members of the group were separating from the slower runners. They had to stop, however, when six vossi emerged from the trees to the left to block their path on the track.

The danger was obvious: if they did not get past, and quickly, they would be caught by the vossi behind them.

Gyrmund and the others drew their weapons and charged the vossi. Fortunately, it was over in seconds. First one, then two, then all the vossi broke away and ran back to the safety of the trees. One lay dying on the ground, and others had received injuries, but none of Belwynn's companions had been hurt.

The brief melee had wasted valuable time, however. Gyrmund was searching the surrounding terrain, a look of anxiety plainly visible on his face.

What's he looking for? Belwynn asked her brother.

Somewhere to make a stand, came the reply. *We can't outrun them.*

A feeling of dread came over Belwynn, since it was plain that they couldn't outfight them, either. There were too many of them.

Soren grabbed her wrist. 'We're off!' he shouted.

Gyrmund had apparently made his decision and was taking them in the very direction from which the six vossi had attacked them. Flanked by Clarin and Herin, he made his way from the track into the forest.

The vossi backed away, albeit screaming their defiance.

Gyrmund pointed towards a mound, barely a hundred yards away, as he was talking to the two brothers.

As Belwynn followed on, she could make out Herin nodding his agreement at Gyrmund's proposition. Everyone made a dash for the point of defence. The vossi were now within missile range and their eagerness made them discharge whatever long-range weapons they had. Now that they were back in the forest proper, the trees gave them enough cover, and the group made it to the mound without injury.

Once there, Herin began shouting instructions to everyone for the defence of the mound.

Two large oak trees dominated the south-east side of the mound, facing the oncoming vossi. The central point of defence was between the two trees, and here Herin positioned himself, Clarin, and Gyrmund. Clarin, whose large shield could defend from missile attack, stood in the centre. Herin and Gyrmund stood either side of him, able to use the trees as shelter if necessary, with a good view of the approaching vossi, in order to use their longbows to best effect. On the other side of Gyrmund's tree, to his right, Herin had positioned Moneva, and next to her was Kaved. His job was to prevent the vossi coming from the flank. Such a task was more than difficult considering the numbers of the enemy. To Herin's left stood Dirk, waiting in the shadows of the tree, and next to him was Rabigar, who had the same job as Kaved. Herin had asked Belwynn, Soren, and Elana to stand behind this line of seven, further up the mound, and to intervene wherever needed.

The mound was in a small clearing in the forest, and as the vossi approached, they stopped short of entering the clearing, preferring to gather in the trees beyond it. Now that Belwynn and the others had stopped running and made their stand, the vossi seemed more agitated than ever. They seemed more confused than aggressive.

Why are they acting so strange? Belwynn asked Soren.

I think we might have stumbled onto one of their burial mounds. They seem nervous about coming closer, although it looks like they're beginning to overcome any doubts.

Some of the vossi leaders had now appeared on the scene and were screaming orders at their soldiers, but the whole approach to the mound seemed very disorganised.

Still, they're in no rush, thought Belwynn, and it was her companions who would feel the nerves as time went by and the ranks of the vossi continued to swell.

Individual vossi were now running into the clearing and approaching the mound, screaming their defiance before backing away again. Herin and the others kept to their positions as the bizarre antics of the vossi continued. One of the braver vossi exposed his genitals to those present on the mound before returning to the safety of the trees on the outskirts of the clearing, to the apparent congratulations of his comrades. The success of this exploit provoked a spate of similar gestures and taunts amongst the vossi.

What are they doing now? asked Belwynn, unsure whether to be intimidated or amused.

I don't know, replied Soren, sounding equally bewildered. *They might be trying to provoke us into attacking them, but surely, they don't think we're that stupid.*

The vossi tactics were now challenged by Herin who, evidently getting bored with the impasse, fired an arrow straight at one of the demonstrating vossi, striking it full in the chest; the creature keeled over in the middle of the clearing. Herin quickly grabbed another bolt and pulled back the string of his bow, threatening to repeat the attack. This gesture caused the clearing to empty again as the vossi retreated to the treeline.

The screaming amongst the vossi now resumed, and soon large numbers were being pushed forwards towards the mound. A barrage of missiles descended upon the defenders as they were forced to take cover behind the two oak trees. Belwynn, Soren, and Elana knelt as stray stones hurtled in their direction. Clarin also knelt and, rather than using a tree as cover, he placed his body behind his shield. This seemed to invite attack, and the vast majority of missiles were now raining down on the large warrior as the vossi sought to penetrate his defence. However, the vossi had used many of their long-range weapons already this day, and they did not seem to have either the amount of ammunition or the skill to get past Clarin's shield.

From the cover of the trees, Herin and Gyrmund now shot back at the vossi. They picked off their targets without putting themselves in too much danger. Herin had an upright style, pulling the string to his chest and looking around before he let go. Gyrmund pulled his string all the way back to his ear, carefully aiming the flight of his arrow so that he was as accurate and deadly as possible.

It wasn't long before the vossi leaders realised the missile contest wasn't getting them anywhere and screamed new orders to their troops. The vossi stopped shooting altogether, and a short period of silence followed, interrupted by the hard *twang* of Herin and Gyrmund's bow strings as they continued to take advantage of the sitting targets.

Then, one by one, the vossi screamed their defiance to those on the mound until every single warrior joined in the chorus.

'Prepare yourselves,' shouted Herin above the cacophony.

As the words left his mouth, the vossi charged. It was a disorganised mess, since many of them didn't seem sure which part of the mound they should attack, but it was a frightening sight, nonetheless. Herin and Gyrmund had a few seconds to release their last arrows before discarding their bows and drawing their swords.

The vossi reached the centre of the mound first. Once they were only a few yards away, Clarin led a counter-charge into the enemy. Shouting twice as loudly as any of the vossi, he used his shield as a battering weapon, shoving it into the vossi at face height and then bringing his sword over his shoulder in a high arc so that it crashed down into his chosen victim with such force that it almost cleaved it in two.

Herin and Gyrmund followed his move, slashing into the vossi with speed and strength while retaining enough manoeuvrability to dodge the returned blows. The vossi who had reached the mound first now looked like they regretted it, but the ranks behind them pushed them onwards, forcing the three defenders to back away to their original places in between the two great oaks. This was no bad thing, since the vossi could no longer outflank Herin or Gyrmund, but had to come at them face on.

In the meantime, more of the vossi had reached the two sides of the mound. To Belwynn's right, Moneva was parrying and defending her position on the other side of Gyrmund's oak tree, while Kaved was hacking and slashing at the vossi with sufficient aggression to keep them at bay. Belwynn turned her attention to the left, where the vossi were just reaching Rabigar and Dirk. As the first vossi approached, Dirk took an enormous back-swing with his mace and aimed a blow. The weapon connected powerfully with the face of its target, leaving the vossi in a crumpled heap on the floor, its head lolling at a strange angle away from the rest of its body. Unfortunately, the force of Dirk's blow was so powerful that it pitched him forwards, and, as the next vossi came towards him, he didn't have enough time to pull back the mace to defend himself from the blow.

The vossi thrust a wicked looking blade towards Dirk's midriff and the best the priest could do was to twist his body away and try to avoid the impact. He could not escape the blow, however, as the vossi lunged forward and stabbed into his side.

The blade penetrated deeply, before the vossi withdrew the weapon, leaving a deep gash pouring with blood. Dirk staggered backwards, then collapsed to the ground. As the vossi stood to full height, the blade of Rabigar's sword sliced into its neck, killing it immediately. The Krykker swung his weapon in deadly circles, forcing the other vossi to back away as he inched forwards to stand over Dirk's body.

Belwynn rushed forward to help and grabbed Dirk under the arms, trying to hoist him further up the mound. Soren and Elana joined her, and between them they pulled the priest away to relative safety.

Elana began tending to Dirk, but it was clear to Belwynn that he was in a bad way. *Can't you use your defence spell again?* she pleaded to her brother as she watched Rabigar slowly being forced backwards by the vossi. The vossi had found themselves a weakness in the mound's defences, and although they rightly feared Rabigar's whirring blade, they also knew it was only a matter of time before they pulled him down.

I'll use it if I have to, Soren replied, *but it will run out eventually and then I'll have nothing left.*

'Then think of something!' Belwynn screamed aloud at her brother, before drawing her sword and rushing down the mound to help Rabigar. Belwynn immediately regretted her words: she shouldn't have handed all the responsibility over to Soren. They were all in this mess together, and shouting at each other wouldn't help—only cause panic. There was no time to apologise, however, as Belwynn gingerly entered the melee, prodding and then thrusting at the vossi, causing them to back off a little and giving Rabigar some time and space to regain a measure of control over the situation.

There was little the Krykker could do against such numbers, however, and Belwynn soon realised that one false move could result in a death blow from the vossi. As they swung and shoved their weapons towards her, Belwynn was forced to retreat up the mound, and Rabigar went with her, standing shoulder to shoulder. It seemed painfully obvious to Belwynn that the vossi could easily move round the bottom of the mound and climb it from the other side, surrounding the nine remaining defenders, but right now the vossi seemed too intent on striking at the nearest enemy to consider that.

As she gave more ground, Belwynn took a quick look around. She was now almost above Herin's position on the mound, and the vossi would soon attack him from the side. Belwynn realised that such an attack would spell the end of Herin's defensive ring, and she resolved to stand her ground and not give the vossi a further inch. Another quick look behind her and she saw that Kaved and Moneva were also being forced to give ground to the vossi, though they were not yet in quite so perilous a position. As she turned back, Belwynn was quick enough to see that one of the vossi had decided to end the deadlock.

It charged straight up the mound, heading for Belwynn. The whole attack lasted seconds, but for Belwynn it happened in slow motion: he vossi leapt towards her, spear held in front and aimed for her heart.

Belwynn's body seemed to react to the threat independently of her mind, primeval instinct taking over. Gripping the sword so that it angled downwards towards the tip, just as Clarin had made her grip it time after time until it was second nature, Belwynn took a stride with her left leg down the slope and knelt on her right knee whilst, in the same movement, extending her sword forwards. The vossi's spear passed harmlessly overhead, while its charge propelled it onto her blade, the sword slipping easily into its guts. Its momentum nearly knocked her over, but she had the strength to keep her kneeling position, shoving the creature onto the ground in front of her, its weapon dropping from its lifeless hand.

Belwynn wrenched at her own blade, which had become embedded deep into her attacker. It came free, bringing with it the stinking entrails of the slain vossi, but not quickly enough.

One vossi had followed up the attack and now dove towards Belwynn, its face contorted into a vicious snarl. Belwynn thought it must be too far away to reach her, but as it threw itself to the ground, the creature stabbed a knife into her foot.

The impact and pain of the injury threw her into a state of shock. It felt as though the knife had torn right through her foot and impaled her onto the mound. Belwynn looked up into the eyes of the vossi, its hand still gripping the handle of the knife with all its might.

Suddenly, from the corner of her right eye, Belwynn detected movement. Her stomach contracted with fear, but she forced herself to turn her head around to face what she expected to be her killer. Instead, all Belwynn saw was a blur streaking past her.

She followed its direction and saw Herin slamming his sword downwards into the prostrate vossi, then clashing one-handed with another vossi while his other hand felt at her foot. Herin removed the knife and then danced backwards, grabbing her around the chest and hurling her further up the mound. She looked up to see Clarin retreating up the mound towards her as he covered Herin's move. This forced Gyrmund to do the same, and as Belwynn scrambled backwards, everyone seemed to follow her, forming a tighter and tighter semi-circle.

Then, behind her, Belwynn heard an almighty scream, the scream of a vossi, yet so loud it didn't seem possible that it could belong to a single voice. Belwynn didn't feel like she could face any more, but she turned around and looked up to the centre of the mound where Soren was.

Or, at least, where Soren had been.

Soren, Elana and Dirk had now been replaced by a swirling distortion of light, a gaseous substance which seemed to take shape whilst emitting the enormous sound.

The shadowy form slowly came to resemble a face, vossi-like in its features, but with burning green eyes and a mouth that, as it opened and closed, let out a scream that must have been heard throughout the Wilderness. Belwynn could now make out what must be words in the vossi language, and she turned around to see what effect the apparition was having on their enemies.

The vossi had stopped their attack on the defenders and were staring up at the face, worry lines creasing their faces, occasional exchanged glances or words passing between them. Clarin and the others looked unsure how to react, nervously looking over their shoulders but keeping an eye on the vossi in case their attention was drawn back to the fight. The vossi were now in a state of confusion, but their leaders rallied their soldiers, shouting in their faces, hitting them and forcing them to renew their advance on the mound.

Just as this seemed to be working, the noise from behind Belwynn got louder, so loud that it hurt her ears, and she dropped her sword and covered them with her hands. The vossi did the same and backed away from the mound.

Then, a beam of light seemed to shine out from the apparition on the mound and strike the vossi warrior standing closest to Clarin.

For a moment, the figure of the vossi was lit up like a beacon, and then flames erupted from his clothing. The vossi struggled in the flames, writhing in agony, and Belwynn caught the smell of burning flesh in her nostrils. Those surrounding the vossi torch, a look of terror in their eyes, turned and ran from the sight. For a moment they met some resistance from their leaders, desperately trying to stop the rout, before every vossi warrior turned their back on the mound and ran, in every direction, into the forest.

As floods of relief overcame Belwynn, she turned around once more to look up at the mound. The image of the vossi face before her was now dissolving, and behind it she could make out the figure of Soren.

He stood facing her, arms outstretched, veins standing out, eyes rolling up into his head in convulsion with a visible streak of blood running from his nostrils.

As the last vestiges of the image disappeared, the convulsions stopped, and he collapsed onto the ground.

AFFLICTIONS

IX

Belwynn gave her foot one final look, marvelling at the scarred tissue that, moments before, had been a gaping wound. She shoved her shoe back on. Elana had dealt with all the injuries. She looked exhausted from the healing she had carried out. But two problems remained.

'They shouldn't be moved,' Elana informed Herin in a tired voice. 'It could cause permanent damage.'

Herin grimaced. Both Soren and Dirk lay unconscious. Soren had not woken since he had collapsed on the ground after the vossi had fled. Dirk had been awake at first, but in agony, crying out in pain: mostly unintelligible, mixed in with pleas for help. He asked for help from the gods, from his mother but, interestingly, not from Toric. After Elana had treated him, he had grown calmer and fallen asleep. Belwynn would have been quite happy to risk Dirk's health, since the priest had been of little help so far, and she knew Herin was thinking the same thing. The vossi had gone, but no-one knew if or when they would return.

No-one else had sustained any serious injuries, but they were all itching to get moving away from the bloody mound. The fact that Soren, who had probably just saved everyone's lives, was now seriously ill, kept them from departing the scene.

'We're going to have to build stretchers,' said Rabigar. 'We'll be able to move them a fair distance before nightfall. Then we can decide what to do in the morning.'

'Agreed,' said Belwynn quickly. She looked around at the group, but no-one disagreed with the plan, even if they wanted to.

'Well, now that's settled,' said Kaved, 'we'd better get a move on.'

The group wasted no more time as Rabigar and Kaved began hacking off adequately sized branches from the trees around the mound. Belwynn and Moneva picked up branches lying around the forest floor and collected those obtained by the Krykkers, bringing them to the centre of the mound, where Herin, Clarin and Gyrmund set about lashing them together to make platforms strong enough to carry the weight of the two men.

They worked quickly, and before long they were gingerly lifting the wizard and the priest onto the stretchers.

'How ill do you think he is?' Belwynn asked Elana.

The priestess pursed her lips. 'I don't know. His affliction seems to be more of the mind than of the body, and the powers that Madria has bestowed on me are not as effective in healing it.'

Belwynn nodded. 'I think the magic that he used on the mound was too great for him to control; he put too much into it. What with the magic he used to get us to the river as well—I don't think he had any energy left.'

'I've never seen anything like that before,' said Kaved with apparent sincerity in his voice.

Belwynn guessed that was the closest the Krykker ever came to saying *thank you,* and she smiled in recognition. The truth was, she hadn't seen Soren do anything like that before, either. It was a different magic to what he had learned from Ealdnoth. It was witch magic.

Gyrmund led the group off in a north-easterly direction while Herin and Clarin carried Soren's stretcher, and Rabigar and Kaved carried Dirk. It was slow going. Everyone was exhausted from the combat on the mound. The adrenaline from the fight had left Belwynn's body, and she felt empty and drained. By nightfall, however, they had covered enough ground to feel that they were a safe distance from the bloody scene, and with little conversation tried to make themselves comfortable on the forest floor. Belwynn lay next to her brother's prone body—still breathing, but dead to the world.

Eventually, she fell asleep.

* * *

PRINCE EDGAR WAS SITTING in his tent with Ealdnoth, his court wizard, and his two bodyguards, Leofwin and Brictwin. They were awaiting the arrival of Wilchard, Edgar's chief steward, with the Cordentine ambassador.

The wait gave Edgar time to contemplate his plans. It had been two days since the attack on Toric's Temple, and he had been busy. The potential threat to the kingdom had led him to raise an army, and he had issued orders to all those in the land who had a duty to provide their prince with soldiers. Even though no threat had materialised, Edgar knew it was a foolish ruler who, once he had an army at his disposal, did nothing with it.

The complication associated with raising an army was that all the grand magnates of South Magnia were there as well, keen to show off the soldiers under their command, eating the army rations at an alarming rate and drinking too much. The inevitable result of such a volatile mixture was confrontation.

Edgar was aware that, with no enemy, he could not hold the army together for long. Men such as Otha of Rystham were already letting their suspicions about Edgar's motives be known. So far, he had spun them along with some vague pronouncements about the robbers of Toric's Dagger having possibly come from North Magnia. Mention of the kingdom's bitter enemies had been enough to keep his nobles on side. The army had marched northwards all day yesterday, albeit at a leisurely pace, and Edgar had let the rumours of a confrontation with North Magnia grow. Aware that he was playing a delicate game, the Prince of South Magnia was not yet ready to show his hand.

Wilchard and Rosmont, the Cordentine ambassador, were shown into the tent by the guards outside. King Glanna of Cordence was a wealthy man and could afford to have several permanent ambassadors in his employ. Their job was to spread Cordentine influence throughout Dalriya and stick their nose into other people's business, reporting all they heard to the Cordentine court. South Magnia was not considered important enough to have its own ambassador; instead, Rosmont's remit was to cover all the lands of south-west Dalriya. Edgar felt he was at court more than enough.

Wilchard bowed to Edgar. 'Your Highness, Lord Rosmont of Cordence.'

'Please sit down, gentlemen,' said Edgar, nodding to some seats prepared for the meeting. Wilchard was the same age as Edgar, an old childhood friend, and now a close adviser.

'Your Highness,' said Rosmont, bowing low. Rosmont began his usual speech, which involved a formal greeting from King Glanna and incorporated a brief history of all the special links and mutual treaties between the two countries. Edgar maintained a fixed smile throughout the proceedings as the ambassador listed what King Glanna believed to be the Prince's most special virtues.

'Please send King Glanna my best wishes,' replied Edgar when, at last, Rosmont had finished.

Rosmont bowed again in acknowledgement. 'I understand you have another ambassador at court, from the newly independent provinces of Trevenza and Grienna?', he enquired.

'Yes, a man arrived late last night, but I have yet to speak to him,' answered Edgar.

'Ah,' came the reply. Rosmont was obviously doubtful of this, but in truth, the ambassador, whom Edgar understood to be a high-ranking cleric of Grienna, had been so tired from his speedy journey that he had been allowed to rest and was due to speak with Edgar after this meeting with Rosmont. The two provinces had only just claimed independence from Persala and were now desperately sending envoys across Dalriya, hoping other states would acknowledge this independence and lend some legitimacy to the move. King Mark of Persala would, of course, treat any such acknowledgement as an attack on his sovereignty.

'I was sorry to hear about the loss of your national treasure the other day,' said Rosmont, moving on to a new subject, 'and shocked to hear that you were personally threatened?'

'Yes, a shocking business all round.'

'And the direction your army is going would indicate that you believe North Magnian agents were behind it?'

Edgar knew Rosmont would be all over these events, but he wasn't about to give him anything here, either. 'Nobody should jump to conclusions over this incident,' he said sternly. 'I have sent my own agents after the robbers to retrieve our treasure. It wouldn't be wise to say anything else at this time.'

Rosmont quickly accepted that no information was forthcoming on this subject and moved on to another, namely rights over the Wilderness. Mention of the place made Edgar think of Soren, Belwynn, and the others. In the past days he had put the loss of Toric's Dagger to the back of his mind and relied on his cousins to retrieve it. He hoped they were doing well.

'...King Glanna feels that such an arrangement,' Rosmont was saying, 'can only be beneficial to both parties.'

The Cordentines were proposing a formal division of the Wilderness between themselves and South Magnia. While those kingdoms that bordered the Wilderness laid token claims over it, in practice the place was a law unto itself, and no-one's authority extended very far into the forest. King Glanna was always trying to win rights and ownership over places, whether by trade treaties or secret understandings. But Edgar could see little advantage in a treaty of ownership with the Cordentines when neither side had any authority over the place they were carving up.

'And what thought has King Glanna given to the Empire's view of such an arrangement?' asked Wilchard.

'King Glanna's view is that Emperor Baldwin will have little interest in the destiny of the Wilderness, particularly if he is drawn into confrontation with Persala.' Rosmont's eyebrows always raised to the corners of his face when dealing in intrigue, and now was no exception. The Cordentines expected a confrontation between Brasingia and Persala over the provinces of Trevenza and Grienna, and while their attentions were turned they could lay claim to the lion's share of the Wilderness; maybe even begin the laborious process of bringing it under the authority of the Cordentine crown.

Edgar nodded in understanding. 'What you say is interesting, Lord Rosmont. You will understand, of course, if I discuss your offer with my ministers first.'

'Of course,' came the smooth reply.

'If we are now finished,' said Wilchard to Rosmont, 'I will escort you out.'

With a deep bow and a few words of gratitude, the Cordentine ambassador was led out of the tent. Edgar rolled his eyes in relief. 'What did you make of that?' he asked Ealdnoth.

'I don't like it,' the wizard replied. 'We offend Brasingia, while Cordence makes a move on the Wilderness. Glanna's soldiers are free, while most of ours will still be tied up defending the northern border. Cordence will have a perfect excuse for building up a large army near our border, and we can hardly object if we have signed a treaty agreeing to it all.'

Edgar had to agree. 'Knowing wily King Glanna, I don't intend signing up to anything with him that isn't in our obvious interest, because it will doubtless be in his. But if he's thinking of making a move on the Wilderness, what's to stop him swallowing it up whole?'

'We could probably frustrate his plans enough to make it too difficult to be worth his while. Plus, if Baldwin doesn't like it, he'll face the wrath of the Empire on his own and may lose some of his beloved trade deals there; I'm sure the threat of that would stop him dead in his tracks.'

Edgar grinned at his adviser. Ealdnoth was not the most powerful of wizards: he admitted himself that Soren had more natural talent, but he was clever and experienced, and was worth as much to Edgar as an adviser as he was to him as a user of magic. Edgar would reject Rosmont's offer, though it might not hurt to string him along for a while first.

Wilchard returned to the tent and immediately agreed with Edgar and Ealdnoth's assessment.

'Can you give me an update on what we know about developments in the north before we meet the Griennese ambassador?' Edgar asked his steward.

'The balance of power there is shifting firmly towards Haskany,' Wilchard began. 'Since he took power, Arioc has won vast swathes of territory from the old Persaleian Empire. Last year it looked like the whole of Persala would collapse when the old Emperor Conrad was deposed by a coalition of generals, led by Mark. However, by rejecting the old title of Emperor, hardly fitting anymore, and by overhauling the army, the new king has secured his position in the country. Mark still has enemies within the country—after all, he seized the throne by force; in the trading provinces of Trevenza and Grienna the people object to paying high taxes to defend what they see as other people's land. Short-sighted, of course, but there you go. It looks like they've decided now is the time to make a break.'

'How do you think Brasingia will react?' asked Edgar.

'Persala has always been an enemy, and if the Empire supports the two provinces with enough force, Mark doesn't have the resources to take on Baldwin—not with Arioc waiting in the wings to swallow him up. Baldwin is not a hasty man and may decide to wait to see how the rebellion develops. He may even have some sympathy with Mark. No doubt he has been weighing up his options.'

If the two provinces were to succeed in their bid for independence, they would need the military support of Baldwin of Brasingia. Edgar realised that the Emperor may have already promised this in an attempt to destabilise his neighbour. Either way, the real momentum in this crisis was going to come from Brasingia, not Magnia.

When the envoy was ushered in, he made offers of money and beneficial trading rights in Grienna and Trevenza in exchange for Edgar's recognition of the two provinces as states outside the jurisdiction of Persala. Edgar's decision was unlikely to alter the balance much either way, but he decided that he would have to let the envoy leave empty-handed. There was no reason to become involved in the conflict, and it was far wiser to wait on Baldwin of Brasingia's response before he came down on either side.

Events in the north were becoming a concern to the Prince of South Magnia, however, and he talked about them with Wilchard and Ealdnoth long after the envoy had left. If war was coming to Dalriya, he had to make sure that South Magnia was in a strong enough position to defend itself.

. . .

THE ORDERS TO raise camp had to be given long in advance because of the cumbersome nature of Edgar's army. It seemed to take an age for orders to pass down the chain of command, and most of the Prince's troops were not professional soldiers, but men who only sporadically became warriors when asked to do so by their liege lords.

Despite this, the main part of the morning was still left when the army of South Magnia resumed its progress northwards. The soldiers would often be greeted by the folk who lived in the villages and farmsteads through which they passed: some simply gawped at the sight, others offered food or drink. All of them were desperate to know where they were going.

As Edgar rode along, never far from his dutiful bodyguards Leofwin and Brictwin, he heard many a soldier claim the Prince had decided to invade his northern neighbour, a claim which he noted was greeted with mixed enthusiasm. While some of his countrymen might delight in taking the old enemy to task, many realised that war meant hardship and taxes, especially for those who dwelt nearest the enemy border.

It was before midday when Farred arrived. Edgar was eager to hear all his news but decided that it would do better to travel a little farther and stop for lunch, when he could sit with Farred, Ealdnoth, and Wilchard to discuss his plans for the day.

After another hour's journey, they came to a suitable location on the outskirts of a sizeable northern town called Halsham. Because of its size and location, Halsham was an important strategic settlement to the princes of South Magnia. Edgar's father, Edric, had encouraged its growth, giving it certain rights to trade and self-governance, and in return the town councillors committed themselves to provide resources to the crown, particularly in times of war. One of the most important of these was providing supplies to the royal army, and Edgar now demanded that the town of Halsham feed his troops while he met with his advisers.

Since Farred's intervention at Ecgworth a few days ago, Edgar had developed an immediate liking to the man. He gave his opinions with honesty and intelligence, and he was not afraid of action. Edgar had decided he would be the perfect man to undertake a special mission to the court of Edgar's neighbour, Prince Cerdda of North Magnia.

The biggest danger to both Edgar and Cerdda was from their own nobility, and it was with this in mind that Edgar had sent Farred to meet with Cerdda. In the borders, both princes were dependent on their followers to defend their territory, and this dependency had long been taken advantage of.

The individual who offered the biggest threat to Edgar was Harbyrt the

Fat, Marshal of the Northern Marches. Harbyrt owned vast stretches of land on the northern border and had many men in his power. Few in the region could stand up to him, and those that tried would more than often end up dead, their lands confiscated by Harbyrt as he used his military powers to brand them a traitor. The problem for Edgar was that he could do little to curtail Harbyrt because of the ever-present threat of war with North Magnia. Harbyrt would have little compunction in transferring his allegiance to Cerdda, which would give the North Magnians a big advantage in terms of territory and military strength.

Edgar had thus been forced to accept several indignities from Harbyrt the Fat. He had once sent a trusted friend to the region to act as royal sheriff to impose his will on the region. Harbyrt had continually frustrated his efforts, and, as the conflict became violent, Edgar had been forced to withdraw his sheriff and replace him with one who could work with Harbyrt.

The problem had become more sinister in the last year; Harbyrt had married his son to the daughter of Earl Sherlin of North Magnia, who held similar powers to Harbyrt. These men, who were supposed to be enemies, had developed a powerful alliance and were now strong enough to ignore their notional superiors. Harbyrt had sent no soldiers for Edgar's army, despite being one of the richest barons in the land. While men like Otha of Rystham might frustrate Edgar, Harbyrt the Fat had come close to rejecting his authority, and Edgar had long resolved to deal with him. With an army at his disposal, Edgar saw an opportunity to put Harbyrt in his place. He had sent Farred to Cerdda to explain the army's proximity to the border and gain his support for the plan. What Edgar didn't want was for the North Magnians to react aggressively to the move and set back the already-difficult relations he had with them. Since Farred was descended from Middian tribesmen, with no family history of enmity with North Magnia, Edgar had chosen him to act as something of a neutral go-between.

'How did they react?' asked Edgar, as they sat down to eat.

Farred grinned. 'Positively, Your Highness. However, Prince Cerdda did insist on changing your plans slightly.'

Edgar raised his eyebrows, but allowed Farred to tell his story.

'As you had hoped, Cerdda is just as frustrated with Earl Sherlin as you are with Harbyrt. The alliance between the two has made Sherlin a rival power to Cerdda within the country—some men apparently give their loyalty to the Earl above the Prince. There are even rumours within North Magnia that the two magnates intend to formally unite their lands and declare themselves independent of both South and North Magnia, effectively creating a separate state.'

'They wouldn't do that,' interjected Wilchard. 'They are in a perfect situation now. Subjects in theory, independent in practice. If they tried to go their own way, they would have to fight for what they already own.'

Farred shrugged. 'No doubt that is true, but arrogant men such as these soon tire of even the pretence of subordination. Either way, this is the background in which Cerdda reacted to my visit, and he was eager to join in the fun. As we speak, he is now raising his own army, and intends to enter the lands of Earl Sherlin whilst we move north to meet Harbyrt. He is using the presence of our army as his reason for the action. He intends to deal with Sherlin and says he would be only too happy to offer any assistance with cutting Harbyrt the Fat down to size.'

Edgar smiled. His plan seemed to be working. Ealdnoth, however, did not look so pleased.

'Do we know we can trust Cerdda?' asked the wizard. 'And even if his intentions *are* the same as ours, the presence of two armies, both of which believe they are there to fight each other, is asking for trouble. Events can soon spiral out of our control.'

'I believe we can trust Cerdda.' answered Farred. 'One problem, however, might be his younger brother, Ashere. He seemed hostile to any agreement with South Magnia.'

Edgar nodded. 'By all accounts, Ashere has never forgiven his brother for failing to attack me when I was at my most vulnerable, just after my father died. He may try to sabotage the plans; it would be all too easy to lead an attack on our troops and provoke a retaliation. However, I must trust that Cerdda can keep his brother in check. The opportunity we have here is too great to pass up. My magnates would never allow me to move against one of them: it would be an infringement on their power. This way, before they know it they will have taken part in a show of strength against Harbyrt the Fat. If Cerdda does the same with Sherlin, we will have stopped a potential threat to my sovereignty in its tracks and improved relations with our neighbours. There are risks involved in this, but the potential benefits are worth it. I don't intend to spend the rest of my reign circumscribed by men like Harbyrt the Fat.'

When Wilchard advised Edgar's generals that Cerdda was raising an army in North Magnia, their support for the campaign was renewed, and the entire army prepared itself for battle.

Edgar visited with the mayor of Halsham, a landowner and trader named

Oslac, at his impressive town-house. Oslac had recently been elected mayor by the council of Halsham for the third year running, and Edgar had worked with him in the past. Halsham was a proud town which resisted the influence of Harbyrt the Fat in its affairs, and Edgar had done his best in the past to give Oslac sufficient powers to continue this resistance. When the Prince confided to the mayor his plans for Harbyrt, Oslac was pleased to offer whatever help he could.

Edgar's problem was that Prince Cerdda had asked for two days to raise a sufficient force to carry out their plan, while Edgar's own nobility wanted to press on, before the North Magnians could prepare for their arrival. In addition, Edgar did not want to arouse the suspicions of Harbyrt the Fat.

Edgar had hoped that he could march his army straight to the heartlands of Harbyrt's estate and punish him before anyone had realised what was happening, but while Cerdda's involvement might result in a more complete victory, it also complicated the picture. What Edgar needed to do was freeze time in South Magnia for a day or two, so that his troops and Harbyrt's stayed apart, while in North Magnia Cerdda got his own force together. He had decided that Oslac and his town residence could help him do just that.

UNDER THE INFLUENCE

X

Belywynn stood, exhausted, taking in the town of Vitugia. It was a small border-trading town, situated in Cordence but close to the Empire and the Midder Steppe. Goods bought and sold here might be sent north up the Great Road or taken south to the long Cordentine coast, where they could be transported by ship.

Back in Cordence, then. It was a week now since their brief trip to Vincente's town, and Vitugia had a similar feel to it. A few big houses for the rich, and lots of very poor ones. A rather mean-looking inn, where Herin was negotiating their accommodation. Although Magnia and Cordence shared a border, they were very different countries. Belwynn knew that history had played its part in this. Magnians were proud that they represented the only humans of Dalriya to have resisted the Persaleian Empire at its height. Cordence, despite the distance between them, had been the most loyal of Persaleian provinces. Whereas the Brasingians had fought bitter wars to overthrow Persaleian rule, Cordence had never rebelled—just drifted into independence when it found itself geographically cut off from its mother. The Great Road still connected Cordence and Persala and the Cordentines were a nation of traders, always keen to get the best deal and get one over on their neighbours. Magnians, on the other hand, were a nation of farmers, and, to Belwynn's mind, had more of a sense of community. That was why Magnian inns were friendly and welcoming, and Cordentine inns were mean and penny-pinching.

Herin poked his head around the door and made a small signal with his forefinger that everyone could come in. Belwynn hobbled after him, eager to get inside The Grape and Goat and spend the night under a roof for the first time in days.

It had been a long day, dragging Soren and Dirk through the undergrowth of the Wilderness. But they had not been troubled by the vossi, and eventually Gyrmund had led them out of the forest and into Cordence. Everyone's spirits were raised by leaving the place, especially Moneva's. She became positively gregarious, speaking in full sentences again, rather than the series of grunts and swear words she had deployed over the last few days. While Belwynn was glad to have left the Wilderness, she was not in the mood for chat, and it had fallen to Gyrmund to entertain Moneva, which he didn't seem to object to.

He had established that Gervase Salvinus and his mercenaries had passed this way in order to connect with the Great Road, and by offering the chance of sleeping at an inn this night, he had persuaded everyone to keep going at a fair pace. Dirk made a speedy recovery from what had seemed, yesterday, to be a fatal wound, and they had discarded one stretcher. Soren, however, remained unconscious, though sometimes he could be heard to mutter some incoherent speech out loud before returning to silence.

Herin had organised rooms for everyone, and Belwynn was grateful that he had arranged for her to share with Soren. Elana came in to check on him before retiring to her own room, but the priestess seemed unable to help. Belwynn knew Soren had exhausted his powers back in the Wilderness, and she knew, too, that her brother might not recover from the expenditure.

Belwynn heard a knock on the door and realised that she must have fallen asleep. After checking on Soren, she opened the door to Moneva.

'We've arranged for us all to have some supper,' she said. 'The landlord is putting it out now. No change?' she enquired, nodding over to where Soren lay.

Belwynn shook her head in response. Moneva waited as Belwynn splashed some water on her face to wake herself up. They had only known each other for a few days, but they already had the easy familiarity that comes with travelling together and sharing danger.

Belwynn felt guilty for having gone to sleep and allowing everyone else to organise the food and accommodation. She went over to Soren and took the money which Prince Edgar had given them for their expenses from her brother's inside pocket. With Soren unconscious, she had to take charge of the situation. Edgar had entrusted the retrieval of the dagger to them, and so far, they had failed him.

Belwynn and Moneva went down to the main room of the inn and joined the others in a welcome hot meal. Belwynn immediately noticed that most of her companions had begun drinking, and they continued to do so throughout the meal. She could understand their desire to celebrate escaping with their lives. The inn was very busy with the arrival of their group of ten from the Wilderness, and the landlord apologised that he didn't have as much food available as he wished. The soup was watery, and the inn lived up to half of its name by providing goat as part of the main meal. It was stringy and tough to eat, and Belwynn haggled down the price of the nine meals because of it. The fact that Clarin, Herin, and the others all wore their weapons to the meal no doubt helped, and the landlord seemed very keen not to upset his guests. Belwynn was happy that he seemed to be a man who asked very few questions so long as he was paid promptly, which she made sure he was.

The food and drink lifted the mood of the nine companions and Clarin persuaded Belwynn to try some of the wines available. Everyone was keen to indulge themselves after the threats they had all faced in the Wilderness, and it surprised Belwynn to see Dirk knocking back his fair share of drink, especially so soon after his injury. Elana, too, seemed to want to make the effort to join in with the group, though she drank only a little watered-down wine and took it in turns with Belwynn to check on Soren. Soon Belwynn was laughing at the antics of Herin and Kaved despite herself, and also found herself warming to her new companions. Their time in the Wilderness had brought them closer together.

After a while Herin and Kaved seemed eager to leave the inn to find amusement elsewhere. 'When you get a close brush with death like that—' Kaved seemed to be addressing everyone in the inn—'you realise what's really important in life...and that's why I intend to couple with as many women as possible tonight.'

'And my investigations this afternoon—' if anything Herin was louder, 'established that Vitugia is not quite as dull as first meets the eye.'

Belwynn realised that the two of them had spent their free time looking for prostitutes and had obviously struck lucky. 'Why is it that after any crisis men find the need to sow their seeds? Believe me, if you two had perished in the Wilderness, mankind and—Krykkerkind? —would have managed well enough without you.'

'Perhaps someone's feeling a little bit jealous?' leered Kaved.

'No human woman is going to sleep with you, Kaved,' Moneva joined in. 'You should stick to your own species.'

'I think they will,' answered the Krykker, producing a few gold coins from his pockets and waving them at Moneva. 'And I've found that one must take companionship wherever one finds it.'

'Who else is coming?' asked Herin. 'Clarin?'

Clarin glanced sideways at Belwynn, stared into his drink, and shook his head.

'Looks like he's got other plans for tonight,' Kaved smirked.

Belwynn felt her cheeks flush red with embarrassment and stood up sharply. The speed with which she got up made her feel dizzy and made her realise how much she had been drinking.

'I'm going to check on Soren,' she declared, and left the table without looking at anyone. As she made her way to her room, she berated herself for going red, and berated Clarin for looking in her direction that way. She had known for a long time that Clarin was interested in her, but he didn't need to make it so obvious to everyone else. She was sure that he had slept with plenty of whores in the past and didn't see why he had to stop himself tonight on her account.

Belwynn entered the room and went straight for the window, which she opened, and then gulped in some night air to cool herself down. She then went over to where Soren lay and took his hands in hers.

Oh, Soren, hurry up and get better. I need you, Belwynn said.

Belwynn.

Belwynn heard her brother's reply, but there was no movement from Soren's body.

Soren, are you awake? Soren!

There was no reply this time, but Belwynn had heard her brother's voice, and to her that meant he was getting better. She lay next to him for a while in the hope he might wake, but he didn't stir again.

Belwynn knew Soren wouldn't have approved of the drinking downstairs. She remembered the fights he used to have with their father. Father would sit alone until late into the night, drinking and brooding. 'There was nothing I could have done,' he would always say, sometimes repeating the words over and over. Belwynn would agree with him. She hated that he blamed himself. She knew he needed forgiveness. From his children? From himself, or his dead wife? Soren would shout at him, and their father would shout back, calling Soren sinful and wicked for his dabbling in magic.

'There was nothing I could have done,' their father would say, until one night Soren shouted back, 'I will become so powerful that I can stop it! I'll be able to stop things like that ever happening again!'

'Get out!' her father had roared at him. Soren had gone and never come back.

Belwynn returned downstairs to tell everyone that Soren had spoken to her. It was now a lot quieter after the departure of Herin and Kaved. Gyrmund and Moneva were talking to each other, slightly apart from the rest of the group. From the corner of her vision, Belwynn saw Dirk stumbling over from the bar in their direction. As he approached them, he sank down on his knees in front of the priestess.

Dirk pulled up his shirt and showed Elana the scar where the vossi blade had punctured his body.

'You have saved my life by a miracle of healing,' he solemnly pronounced to the priestess. Despite being obviously under the influence of alcohol, Dirk was speaking clearly.

'I didn't save your life, Dirk. It was Madria, Goddess of this land, who healed your wound.'

Dirk nodded at this statement in acknowledgement, his head bent slightly forward, in deference to Elana, or Madria, or both. 'Yes. Madria has blessed me in a way I have never felt before. By saving my life, she has asked that I now devote it to her. Therefore I renounce my allegiance to Toric and turn to the one true goddess. Elana, I submit my soul to Madria's keeping, and ask that I become your disciple.'

'This is what Madria wishes,' replied Elana. 'Dirk of Magen, you shall be my first disciple.'

Elana touched Dirk's forehead and then raised him to his feet.

Belwynn caught eyes with Clarin, who looked as surprised about the episode as she felt. She felt that something significant had just happened, and was reminded that Elana had led an attack on the Temple of Toric to get the dagger for herself.

This softly-spoken priestess had an agenda all her own with regards to its recapture. Now she seemed to have converted a priest of Toric to her own cause.

Belwynn resolved to keep an eye on the life-giving priestess of Madria.

BELWYNN'S MORNING was filled with joy because, when she woke, Soren was already awake and sitting up in bed. He was still weak, but strong enough to resume the journey north. In fact, Soren looked in better shape than some of his companions that morning—many of whom were now paying for the excesses of the night before.

Herin, Clarin and Kaved had spent the early hours of the morning finding ten suitable horses for the journey along the Great Road into the Empire. They had been forced to pay above the odds, but Belwynn and Soren were grateful for their efforts and happy to pay over a large portion of Edgar's money in order that they renew their chase of Salvinus' mercenaries on horseback. When Belwynn tried to express her thanks, however, her companions responded with a strange series of grunts, which was apparently the only form of communication they were capable of for the rest of the morning.

Dirk, too, seemed to be suffering from a hangover, as he rode next to Elana with slit eyes and a pale, slightly grey complexion. Sometimes keeping the horse in the right direction would prove too much, and he would veer off the track into the grassy verge by the side before awkwardly returning to the group. The entire episode between them from the previous night seemed even stranger this morning, as if it had been a dream.

Elana was involved in a running argument with Kaved. 'Well, surely,' the Krykker was saying, 'if your great goddess 'Madigar' can heal up this man's wound—' Kaved gestured in Dirk's direction— 'she can cure me of a bloody hangover!'

Elana finally lost her patience. '*Madria* certainly does not respond to foul language. But that is not the point. Maybe I could rid you of it...but I think it is a good lesson for you not to indulge in excessive drinking in the future.'

'A lesson!?', exploded Kaved, and then wished he hadn't, grabbing each side of his head with his hands as if it would split open without being held together.

'Well, you're both making me feel a lot worse,' interjected Herin. 'Let's have some peace for a while.'

Kaved muttered something under his breath about suffering in silence, but kept relatively quiet.

Belwynn and Moneva, on the other hand, were in high spirits, and took great delight in increasing the irritability of their comrades by reminding them they had brought it all upon themselves. Gyrmund and Rabigar rode with Soren at the front and soon connected the group onto the Great Road.

The group had decided that Gervase Salvinus had most likely headed back to his own power-base in the duchy of Barissia. There were many travellers on the Great Road, but none of those questioned could confirm whether or not their decision was sound.

The plan was to continue north along the Great Road and then take the Barissian Road west into the duchy, heading for its capital, Coldeberg, where they were sure to get some information on the whereabouts of Salvinus.

Many of the group were eager to question Soren about the events on the mound in the Wilderness, in particular his apparition, which scared off the vossi tribesmen.

'What exactly was the image you conjured up?' asked Moneva.

'When the vossi were reluctant to approach us at first, it made me realise we had stumbled onto a vossi burial ground. The vision I created was one of their gods, Riktu, who is lord of the vossi underworld. I made him berate them for making war on his sacred site. He eventually persuaded them to leave.'

'Well, I think we all owe you one,' she replied.

'I used to think that all wizards were con-artists,' interjected Kaved, 'but you're different. Where does that kind of power come from?'

'I have always had magic within me, Kaved. The Caladri have long used and accepted magic, while the Isharites control powerful yet terrible sorcery. For my part, I have been blessed with some power which I had to learn how to use and control. I've spent my time learning from masters of the craft, just the same as you have spent yours learning how to fight and to use your weapons in battle.'

'I find it interesting, Soren,' said Rabigar, 'how you distinguish yourself from the likes of Elana. It is obvious to us all that you both have extraordinary powers at your disposal. Elana freely admits that her powers come from a superhuman being, her goddess Madria, yet you say your powers all come from within. We Krykkers have long held the belief that there can be no such distinction. Whether or not you know it, your powers have been given to you by spirits not of this world, in just the same way as Elana's. I do not agree with allowing interference into our world from unknown forces outside it, however well-meaning your intentions. It is dangerous.'

Kaved made one of his smirks at this statement. 'All that rather depends on what you call extraordinary powers, does it not, Rabigar?' he asked enigmatically.

Rabigar shrugged the question off.

'Well, it is certainly dangerous,' Soren replied to Rabigar. 'You have all witnessed that. As for the powers coming from outside forces, that is very far from the truth. They come at a considerable cost to myself.'

Rabigar didn't reply, and the group rode on in silence for some time.

Elana insisted that, for Soren's sake, it would be best if they had a brief rest for lunch, but they were all soon back in the saddle again. The nature of the Great Road meant that they were eating up the miles, and Gyrmund suggested they might even make it to Barissia by the end of the day.

It was mid-afternoon when the group came upon the lone rider sat on his horse by the side of the road. As Gyrmund and Rabigar approached the stranger, it seemed that the man was actually *waiting* for them to arrive. He had a stunning appearance, jet black hair down to the nape of his neck, a black silk cloak which reached to his knees, and the most expensive-looking stallion Belwynn had ever seen.

What really drew attention, however, were his eyes. They were red.

Belwynn had never seen anything like it. Deep red eyes, as if they were on fire, and they were looking at the approaching group with an unreadable expression. Belwynn sensed power in this man. She looked back to his cloak, the hems of which were decorated with runic inscriptions.

He's a wizard, Belwynn almost hissed to Soren, as if, by thinking too loudly, Red-Eyes would hear it.

Yes. A powerful one. We're going to have to be very careful here.

'Well met, friend,' Gyrmund greeted him nonchalantly, as if he had already met several red-eyed travellers on the road that day. It was a neutral welcome, except for the fact that Herin, Clarin and Kaved had all ridden from the back of the line to the front, hands stroking the inches of air separating them from the hilts of their weapons.

The man gave a friendly smile, revealing white, polished teeth. 'Well met, friends,' he began, his voice strong, resonant and confident. 'I saw you approaching and wondered if I might accompany you along the road for a short while. I fear it can be dangerous to travel on one's own these days.'

The words raised Belwynn's concerns higher. Surely little in this world could provide much of a danger to this man.

'We travel alone,' said Herin coldly, not fearing to stare into those red eyes for signs of dissent.

Before the stranger could respond, however, Soren contradicted Herin's decision. 'I think in this case we could make an exception, Herin. It will not cost us anything to travel with an extra companion for a short time.'

Herin looked at Soren. Belwynn knew her brother was probably the only person who Herin might allow to overrule him. With a raised eyebrow, he conceded to his wishes.

'If you think so, Soren,' he said.

'You are all most gracious,' said Red-Eyes, inclining his head, as if he were oblivious to any undercurrent of tension in the group. 'My name is Pentas. I am pleased to meet you all.'

Soren introduced himself and his companions, using their real names, which raised further eyebrows, but no comment from the rest of the group. 'Where are you headed?' he enquired of Pentas.

'To Persala,' he replied, 'I felt that I must return to my home there, because of all the recent troubles.'

'What troubles are those?' asked Belwynn. 'I'm afraid we've heard little of events to the north in recent days.'

Pentas nodded, though Belwynn thought he looked a little surprised. 'Well then, I must report to you that Trevenza and Grienna have broken away from Persala in a pact of independence. I fear that war must be inevitable. Of course, such a situation will be of more concern to myself than to a Magnian.'

Belwynn knew that her accent was unmistakably Magnian, but she had travelled enough to know that Pentas's was not strong enough to place, and so she reserved judgement on whether he was Persaleian or not.

'And where are you headed, friends?' Pentas asked.

It was an awkward question, since they didn't want to tell this stranger exactly what they were up to. Herin looked about to tell the wizard to mind his own business, but instead turned to Soren.

'Coldeberg,' replied Soren.

Herin frowned, unable to understand why Soren was deferring to this man, but he kept his mouth shut.

'Interesting,' replied Pentas. 'I thought you would be heading south, back to Magnia.'

He looked at Dirk as he said this, red eyes fixed on the priest. Dirk looked troubled under that glare and turned to Elana for support.

'No,' she replied. 'We are heading north.'

Pentas now turned his gaze on Elana, but the priestess looked straight back at him without wavering. He nodded.

'Very well. It is very kind to let me ride with you as far as Coldeberg.'

What was that about? Belwynn asked Soren.

Not sure, he replied.

Soren still looked tired from his exertions in the Wilderness, and Belwynn suspected he was hiding the extent of the damage done. She had to ask another question of her brother, however.

Why did you let him ride with us?

I don't think we had much of a choice in the matter, Soren replied.

You mean he's a more powerful wizard than you?

You could say that.

Soren sounded down, almost bitter; Belwynn decided to leave it at that.

The group continued their journey north, and Pentas did not hinder the speed of their progress, but rode along comfortably in the middle of the group, as if he were out on a ride with friends. He behaved as if he were blissfully unaware of the nervous looks that some of the others gave him, but Belwynn knew it was an act and kept her eyes on him.

It was early evening when Gyrmund advised the group that they would shortly turn off the Great Road onto the Barissian Road, which led directly to the capital, Coldeberg. Before anyone could respond a hissed whisper from Rabigar got the group's attention.

In front of them was the second lone mounted figure they had come across that day. Belwynn was unsure where he had come from—suddenly, he was there, in the middle of the road. Pentas had been an arresting sight, but this newcomer managed to trump it. His mount and his clothes were just as expensive, but instead of red eyes, he wore a mask which covered his face.

It was a death mask, a human skull stripped of flesh and skin, frozen in a contorted howl of pain.

It sent shivers down Belwynn's spine, and she could sense from behind the empty eye sockets the malevolent presence of the wearer, studying them.

The figure nudged his horse and trotted slowly towards them. Belwynn felt the saliva in her mouth dry up as Herin, Clarin and Kaved once more moved from the back of the group to face the danger.

'Give me the dagger,' demanded the skull in a rasping voice, as if the figure behind the mask was indeed a corpse, raised from the dead and given the power of speech.

In response, Herin and the others drew their weapons and spread across the road in a fan shape, readying themselves for an attack. The masked figure stopped his advance and waited, as if daring them to try anything.

'Be careful,' warned Soren in a tense voice.

Belwynn could see a scabbarded sword at the right thigh of the figure, but he had made no attempt to reach for it. As she had with Pentas, Belwynn could sense the power emanating from the creature in the mask.

Just as she thought of the red-eyed wizard, he trotted his horse past her and towards the confrontation. Clarin and Gyrmund turned around in surprise, but allowed him to move between them and out onto the road to face the waiting threat.

Belwynn's mind was racing. She wanted to shout out that they didn't have the dagger, but no-one else had offered that information, so she decided it was best to keep her mouth shut.

'You,' said the masked figure as Pentas approached, in a voice filled with hostility and disdain. 'You would do best to stay out of my way, Pentas.'

'I got here first, Nexodore. You're too late. The dagger is now my responsibility.'

Nexodore cackled, but there was no humour in the laugh. 'These matters will never be your responsibility, Pentas. I will not think twice about casting you down if you stand between me and my duties.'

'Then there is nothing left to say,' answered Pentas.

His voice was firm and betrayed no emotion. For a moment Belwynn wondered whether anyone in this world would dare do anything even to displease this red-eyed man, whose presence was so powerful. She half expected this Nexodore to turn around and ride back from where he came, but both men sat still, facing each other across a few feet of road. Belwynn felt a buzzing sensation in her head, which grew by the second as the hairs on her body stood on end.

They're testing each other out, trying to find a gap in each other's defences, said Soren.

What can you do? asked Belwynn.

Nothing.

Belwynn looked at her companions and saw that they, too, were feeling the side effects of this magical duel. Even the horses whinnied nervously.

Then, suddenly, wave upon wave of power surged from the two figures. Belwynn turned back to look at the two wizards and nearly wretched with the effort as the magical forces at work surged into her body. They were still sitting perfectly still, in the same position, but something told Belwynn it was Nexodore doing the attacking.

Then, from the corner of her eye, Belwynn noticed a flash of metal. Herin's drawn sword seemed to be sucked from his grasp, and the weapon flew straight towards a point between Pentas's shoulder blades. Just as the blade was about to sink into the wizard's back, its flight was halted in mid-air and it clattered harmlessly to the ground.

Pentas had stopped an attack, but his concentration, it seemed, had been affected. Almost as soon as Herin's sword hit the ground, Pentas's horse collapsed. It seemed to Belwynn as if the stallion suffered some kind of internal haemorrhage. With a sudden jolt, it spasmed and then its legs gave way, causing Pentas to topple forward off his mount. Nexodore held his hand above his head, ready to finish his defenceless opponent, when an arrow whistled past his head.

Instead of sending the spell to Pentas, he quickly adjusted, and the power was instead directed at Herin, who had tried to make up for the embarrassment of losing his sword by taking out the wizard himself. Herin was hurled from his mount by the power of the blast, shooting into the air for a few feet before crashing to earth.

Pentas had been given the precious recovery time he needed, however, and he slammed his palms onto the Great Road. There was a deafening, tearing sound of rock on rock, and then the ground between the two wizards opened. Pentas had created a crack along the road, allowing hot steam to billow forth from the fissure. Now it was the turn of Nexodore's mount to lose its footing, and both horse and rider tumbled into the widening hole which Pentas had rent in the earth.

Pentas had no time to gloat, however, as the ground beneath him also gave way, and he was dragged into his own trap, followed by the carcass of his horse. Clarin, who had moved forward after his brother had been attacked, was now forced to quickly backtrack to avoid joining the two wizards. They all quickly moved to safety, Gyrmund grabbing the reins of Herin's horse to pull it away.

The cracking of the ground ceased, though it continued to smoulder.

As the others went over to check on Herin, Soren and Belwynn went to look at the hole. Soren gingerly peered down, but shook his head. Belwynn looked for herself, but could see no trace of any of the bodies which had been sucked in, surely to their deaths. The fissure stank of rotten eggs, and they reluctantly walked away.

Herin was a little dazed, but had no serious injuries. He did, however, get upset when Clarin ruefully informed him that his sword had joined the two wizards in their deep grave.

'Don't tell me I've lost another one!' he groaned.

'Well, what was all that about?' asked Kaved, and everyone looked at Soren for an answer.

The wizard, however, shrugged his shoulders. 'I can't tell you much. Nexodore is a name I know, a man of great power who serves Erkindrix of Ishari. I don't know the name Pentas. But what I do know is that we've just been involved with two of the most powerful wizards of Dalriya. For both of them to come looking for us, personally...I don't know. I don't know what's going on. But any wizard of real power in Dalriya will have heard what went on here; the expenditure of magical power was incredible, and if these two came looking for us, then anyone else will now know exactly where we are as well. I suggest we get as far away from here as possible, as quickly as we can.'

'I'll not argue with that,' said Gyrmund. 'We might not make it to Coldeberg before nightfall, but I'm all for giving it a try.'

A CROWN AND A HAT

XI

They didn't make it to Coldeberg, instead spending the night outdoors. Everyone agreed it was safest to keep a low profile and avoid possible detection.

Belwynn was tired, but couldn't get to sleep. Night noises sounded like they could be people out in the dark, looking for them. When she did finally drift off, she dreamed of being chased by a man with red eyes. When he caught her, he turned into a skeleton and dragged her underground, to the land of the dead.

Belwynn awoke the next morning feeling little better for the few hours of sleep. Gyrmund and the others had taken shifts, keeping watch through the night. Nothing had happened. But everyone was still on edge. Just as in the Wilderness, the group felt as if they had now somehow become the hunted rather than the hunters. It was clear that they had become involved with the dark powers of Ishari, yet no-one could put their finger on how or why. They hoped to find answers in Coldeberg, both to the whereabouts of the dagger and to the reasons why it had been stolen.

Coldeberg was situated in the middle of the duchy of Barissia, and it would take most of the morning for the group to get there.

'What is the city like? I've never been,' Belwynn asked, to no-one in particular.

'Bigger than anything in Magnia,' Herin replied, 'but not the same size as Essenberg. No real reason for traders to go there rather than Essenberg. It gets a few from the Steppe, selling cattle; some from Guivergne who come down by river. But a lot of the Middian tribes aren't that keen on Barissians, not after Emeric's wars there.'

'Can't blame them, either,' added Clarin.

Belwynn knew that the two brothers had fought for Emeric as mercenaries a few years back, and that they had bitter memories of it.

'Barissia's farming country,' said Moneva, sounding dismissive in a way that Belwynn didn't much appreciate. 'Wealthy enough, but insular.'

No-one was really selling the place, and as they approached the city along the Barissian Road, Belwynn picked up on an uneasy atmosphere. They were greeted with unfriendly looks more than she had expected—far more than they had received on the Great Road.

There seemed to be a lot of soldiers on the road. They wore the livery of the dukes of Barissia, the charging boar. They were almost always challenged for their business by these soldiers, and they soon learned that the best answer was that they were on their way to Coldeberg to enlist with the army. Since everyone seemed to be either in the army or on their way to join, they were greeted with much less suspicion.

Coldeberg was built on a hill, so that the northern part of the city became visible from the road first. As they got closer, the southern half of the city came into view, the whole place enclosed by steep, grey stone walls.

They arrived at the main gate, where city guards were questioning those who came in or out. Flags had been positioned on each side of the gate. One had the charging boar of the dukes of Barissia, the other a large golden crown on a red background.

When it came to their turn, the guard on their side of the road looked them over, frowning, not quite sure what he had in front of him.

'We're here to join the army,' stated Kaved, as if it was a momentous occasion that required a fanfare.

The guard looked a little underwhelmed. 'You all together?' he asked. He was smartly done out, and it looked like he was expected to do a thorough job of monitoring the traffic coming in to the city.

'Not really,' replied Kaved. 'Us two are,' he said, indicating himself and Rabigar, 'and we hooked up with these poor souls on the road,' he finished, gesturing at everyone else.

'I'm not sure that the army has Krykkers.'

'It does now,' said Kaved, so mean-looking and full of confidence that the guard quickly moved on.

'Are all of you joining the army?' he asked, looking doubtfully at Belwynn,

Elana and Moneva. It wasn't unusual for women to accompany their menfolk in the army life. Indeed, they were very useful when it came to the myriad jobs that needed doing to keep an army on its feet. It was much less common for women to be employed as soldiers, though it did happen.

Moneva scowled, fingering the two swords at her hips.

'You saying I can't?' she demanded.

'I always travel with my wife,' explained Herin, grabbing Belwynn by the waist. 'I can't leave her behind. We're too in love.'

Belwynn silently fumed as Herin pulled her in close, feeling self-conscious and trying not to blush, knowing that inside Herin was laughing.

'Where do we sign up, anyway?' he asked the guard.

'Up at the castle,' said the guard, looking at them all with a certain distaste before waving them through into the city.

'You can get your hands off now,' said Belwynn irritably.

'Of course,' Herin agreed mildly, with a smirk on his face. 'Just trying to make us look convincing.'

Dirk knew the city well, and he suggested they find rooms at The Boot and Saddle, a large inn in the north-west quarter of the city that was hospitable to foreigners. He considered it to be one of the best places for keeping a low profile. Once through the gates, the Barissian Road they had arrived on became the main street of the city, running east to west.

Immediately to their right sat Coldeberg Cathedral, home of the Bishop of Coldeberg, who had the exclusive right to worship all the Brasingian gods. But on their way, they passed several other temples to specific gods. Sibylla, goddess of health and prosperity, was popular with townspeople. Gerhold, lord of war and friendship, was favoured by soldiers. Belwynn spotted a smaller temple for followers of Toric, the Magnian sun god.

Many smaller streets ran off the Barissian Road, where specialist traders sold their wares. Tanners, metalworkers, cloth-workers, grocers, bakers, more and more. Dirk informed her that the market was in the downtown part of Coldeberg, to the south.

Towering over everything was Coldeberg Castle. Located at the highest point of the city, the northern city walls doubled as the castle's outer wall, and the structure then sprawled down towards the Barissian Road in an irregular hexagonal shape with six large towers and a massive gatehouse. Its looming presence emphasised that the dukes of Barissia were in charge of the city and made it feel like they were watching everything that was going on.

The streets were busy. Most of the people here weren't residents of Coldeberg, but had come in from the surrounding villages to buy goods they couldn't get at home and perhaps to sell their own. A conspicuous presence on the streets were the groups of mercenaries who had been recruited by Duke Emeric. They hung out in small groups, watching everyone else at work while they lounged around, drinking and playing cards, moving from one inn to the other, arguing with each other or passers-by or shopkeepers. They added an unpleasant ingredient to the city's atmosphere, and Belwynn was pleased to be with Clarin, Herin and the others, whose physical presence and grim expressions ensured they were given a wide berth.

Dirk took them almost as far as the western gate of Coldeberg before turning right and taking them up some twisting, narrow streets. Then they were there, in the courtyard of the Boot and Saddle.

It was a large, well-maintained building with a sizeable stable where they left their horses.

'The landlord goes by the name of Bernard Hat, on account of his large collection of hats,' explained Dirk with a straight face as they made their way into the establishment.

It was busy inside. According to Dirk, this was the most cosmopolitan of the inns in Coldeberg, and Belwynn noticed a few foreigners, especially Middian tribesmen, whose dark skin and long, tied-back hair made them distinctive. Mercenaries and soldiers dominated the clientele, however—drinking early in the day and creating a rowdy atmosphere. They had to squeeze past tables and through knots of drinkers to make it to the bar.

'You must be Bernard,' said Moneva to a man serving behind the bar. He was wearing a green beret tastefully decorated with two feathers. 'I love your hat!'

Bernard beamed at the compliment, and was an attentive host, getting their orders in quickly and making sure that he found them seats.

'Theodoric!' he exclaimed to a man occupying a table with only one companion. 'I've brought you some interesting conversation while you have your lunch!'

'Ah! Sit down, grab a chair, that's right,' said Theodoric welcomingly. Bernard made sure that his guests were all seated before rushing off back to the bar.

As they waited, Herin struck up a conversation with Theodoric, a lean man who introduced himself as a linen merchant from the duchy of Thesse.

'I'm waiting on a final sale, and then I'm back home,' he said, perhaps by way of explanation as to why he was sitting in the inn at midday, already a little worse for wear. He was sitting with what Belwynn assumed to be his assistant, a large man about the size of Clarin, who was gawping at a spider in the corner of the inn, apparently oblivious to the conversation going on around him. Belwynn also assumed that Theodoric paid his assistant criminal wages, that his assistant probably did not know or care, and that both were happy with the arrangement, except that Theodoric naturally craved a bit of conversation from time to time.

'Has business been bad?' enquired Herin.

'Business is never bad if you have a brain in your skull,' answered Theodoric, and proceeded to flap his forefinger in thin air a few inches from his ear, which everyone understood to be an attempt to tap the part of his anatomy he had been referring to. 'I'll tell you this, though.' Theodoric's voice lowered to what he believed to be a conspiratorial whisper. 'When I come back, I won't be bringing linen.'

There followed an uncomfortable pause, until Herin realised he was supposed to respond. 'What *will* you be bringing?' he reluctantly asked.

'Weapons. Swords, armour, bows, arrows. They're all cheap in Thesse, nobody wants 'em there, you see. But here in Coldeberg, of course, demand is sky high.'

Herin made a face at Rabigar, who was listening attentively.

'Why is that?' Herin asked.

Theodoric frowned at Herin, tried to focus on him but then gave up. 'Are you new here or something?'

'Yes.'

'Oh. Oh, well then, you haven't heard.'

Another uncomfortable pause. 'No.'

'Rumours at first, but then you get the more official announcements. Until the day before yesterday there was a formal ceremony in Coldeberg Cathedral. A duke isn't good enough for Barissia anymore. Oh no. If us Thessians have a duke, then these Barissians can't possibly settle for a mere duke themselves, can they? So Duke Emeric is now no more—long live King Emeric! Unbelievable! These Barissians.' Theodoric shook his head at the Barissians. 'Of course, you know what this means now, don't you?'

Herin and the others shared astonished looks at the news. Theodoric, however, was still expecting an answer, so Herin shrugged his shoulders at him.

Theodoric shook his head again, this time at Herin's apparent slowness. 'It means war! When Emperor Baldwin hears about this, he's going to march his army straight at these Barissians. That's why there's all these soldiers around and that's why demand for weapons is so high. These Barissians are preparing for war! Unbelievable!'

Herin had a foul expression on his face and interrogated Theodoric about the best place in the city to pick up a quality sword to replace the one he had lost. Everyone else, meanwhile, huddled together to discuss the news.

'I don't like this,' said Soren. 'Gervase Salvinus, a Barissian, steals Toric's Dagger. Emeric of Barissia declares himself king. And behind it all, I see Ishari at work. I don't know how yet, but it's all linked somehow. We need to spend this afternoon gathering information.' Soren looked at Dirk. 'What do you know of Emeric?'

Dirk shrugged. 'Arrogant, ambitious—but not stupid. He wouldn't attempt anything like this without knowing that he had support from someone else. I guess that Ishari and Haskany are the most likely candidates.'

'Pentas mentioned trouble in Persala,' Belwynn reminded everyone. 'This could extend beyond the Empire.'

Soren nodded. 'Right. I suggest we go about our business in ones and twos so that we attract as little attention as possible and meet back here this evening. I've got something I need to do on my own.'

Belwynn felt a little taken aback by the abrupt statement, but chose not to pry. 'I've got something I need to get as well. Clarin? Will you come with me?'

'Sure,' replied the huge warrior.

'We need rations getting. Moneva and I will do that,' volunteered Gyrmund.

'I'll go with Herin to get his sword,' said Kaved.

'Right,' began Soren. 'If you three don't need anything, it might be best for you to stay put and look after our gear. The more of us who go out there, the more chance we have of finding trouble.'

Soren's implied message was that a Krykker and the two founding members of a strange new religious sect might attract more trouble than was average.

'Well, I'd like to get some clothes, and I might be able to get in touch with some contacts in the city,' replied Dirk. 'I don't mind picking up anything for anyone else, though.'

With that agreed, eight of the group made their way into the streets of Coldeberg, leaving Rabigar and Elana behind at The Boot and Saddle.

TRIMMING THE FAT

XII

Edgar sat on Oslac of Halsham's bed, awaiting news. A messenger from Cerdda of North Magnia had arrived and was currently meeting with Wilchard before the news was brought to Edgar.

Edgar, of course, had been ill since yesterday morning. Officially ill, that is. Unofficially, he was feeling great.

To buy himself and Cerdda time, Edgar had decided to fall ill. Oslac, at whose house Edgar was staying, rushed to find Ealdnoth. Ealdnoth immediately diagnosed the illness. It was a rare illness that no-one else had heard of before; it had a long and unpronounceable name, and worst of all, it was extremely contagious.

Rumours flew around the camp, many suggesting foul play by the North Magnians. The campaign was halted in its tracks just as conflict with the old enemy seemed imminent. Edgar was confined to his room; only Ealdnoth and his two bodyguards daring to stay with him. Leofwin and Brictwin took turns in keeping guard outside the room; the other sleeping with their prince in the room. The loyalty of the two men was commended by many, though the commending was carried out at a healthy distance. Edgar's room was given a wide berth. Many sympathised with Oslac over the disruption caused to his house and the fact that Edgar had dined with him and his young family the night prior to the illness taking hold. Many gave Oslac and his family a wide berth, too.

Ealdnoth let it be known that Edgar had asked for Wilchard to take charge of the army during his illness. For some reason, Wilchard had never been so popular. Many a grand nobleman of South Magnia took time from their busy schedule to speak personally to Wilchard, to praise him on the fine job he had done for his prince over recent years and to remark on how well he handled the onerous duties of managing the army. They even confided to him their own fears for Prince Edgar's health, and what might befall the kingdom should he tragically succumb to illness. Edgar had no heirs, and there was no obvious successor to the throne. Many a grand nobleman gave Wilchard their own opinions as to who would be best placed to take over the leadership of the kingdom in such a grave situation. Wilchard listened politely and passed on everything he heard to Edgar. Edgar wondered if he should be ill more often.

The ruse had worked well. Harbyrt the Fat had doubtless heard about the fate of his prince. He and his following had still not joined up with the royal army. Edgar knew that Harbyrt's scheming mind would be working overtime. If Edgar died now, it would be the perfect opportunity for him to declare his independence. South Magnia would be in chaos, and there would be no one to stand in his way.

Of course, what Harbyrt didn't know was that Edgar was biding his time until he was ready to confront his wayward vassal in person.

There was a knock at the door. Brictwin stood up from his prone position on the floor, where he had been catching up on some sleep, and Edgar called for his visitors to enter. Leofwin opened the door from the outside, let in Wilchard and Ealdnoth, and closed it again.

'Take a seat,' said Edgar, motioning to Oslac's bed, upon which his councillors duly perched.

'Important developments,' began Wilchard. 'Last night, Ashere, Prince Cerdda's younger brother, led a surprise attack on Earl Sherlin. Apparently, it was a complete success. Sherlin was captured, and before his men knew anything about it, Ashere had delivered him up to his brother to stand trial on charges of treason. Cerdda has raised a small army and is currently located just a few miles north of the border. He sends apologies for not advising you of Ashere's attack, but because it was a risky venture, he preferred to wait on its result and then report to us on the current situation. He advises you to strike at Harbyrt soon. There is a good chance he knows nothing of these events yet.'

Edgar stood with excitement. 'Yes. We move now and we move fast. Wilchard, I'm suddenly feeling a lot better, and feel good enough to resume command of the army. We leave within the hour. If anyone feels their men cannot be mobilised before then, they will have to stay at Halsham.'

With a little grumbling aside, all of Edgar's commanders had their troops ready on time. His recovery was seen by many as a sign of Toric's blessing on the campaign. The official line was that Edgar wished to link up with Harbyrt to share information and combine forces before pushing into North Magnia.

It was only a few miles from Halsham to Harbyrt's castle at Granstow, the largest of half a dozen strongholds in the northern marches which were in his keeping.

It was mid-afternoon by the time it came into view. Well-positioned on a hill overlooking the surrounding territory, Granstow was one of the largest border castles. Nonetheless, it was designed to be effective rather than grand-looking. The regular garrison would only be about fifty strong, though that was enough to be a considerable drain on food and wages. It could hold considerably more people when necessary. The central keep, perched high on an earth mound, was stone-built, but the rest of the fortifications were constructed from wood from the local area.

Edgar pitched his army's camp a mile away from the castle. It left something of a no-man's-land between the two forces. The prince wanted Harbyrt to be the one to cross it.

It was some time before a messenger from Harbyrt arrived. The messenger turned out to be Kenward, officially royal sheriff of the region, but in reality, securely in Harbyrt's pocket. He was a man about the age Edgar's father would have been: bushy, grey hair topping a large-featured, flat face that Edgar didn't like very much. Kenward was taken to Edgar's tent to talk with the Prince.

'Greetings, Your Highness,' began Kenward, 'we did not expect your visit, I am afraid, but arrangements have been made at the castle for your entourage to stay.'

'You did not expect my visit, Kenward?' enquired Edgar in a quiet voice. 'In time of war with the Northerners I would hope my marshal and sheriff would expect to be involved a little.'

Kenward inclined his head at the prince's response, but offered no apology. 'Of course, both Marshal Harbyrt and myself have been busy, stockpiling and garrisoning our strongholds and raising our soldiers. I merely explain that we did not receive notice of your plans to march the army here—in fact, the last message we received was that Your Highness was gravely ill.'

Edgar didn't like the sheriff's words, demeanour, or his tone of voice, and felt like smashing a gauntleted fist into his face. But he controlled his emotions. After all, this man wasn't the target today. 'Thank you for asking after my health, Sheriff. I am fully recovered and feel no need to impose on Harbyrt at Granstow when I can spend the night here amongst my soldiers. I would, however, very much like to speak with Harbyrt regarding the forthcoming campaign, and would be grateful if you could fetch him for me.'

'Of course, Your Highness,' replied Kenward, doing his best to hide his discomfort. 'Do you intend to strike at the enemy tomorrow, sire?'

'You will understand, Kenward, if I keep my plans to myself and my trusted councillors for the time being. It would be a blow if they were to find their way into enemy hands.'

'Of course, Your Highness,' repeated the sheriff before bowing and leaving the tent.

Satisfied with his strategy, Edgar called a meeting of the Royal Council. Since many of the most powerful men in the kingdom were present with their retinues in the army, it was difficult for Edgar to keep the council manageable in size without putting people's noses out of joint. Thus, along with loyal supporters like Wilchard, Ealdnoth and Farred, this meeting also involved men whom Edgar had been obliged to invite. Otha of Rystham, probably Edgar's wealthiest vassal, was there along with his brother Wulfgar, High Priest of Toric. Aescmar, the bulk of whose lands were held by the Magnian coast where he had responsibility for the kingdom's naval defences, was also present. He was a man who kept himself to himself, happy not to interfere with Edgar's plans if Edgar did not interfere with his.

Harbyrt took his time to get from his castle to the camp. No doubt his lack of haste was a reminder to his Prince that he would not be treated like a wayward lackey. The facts of the matter were, however, that the Marshal could offer little resistance to Edgar when he had the kingdom's army with him, and wasting time now just served to irritate his peers.

When Harbyrt eventually arrived with a small entourage, he was immediately taken to the royal tent. He bowed to his Prince and clasped hands with the others present, as if nothing was amiss. Farred's face was the only one he did not recognise, and when introduced, he made a jest about Steppe tribesmen attending Royal Council in an obvious attempt to reduce the standing of someone he correctly guessed to be a royal loyalist. The dangers of councils, as Edgar and his father before him had found out, was the tendency of the nobility to stick together as a group to defend their own rights and privileges, and to see the prince as something of a threat to these.

'I have called this meeting,' began Edgar, 'in order that we discuss our plans for the next phase of this campaign.'

Wilchard, on cue, was the first to respond to this announcement. 'First, I feel I must speak my mind on some aspects of the campaign so far. It is my opinion that, in the grave situation in which we find ourselves, the support of Harbyrt as Marshal of the North has been totally inadequate.'

'How dare *you* pass judgement on *me*?' Harbyrt stared around the tent in incredulity, looking for support, his face and neck mottled with red blotches as his anger boiled over. 'You're nothing but an upstart royal boot polisher!' Harbyrt roared at the chief steward, spittle shooting in Wilchard's direction.

Edgar surveyed the assembly. Normally, Harbyrt's bluster would have been enough to see off the attack from Wilchard. Wilchard was not from a great noble family, and many of those present did resent the power he wielded in the kingdom, whereas Harbyrt was one of them, and therefore should be defended at all costs. These were not normal times, however. This was time of war, and survival was of vital importance. Wilchard had shown himself to be an able commander; he oversaw the army logistics and had made sure it was fed and well supplied. He had kept the peace in an army which seemed to have as many officers as soldiers with a mixture of discipline and diplomacy. Harbyrt, on the other hand, a man who was supposed to be a key leader in times of war, had not figured at all, and was resented for this. Edgar's Council was not sure who to side with and looked to their Prince for a decision.

'I think we should hear Wilchard out, Harbyrt, and then you may defend yourself.'

Harbyrt looked around the tent again, but found that he had no overwhelming support as he had hoped. On all previous occasions when Edgar had tried to corner his marshal like this, Harbyrt had simply walked away, retreating to his northern power base and daring Edgar to do something about it—which, of course, he couldn't. Now, however, as much as he no doubt wanted to walk out, Edgar had an army with him. That changed the dynamics more than a little.

Wilchard continued. 'Four days ago, Prince Edgar sent out orders that every magnate should raise his quota of troops because the kingdom's most precious treasure, the Dagger of Toric, had been stolen, and it was feared that an invasion would follow,' began Wilchard, making sure that he mentioned the dagger in order to get Wulfgar on side. 'Since that time, we have heard nothing from Harbyrt, despite two further attempts at communication. When we approached your lands, the least I expected was information on the situation in the borderlands and confirmation that your forces and strongholds were ready. I would have expected you to join up with the royal army long before now.'

Wilchard's words were greeted with the odd murmur of approval from around the Council, but Harbyrt was ready with his comeback.

'Your words display a totally unjustified lack of faith in me, steward. My soldiers have been working for days on preparing the kingdom's northern defences for sieges, a task which may prove vitally important. I have sent scouts across the border to monitor enemy activity. Why would I join up with you when we need a force here on the border, ready to react to the enemy, should they make an incursion before the royal army approaches? While you have been camped out in Halsham, it is my forces who have been working tirelessly for the kingdom. I didn't expect gratitude, but all I have found is accusation!'

'Nobody is accusing you of anything less than total commitment to the kingdom, Harbyrt,' began Otha of Rystham, slithering into the argument. 'We are all grateful to have you working so tirelessly for us all. Perhaps all this really boils down to is the lack of...communication on your part, simply to reassure us that all was well in the north.'

'Well, perhaps I could have spared some time to keep you better informed,' Harbyrt conceded gruffly. 'If you all feel that I have failed in that regard, please accept my apologies.'

Otha had taken the fire out of a confrontation which Edgar had hoped to stoke up. He would not let his chance slip away, however.

'Apologies are all very well, Harbyrt, but I need to be totally confident that the administration of my northern provinces is being handled correctly. Your recent conduct has only added to feelings of unease which I already held. It is my opinion that authority in the northern marches needs to be re-organised.'

'What do you mean, *re-organised?*' barked Harbyrt as the red blotches returned to ruin his complexion.

'Since my father's time, responsibilities in the north have been shouldered by just one man. I think that after this campaign is over, it will be the perfect opportunity for me to take a fresh look at arrangements here and share out some of this responsibility.'

Harbyrt's temper boiled over again. 'You can't get rid of me, Edgar. I have rights in this kingdom. My lands aren't yours to give away.'

Edgar quickly responded before Otha of Rystham gave a sermon on the laws of the kingdom. 'Harbyrt, I do not intend to take any of your own lands from you, and I still intend for you to be one of my leading magnates in the region. I simply require other leaders as well. Yesterday I was gravely ill, and that led me to think about what the consequences would be if you were to take ill similarly. If I had other lieutenants in the region, my peace of mind would be far greater. As for lands, a large proportion of those which you control are royal lands, given to you by virtue of your title as marshal. I intend to redistribute some of those...perhaps amongst some of your fellow councillors here.'

That was the clincher. Several of Edgar's magnates had looked slightly unhappy about this public curtailment of Harbyrt the Fat's power, even though it was generally understood to be in the kingdom's interests, simply because, if he could do it to Harbyrt, what was to stop him from doing it to them? The possibility of some lands being shared out now meant that many in the room seemed to be on side with the idea of re-organising things in the north.

Harbyrt was ordered to stay with the army. The Council agreed that the current position, just a few miles from the border, was basically sound. The camp was now to be fortified with a ditch and wall of stakes.

Edgar took personal control over Granstow Castle. Ealdnoth's suggestion that they should send a messenger to Cerdda of North Magnia was unanimously agreed with. After all, if they could get to the bottom of this conflict and end it without going to war, it really would be much better. Edgar knew that the thought of all those lucrative northern estates being pillaged by North Magnians had nothing whatsoever to do with this sudden desire for peace. A messenger was sent immediately, and Edgar's army entrenched its position while it waited for a reply.

The South Magnian request for peace talks was answered promptly. Ten North Magnians, including Prince Cerdda himself, were making their way to the giant ash tree in Adingley, a well-known meeting place for the people of the area for generations. Edgar decided that he too would travel there himself. As well as Leofwin and Brictwin, he chose as his companions Ealdnoth, as Chancellor; Farred, who had already met with Cerdda, though that meeting was always to be kept a secret; Wulfgar, as the leading prelate of the kingdom, and the high-ranking noblemen Otha of Rystham and Aescmar. Finally, Edgar thought it might be wise to take Harbyrt the Fat and Kenward, his sheriff, just to make sure that no mischief was caused while he was away.

Wilchard was left in charge of the army, and Edgar's party made their way to the prearranged spot.

Harbyrt seemed to have been struck dumb by the sudden turn of events he had experienced this day, but Edgar hoped he wasn't plotting his revenge. It seemed that the Marshal had not yet heard about the arrest of Earl Sherlin in

North Magnia, and Edgar had chosen not to mention it. If revenge was on his mind, he would soon find out that he no longer had the allies or resources to mount a challenge to Edgar's authority.

They arrived at Adingley in good time, and Edgar was relieved to see that Cerdda was already there with nine companions, waiting by the ash tree. While the hostilities between the two kingdoms had been a pretence, meetings such as these were always dangerous, since it was the perfect opportunity to isolate an enemy with a few followers and ambush them.

This was the first time the two princes had met. Cerdda, unlike most Magnians, was dark-haired with amber-coloured skin. Edgar remembered his father telling him that Prince Bradda's three children had got their dark looks from their mother, Mette, whom he used to say was the most beautiful woman of her generation.

The two clasped hands and introduced each other to their companions. Cerdda's brother Ashere had come as well. He was almost a mirror image of his older brother, except for his more youthful looks, and the fact that he smiled a lot less.

Edgar suggested that he and Cerdda talk alone for a while, leaving their followers to enjoy a few bottles of wine together.

'I see you've brought Harbyrt with you,' began Cerdda, once they were out of earshot.

'Yes. I have reduced his power in the north, but he will still have a significant estate. I did not want to humiliate him totally and force him into a rebellion.'

Cerdda pursed his lips. 'Edgar...yesterday Ashere intercepted a letter which was intended to reach Earl Sherlin.' Cerdda produced a piece of parchment from inside his tunic and handed it over to Edgar. 'We captured the bearer of the letter: one of Harbyrt's men. Sherlin admitted to the conspiracy, admittedly under some duress.'

Edgar scanned the few lines of scrawled writing.

'Greetings, brother. The time may be at hand to bring our plans to fruition. The fox cub has fallen seriously ill. Prepare and wait for further news. Patience now may soon be rewarded.'

Edgar had no doubt that he was the fox cub referred to, a choice of words which galled him. Harbyrt's seal was not on the letter, so there was no definite proof that it was his. It was quite possible that Cerdda's zealous brother, Ashere, had composed it himself. Edgar, however, had no doubts that Harbyrt and Sherlin had conspired along those lines, and he was quite prepared to use the letter as evidence.

'Where is Sherlin now?' he asked the Prince of North Magnia.

'Dead. I executed him this morning. The man was too dangerous to leave alive. It is difficult to say how many people in my kingdom were embroiled in his treacheries. My enquiries thus far have suggested more names than I had expected.'

Cerdda spoke with some bitterness, for which Edgar did not blame him. 'You had no choice, Cerdda, and from this letter, it seems that I have none either. Know that you have my support should anyone try to avenge Sherlin's death.'

Cerdda nodded in thanks. 'I do not pretend that I have received no positives from these events—an important one being your friendship, Edgar. I had a grin on my face for hours after Farred left. Our little intrigue has been productive. Your father was always honourable towards me, and you have been, too. Magnia has spent a generation embroiled in internal jealousies—it is high time we took steps to retrieve our standing in Dalriya.'

Edgar smiled. 'Your feelings match with my own, Cerdda. On the subject of Dalriya, Farred told you of the theft of Toric's Dagger?'

Cerdda nodded gravely. 'He did. Is there any more news?'

Edgar shrugged. 'I sent a group to follow the Brasingian robbers. At the least, I hope they will tell me where it is and who has it. I have heard nothing so far, however.'

Cerdda gestured towards Ealdnoth. 'Is that man your wizard?'

Edgar nodded. He knew Cerdda did not have a wizard himself; many rulers of Dalriya considered them to be a dangerous, untrustworthy sect, and had anyone who possessed such skills killed. 'He is one of my most trusted advisers, Cerdda. And very useful. You should get yourself one.'

Cerdda smiled. 'Maybe.'

'Perhaps we should join the rest of them. We *have* agreed to peace, haven't we?'

Cerdda grinned. 'I suppose so. I must admit, however, that the first war of my reign has not been quite how I imagined it would be.'

'Mmm... you expected more fighting, perhaps?'

'A bit more, yes.'

The two princes strolled over to their followers and announced that peace had indeed been agreed. Both sides showed genuine relief and felt able to relax into some more unrestrained drinking.

Edgar took an opportunity to pull Otha of Rystham to one side.

'What do you make of the peace, Otha?'

'Good news, of course. It would appear that the North Magnians were not involved in the theft of Toric's Dagger, then?' enquired the magnate pointedly. Otha wasn't stupid. No doubt he had suspicions about the game Edgar had been playing. But Edgar was still one step ahead.

'Not entirely. We may never know, but it is quite possible that Earl Sherlin of North Magnia was involved.'

'Sherlin? Really?'

'Yes. I'm sure it won't have escaped your attention, Otha, that Harbyrt and Sherlin have grown close recently.'

'Well...Harbyrt's son married Sherlin's daughter...'

'Without my permission. I have long had suspicions, Otha, and Prince Cerdda has, too. Sherlin was executed this morning.'

'What!?' gasped Otha.

Edgar put a finger to his lips. 'For treason,' he murmured. Now Edgar produced the piece of parchment from under his tunic. 'This was picked up by the North Magnians, apparently in the possession of one of Harbyrt's men, on the way to be delivered to Sherlin.'

Otha perused the document. His expression was grim. 'There's no evidence that Harbyrt issued this.' The words were Otha's, but they lacked his usual conviction.

'No conclusive evidence, perhaps. I cannot claim to be surprised by its contents, however. Harbyrt has shown a total absence of loyalty since I came to the throne. I cannot tolerate the situation any longer. I need your support, Otha. Emotions will run high if I execute my own marshal. I need you and Wulfgar to support my decision publicly. United, we can stifle any opposition.'

Otha looked as if he were in physical pain. 'This is a difficult situation, Edgar. We cannot legally deprive Harbyrt of life or land without a fair trial. I cannot be seen to endorse the denial of a lord his rights.'

'He cannot be allowed to live, Otha. As for his lands, however, there is no evidence of his son's participation in the plot, and I intend to let him inherit his father's estate when he comes of age. In the meantime, the estate must be administered on his behalf, and I see you as the perfect choice for this. You can fill the vacuum of power in the north caused by Harbyrt's removal and lend some stability to the region. What do you say?'

Otha was being offered a fortune. For the next few years he would have control of the resources, revenues and men from Harbyrt's lands. With this addition to the lands he already held, it would make him unquestionably the greatest noble of Magnia.

Otha looked over to where Harbyrt was standing uncomfortably with Kenward, the sheriff. 'He has to go. I will support you, Edgar.'

Edgar had judged correctly. Harbyrt's fate was now sealed. He was just about to offer Otha his thanks when the sound of a horse riding at full gallop caught his attention.

It was a single rider, who pulled up by the ash tree where everyone was congregating. Edgar and Otha walked over to see what was happening.

The rider jumped off his horse and bowed to Cerdda. 'Your Highness, I bring news from the north. Your mother instructed that I should find you and relay it immediately.'

'Of course. You can tell us all unless it is of a private nature.'

'My lords, there are early reports of an invasion of Persala by King Arioc of Haskany. It took place yesterday and they say that the capital, Baserno, has fallen to him.'

There were gasps all round, and Cerdda let out a whistle. 'If Baserno has fallen, then the entire kingdom may be lost. What of Mark?'

'It is unclear whether the king is dead or alive, captured or escaped. I believe there have been conflicting reports.'

Edgar, like everyone else, was in shock. Persala was the great founding state of humankind; history had begun with its rise to greatness. Magnians defined themselves in relation to Persala, being the only people of Dalriya to resist the Empire at its height. In more recent times, Persala had lost its dominance to Brasingia, and was not even the strongest power in the north any more, as province after province had been torn away. But for it to be conquered in one day? It was difficult to comprehend.

Cerdda caught Edgar's eye and interrupted his thinking.

'Well, my friend, it looks like we may have a busy time ahead of us.'

Edgar could only nod in agreement.

THE BOAR STRIKES

XIII

'Two thalers per arrow!' exclaimed Gyrmund, genuinely shocked at the charge.

The fletcher, on the other hand, maintained his disturbingly cool composure and smiled back. Gyrmund was sure that he could even detect a hint of pity in the man's face. He turned around to Moneva for support, but his companion did not seem particularly interested in the price of arrows.

'Seventy-five marks for forty,' stated Gyrmund, in a voice that suggested he would not take no for an answer.

The fletcher let out a puff of air and then screwed up his nose as he considered the offer. Eventually, he nodded his consent, and Gyrmund left the man, having spent twice as much as he had planned.

'This is ridiculous!' began Gyrmund, as he and Moneva made their way back to The Boot and Saddle. 'Emeric's army is swallowing everything up. Arrows I can just about understand, but how much did we have to pay out for a bit of bread and cheese?' Gyrmund could feel himself getting hot.

'What's the matter with you, Gyrmund? I haven't seen you get this stressed before, and I think we've been through some worse experiences recently than getting overcharged! There's nothing we can do about it, so just forget it.'

'It's this city. There's too many people milling around. I'll be glad when we get out of here.'

Moneva laughed. Gyrmund couldn't remember hearing her laugh before.

'What's so funny?'

'We're like chalk and cheese, you and me. I spent three miserable days in the Wilderness, sleeping on the forest floor, being permanently uncomfortable, getting chased by those creatures, seeing nothing but trees all day. You seemed to have a great time. Now, I'm back in civilisation, looking at the stores, looking at all the people and what they're up to, enjoying a bit of city life, and you're moaning about it and can't wait to leave!'

Gyrmund smiled. 'I didn't realise you had such a bad time back there.'

The conversation paused as they separated to either side of the road to allow a horse and cart to pass by.

'So, you've been to Coldeberg before?' Gyrmund resumed.

'Yes. I spent some time here a few years ago. How about you?'

'I've passed through a few times.'

Moneva laughed again.

Gyrmund didn't think he was being funny and decided that Moneva must simply be genuinely happy to be here. 'So, you've got fond memories? What did you do here?'

'I worked for a merchant who did business here. He had interests all over the Empire, so I travelled about a bit.'

What did you do?'

Moneva sighed. 'Well, I spied on his rivals, I spied on his business partners. I sabotaged his rivals' plans, I sabotaged his partners' plans. It was good money, but in the end, it got boring. A bit too easy. In the end I was charging so much for the tiniest little things that even he decided I was too expensive.'

'So why did you take up this little assignment?' asked Gyrmund.

'Well, there's the money, of course. But really, I thought it would be interesting. I suppose I can't complain on that score.'

'Good answer,' said Gyrmund approvingly.

Moneva raised an eyebrow, but said nothing.

'So, how long have you known Herin?'

'Why do you ask?'

Gyrmund shrugged. 'Just asking.'

'I met Herin and Clarin while I was working here, as a matter of fact. They were fighting as mercenaries for Emeric in his war with the Black Horse tribe. He already had a sizeable army back then, and the merchant I was working for squeezed a tidy profit out of the whole affair. Herin and I made sure we did alright as well; the army structure was totally disorganised, and so it was quite easy for him to get his hands on provisions, which I could sell on. Since then I've bumped into them a couple of times. Last time was when I was working in Cordence. For another greedy merchant. I'm wondering now whether I wish I hadn't bumped into them again.'

'Yes, I know what you mean. I wasn't quite expecting things to turn out as they have.'

Gyrmund and Moneva fell silent. They rounded a corner and found themselves back at the Boot and Saddle.

'Pretty quiet,' commented Moneva, as they walked in.

Gyrmund looked around. There were no customers in the bar area and even the owner, Bernard Hat, was absent.

'Well, I'm going to put this food away and see if Rabigar is about. I expect they've booked rooms upstairs.'

Moneva nodded. 'I hope so; a bit of rest would do me the world of good. Be careful, though. It's eerily quiet around here.'

Gyrmund made his way behind the bar and into the kitchen at the back. There was no sign of any staff here, either. What was more, the room had been left in a mess, pots unwashed and food lying about. He looked around for somewhere to store the provisions he had bought. He heard footsteps behind him and turned, half expecting that Moneva had come to investigate.

She hadn't.

Three soldiers had followed him around the bar and into the kitchen, weapons drawn. Gyrmund dropped his stuff and grabbed his sword. He made a move for the exit at the back of the kitchen. But as he approached the door, it burst open from outside, and three more soldiers entered the kitchen, trapping him.

'Drop it!' one of them shouted at Gyrmund.

But he was not eager to part with his weapon so easily. He looked around the room: there was a window, but he had no chance of escaping through it in time. He was caught between the two groups of soldiers, and six blades were pointing towards him. They were all dressed in the uniform of Barissian soldiers.

'You are under arrest by royal order,' explained the man at the front of the first group. 'If you do not drop your weapon, we will take you by force. I advise you not to take that option.'

The man spoke with confidence, and Gyrmund realised he was in a no-win situation. It was better to submit to the soldiers than die pointlessly in the kitchen of this inn. If they wanted him dead, he would be. Gyrmund knew that Herin, Soren and the rest were now his best hope of staying alive. He dropped his sword and allowed the soldiers to take him.

As soon as his sword left his hand, the soldiers pounced, beating him to the floor and pulling his hands behind his back so that they could tie them together with rope.

'It would have been better for you if you'd died with some honour here,' whispered one of his assailants in his ear, and Gyrmund felt a sick feeling in his stomach. He berated himself for walking into a trap, for entering this damned city in the first place.

He thought of Moneva, which made him feel even worse. If it was better for Gyrmund to die now, then it was doubly true for her. He had no illusions about the standard treatment of female prisoners by soldiers in this part of the world.

Gyrmund was led out into the rear courtyard of the inn, where he was surprised to see another two dozen soldiers waiting. It was obvious that these soldiers had been lying in wait for them to arrive. His captors shoved him in front of the man who must be their leader. He wore no distinctive clothing, but he was sat astride a powerful looking warhorse, emanating a sense of authority over the proceedings. Gyrmund noticed a scar running down the left side of his face, from ear to chin.

'Here's the man, General Salvinus,' said Gyrmund's captor with pride.

Salvinus? Gyrmund could hardly believe that the man they had been chasing was now sitting opposite him. His look of surprise was picked up by the rider, who smiled maliciously at him.

'Help them get the woman, then,' Salvinus shouted at his officer, and the men quickly hurried back to the inn. 'And be quiet! More of them could come at any moment!'

Salvinus turned his attention back to Gyrmund.

'You recognise my name, then?' he grinned.

Before Gyrmund had time to reply, Salvinus had kicked out at him, his boot smashing into Gyrmund's chin and sending him crashing to the floor. Gyrmund landed badly on his back because of his tied hands, pain shooting up and down his spine. He turned back to his attacker, who was sliding off his horse, to the cheers of his soldiers. He turned around at his men with a look of anger and put a gloved finger to his moustache, silencing the noise immediately.

Salvinus moved over to Gyrmund and crouched down next to him so that they could talk in private.

'So, you're the one who tracked me through the Wilderness, eh?'

'Yes. You make it sound more difficult than it was, though.'

Salvinus smiled and produced a knife, which he proceeded to push against Gyrmund's throat, drawing blood.

'Do you have the dagger?'

Gyrmund looked up blankly, not comprehending the question. Surely Salvinus had the dagger—wasn't that the whole point? The question reminded him, though, of the sorcerer Nexodore, who had demanded the dagger from them on the Great Road. Something wasn't right, but he was at a loss to know what.

Gyrmund could see Salvinus's eyes studying his reaction, and he brought the knife away from Gyrmund with a look of half-hearted disappointment, as if he had been expecting Gyrmund would be unable to help.

Salvinus was interrupted by the return of his soldiers. Gyrmund turned around to look for Moneva, but she wasn't with them. About a dozen soldiers were now reporting back to him, and he felt foolish for not noticing their presence in the inn. Hopefully Moneva had.

'What's the matter?'

'She's not there, general,' Salvinus was informed.

'What do you mean? I saw her go in with my own eyes, you idiot.'

Salvinus turned back to Gyrmund and replaced the knife at his throat. 'Where is she? I'll slit you open if you don't tell me. King Emeric wants you alive, but if you put up a struggle...what can I do?'

'I don't know where she went...we split up when we got inside.' Gyrmund felt some shame for blurting it out, but the man already knew that Moneva had gone inside the inn.

Salvinus waited a moment and then withdrew the knife a second time. 'I'm bored with talking to you,' he told Gyrmund. 'Curtis, search him, mount him up, and take him to the castle. We'll teach these foreign bastards not to interfere with the Kingdom of Barissia.'

Curtis stepped forwards and lifted Gyrmund onto a horse, shifting him around until he could sit upright. Salvinus, meanwhile, had returned his attention to the search for Moneva.

'I'm going in there myself and you lot are coming with me. She went in, she hasn't come out, so she's still bloody in there!' He turned around one last time to look at Gyrmund. 'Oh, I nearly forgot. Just to get you in the mood for your stay in the castle dungeons, you should look at the landlord of this inn. When I arrived, he decided he would rather take sides with you than help me carry out the king's business. I loosened his tongue eventually, but I was still not satisfied with his loyalty.'

Curtis grabbed Gyrmund's reins and led him out of the yard entrance, escorted by three more soldiers.

There the Barissians had erected a stake, and when Gyrmund looked, he saw that placed on top of it was the decapitated head of Bernard Hat, still adorned with his green beret.

* * *

BELWYNN HAD BEEN ENJOYING her afternoon in Coldeberg. Clarin was undemanding company, and she began to relax after the stresses and strains of recent days. As far as information gathering had gone, they had achieved little except to find that the name Gervase Salvinus was familiar to many in the city: he had been chosen by Emeric as the general of the army which was being raised in Barissia. While people in the city were overwhelmingly loyal to their new king, there did not seem to be much genuine enthusiasm for war. Like Belwynn herself, the citizens of Coldeberg did not seem to understand why Emeric had declared his duchy independent of the Empire.

Having asked several questions of the tight-lipped citizens, Belwynn and Clarin headed back to the Boot and Saddle. She was still worried about Soren. He seemed to have recovered physically from his ordeal in the Wilderness, but he was not himself, and had been eager to leave the inn on his own. Belwynn wanted to communicate with him but sensed that he wanted time alone.

She was slightly surprised when he contacted her.

Belwynn, where are you? The tone seemed urgent.

We're just on our way back now.

Stop.

Belwynn sensed fear in her brother's thoughts and came to an abrupt halt. She grabbed Clarin's arm to make him stop as well.

'What is it?' asked the big warrior.

'It's Soren. Something's wrong.'

Clarin looked around them and placed his hand on the hilt of his sword, but seemed content to let Belwynn continue her private conversation.

Emeric's troops are swarming all over the Boot and Saddle. It's not safe there. I'm in an alleyway off Orchard Lane, two streets before the inn. Meet me there.

The instruction was simple enough, and Belwynn relayed it to Clarin, who grimaced but nodded his consent. Orchard Lane was the next street on their right, and they entered it warily, on the lookout for soldiers. Belwynn spied Soren signalling from his alleyway, and they quickly met up with him.

'What's happening?' Belwynn and Clarin asked the wizard in unison.

'I nearly walked straight in,' began Soren. 'I've been to the north-east of the city this afternoon, and I was returning to the inn via the back yard rather than the front.' Soren's face was grim. But Belwynn just wanted him to spit out the news. 'The head of Bernard Hat has been placed on a stake there. I tried to get a glimpse of what was going on without being seen and saw soldiers in the yard. I skirted round the edge of the inn and I'm pretty sure they're inside as well. I think they're waiting there for us to return. We left Rabigar and Elana in there,' he said, sounding worried. 'Some of the others might have returned already.'

Belwynn swallowed hard. If Bernard Hat had been decapitated, what had been done to the other members of their party?

'Why are they after us, Soren?'

'Emeric is obviously linked to the dagger—'

'Yes, but how did they know where we were?' Belwynn was having trouble getting her head around this new turn of events. She looked at Clarin. Concern was plainly visible on his face, no doubt concern for Herin's whereabouts, but he was saying nothing. The three of them were used to working together in these situations. Soren did the thinking; Clarin would agree with his course of action.

'I think,' began Soren, responding to his sister's question, 'we've been betrayed. Someone's told Emeric of our whereabouts. Those soldiers seemed to know that if they waited in the inn, we would be coming back.'

'I've just seen Dirk walk past,' interrupted Clarin, who had been keeping an eye on the top of the street.

'Dirk?' Soren sounded surprised. 'Go and grab him, Clarin.' The big warrior dutifully ran off back to the top of the street to stop Dirk from walking into the trap which had been set for them.

Belwynn watched Clarin go and then turned back to her brother.

'Betrayed? But who knew that we would come back now?'

Soren shrugged. 'No-one else did.'

'You mean you think it was one of us?'

'Most of us have had a chance to get in contact with Emeric's forces this afternoon if we'd wanted to.' Soren looked up at Clarin and Dirk, who had turned into the street and were walking over. 'And here comes my prime suspect.'

Clarin had taken Soren's instructions to grab Dirk, quite literally. He still had a hand on the priest's shoulder, and the pair had the appearance of a wayward son and his father.

'What's going on?' asked Dirk.

'Where's the dagger, Dirk?' asked Soren.

Belwynn and Clarin shared confused glances, but allowed Soren to continue without interruption.

'What do you mean?' began Dirk, but he looked into the wizard's eyes, boring into his own, and seemed to think better of continuing.

The priest put his hand inside his tunic, fumbled around a bit, and produced a knife. It had a jewel-encrusted hilt, a thin blade, and ended in a sharp needlepoint.

Toric's Dagger.

'I think you've got some explaining to do,' said Soren.

* * *

GYRMUND WAS TAKEN DIRECTLY to Coldeberg Castle. He was given no opportunity to escape, his attempts at conversation were met with a stony silence, and before he knew it he was being led through the keep into the main courtyard.

The castle was heavily defended. Gyrmund was shocked at the number of soldiers moving around the structure. His hopes of getting out of his situation alive were diminishing by the second. At first, he had castigated himself for allowing Salvinus to catch him so easily, but now he had come to terms with the fact. His thoughts had turned to escape. Gyrmund realised that his best hope lay with being rescued by the other Magnians. He just hoped that some of them had evaded Salvinus's trap.

Curtis shoved him off his horse. His hands still tied, Gyrmund fell badly off the beast. He twisted his body around to land as best he could, but his right shoulder took the impact and was snapped out of place. As he landed, pain lanced up and down his spine. He cried out in agony, leading to much amusement from the soldiers watching in the yard. Curtis yanked him to his feet. The pain in his shoulder didn't stop. He worried it had been dislocated, but he refused to give the Barissians any more satisfaction by letting them know.

Curtis prodded him over to a doorway in the corner of the yard, and Gyrmund entered the castle proper. Curtis led him along a stone corridor, decorated thickly with tapestries on both walls, while behind him three other soldiers continued to guard his progress. He could not help but be impressed with the small part of the castle he was being shown. Both as a fortress and as a display of wealth and power, Coldeberg Castle came second to few. Certainly, thought Gyrmund, nothing in Magnia was a match.

In the Brasingian Empire, though, things were different. Impressive as

Emeric's castle and army seemed to be, he was no match for Emperor Baldwin, and Gyrmund took some consolation from the joy he would feel when Baldwin burned the place to the ground. If he was still around when that happened.

Gyrmund's spirits dropped again, however, with the arrival of the moment he had been dreading. Turning the corner, Curtis took him past a couple of armed guards and began descending a stairwell. They were now headed for the dungeons. A genuine feeling of dread passed over Gyrmund.

As they descended deeper into the bowels of the castle, the air became stale and his feeling of confinement began long before he was placed in the irons that he knew would be waiting for him. The twisting staircase took them even farther down than Gyrmund had expected. The journey finally ended and Gyrmund alighted from the last step into a stinking smell of sewage. Torches adorned the walls, but they did little to break through the underground gloom. The grimy, squalid bits of the dungeon which Gyrmund could make out made him think that was probably a blessing.

'Herman!' shouted Curtis into the murk.

The address was met with silence. Gyrmund looked at Curtis, but he didn't seem moved to try again, so they waited. His shoulder throbbed with pain. He worried that if he had to stand for much longer, he would faint.

Eventually, Gyrmund could make out a shuffling sound, which was gradually getting closer. Gyrmund was now ready to meet with the deformed, brutish, stereotypical jailer he had been expecting. Such a figure duly emerged out of the darkness. Trailing a crippled leg behind him, the jailer gave Gyrmund a smile full of rotting teeth as he lumbered closer. He was a giant of a man with fists the size of a man's head. Two-thirds of his own head was purple, the skin twisted and uneven, as if it had been held in a pan of boiling water for a very long time. One eye was useless, a milky white colour amid angry purple. This, however, did not seem to be Herman. Next to him was a small, thin man with a sharp nose and a thin black moustache over sneering lips. While his purple-headed colleague seemed positively pleased to see Gyrmund, this man gave him a once-over with hostile, beady eyes.

'Follow me,' Herman ordered, turning around and retracing his steps down the dark corridor. His accomplice gave Gyrmund one last smile and shuffled along next to Herman. Curtis gave Gyrmund a sharp prod in the back to ensure that he followed them and walked along behind. Obviously, he was going to fulfil his duties by ensuring that he didn't leave until Gyrmund was locked up in chains.

Gyrmund's eyes adjusted to what little light there was, and he made out a door to a cell further up the corridor. It had an iron frame and vertical iron bars so that the jailers could look into the room. As they approached the door, Gyrmund could see a man sitting against the far wall, his arms and legs in manacles.

It was Herin. Their eyes met. Herin had a look of icy rage in his eyes. When he realised it was Gyrmund, a look of disappointment passed over his face. Gyrmund understood why; he represented one less potential rescuer.

Herman unlocked the door, and Gyrmund was shoved into the cell. Sitting next to Herin was Elana. On the opposite wall was Rabigar. Both were in manacles, too.

Herman pointed to a place next to Rabigar. 'Over there.'

Curtis pushed Gyrmund in that direction, causing him to crash against the wall and land awkwardly. He could not stop himself from gasping out loud as his injured shoulder flared in pain.

'Get him ready, Greg,' ordered Herman.

The big jailer knelt, grinned at Gyrmund, and pulled him into position. Curtis moved closer and pointed the tip of his sword towards Gyrmund, discouraging a struggle. Greg put one shackle around Gyrmund's ankle, clasping it into place and then locking it, before repeating the process with the second ankle. Herin and the others watched on in silence. Greg then pulled out a knife and lumbered behind Gyrmund to cut his bonds. Curtis leaned closer and rested the end of his sword on Gyrmund's chest. Greg cut through the bonds, but immediately grabbed one wrist and placed it into a manacle. Once he had secured both arms, he pulled back to admire his work. Curtis withdrew his sword.

'Have fun,' he advised Gyrmund, before, with a nod to Herman, he left the cell and made his way out of the dungeon.

A short period of silence followed. Herman was staring intently at him. Gyrmund felt panic rise within him. He couldn't stand the idea of rotting away in this place. The threat of violence hung heavy in the air. He looked over at his fellow prisoners. While it felt wrong, he was relieved that he wasn't on his own. Herin and Rabigar had grim faces, but were not showing any fear; their expressions were more like anger. Elana was a picture of calm. She had no reason to be, but it made him feel a little better.

A rasping noise made him turn his attention back to Herman. The jailer had withdrawn a knife of his own, a wicked looking instrument with a serrated edge. Still staring into his eyes, Herman walked slowly towards him and dropped to rest on his haunches.

He crawled the knife up between Gyrmund's shackled legs until it rested against his manhood. The jailer still said nothing. Gyrmund didn't know how to respond, so he kept quiet, his eyes flicking down towards the knife and back up to look at the jailer.

Herman, eyes still boring into Gyrmund's, put pressure on the knife. The blade sliced through the leather of his trousers. Herman pushed the cold metal up against the inside of his thigh, then against his member. Terror welled up within him but he resisted the urge to shout out or to struggle. He had to keep control. Silence obviously wasn't working. He forced himself to swallow, his mouth dry with fear.

'What do you want?' he asked, trying to keep his voice steady.

'I have been asked, by the King,' began Herman quietly, 'to discover the location of a certain weapon. I do not intend to fail him. I now have five prisoners. You and your prick are therefore dispensable to me. Tell me where it is, or I cut it off.'

Gyrmund's mind raced to find the best answer. He had no doubt that he was dispensable to this man. Would he go through with his threat? Should Gyrmund pretend he knew something? Pressure down below told him that the jailer wanted an answer now.

'I don't have it. I've never seen it and I don't know where it is. I didn't even know that one of us had it...'

Herman's expression didn't change, and the blade remained where it was. Seconds passed; they seemed like hours to Gyrmund. Herman's hand moved. He withdrew the knife and stood up. Gyrmund let out a ragged breath of relief. The jailer looked around the cell.

'Maybe none of you know anything useful. Maybe you do—but I *will* find out either way. When I'm finished with you, you'll be telling me how many times you wet the bed as a child.' His eyes found Rabigar. 'I'm going to start on this one,' he advised Greg. 'You should have stayed with your own kind, Krykker.'

Rabigar looked at Herman as if he were something unpleasant found on the bottom of his shoe.

Greg lumbered over and detached Rabigar's chains from the wall. He held onto them as if they were puppet strings.

'Get up,' ordered Herman.

Suddenly, Rabigar sprang to life. Despite the chains weighing him down, he thrust himself towards the big jailer holding his chains. Greg was taken by surprise, slow to react. As Rabigar dived into him, Gyrmund saw the Krykker snatch the knife which the giant had been using from his belt. Greg grabbed Rabigar by the hair and yanked the Krykker away with an iron grip. Rabigar slashed upwards at his arm, and Greg howled in pain, letting go of the Krykker. However, with his other hand, the jailer yanked at Rabigar's chains, and the Krykker was pulled to the floor. Greg's booted foot slammed down on Rabigar's hand, effectively disarming him.

Meanwhile, Herman jumped on top of the Krykker's back, wrapping one arm round his neck in a headlock and placing his own knife at Rabigar's throat.

'I should kill you now for trying that!' screamed the jailer hysterically. He had got a fright.

Rabigar was breathing hard, down on all fours, with one man on his back and the other holding his chains.

Greg moaned in pain.

Herman smiled. 'To teach you a lesson for wounding Greg, you should be made to suffer as he has.'

In a deliberate movement, Herman withdrew the knife from Rabigar's throat, reversed the blade, and sent it into his eye.

Rabigar roared out in pain, and Gyrmund cried out in shock. The Krykker reared up and knocked the Barissian off his back.

Greg, however, gave the chains another yank, and dragged the Krykker across the floor, towards the door of the cell. Rabigar clutched at his eye as he was dragged off down the corridor.

Herman picked himself up. He bent over, wheezing. It looked like he had some kind of injury. Then Gyrmund realised that he wasn't injured—he was laughing: a silent, breathy noise that made Gyrmund feel sick. He slowly stood up and gave the cell and its prisoners a final look.

'I think the rest of you should reconsider,' he said, gesturing into the corridor. 'I've only just started with him.'

* * *

BELWYNN STARED at Toric's Dagger.

She had seen it once before, when she and Soren had visited the Temple with her father. It had a fancy enough hilt, if you liked that kind of thing, but the blade itself didn't seem that special. There wasn't much of it—just a thin sliver of metal that ended in a thin point for stabbing. Tiny runes had been inscribed onto the blade. It wasn't in a language she understood, and as she stared at them, they began to swim and swirl around in front of her eyes. Belwynn forced herself to look away from the dagger and returned to the conversation at hand.

'...from the beginning, all of it. And make it quick,' her brother was ordering Dirk.

Dirk nodded his acceptance. 'I have been living here in Coldeberg for some years now. I am not a priest, I make my living by—well, mainly by thieving.' He spread his hands as if to apologise. 'For a while now, Emeric has been building up his power, hiring soldiers—he seems to have unlimited supplies of money from somewhere. A few weeks back, the word was spread about to people like me that he wanted Toric's Dagger. There would be a reward of thirty thousand thalers, a small fortune. I wanted that money.' He shook his head, seemingly in disappointment at himself.

'I decided that the best way to gain access to the dagger was to become a priest of Toric. It took a while, but I was accepted, just about a week ago. I sneaked into the Temple during prayers and took it. It was easy. I was planning my escape when Salvinus and his men broke in. Obviously, he was too late, and he never got the dagger. But everyone assumed he had. The suspicion was totally off me. If I had left of my own accord, it might have awakened some suspicions. By volunteering to go with you, I could leave freely and get protection on the way back to Coldeberg, where I knew Salvinus would be heading.'

'You had it *all the time*?' Clarin blurted out. 'In the Wilderness, on the Great Road when that sorcerer attacked us—'

Words failed the big man, and he grabbed Dirk by the throat.

'Leave him be,' snapped Soren.

Belwynn could tell that her brother was just as angry as she and Clarin were. That he had put them all in unnecessary danger was bad enough, but it was the fact that he had made fools of them all which rankled the most.

'So, this afternoon,' Soren began. 'Why didn't you take the dagger straight to Emeric when you had the chance?'

Dirk had the gall to look affronted by the suggestion. 'I would never do that, not now. Now I understand why it is so important. Elana has explained it all to me.'

Something in that comment made Belwynn uneasy.

'Does Elana know that you've got the dagger?' she demanded.

'Yes,' replied Dirk meekly.

'Gods!' thundered Soren. 'Who else knows?'

'Just her and me—and now you three,' answered Dirk defensively.

Soren pushed his hand through his hair as he tried to take control of the situation in his mind. Belwynn felt the same way; her head was spinning. The attack on the inn, their friends captured. Dirk and the dagger. What should they do now? 'So what have you been doing today?' she asked the thief.

Dirk shifted his pack off his shoulder and opened it up. He shoved his hand inside and pulled out a white cloak. 'I bought this, so that I can look like a proper disciple of Madria,' he said, holding it up for Belwynn to see.

Soren groaned and rolled his eyes up in his head. 'You do realise that Elana has probably been captured by Emeric?' he demanded of Dirk.

The thief-turned-disciple looked shocked. 'What do you mean?'

Belwynn realised they hadn't told Dirk about the situation. Soren, however, looked impatient to get moving.

'I'll fill you in as we go along. We need to establish what exactly has happened and, if necessary, think of some way to rescue the others. Meanwhile, I still think we've been betrayed, and you,' he said, pointing at Dirk, 'are the most likely candidate, despite what you've said.'

He stared balefully at the Barissian, took a step towards him, and snatched the dagger from his hand.

'And I'm keeping hold of this.'

ARIELLA & TIVIAN

XIV

Time had passed. How long, it was hard to say. Gyrmund had been sitting in silence with Herin and Elana, none of them knowing what to say after Rabigar had been dragged away.

Herin shifted his position. 'How did you get caught?'

Gyrmund turned his thoughts away from Rabigar and the jailers. 'Moneva and I returned to the inn. They were waiting for us. They cornered me in the kitchen, but they couldn't find her. Hopefully, they won't. Do you know it was Salvinus?'

Elana nodded. 'He came for Rabigar and I at the inn. He wanted to know where the rest of you had gone. When we wouldn't tell him, he sent us here.'

'What about you?' Gyrmund asked Herin. 'He said he had five of us. Is Kaved here?'

'Yes, they got us first. Kaved and I went into town, but then split up while I went to get a sword. I arranged to meet him later in the town square. When I got there, Salvinus himself was waiting for me, with half a dozen men. I had to give up my sword. I'd only just bought it,' Herin fumed, as if another lost sword was the worst that had happened. 'When I got here, Kaved was already in the cell. They took him for questioning. We haven't heard from him since.'

The sick feeling in Gyrmund's stomach returned. He felt like vomiting. Kaved, then Rabigar—who would be next?

Herin was chewing at his lips, studying him. 'Listen, you two,' he began, 'Salvinus knew exactly where to find me. He knew to go to the inn; he knew to wait there for you and the others to come back. Someone's told him. If Gyrmund was with Moneva the whole time, I suppose that rules her out. It wasn't Soren or Belwynn or Clarin. I know that for a fact. But how else would he know where we were?'

Gyrmund thought about it. It made sense. Salvinus seemed very well informed. 'Does that mean it was one of us? He may have had an informer at the Boot and Saddle.'

Herin shook his head. 'The thing is, only Kaved knew where to find me.'

Gyrmund had no reply to that. It was the first time he had seen Herin look unsure of himself. Maybe the Krykker had betrayed them. No doubt he would receive a substantial reward from the new king. Something was still troubling Gyrmund.

'What I don't understand is—why do they think that we've got the damned dagger?'

* * *

BELWYNN AND CLARIN turned the corner and hurried back to the alleyway. Time, they knew, was not on their side.

Clarin held the lute in his big hands, arms out in front of him. This was hardly a sight which made them look less conspicuous, but somehow, they had not been delayed in the city streets.

When they reached the alleyway, Soren and Dirk were waiting for them. Her brother's face looked grim. 'We've been waiting outside the inn, but no-one has turned up. I think we must assume that all six have been captured. That means we have to go in after them.'

Clarin and Dirk nodded in agreement. Belwynn knew that this was a desperate move. At least the two men were committed to it. Clarin wanted to rescue his brother; Dirk was desperate to save Elana. Belwynn dipped into her pack and pulled out the robe she had chosen for Soren, throwing it over. He quickly shrugged it on over his clothes.

'Right, it's best that everyone leaves the talking to me where possible,' he began. 'We'll have to rely on Dirk to locate them. Our movements will be limited. Of course, it is more than likely that we will be recognised. We have to be ready to flee if necessary; it will do no good to the others if we are captured as well.' Soren paused before continuing. 'None of us knows why yet, but the dagger is important to them.' He pulled it out from a pocket of his cloak. 'We are going to be bringing it into the castle. I believe it is better for Dirk to have it for now. He has a higher chance of escaping. If we fail and he escapes, he has agreed to return to Edgar and explain what happened.' Soren sighed. 'Questions?'

'Yes,' said Belwynn. 'How can you trust him like this?'

'I have no other choices, Belwynn. If he was working for them, why would he still have it on him?'

It was a logical argument; she had come to the same conclusion herself. But that didn't mean she trusted the thief. Still, what else could they do?

'Alright, let's get on with it,' she conceded.

Belwynn stashed her sword in the shadows of the alleyway, just in case they had the chance to retrieve it.

Clarin, eager to get going, handed her the lute. He stroked the hilt of his sword and led them out of the alley.

Belwynn followed on, thinking over Soren's plan to get them inside Coldeberg Castle. The four of them were to pose as travelling entertainers: Belwynn, a singer and musician, and Soren a conjurer. This was a variation on a routine they had done more than once, and the twins knew their parts. Belwynn had chosen herself a lovely dress and picked out a suitable robe for Soren which had stars embroidered onto it. Clarin was their bodyguard and Dirk a servant. Quality entertainers were usually allowed into the courts of rich noblemen. Since Emeric was now a king, Soren reckoned he would be even more likely to want to celebrate and provide entertainment for the lords and ladies of his new kingdom. Once they got inside, Dirk could peel off and explore the castle.

Clarin led them on the uphill journey towards the castle. As they crossed a street, Belwynn could see the building looming ahead.

On the other side, a trio of soldiers walked by in the opposite direction. Belwynn's nerves jangled. Coldeberg was crawling with soldiers, and some of them would be out looking for her and her friends. Fortunately, the soldiers were laughing and joking between themselves, and did not seem interested in them. It made her wonder, however, about her twin's rescue plan. There was a fair chance they would be allowed entry. But once inside, it would not be long before they were recognised by someone. They were asking to perform before Emeric himself, for Toric's sake! She knew that they would have to rely, again, on Soren's powers.

How are you, Soren? she asked, concerned about the idea. *How well recovered?*

I'll have to be honest with you, Belwynn, he replied, looking ahead. *Since I woke up after the Wilderness, I've had nothing. I've lost my powers. I burned them out by overextending myself that day. I went to seek help this afternoon but found none. I'm sorry.*

Belwynn didn't know what to say. Her mind was already in bits. And now this? Everything she and her brother had worked for, vanished? And now, when they needed his magic the most, they were about to march into Coldeberg Castle without it? She tried to collect her thoughts and make a reply, but as she did, they turned the corner and came upon the gatehouse.

This stone building controlled access to the rest of the castle. If it was under siege, the drawbridge would be up and the portcullis down. Now, however, two guards stood on the drawbridge to deny entry. As they approached the two young soldiers, Soren moved to the front. They held out their spears in warning.

'What business do you have here?' one of them called out.

Soren approached with an air of friendly confidence. 'Hello there! Well met, good soldiers of Barissia. I am Tivian the Magnificent, a conjurer of the very highest quality. And this,' he said, gesturing extravagantly towards Belwynn, 'this is the Lady Ariella, a minstrel with the sweetest voice in all Dalriya. We have come here—'

'Sir!' interrupted one of the guardsmen, calling into the gatehouse.

After a few moments, a portly, older man emerged from his quarters in the gatehouse. He looked the four of them up and down.

'Well met!' began Soren, and repeated his introductions, word for word, with the same enthusiasm. 'We have come here to help celebrate King Emeric's consecration as King of Barissia.'

The old soldier didn't seem as impressed as he should have been. He stroked at his moustache. 'Who are these two?' he demanded gruffly, gesturing at Clarin and Dirk.

'The big man is our bodyguard. It will not surprise a man of your experience to know that some roads we take could be very dangerous if travelled alone. We have long found it necessary to secure the services of a hired man. In truth, it is a very great drain on our resources, but we have been left with little choice,' Soren explained, with a self-pitying simper.

'What about the other one?' pressed the soldier.

'Oh, he is nothing, nothing but our simple-minded servant.'

The old soldier stroked at his moustache again. 'Well, they have more than enough servants in the castle, and there is no need for a bodyguard here either.'

Soren put on a troubled expression. 'Oh no, we must have our men with us, we must!' He skipped forward towards the soldier and grabbed his hands. Belwynn could just make out a glint of metal as he pressed something into the hands of the soldier. 'Please allow them as well, sir!'

The old soldier pulled his hands away from Soren, but seemed to have a contented expression on his face. 'Well, alright then, but he'll have to hand in his weapon,' he said gesturing towards Clarin.

Clarin unbuckled his sword and handed it to the soldier.

'Dom!' shouted the captain into the gatehouse. Another soldier came hurrying out. He was young looking, with big, bushy eyebrows. 'Take these four to see Master Orlin. If he doesn't want them, escort them back out of the castle again.'

'Yes, sir!' exclaimed Dom. He waved them all to follow him and began marching across the drawbridge.

Belwynn and the others followed behind. The two soldiers on the drawbridge moved aside to let them pass.

They were in.

Dom led them into the outer bailey of the castle. They were now within the walls of Coldeberg Castle. As well as the gatehouse, the castle had six towers between which ran the high walls. Since the castle was situated in the far northern corner of the city, half of the castle walls doubled up as the city walls as well. The bailey was open to the elements, with a few wooden buildings. Belwynn noticed a stable to their left and a training yard in the distance. The other half of the site was taken up by a large stone building, two storeys high. This would be where the residents lived and where Emeric had his hall.

Dom led them towards the entrance to the living quarters. A huge wooden door was open, guarded by a further two soldiers, wearing the livery of the Duke, now King, of Barissia.

'Are you really a conjurer?' asked the young soldier as they continued to make their way.

Soren raised an eyebrow, but stopped and grabbed a coin from inside his robe. He placed it on his thumb and then flicked it high into the air. As it came spinning down, he clapped his hands. The coin had vanished. He took a step towards Dom and placed his hand behind the soldier's ear. When he withdrew his hand, he was holding the coin.

'That's amazing!' said the soldier, his thick eyebrows raised in wonder.

Soren took a small bow. 'Onwards?' he suggested.

Dom nodded and took them to the door. 'I'm taking them to see Master Orlin,' he told the two guards. They stepped aside.

Dom ushered the group through the door and into the stone structure. They entered a sizeable hallway. Candles set in finely worked sconces and intricate tapestries lined the stone walls. On the wall to their left, a fire blazed.

Several people were warming themselves there. On the right hand and opposite walls were doors leading to other parts of the castle.

'Orlin's chambers are upstairs,' Dom informed them, and led them to the corner of the hall, where a set of stone steps led upwards. Next to them, steps led down beneath the castle. These steps were guarded by another couple of soldiers. Belwynn exchanged glances with the others. The significance of that was lost on none of them.

They continued up the steps—narrow, steep, and circled upwards at a tight angle.

'Is Orlin the king's steward?' Belwynn asked the soldier as they reached the top of the stairs.

'He's the royal chamberlain. Runs the castle for the King. Oversees the entertainment for the court. He'll probably want to use you for the evening meal, when King Emeric feasts his lords.'

Once they reached the second-floor hallway, Dom led them through a door on the right and into a corridor. They passed doors to rooms on the left and right, but the soldier led them on until they reached the last door at the end of the corridor. He banged on the heavy wooden door and it was promptly opened. A smallish, balding man with a hooked nose poked his head into the corridor.

'What do you want?' he demanded.

Dom did not seem taken aback by the rather unwelcoming response. 'I have escorted these travelling entertainers here who would like to perform for the King.'

'Hello there! Do I have the pleasure of addressing Master Orlin—' began Soren, but he was interrupted.

'No, you don't,' said the man at the door. 'I work for him, he's busy right now. But it's my job to sort out the riff-raff. What do you do?' he demanded.

'He does really great magic tricks!' Dom answered for Soren excitedly.

Orlin's man did not look impressed. 'Show me.'

Soren produced two coins. He showed the man that both hands were empty apart from the coins. With both coins in his left hand, he put the hand into a fist. He then used his right hand to take one of the coins from the fist and gave it to the man. Soren then opened his left hand again. The two coins were still there in his palm.

Dom gave a little clap. Orlin's man grunted, pocketing the coin. 'What about the others?' he asked, waving a hand at Belwynn, Clarin and Dirk.

'Well,' began Soren, 'these two are mere servants, but this is my sister, Ariella. She has the sweetest singing voice in all of Dalriya!'

'Let's hear it, then.'

Belwynn cleared her throat. She decided to sing a well-known song from the Empire, which she thought would suit the audience. *The Fight for Freedom* was a song celebrating the end of Persaleian rule over the Brasingians.

Even after the first few words, Belwynn's singing had its usual effect. A gift, many people had told her. A singing voice she had been given, capable of melting the hearts of the coldest men of the land. The first line was enough to bring tears to Dom's eyes. After the first verse, the other man had succumbed. His face had a look of wonderment on it, as if he was experiencing emotions he didn't think he had. Belwynn stopped after the first verse and chorus, but that was enough.

'Yes, well, I'm sure you'll do just fine,' mumbled Orlin's man, and fully opened the door to let them enter.

As they entered the room, Dom called out a goodbye and, brushing a tear from his eye, made his way back down the corridor.

Belwynn and the others had entered an antechamber. It was a well-furnished room leading on to two further rooms, but their host gestured for them to sit and wait here. Belwynn sank down into a comfortable seat, and the others did likewise.

'My name is Tivian the Magnificent,' said Soren. 'May I have the pleasure of your name?'

'Urval.'

There followed an uncomfortable silence, during which even Tivian the Magnificent was lost for words. However, Urval eventually broke it.

'I will tell Master Orlin that you're here, but don't expect him to be hurried, he's a busy man.' Urval glanced over at Belwynn with a pained expression, as if he didn't want to be reminded of any emotions he might have felt from her song. 'I'll get you some drinks first,' he said.

'That is very gracious, sir,' responded Soren. 'However, there is no need to get this one a drink,' he said pointing at Dirk. 'While we like to have our bodyguard with us at all times—for my sister's protection, you understand—this one is of little use, to tell the truth. If you have a servant's quarters he would be best off there.'

'Yes, it's downstairs. He just has to say that I sent him. He'll be looked after alright down there.'

'Off you go, Skerit.'

Dirk got up and left the room.

* * *

RABIGAR WAS LYING face down on a table, his hands and ankles bound. He was vaguely aware of his torturers working on his back with a cutting instrument, as if they were trying to remove the scales from his flesh. They were talking, to each other or to him, he wasn't sure. The pain in his head was dominating his senses. It left him feeling nauseous.

The attack in the cell had left him blind and, he thought, dying. He couldn't scream or shout out. Herman and Greg could have done anything to him now; it would not register above the pain caused by his eye wound. Every now and again he would get a woozy sensation, as if he was about to faint. He fought against it, fearing that he would never regain consciousness if he lost it now.

He only dimly heard the knock on the door. His torturers exchanged words. The cutting stopped. It went silent. He heard the door being opened. There was muffled shouting from behind him, and then a sharp, piercing scream to his right. It went silent again. Rabigar concentrated on his hearing, trying to block out the pain so that he could try to understand what was going on.

Then someone spoke to him, a soft voice. 'Rabigar? Can you hear me?'

He hadn't been expecting a woman's voice.

He worked up some spit so that he could reply.

'Moneva?'

A SONG FOR A KING

XV

Belwynn, Soren and Clarin were sitting in Orlin's chambers, waiting.

Belwynn plucked nervously at the strings of the lute. She re-tuned the instrument until it sounded perfect, then adjusted it some more. Every few seconds, one of them would look anxiously at the door. They hoped for the return of Dirk—hoped he had not betrayed them and that he had located their friends. They feared the return of Urval, that their subterfuge would have to continue and put them in greater danger.

Eventually, they heard footsteps and the sound of voices approaching the door. Clarin stood up. The door swung open. It was Urval. He entered the room with another man.

'This is Master Orlin, chamberlain to King Emeric,' he announced gruffly.

Two more men hovered in the doorway. They had swords strapped to their waists. Clarin looked at Soren. Belwynn knew that, with a nod, Clarin would set on all four. But with no weapon himself, that would be a desperate move. Soren hesitated briefly, but decided against it and stood up himself.

'Ah, Lord Orlin, a great pleasure to meet you,' he began, bowing his head towards the floor. 'I am Tivian the Magnificent. My sister, the Lady Ariella, and I have travelled a long way to entertain this great court.'

Orlin snorted. He was an older man, draped in expensive clothes. He had a long face, accentuated by a thin grey beard which ended at a slick point. His eyes were piercing blue, and he studied each of them with the attitude of someone who was continually disappointed with the stupidity of those he encountered.

'I sincerely doubt that your sister is a lady, in which case you should not use the title.'

Tivian the Magnificent laughed nervously.

'It is not my habit to meet and greet every entertainer that passes through this castle. But when informing me of your arrival, my servant advised me that your sister was a very good singer. In the twenty or so years that he has worked for me, Urval has never been so fulsome in his praise. As a consequence, both myself and the King are interested to hear this voice.'

Orlin turned his gaze to Belwynn again.

'If the voice is as pretty as the vessel, it must be special indeed.'

Belwynn blushed and muttered a demure thank you.

'You will perform at this evening's banquet, in about two hours. But first, King Emeric has requested a private audience. This is a great honour I have arranged for you. Do not disappoint.'

No. Belwynn's heart dropped into her stomach. The plan had gone wrong already. They were going to be taken to see the very man who was hunting them down.

'Of course not,' enthused Soren. 'My heart is beating wildly with excitement.'

Orlin frowned at him. 'Most importantly, do not make the mistake of addressing him as a duke. It must be king. That would be more than your life is worth.'

Orlin turned around and left the room. The four men headed back down the corridor. Belwynn, Soren and Clarin followed behind.

At the end of the corridor, they came to the stairs. Belwynn looked around, wishing that Dirk or even Herin would rush up to intervene. But no-one did. They continued towards their destination, Belwynn's sense of dread growing with each unavoidable footstep.

Instead of going down the stairs, they went through a second door. This opened into an antechamber. Two armed soldiers watched them walk straight past. Urval opened a large wooden door and ushered everybody through.

Emeric's chamber was not large; his main hall would be downstairs somewhere. Belwynn had been expecting more people, but only two were waiting for them.

Sitting on a large chair at the end of the room, facing them, must be Emeric. Belwynn had to admit that he carried himself like a king. He was not tall, but well-built, had mid-length jet black hair, which he pushed back, and a pale complexion. He was wearing leather and looked like he had just come back from, or was about to go, hunting.

Standing next to him was an unusual looking man. That was, he looked unusual at first sight, but on second sight Belwynn found it difficult to decide why. Certainly, he did not dress like a Brasingian nobleman. He wore a long fur cloak with inscriptions sewn into it around the edges. He did not carry a weapon. He was clean shaven, with closely cropped dark hair. It was his eyes, maybe. They were a dark, strange colour, close to violet, she thought. When Belwynn looked at his eyes, they gave nothing away: no expression or emotion.

Watch out for Emeric's friend, advised Soren. *I think he's an Isharite. He could be a wizard.*

'Your Majesty, the songstress Ariella, at your request,' introduced Orlin.

Belwynn curtseyed, and Soren gave a deep bow.

Emeric looked Belwynn over. 'Very nice. Who are these?' he asked, waving a hand at Soren and Clarin.

'Greetings…' began Soren, but he was cut off by Orlin.

'This is the brother, the conjurer. This is their guard.'

'Did I ask to see them?' The question was put innocently enough, but Belwynn could sense the steel underneath.

'No, sire, you did not. My apologies. I will ask them to leave,' replied Orlin.

'No. They're here now. They may stay,' announced the king magnanimously.

At a prompt from Orlin, Urval moved over to the side of the chamber and grabbed a stool, which he carried towards Emeric. He deposited it about twelve feet away from the king. Orlin and Urval then moved over to stand by the wall on one side of the room. The king gestured for Belwynn to sit on the stool. Belwynn, carrying her lute with her, did so. She sat down, facing only Emeric and his friend. Meanwhile Soren, Clarin and the two soldiers were left to find standing positions along the second wall.

Choose a long one, advised Soren. *Try to keep it going until the others get here.*

If they get here, thought Belwynn. Dirk had betrayed them and warned the Barissians of their presence, but that did not mean that he would or could locate and free the others. Unfortunately, that prospect appeared to be all they had. Emeric inclined his head towards her, indicating that she should begin.

With his dubious position as a newly crowned king in mind, Belwynn decided that it was best to steer clear of any songs connected to the Empire. She settled on the neutral song of *Celandine the Slave Queen.*

Celandine was a girl from the coast of Kalinth during the time of the

Vismarian Onslaught. The local knight, Hector, had failed to defend his people and instead paid tribute to the Vismarians to stop their attacks. He took Celandine from her home and sold her into slavery to the rovers of Vismar. She became the slave of Bringar, a fierce warrior, who took her back to his home. Over time, however, Bringar fell in love with Celandine, and made her his wife. To honour her, he returned to the shores of Kalinth with his war band. There he won a great victory over the Knights of Kalinth. Hector and many of his allies lay dead, and Bringar established a Vismarian kingdom there. Celandine returned to her homeland to be crowned queen.

Belwynn sang, playing the lute to support her voice. She used her voice to throw out patterns, to entice and entrance the listener and dominate their senses. She pulled them into the song so that all they were aware of was the music, the story, and her.

It did not take long for Emeric to lose himself in her voice. She could tell the signs by now. The eyes were the best guide. Emeric's became transfixed, focusing on some object in the distance, looking at her but through her at the same time. Frowns of concentration on his forehead eased away and his facial muscles relaxed. A light smile appeared on his lips.

Others soon followed: the two soldiers, Urval, even stern Lord Orlin.

But one man did not lose himself in Belwynn's song. The man from Ishari was indeed looking at her, but very differently from the others. His strange, violet eyes were staring into hers, as if he could see through into her mind and her soul. He made no facial gesture other than the stare, and once Belwynn noticed that, it became difficult to concentrate on anything else.

As Belwynn sang and strummed the closing notes of the song, the Isharite began clapping, making stilted, discordant noises.

'Very good,' he pronounced as he clapped, though his sneer said otherwise. This had the effect of waking the others from their reverie. Emeric flashed his companion a look of anger for making the sound, but it passed quickly. He shook his head, as if waking up from sleep. The other listeners did the same.

'Ariella, come here,' beckoned the King.

Belwynn placed the lute on the floor and stood up from her chair. She walked over to him. Emeric remained seated. The Isharite still stood beside him, watching her, his sneer not far from his lips.

'That was wonderful, Ariella,' Emeric declared in a quiet voice. He offered Belwynn the palm of his hand. She placed her own in it. Emeric raised her hand and gave it a kiss, lingering just a touch longer than politeness allowed. He returned it with reluctance. Emeric's eyes glanced over towards Soren.

'This conjurer,' he began, keeping his voice to little over a whisper, 'he is your brother, yes?'

'That is right, Your Majesty,' replied Belwynn.

'Ah…' Emeric looked pleased. 'You must stay at court for a while. Both of you, of course.' Emeric's eyes moved from hers to appraise her body, looking at her breasts, her hips, and her legs. There was no doubt why he wanted Belwynn to stay around.

Belwynn forced herself to continue with the routine. She had to hope that this would soon end. 'You are most generous, Your Majesty.'

From the corner of her eye, Belwynn saw the Isharite smirking.

Emeric followed her gaze. 'Don't mind Tirano. He can be tiresome, but he has his uses.'

Emeric indicated Belwynn should step to the side as he turned his attention to the small gathering in the chamber. 'I am well pleased with this performance. Ariella will be invited to sing more of her songs at supper tonight. Her brother will also perform,' he added. 'This song of Celandine has much to teach us. This Bringar of Vismar was not born a king, but he made himself one. Those men who cannot defend their people, men such as this Hector, will have their titles stripped away. Soon there will be many changes in Dalriya. We in Barissia are the ones who will rise to glory.'

Everybody in the chamber politely applauded Emeric's speech, including the Isharite, Tirano. Belwynn noted that he even nodded in agreement with the king's words.

Then the door opened. One of the soldiers from the antechamber outside had pushed it open, and he now leaned into the chamber.

'Kaved the Krykker,' he announced.

Before Belwynn could take in what was happening, Kaved sauntered into the room. He took a few steps and then stopped dead. For a moment he stared at Belwynn, then at Soren and Clarin standing by the wall.

'What the fuck is happening here?' he demanded.

Then everything happened very fast.

Belwynn's head started swimming. Kaved was the traitor, and he was about to blow their cover.

'How dare you burst in here and speak to the King like that?' Orlin was demanding of the Krykker.

At the same time, Kaved was speaking. 'That's them, you idiots! They're the ones with the dagger!'

Now it was time for Emeric and the others to look around in bewilderment.

Belwynn grabbed the opportunity. She leant down and grabbed the knife she had been concealing in her boot. Before he had time to react, she grabbed Emeric off his chair and put the knife to his throat. Tirano grabbed at the arm of the king as if to pull him away.

'Let go or he's dead!' screamed Belwynn, more hysterically than she had intended.

Tirano let go and backed off. The two soldiers along the wall had drawn their own swords and now faced her. Meanwhile, Kaved and the two guards from the chamber were closing in as well.

Belwynn pressed the knife edge into the king's neck, drawing blood. 'Tell them to stop or I'll do it!'

'Stop! She's got a knife,' shouted Emeric hoarsely.

'Do as the king says. No closer,' Tirano commanded Kaved and the soldiers.

The soldiers—even Kaved—did as they were asked, but still held their swords. Belwynn had bought them some time, but they were outnumbered and the longer the face-off went on, the more likely the rest of the castle would hear. Her knife hand was shaking, causing Emeric to utter a fearful *careful* as it scratched against his throat.

What are we going to do? she asked Soren.

'Give it up, Belwynn,' shouted Kaved. 'They won't hurt you. They just want the dagger.'

'Shut up, traitor,' Clarin shouted back at him. 'Where's my brother?'

'Here I am,' came a shout from the door.

Belwynn peered over to the doorway. Standing in the entrance, sword in each hand, stood Herin. *Don't say he's betrayed us as well,* she thought.

He raised one sword so that it was pointing at Kaved's head. 'And now you pay for your treachery.'

Herin rushed into the room, throwing one sword to Clarin while lunging at the Krykker with the other. Kaved met his sword stroke and the clash of steel rang out in the room. Then, behind Herin, Belwynn saw Moneva enter the room.

'This way,' Moneva shouted over to them.

Belwynn tried to pull Emeric toward the doors at the far end of the chamber. Her knife hand, however, was now shaking violently; she could no longer control it. She looked over at Tirano and saw him staring intently at her. He was using magic. Her hand began to jerk away from Emeric's neck, so that the knife was no longer pressed against him.

The king took his chance. With one hand he grabbed Belwynn's wrist, pushing it away, and then smashed backwards with his other elbow. Emeric caught Belwynn in the face and she fell backwards, dropping the knife.

Belwynn landed sharply on her backside. Her nose throbbed, and she felt dazed. She could hear shouting all around her and the clash of swords. Then arms grabbed at her, half dragging, half lifting her to her feet.

It was Soren. He was pulling her over to the doors. Herin was slashing wildly at Kaved and had pushed him backwards into the room, but the Krykker was resisting. Closer to the doors, Moneva was clashing swords with one of the guards; another lay on the floor, clutching his chest.

'This way,' came a shout, and there was Dirk, beckoning them out of the room. Belwynn and Soren passed through the doors and turned around to look for Clarin. The big warrior was walking backwards in their direction, fighting against Orlin's soldiers. Belwynn could see a body lying on the floor and thought at first that it was Emeric, but she could see him by his throne, along with Tirano and Orlin. She realised that the body must be that of Urval.

Then Emeric, Tirano and Orlin began moving towards Clarin, and Belwynn could see swords in their hands. 'Clarin, watch out!' she called. Dirk responded by running over to stand by Clarin, but they were too heavily outnumbered.

'Herin!' shouted Soren. 'We've got to go!'

Herin had pressed Kaved back and back, but had not found an opening in his defence. He took a step back and looked around at the room. After a brief respite, he pressed on at Kaved once more, but after three strokes he suddenly pulled backwards. In a fluid movement he spun around and moved on the soldier who was fighting Moneva, swinging at him from behind. The soldier never saw the blow coming as Herin's sword sliced into his neck. Moneva stepped over the body and, together with Herin, moved in to help Clarin and Dirk.

Belwynn looked behind her, through the next set of doors, towards the stairs. There was no-one there, but it was only a matter of time. 'Hurry!' she shouted back into the room. They were moving towards the door but still facing outwards to defend against the Barissians.

'I'll come back for you,' Herin snarled at Kaved.

'You'll finish it now, unless you're craven,' Kaved barked back.

Moneva turned around and skipped through the door, past Belwynn and Soren. 'Follow me,' she called without stopping. Belwynn and Soren ran after her and soon made it to the stairs. Moneva was already halfway down. Belwynn began descending the thin and winding steps, Soren close behind, and Dirk behind him. At the bottom Belwynn arrived in the castle hallway where the fine tapestries hung, with the fire still blazing. Thankfully, nobody was standing around it any more. She wondered why, and turned around to ask Moneva.

'We've dumped the bodies down the stairs,' she answered, before Belwynn got her words out.

'This way,' said Dirk.

Rather than attempt to leave via the bailey and through the gatehouse, Dirk took them in another direction. They ran behind him, down a long corridor with rooms on either side. The corridor ended in an opening into a room from where Belwynn could hear clanging noises and the occasional shout. Dirk ran straight in, and she followed.

The room turned out to be the castle kitchens. There were a dozen people working there: kneading bread, filleting meat, boiling stew, washing and carrying pots, pans and utensils. When Dirk entered, there were shouts and challenges. After he had waved a sword at them and Belwynn and the others entered the room, they piped down.

Dirk took a second to get his bearings and then moved to the far end of the room. He dropped his sword and began moving a huge set of shelves containing pots and pans, crockery, tubs of sauces and bags of flour and salt. A couple of plates fell off and smashed onto the floor. Soren rushed over to give him a hand, and they shifted it out of the way. They had revealed an iron gate, which Belwynn hadn't even noticed behind the shelves. Soren pushed and pulled at the gate, but it was secured with a lock. They didn't have a key.

Dirk fumbled in his pockets and pulled out a slim piece of metal, which ended in a short curvature. He inserted it into the lock and then wriggled it about inside. Meanwhile, Clarin and Herin had entered the kitchens, looking behind them for any potential pursuers. After a few moments Dirk gave it a full twist and pushed open the gate, which moved with a rusty screech. He rushed through and Soren followed behind him.

Belwynn followed her twin into a small, round stone room. She briefly glanced up and realised that she was in one of the castle towers. Two feet above them was a grate, forming a murder hole through which burning oil or other material could be poured down onto attackers. It was more than likely that there were some guards in that room now. Dirk moved directly to a postern gate in the opposite wall and jiggled his skeleton key in the lock before it clicked. They burst through the door and found themselves outside the city walls, on a long grassy slope leading downwards. Beyond, they could see meadows and fields.

'Keep moving,' said Herin. 'Get away from the walls!'

They ran down the slope, Belwynn's legs going so fast that she thought she would fall over. She turned back to see some guards lining the walls looking at them, but there seemed little they could do from up there. Then, a file of soldiers emptied out of the gate they had used and called out a challenge before pursuing them down the hill.

'Where are we going?' shouted Soren, his breath ragged already.

'Just keep going,' Moneva shouted back. 'With some luck, Gyrmund will meet up with us. If not, this could be the briefest escape in history.'

They kept running away from the city. Belwynn's lungs were burning. She could see, up ahead, there was farmland, and to the right a rough track.

Then she heard the horses coming. How could they have got a mounted force here so quickly? She had to turn around to look.

A group of half a dozen horsemen were coming towards them from the west side of the city. She could see the lead soldier wore the livery of the dukes of Barissia. Belwynn took a second look. Rather than six horsemen, there were in fact only three of them, each one riding a mount and bringing a spare with them.

The man in the lead, wearing the soldier's uniform, was Gyrmund.

He drew up, gritting his teeth as if he was in pain, as Belwynn and Moneva ran towards him. Moneva climbed up onto the spare horse and held out a hand for Belwynn to climb on with her, since there weren't enough horses for one each.

Behind Gyrmund came Elana, not finding the task of riding and holding the reins of another horse quite so easy. Rabigar was even further back. There was something over his eye—no. On closer inspection, she saw he had no eye any more, just a bloody socket where it had once been.

'What happened to Rabigar?' Belwynn blurted out.

Gyrmund screwed up his face as if he was about to cry. 'They took his eye,' he said, almost choking on the words.

Belwynn physically flinched at the news.

Clarin swore out loud.

'How is he?' Soren asked Elana.

'His eye is gone. I have done what I can for him.'

'Can't you fix it?' asked Belwynn.

'I can't grow back an eye,' responded Elana. 'He needs rest for his body to cope with the shock.'

'We can't give him rest,' said Soren. 'Not now.'

As Rabigar pulled up, Herin quickly clambered on in front of him and took the reins. Rabigar put his arms around Herin's waist and slumped forwards. Clarin and Soren took the remaining spares. The soldiers were only a couple of hundred yards behind them, but it looked like they had already given up on the chase.

'Come on,' said Herin, 'we have to assume they'll be sending a force after us. We can talk later.'

Moneva kicked their horse on and Belwynn was forced to hold on to her waist. Belwynn realised they were on her own horse, the one they had bought back in Vitugia. Gyrmund and the others had somehow gone back to the Boot and Saddle to collect them. There was a lot of explaining to be done at some point, but for now Belwynn was content to look back as Emeric's soldiers and castle receded into the distance.

They were still in danger, she knew, but she felt a sense of relief at leaving the place behind. Belwynn thought she would be quite happy if she never saw Coldeberg again.

THE IMPS

XVI

Gyrmund took them across the open land north of Coldeberg, onto a track that headed in a north-easterly direction and would take them to the Kellish border. It was certainly the shortest route out of Barissia. The track was narrow and uneven, not nearly as fast as travelling on the Barissian Road; but if they tried to cut east, they would almost certainly run into Emeric's soldiers. Meanwhile, they had to assume that a force would come after them, and at a faster pace, given that many of them were sharing horses. Rabigar had his arms around Herin, his one eye closed and his face deathly pale, with a pained expression. He obviously needed to rest, but they simply couldn't afford to.

They passed through Barissian farming land, gently rolling terrain with fields of grass, crops and grazing animals, not unlike the Magnian lands Belwynn had grown up in. They were rich lands, but she knew all too well how much work the farming folk who lived here had to put in to keep them that way. She wondered what they thought about their duke spending all their taxes on mercenaries and threatening war with their neighbours. She knew from her own bitter experience what civil wars did to places like this.

'Look there!' shouted Clarin, pointing behind them. Belwynn could see that the land they had travelled across gradually declined and, on the horizon, from the direction of Coldeberg, was a large group of riders, perhaps two score in all.

'Can we get to the border in time?' Belwynn asked.

Gyrmund pulled a face. 'I don't think so.'

'Herin and I could hold them up for a bit,' suggested Clarin. But even he sounded doubtful.

'We'll carry on for now,' said Soren. 'Let's not do anything reckless until we know we have to.'

They moved on again. But that sick feeling had returned to Belwynn's stomach. The others were probably hoping that Soren could help get them out of the situation again. She knew he couldn't.

They rode on. Afternoon was turning into evening, but it was a fine summer's day and Belwynn knew they wouldn't be saved by the drawing in of the night. It didn't seem like they would reach Kelland before the end of the day, either. As each minute passed, things got a bit more desperate. When she looked back, she saw that a smaller group of riders, about half a dozen, had detached itself from the main group and were gaining on them much faster. As soon as this faster group caught up with them, they would be forced to stop, and then the main group would be on them too.

Ahead, Gyrmund slowed down.

'What is it?' shouted Herin.

'Soldiers.'

'Barissians?' Belwynn asked. 'How could they have got ahead of us?'

'Not sure who they are,' said Gyrmund.

They trotted forwards, unsure whether they were about to be trapped between two forces and if they should make a break for it across country.

Belwynn peered over Moneva's shoulder to look. There was a sizeable force of riders spread across the track and to either side of it, at least as many as the chasing Barissians, who were now catching up fast. This second force wasn't moving, however. They seemed content to watch.

Belwynn turned around. The leading group of six riders was very close now; she could make out their individual faces.

'We've got to do something!' she said.

'Let's risk it, then!' replied Moneva.

Moneva spurred her horse on towards the waiting group of soldiers.

'Moneva, wait!' shouted Gyrmund, but she ignored him.

Sitting at the front, a few feet ahead of his troops, seemed to be the leader of the small force. He was approaching middle age, had close-cropped black hair and stubble. Neither he nor his soldiers wore any identifiable markings—just simple-looking leather armour—but their weapons and their horses looked expensive enough.

'Who are you?' demanded Moneva.

It was a little too bold an opening for Belwynn's taste, and the man seemed to think so, too, as he reacted with a frown and a half smile.

'I am Walter, Marshal of the Empire,' he replied. 'And I was wondering who you might be, too.'

'Thank the gods!' declared Moneva and rode the short distance over towards him.

Some of Walter's troops moved forward, as if they saw Moneva as a threat, but he held up an arm and they stayed in position. Gyrmund and the others, hearing his reply, joined them. Meanwhile, the first six riders of the Barissians had pulled up, looking warily at Walter's war band themselves.

Walter? Isn't that Baldwin's brother? Belwynn asked Soren.

Yes, he replied. *We may have just been saved.*

'We've just escaped from Coldeberg,' said Moneva, apparently neither shy nor hesitant about explaining the situation to him. 'Those are Barissian soldiers after us. Did you know Emeric has made himself king?'

'Yes, I had heard,' replied Walter, still finding something amusing about the encounter. 'That's kind of why I'm in the area.'

The rest of the Barissians had now caught up with the lead group, and they sat as their mounts drew breath, staring balefully at Belwynn and the rest of them. One of them trotted forwards from the group, stopping when he reached the halfway point between the two forces. He had a mean-looking scar from ear to chin and sat there, an air of confidence about him.

'Salvinus!' hissed Gyrmund.

This was the man they had been chasing? Belwynn felt almost pleased to put a face to the name at last.

'Have you come for a fight, Salvinus?' Herin shouted towards him. 'I'm ready for you, if so.'

Soren had to reach over a restraining hand to stop Herin moving forwards. Belwynn wondered if Herin would have been quite so full of machismo if he wasn't sitting with about fifty imperial soldiers. He probably would, she decided.

Salvinus ignored Herin's invitation.

'Walter,' he said, nodding at the marshal.

'Gervase,' came the reply.

Suddenly Belwynn was filled with doubt. They were on first-name terms. Might they be allies?

'This group you've apprehended are escaped prisoners from Coldeberg. They tried to assassinate Emeric today. I am taking them back there.'

'Indeed, so they tell me. Why don't you tell me something, Gervase? Did they try to kill Duke Emeric or King Emeric?'

'King Emeric.'

'Indeed. That puts a rather different perspective on the situation.'

'I don't see what it has to do with it.'

'You don't see?' Walter's tone moved from genial to outraged in three words. 'You don't see how that makes him a traitor?'

For the first time Salvinus looked a bit disconcerted. He tried to shrug the issue away. 'A title is a title, to me. I know Emeric meant no offence to Baldwin over it. He still recognises his authority as his liege lord and emperor.'

'A subject receives his title from the emperor. He doesn't presume to take one himself. We both know what Emeric has done, so don't play the innocent, Gervase.'

'Look,' said Gervase, still all reasonable. 'That business needs to be settled between Emeric and Baldwin. Fair enough. Our business here is about these prisoners. You're on Barissian soil; that can be overlooked. But you don't want to get personally involved in this, Walter. You don't want to make a personal enemy of Emeric. Believe me.'

'He doesn't want us,' said Soren. 'He wants something we have. I think Emperor Baldwin would be very interested in it.'

Walter raised an eyebrow at that. 'Thing is, Gervase, I'm on Imperial soil, and I'm Marshal of the Empire. Unless you want to make a fight of it, which I don't recommend, you'll have to run back to Emeric without your prisoners. And you can take him some personal advice from me. He better come crawling to Essenberg with an apology soon if he wants to keep his duchy.'

'This is very stupid, Walter,' said Gervase, at last flashing some anger of his own. 'We'll get what we want in the end. You don't know who you're dealing with.'

'Oh, you might be surprised about what I know,' responded the Marshal.

Gervase turned his horse around and left without another word.

He passed his men and carried on back down the track towards Coldeberg. Turning their mounts around, the rest of the Barissians followed him. Belwynn and the others watched them go until they were left alone with Walter and his soldiers.

'Thank you so much,' said Belwynn to him, meaning every word.

'Well, you're welcome. This has been an unexpected end to the day. But I should warn you, based on what I've just heard, the Emperor and his ministers will want to hear about this. If you were planning to go to to Essenberg anyway, well that's just fine, and we can all stay friends. But if you had other plans, I have to tell you, they've been changed. You're coming with me to see my brother. Whether you like it or not.'

'It was Kaved,' said Moneva. 'He betrayed us to Salvinus.'

The inquisition had begun, then. And maybe the recriminations.

Yesterday Walter had taken them another two miles along the track to his camp, and most of them had collapsed into the beds he had provided for them without saying a word to each other. Belwynn certainly had. But now that they had slept and Walter had seen to it they were provided with some army rations for breakfast, she got the feeling that the talking would start. Personally, Belwynn had little appetite for either.

Everyone had taken up a seat around a dead fire as Walter's men broke up camp and prepared to set off for Essenberg. Herin was grim faced. Rabigar had been treated again by Elana, and she had cleaned the eye up a lot, so that it didn't look half as bad as yesterday. It still looked terrible, though. She wondered why they hadn't covered it with anything. But why should he? To make Belwynn feel better?

'How do you know?' asked Gyrmund.

'He came in as Belwynn was entertaining Emeric,' said Clarin, who recounted the brief adventures of Tivian and Ariella.

Gyrmund's eyes opened wide.

'Yes,' said Clarin with a chuckle, 'you missed out on some fun there, Gyrmund.'

'So Kaved's still alive, then?' Gyrmund asked.

'Yes,' said Herin, his voice steely, 'but I'll make sure he pays for what he's done.'

'Why did you bring him?' asked Rabigar. His voice sounded like he looked: injured, and hurt. 'I knew he couldn't be trusted...'

Belwynn felt desperately sorry for the Krykker, but she felt sorry for Herin, too. He could hardly look at Rabigar, but he made himself.

'I'm sorry, Rabigar. I swear to you—I'll make him pay. I'll get revenge.'

That was perhaps the first apology Belwynn had ever heard Herin make. She could tell that there was a part of him who wanted to turn around and head straight back to Coldeberg right now.

'Why did you ask me to come with you? Why didn't I say no and stay where I was?'

Rabigar sounded miserable. In mourning. Elana had apparently stopped the pain from his eye, but she couldn't heal the loss he was suffering. That would take time, but right now it was raw and there for all to see.

'I'm sorry,' repeated Herin, his mouth dry. 'What else can I say?'

There was a horrible silence. Eventually, Soren filled it.

'So, you know what happened to us; our meeting with Emeric. What about the rest of you?'

'Moneva freed us,' began Gyrmund. 'She won't tell us how...'

Moneva shrugged. 'Getting into places without being seen is what I do. Carry on with the story.'

'Then Dirk found us,' continued Gyrmund. 'He told us you were upstairs and that he knew the way to a postern gate on the north side of the castle. We agreed that some of us needed to get out and pick up the horses or we'd never get far, even if we did make it out of the castle. We had to risk going back to the Boot and Saddle.'

True enough, considered Belwynn; without the horses they would almost certainly be dead by now. They would also have needed to get Rabigar out at that point. She shuddered to think what state he would have been in.

'He then saw this soldier he recognised,' said Gyrmund, handing this part of the story over to Dirk.

'Do you remember the soldier who took us to Orlin's rooms?' asked Dirk.

'Yes...Dom, wasn't it?' said Belwynn. 'A funny little chap.'

'Well,' said Dirk, 'Gyrmund had put on a soldier's uniform, so I told him to ask Dom to help him take some prisoners back to see Salvinus.'

A soldier's uniform taken from some dead soldier Moneva killed, no doubt, Belwynn said to Soren.

She got them out, didn't she? he replied.

'He was a very helpful fellow,' said Gyrmund. 'We walked straight out through the gatehouse entrance; Dom did all the talking for us. When we got to the Boot and Saddle, we went straight for the stables. I don't know if Salvinus or his men were still there, in the building or out the back. Didn't seem like it. No-one came out to challenge us, anyway. We simply rode out and carried on through the West Gate.'

'What about Dom?' asked Belwynn. She was soft, she knew, but she didn't want them to have harmed him.

Gyrmund smiled and shook his head. 'We gathered up six of the horses. I told him they were the prisoners' horses and that Salvinus would want to inspect them. When we rode away, we left him standing there, a puzzled expression on his face.'

'Well, thanks for coming back for us,' said Belwynn.

'Yeah,' said Clarin, 'and at least we know we can trust Dirk now after the dagger thing.'

'What dagger thing?' asked Gyrmund, frowning.

Clarin shook his head. 'I clean forgot,' he said. 'Most of you still don't know!'

'Don't know what?' said Herin through gritted teeth.

Belwynn suddenly had a bad feeling.

'Dirk had it all along!' said Clarin, seemingly oblivious that this might not go down too well.

'Hold on a minute,' said Herin, his voice getting loud. 'What do you mean he had it all along?'

The two brothers both looked at Dirk.

'I—I stole it from Toric's Temple before Salvinus got there. He never had it.'

Herin slowly stood up. 'You mean all this,' he said, waving his arms around, 'all this happened because they knew we had the dagger? You let us blunder into Coldeberg unprepared when you knew they would be after us?'

He began walking towards Dirk and slid his sword from its sheath as he did.

'Herin, that isn't getting us anywhere!' shouted Belwynn.

Clarin quickly shot up and moved between Dirk and his brother.

'Get out of my way, you idiot!'

'No, Herin.'

Herin pointed his sword at him.

'Get. Out. Of my fucking way.'

Clarin drew his own sword. 'You're not getting near him.'

It was said in a matter-of-fact way, but Belwynn had rarely heard Clarin deny his older brother anything. The two men stared at each other.

'This is ridiculous,' began Gyrmund.

'Shut the hell up,' Herin interrupted him.

'I told him not to tell anyone,' said Elana quietly.

Everyone turned to look at her.

'You knew all along, too?' demanded Herin, still brandishing his sword.

'When Dirk told me, I wasn't sure if we could trust everyone. He has kept it out of the hands of Ishari. That's the most important thing.'

'But we were supposed to be taking the dagger back to Magnia,' said Soren. He looked angry himself now, just in a more controlled way than Herin. 'That was what the rest of us were trying to do. You weren't, though.

Were you ever going to tell us you had it, I wonder? I don't see how you dare talk about trust.'

Elana nodded. 'Yes. I'm sorry. If you had found out that Dirk had the dagger, you would have insisted on taking it back to the Temple. It wasn't safe there. Ishari would have just come back for it.'

There was clearly something in what the priestess was saying, Belwynn had to admit.

'So where should the dagger go?' she asked Elana, intrigued.

'I don't know where, exactly, for sure,' began Elana apologetically.

'I'm not listening to any more of this,' said Herin. 'She's either got a screw loose or she's lying. If you were a man, I'd have given you a smack in the teeth by now.'

Herin's tantrum was irritating Belwynn now, but she held her tongue.

'Madria doesn't tell me everything!' Elana tried to explain. 'She speaks to me in visions, in instinct. I know that Dirk should have the dagger. I know we should go to Essenberg, not back to Magnia. I don't understand everything that is happening, though.'

It sounded heartfelt enough, but it left everything totally in the dark, nonetheless.

'What are we going to do?' asked Belwynn.

Everyone looked at each other; no-one seemed to have a quick answer. Soren puffed out his cheeks and let out a deep breath.

'It looks like we're going to Essenberg, anyway. It may not be a bad thing that the Emperor hears about all of this. After that...we'll have to wait and see.'

'In the meantime, are we trusting this little shit with the dagger?' demanded Herin, pointing his sword at Dirk.

'He hasn't behaved as if he's working for Ishari, Herin,' Soren said mildly. 'In fact, quite the opposite.'

'No, not at all,' responded Herin sarcastically. 'He's only robbed our nation's treasure and taken it to Coldeberg.'

'Well,' said Soren, losing patience, 'do you want it?'

'I don't particularly want the thing,' snarled Herin, taken aback, 'I just don't want him to have it a moment longer. You take it, Soren.'

'Shush,' said Moneva, flicking her eyes over to the side.

Belwynn looked over and saw Walter approaching. He and a few of his men were leading some horses over. Nine in all.

'Morning,' he said, looking around the group. That faint smile hovered at the corner of his mouth again. Had he heard any of their conversation? Belwynn wondered what he was thinking.

'I've brought over your mounts for the ride to Essenberg, plus three spares.'

He seemed to be the kind of person who never went anywhere without spares of anything. Belwynn guessed that probably made him a good general.

'We owe you thanks,' said Soren. 'Not only for the horses.'

'Well,' replied Walter, 'when we got word of Emeric's coronation, my brother sent me off to investigate and bring back intelligence. Potentially a dangerous mission. We're both lucky that one of my scouts spotted you when he did. You're my intelligence. So thank *you* for showing up when you did. Are you all ready to ride?' he asked, his eyes lingering over Rabigar and his damaged face.

'Aye,' said the Krykker. 'I think we've done enough blathering here.'

THEY HAD a full day's ride ahead of them to reach Essenberg. It was another cloudless day, and everyone seemed confident that they would sleep indoors tonight. Everyone seemed to have had enough talk for a while, and they mostly rode in silence, each lost in their own thoughts, and not necessarily the cheery ones. Herin brooded over Kaved's betrayal, and Clarin, who had stood up to his brother earlier, was unusually quiet. Rabigar was distant and withdrawn. Soren was dealing with his own inner demons over the loss of his magical powers since the fight in the Wilderness—an issue that he had kept from everybody except Belwynn. Dirk, who for now still kept Toric's Dagger in his possession, also looked troubled. Gyrmund and Moneva were perhaps the only exceptions, talking quietly to each other every now and again. No doubt Gyrmund felt some relief at no longer having to think about where they were going or worry about enemies behind or ahead. Walter was in charge today, and the marshal seemed happy enough to leave them alone as long as they didn't cause him trouble.

His soldiers knew their jobs, and everything was performed to military precision, as if they were in hostile territory rather than on the road back to their own base. The scouts rode out to survey the terrain in all directions. Walter himself stayed at the front of the line and was regularly reported to by the scouts. A rear-guard of ten soldiers ended the line, keeping Belwynn and her party in the middle. Protected—or contained, whichever way one wanted to look at it.

After a few hours they were well inside Kelland and Walter ordered his men to wear the uniform of the duchy, showing the eagle symbol of his own family. The track they had started on had now become a road. The villagers in this area sold their surplus crops in Essenberg, and the traffic heading into the city became steadily heavier. They passed small groups of farmers and merchants who were expected to make way for the imperial army. Walter offered the odd greeting as he passed, but he was only interested in getting back to the capital, and his men left these travellers to their own business.

They made a brief stop for lunch, and Belwynn took the chance to stretch her legs. Clarin joined her and they walked a few feet from the road in silence, stopping at a stone wall that kept in a herd of cattle, looking out over the Kellish countryside while the sun shone down directly overhead. It was a peaceful, idyllic little scene.

'Reminds me of Beckford,' said Belwynn.

That was where she had met Clarin and her brother. She had been living with Soren at the house of the marsh witch, Delyth. It was an awful place. It stank to high hell. There were no humans nearby; instead, the lizard men who infested the Gotbeck marshes were regular visitors, and the old hag, Delyth, acted as if she were their queen. Then, one day, Soren had sent her home. Told her not to contact him. Didn't tell her why, and she still didn't know to this day.

She returned to Magnia and lived by herself in Beckford for a year, waiting for him to return from his apprenticeship with Delyth. She busied herself with estate business. Herin and Clarin's father lived nearby, and she met them when they returned home to see him. Their father had been sick and died shortly after they returned. A neighbouring landowner was giving her unwanted attention and asked her to marry him, refusing to take no for an answer. The brothers scared him off for her, and they had become friends. Looking back, it seemed to her now not to have been such a bad period of her life, even though she had thought herself miserable at the time.

'Do you ever wonder where you'll end your days?' she asked the warrior.

Clarin looked over the farmland. 'Yes. Somewhere like this, I hope.'

She turned to him. 'Really? I didn't think you'd be the farming type.'

'Why not? When I'm too old for this nonsense,' he said, patting his scabbard, 'I'll need to settle down. Buy a piece of land, start a family. That's what most men want, isn't it?'

'Maybe,' said Belwynn. 'It's what most men tell themselves they want, perhaps. But look at you; Herin; Soren. After this, are you all going to club together and buy a farm? I don't see it.'

Clarin laughed. 'Yeah, that does seem kind of hard to picture. I can't see your brother on the farm. Or Herin, for that matter. I can picture myself there, though.'

Belwynn looked at him. Maybe he could. Maybe she could, too.

They looked out over the fields a while longer.

Footsteps coming towards them made them turn around. It was Walter. Coming to check on them? Belwynn wondered whether he was really interested in them or whether he was just being the good general, checking that all his pieces were in place, looking out for obstacles in the plan.

'Nice view, isn't it?' he asked, joining them to look over the wall.

'Very,' said Clarin.

'I hope it stays that way,' the Marshal commented.

'You mean if there is war with Emeric?' asked Belwynn. 'Do you think that's likely?'

'Likely? Let me put it this way. If it wasn't for the troubles in the north, we'd have been taking an army to Coldeberg, not fifty men.'

There was a pause.

'You haven't heard?' he asked, studying their faces.

Belwynn remembered the cryptic comments of the wizard with red eyes, Pentas, about Persala.

'Nothing concrete,' she said. 'We've been on the road a long time.'

'Right,' he said. 'Well, it's no secret. A few days ago, two states, Trevenza and Grienna, declared independence from Persala and made a request to join the Empire. We didn't commit to anything at the time. Then, just before I left Essenberg, we heard the news that a Haskan invasion of Persala had taken the capital, Baserno. The Persaleian army is destroyed.'

At first Belwynn assumed Walter was joking, but he said it in such a matter-of-fact way. Persala was the dominant power in the north, even if it had lost control of the south of Dalriya some time ago. It had been a great power for hundreds of years. For it to lose its capital and its army in an instant didn't seem possible.

'Where does that leave your brother?' Belwynn asked.

'He's in a difficult situation. Does he allow the Haskans to take these two provinces and let Arioc's army reach the northern border of the Empire? If he stands up for them, he risks immediate war with Haskany.'

'And this is the moment that Emeric declares himself king,' added Clarin. 'Hardly a coincidence.'

'No, it can't be,' agreed Walter. 'Which is why anything you've learned about what's going on in Coldeberg will be very much appreciated by the Emperor.'

. . .

THEY RODE on for the rest of the afternoon and early evening. Despite herself, Belwynn was excited about visiting Essenberg and meeting the Emperor. They had all gone to the city last year: she, Soren, Herin and Clarin. On one of their adventures working for a merchant. The job had been little more than a glorified shopping trip: taking some valuable jewellery there to be sold and bringing back the money, without losing either. Soren had disappeared one night on some mysterious mission, and she had gone drinking with Herin and Clarin. She had ended up in bed with Clarin at the end of the night. The next morning had been awkward. Neither of them had mentioned it since, and that was that.

Essenberg itself was considered by many people to be the greatest city in Dalriya, and, Belwynn reflected, had perhaps lost its biggest competition, now that Baserno had fallen to the Haskans.

Belwynn thought of Essenberg as a beating heart, with many arteries giving it life. The first to give it life must have been the river Cousel, since the city featured an island in the middle of the river, which made it an ideal crossing place. The Cousel ran from the Krykker Mountains down through Guivergne and the Empire and emptied into the sea where the southern Caladri lived. It was the biggest river on the continent and an important trading route as river barges passed up and down it, easily carrying heavy goods by water that would have been much more difficult to transport by land. Just as important now was the Great Road that passed through Essenberg. It was where north met south and where traders from all parts of the continent could meet and do business in safety, with the emperor's soldiers there to enforce the law. Essenberg also enjoyed a central location within the Empire itself, with roads from Coldeberg, Witmar and Guslar all meeting there. In short, Essenberg's location made it almost destined for greatness.

Eventually they saw the walls of Essenberg ahead of them. Most of the buying and selling was done for the day, and there was no queue for entry as they reached the Coldeberg Gate. Walter's status meant that they were all waved through without challenge, and they passed into the city.

They were in the Market Quarter of the city, where the Great Road, the road to Coldeberg, and the road to Valennes in Guivergne all converged on the south side of the river. This part of the city had been given over to the merchants and farmers who brought their goods from all over Dalriya to sell. Most of the stalls were now empty, and the local farmers had left for their homes, but some citizens were still plying their trade. Hot food was on sale for those who needed their dinner, and Belwynn's stomach rumbled at the smells of fresh-baked bread and sizzling meats. Some stallholders, perhaps those who most needed the money or hadn't got rid of their produce, remained, shouting out their final offers. The crowds had died down, but the numbers were still healthy as people strolled along in pairs and small groups, enjoying the summer evening.

Their route took them straight to the heart of the market where, ahead of them, Albert's Bridge, a hugely impressive stone and concrete construction, spanned the river. It was wide enough for people to walk six abreast, and Belwynn could see that several vendors had taken up positions along the bridge, selling jewellery and trinkets to rich men's wives and girlfriends. To their left was Baldwin's Bridge, a military bridge that formed part of the circuit of the city walls and defended Essenberg from a potential attack downriver by the Guivergnais. It was reserved for use by the army rather than civilians and was linked to two towers that had been built on either side of the river, so that defenders could move on and off the bridge with ease. Two catapults were stationed on the bridge, so that boats could be sunk before they reached the city.

Instead of going in this direction, Walter took them right onto the Great Road. This led them into the Army Quarter, where the Imperial Headquarters was located—colloquially known as the Imps. It had a large rectangular site on the far side of the city, next to the river. This stretch of the river featured the First Bridge, made up of two separate bridges that each crossed from one side of the river bank to Margaret Island, in the middle of the Cousel. Elsewhere in this part of the city was the lion's share of the residential buildings, crammed in between the Great Road and the city walls.

Their route took them close to the First Bridge, so that Belwynn could see the trees on Margaret Island, before turning right to the Imps. The perimeter was marked out by wooden stakes but there were no defences and no guards. When Walter arrived, a few orders were barked out, and a group of boys came over to take the horses to the stables. Belwynn dismounted stiffly and handed over the reins to one of the boys, who she supposed were in training to become soldiers.

'Till!' Walter called over a boy. 'Take our guests to the dining hall and tell the cooks that I said they should be fed.'

Walter turned to them. 'I will see to it that you all get a bed for a night, too, in the barracks. It may not be the most comfortable accommodation, but it will be the best we can do on short notice. Then I'll have to go over and see Baldwin. You'll get an appointment some time tomorrow.'

'How safe are we here?' Elana asked him.

To Belwynn's mind, the priestess was being unnecessarily fearful, and she shared a look with Soren. Herin was less subtle, rolling his eyes for all to see.

Elana picked up on the response. 'The Barissians could have people in the city now, could they not?'

'They do,' said Moneva. 'Emeric will have sent his followers to the Great Road as soon as we escaped. They'll be here by now.'

'Relax. You're in the middle of the Imps, surrounded by soldiers,' said Walter, waving his arms about him with a smile. Elana still looked less than convinced, and the marshal's face grew more serious. 'If I'm not around, ask any soldier for help. If the worst happens, you can seek refuge at the castle. Or at the cathedral, with Archbishop Decker. He can be completely trusted. But listen—you'll be perfectly safe here.'

THREE COFFINS

XVII

'It's not safe here,' said Moneva.

They were in the dining hall of the Imps, where neat rows of benches and chairs were laid out and the soldiers garrisoned here got their three-square meals. They had arrived too late for dinner and a grumbling cook had served out watery soup, dry bread and waxy cheese.

'The food's not that bad,' joked Clarin.

'How so?' Soren asked Moneva in a tired voice.

He sounded like Belwynn felt—ready for bed and not in the mood for paranoia.

'We were seen coming in through the Coldeberg Gate. Two men were sat down, chatting by the side of the road. One of them followed us into the market. A third man tailed us from there to here. He's probably watching the Imps now, or someone else is.'

That changed things somewhat.

'Barissians?' Soren asked Moneva.

'I presume so.'

'Why didn't you tell Walter?' asked Gyrmund.

Moneva shrugged. 'We all trust him now?'

'You were quick to trust him when the Barissians were after us,' pointed out Gyrmund.

'We were about to get killed!' retorted Moneva.

Belwynn looked around at everyone. Tired faces, struggling to think straight. They had all been through a lot in the last few days.

'We need to be careful,' said Soren. 'If this is true, we don't know how many of them there are. Emeric also had a wizard with him, called Tirano. It's possible he is here, too.'

'*If* it's true,' said Belwynn doubtfully.

'Why would Moneva make it up?' demanded Gyrmund heatedly.

'Whoa, no need to fight about it,' said Moneva. 'I understand if people want some proof. I'll take Herin with me and we'll find the spy watching us. Will that do?'

'Yes,' said Belwynn, feeling slightly ashamed. 'Sorry.'

'Don't be sorry. We all need to be careful.'

'We need to decide what to *do*,' said Herin impatiently.

'We could ask Walter's troops to post a guard,' suggested Soren.

Moneva made a face at that. 'Assuming they're Emeric's people and they're after the dagger, they'll want to come for it while they know where it is and while it's not under lock and key somewhere else. This could be their best chance. Most likely in the night while we're asleep. It could get dangerous here.'

'What do you suggest?' asked Soren.

'If it were up to me, I'd move out of here, so they don't know where we are anymore. It's safer.'

'What about this wizard, Soren?' asked Herin. 'Can you handle him?'

'No,' said Soren, looking around at everyone. 'No. It's time I come straight with you all. I haven't been able to use my powers since I lost consciousness in the Wilderness. I won't be any help here.'

There was an awkward silence after Soren's revelation.

'I'm sorry, Soren,' said Clarin. 'Will it come back?'

'Thanks. I hope so. But we need to focus on this now.'

'I think we should try to leave without being seen,' said Elana.

'Agreed,' said Gyrmund.

'Herin?' asked Soren.

Herin looked in two minds, which was unusual for him. 'Kaved might have come with them,' he said.

Belwynn hadn't considered that.

'We need to focus on our safety, Herin,' said Rabigar. 'We can get our revenge another time.'

'Alright,' said Herin, relenting. 'What now?'

'It's already getting dark, 'said Moneva. 'You and I are going to find out who, if anyone, is watching us. Ideally, eliminate them. Then get out of here.'

'Where to?'

'Margaret Island. It's not inhabited at night time.'

'Very well,' said Soren. 'Moneva knows Essenberg better than anyone else. We'll spend the night on the island. Then, in the morning, we need to make our way to the castle as soon as they open the gates.'

THEY HAD BEEN ALLOCATED a barrack hut to themselves, and they stripped the beds of blankets so that they would be warm on the island, which might get chilly overnight.

So much for a sleep in a bed, complained Belwynn to Soren.

When Herin returned with Moneva, he swiped a flat hand across his neck. No-one was keen to ask questions about it.

Instead, they made their way out of the Imps, Moneva leading them out the back way towards the river and then following it along towards the First Bridge. They travelled by moonlight. Moneva held up a hand for them to stop.

She peered towards the bridge and then hastily signalled that they move towards the river. Belwynn crept slowly towards the bank, fearful lest she trip over, then sunk down onto the ground. Everyone lay or crouched down and looked in the direction of the bridge.

Presently, they heard voices from that direction that got steadily louder, until a group of about a dozen came into view. It was an eerie feeling, watching them in the darkness. Belwynn wondered if anyone was out there watching them.

It was too dark to make out faces or to tell whether any of them were looking in their direction. They all looked like men, some clearly carrying weapons. They walked with purpose, not as if they were revellers who had been drinking all evening. An icy feeling clutched at Belwynn. Everything about them suggested they were here for them; and they had nearly walked straight into them.

They waited by the bank as the group continued past. They could have been innocent men going back to their homes, but they were heading for the main entrance to the Imps.

'We can't wait here all night,' hissed Herin.

'I'll look,' said Moneva.

She set off, moving in a crouched position towards the bridge. Belwynn watched her peering around before she made her way onto the bridge. Then she disappeared.

The seconds passed like hours. Had those men found the dead body of the spy, or found him missing? Had they gone to their hut and found *them* missing? Belwynn looked back the way they had come, worried that they might be followed to the river.

Eventually Moneva returned and waved them forwards. They shuffled over towards the bridge, Belwynn looking nervously around in all directions.

'It's clear,' whispered Moneva.

Belwynn hoped she was right. They walked along the wooden First Bridge, which was only the width of two people. In the daytime, users of the bridge had to go single file so they could pass people coming the other way. Moneva set a fast pace so that they weren't out in the open for too long. She moved like a cat, making no noise, but the same couldn't be said for everyone else. Despite his efforts, Clarin clunked along like a giant learning to play the drums. Still, the sound of the Cousel flowing beneath them was surely loud enough to drown out the noise of their movement.

Then, they were off the bridge, onto the soil of Margaret Island.

Moneva didn't hesitate, taking them left into the trees that covered the north side of the island. Belwynn hoped she wasn't going to take them too far, since she was sure that at any moment she would walk into a hole or a tree.

Something ran off to her left.

'There are creatures here!' she exclaimed.

'Rabbits,' said Moneva.

'How did rabbits get here?' she whispered to Clarin.

'Hopped across the bridge?' he suggested.

Finally, they stopped at a grassy ridge with a decent view back to the bridge, but far enough away not to be seen.

'Is this it?' asked Herin.

'Yes,' said Moneva, 'I hope you like it,' she added sarcastically.

'Do you think those men we saw were Barissians?' asked Belwynn.

'Yes,' replied Moneva. 'Almost certainly sent to kill us. Sweet dreams.'

BELWYNN TOOK a long time to get any sleep. It felt strange on the island at night, and her mind refused to relax. Rabigar slept badly, and she heard him cry out more than once.

As soon as she nodded off, everyone else had woken up and was ready to go. A sparkling white sunrise was blasting its way in between the trees on

Margaret Island. If she didn't have such a pounding headache, Belwynn thought she might have found it a beautiful sight.

The plan this morning was simple enough: head straight for Essenberg Castle and ask for admittance. The unknown was whether the Barissians would be waiting in ambush somewhere. Soren made it clear that if they couldn't get there safely, they would have to leave the city without seeing the Emperor.

They left Margaret Island via the other bridge, arriving on the north bank of the Cousel. The bridge fed into a street which ran straight to the Witmar Gate and became the Witmar Road, taking travellers to the capital of Luderia. They were now in the Cathedral Quarter of Essenberg. Up ahead and slightly to their left, they could see the spire of the cathedral, the tallest building in the city. Not far to the left of the cathedral stood Essenberg Castle, which dominated the Castle Quarter of the city.

It was towards the castle that Moneva led the group. This was the part of the city where most of the more established shops were located, but the city was still waking up and the streets were nearly empty. As they got nearer to the castle, they passed the houses of the wealthier citizens of Essenberg, keen to get locations close to the seat of power. Several of them were being rebuilt or extended, testament to the period of prosperity they were enjoying.

They turned a corner and opposite them was the central square that held the castle. The building was an impressive piece of construction, and that was perhaps its primary purpose. Whereas Coldeberg was stronger defensively, Essenberg Castle was more graceful. A square structure with four square towers on each corner, from whichever angle you looked at it, you saw clear geometric lines. Its walls were whitewashed so that it gleamed amid the muck of city life. The crenellations along the top looked almost too perfect, as if they had been made to make the castle look pretty rather than to be used for the dirty business of war. The eagle flag of Kelland fluttered in the breeze on the roof, but so too did the stag, symbol of the Brasingian Empire. Its seven antler tips represented each of the seven duchies and emphasised their unity. The Emperor's Castle spoke of truth and justice, ideas that, in their own way, were just as potent as the mercenaries Emeric had bought and the new crown he had on his head.

Belwynn felt an urge to get to the castle and meet with the Emperor. Moneva, however, didn't look so keen. She was peering into the square.

'There's a group of men sitting in the corner,' she said. 'Armed. Hard to say whose men they are, but they're not wearing uniforms.'

'How many?' asked Herin.

'Eight.'

'We could fight our way through them, if necessary,' he suggested.

Moneva screwed up her face. 'Maybe, but there could be more of them in the streets off the square...'

'Someone's coming,' interjected Gyrmund sharply.

They turned to face the threat, what weapons they had appeared in hands.

A lone figure had detached itself from the shadows of a house and edged towards them. It was a young man, wearing the vestments of a priest. He stopped, eyeing up the group and their weapons. He seemed to be unsure how to proceed.

'Hello. My name is Ancel,' he began. When he spoke, he had a smooth, confident voice. 'I work for Archbishop Decker. He sent me to find you,' he said, glancing towards the square. 'He asked me to take you to the cathedral. It's not safe for you here.'

'Why not?' asked Soren. 'Doesn't the Emperor have control outside his own castle?'

'Orlin, Duke Emeric's chamberlain, is here in Essenberg. He arrived yesterday and went straight to the Emperor, asking him to apprehend a group of your description if you should arrive. There are other men from Barissia here as well. I don't know how many—some in groups, some alone.'

'What is your interest in this?' Soren responded.

'His Grace spoke with Marshal Walter about you. He wants to keep you safe.'

'Walter said we could trust the archbishop, remember?' said Belwynn.

'But can we trust Walter?' asked Herin.

'The longer we stand around discussing it, the more conspicuous we get,' said Moneva impatiently.

'Alright,' said Herin irritably, 'back to the cathedral, then. I'm tired of all this skulking around.'

Ancel turned around and led them down a narrow street. If he was planning an ambush, this would be a perfect place, thought Belwynn. Instead, he turned right, and they could see the spire of the cathedral ahead of them.

'Don't turn around,' Moneva whispered harshly from the back. 'We're being followed. Two of them. They've probably watched the whole thing.'

'Two isn't enough,' said Clarin.

'It's enough to find out where we're going and get others,' replied Gyrmund.

'Don't worry,' said Ancel, turning behind him. 'We're nearly there.'

They picked up their pace but didn't run, moving along a street with residential housing on each side. They were now approaching the tall walls of the cathedral from its west side. Then Belwynn noticed a small wooden door in the cathedral's west wall. Ancel made straight for the door. He rapped on it four times.

'It's Ancel.'

Glancing behind, Belwynn could see two men halfway up the street, looking in their direction.

The noise of sliding bolts came from behind the door, and it opened inwards. They dived through; the men had to bend down to get under the lintel. They found themselves in a small antechamber, just off the main nave of the cathedral. Another young priest waited until they were all through and then shut the door, slamming home a series of bolts.

Belwynn and the others wandered into the nave. The ceiling stretched high above them, decorated with holy images of the various gods worshipped in the city.

Great pillars separated the open space into areas where each god was isolated and could be worshipped by their followers. Lars the Creator held the world and the planets in the palms of his hands. Lady Alexia, the Protector, could be asked for help from those in need. Justus, God of Death and Justice, held a sword and scales, and could deliver his verdict on a supplicant's enemies. Sibylla, goddess of Health and Prosperity, might be called on by a young wife hoping to conceive, or an old man with money problems. Some visitors came to see one of the gods; some came to see several. But all visitors were equal, and all gods were equal. All prayed under one roof. All religious service was carried out under the watchful eye of the Brasingian Church, which had won a measure of control over the different sects in the Empire by establishing these united cathedrals in the major cities.

Ancel had not stopped to look around, but had marched on, into the nave and towards the rear of the cathedral. He turned around to wait for the others to catch up.

'The private chambers of the cathedral are behind here,' he said, pointing up at a large, red set of curtains. 'His Grace will be waiting for us,' he added.

Pulling aside a section of curtain, Ancel walked through, holding it up for the others to follow. Within a few yards, the wide expanse of floor narrowed into something more like a corridor, with stone walls on either side where separate rooms had been built. As Ancel entered the corridor, he was challenged by an older priest.

'Archbishop Decker asked me to bring these people to him as a matter of urgency,' explained Ancel.

The older priest frowned at Belwynn's group. 'You're not going in with those weapons,' he stated.

'We're not dropping our weapons,' retorted Herin. 'We don't even know why we've been brought here.'

The older priest's face looked aghast. 'You can't barge into the Archbishop's chamber armed like a bunch of killers!' he exclaimed.

A door further up the corridor on the right slowly opened. Everyone turned around. A third man, even older, now appeared, moving with small steps into the corridor. Belwynn noted he was at least seventy if he was a day.

'It's alright,' he said, his voice shaky with age. 'They are welcome to come in. Well done, Ancel.'

Archbishop Decker had a large, well-furnished chamber in the cathedral, as befit his rank. His official residence was by the river. Like most powerful men, suspected Belwynn, Decker knew he was better off closer to the centre of power. Here he was a short walk away from the imperial court.

Decker sat his guests down. He nodded over to Clarin.

'I was a soldier once,' he said in his reedy voice. 'A long time ago now. You might find that hard to believe.'

'A little,' said Herin, looking him up and down.

Decker smiled at that, showing what was left of his teeth.

'Ha, no doubt! I made the right decision, though. Here I am, three score and ten; another war is coming, and I'm set to outlive another generation of young men.'

'Fair enough, if your goal is simply to live as long as possible,' said Gyrmund.

Decker widened his arms, encompassing the cathedral. 'I've done a bit better than just live, wouldn't you say?'

Belwynn was regretting their decision to come here to bandy words with a half-dead archbishop.

Emeric's spies are probably bringing a troop of soldiers this way right now, she said to Soren. *If we had gone straight to the castle, we could have got in there by now.*

'Anyway,' Decker continued, 'young men with swords don't listen to old bishops; there it is. I spoke with Walter about you and thought you might have something important to tell us all. But when he got back to the Imps, you had gone. Meanwhile, Master Orlin arrived straight from Barissia with who knows how many underlings, wanting you caught and handed over. At that point I *knew* you were of importance and needed to be found. If you weren't already dead. And, here you are.'

The Archbishop stood up, taking the manoeuvre slow and steady.

'I think it's now time to show you all something,' he smiled, almost mischievously.

What now? A tour of the cathedral? Belwynn fretted.

Decker exited the chamber and turned right, taking the group further down the corridor. It ended in a circular shaped expanse of floor with a metal pole in the middle, which the Archbishop headed for. Decker looked at his guests and beckoned Clarin over.

'Could you do the honours?' he asked, pointing at the stone floor.

Clarin frowned, but obligingly studied the floor. The big man's frown deepened, and he knelt down by the pole. Finding a gap in the stone floor, he placed both hands in and pulled upward, bringing a stone slab with him. He manoeuvred the slab away and carefully laid it down.

Belwynn couldn't help moving closer to look. The slab concealed a set of stone steps, which wound their way down into a cellar.

'The Crypt of the Dukes of Kelland,' announced the Archbishop.

Picking on Clarin again, he gestured to the wall where a lighted torch was hanging.

'You may lead on, sir,' he said.

Clarin picked up the torch and began the descent, holding on to the pole as he twisted around the thin steps. As he disappeared from view, Decker followed behind. The archbishop went incredibly slowly, leaving Belwynn and the others standing around at the top.

Eventually, they made it down into the crypt. Clarin had used the torch to light several lanterns before hanging it up. Decker asked Herin to place the slab back over the top of the stairs. The lanterns cast an eerie, flickering light in the cold, humid crypt, picking out recesses in the rock and creating dark shadows. As Belwynn's eyes adjusted, she saw that along the walls, to the left and right, were the rectangular stone coffins of the three previous Dukes of Kelland.

Each one had a carved likeness of the duke on the lid, looking sternly out from their rest, still grasping their favoured weapons in different poses with which to defend their territory. Their names had also been carved into the stone beneath their feet, so that Belwynn could read along: Manfred the Great gripped a great sword with both hands, laid along his chest and legs; Duke Bernard, Baldwin's father, held sword and shield in battle-readiness; Duke

Albert had his sword buckled at his waist and his palms pressed together on his chest in prayer.

Belwynn brought her attention back to Archbishop Decker, still wondering why he had brought them down here. He was at the far end of the crypt with Clarin. He pointed to another gap in the wall, again big enough for Clarin to place both hands in. Clarin pulled, then pushed. Nothing happened.

'This way,' said Decker, using his hands to make a circular motion towards the right.

Instead of pushing away or pulling towards him, Clarin used his grip to push upwards on the wall. He briefly strained with the effort, and then the mechanism kicked in, a section of stone wall rolling away to the right like a wheel.

When the stone disc stopped moving, there was a gap in the wall big enough to walk through. It was dark, but Belwynn could make out a passageway.

'The underground route into the castle,' announced Archbishop Decker. 'Very useful over the years for the dukes to have a secret way in and out. And today, very useful for us.'

AN AUDIENCE WITH THE EMPEROR

XVIII

Belwynn looked at the mirror again. She was about to meet the Emperor of Brasingia, and no amount of cosmetics or changes of hairstyle altered the fact that she looked a tired, haggard mess.

It had taken him a while, but Archbishop Decker had led them through the short tunnel from the crypt under Essenberg Cathedral to the wine cellar of Essenberg Castle. He had immediately taken them to Baldwin's chamberlain, Rainer, who explained the situation to them more fully.

'The Emperor is due to meet with Orlin for a second time this morning. Before you start to worry, we already know, in a general way, the state of affairs in Barissia. For the time being it suits us to keep our knowledge of events in Barissia to ourselves. So, the Emperor meets with Orlin, agrees to hand you over if you are found, and Orlin leaves.' Rainer waved his hand, as if Orlin were a fly he was swatting away.

Rainer wanted to know the details of their time in Barissia. Soren gave him the bare bones, but demanded an audience with Baldwin himself. Rainer politely nodded.

'Yes, yes, the Emperor will want to speak to you today. He is also meeting with a Haskan envoy from King Arioc this morning. As I'm sure you'll be aware,' Rainer continued, forcing a smile, 'there is much to talk about there. So, I propose a meeting this afternoon. In the meantime, I can arrange a suite of apartments here in the castle for you to rest in. Not as spacious as would ordinarily be the case, but we have a lot of visitors in the castle at the moment.'

Soren and the others had agreed to the afternoon meeting. They also agreed that not everyone need go. As well as the twins, Herin, Gyrmund and Moneva were to come. Despite being related to a prince, being given a meeting with the Brasingian Emperor gave Belwynn a bit of a thrill. The afternoon slot also gave them time to get some rest and take stock of the situation.

As it was, Belwynn had fallen asleep, and had woken up with little time to get ready. Rainer had sent an aide, who told them to be ready to meet with Baldwin.

The door opened.

'All well?' enquired Soren, taking a step into the room.

'I suppose so,' Belwynn replied, staring unhappily at her reflection.

Moneva, who had been sharing the room with Belwynn, got off the bed and joined them. She took a brief look in the mirror herself, smoothing down her chin length jet-black hair in five seconds.

'I hate people like you,' said Belwynn grumpily.

Moneva smiled and gave her cheek a pinch.

'She looks beautiful, doesn't she, Soren?'

'For Toric's sake, haven't we got more important things to worry about?'

Moneva shook her head at him. 'A *yes* is what we were looking for.'

The others were waiting in the corridor, along with an aide sent by Rainer.

'We're ready,' said Soren. The aide wordlessly turned around and walked ahead, leading them to the great hall where Baldwin did his meeting.

'This guy's so full of himself he gets his servant's servant to collect us,' said Herin.

'You are going to behave, aren't you?' asked Belwynn.

Herin snorted in disgust at the question.

At the end of the corridor they went down a flight of stairs to ground level. Here they briefly went outside into a courtyard. There was some evidence of military preparations here. At the far wall Belwynn could see three wagons being loaded with food, weaponry and other provisions. The Kellish war machine was slowly rousing.

After a check that they were unarmed, Belwynn and her four companions were allowed into the hall by the two sentries. The hall was designed to impress the visitor. Tapestries depicted the great events of imperial history. All four emperors were shown. Manfred the Great was shown as both a warrior and peacemaker, forging the Empire. Emperor Ludvig, Duke of

Rotelegen, was a pious figure, uniting the disparate faiths in one church. Bernard was a defender against enemies abroad. Finally, Baldwin was an architect, building a new age of prosperity.

Four pillars stood in a rectangle shape in the centre of the hall, supporting the roof. It was big enough to hold dozens of people for feasts or formal ceremonies. Now, however, it held only twelve. At the far end of the hall, there were two tables. Off to the side, the smaller one seated six bodyguards, bearing different liveries, all fully armed. At the larger main table, a further six people stood up from where they had been seated as Belwynn and the others approached.

Welcoming them, Rainer stepped forward to do the introductions.

'His Imperial Majesty, Emperor Baldwin; His Grace Ellard, Duke of Rotelegen; His Grace Decker, Archbishop of Kelland; His Lordship Walter, Marshall of the Empire; His Lordship Gustav, Archmage of the Empire.'

Belwynn muttered a *my lord* after each name was announced and nodded in what she thought was the right direction.

Rainer began the other set of introductions, impressing Belwynn by remembering their names.

'Soren and Belwynn, cousins to Prince Edgar of South Magnia; Herin of South Magnia; Gyrmund of South Magnia; Moneva of…?' Rainer hadn't been told where Moneva was from.

Moneva's lips twitched in amusement.

'Of Dalriya,' she said.

Baldwin smiled. 'Quite right. None of our business. Though your accent sounds more than familiar. Sit down,' he said gruffly, gesturing at the opposite end of the table. 'That's the formalities over with. I understand that you've already met a good number of our group already, one way or another.'

He spoke with the same trace of humour Walter did, as if they were all sharing a joke amongst themselves.

Belwynn and the others found a chair and everyone sat down. Feeling a bit more relaxed, Belwynn took another look at the Emperor close up. Baldwin was essentially an older version of Walter. He had a powerful build and a strong face, surrounded by cropped, dark hair which also contained flecks of grey. He had more lines on his face than his brother, no doubt caused by the years of extra responsibility.

Belwynn briefly examined the other unfamiliar faces. Duke Ellard was perhaps ten years older than the Emperor. He had a soldierly look to him, as if he were used to giving out orders, though he looked less than interested in Belwynn and her companions.

Gustav was a different kind of man. While tall, he was no soldier; his body had been left slim while he pursued his magical gifts. Soren had told Belwynn a bit about him over the years, though her twin only knew him by reputation. He was perhaps the most powerful human wizard in Dalriya. Born in the Empire, Baldwin had wanted Gustav's services at court. He eventually got them, but Gustav had come at a high price. Not only money and property, but an official title—Archmage of the Empire. This had brought the Emperor into conflict with the Church and others who despised magic as an abomination and objected to any official recognition. However, imperial recognition for Gustav had made the position of wizards in the Empire and its neighbours safer than they had been for generations.

'I should apologise,' began Walter, looking at each of them. 'Last night I should have brought you to the castle immediately. I didn't imagine that the Barissians would be so brazen as to send such a significant force into Essenberg after you.'

'There's no need to apologise, my lord,' responded Soren. 'You weren't in full cognisance of the facts and, for that, we apologise. There are certain things we felt we needed to tell the Emperor to his face.'

'Well, I am all ears,' said Baldwin. 'You have news from Barissia, perhaps very important, since Emeric seems desperate to get his hands on you. Rainer also tells me you bring news from Magnia.'

Before the meeting, they had agreed on two things. First, that Soren would do the talking, and second, that he would be completely honest. Baldwin and his advisers already knew much, and they needed the Emperor's support in their current situation. Hiding things from them could jeopardise that.

Soren began by giving an account of the attack on the Temple of Toric and Edgar's decision to send them to retrieve the dagger. He outlined the pursuit through the Wilderness, not hiding the fact that he was a wizard. He explained, as best he could, the encounter with Pentas and Nexodore on the Great Road. Naturally, this sparked an interest.

'Gustav?' Baldwin enquired, seeking elaboration.

Gustav had leaned forwards in his chair at Soren's description of the fight between the two wizards.

'I know the names. They are lieutenants of Erkindrix. I believe that both are on his Council of Seven, meaning that they answer to no-one but him. Arioc of Haskany is another member—that is the level we are talking about. Why they should fight with each other is, therefore, beyond me. We could speculate that they both wanted to be the one to take this dagger to Erkindrix and win his favour. But the fact that they both became personally involved in this is remarkable. In that sense, it makes the dagger a bigger issue even than Emeric.'

Ellard snorted, a look of disgust on his face. 'A poxy dagger won't seem a bigger issue when Emeric decides to move his army.'

'Can I see it?' Gustav asked, ignoring the Duke.

Soren handed it over. Gustav peered at it, studying the writing. He traced his forefinger up the length of the blade and handed it back with a slightly disappointed look.

'Interesting. I'm not sure what to make of it. Where did the dagger come from originally?'

'In our country the legends say that the Magnians defeated the Lippers and took the dagger as spoils.'

'Nothing to do with Toric?'

'I think he was given the credit by the Church.'

'Have you held the weapon? Felt any kind of reaction from it?'

'No, I—' Soren seemed unsure what to say. 'I have lost my powers. It happened when we were going through the Wilderness. I overextended my powers.'

Gustav's eyebrows rose slightly, and a look of sympathy appeared on his face. 'I see. Perhaps you and I can talk about that later, Soren. I certainly felt nothing, anyway.'

Soren continued. He told them about Kaved's treachery in Coldeberg and Dirk's revelation that he had been in possession of the dagger all along. He finished the tale with the escape from Coldeberg and their recent adventures in Essenberg.

'Thank you for being so frank, Soren,' said Baldwin. 'I will repay you in a moment by updating you on recent developments here. You may wish to carry this news back to Edgar. First, I want to get the nature of Emeric's rebellion straight in my head. You say this wizard, Tirano, is an Isharite. In that case, Emeric could have given his allegiance to Ishari, and may be preparing a coordinating attack from the south.'

'That would be my guess,' said Walter. 'He's been recruiting every sell-sword in the Empire for weeks now. I wouldn't be surprised if Arioc, or whoever, has offered him the Empire in return.'

'Possibly,' agreed Baldwin. 'All of this is confirmation of our suspicions that Emeric's actions are a bit more than opportunism, and he may not be easily bought off. I have received a letter from Coen, informing me that Prince Edgar is holding some kind of Conference of the South,' said Baldwin, changing the subject. 'When is it, Rainer?'

'Two days' time.'

'He aims to secure an agreement for the southern states of Dalriya to send us help. I am very grateful for this. I am sending an ambassador out today. I don't know whether you intend to return to Magnia now. But you are welcome to write a letter to Edgar yourselves if you wish. My ambassador will ensure that it is delivered.'

'Thank you,' said Belwynn. 'We will.'

'You have told me of events in the south, and so I will pass on what we know of events in the north. Walter?'

Walter nodded and unfurled a map of Dalriya on the table so that everyone could see.

'The threat from Ishari really only began about a year ago,' continued Baldwin. 'Everyone knows they control the Drobax—potentially a fearsome threat, but they have been relatively quiet the last ten years. Three years ago Arioc took the throne of Haskany. King Harel died suddenly with no male heir. Arioc had a claim through marriage to a relative.' Baldwin shrugged. 'It happens. Suddenly, Ishari was in a stronger position. We became worried, but not overly concerned. Haskany raised troops, but only to fight a long, drawn-out campaign against the Barbarians of the east coast. The Kharovians allied with Ishari, probably out of fear of the Drobax. Last month they took the island of Alta from Vismar. These were minor events. No, it was the fall of Persala that took us by surprise.

We don't know what Erkindrix and Arioc's ultimate intentions are. But I couldn't let them take Trevenza and Grienna as well. That would put Arioc right on our border. So, yesterday, Trevenza and Grienna were both fully incorporated into the Empire. I've made my move. Will it make Haskany think twice about pushing further south? Or will they take it as a cause for war? The evidence now suggests that they've been planning for a war for a long time.'

'We've just had Arioc's envoy in before you,' said Ellard, interested in this part of the conversation. 'They refuse to accept the status of the two provinces as belonging to the Empire. They claim them for themselves, as part of Persala. That doesn't sound like backing down to me.'

'If war comes—' Baldwin took over again, 'we are in real trouble. With Emeric's army, they have us caught on two fronts. If I take an army north to fight Haskany, it leaves the Empire open for Emeric's army, and vice versa. That's why we're having to play it cagey—tolerate Orlin and the Barissians, despite the fact they've put soldiers onto the streets in my city.'

He raised a fist, as if he was going to bang it onto the table, but controlled himself, gradually relaxing his hand.

'If Emeric had any sense of strategy, he'd have sent his army to Essenberg already, but he's never had sense, thank the Gods. But it's not just the Empire,' the Emperor continued, sounding passionate. 'If the Empire falls, Guivergne, Cordence, even Magnia—they will all follow. We are heavily outnumbered, and allies are scarce. Our relations with Guivergne are not good. They will not lift a finger to help. Neither will the Confederacy. King Jonas of Kalinth is weak, too fearful of the Drobax to act. I send him a message of support against Ishari, and he wrote back to say that he has good relations with Erkindrix! There is no stomach for a fight there.

'Where does that leave me?' said Baldwin, looking at the map of Dalriya, emotion returning to his voice. 'The Krykkers. The Caladri. I have little contact with them and know nothing of their ways. This is why the support of the Southern states is so important to me. I have decided to send a formal request for help to this conference Edgar is holding. As for the Empire, I sent instructions for each duke to raise his army.' Baldwin smiled grimly at this, as if he had just made a sour jest.

'Well,' he continued, 'each duke has raised his forces. At the moment, however, Ellard's is the only one within range of Trevenza and Grienna.'

'Under the control of my sons,' Ellard added proudly.

'Walter has my forces prepared, but we are wary of moving into Rotelegen for fear of leaving Kelland undefended against Emeric's army. Arne, to be fair, should move his forces today. But the rest...'

Belwynn didn't quite know where to look. The Emperor was criticising the dukes of Brasingia in front of them. Perhaps he found it easier to unload his problems onto strangers. It was a brutally frank analysis of the situation. She felt a little disappointed by it all the same. It seemed that emperors were just men with their own problems, like any other.

'Anyway,' resumed Baldwin, 'I won't go on any more, but you see my dilemma. Perhaps if you return to Magnia, you could help explain the situation to people there.'

'That would no doubt be of value,' said Gustav, 'but we must not overlook this dagger in their possession. Simply returning it to Magnia may not now be the right thing to do. I need to discuss this further with them.'

'I will leave you in the hands of Gustav regarding the weapon,' said Baldwin. 'You have agreed to write a letter to Edgar. Whatever else you and Gustav decide you should do, it has my blessing. Ellard is returning to

Rotelegen tomorrow, and we need to plan our next move. Thank you for your help.'

With that, everyone was suddenly standing up. Before she really knew it, Belwynn was leaving Baldwin's hall. Gustav and Rainer followed them out into the courtyard.

'The Emperor sounded down in there,' said Rainer. 'He is not usually like that. He's had to listen to the ambassadors from Haskany and Barissia lying to him all morning, pretending he doesn't know what they're up to. Don't worry. Whatever else he is, Baldwin is a fighter.'

Gustav gave a cough. 'I would like to speak to you, Soren. About the dagger, and about your powers.'

'I would appreciate your guidance, Gustav.'

'Very well, we can go to my rooms,' said the Archmage.

'Would anyone be able to write that letter now?' asked Rainer.

'Sure, I can do it,' Belwynn agreed.

'Thank you. Follow me, please, if you will.'

As Rainer led Belwynn in one direction, she watched Soren and Gustav head off in another, wondering what kind of guidance Archmage Gustav was about to give her brother.

* * *

SOREN AND BELWYNN looked out over the battlements of Essenberg Castle as the sun rose. Soren was staring down at the early morning streets of the city and gazing beyond the city walls to the southern horizon, imagining briefly that he could see all the way to Magnia.

He turned to his sister.

'I spoke to Gustav for a while last night. I've slept on what he said and come to a decision on what I want to do now. I'm going to tell the others in a moment, but I wanted to talk to you first. I don't mind what the others do now, but I want you to agree—to come with me.'

'Soren,' Belwynn said, her voice showing a trace of dry humour, 'you haven't said where you want to go yet.'

'The Blood Caladri.'

Belwynn said nothing, waiting for an explanation.

'I have two good reasons. First, the selfish one. Gustav had some knowledge of overextension, which I didn't. You know that overextension breaks the bonds, the bonds that you build up between yourself and the magic you try to control?'

'Yes, you've explained that.'

'Gustav has heard of a method which can repair the bonds. A second wizard can charge their power into you and repair the bonds. Gustav has never done it himself—he says it is a highly dangerous piece of magic. It would be too risky for him to try. But he said the Caladri wizards would know more of the technique. He has spent some time with the Blood Caladri himself.'

Soren produced the insignia Gustav had given him. It was a delicately crafted silver hawk with runes inscribed upon it. Soren had recognised the runes as Caladri, but could not completely decipher it, though the first line read *Gustav the Hawk*. He handed it to his sister.

'He says they would recognise his symbol and grant us passage.'

Belwynn stood for a while, absent-mindedly looking at the silver emblem. Soren knew what his sister was thinking. They were close, and not just because they were twins. They had lost both their parents when young and struggled to keep their family's estates. They had struggled, also, with Soren's gift. It had marked him out as different from a young age, and Belwynn had often had to act as an older sister or a parent, protecting him and hiding his secret.

Soren had needed help with controlling his magic powers. He had been lucky, in the end, to have found Ealdnoth. Wizards were a rare species. To have another living close by was one thing. For Ealdnoth to be open about his magic, to be friendly towards Soren, to be prepared to teach him—that was another; and Soren sometimes wondered what would have happened to him without Ealdnoth.

The master and pupil relationship ended. Ealdnoth had taught him everything he knew. Meanwhile, Edgar had befriended the older man through Soren and invited him to his court. Soren knew that to improve, to enhance his powers, he had to learn from other wizards who could teach him new skills and knowledge. He was ambitious. The desire to master magic burned through him. That ambition had led him to go to Delyth, the marsh witch. It had been the right choice as far as his development was concerned. But the experience had changed him, and his relationship with Belwynn had suffered.

Belwynn's voice interrupted Soren's train of thought.

'What is the other reason?'

Soren knew Belwynn didn't understand his ambition; that she even resented it. Part of her would prefer it if he never tried to get his powers back. She certainly believed that it wasn't worth risking his life over, that he should be happy just to have his health. But Soren also knew that Belwynn would do what he wanted.

'The dagger. Gustav studied it, for a long time. I think he was hoping for a reaction when he touched it a second time, but there was none. He even looked it up in some of his books, but found nothing. But he still feels that it is important, and I agree. He suggested I take it to the Caladri and see what they know of it. They have texts which go back hundreds of years, learned men who could examine it. Once we know what it is, why Ishari would want it, then we can make sensible decisions about what to do with it.'

Soren knew that Gustav had made sense on this. He also knew that Belwynn wouldn't want to walk away after all they had been through. She was as curious about the dagger as he was.

'So be it, Soren. I will come,' she said. 'Let's explain this to the others.'

The conversation with the rest of the group was shorter than Soren had expected. He began by putting forward the case for taking the dagger to the Blood Caladri. Herin and Clarin nodded, as if there was nothing unusual in Soren's suggestion. Elana, in that mysterious way of hers, agreed immediately. She and Dirk would go with them. Gyrmund was not so sure.

'Our task was to take the thing back to Magnia, and its resting place in the Temple of Toric. I don't see where this is all going.'

Belwynn answered him. 'Look, we've completed that task of recovery. I have told Edgar this in my letter. If anyone chooses to go back to South Magnia now, I am sure that Edgar will pay the reward in full. You've done what was asked. No one is expecting you to do any more. It's just that some of us need to know what this dagger is.'

Gyrmund looked over at Moneva.

'We need to discuss this,' she said.

Gyrmund and Moneva walked out of the room. Until now, Soren had not really noticed those two becoming so close.

'Soren,' said Rabigar, leaning against the wall, his new eye patch a reminder of the terrible injury inflicted on him in Coldeberg. 'I've made a good physical recovery, thanks to Elana. I can walk and ride fine. I don't know how much use I'll be with my sword any more. I've decided that I would like to see this thing through to the end. It would make things...' The Krykker struggled—to find the right words, perhaps. To control his emotions. 'It would make things seem like there was a purpose. But if you feel I wouldn't be of any help, you only need to say so. I will understand.'

'No,' said Soren immediately. 'I would like you to come.'

'Then I will,' replied Rabigar.

Gyrmund and Moneva re-entered the room.

'We'll go with you to the Caladri,' Moneva said, flashing a quick smile.

Soren felt himself smiling, a bit foolishly, at the show of solidarity from this group, many of whom had been strangers to each other only a week before.

'Well then…' he began, but didn't really know what he was going to say.

'I think everyone should get ready immediately,' began Belwynn, jumping into the silence in her slightly officious way. 'I'm going to see if I can find Rainer and add something to the end of that letter, if Baldwin's ambassador hasn't left yet. Edgar should know what we're up to.'

Belwynn found Rainer in time and got much more from him besides. Their mounts were sent for from the Imps, and he arranged for supplies and equipment to be provided, including the weaponry of their choice. He also explained that they would have an escort. Duke Ellard and twenty of his retainers were leaving Essenberg, heading back to Guslar, the capital of his duchy.

It was still morning when Soren, his sister, their friends, and the men of Rotelegen set off north along the Great Road.

THE ROAD TO WAR

XIX

Shira walked slowly along the stone corridor, her footsteps echoing around the cold, desolate fortress.

She was feeling queasy. She was tired, for one. Yesterday, she had led her Haskan troops through Trevenza and Grienna. She smiled to herself. *Like a hot knife through butter.* The Griennese were good talkers, and maybe they had brought the Empire into the fight. But that was all they could do: they barely had an army, and what they had soon melted away when faced with the numbers at Shira's disposal.

She made a left turn, becoming more apprehensive as she went. When she had been given the news that Erkindrix demanded her presence here the next morning, she had laughed. How was she supposed to get to Samir Durg within a matter of hours? Now she knew better. Shira mistrusted magic. When the Isharite magi who accompanied her army had explained that they would teleport her to the meeting, she had told them where to go. Empty words, of course. Everyone knew she would do it, for who would refuse the demands of Erkindrix of Ishari?

The magi had worked together on the spell and sent her off. It had lasted hours—hours upon hours of stomach-churning movement. As soon as it began, her vision had left her. When she'd opened her eyes, they would not work, unable to focus on anything as strange lights shot past. She felt the wind on her face, the same sensation as when galloping a horse. Her sense of balance had gone, too. She had the sensation of travelling, but whether she was lying down, upside down, or in some other position, she had no idea. When it stopped, Shira found herself lying in a crumpled heap outside the walls of the fortress. She had retched on the ground. She had retched again, until there was nothing left to bring up. It was morning, and she had traveled all night without sleep.

But Shira was a soldier. She stood up and walked to her meeting.

At the end of the corridor, the iron gates of the throne room loomed large. Shira made out a figure waiting in the shadows. It was Arioc. So, he had been summoned too. After their successful invasion of Persala, Arioc had been ordered to complete the occupation of the country, destroying any remaining opposition. Shira had been given the task of completing the conquest by taking Trevenza and Grienna. Although only brief, it had been the first time she had been put in sole charge of a campaign. She was edging out of Arioc's shadow.

Shira had first met Arioc in her home country of Haskany. She had been attracted to him from the beginning. She was attracted to powerful men, and he was the most powerful she had ever met. Arioc was a great warrior and war leader. Well over six feet tall, he stood above most men in height, but stood above all in sheer presence. Only a few did not succumb totally to his authority. And there was Arioc's Isharite heritage. His legend said he was the son of Erkindrix. If so, he had inherited his father's magical abilities. Shira knew little of magic, but she knew Arioc had few peers as far as that went.

When she had first met him, nothing had happened. But soon, Arioc's ambitions and those of her family united. Shira's uncle became a close ally, plotting with him to secure the throne upon the death of King Harel. It had been Uncle Koren who had first suggested their marriage, to lend legitimacy to Arioc's seizure of the throne. But playing the part of the good wife had little appeal. When the fighting started, Shira played her part as a soldier. It was only once they had fought together that Arioc and Shira became true lovers.

Shira knew that becoming Arioc's wife and lover might bring her power, but she was unprepared for what followed. Arioc proposed to Erkindrix that she become the new member of the Council of Seven. He had a good argument. The people of Haskany respected, or feared, Arioc. But they could love Shira like they could never love him. Having no magical powers, she posed no real threat to anyone in Ishari, either. For Arioc, of course, it would strengthen his position on the Council.

Since becoming King of Haskany, Arioc was increasingly establishing himself as second in command in Ishari. He got his way and Shira—a human, a woman, with no magic—joined the Council of Seven. In a formal meeting of the Council, she was appointed by Erkindrix himself. It was the only time she had met with the leader of Ishari before today. Shira had never felt true fear before that day.

Shira was feeling queasy, but not just from her journey. From dread at what lay beyond the gates.

'I hear congratulations are in order,' said Arioc drily, as Shira approached the doors. 'I've heard about Trevenza and Grienna. You look like shit, by the way.'

'Yes,' replied Shira, barely taking in what he was saying. 'What are we here for? Is it a meeting of the Council?'

Arioc shrugged. 'I don't know why we're here. It's not a Council meeting, though. Just you and me.'

Arioc smiled, appreciating the look on Shira's face as she realised that meant an even closer, more intimate meeting with Erkindrix.

Shira felt angry at his pleasure in her weakness. She asked Arioc a question she had not dared to ask before. 'You are his son, aren't you?'

The question hung in the air for a while. Eventually, Arioc shrugged again, his face showing little emotion. 'I don't know,' Arioc paused. 'I've never asked.'

An unbelievable answer, but Shira believed it all the same. For a second time, Arioc smiled at the reaction on her face. 'Time to go in,' he said.

Before Shira could say anything, something which might delay proceedings for a few seconds more, Arioc pushed open the gates and entered.

* * *

EDGAR WAS FEELING pleased with the day's proceedings so far.

The response from his neighbours had been good. Prince Cerdda had come himself. Lord Rosmont, the Cordentine ambassador, was here to represent King Glanna. From the Midder Steppe, two chiefs, Brock and Frayne, had come. Emperor Baldwin's ambassador, Lord Kass, had arrived this morning. He was a heavy-set man with a large stomach and a handlebar moustache that gained a life of its own whenever his mouth moved.

Guivergne had also sent a representative. Bastien, Duke of Morbaine, was brother to King Nicolas. Bastien himself was not here, but he had sent a rather brusque, red-headed man named Russell. At first, Edgar had not taken to Russell, who seemed to be a soldier by trade rather than an ambassador. After a while, however, he took his presence as a compliment. Russell was not here to play with words or waste time. He was here to tell Edgar and the others the truth, then report back to the Duke.

Edgar had wanted the numbers at the Conference to be kept down to a minimum, and this had been achieved. He himself had excluded all the nobles of South Magnia, such as Otha and Wulfgar, who had both requested a seat at the table. Ealdnoth and Wilchard were his only advisers.

His guests had followed Edgar's lead. Altogether, only twelve men sat around a table in Edgar's castle at Granstow, on the border between South and North Magnia. It was a suitable location for the Conference, but also it made Edgar feel good to be here—the castle which, until recently, had been held by Harbyrt the Fat.

He had sent out invitations for the Conference on the same day he had Harbyrt beheaded.

Edgar was also pleased because Lord Kass had passed on a letter from his cousin, Belwynn. It was the first communication he had received from the group since they had set off over a week ago.

He had not fully digested the contents of the letter. Parts of Belwynn's story sounded strange, and he did not fully understand why she and Soren had decided to head further north rather than bring Toric's Dagger back to Magnia. But the central facts: they had the dagger; they were safe. This was good news.

Lord Kass began the proceedings with a formal request for help from Emperor Baldwin. He then outlined the position the Emperor faced: an enemy much larger in numbers, a divided Empire, and little prospect of help coming from anywhere else. The Magnians and the Steppe chiefs were eager for all the information from around Dalriya they could get. Lord Kass and Lord Rosmont were often the better informed, and therefore did more of the talking.

'In the margins, Ishari has been flexing its muscles for some time now,' Rosmont was saying. 'In the east, the Barbarians have gradually been subjugated by Ardashir, a member of the Council of Seven. He is now pushing into the territory of the Bearmen. The Shadow Caladri have allied with Ishari and are waging war against the Blood Caladri.'

'We believe that King Dorjan of the Shadow Caladri is another member of the Council of Seven,' added Kass, his moustache bouncing about.

'In Halvia, Drobax are raiding the kingdom of Vismar,' continued Rosmont. 'The Vismarians have already lost Alta island to the Kharovians, who now have mastery of the western sea. In the north, King Jonas of Kalinth has all but handed his realm over to Erkindrix. But now Erkindrix and Arioc are putting their cards on the table. The conquest of Persala has drawn Baldwin to the brink of war. The intentions of Ishari are becoming all too clear. They want the whole of Dalriya.'

'The trouble,' began Kass, 'is that the rest of Dalriya is not ready. The Empire is perhaps as much to blame as anyone. The danger from Ishari had become a thing of history. We have become obsessed with our own petty quarrels. Brasingia has warred with Guivergne and the Confederacy. Magnia has fought itself. The Caladri and the Krykkers have left the humans to themselves and become insular. Now that the threat has returned, there is no alliance to withstand it. My Emperor, Baldwin, has realised this. He hopes it is not too late.'

Edgar nodded. 'As do I, Lord Kass. I want to ask: you refer to the previous threat Ishari posed this land. For me, this is a story passed down from so long ago it has more the feel of legend than history. But I feel we should now learn all we can from it.'

Kass chuckled. 'I agree, Prince Edgar, but the legends I was told round the fire of an evening are likely to be no more illuminating than yours. If anyone here can teach us, perhaps it would be Lord Ealdnoth?'

Ealdnoth nodded. 'It is history, not legend. But it is a history from hundreds and hundreds of years ago. A time before humankind recorded events through writing—or at least such writing has not survived. If written accounts do survive, they were written by the Caladri.'

Ealdnoth took a breath, pausing before recounting his knowledge.

'This was a time before the humans had spread throughout Dalriya as they have now. Before the Persaleian Empire was created—perhaps before Persala itself. The Caladri held lands that stretched from north to south. The Krykkers built their kingdoms in the north and west. The Lippers cultivated much of the south, including modern-day Magnia. And, of course, Dalriya was much larger than now, for she and Halvia were one.

'The Isharites invaded. Humans arrived in Dalriya by sea. The Isharites arrived from another world, transporting themselves here by magic. A terrible war of survival followed, when the Isharites aimed to take Dalriya for themselves. The people of Dalriya united. If I were to stick to true history, then I know nothing else for sure except the end of this war. A great battle between the two sides was fought. Incredible magical forces were released. The cracking of the world was the result. In the stories, we are victorious. But what does history really tell us? This great conflict seemed to end the war, but it was not decisive. We survived, but so did Ishari. Not a victory, then. More like a bitter truce. That truce has lasted hundreds of years, but the Isharites, it seems, have not forgotten. They have been waiting. The truce is over. I don't know why it has happened now. But we should know that Ishari wants total victory—Dalriya for themselves only.'

THE FORMAL MEETING lasted until the end of lunch. Then there were smaller meetings where deals might be made. After talking with Cerdda, then with Russell, Edgar found himself alone with Ealdnoth, waiting for news from other quarters.

'No one has really needed persuading that Ishari represents a threat to all of us,' Ealdnoth commented.

'Yes,' agreed Edgar. 'But does that mean they'll do anything about it? I want them to commit troops. Russell has already said that Bastien will not send any without the agreement of King Nicolas.'

'That was always likely, Edgar,' said Ealdnoth. 'Guivergne were never going to give any of its soldiers to Baldwin. To be fair, Nicolas will doubtless be concerned about his own borders.'

Wilchard entered the room.

'Well?' Edgar demanded.

'I've just spoken to Prince Cerdda. Seems like he's been testing out Lord Kass. He's drawn a commitment from Kass—Baldwin will pay half the wages of any troops we send once they arrive in Brasingia. Cerdda says he'll discuss precise numbers with us, but he is prepared to match ours, within reason.'

'Great,' said Edgar. 'A fair enough demand, since Baldwin will in reality have command over any soldiers we send. Go back; see if he'll agree to two thousand each. What about the others?'

Wilchard frowned. 'Well, I'm not sure yet. Brock and Frayne are in a private meeting with Rosmont. I tried to find out what was going on. Rosmont was polite enough, but beneath all of his pleasantries, he basically told me to get lost. I don't know what they're up to.'

'Speak to Cerdda. Ask him whether he has a leader for his forces in mind. Do your best to find anything else out.'

The North Magnians were on board. Edgar waited. Wilchard came back and forth, but there was no more news from Rosmont and the Middians. Edgar wanted them to commit. If King Glanna were to send troops to fight for the Empire, it would effectively be a declaration of war against Ishari and Haskany. Edgar wanted as many rulers as possible to join with the Empire now. It would encourage the other powers in Dalriya to do the same.

But Edgar waited, and no news came. Wilchard would enter the room and shrug. Lord Rosmont would not be disturbed. And then Wilchard arrived a final time. His shoulders did not shrug this time, and his mouth was twitching into a smile.

'Lords Rosmont, Brock and Frayne send news,' he began. 'They are making us privy to a private agreement between Cordence and the two tribes. It amounts to this. The Middians match our commitment and provide a total of two thousand mounted fighters, which Brock will lead himself. Cordence has agreed to pay for all expenses incurred.' Wilchard smiled sardonically. 'The sum involved was not disclosed.'

Edgar nodded. 'I shouldn't be surprised. The Cordentines have got on board without actually sending any troops. The Middian chiefs are making a profit out of it. So be it—the result is a substantial number of well-trained fighters. Wilchard, can you organise a final meeting with everyone present? We need to sort out logistics.' Edgar smiled grimly at Ealdnoth and Wilchard. 'The second army I will raise in the space of two weeks. And unlike the first, this one is going to see action.'

* * *

THE VAULTED CEILING of the throne room rose so high above them that Shira almost felt herself losing her balance when she looked upwards. At the top, it was finished with a gold dome that could be seen from virtually anywhere in the fortress of Samir Durg. She turned her attention to the throne itself.

Situated in the centre of the room, the carved red crystal shone uninvitingly, drawing the eye nonetheless. Shira felt her feet move in that direction, alongside Arioc. Her eyes flicked to the small, crumpled figure occupying the throne before she forced them to look at the second figure present, standing to one side. Siavash, High Priest of Ishari and fellow council member to Shira and Arioc, was wearing the hooded black cloak of his order. The Order of Diis was a powerful but secretive sect in Ishari. Shira knew little of their ways, but understood that they had a special relationship to Erkindrix, making Siavash a commanding figure. Even Arioc treated him with care.

Before she knew it, Shira and Arioc were standing before the throne. The fetid smell of decay assaulted her nostrils, and it was all she could do to stop herself from gagging. Someone had scented the throne, or Erkindrix himself, with a sweet, cloying perfume, but it did nothing to hide the smell.

Erkindrix was living in a dying body. It had been rotting away for years, kept alive only by his immense magical powers. It was clear to Shira, however, that even such magic could not hold back time forever.

Erkindrix turned to look Shira full in the face. Shira now had to return his look without revealing her disgust. His flesh was not lined and wrinkly like the elderly she knew in Haskany. Mostly it was grey and waxy, but frequently interrupted by red and black sores. Shira could see a sore on his neck oozing with yellowish-green pus. This was unpleasant, but Shira had seen much worse after a battle.

The eyes, which looked at hers, were grey and watery, almost lifeless. But once Shira looked into those eyes, she could see the second pair staring back. Like burning black coals, they fired alive once they realised they had been seen.

Shira felt them boring into her, feasting on her, as her chest tightened. The black eyes would know everything about her. Hard and bruising, they interrogated her. Her body, her private parts, her private thoughts—nothing could be hidden from them.

The eyes abruptly withdrew. Shira controlled a little convulsion. She wanted to scream out, turn around, and run. Now she could see more of the second face, moving and rippling beneath the pallid grey surface of Erkindrix's skin.

Shira experienced what true fear was. A fear that no human could ever cause or recreate, deep and primeval, spirit-sapping. Shira's being knew instinctively that this was a creature she should never have met.

'You have my congratulations, Shira,' said Erkindrix, his voice stronger and harder than should have been possible when one saw his weak and crumpled form. He dribbled as he spoke, as if he had too much moisture in his mouth.

'Thank you, My Lord,' Shira responded. 'Trevenza and Grienna are secure. We need to fortify our position on the Brasingian border.'

Erkindrix turned away, as if he had not heard her. He fixed his gaze on Arioc. Shira turned to look at Arioc and wondered at his ability to remain composed and nonchalant in front of such a sight.

'You have not found King Mark.'

'No,' replied Arioc. 'Persala is secure, but Mark has not been found. I don't know if he's alive or dead.'

'Persala is not secure if King Mark is alive,' retorted Erkindrix sharply.

Arioc said nothing.

'Our enemies are becoming aware of our power and may try to unite against us,' began Erkindrix. 'The time for secrecy is now over. We must finish the process quickly. I have decided to move against our two greatest enemies simultaneously. Arioc, you will leave Persala and plan the destruction of the

Grand Caladri. The magi of Ishari and one third of the Drobax will be at your disposal.'

Shira could not help but take a sharp intake of breath. The Grand Caladri were the greatest of their race, heirs of a civilisation which had stood in Dalriya for centuries, a place of great learning and magic. Erkindrix had dismissed them to oblivion in a sentence. Even Arioc showed surprise, his expression changing to pleasure as he considered the enormity of the task given him.

The leader of Ishari turned back to Shira. 'Shira, you will continue south and occupy the Brasingian Empire.'

A thrill coursed down Shira's body. What an honour! This was better than Persala. Persala had been an overripe fruit, easy to pluck. Its greatness was in the past. The Empire would be a different, far worthier opponent. And in Persala, she had been Arioc's number two. This time Shira, a girl from Haskany, would be the one to bring the Empire to its knees.

She trembled again at the thought. This was too good!

'You will command the Haskan army. I will also divert one third of the Drobax to your command.'

Shira reacted instantly. Her disgust at the thought of commanding those creatures prompting her to challenge the dread Erkindrix. 'I don't need the Drobax. They are not soldiers. I can take the Empire with the Haskan forces.'

'You misunderstand me. The time for human warfare, for pitched battles and sieges—that time is over. This is Ishari's war. You will use both the Haskans and the Drobax. The fall of the Empire must be quick, decisive, and inevitable. The humans' defiance must be totally crushed.'

Shira nodded her acquiescence, not quite believing that she had dared to argue in the first place. Her excitement at the charge given her had been dulled slightly by the knowledge of how it would be done. One thing was certain, however.

The Brasingian Empire would fall.

SECRET PATHS

XX

Gyrmund's excitement mounted as they left behind the last traces of human habitation and moved ever closer towards the alien lands of the Caladri.

It had been a tiring two days of travelling. On the first day, Duke Ellard of Rotelegen had led them at a hard pace, northwards along the Great Road. He was a tough old boot of a soldier and had a clear schedule which he always kept to when travelling between Essenberg and Guslar. At midday they stopped at the town of Appen, where he had his own stables. He had enough spares to swap everyone's mount before they headed off again. By the end of the day, they had reached Herdorf, not far from Ellard's duchy.

The next morning, they set off at the same pace, leaving Kelland for Rotelegen. To the west, they could see the formidable, brooding presence of Burkhard Castle. As the castle retreated into the distance, they were met by a small group of Rotelegen soldiers, bearing weighty news for their duke.

The Haskan army had invaded Trevenza and Grienna and the vanguard was stationed on Ellard's northern border. Given that the two provinces had recently been incorporated into the Empire, the two states were now at war. If the Haskans continued further south, Rotelegen was clearly the next target.

It was at this point that Ellard curtly made his farewell and his force galloped off at an even faster pace. The threat from Ishari and Haskany suddenly seemed very real to Gyrmund. Although he and the others went their separate way, Gyrmund at least felt that what they were doing was part of the same fight that Ellard was involved in.

Gyrmund took his group at a slower pace than the Duke had led them. There was no point pushing them to reach the land of the Blood Caladri that evening. It was better to give them one last night in a decent bed before stepping into the unknown.

They headed east, entering Luderia by midday. The roads turned into paths as they pushed into the sparsely populated northern part of the duchy. Gyrmund was familiar with this part of the Empire and knew it to differ from the farming regions of Barissia and Kelland. The Luderian Forest covered the land—miles upon miles of pine trees, inhabited by only a few woodsmen. To the east, the run-off from the Karnica mountain range had created wetlands. Here lived the Sparewaldi tribe, largely independent from the rest of the duchy. Gyrmund had spent half a year living with the tribe. They lived a good life from river and lake fishing and burned peat for fuel. The quiet, slow pace of life had done him good, and he still felt a sense of regret for having left.

It was evening when they reached the village of Guben. The White Boar Inn had been recommended by a couple of travellers as one of the last places big enough to sleep and feed them all with comfort.

The White Boar served a simple vegetable pottage with huge chunks of dark bread. They were so famished that they wolfed it all down. Gyrmund could see that Elana could barely stay awake long enough to eat. She went to bed immediately after the meal, as did Rabigar and Dirk. The others stayed up a while to talk with the innkeeper and his guests.

It was only natural for them to ask Gyrmund and the others where they were going. When Herin confidently replied that they were headed to the Blood Caladri, a lively conversation followed, with much advice given.

The innkeeper seemed worried for them. 'You're not invited? If you're not invited, you won't be coming back. The Caladri don't let strangers come and go in their lands—you must know that. They want to protect their secret paths, don't they? To their cities.'

'He's right,' joined in one of the regulars, who seemed to be glued to a stool at the bar. 'There's a few in these parts disappear each year. They get too far into the forest and aren't heard of again.'

'Some say they don't kill 'em. They just don't let them leave. Have to live amongst the Caladri 'til they die.'

'Well, anyone who gets caught by the Caladri is plain stupid,' said an old man, nestled by the fire. 'They've got poles up in the forest, marking their territory. There's writing on 'em, in their own language sure enough, but the message is plain and simple. Don't go any farther. If you go farther, you're invading their territory. Shouldn't expect to come back alive.'

'Whose side are you taking, Trevor?' countered an angry woman. 'We want Duke Arne to show his face round here with an army at his back. That would sort the Caladri out.'

'You ignorant woman,' responded Trevor. 'We've had peace here for generations. It works because we respect them and leave them alone, and they do the same. You all know what happened to my brother. Now there was a stupid man. We was out hunting in the forest and he got himself too close to a boar. Nearly sliced him in two. I couldn't move him. He was dying on me. Then three Caladri came along and dressed up his wounds. Used these special medicines on him. I seen them do it with my own eyes. They're an old, wise people.' The old man turned to face Gyrmund and the others. 'They don't need folk barging into their lands for no good reason.'

'We've got good reasons,' Gyrmund heard himself say, almost before he realised he was speaking. 'You know the Empire is under threat. We may need the help of the Caladri.'

'Hmm...' pondered the old man. 'I can understand that. I just don't see why they should stir themselves to help us out.'

* * *

Farred turned in the saddle to look behind him. Over a thousand mounted troops waited there. His army.

He had burst with pride when Prince Edgar had first asked him to lead the South Magnian troops. It was a sign of how close they had become since the attack on the Temple of Toric ten days ago. Edgar had turned down several other noblemen who had demanded the position. He had insisted on Farred being the right man for the job. The good relationship Farred had built with Cerdda was also important, given that troops from both countries would have to work together. His Middian heritage was another quality in his favour. It was the chance he had been waiting for, to rise above his position as a middling lord on the outskirts of the realm.

After a while, other thoughts had crept in to Farred's thinking. His prince had given him a difficult mission. The Empire was in serious danger from Haskany and Ishari. Farred and his men would soon be in the middle of that. What would happen when Farred and his men reached the Empire? How would Emperor Baldwin treat them once they were there? There were uncertainties ahead. But there was doubtless action as well. And Farred was ready for it. He thought of Gyrmund, journeying around Dalriya on his adventures. Now it was his turn.

In recent hours, he had enjoyed little time for further reflection. Farred wanted as large a proportion of the South Magnian troops to be as personally loyal to him as possible. He travelled to his homeland on the border between Magnia and the Midder Steppe. The fighting men from his own estate formed the nucleus of his force. He then recruited from his friends and neighbours, men who could be vouched for and who knew him. Edgar was offering excellent wages for recruits, but insisted that each supply their own mount, armour and weaponry. This reduced the pool of potential soldiers, but ensured that only those with a decent level of training were likely to sign up.

When Farred returned to Bidcote, Edgar had also raised around five hundred mounted soldiers. They were mostly young sons of noblemen, eager for glory. This made them naïve but well equipped, and in the main, well trained. This combined force was now ready to head north. Wilchard, Edgar's steward, had ridden north immediately after the Southern Conference. He had been given the task of raising around another thousand soldiers. This was to be done by gathering the only permanent army in the kingdom: those men who were stationed as guards in the castles on the border with North Magnia. These men would be career soldiers, though perhaps, thought Farred, less than keen to leave their easy existence for the obvious dangers in the Empire. Since Edgar already paid their wages, however, they had to go where he asked. Cerdda of North Magnia was using his border soldiers for the same purpose, leaving both sides of the border undefended.

This would become the full contribution of troops from South Magnia. The Conference had agreed that all troops raised should be mounted, since it would be a long journey north. Farred would lead his force to the north-east corner of the kingdom. Here the forces of South and North Magnia and the Steppe would combine to make six thousand. Prince Cerdda's own brother, Ashere, was leading the North Magnians, and Brock was leading the fighters from his tribe. It was hoped that Bastien of Morbaine could arrange safe passage for the force to travel through Guivergne on its way to Kelland. This would help them to avoid trouble from the rebellious Duke Emeric.

The moment to leave had arrived fast. Farred trotted forwards. Ahead, a scaffold had been erected. The flag of Magnia, the Sun in Glory, had been draped around it to create a kind of rostrum. It was an image rarely used in recent years, since it represented the whole of Magnia; neither Edgar nor Cerdda had been willing to use it very often. But Edgar had requested it for this occasion, since troops from both countries would fight together in one army.

He waited on top of the scaffold with other notable persons of the realm, ready to give his blessing to Farred's army. Underneath it stood the more ordinary folk of Magnia, seeing off their loved ones. Farred nodded to the noblemen and churchmen atop the scaffold, some of whom solemnly nodded back; others gave an encouraging welcome; yet others studiously ignored him. Succeed in this venture, thought Farred, and they could not afford to ignore him in the future.

Edgar moved forwards, and they clasped hands.

'Are you ready, Farred?' asked the Prince.

Farred nodded. 'Ready.'

'You will meet up with Prince Ashere soon. You must make sure to give him every courtesy as befits his rank. Defer to him when possible, but control over my troops ultimately rests with you. In the Empire, the same applies in your dealings with Baldwin. Is that clear?'

'It is clear, Your Highness.'

Edgar grasped his shoulder. 'Good luck.'

Farred nodded. He walked his horse a few feet away from the rostrum. He drew his sword and held it in the air. A cheer rose up. Farred's army began to move.

* * *

'This is as far as we go,' said Trevor.

Belwynn and the others looked at the old man they had met last night in the inn. They had been travelling for about three hours. He and a couple of younger men from the inn had taken them along a route which they had said would get them to the lands of the Caladri quickly. They had passed by the odd cottage at first, where woodsmen eked out a lonely existence. The countryside north of the inn was not suitable for arable farming, but Belwynn observed that most people kept pigs, who were left to their own devices to forage and root amongst the trees. As they moved farther into the forest, human habitation ended and any pigs they saw were wild ones. The going got slower and slower as their horses were forced to pick their way through denser and denser cover.

Trevor nodded ahead. 'Up there, you can make out one of the Caladri poles.'

Belwynn could just make out a light brown wooden pole which had previously blended in with the surrounding trees. She looked at Soren, and he nodded back.

They all dismounted and took what they needed from the saddlebags of their mounts. They were leaving yet another set of horses behind. Trevor had agreed to take the horses in return for guiding them here. He had also promised to sell them back at a reasonable price if they came back, but he didn't seem very convinced that was likely to happen, and Belwynn had the same feeling.

Trevor and his two colleagues gathered the nine mounts. 'Good luck,' he murmured, the others nodding silently in their direction. With that, they turned around, looking relieved to be heading back in the direction they had come.

Belwynn watched them leave until they were no longer visible before turning around to the others. They stood looking at each other, less than eager to press on. To Belwynn, they looked like nine little children who had got lost in the woods.

'Let's take a look at this pole, then,' suggested Herin.

He marched off in that direction.

One by one, they followed him.

As Belwynn approached the pole, she could see that it stood in a small cleared circle within the forest, suggesting that it was maintained fairly regularly. It stood approximately two-thirds the height of the biggest trees around it. Gyrmund was talking to Clarin and pointing to his left. Belwynn followed his finger and could just make out a second, similarly designed pole in the distance. Curious, she looked in the other direction and saw yet another.

Soren was studying the inscriptions on the pole, carved and coloured with inks. There were a series of pictures running down it. At the top of the series was the largest image—a three-dimensional face. Belwynn was struck by it, for in many respects it resembled a human face, and yet clearly it was not. She knew she was looking at the carved face of a Caladri.

She took a while to study it and identify what made it different. The face was tilted upwards slightly. It began with a pointed chin and thin lips. The nose was hooked and the eyes full circles. Belwynn felt she could stare at this alien face for hours and remain fascinated, but she made herself look at the other carvings on the pole.

Beneath the face were three smaller and less detailed pictures: a skull; a knife dripping with blood; another face, neither human nor Caladri, but some kind of devil with glaring red eyes. Clearly, these were designed to scare off or warn people who came across them.

Beneath the pictures was a short piece of carved writing, but the characters were undecipherable to Belwynn. Soren was studying it.

'Do you know what it says?' she asked him.

Moneva and Dirk looked up at the question and moved closer. Belwynn felt a certain amount of pride in her brother, since both held expressions of surprise at the idea that Soren might understand the strange looking characters.

'Just about. It is mostly straightforward. The first line says *Turn around, walk away, do not look back and you will live*. The second is *Or face ahead, walk on and you will...* I don't know what the last word means.'

Dirk shrugged. '*You will die* seems to fit.'

Soren smiled. 'Yes, that's possible...but it's not a word for death that I've come across.'

'Well,' said Moneva, 'seems to me a bit of a waste of time to carve a message in characters which no one will understand.'

Moneva had a point and, growing bored with the pole, the group pressed on into the lands of the Blood Caladri. Gyrmund, as usual, led from the front, though Belwynn wondered why; he had already admitted that this was one part of Dalriya he had not visited before. Rabigar walked next to him. Soren had suggested that the Blood Caladri might be curious if they saw a Krykker in the party and be more likely to refrain from killing them on the spot. Rabigar had looked at him sceptically, but took his position at the front willingly enough.

They walked into the forest for three hours. There were no paths, since humans did not enter the lands of the Caladri and, according to the folk at the inn last night, they did not leave either. Gyrmund took care to follow the easiest route, but the going was difficult. The forest itself was pleasant enough, having nothing like the oppressive quality of the Wilderness. After travelling so far, so fast on horseback, however, Belwynn found the current pace frustrating. The knowledge that they did not actually know where they were going made things worse. The others were getting equally fed up and Belwynn asked for a rest.

'This is hard work,' she commented. 'We may have a long journey before we reach the inhabited part of the forest.'

'This was a stupid idea,' said Herin, less constructively. 'We've only gone a mile or two in all this time. We're bumbling around like a bunch of idiots.'

'If you have a better idea where we're going, feel free to take the lead,' said Gyrmund defensively.

'That's the point, isn't it?' replied Herin irritably. 'None of us know where we're going. We don't know of a town or city. Finding a settlement in this forest is like finding a needle in a haystack. We could spend the next month here walking around and not find one stinking Caladri.'

'True,' said Gyrmund. 'We're going to have to wait for them to come to us.'

'And if they don't?' asked Clarin.

Gyrmund shrugged.

'They'll have to find us first,' Belwynn considered, thinking that they might have to do something to draw attention to themselves.

'They already know we're here,' said Gyrmund.

'What do you mean?' said Belwynn.

'What are you talking about?' demanded Herin.

'I think they've been following us for a while now,' explained Gyrmund.

'Why didn't you bloody say so?' shouted Herin, getting increasingly angry.

'You didn't ask,' Gyrmund responded calmly.

Herin drew his sword.

'Oh Toric, not more hysterics, Herin,' complained Belwynn.

Gyrmund backed away, his hand on his sword hilt.

'I haven't seen anyone, and my eyesight's as good as yours,' said Clarin.

'Perhaps, but do you know what you're looking for?' asked Gyrmund.

'This idiot is pushing us too far,' growled Herin, pacing forwards as Gyrmund walked backwards. 'How do we know he's seen anyone?'

There was sudden movement about them.

A form appeared out of the forest behind Gyrmund, and before Belwynn could shout out, the ranger had a knife at his neck.

There were about a dozen other figures surrounding them, with bows drawn and arrows aimed at them. The Blood Caladri had found them.

'Now do you believe we're here?' asked the Caladri, who had his knife pressed against Gyrmund's neck.

Belwynn looked about her, fearful that with one word the arrows pointed at them would be loosed to find their targets. She was still able, however, to take some pleasure in the look of total surprise on Gyrmund's face.

Soren fumbled about in his cloak; two Caladri were training their arrows on him should he try something.

He produced Gustav's signet, the silver hawk with runic inscriptions, and handed it to the nearest Caladri. The Caladri soldier studied it briefly and showed it to his leader, who still had his knife at Gyrmund's throat. The leader had a look himself before turning back to Soren.

'What are you doing here?' he demanded.

'We are representatives of Emperor Baldwin of Brasingia and of Prince

Edgar of Magnia. The primary purpose of our visit here is to discuss with King Tibor the shared threat from Ishari, and how our peoples can help each other.'

The head Caladri stared at Soren for a few seconds, as if doing so would tell him whether or not Soren was lying.

'It appears you have important business,' he decided. 'King Tibor is a long way from here. His son, Prince Lorant, is close by. We will escort you to *him*.'

With that, and with no other introductions, the Caladri leader released Gyrmund. 'We require that you give your weapons to us.'

Rabigar acted first, handing his sword to the nearest Caladri soldier, who decided it was easiest to sling his bow over one shoulder and carry the sword in his hands. Belwynn and the others followed his lead.

Satisfied, the Caladri turned around and headed in a north-westerly direction. They spread out in a fan shape, not bothering to give Belwynn's group a second look.

'Right,' said Soren, seemingly to himself as much as to anyone else. 'We'll just follow them. Be careful. I think that little argument between Herin and Gyrmund was …*encouraged*. They have at least one wizard amongst them.'

Herin and Gyrmund glared at each other, but the anger seemed to have gone.

So, Belwynn thought to herself, we're walking through the forest again. At least they were now being led by the Caladri to a specific location. Despite carrying two sets of weapons, while Belwynn and her friends carried none, they set a quick pace.

As she settled in to her walking again, Belwynn took the time to study the first real-life Caladri she had seen.

The carved face on the pole she had examined was a very accurate representation. Indeed, she could see that, compared to humans, their faces were tilted at a slight angle, giving the impression that they were always looking down their noses at people. To them, she guessed, humans might appear to have rather flat faces. Their hair, like humans, could be blonde or dark or red, but the fashion among these male Caladri was to grow it long to their shoulders. Most of them tied it up or braided it to keep it out of their faces.

The body structure of the Caladri was also different. Most noticeable were the feet: four long digits ending in claws. They walked barefoot and put their weight on these four toes rather than on the rest of the foot. It gave them a more broken, bird-like gait than the smoother walking motion of Belwynn's group, but it seemed to allow them to travel at a quick pace. They were, on average, a couple of inches smaller than humans, and had noticeably thinner frames. Their arms and legs looked so thin to Belwynn that they might snap if pressed too hard, yet clearly, they were strong enough. One of them was carrying Clarin's huge sword, resting the flat end on his shoulder as he navigated his way through the forest.

The Caladri did not stop for rest or food, and Belwynn and the others ate their lunch as they walked. The interest Belwynn had in the Caladri eventually waned and the journey once more became a drain. The Caladri, clearly forest dwellers, were used to the dense foliage and seemed able to find obstruction free pathways without even looking for them. The others, save perhaps for Gyrmund, were not doing so well. Although they were, in theory, simply following the path the Caladri at the front were taking, they tripped on snags and undergrowth, slipped in the permanently damp forest floor, and jammed their feet in holes in the ground, which the forest seemed to have deliberately covered over with leaves. Belwynn noticed that Moneva, in particular, was increasingly swearing under her breath. When Gyrmund reached over a hand to guide her along, she snatched her arm away from him and continued to run through the long list of expletives she knew.

Then, sometime around mid-afternoon, Belwynn found the Caladri had led them onto a stone path. It was more than a path worn into the forest floor by feet; it had the look of something deliberately created, being wide enough for five people to walk side by side. Belwynn supposed it was the equivalent of a road.

None of the Caladri made any comment on the introduction of a new surface to their guests. They didn't talk amongst themselves, either.

The journey continued on foot on the Caladri path in silence. The Caladri still walked in a kind of triangular formation, so that while the leaders at the front walked on the road, most of the Caladri were scattered to either side, seemingly happy enough to keep walking on the forest floor.

They reached a way station. A large timber building had been constructed a few feet from the road, along with several smaller ones. In the yard between the road and the building there waited a couple of huge carriages. Four powerful-looking male gaur were connected to the front carriage, which was attached to the rear one; both of them large-wheeled, roofed, and luxurious looking.

The group stopped on the road while the leader of the Caladri soldiers walked over and entered the building. Time passed in silence. The remaining Caladri soldiers seemed disinterested in the proceedings and in their human guests. Belwynn found this surprising, since she and the others could not stop themselves from staring at the strangeness of them.

The leader returned. He uttered a few commands to his soldiers; each of them walked over and handed back the weapons they had been carrying to their rightful owners. The Caladri, who approached Belwynn, held up her sword, balanced on his palms.

'Thank you,' she said, taking the handle and lifting the weapon.

The Caladri inclined his head in recognition, but said nothing.

'We are leaving you here now,' the leader said to everyone. 'Good day.'

With that, the troop of Caladri soldiers turned around and walked back in the direction they had come. Belwynn turned around again to look in the building's direction, anticipating that they were a responsibility which had now been passed on to someone else. Sure enough, there was another Caladri, now waiting to greet them. He stood by the gaur, where steps on the carriage led up to the driver's platform.

'Greetings,' he began. This Caladri was not dressed as a soldier, but wore leather leggings and top. 'My name is Gyuri. I will now transport you to the camp of Prince Lorant. You are most welcome in the lands of the Caladri. I may apologise if, so far, you have not been treated as honourable guests.' Gyuri waved in the direction of the departing soldiers. 'They are warriors, yes? Not diplomats.' Gyuri smiled. 'We will load up this carriage and then depart. If there is anything you want, please ask us. We have toilets inside, if you wish,' he added, gesturing at the buildings.

As Gyuri finished speaking, six more Caladri arrived by the carriage: three men and three women. Belwynn was approached by one of the women and ushered over to the second carriage.

'Hello, my name is Marika. The ladies will be travelling in this coach.'

Moneva and Elana had joined Belwynn, each of them gathered by the other two female Caladri.

'Toilet?' asked one of the women.

Moneva rolled her eyes. 'Yes,' she said bluntly.

Moneva and Elana were taken towards the timber building, while Belwynn and Marika stood outside the carriage. Belwynn looked over to the first carriage, where the men were being organised in the same manner. She turned her attention to the gaur. Gyuri was patting their heads and talking to them, seemingly in preparation for the journey.

'You like?' asked Marika, smiling sweetly. 'Come.'

Marika took Belwynn's hand in hers and walked her over to them. Belwynn was taken aback by the physical contact, especially since the Caladri soldiers had been so aloof. She allowed herself to be led, however. Marika stroked the neck of the nearest gaur, whispering into its ear. They had big, strong shoulders and curved horns on their heads, and Belwynn approached with care. Their tails whipped constantly, and they panted heavily. Encouraged by Marika, she stroked the neck of the same animal. It turned its head to look at her and she felt its breath. As she made eye contact, Belwynn felt she sensed a greater intelligence there than in human-bred cattle.

Once everyone was ready, they entered the two carriages—men in the front and women in the rear. The six Caladri accompanied them, while Gyuri clambered up into the driver's seat and led them off.

The wooden interior of the carriage was painted in a floral design. It could hold perhaps ten or twelve passengers and was therefore spacious, allowing everyone to relax on the upholstered benches and cushions. It had been perfumed with an exotic smell that Belwynn had never come across before. Belwynn sat with Moneva and Elana on one bench, facing the three Caladri women.

The Caladri introduced themselves. Beside Marika sat Dora and Emese. They explained they were all young women who worked on the transport system. This involved looking after the animals, supplies, and the needs of travellers.

'How old you are?' asked Moneva in her direct manner.

'We are all in our thirties,' answered Dora.

'But,' added Marika, 'Caladri live longer lives than humans, don't they?'

Her two friends nodded.

'How long?' demanded Moneva.

'On average, perhaps one hundred and fifty years,' replied Dora.

Belwynn took a sharp breath. 'That's more than twice as long as humans,' she said.

The three Caladri looked sad for the human women. Marika leaned over and stroked Belwynn's hair, seemingly to make her feel better. It was the second time the Caladri had been a bit overly familiar. Belwynn looked over at Moneva and Elana, who held the same quizzical expressions on their faces as she did.

'Maybe Caladri mature more slowly than humans?' suggested Elana.

'Then you are the equivalent of human teenagers?' Belwynn asked Marika.

She shrugged. 'Perhaps so.'

The Caladri provided them with drinks and food. There was water and fruit juice, which the Caladri mixed together. To eat there was more fruit, as well as nuts and seeds. As the carriage gathered pace, they ate and drank and grew more comfortable with each other, the conversation becoming more relaxed and wide ranging. Unlike the male soldiers, these women were at least as curious about Belwynn and the others as she was about them. They asked about their families, about the human cities and kingdoms, and their way of life. They were curious about their looks and not shy about it. More than once, one of the Caladri would reach across and touch someone's hand, hair, or face with an almost childlike curiosity. They giggled a lot, confirming Elana's perception that they were in some ways younger than their thirty years.

Marika asked which of the men were theirs. It was an interesting question. In the event, Moneva answered that none of the men were 'theirs' in the sense of being a partner. The Caladri were confused by this, wondering aloud why three women were travelling with five men who were not their spouses or relations. Belwynn confirmed that this was unusual in human society as well. It became clear that the three Caladri men in the next carriage were the partners of the three Caladri women, but not yet, they made clear, married husbands. They would wait awhile for that ceremony which, as with humans, meant that they were committed to that person for life and would have children.

Belwynn wondered idly, to herself, about Marika's question. The answer to it was more complicated than Moneva's answer had admitted. If she were to pick a partner for Moneva, she would have immediately answered Gyrmund, for it was clear to Belwynn and to most of the others that the two had formed a special friendship. For Elana, perhaps it would be Dirk, since he was an attentive follower of hers and, Belwynn sometimes wondered, perhaps had deeper feelings for the priestess. And her man? It could be Clarin. He had made it clear, in his own way, that he was interested in her. He had not, though, done anything in particular about it. Belwynn, she admitted to herself, was confused about what she wanted. Their relationship, therefore, was one of perpetual, albeit buried, tension.

As the conversation in the carriage died down, and Belwynn found herself getting drowsier, she was content to gaze at the three Caladri women. All three were beautiful creatures, slim and delicate in body and features, and she wondered if they would be attractive to most human men. The clawed feet were surely a bit of a turn off. The Caladri men certainly held no appeal to her. Their thin yet powerful bodies, their pronounced features, while arresting, could hardly be considered physically attractive. She wondered what the Caladri made of them.

It was in this cosy and contented frame of mind that the last part of the day's journey passed. Before Belwynn knew it, they had stopped, and Marika was helping her down from the carriage.

Outside, the light was fading. They found themselves in a part of the forest which, to Belwynn, looked exactly the same as that which they had left. In the distance they could see triangular tents, presumably the camp of Prince Lorant. Marika and the others said goodbye, but promised that they would try to visit with them again tomorrow. They, and their three men, stayed behind to sort out the carriage and gaur. Gyuri led them off towards the camp.

Belwynn fell in stride next to Soren.

'Did you have a good journey?' she asked.

Soren smiled. 'Yes, thanks, very comfortable.'

'And your hosts?' Belwynn asked.

Soren's mouth twisted to one side. 'They were very friendly, just—maybe a bit too friendly.'

Herin, walking in front, turned around. 'One of them tried to give my legs a massage!' he exclaimed, his face a mixture of anger and concern as he recalled the encounter.

Soren and the others chuckled at the incident.

Belwynn smiled. It sounded like the men had enjoyed a similar experience to theirs.

They approached the Caladri tents. They comprised of long strips of timber formed into a circular shape at the base. At the top, they leaned into each other to form a roof and were tied off with rope to keep secure. Finally, a large strip of canvas had been placed over the top, with a hole which fitted over the pointed roof. Each was individual, being a different height, width and colour from its neighbour. Many of the Caladri were sitting outside their tents in small numbers, with individual fires burning. They talked quietly or listened as others played music and sang.

Gyuri passed without comment, leading them towards the centre of the camp. Many of the Caladri stopped what they were doing as they passed, staring at the Krykker and the humans and whispering to one another.

They approached a large tent guarded by soldiers. Gyuri and one of the soldiers went inside, presumably to fetch the prince. Instead, he returned with a female Caladri.

She approached the group. 'Greetings, visitors,' she said. 'My name is Hajna. I am the wife of Prince Lorant.'

She was blonde and blue-eyed, older, and carrying more authority than Marika and the others. Belwynn found it difficult to guess her age, but felt sure that she was the most captivating looking woman she had ever seen. Hajna smiled and nodded politely as she waited for Belwynn and the others to introduce themselves in turn. Finally, she spoke. 'Prince Lorant is not here tonight. He is further west, on the borders of our lands. He will be here tomorrow morning, when he will devote himself to speaking with you. Is there anything you need to tell me about immediately?'

Belwynn and the others looked at each other, tired and sleepy after their journey.

Soren responded for them. 'We can wait until tomorrow, Your Highness,' he assured the princess.

Hajna smiled again. 'Very well. Night is falling,' she said, gesturing towards the sky. Everyone followed her gesture and looked upwards, as if it was the first time they had realised this was the case. 'We will find food and shelter for you here tonight.'

Hajna busied herself in organising the appropriate accommodation for her guests. This was achieved in a matter of minutes. As before, Belwynn, Moneva and Elana were accommodated together, separate from the men, in a small tent. Belwynn quite liked the arrangement—having some time away from the men. They spent a few minutes chatting idly about the Caladri, laughing at the thought of the tactile Caladri men in the carriage with Herin and the others, wondering together at the beauty of Princess Hajna of the Blood Caladri.

Soon, though, they became too tired to speak. The food provided by the Princess lay largely untouched in the corner, and they went to sleep.

A HISTORY LESSON

XXI

Soren woke as the early morning light filtered into the tent he was sharing with Clarin and Herin. He was wet with sweat. He knew his dreams had been troubled.

One had been about his mother. She was being attacked by vossi-like creatures, and when he had gone to help her with his magic, he had been powerless. The whole tent was damp from the three of them sharing such a confined space, and as the other two men slumbered on, Soren clambered out of the cloth doorway.

Outside, a sea of Caladri tents dominated the view. The early morning forest air was chilly on his damp skin and he rubbed himself before stretching out his back and legs. Today, thought Soren. Maybe today. He hoped so. It had been about ten days since he had woken in Vitugia without his powers. But it felt like a lifetime. If, somehow, the Blood Caladri could restore them, it would feel like a new start. Like a rebirth. Soren looked out over the forest, eager for what the new day would bring.

He had to wait awhile until Joska, one of the carriage attendants from yesterday, came to collect them.

'Prince Lorant is ready to meet with you,' he said simply, and led them back to the large tent in the centre of the camp.

On the way, they met up with Belwynn, Elana and Moneva, who were being led in the same direction. Once there, Joska held open a flap in the tent and gestured for them to enter. Soren ducked his head and walked in.

Rabigar, Gyrmund and Dirk were already seated in the middle of the tent on one side of a small fire. Opposite them sat Princess Hajna and two other men, one seemingly much older than the other. Soren found a space by the fire and sat down. As he waited for the others to sit, he pushed his hands to the fire, rubbing them together. The smoke drifted upwards towards the hole in the roof.

'Hello again, friends,' welcomed Princess Hajna, once everyone was settled.

'Greetings,' said the younger man. 'I am Prince Lorant, son of King Tibor of the Blood Caladri. You have all met my wife,' he gestured to his right. 'This is my chief adviser, Szabolcs,' Lorant continued, now gesturing to his left. 'He is a learned man, much wiser than I. I trust these two to hear all that you have to say. You may trust me to tell my father your news. He is currently in the north of our country, waging war against the Shadow Caladri.'

Everyone introduced themselves. Prince Lorant had a more formal manner compared to his wife, but Soren supposed he was naturally wary of them. He had blonde hair, tightly plaited to his head, sea-blue eyes and an athletic build.

'How long have you been at war with the Shadow Caladri?' asked Soren.

'This war began two years ago and has been fought with varying intensity ever since. Recently, King Dorjan has increased the severity of his raids. It feels like a preparation for an invasion. He is working closely with Erkindrix of Ishari. We had feared that the army of Haskany, which has invaded Grienna and Trevenza, might now turn against us. That is why my forces are currently based in this region. It seems, however, that the army is meant for the Empire.'

'That does seem to be the case,' agreed Soren. 'And that is one reason we are here.'

'I see. Now that the humans are under threat, they want our help, when they have given us none for two years?'

Soren let the question hang in the air for a while. He could not afford to offend the Prince. The Blood Caladri may well have just cause to be bitter if they had been fighting alone for two years.

Elana spoke up. 'The peoples of Dalriya must unite to stop Ishari. Some have been slow to see this, but we must look forward, not behind us.'

Lorant made a motion with one arm towards Elana, which Soren read as an acceptance of the point she had made.

'Very well,' replied the Prince. 'I do not intend to blame any of you directly for diplomatic failures. Let me hear what Baldwin of Brasingia and Edgar of Magnia have to say.'

'Well,' said Soren, warily re-joining the conversation. 'I think it best for us to start with the events of two weeks ago. This way you will better understand who we are and what we have to ask.'

Soren explained the events surrounding Toric's Dagger and recounted their experiences in Coldeberg and Essenberg. Half way through, Szabolcs, the old Caladri, stood up and shuffled over to the corner of the room, where he began rummaging through some books. Picking up three, he returned to the fire and began flicking through the pages while Soren spoke. Soren finished by passing Lorant the insignia that Gustav had given him.

'Gustav is a friend of the Blood Caladri,' said Lorant. 'I understand Baldwin needs allies. He cannot stand up to Ishari and Haskany alone. The truth is, however, that the Blood Caladri make poor allies now. Erkindrix has made sure that we are tied down in war with the Shadow Caladri. We cannot spare troops to help him; he cannot spare troops to help us. We must work together in some other way.'

'Can we see the weapon?' asked Hajna.

Dirk produced the dagger from inside his cloak.

The princess examined it. 'Beautiful,' she commented, before passing it over to Szabolcs.

The old man studied it intently for a long time, saying nothing.

If Caladri live to a hundred and fifty, Belwynn said to Soren, *he must be nearly there.*

Szabolcs did indeed seem to be a man of great age. His skin was wrinkled; the hands that held the stone were gnarled and gently shook. Soren, however, could tell that this was a wizard of significant power. Despite the current topic of conversation, he could not help thinking of his own magical powers and holding onto hope that this man could restore them.

'I think I know what this is,' Szabolcs said slowly.

He looked up at the others, as if waking from a dream and readjusting to the waking world.

'This is an old story. I don't know it all. But it goes back to the Cracking of the World. This occurred hundreds of years ago when the Isharites first arrived in Dalriya. They came from another world, sent by a dread demon to take ours.

Our Lady Onella created seven weapons with which to defend the land. To the Caladri she gave a staff with magical properties. Each other race of Dalriya was given a weapon. I believe that this is one of them. But the demon did the same, and poured his own magical power into seven weapons, granting them to his servants. The war culminated in a great battle. The two sides met in the middle of Dalriya. The champions of the gods met in combat, armed with the weapons. A great magical energy was released when the two sides clashed. The continent collapsed into two. The soldiers of each army were drowned in the flood.'

'Who is this Lady Onella you talk about?' asked Elana quietly.

'Onella is Dalriya's goddess, who protects all of us,' answered Hajna simply.

'I…,' Elana started, and Soren detected emotion in her voice, which was usually so controlled. 'I believe I serve this Onella, though she calls herself Madria to me.'

'Our Lady is known by many names,' said Hajna. 'In the Brasingian lands she is known as the Lady Alexia.'

'And these seven weapons are hers?' Elana asked Szabolcs.

'Yes.'

'Madria wants us to find all of them,' said Elana firmly. 'We need them to defend against Ishari.'

'Why didn't you mention this before?' asked Herin sceptically.

'I cannot speak to Madria in a normal conversation,' Elana answered him. 'I cannot ask her every question I have and get an answer. But she guides me. These weapons are vitally important; I am sure of it.'

'Szabolcs,' said Soren, 'do you know where the other six are?'

'No, I don't know where they are; I don't even know *what* they are. With one exception. Onella's Staff is a precious treasure, kept by the Grand Caladri in Edeleny. I don't know what happened to the others after the Cracking of the World. But we may have the story in our histories.'

Szabolcs opened one of the books he had been flicking through before. 'There is a chance that I can get answers in here. *Zoltan's History* was written when the Caladri were still united.' Szabolcs began reading. Some time passed in silence.

'While we wait,' began Belwynn.

Soren smiled, knowing that watching someone read would not hold his sister's attention for long.

'May I ask about the Caladri?' she continued. 'They were once united? Why did that come to an end?'

Lorant and Hajna looked at one another. The prince smiled and gestured that his wife should answer.

'Our history in Dalriya,' Hajna began, 'goes back much further than the humans does. When they first arrived, we were the strongest people in the land, and lived across the continent. Our strength lay in our magic. A great number of our children are blessed by Onella with magic. For humans, this is very rare. For Krykkers—' the Princess smiled at Rabigar—'never?'

Rabigar solemnly nodded his agreement.

'We like to think that we taught many of our skills to the humans who arrived. We gave them our language,' Hajna continued, with a slight shrug; 'maybe they would have described it differently. Either way, the power of the Caladri began to fade as the humans grew stronger and more numerous and the Isharites pressed us from the north. There appeared a faction within the Caladri who argued that we should fight against this decline with magical forces, which we had never touched before. They believed we should tread the same path as the Isharites and gain extra power by contacting demons from beyond our world; that this was the only way to save our civilisation. This faction became the Shadow Caladri. An opposition faction emerged, who believed that this dangerous practice should be forbidden, that it threatened the power of Lady Onella. This was our faction, the Blood Caladri. We pressed the elites of our society to put a stop to the Shadow Caladri, but they did not intervene. Civil war between the Shadow Caladri and the Blood Caladri erupted. Both groups were condemned and exiled by these elites, who are known as the Grand Caladri. A fourth faction eventually came to settle in the far corner of Dalriya, becoming the Sea Caladri. As time went by, human kingdoms took away lands from all four realms. The Persaleian Empire became the dominant force in Dalriya, driving us into the forest. By that time our divisions were too entrenched to unite and we each, in our own ways, accepted our new place.'

'Thank you,' said Belwynn. 'So, the Shadow Caladri and Blood Caladri have been at war ever since?'

'No,' answered Lorant. 'Initially we fought long and hard, but neither side won, and meanwhile we had weakened ourselves against outside enemies. So, many years of truce followed—necessary to ensure our own existence. But there can never be true peace when each side opposes every principle the other stands for. The current war is a very recent reopening of ancient hostilities.'

Szabolcs cleared his throat. 'It may take me some time to find the information I am looking for.'

'Yes,' agreed Lorant, 'there is no point in us all sitting here wasting time.'

'I suggest we meet up here again at midday,' added Hajna. 'There are several things we can offer our guests in that time. However, if Rabigar would agree, I would like to spend some time with him. I have experience in helping soldiers recover from injuries. I know certain exercises that help to improve strength and coordination after losing an eye. I could teach them to you this morning, for you to use in the future.'

'I would be much obliged with such help,' answered Rabigar.

Hajna then began assigning activities to the other members of the group.

Soren decided to get in his request early. 'I should like to stay with you, Szabolcs, unless you feel I would disturb your concentration. I have some questions I would like to ask of you...' Soren found his sentence trailing off.

Szabolcs nodded his agreement, hiding any curiosity or irritation he might have felt, and continued to flick through his book.

Everyone began to leave the tent in twos and threes, as Princess Hajna allocated them to a Caladri guide who would see to their needs.

Eventually, Soren and Szabolcs were left alone.

* * *

Belwynn emerged from the tent and drew a deep breath of the forest air, gazing up to the canopy of trees, where sunlight dappled down through the gaps to reach the floor. She turned around to find out what was in store for her this morning.

Soren had stayed behind in the tent with Szabolcs, and Belwynn knew he would be asking the old wizard about his own magic powers. Elana stood talking to Prince Lorant, with faithful Dirk a couple of yards apart from them, content to stand close by rather than join in the conversation. Princess Hajna was talking to a group of Caladri, whom Belwynn recognised as Marika and the other attendants who had travelled with them on the carriage. Hajna sent them over toward Belwynn and the others, while the Princess herself walked over to Rabigar and, with a quick word and gesture, led him away from the tent. Meanwhile, Lorant, Elana and Dirk began strolling away in the opposite direction.

The six Caladri attendants approached the entrance to the tent where Belwynn and the others stood, waiting.

'Princess Hajna has asked us to show you something of our home,' said Marika, a pleasant smile on her face. 'Do any of you have any requests?'

'The Blood Caladri are known for their archery,' Herin said. 'Do any of you use a bow?'

'Elek is the best archer here,' said one of the men.

'I will teach you what I know,' agreed Elek. 'You come too, Joska.'

'Since our men are leaving us,' said one of the girls, whom Belwynn remembered from the carriage ride as Dora, 'Emese and I shall show you two a lovely walk.' Dora reached out and took Moneva's hand. Emese then linked elbows with Gyrmund and began to walk off.

Belwynn found herself left with Clarin. Remaining with them were Marika and another male, Caladri.

Marika introduced herself to Clarin.

'I am Vida,' said the man to Belwynn.

Clarin and Belwynn, looking at each other a little uncertainly, exchanged introductions.

'I can think of a pleasant walk, too, if you would like to come?' asked Marika.

Belwynn and Clarin accepted the invitation. Marika led the way, and Belwynn stepped in next to her. She explained that to the east of the camp, Prince Lorant had established a temporary exercise camp for physical training. That is where Rabigar and Herin had been taken. To the west was a garden, which the local inhabitants had created and maintained. Gyrmund and Moneva had been taken in that direction.

'We are going south, though,' said Marika, an ever-present twinkle in her eye. 'This is a beautiful walk, but made by nature, not ourselves.'

They walked past the tents of Lorant's people; occasional stares and whisperings directed at Belwynn and Clarin, by those who were working there. Some cooked food; others mended tools or weapons.

'Is this an army?' Belwynn asked Marika.

'Yes. Not everyone is a fighter—some people are here to support, looking after food or animals. But most of them will do battle if Prince Lorant orders it.'

'There are a lot of women.'

'Human women do not fight?'

'Some do, but not many.'

'Hmm,' considered Marika. 'Perhaps that is because there are fewer Caladri than humans, and the women need to fight. Several people fight with magic.'

'How many Caladri have magic in them?'

Marika breathed out heavily as she thought about this question. 'Perhaps… one in every few hundred are born with the gift. For humans, this is much less?'

'Yes,' agreed Belwynn.

Behind them, Clarin had struck up a conversation with Vida about military tactics. It was not a subject that particularly interested Belwynn, but she heard the Caladri man explaining the value of every soldier being armed with a bow and arrows. Clarin, meanwhile, defended the human custom to fight in heavy, metal armour.

They left the camp behind them and entered the thick forest. A footpath carried them in a winding, uphill direction. The conversation petered out as Belwynn looked about her and used her breath to help her legs make the climb.

After an hour's walk, the path emerged at the top of a ridge.

Belwynn gasped as she looked out over the ridge. The position gave her a 180-degree view down over miles of the Caladri lands. Most of it was forest—what Belwynn knew to be great trees looking like tiny little models of the real thing. But she could see that the forest was occasionally broken up by areas of grassland or scrub. Rocky outcrops dotted the ground, rising and falling in gentle waves. Belwynn could also make out tiny settlements. She could see half a dozen of them, the wooden buildings clinging to the edges of the tree line.

Clarin arrived to take in the view.

'Those are your villages?' Belwynn asked Marika, pointing below her.

'Yes. Most are very small, with only a few families. At times of war like this, the youngest and oldest are left behind in the safety of the forest. Our settlements are safe from invaders. They are very difficult to find.'

Vida joined Marika, and they walked on ahead, hand in hand. The path continued along the ridge, enabling walkers to keep the view below to their right. After a while, Belwynn and Clarin followed after them, some distance behind.

'I never imagined that I would ever visit the lands of the Caladri,' Belwynn said as they idly walked along.

Clarin smiled ruefully. 'This is turning into our biggest adventure yet. Magic weapons, meetings with kings and emperors...'

'It's the most serious, Clarin. If Ishari wins, then this place will be destroyed. Magnia will fall eventually. Our whole way of life...it will all be gone.'

Clarin shrugged and then patted the sword strapped to his waist. 'We won't let that happen.'

Sometimes Belwynn found Clarin's confidence and unlimited, misplaced optimism infuriating. Now, though, she found it reassuring. She reached for his hand.

He looked down in surprise, but then smiled and took her hand in his.

They walked on in silence.

* * *

GYRMUND COULD NOT HELP himself smiling foolishly at the young Caladri women, Dora and Emese. They had brought Moneva and himself to a garden, about a mile to the west of the camp. A stony path snaked its way through plants, lined by trees and flowers on either side. Further on, cut stone steps took them higher, until they reached a small, trickling waterfall, which emptied into a large pool where fish swam. Dora and Emese dipped their hands over the side of the wall into the pool and splash water at each other, cackling and giggling as they did so.

A month ago, Gyrmund thought to himself, he would have found such a sight alluring. He had been a single man for a long time, but he had never found it difficult to make women like him. The two young Caladri women were attractive in their own way. But now he had eyes for only one woman.

She was next to him. Sitting on the wall at the edge of the pool, Moneva had placed her hands palm down on either side of her and looked out over the gardens. Gyrmund liked the fact that they could now relax in each other's company. After an eventful two weeks, they were both content to be still and silent.

The wind gently lifted Moneva's dark hair, which was usually kept rigidly straight to her neck. Gyrmund found himself looking into her dark eyes as she turned her head to look back at him; her raised eyebrow was her only comment on finding him gazing at her. Gyrmund felt like a teenager caught staring too long at the source of his infatuation, but he enjoyed the feeling.

The moment was then broken as Gyrmund received a splash of cold water on the back of his neck. He stared at Moneva for a moment, who shook her head in mock despair, as if indicating there was nothing she could do about the situation.

Gyrmund turned to his attacker, Dora, and launched handfuls of water in her direction. Overwhelmed by the volume of water Gyrmund was splashing at her, she screamed, turned, and ran away. Gyrmund gave chase as she darted away from the pool and behind the rise of rocks from which the waterfall coursed. Gyrmund followed and quickly caught her, which only made the screams grow louder.

Eventually, Dora controlled herself. Gyrmund let her lead him further round the corner. An archway had been created in the stone, so that Dora and

Gyrmund could walk underneath the waterfall. The drumming sound of the water could be heard above.

'Under here,' began Dora, 'all questions have to be answered truthfully.'

Gyrmund nodded cautiously, deciding to go along with the premise, though he considered it highly likely that the girl had just made it up.

'Do you love Moneva?' she asked, her face a sudden picture of seriousness.

Gyrmund felt his face growing hot at the personal nature of the question. Whether it was the location, or the apparent innocence of the questioner, he was not sure, but he found himself answering honestly.

'Yes, I—have fallen in love with her.'

Dora nodded encouragingly before her next question. 'Are you going to make her yours?'

Gyrmund was not entirely sure what was meant by the question. He decided on a vague answer.

'We cannot marry. We are very busy. We are both independent. We have not known each other long.'

Dora nodded slowly, as if digesting each word. She crooked a finger at Gyrmund to follow. They walked through to the other side of the arch. Dora then abruptly stopped.

By the rocks was a patch of plants Gyrmund did not recognise. The plants were thin, ending in small white flowers, and the tallest reached as high as his knee. They had bright green leaves with a shiny texture. Dora knelt down and, one by one, carefully picked about a dozen leaves from the plants. She stood up and offered them to Gyrmund, who dubiously accepted them.

'Joska and I cannot yet join as husband and wife. This means that we are not yet ready to bring children into the world,' Dora paused, to make sure that Gyrmund was following what she was getting at. 'We still wish to be together as man and woman, though.'

Gyrmund felt even more embarrassed at the turn of the conversation, but allowed her to continue.

'You must take two of these leaves and crush them. Then add hot water to it and make it into a drink. When a woman drinks this, she cannot produce children.'

Gyrmund understood what she was saying. 'Thank you, Dora,' he said, stuffing the leaves into a pocket.

'You are welcome.'

Dora led Gyrmund back round to the pool, where Moneva and Emese were talking quietly. As they approached, Moneva looked up at Gyrmund and blushed. He had more than a suspicion about what they had been talking about.

* * *

For some time, Soren and Szabolcs sat in silence, the Caladri wizard intent on finding any relevant information he could. While he spent most time on *Zoltan's History*, he would occasionally cross-reference something from one of the other books. Soren would have offered to read something, but while he might have been able to decipher the characters, he would have been slow and unsure; little real help.

After a while, Szabolcs looked up at him.

'I have found a relevant passage. Not as complete as I would have hoped, but it tells us something. Before that,' he continued, focusing more intently on Soren, 'you have a question?'

'Yes,' said Soren. 'I'll get straight to it. On our journey through the Wilderness, we were attacked by vossi. I used too much magic in the encounter and overextended. I haven't been able to do anything since, not the slightest thing.' Soren took a breath as he heard the despair in his own voice. 'I spoke to Gustav. He said that wizards amongst the Caladri might be able to help me. He said he'd heard of powerful users being able to channel their power into another, in order to repair the broken bonds.'

'I see,' said Szabolcs, a look of pity slowly crossing his face. 'I believe that I have spoken to Gustav about such a practice myself. I have to tell you; I have only known one such case in my lifetime. This is because it is rare for enchanters to survive overextension. About thirty years ago, a young male enchanter, while warring with the Shadow Caladri, overextended, and somehow survived. No one knew how to treat him. In the end, he travelled to the lands of the Grand Caladri. An enchanter there knew how to perform the healing you describe. It worked, and he returned. This enchanter is still alive; he is part of King Tibor's retinue. That does not mean he could perform the task himself—I doubt whether he could. No other enchanter amongst the Blood Caladri has been involved in such a healing, to my knowledge.'

Szabolcs paused. 'I know what it is to be blessed with magic. I also know that it can be a curse. The desire for knowledge can become all consuming. I have lived a long—some would say useful—life. But I have never had a wife, or a family.'

Soren knew that Szabolcs' words were true. If not for the determination of his sister, and the link they shared as twins, he would likely be a very lonely man already.

Szabolcs looked him in the eye. 'As I say, I know what it is to have the hunger for magic. If you are desperate to regain your powers, I suggest travelling to the Grand Caladri. If there is an enchanter who has the skill, you will likely find them there.'

Soren's stomach lurched. He had hoped to find a cure in these lands. Indeed, he had hoped that Szabolcs might be his saviour. Now he had to make another journey, with little certainty that he would find anyone to help at the end of it. It was a desperate move, but one he knew he would take.

Soren had done worse for his magic. When Soren had requested to study with Delyth, the marsh witch, it was to develop his skills after his apprenticeship with Ealdnoth had come to its natural end. Her magic was totally different to Ealdnoth's, and he was quickly learning new things. But Belwynn had come with him. Soren had begun to realise that Delyth resented his sister's presence. She wanted Soren all to herself. She was a dark and dangerous character, totally different to Ealdnoth. Soren had been naïve to think otherwise. Belwynn hadn't seen the threat at all.

Soren had told Belwynn to leave, for her own safety. It had hurt her, he knew, but she couldn't have stayed any longer. When Belwynn left, Soren gave Delyth what she wanted, and they had become lovers. The sex had repulsed him, yet he knew he was learning more about his craft, faster than he ever had. All the time he knew Delyth would never let him leave, that she wanted him to stay with her forever. He went along with it. When it became clear that she had nothing left to teach him, he only had one option.

She was taken by complete surprise. He turned on her before she had a chance to defend herself. Under the cover of night, he had dumped her body in a bog and fled, returning to Magnia.

He couldn't explain any of this to his sister. She was the same Belwynn when they met up again, only too pleased to see him. He had changed, however. Their year apart had created a distance between them that hadn't been there before.

'There is another reason for you to go there, too,' said Szabolcs slowly, bringing Soren's thoughts back to the present.

'What is that?' asked Soren calmly.

Szabolcs located the passage he wanted in his history book, placing a finger under the words as he read. 'Zoltan says the great battle of which I spoke took place in the high mountains of the Krykker kingdoms.' Szabolcs traced the lettering with his finger. 'He says that both sides had seven champions, armed with a weapon each.' Szabolcs looked up at Soren. 'I wonder if Erkindrix's Council of Seven is more than coincidence? It could be that as well as looking for Lady Onella's weapons, Erkindrix has been looking for his own.'

Szabolcs bent his head down to his book again. 'This is where Zoltan is vague. He says that the seven allies who fought at the great battle each returned to their homeland, to guard their weapons and to make sure that they would not fall into the hands of any one person unless needed again.'

Though vague, this was an interesting piece of information to Soren. 'That makes sense. Our legends say that Toric's Dagger was taken by King Osbert of Magnia from the Lippers. So they may have been one of the allies in the battle.'

Szabolcs nodded. 'Unfortunately, Zoltan does not specify any more. Apart from saying that the Caladri took their staff home and kept it in a place of honour in Onella's Temple.'

'I guess,' said Soren dryly, 'that Onella's Temple is in the lands of the Grand Caladri?'

'Yes. There are other histories I can read which may say more, but I don't carry them with me.'

'Still,' replied Soren, 'that tells us quite a lot. If Elana is right, we need to find all seven of them. We already have one. We know the location of a second. The battle was fought in the lands of the Krykkers, so presumably they had a champion and a weapon themselves.'

'Yes,' agreed Szabolcs. 'The humans were present in Dalriya at this time. It is likely that they were one of the seven allies, too. As for the other three, I would only be guessing.'

'Well,' said Soren, as the information Szabolcs had given him sank in, 'it looks like you have given me two good reasons to go the Grand Caladri.'

* * *

As HE WALKED a discreet distance behind Elana and the Prince, Dirk peered closely at the flora of the Blood Caladri kingdom. In truth, he admitted to himself, he had never had much interest in such things. He was, in fact, listening intently to the conversation ahead of him. Listening. Gathering information. That was what he had always been good at.

Lorant had led them through the gardens to the west of the camp. The conversation there had been limited. The Caladri Prince would occasionally stop to comment on a flower or plant as they walked past. Elana would make some appreciative noise. Dirk, following a few feet behind them both, wondered whether she was as bored by it as he was.

After they left the gardens, where no other ears could hear, Lorant turned the conversation to weightier matters.

'I believe you entirely, Elana,' Lorant was saying. 'Onella, or Madria, does appear to be communicating with you.'

Dirk noticed how Elana relaxed and, turning slightly to her left, gently smiled at the reassuring words.

'But you must understand,' Lorant continued, 'that you are the first person I have heard of who can communicate, in such a direct way, with the Goddess. No one in our lands has been gifted in such a way. I want to know what she has told you to do.'

'As I said earlier, I don't have a direct conversation with Madria. But I now know that it is my duty to find and collect her weapons. They must be used to defend Dalriya, just as they were before.'

'But that will never happen.'

The words rang out, cold and hard and loud, and floated in the air around them.

Ahead, a tall, black figure emerged and walked on until he stood facing them.

It was Nexodore, the wizard who had attacked them on the Great Road. A feeling of dread and panic rose in Dirk. He forced himself to control his roiling stomach.

'Nexodore?' asked Prince Lorant, with disbelief in his voice. 'How have you invaded our realm?' he demanded.

'With ease, Prince,' replied the sorcerer dismissively. The voice leaving the death mask sounded like rock grinding on granite. Nexodore turned to look at Elana. 'My master gave me the task of watching the other lands, to find the whereabouts of the lost weapons and to discover who She has chosen as his enemy.' The sorcerer made an unpleasant noise, which Dirk surmised was laughter, but it was so devoid of emotion it could hardly be called that. 'A clever choice by your goddess,' he said grudgingly, 'to choose a nobody. It has made it more difficult for me to find you. However,' he continued, and drew his sword, a cruel scrape of noise as it left the scabbard, 'now I have.'

The drawing of the sword seemed to prompt Lorant into action. Drawing his own, he launched himself at Nexodore, shouting spells as he went. Two vines thrust themselves out of the ground and clasped themselves around the legs of the sorcerer. 'Run!' shouted the Caladri.

Dirk rushed forward to grab Elana and escape with her back to the camp.

However, by the time he reached her, Nexodore had responded to Lorant's attack. One scream of a word and the vines securing him withered and died. In the same breath, he hurled his own sword at Lorant's approach.

The prince had made up half the distance between them when the hurtling sword came straight for him. He blocked the weapon with his own just in time, sending it flying into the forest floor. There was no time to react further, however, as Nexodore slammed an open palm towards him and sent a powerful blast of magic in his direction. Dirk could feel the force of it as a tremor in the ground and a blast of warm air on his face. Lorant just had time to surround himself with a glowing, light blue shield. But this defence was to no avail. The magic blast was too strong for him and he hurtled through the air until his body slammed into a tree.

Nexodore wasted no time and marched towards Elana, his mask of death implacable.

Elana shivered. She seemed unable to move.

Nexodore's march ate up the space between them in seconds. Dirk found himself releasing his grip on Elana and backing away, to one side. Elana began to pray to Madria.

Nexodore stopped in front of her. He stretched out his hand in a grasping movement and his sword, which Lorant had knocked aside, came flying back into his grip.

Through his fear and shock, Dirk was surprised to see the sword was not made of steel, but some kind of black crystal. Almost subconsciously, Dirk pulled out the dagger from inside his cloak.

'Your goddess cannot help you.'

Elana looked up into the mask as Nexodore raised his black sword behind his head.

This was the moment to act. Dirk forced his body to follow his orders. He hurled himself at the sorcerer and planted Toric's Dagger into his groin.

Nexodore screamed out in pain, and his sword fell out of his hands. He had not seen Dirk's attack coming. Dirk looked up to see the mask staring down at him. He twisted the dagger further into his enemy in defiance. Nexodore had made a mistake, and Dirk intended to punish him for it.

Nexodore's gauntleted hand smashed into Dirk's face. He fell flat onto his back, the impact knocking his senses out of him. Dirk struggled to sit up. He saw Nexodore rip the dagger from his body, toss it aside, and then pause with his hand over his groin area, looking in Dirk's direction.

Dirk struggled to make himself stand up, swaying on his feet as he did.

Nexodore advanced quickly and grabbed Dirk by the wrist.

Dirk yanked and punched and kicked, but Nexodore's grip was like a vice. Pain shot through him, from his wrist, down his arm and into his body. He could no longer struggle or move, except to scream in agony. It felt like the sorcerer was burning him alive, sending fire through his body. Within seconds he could no longer even scream—his mouth held rigid in a rictus grin, his vocal chords frozen in place; but Nexodore's grip still held him.

Dirk felt like his insides were slowly being cooked. Then, just out of the corner of his eye, he could see Elana pick up the knife that Nexodore had discarded. She ran at the sorcerer, but he was aware of her approach. He turned towards her and, with his free hand, slammed a fist into her head.

Elana collapsed and crumpled to the floor. It was a horrible sight; Dirk hoped the blow had killed her, that she would avoid any further suffering.

Nexodore turned his full attention back to Dirk. The burning sensation increased and Dirk could feel himself dying. He kept his eyes fixed on Elana's body, but his own could no longer cope with the pain he was experiencing. His body spasmed and a shower of blood spurted from his mouth onto the sorcerer.

Dirk looked up to see the death mask's expression remain fixed as Dirk's blood trickled down its face.

Then, suddenly, something seemed to erupt from the Isharite's right eye. The energy entering Dirk's body stopped. Nexodore's grip loosened and Dirk fell to the ground.

Dirk tried to concentrate on breathing, but his insides seemed burned away, leaving a crumpled husk of skin and bones. His breathing rattled around in his head. He forced himself to look up.

Nexodore had his back to him, and poking out of the back of his head was the point of an arrow.

Beyond him came Lorant, bow in hand, and a second arrow nocked and ready to be released.

'A nice trick,' came the grinding voice from behind the mask. 'But I've survived the fires of the underworld. Your bow and arrow and petty magic can't do me harm.'

The Dagger, thought Dirk. *The Dagger harmed him.*

'Maybe I can take your other eye,' said Lorant viciously, and fired his second arrow, chanting more magic as he did. The bolt flew towards its target but Nexodore casually waved a hand, and it disintegrated.

Dirk made himself sit up, pain wracking his body so that he had to bite down on his tongue to keep from screaming out. Lying next to him was Elana: out cold, but breathing. He grabbed the Dagger that she had dropped.

He forced himself to stand up, his legs threatening to give way. If he didn't act now, Elana was doomed.

Nexodore fired a blast of magic at Lorant, forcing him to dive to the side to escape, dropping his bow as he did. Nexodore followed his target, winding up another assault.

Dirk launched himself at the sorcerer, holding the dagger in both hands and driving its thin point into the back of his neck.

Then Dirk's vision blurred, and all was dark.

GOOD NEWS

XXII

Baldwin had seen his scouts riding up to the front of the column. A halt had now been called. Clearly, something was happening.

'I'm going up to see what's going on,' he said to Rainer, who was riding next to him.

'Very well, Your Majesty,' replied his chamberlain.

They detached themselves from the line and made their way to the front, a hundred yards ahead, in no particular hurry. An army needed a good organiser, and Baldwin had therefore brought Rainer with him to oversee logistics. He had some reservations about this decision. He had a great fondness for his Queen, Hannelore. She was a loyal wife, but not a politician. Rainer would have been useful back in the capital. He hoped that Archbishop Decker would keep his wife safe in Essenberg while he was away.

Baldwin had decided that he had to head north with his forces, even though most of his dukes had not. He could not expect Ellard of Rotelegen to hold the border by himself. He had to be seen to be defending his Empire. But he was uneasy about leaving his own duchy of Kelland virtually undefended with the treacherous Duke Emeric and his army waiting to pounce. He hoped he could rely on Coen of Thesse to keep Emeric pinned down. He hoped that his other dukes would heed his orders and bring their armies north.

Baldwin looked up, not for the first time that day, at the towering presence of Burkhard Castle, only a mile away now, to the north-west. It was the key to the Empire's defence against invasion; legendarily never taken by an enemy force. Despite this history, a shiver ran down Baldwin's spine at the thought of it all. The idea of being trapped in there by the superior forces of Ishari and Haskany; of it becoming his grave. These thoughts were bad enough. But the prospect of being the first emperor to lose the castle, and the lasting shame that such a loss would bring to his name—such thoughts were far worse.

'What's going on?' he snapped when he and Rainer reached the front.

'Riders approaching ahead, Your Majesty,' quickly replied one of his scouts, sitting straight to attention.

'Numbers?'

'About thirty, sire,'

Baldwin peered ahead. He could make out a group approaching, but the sun was in his eyes.

'Banner?'

'The tree of Luderia, sire.'

'Luderia, eh? Then maybe Duke Arne has beaten us to the castle. I hope my brother has made him welcome.'

Baldwin had sent Walter up to the castle a few days before to speed up preparations. Parts of it needed repair, and large amounts of supplies had to be brought in to feed the size of the force he intended to keep there.

Baldwin waited for a few minutes. Sure enough, his father-in-law, Arne, rode at the head of around thirty Luderian noblemen. Arne was not getting any younger, mused Baldwin; nor was he getting thinner. Baldwin knew himself that as the years went by, iron discipline was needed to keep in the same physical shape as a young man. His father-in-law had let his discipline slide for a few years now; the size of the gut resting on the saddle was testament to that.

When they arrived, there was much shouting, hugging and shaking of hands as Baldwin went out of his way to thank every man for being there, and each nobleman made sure that they clasped hands and were acknowledged by their Emperor.

'And how is my daughter?' Arne bellowed, perhaps to remind anyone who had forgotten that he was father to the Queen.

'She gets more beautiful every day,' Baldwin answered, with the expected charm. 'It was a wrench to leave her back in Essenberg.'

'Quite, quite,' replied Arne. Baldwin could almost detect a tear in the older man's eye.

'But I've got news to cheer you up, my son,' said the Duke, a term of address that Arne always used and that Baldwin had never got used to. 'When you were spotted on the road, I insisted that I ride out and be the first to tell you. Our cousin Duke Ellard has been busy since he left you at Essenberg. When he arrived in Guslar, he wasted no time in raising a force of his own men and headed north yesterday. The Haskan forces were camped out in Grienna, idly waiting for orders from Ishari. They weren't expecting us to take the fight to them! But that's exactly what Ellard did, riding his force in and engaging the bastards. The Haskans put up a fight for a while, but then turned and ran! I don't want to build this into something more than it is: they were routed, but they'll be back. Still, a victory is a victory!'

By this point, Baldwin himself had a genuine, beaming smile on his face at the news. This was exactly what his nervous Empire needed. Bless Ellard!

'It certainly is,' he replied. 'Rejoice!' he shouted, 'and spread the word down the lines!'

A cheer rose up, and his soldiers did as they were told, retelling the story of how their fellow Brasingians had given the army of Haskany a bloody nose. Baldwin fell in next to Arne and the army continued towards Castle Burkhard.

Looking up, Baldwin could no longer think why the sight of his mighty stronghold should have made him feel grim at all.

* * *

WAKING up was a gradual process and took several minutes.

Dirk was first aware of a sickening, pounding headache. He focused on his surroundings. He was lying on a bed, his head propped up by pillows. It was in one of the canvas Caladri tents. Sitting at the foot of the bed was Elana. Her head was resting on her hand. He couldn't tell whether or not she was asleep. He looked at her awhile. He became aware of a great pressure in his bladder, but Dirk supposed that he would have to wait a bit to relieve himself.

'Elana.'

His voice croaked out the name, practically giving up on the final syllable.

He saw Elana raise her head and look at him.

'Dirk?'

Her concerned face caused him to remember, with a jolt, his last waking memory. Nexodore had attacked them. He had forced a burning magic into Dirk's body, and then...

'What happened?' he asked.

'He was holding you and...damaging you in some way,' Elana said. 'I tried to stop him...'

Dirk remembered Nexodore's fist crunching into Elana's head, and how he had wondered if the blow had killed her.

'...but I couldn't. I blanked out myself after that. But Prince Lorant survived the blast from Nexodore. He woke up to see Nexodore attacking us. He fired an arrow—luckily for us, it hit the mark. When Nexodore's attention was turned to the Prince, you used Madria's Dagger to kill him.'

Dirk had no memory of the last bit; his head felt foggy. 'What about your injury?' he asked.

'I had a headache for the rest of the day,' Elana smiled, 'but I am fine now.'

A thought occurred to Dirk. 'How long have I been here?'

'Two nights have passed. It is now early morning. The Caladri, including Princess Hajna herself, helped me to tend you. We all thought it likely you would die at first. You have still sustained serious injuries, though. You will never be fully healed, Dirk.'

Dirk nodded briefly to acknowledge the information. He certainly felt like he had been seriously damaged. He remembered the burning sensation of his insides. At the time, he had assumed Nexodore had killed him. Elana had saved his life for a second time. He hoped his actions had gone some way to repaying the debt.

Elana walked over to the bed and picked up a jug from the table in the corner. She carefully poured some of the contents into a mug.

'The Caladri have prepared this for you. It will help with recovery and with the pain.'

She reached over to let him drink it, but Dirk insisted on reaching out to take it himself. He gave it a brief smell, but his stomach roiled in protest, so he decided to take a quick gulp. As soon as the liquid hit his stomach, he received a piercing, shuddering pain. It was as if the acids in his stomach were attacking him. He cried out in pain and doubled over as his stomach cramped, spilling the rest of the drink onto the bed. Gritting his teeth, Dirk controlled himself and sat back up, red faced.

'Are you alright?' asked Elana. Her voice did not sound unduly concerned, and that helped Dirk to calm down.

He nodded, 'Yes.'

'You will have that kind of reaction to anything for a while. This drink will help to heal your insides. But I think you have permanent damage there. You must eat and drink only the blandest of foods. And drink water instead of beer or wine.'

'Very well,' agreed Dirk. What else could he say? 'What's been going on while I've been asleep, then?' he asked, hoping that a change of subject would make him feel better.

'Szabolcs, Prince Lorant's adviser, has identified the location of another of Madria's weapons. It is in the hands of the Grand Caladri. I asked Soren to wait until you had regained consciousness, which he agreed to. But now that you have, we will make our way there immediately. Nexodore's comments were worrying. If Ishari knows of the existence of Madria's weapons too, we are in a race to collect them all.'

'I am going with you,' said Dirk, worried that Elana was implying that he was to stay put and recover. He knew he was in no physical shape to continue the journey at the pace they travelled. But he was desperate not to be left behind here with the Caladri.

Elana frowned, as if she was about to deny his request. However, something seemed to make her change her mind and her face relaxed.

'Very well,' she said, giving a nod in acceptance. 'I will go to see Soren about it. You need to get ready immediately, then.'

Dirk nodded. *First, though,* he thought to himself, *I need to empty my bladder.*

* * *

IT WAS NIGHT-TIME. The sun had set about an hour ago. Farred sat at his table in his tent. A couple of candles shed a bit of light about him and cast some flickering shadows, but the rest of his tent was shrouded in darkness. The united army of North Magnians, South Magnians and Middians were camped in the relative safety of Kelland. Farred and his men had made speedy progress since leaving home, successfully meeting up with the forces controlled by Prince Ashere and Brock, the Middian chieftain, at the agreed location.

Things had become more difficult since then. First, Bastien, Duke of Morbaine, had been unable to persuade his brother, King Nicolas of Guivergne, to allow their force passage across Guivergnais territory. Wary that they should respect this, Farred and the other leaders had agreed to march from the Steppe to Kelland across the northern part of the duchy of Barissia. This meant moving across what was effectively enemy territory, since it was now well known that Duke Emeric had declared his duchy to be an independent kingdom from the Empire. Emeric had raised a large army which, although based in Coldeberg, could destroy their force of six thousand if they encountered it. They had decided that today they should ride across the duchy in one day. This was a tall order, but they were a highly mobile force, since most soldiers had their own mount. Those without shared mounts. They had been successful, though it had been a long and tense day.

Second, relations between the soldiers were not good. Many had, a week before, literally been enemies. Soldiers amongst the North and South Magnians had been stationed on either side of a hostile border. They were now expected to be comrades in arms. The tensions of the day had perhaps added to the problem: a fight had broken out this evening. A soldier of North Magnia had been stabbed. Luckily, the injury was not fatal, but Farred needed to restore order now or it would be lost forever.

The tent flap, facing Farred, was pulled aside. Burstan walked in.

'You wanted to see me?' he grunted.

Burstan was the captain of the troops who had been stationed on the Magnian border, about one thousand in all. This was about one half of all the troops under Farred's command. Although Burstan had not directly disobeyed an order, he had made it quite plain that this experienced core of the army were *his* soldiers, challenging Farred to act otherwise. Since it was clear that he did command the loyalty of his men, Farred had avoided a confrontation over the issue. Until now. Burstan had been present at the confrontation earlier this evening and, according to accounts, had done nothing to stop it from taking place.

'Yes, I sent someone for you about a half hour ago,' Farred replied to the captain's question. 'Take a seat,' he suggested, offering the chair opposite him.

Burstan sat down, a nonchalant air about him.

'I'll get straight to the point,' said Farred. 'As you know, there was a stabbing a couple of hours ago. By one of your men. Apparently, you were there. I've heard mention that you did more to stir up the antagonism than stop it. I shouldn't have to remind you that we need to maintain unity amongst our forces so that we are an effective fighting force against the Haskans.'

'Anyone who says I was stirring up trouble is a liar. I want a name,' demanded Burstan angrily.

Farred remained quiet. With no name forthcoming, Burstan continued.

'What you don't understand is that for my men, most of whom 'ave served their country for years, it's the North Magnians who are our real enemies, who are responsible for spilling South Magnian blood. Haskany poses no threat to us. That's the way my men see it, and then they see you licking the arse of their Prince.'

The insult was meant to provoke, but Farred kept cool. 'That sounds like treason to me. It's Prince Edgar who decides who our enemy is, not you.'

Burstan's face reddened. 'I'm passing on to you what my men are thinking, that's all. And my men,' he continued, 'make up half of our army, so I suggest you start listening to 'em. Cos they won't tolerate you accusing me of treachery.'

The gauntlet was being thrown down, much more obviously than before.

'What you fail to appreciate, Burstan,' Farred replied, keeping his voice neutral, 'is the fact that there are four thousand other soldiers in this army besides ours. One of ours has stabbed one of theirs. Prince Ashere is outraged; Brock supports him. They came to see me about one hour ago. It's all around the camp that you were there at the time. They're asking for your head, since you were the officer in charge. And while you may have the support of your thousand men, that's not enough to fight off four thousand.'

'They want my head? What for?' demanded Burstan. 'I don't believe you.'

Farred could see in the man's eyes, however, that he almost did. 'How did you expect them to react?' he asked, almost gently.

Burstan thought about that for a while. 'Look, I didn't do the stabbing. It was Vanig. I didn't encourage him, neither. I'm not that stupid.'

'I believe you, Burstan. That's what I said to Prince Ashere.'

Burstan looked at Farred gratefully. Farred almost felt sorry for him.

'You're a good soldier with a fine record. Prince Edgar told me as much himself. But we're in a situation here. This attack can't go unpunished. You know what has to happen.'

Burstan breathed out slowly. 'Vanig's not a child. He knows that something like this can get you killed. But he'd been drinking, and he was provoked—he didn't kill the other lad after all, did he?'

'No, but what's the message, Burstan? Stab a comrade and get away with it if you're a bit tipsy? I'm not going to stand for that; neither are Prince Ashere and his troops.'

'Alright, discipline is discipline,' responded Burstan gruffly. 'Death it is.'

'There's one more thing, Burstan. I told you that Ashere and Brock wanted you punished as well. I told them no, that you believe in discipline. But you're going to have to prove it.'

Burstan didn't understand at first. He frowned, then shrugged, as if to say that he kept discipline amongst his soldiers anyway. Then his face went pale as he realised what Farred was saying. 'You mean—you want me to do Vanig in myself?'

'You have to. You're his commanding officer. You need to show that you're in charge.'

Burstan said nothing for a while, his mouth open as he thought about his situation. 'So be it,' he said finally, his voice thick. 'I'll do it.' There was a pause. 'May I be dismissed now?' Burstan asked, not looking Farred in the eye.

'Of course.'

Burstan stood up and made his way out of the tent without looking back. Farred was left in darkness. He turned around to look at the far corner of the tent. Prince Ashere was sitting in the shadows.

'You handled that well,' he commented, his voice a soft whisper.

Farred sighed. 'We've maintained a united front for now, that's the main thing. I'm thoroughly sick of this day.'

'This is the hardest part: controlling the troops when there's no fighting to be done. I tell you, it will be a relief when we reach Castle Burkhard and meet with the enemy. Things will be easier then.'

Farred gave a brief smile, for in the darkness he could not tell whether the Prince was making a joke or not.

DARK TIDINGS

XXIII

Dirk had been given a few moments to prepare himself, and then they had set off. Prince Lorant, still recovering from his own encounter with Nexodore, had given them fresh mounts and loaned them the use of a couple of Caladri soldiers to make their journey out of his lands speedier. The soldiers knew the route, so the group could concentrate on setting a good pace.

For Dirk, the journey was intolerable. The physical pressure on his battered body made his head pound like someone was smacking it with a hammer. He felt nauseous and faint. Princess Hajna had given on him plenty of herbs and medicines which might help his condition before he had left. She had been very gracious, calling him a hero. Dirk had never been called a hero before, and it had made him feel better for a while. There was plenty of the drink which Elana had introduced him to this morning. He took an occasional swig of it as they rode. His stomach protested at having to digest it, but it did keep the direct pain from his injuries down to a minimum. The bitter after-taste he could live with. He found that chewing on some herbs, from a pouch which Hajna had provided, eased his nausea. Not, he thought grimly, that he had anything left inside him to expel.

After days of sunshine, rain clouds had rolled in, depositing a steady drizzle onto their heads, making Dirk's mood even worse. The forest glistened, and the water soaked into his clothes, making them stick to his skin. They stopped briefly for a rest at lunchtime. Dirk immediately swung down from his horse, hoping that someone else would see to its needs. He staggered off into the trees. By this time, his limbs were shaking from his exertions. Dirk gritted his teeth and insisted his body do what he told it to for a while longer.

After he had gone a distance which he thought was far enough to avoid people overhearing, he allowed his body to take over. His insides convulsed sharply, and he doubled over in pain. He then faced a wracking series of coughs which resulted in dark-coloured blood coming up, spattering the leaves and grass on the floor. Another bout of coughing followed, and more came up.

He wiped his sleeve over his mouth and headed back to the others. He knew that Elana would be keeping an eye on him, and he didn't want her to see. He was enough of a liability as it was. If Soren and the others knew how ill he was, they would doubtless have left him behind; for his own good as much as anything else, he knew. But he couldn't leave Elana on her own when he was her only disciple. He had to deal with his injuries.

As he returned to camp, he met eyes with Elana, who was nervously looking out for him. He nodded in her direction. She would think he had gone into the trees to relieve himself. He had been doing enough of *that* lately.

Dirk went over to the saddlebag and rummaged around until he found a Caladri bread roll, dark brown and savoury to the taste. He took a bite and chewed thoroughly, making sure he didn't swallow any of it until he had turned it into a watery paste. He swallowed, feeling the food go all the way down. His insides protested at solid food. It was the first thing he had eaten for two days. He kept it down. That was important, and he was hopeful that it would get better over time. He couldn't face eating anything else, however, and returned the roll to his bag.

Before long, they were travelling again. The two Caladri soldiers led them onwards, as efficient and as serious as they would be on any military mission. After a couple of hours, they informed everybody that they had moved into that indistinct part of the forest where the lands of the Blood Caladri ended and those of the humans of Grienna began. They had to be more on their guard from this point onwards.

They carried on into the evening, deliberately skirting around any signs of human habitation. It would be easier if they were not seen by the local inhabitants at all. Eventually, and to Dirk's relief, the two soldiers stopped them in a suitable clearing.

'Half a mile in that direction and you will find yourselves on the brow of a small hill,' one of the soldiers told them. 'If you look down from there tomorrow morning, you will see the Great Road and several settlements. The Road is only about three miles from here. You can work out your favoured route then. I suggest you try to head due west as much as possible, while avoiding settlements. Be careful of the Road. We know that large armies have passed south along it. But it is still being used to carry supplies south to the Haskans.'

The two soldiers did not hang around. Their orders were to head straight back that night. After they left, taking the horses that Lorant had loaned them, Herin said that he had suspected Lorant's army was ready to move out. He added, in his typically dark manner, that Lorant wouldn't have shared such information in case any of them were captured and revealed the destination under torture.

That night Dirk retreated into the trees again and coughed up more blood. This time it only happened the once. He was too tired to worry about it and went straight to sleep, as everyone else around him busied themselves with making camp and dinner.

The next morning, Dirk was one of the first to wake. Gyrmund and the others had constructed a basic shelter from the branches they had found in the forest, which had kept them all dry. Outside the shelter, it looked like it had rained all night. The ground had become soggy and muddy.

Hunger pangs afflicted him, preventing him from resting further. Dirk collected his bread roll from yesterday and a flask of water. He sat down and ate. He took one bite from the roll and a sip of water to go with it, to help him work on the hard bread. Like a child or an old man with no teeth, Dirk thought to himself. But he persevered, forcing himself to complete his breakfast. It was a long process and by the time he had finished, the others were up and preparing to go.

Gyrmund had followed the advice of the Caladri soldiers and surveyed the plain below them. He led them along a route he had planned out from the viewpoint. They headed west, for the woodland and rugged terrain which lay between the settlements of the Griennese dotted around the countryside. Dirk could tell that these settlements they skirted around were getting progressively larger the farther they went.

They smelled the Great Road before they saw it. At first, it was an unpleasant odour on the wind which one or two of them would catch before it disappeared. But as they walked onwards, it became a consistent stench. Dirk's nausea returned. He tried chewing on the herbs he still carried, but the smell in the air mingled with the taste in his mouth and he had to spit them out. In the end, he resorted to holding a piece of cloth over his nose and mouth.

The countryside had now become flatter, the trees replaced by grassland. This was man-made scenery. The woodlands had been cut back from the Great Road to prevent robbers from waiting in ambush. The Great Road appeared on the horizon up ahead. There was no traffic on it, but the smell in the air made the group wary.

'Smells like shit and rotting meat,' Herin suggested.

The comment didn't make Dirk feel any better.

As they approached the road, they found that Herin's identification of the smell was accurate. The road itself, and the trampled grass to each side, was dotted with faeces.

'It's not animal droppings,' said Clarin, screwing his nose up at the smell.

'I don't think it's even human,' added Rabigar, his one good eye studying the ground carefully.

Dirk waited a few yards away as the others strode over to the road to inspect it more closely. He feared losing his breakfast if he were to do the same.

'I would say Drobax,' Gyrmund added, confirming Rabigar's thought.

'How do you know? You've travelled that far north?' asked Moneva.

'I have, briefly. Look around us. What else would have left a trail like this? But the sheer numbers of them that must have passed through—I can't believe it.'

'Has anyone else seen Drobax before?' asked Soren, trying to establish the facts.

A few heads were shaken, but Rabigar spoke up. 'I have, many years ago now. If this is what it looks like, countless thousands have been marched through here.'

'Look at this,' said Herin, who had walked down the road a few feet.

Dirk looked at what he was pointing at. At first, it was an indistinct blob by the side of the road. Curious, he followed the others to look.

Suddenly, he realised what it was. A dead baby. But not human. It was a greyish colour, with a sharp, grotesque looking face. It looked like it had been trampled on repeatedly, lying flat to the ground.

Dirk couldn't look any more. He turned away, but it was too late; the sight of the baby and the smell combined to make his damaged body spew out the contents of his breakfast on to the ground. Elana edged over towards him, but Dirk waved her away.

Belwynn made an upset noise as she, too, recognised what it was. 'What is it doing here?' she demanded.

Nobody seemed to have an answer for her.

Then Rabigar spoke up. 'The Drobax are unlike any other race in Dalriya. They are so numerous and yet so despised by their masters in Ishari that, when they march to war, everyone goes. Not just male adults, but everyone—even infants. If a few thousand die on the way, no one cares. So many have marched through here. If you were to follow in their path you would find many bodies along the way.'

'Thousands of them,' said Gyrmund. 'What can the Empire do to stop that?'

No one answered him.

'It can't,' said Herin finally.

'Do all the Drobax...look like that?' asked Moneva, gesturing towards the baby, though keeping her eyes fixed away from it.

'Their skin is grey in complexion. Adults are often hairy. The strongest will wear armour they have taken from somewhere, but many wear nothing. They can reach five feet in height, thin looking, but that hides their strength. They are a created race,' Rabigar continued, 'by the wizards of Ishari. They bred them for their own purposes. Stupidity and base instincts make them easy to control. But they can be cunning and cruel. They have as strong an instinct for self-preservation as any living thing. That makes them dangerous. But they are a blunt, imprecise weapon. If Erkindrix has sent them to take the Empire, it means he has decided on a speedy destruction. Nothing much will be left surviving afterwards. These are new tactics from him.'

'New tactics?' asked Belwynn.

'Up to now Erkindrix has used the people he has conquered. Arioc was made King of Haskany, and their soldiers now fight for Ishari. The Drobax have hardly been used. Their use now suggests that Erkindrix isn't that interested in the Empire as a rich resource to be exploited. He wants total victory, whatever the cost, and soon.'

Soren nodded. 'What you say makes sense, Rabigar. I wonder if anything has prompted this change in approach.'

Nobody seemed to have any suggestions, so Soren's question was left unanswered.

'I'm going to bury that baby,' said Belwynn suddenly.

'Belwynn—' began Soren.

'I know, it may be stupid,' said Belwynn, interrupting him, 'but I'm not leaving it like that.'

She walked over to the body. Clarin followed her and offered his help.

Everyone waited in uncomfortable silence, but the big man dug out a shallow grave quickly enough.

Gyrmund wordlessly led them off away from the Road. Everyone followed in silence. A sombre mood had fallen on the group, and everyone seemed lost in their own private thoughts.

As he struggled on at the back of the group, Dirk tried to imagine a horde of these Drobax descending on his homeland. *Maybe I hadn't fully realised,* he admitted to himself, *what was at stake. I have to force this broken body to help Elana as much as possible. Only she can save us.*

* * *

FARRED FELT a sense of foreboding as the combined forces of Magnian and Middian soldiers arrived at their destination: Castle Burkhard. It had been a looming presence in the distance for the last few hours, and the closer they had got to it, the more formidable it seemed.

Two giant rocks shot upwards from the ground, dwarfing the countryside around. Brock fancied they looked like the bent knees of some immense sleeping giant. The slightly smaller rock, where they were now heading, was thinner and irregular in shape, while the larger rock was shaped like a pyramid. Both had stone-built structures on top of them, and Farred had noticed a bridge connecting the two about three quarters of the way up. Coming to it from the east, which most people would do, would make it even more formidable looking, he considered. The land to the east, including the Great Road, was relatively flat and featureless. Castle Burkhard dominated this territory. To the west, from where Farred and his soldiers had come, the land was rocky, tough, barren and virtually unsettled by humans. They had, in fact, seen more impressive slabs of rock on their journey. None of which, of course, had a stone castle built on top of them.

At the base of the castle, they were met by Rainer, the imperial chamberlain. There was a small village here which must have found itself suddenly overwhelmed with soldiers. The road which ran through the village and approached the castle was a muddy mess after the comings and goings of so many soldiers. Their force had been allocated a temporary barracks to the south, which was adequate enough.

There was no time to rest, however. Rainer led the way up to the castle, followed by Prince Ashere, who was flanked by Farred and Brock.

They followed the path and reached the base of the first rock. Farred was keen to study the defences of the famous fortress, which they might have to help to defend. This first rock, even more so than the other, was a virtually vertical climb upwards, and so the path, which had been hewn into it, wound its way upwards around the rock. Any defenders were automatically given a height advantage on the path itself, but more than that, could hurl down onto the attackers all manner of unpleasant objects. Rock, thought Farred, being the most obvious.

Half way up, a massive boulder was positioned just off the path, kept in place by a wooden buttress. When released, it would roll down the path, squashing anything in its way. They stopped for a brief rest.

'The castle atop this crag is known as the Duke's Keep, traditionally occupied by the dukes of Kelland,' said Rainer, breathing hard from the steep climb. 'It's linked by the bridge to the Emperor's Keep. Duke Burkhard built both structures here as a defence against the Persaleian army, which couldn't be beaten in a pitched battle. How times change, eh?' he said wryly. 'Baldwin has garrisoned the Emperor's Keep; his father-in-law Duke Arne has his forces in the Duke's Keep.'

'Are you expecting the other duchies to send forces here?' asked Ashere.

'Yes...' Rainer replied, though he sounded unsure of himself. A look of worry crossed his face. 'I'll let the Emperor explain all that to you.'

They walked on, and Farred began to feel the effects of the upward climb in his thighs, especially after all the riding they had done. 'This is one hell of a thing to climb up when you've got people trying to kill you every step of the way,' he commented.

Brock chuckled and slapped him on the back. 'Good job we picked to fight with the defenders, my friend!'

'We're here, Your Highness,' said the chamberlain, stopping to catch his breath.

It must have taken them close to an hour to reach the summit, and all four men were perspiring freely after the steep upward climb. To attack such a place, thought Farred, must surely be madness. At this point, the path divided into three ahead of them, while, in-between and to the side of each path, sheer rock walls loomed above. Even now, the Brasingians had stationed some men here on guard duty, but in a real attack these defences would bristle with soldiers.

Rainer began towards the left path.

'Does it matter which path is taken?' asked Ashere.

'Only the left path takes you to the top,' said the chamberlain, turning around and resuming the last ascent.

They followed behind and reached the top. Although it was a mild day, the wind whipped about them at this exposed height and soon cooled off Farred's sweat. To their right lay a stone-built fortress which perched close to the far edge of the summit: the Duke's Keep. Farred counted five towers, the farthest one being the tallest, soaring above the walls as if trying to reach the sky. To their left was the bridge, which Farred had noticed from the ground. Rainer took them in this direction. As he approached, Farred let out a whistle.

'It's made of stone!' he marvelled.

The bridge arched across the divide between the two rocks as if held there by magic. On the other side of the bridge, and slightly higher up, stood a larger fortress which took up the whole of the opposing summit. Below was a sheer drop of several hundred feet. Farred had only seen a handful of stone-built bridges in his life. To see one here, spanning these huge crags, was stunning.

'How did they—' he began.

'I've got no idea how they built it,' Rainer interrupted, obviously expecting the question. 'Marshall Walter, the Emperor's brother, might know. He seems to have studied this place as much as anyone. My job is to lead you across. Emperor Baldwin's hall is in the Emperor's Keep opposite. I advise you not to look down.'

With that, Rainer placed his first foot on the bridge. He walked steadily, if carefully, across it. Farred and his companions exchanged worried glances.

'I'm staying here,' announced Brock, folding his arms.

'If you do,' replied Ashere, placing one foot and then the next onto the bridge, 'I'll have to tell your men that you were too scared to cross.'

Farred held his breath and joined Ashere on the bridge. The bridge did not, as he had half expected it to, suddenly collapse.

'Oh, shit,' swore Brock, and, after a moment's hesitation, followed on.

EMPEROR BALDWIN HAD INVITED ONLY Ashere to the Royal Council, but the Prince had insisted that Farred and Brock attend as well, since he could not speak alone for all the soldiers in their force. Rainer had assented, but was clearly in a rush.

'This is the main hall,' he said breathlessly, before barging open the double doors and entering what must be the largest room in the fortress. Like everything else, it was designed with functionality rather than elegance in mind, but it impressed with its size. No doubt it would have looked larger, but most parts of the hall were being used for temporary storage. Pieces of armour, for every part of the body, had been unceremoniously dumped in one corner. In another, barrels of food and drink had been stacked. It was at the far end of the hall that the meeting was taking place.

Rainer led them over to the small group of men sitting at a plain wooden table. As they approached, the men stood up to greet them.

'Your Majesty, I present His Highness Prince Ashere of North Magnia and the lords Farred and Brock.'

Farred looked to see who Rainer directed the introduction to.

Emperor Baldwin looked confident and physically fit, his hair dark but studded with grey. This was the man responsible for the deployment of Farred's troops and the defence of the lands of the South. On first sight, Farred could not be disappointed. He detected a slight look of anger in his eyes and jaw, presumably at the fact that Farred and Brock were attending as well. It was a small war council, and no doubt Baldwin would rather have had men around him that he knew he could trust. Still, the Emperor hid his annoyance. Farred didn't mind the anger. It showed a man used to having his orders followed.

'His Imperial Majesty, Emperor Baldwin; His Grace Arne, Duke of Luderia; Lord Walter, Marshall of the Empire; Lord Gustav, Archmage of the Empire.'

Baldwin moved and shook Ashere by the hand, thanking him for coming. Everyone then made sure they shook a hand or nodded an acknowledgement before they were quickly seated.

'I hope you will excuse our grim faces and lack of hospitality this day,' began Baldwin, 'but we have bad news and hard decisions to make.'

'We expected such a situation, Your Majesty,' replied Ashere. 'That is why we are here.'

Baldwin nodded. He let out a breath of air, as if deciding which bad news he should relate first.

'Two days ago, Duke Ellard of Rotelegen made a second raid on the Haskan forces positioned just over the border in Grienna. It seems that the first time he caught them by surprise. But on the second, the tables were turned. They were waiting for him—probably lured him into a trap. He was killed.'

Baldwin paused a few moments to let that news settle in. Farred felt a tingle along his spine. This was important news of war, but it was magnified in that it had happened only miles away from where they were now.

'Most of his army was slaughtered, including his three eldest sons. A few escaped to bring back the news. His youngest and only remaining son, Jeremias, was left back in Guslar. He is now duke. Only sixteen, we think.'

Walter, Baldwin's brother, nodded grimly in confirmation.

'So, in most ways that matter, we have lost the army of Rotelegen. The duchy is indefensible...' Baldwin's voice trailed off a little.

Indefensible. Farred wondered what that meant, what decisions had already been made.

Baldwin gathered his thoughts together. 'Gustav had just begun to tell us his news. If you could go over that again, Gustav.'

The other three men were dressed in the leather armour of soldiers, as if ready to ride and fight at a moment's notice. The brothers, Baldwin and Walter, looked the part. Duke Arne of Luderia didn't. In fact, the man looked ill, his face pale and his eyes baggy. They seemed to wander around, as if he were not really involved in the conversation. The fourth man, Gustav the Archmage, was wearing knee-high black leather boots and a yellow robe with a patterned hem, belted at the waist. He began to speak.

'On hearing the news of the battle yesterday, I went to Grienna to see for myself. To check on the facts of the battle as they were reported to us. The facts are true, I am afraid. However, once there, I discovered yet worse news. The Haskan army has now been joined by a force of Drobax from the north. The size of this force is beyond imagination. It sits like a plague on the edge of our lands. Perhaps less than half of these Drobax are fighters, as we would call them. For Ishari has sent all of these creatures, be they male or female, old or young, healthy or ill. As for numbers, I could guess, but it would be meaningless. Millions. When it is in those numbers, you cannot count or assess size.'

'Millions?' Brock let out, his voice incredulous.

Gustav simply nodded. 'It is not a military force, as we would understand it. They are not trained fighters, but beasts who would do Ishari's bidding. They are not even being provisioned. Supplies come in for the Haskan soldiers, but hardly any for the Drobax. They steal what they can from any Griennese stupid enough to get caught. But mostly they eat each other.'

Farred gasped, an involuntary sound.

'To me, it seemed a practice the Drobax were familiar with. The smallest and weakest are killed and eaten. And yet at the same time, more are produced. I could see them fornicating; I could see pregnant Drobax females walking around. In one sense, it is the ultimate army, capable of feeding itself. The commanders seem not to worry about logistics or keeping them alive. Each day they are there, many thousand will perish. But that is something hardly worth caring about, since such mortality hardly takes away from the overall number. Soon, they must unleash this force on the Empire. When one combines it with the large and well-organised army of Haskany and the Ishari sorcerers they have gathered there, I am afraid it is unstoppable. To put an army against it in the field would be laughable. A fly attacking a horse.'

'So,' said Ashere, speaking slowly, as if still absorbing this terrifying information, 'Rotelegen is virtually defenceless, while there is such a force on its border ready to invade. Have you any ideas about how to respond?'

Baldwin gave a pained smile, as if the question were a cruel joke. 'I know how I will respond. Unfortunately, it is not a response which holds out any real hope. That, I am afraid, is beyond me.'

Baldwin paused. Farred wondered whether he hoped that someone would interrupt, and demand that there was cause for such hope. But how could there be?

'I have already sent word to Jeremias and his advisers in Guslar. Rotelegen is to be evacuated. The whole duchy. Everyone there is at the mercy of Ishari. I'm not going to waste what force I have left on making a vain gesture. I'm going to make it as hard as possible for the fuckers.'

Farred liked what he heard.

Ashere seemed to agree. 'Yes. Give them the hardest fight you can. That is all you can do.'

Baldwin seemed to take some encouragement from those words. 'What forces Jeremias has left he will have to use to make their people leave. Arne's troops will help. Those who can fight will be sent here. Those who can't will go south to Essenberg. Any source of food or water for the invaders will have to be destroyed or poisoned. We're not giving them one free meal. Walter will finish the defences here. I pray to Gerhold and any other god who will listen that the other duchies of the Empire send their troops in time. And then we hole ourselves up in here and last as long as possible.'

Ashere nodded. Farred wondered how he could, since Baldwin of Brasingia had just spelled out a nightmarish end to his Empire: its army holed up in this castle, its people scattered to the south, utterly defenceless against Ishari's armies.

'May I ask,' said Ashere, 'whether you have found a role for our small force?'

Baldwin smiled. 'Thank you for coming to help us,' he said, making sure that he met eyes with both Farred and Brock as well as with Ashere. 'You have arrived sooner than most of my dukes. I would like to think I would have done the same for your countries, but...anyway, I owe your people a debt of gratitude. To answer your question, Your Highness: yes. I have a role for you. You are to check the advance of the enemy while my people escape.'

SWIFT MAGIC

XXIV

Belwynn did her best to put the sights of the Great Road behind her as the group continued on their journey westwards. Everyone was quiet, however, and that did not make it easy. The whole experience had been very unsettling. The Drobax were a disturbing intrusion into the world she thought she knew.

Grienna was not a large state, and it did not take them long to travel the width of it. The major settlements were clustered around the Great Road, which fed their economies. But travel a few miles either way and the ancient forests of Dalriya reclaimed their dominance of the landscape. It was not long after midday that they found the terrain getting more difficult and the signs of human habitation disappearing.

They pressed on. As was usual by now, Gyrmund led the way. He was taking them in a north-westerly direction, hoping to cut into the centre of the lands of the Grand Caladri and find the inhabitants. The forests of the Grand Caladri were larger than those of the Blood Caladri. That meant they would be even more sparsely settled. Soren pointed out that finding the Caladri would be almost impossible. They would have to hope that, instead, the Caladri would find them.

As time went by, Gyrmund began muttering to himself. Then he abruptly stopped. 'We've been past here already,' he exclaimed angrily.

'Are you sure?' asked Belwynn.

'Yes. I've had the feeling awhile. At first, I thought I was going mad. So I snapped a twig.'

Gyrmund pointed to a low-hanging branch of a tree a few feet in front of him. A twig lay hanging down from it at head height, snapped but still attached.

'Well, stop taking us the wrong way,' suggested Herin.

'I'm not!' shouted Gyrmund.

'Calm it,' said Soren. 'This is the work of the Grand Caladri. They are stronger magic users than the Blood Caladri. They have always used magic to defend their boundaries rather than weapons. They obviously confuse anyone who tries to get too far.'

'Then how can you stop it?' asked Gyrmund.

'I can't!' snapped Soren. Now he seemed to be losing his temper. He held his hands up in an apology and took a deep breath. 'Sorry. It's happening again. They are casting a subtle sort of magic which encourages people to fight with each other. I suspect that most unwanted intruders end up killing each other so that the Grand Caladri don't have to bother. Anyway, we'll have to control ourselves and be careful. Especially you two,' he said, gesturing at Herin and Gyrmund.

Herin and Gyrmund stood sour-faced but said nothing.

'So, Soren,' began Belwynn carefully, 'any ideas what we should do?'

'Not really. There's no point carrying on. I guess we just wait here and hope they come to us. That's the trouble with shutting yourself away from the world. You cut off potential friends as well as enemies.'

'Why should they come to us?' asked Moneva.

Soren shrugged. 'Perhaps we look more interesting than the usual visitor?'

'Well I would think so,' said Herin. 'A one-eyed Krykker for a start—' Herin realised what he had done in mid-speech and clapped a hand over his own mouth. 'Sorry,' he said to Rabigar.

Rabigar shrugged the insult away.

'I think I'll go for a walk and cool down,' Herin said.

'I wouldn't,' said Soren. 'You might never find us again. I think we should all rest up here for a while. Gyrmund, maybe you could start a fire?'

The group sat down around Gyrmund's fire. There was an uneasy feeling amongst them, and most people took the chance to eat their midday meal in relative silence.

Perhaps an hour went by before the Caladri arrived. Where the Blood Caladri had intercepted them with an armed group of soldiers, the Grand Caladri had apparently sent only one person.

He was dressed in loose tunic and trousers and carried no weapons that Belwynn could see. Belwynn knew that didn't necessarily make him any less dangerous.

Wizard, said Soren, confirming her suspicions.

The Caladri wizard approached from the direction they had been heading in. He walked slowly, but with the same jerky motion Belwynn had noticed amongst the Blood Caladri. He had a long, grey beard that covered his facial features and went down to his chest. It was difficult to place an age on the Caladri they had met, since they had longer life spans than humans. But Belwynn guessed that this man was of the generation between Szabolcs and Prince Lorant.

The group hastily stood up as he approached. He stopped a few feet from them and stood still for a while, observing. Did Belwynn feel a feather-light touch on her mind? She couldn't be sure.

No one said anything. The group had become accustomed to taking the lead from Soren in these situations. He seemed content to wait for the Grand Caladri to speak, and so everyone waited.

'You are not from Ishari.'

It sounded like a statement rather than a question, but Soren nodded to confirm it.

'You bring news of the invasion?'

The invasion? Does he mean Ishari has invaded the Empire? Belwynn asked her brother.

I don't know what he means.

'We bring news from Prince Lorant of the Blood Caladri and from Emperor Baldwin of Brasingia,' said Soren. 'This news is about the threat from Ishari. However, we have been travelling, and have not heard from the south for a while. Has the Empire been attacked?'

'Quite possibly, but I have no news of that myself. I speak of the Ishari attack on our lands. They are mounting their challenge now. The news you bring us is perhaps redundant now?'

'I don't think so,' replied Soren. 'I think it's vitally important.'

'You must understand,' said the wizard. 'Time is short and all enchanters are needed for the defence. Why should I expend my energies on bringing you into our lands when they are needed to defend them? You must give me an acceptable answer.'

Soren thought about it. Before he came up with a reply, Elana answered for him.

'We bring tidings from Lady Onella. She has told us how to defend Dalriya from Ishari.'

The wizard's eyes widened a little at the answer to his question. He stood looking intently at Elana for a while. Again, Belwynn wondered whether he was using magic to search within her, checking on the truth of what she said.

'Very well,' he said eventually. 'Your presence may be important. We have no time to go by foot. I must transport you inside. I will get little help to do that, and it is costly. The more people I transport, the more difficult it is. Must you all enter our lands?'

They all looked about at each other. How could they decide who was important and who wasn't?

'I think we all should go,' said Belwynn honestly.

The wizard nodded his acceptance of this.

'My name is Ignac. Please follow me.'

Ignac led them back in the direction that he had appeared from, past Gyrmund's broken twig. Except this time, instead of more forest, they came upon a wooden pole. It was just like the one they had found when they had entered the lands of the Blood Caladri, with similar markings on it.

'Place at least one hand on the pole,' instructed Ignac.

'It's a form of transport?' asked Soren wonderingly.

'Yes. They help us guide a transportation from one location to the next.'

They all crowded around it. Belwynn sat down on her haunches so that she could grab a lower section of the pole and leave room for everyone else.

Ignac recited some words under his breath, and Belwynn felt her stomach lurching. Lights swirled around them and her vision receded until all she could see was her friends clasping the pole. Then she could see nothing.

She gripped the pole tightly as she experienced the sensation of moving. She thought she could hear speaking or shouting, but they seemed like faraway sounds. Her stomach roiled as she moved, cut off from most of her senses. Then she stopped. She saw her knuckles, white from clinging on to the pole. Her vision expanded. Soren and the others were there. She took a deep breath and tried not to vomit. Clarin didn't manage it, staggering off to the side and hurling against a tree. Dirk had a coughing fit that brought up blood and mucus.

Belwynn used the pole to lift herself to her feet. She realised this pole must be a different one, because they were now in a new location, but at no point had she let go of the original.

Ignac had taken them to the outskirts of what looked like a sizeable settlement by Caladri standards.

'Are we ready?' he asked.

The group gathered themselves together.

Are you alright? asked Soren.

Yes, why?

Nothing. You just look very pale.

Looking around, she saw she wasn't the only one. Dirk looked dreadful, but Elana was tending to him, and he gave a weak thumb up to indicate that he was ready to move on. After hearing how he had killed Nexodore three days ago, Belwynn found she had a completely different opinion of the man, and she admired his bravery in continuing their journey despite his obvious physical frailty.

Ignac led them towards the settlement. The Caladri did not appear to engage in arable farming at all, so there were no fields or such signs of habitation, as Belwynn would expect to see in human lands. There was a Caladri road, however, and on each side sat timber buildings, nestling in amongst the trees of the forest. The settlement was designed, it seemed to Belwynn, to blend in to the natural surroundings as much as possible.

She worried, however. There were no signs of defences here. The bigger towns of the Empire and even of Magnia all had some kind of walled defence, of timber if not of stone. The Caladri, it seemed, did not feel the need for such defences. Yet Ignac had told them that Ishari was about to invade their lands.

He led them along the road towards the settlement. Coming in the opposite direction were about a score of Caladri, a mixture of males and females. As the two groups approached each other, they slowed down and stopped. One of the male Caladri left his group to approach them. Belwynn thought he looked about the same age as Ignac. Ignac fell to one knee.

'Lord Kelemen,' he began.

The man he addressed made a wristy movement with one hand. Ignac stood up again. Kelemen looked Belwynn's group over.

'This is a delegation, apparently from Prince Lorant and Emperor Baldwin,' explained Ignac.

'With what purpose?' asked Kelemen.

'We bring news of a threat from Ishari,' explained Soren.

'Ha,' Kelemen laughed bitterly. 'A little late.' He looked them over. 'Rather a strange group to be representing the Blood Caladri and Kellish. May I ask what you are doing in this company?' he said, directing the question at Rabigar.

'I am exiled from my homeland. I do not represent the Krykkers.'

'I see,' said Kelemen. 'I will be frank with you all, since you arrive at a serious time, when our presence is needed elsewhere. We are the ablest enchanters of this region. We go to our capital, Edeleny, to defend the borders of our realm. The forces of Ishari are preparing to attack them. An army is poised to invade from the north should our defences be breached. As a leader of this region, it is my duty to bring my enchanters to Edeleny as soon as possible. Ignac says you have news of the threat we face. I must hear this news quickly.'

Soren spoke for the group, going as quickly as he could. He told Kelemen what they had learned of the weapons of Madria from Szabolcs of the Blood Caladri. He explained how they came to be in possession of one of them. Finally, he told Kelemen that they believed Ishari posed a threat to the whole of Dalriya. 'So,' he concluded, 'this attack on the Grand Caladri is part of a greater scheme that Ishari has. I believe that to defeat Ishari, we need these weapons. And I fear Ishari has grown in power. How sure are you that your magic defences will hold against them?'

'They have never been breached,' replied Kelemen simply. 'May I see the weapon you have?'

Dirk fumbled in his cloak for a while before producing Toric's Dagger. He looked nervously at Elana, who nodded at him, before he passed it over to Kelemen. The Caladri studied it closely, tracing a finger along its edge.

'Of course, you are interested in Lady Onella's Staff, in the temple at Edeleny. That is partly why you are here,' he said, making it a statement rather than a question.

Soren nodded.

'You intend to take the staff from us just like you have taken this dagger?' the Caladri said, in accusing tones.

'The Lady Onella, or Madria, as she names herself to me, needs the weapons to fight Ishari,' interjected Elana. 'We do her work.'

'Onella speaks to you?' demanded Kelemen.

'Yes,' replied Elana simply.

Kelemen looked at Elana for a good while, with a reflective expression. 'You may come with us to Edeleny. Perhaps your words should be passed on to the elders of the Caladri. Any decision is for them to make. But Edeleny is under attack. I cannot guarantee your safety if you come with us.' He gave the dagger in his hands another look. Belwynn saw the look in his eyes.

He wants to keep it, she warned Soren.

A few moments passed before Kelemen offered the weapon back to Dirk. He had obviously decided to return it. For now.

Soren looked around the group. 'Not everyone has to come,' he advised them.

Indeed, not everyone looked sure that they wanted to go. But the alternative, stuck in an unknown part of the Grand Caladri forest, didn't seem too appealing, either. Belwynn knew everyone had made their decision back in Essenberg, for good or ill. No-one was about to change their mind now.

'Are you still strong enough to help us?' Kelemen asked Ignac.

'Yes, My Lord,' Ignac replied.

Kelemen pointed towards the pole they had arrived at. 'Then we will all go on to Edeleny at once.'

With a gesture towards the other Caladri, Kelemen led them on to the pole. They were now about thirty in number. Kelemen decided they would travel in two groups. He asked Belwynn's group to split into two, so that there would be sufficient magic users in each group.

Kelemen and half of the other Caladri placed their hands on the pole. Belwynn joined them, along with Soren, Rabigar, Elana and Dirk.

As before, Belwynn felt a strange lurching sensation in her belly first, then the rest of her senses began to be affected as the teleportation began. She felt a kind of itchiness inside her head, then her vision left her and the feeling of nausea kicked in. They were travelling faster than before, and she felt the sensation of speed on her body. They were also travelling further this time, and the longer it went on, the more tiring and difficult it became. Then, without warning, they had stopped. Belwynn felt like the world was spinning around her. She was physically sick. She actually felt better for it. A hand brushed her hair back.

'Belwynn? Are you alright?'

It was Soren. She opened her eyes. She couldn't focus on anything properly. Soren helped her pull herself up. The spinning sensation returned as she stood up, but she gradually recovered. Rabigar had put Elana into a sitting position and was murmuring to her. It looked like she, too, had been sick.

Then Belwynn saw Dirk. He was still lying in a prone position, unconscious. He had also been sick, but it was stained red with his blood.

'The teleportation must have affected him badly,' said Soren. 'He has not recovered from the injuries Nexodore gave him. Not nearly recovered.'

A female Caladri was crouching over Dirk, while feeling his forehead and the pulse in his neck. When Elana saw him, she gave a little cry and crawled over to check him herself.

'Will he be alright?' asked Belwynn.

'I'm not sure,' said Elana. 'He's breathing...'

The female Caladri, crouching next to her, reached up to receive an item passed down to her. Belwynn could see that it was a small vial. The Caladri worked away a stopper at the top. She then delicately passed the vial under Dirk's nose.

Nothing happened for two seconds, then Dirk suddenly jerked awake. He gave a horrible, rasping cough, and more drops of blood were expelled. He fought to breathe in air for a while, looking like a fish that had been pulled out of the water. Elana whispered quietly to him and slowly his breathing steadied and he opened his eyes. Dirk was helped to his feet, and everyone moved a few feet away from the pole to make space for the arrival of the second group.

Belwynn looked about her. They were in another forest clearing, but close by she made out a Caladri road. Following its path, she could see what must be Edeleny in the distance. Peaks of tall buildings rose as high as the trees, and she thought she could faintly hear the noise and bustle which always emanates from large settlements.

The second group arrived at the pole. It was fast, but Belwynn's eyes detected movement, as if they had arrived *from* somewhere, to the east, rather than appearing from nowhere. The Caladri seemed immune from the side effects of the teleportation, but Herin, Clarin, Gyrmund and Moneva were all affected in the same way she had been. They lay in a confused state, clutching their disturbed stomachs, before they slowly recovered.

It was another few minutes before everyone was ready to walk the short distance to Edeleny. Dirk said he felt better, but he was still pale and fragile-looking. They connected to the road, and as they walked, Belwynn got a better view of the capital.

It was smaller by far than human cities such as Essenberg or Coldeberg, but Edeleny did stretch out over a reasonably large area. The buildings were bigger and more substantial-looking than she had seen elsewhere in the lands of the Caladri. They walked past small, one-storey houses, made from timber with thatched roofs. They all had the same conical shape and were virtually identical in size. Kelemen had intimated that wizards would arrive here from all over the lands of the Grand Caladri to work together in its defence. Belwynn wondered whether some of the accommodation they passed was built to house visitors to the capital, rather than serving as people's permanent homes.

Belwynn regularly caught glimpses of the taller buildings of the settlement, which all had a central location. These were white, looking as if they had been made of marble. It gave them a delicate, ethereal look. As they neared, Belwynn found that many had been constructed in and around trees. Tree trunks and branches somehow mingled with the white walls of the buildings. It looked as if the Caladri had used the trunks as central pillars for construction. The wide, sturdy branches were used to build the floors of the buildings. The largest had many floors, each with wide windows that allowed Belwynn to see through and get a look at the interior.

There was little sign of habitation. Some looked like industrial buildings, with spinning machines inside. Gyrmund brushed his hand along one of the white walls, then gave it a knock.

'Wooden,' he said, when he noticed Belwynn taking an interest. 'It looks like it's been treated with some substance that turns it white and reinforces it.' He gave it another slap. 'It feels as strong as stone.'

They passed Caladri, all of whom seemed busy on some errand. Some were guiding people to various locations; others carried food or wooden boxes.

None of them carry weapons, or wear armour, Belwynn said to Soren.

They seem totally confident in their magical defences, he replied. *I fear it is overconfidence.*

The main road they were walking on now joined into a central square, which had three other roads running off it at parallel points. The square surrounded by the roads seemed to be a gathering place, mostly covered in grass; wooden seats and a garden were located in the middle. At its centre, a fountain sprayed water into the air in beautiful, frothy arcs. But no one talked by the fountain or walked through the gardens now.

Kelemen pointed to a large, one-storey building roughly opposite them.

'That is Onella's Temple,' he said. 'Her staff lies there.'

Built of the white wood material, the temple comprised several wings connected to each other at right angles so that it took up an extensive amount of space on the ground.

'We are going to the Temenos,' continued Kelemen, this time pointing to a building sited on the left-hand side of the square. This had been constructed around one enormous tree, which rose through the centre and was the tallest building in the complex, presumably comprising many floors. It was cylindrical, the white wood punctured in various places to allow certain branches of the tree to continue out of the structure. The tree, and possibly the building, must have been hundreds of years old. The building gave off an aura; almost as if it was alive.

Outside, eight Caladri soldiers stood guard. They wore brightly polished armour and carried impossibly long pikes, at least twenty feet long, all held at the same angle. They looked straight ahead and were perfectly still, as if they were not living creatures but statues. The spikes and blades on the end of the pikes looked viciously sharp. They were the first soldiers Belwynn had seen in the lands of the Grand Caladri, but their presence seemed as much ceremonial as practical.

The large wooden doors of the circular building were open, and as Kelemen approached them, another Caladri came out to meet them. He wore a plain white outfit and had white hair which was tied up in a ponytail.

'Hurry!' he said, jerking his arm vigorously to get them into the building. He then stopped short as he noticed the strangers in his capital.

'What are they doing here?' he demanded, sounding almost hysterical.

'They are messengers from Baldwin of Kelland,' explained Kelemen, not looking happy at how he was being addressed. 'Lorant of the Blood Caladri sent them here.'

'Who is he?' Belwynn asked Ignac in a whisper.

'That is Agoston, one of our elders,' replied the Caladri.

'...haven't got time,' Agoston was saying, lecturing Kelemen. 'Whatever Baldwin and Lorant have to say will not change anything.'

'I have spoken to these people myself,' replied Kelemen, standing his ground. 'I believe that Lady Onella has directed them here.'

In the end, Kelemen got his way. The white-haired Caladri elder waved them in.

THE TEMENOS

XXV

The temenos was unlike anything Belwynn had ever seen. The whole of the ground floor was taken up by one large circular room, while a flight of stairs twisted around the wall to the next level. The great trunk of the tree rose in the middle of the floor and carried on through a massive hole in the ceiling. Around the circumference of the trunk, a large circular table had been constructed. Nearly a hundred Caladri sat on chairs around the table. All the chairs seemed to be filled. There was a mixture of Caladri: old and young, male and female; all sat calmly, as if in meditation. Some had their eyes closed; others had their eyes fixed on the giant tree in front of them. Agoston led them around the table and took them upstairs to the next floor.

As they ascended, Belwynn noted that two great branches of the tree stretched along the full length of the ceiling. She surmised that the Caladri must have shaped the growth of this giant tree over the years to suit the design of their building.

'Well, this is peculiar,' Belwynn heard Clarin mutter ahead as he reached the next floor. When Belwynn got sight of the room, she had to agree. It was set up in an identical fashion to the room below. Most of the chairs around the table were filled with Caladri, sitting in silence.

Are they all wizards? she asked Soren.

There was no answer. She looked behind her. Soren was staring at the room. She sighed. Sometimes he would nod or shake his head in answer to a question without realising that she couldn't see it.

Are you going to answer me? she demanded testily.

Sorry. Yes, all of them are wizards. Some will be very powerful, some less so. I'm just wondering how many floors there are. I've never imagined this many wizards present all in one place.

It looked like Soren would find out. Up they went, past the third to the fourth floor, each room identical, except that the trunk of the tree became gradually narrower and the rooms therefore slightly less cramped. On the fourth floor there was a group of empty chairs, and here Kelemen's group of wizards, including Ignac, took their seats.

Agoston led the rest of them all the way to the seventh and final floor.

Kelemen turned to them. 'The Grand Caladri are unlike most other peoples. We have no kings or emperors to rule over us. We make our own decisions. But we do have three elders in our society: the wisest of our people who reside in Edeleny to guide our affairs. These are the people who wear the white. They must hear what you have learned about the weapons of Onella.'

The last step brought them into the highest room in the Temenos. The tree was thinner at this height, which meant that there was a bit more space around the edges of the room. This was taken up by shelves, mostly containing books and scrolls of parchment. There were only about thirty Caladri here.

Two of them stood apart from the rest, wearing the same white garments as Agoston. They were facing the direction of the stairs, as if waiting for their arrival.

Agoston spoke with his comrades. 'Kelemen intercepted this group on his way here. He insists we need to listen to them.'

One of them, a brown-haired man with fierce eyebrows, riled at the suggestion. 'The attack has begun. We need to respond now.'

'They should go,' said the second, a woman who held her chin so high it gave her an arrogant demeanour. 'They could interfere.'

'I wouldn't have brought them here if I didn't think it was important,' said Kelemen, holding his ground.

'Very well, Kelemen,' the first man responded. He turned to face them. 'We still have our manners, even on a day like this. My name is Odon. This is Dorottya. We will hear your news.'

Elana spoke to them, explaining her relationship to Madria as clearly as she could. The three elders seemed to listen to what she said. Dirk produced the dagger, and it was briefly passed around.

'Clearly, this information is important,' said Odon when Elana had finished. 'Our current situation makes it clear that we are as guilty as anyone else of underestimating the threat from Ishari. We have been deceived; or deceived ourselves. The other weapons should be found and brought together again.'

'We can discuss this further after the attack,' Agoston added.

'No,' said Elana, surprising Belwynn with her defiance. 'There is no time to lose. We must take the Staff now, before it is lost to Ishari.'

'Don't worry about that,' said Odon reassuringly. 'They have an army out there, but it won't be able to get into our lands. If they try to invade, we will ensure that they wander in our forest, lost, until they drop from exhaustion.'

'You are missing the point,' interrupted Soren. 'Erkindrix can call on far more wizards from Ishari than even you can muster on your own. I fear your defences will not hold against a committed attack. You need to prepare your military forces as well.'

'This is nonsense,' said Dorottya. 'Our defences have never been broken. If Ishari attacked us with all their wizards, they would suffer as well. Wizards from both sides would perish. What would they have to gain from that? They are testing our defences, that is all. But they will find them as robust as ever.'

'We have not threatened them,' Agoston added. 'We have remained uninvolved in their affairs for centuries.'

'But,' argued Kelemen, 'the objective of Erkindrix has now changed. He wants all of Dalriya. Including our lands. He may well be prepared to lose some of his forces to defeat us. What if he did? Our people in the north would be totally defenceless. We must act now. Give the order to raise an army to meet the invaders.'

'Listen, Kelemen,' said Odon. 'Our magic is our only hope. Do you know what waits for us on the northern border? Drobax. Thousands upon thousands upon thousands. If you raised an army, you couldn't stop them anyway. When was the last time the Grand Caladri fought in a war? We must rely on our magic. It has ever been thus, because we cannot hope to match them any other way.'

'Then evacuate,' said Rabigar. 'Tell your people in the north to move south now. Get a message to the Krykkers. They will take your people in. But you must do something. It is your duty to protect your people.'

'Don't tell us how to protect our people, Krykker,' said Agoston angrily. 'You do not understand magic and so cannot understand how strong our defences are.'

'This is getting us nowhere,' insisted Kelemen. 'Authorise me to raise an army and begin evacuations. If you can stop the invasion here, well and good. But let me put a contingency plan into operation.'

'If you wish to leave we cannot stop you, Kelemen,' said Odon. 'Though we could do with your help here. And that of your wizards.'

Kelemen nodded. 'I will give them a free choice. They may stay here or come with me.'

Odon spread open his hands, as if there was nothing more he could do or say. 'You are free to go, Kelemen. But these visitors and their weapon must remain. We cannot afford to let it leave. It must be properly examined.'

'You can't keep us here!' shouted Herin, his hand moving to his sword hilt.

Odon turned to him. 'This is the safest place in Dalriya. Until we decide what should be done about the dagger you have, here it stays. You are guests here, not prisoners.'

Belwynn and the others looked to Soren for a lead. He shrugged. 'Very well, we stay.'

Herin didn't like it; nor did Gyrmund and Moneva. But they trusted Soren enough to follow his lead.

Soren turned to Kelemen and held out his hand. 'Good luck.'

Kelemen took his hand. He nodded to the others. 'I wish it hadn't turned out this way. But if the worst should happen and Ishari breaks through, know that your coming here will have helped to save some lives.'

With that, Kelemen turned away and left. Belwynn watched him go, a sinking feeling in her stomach. She then turned back to the Caladri elders. Agoston was instructing a couple of Caladri to fetch something from a corner of the room.

'I am sorry,' he said, 'that this room is not very comfortable for you. But it is the best place for you to stay for now. We have refreshments.'

A couple of Caladri men brought over some trays containing biscuits, fruit and jugs of water.

'We must resume our places at the table for now,' Odon explained.

Soren sat down on the floor. Reluctantly, Belwynn and the others did the same, though Herin muttered darkly about their predicament. Belwynn herself was worried about the turn of events, though curious about what they would see take place in this room. She knew that Soren's curiosity would be tenfold. She also knew that he still hoped for a magical healing of his overextension. He would never get a better chance than this, in the presence of hundreds of Caladri wizards. Soren was clearly happy enough to stay here for now, but the threat from Ishari hung heavy in the air.

Others weren't so happy to stay.

'This building might become the site of a battle,' Gyrmund whispered to the group, 'and the fact that it would be a magical one doesn't make me feel any better, since Toric only knows what that will involve.'

'Let's see what happens,' Belwynn whispered back. 'We can always try to escape if we need to.'

They sat in silence, watching the wizards on the top floor prepare the defences of their realm. Belwynn wondered whether this group somehow channelled the power of everyone else in the building and sent it out to hold up the barrier around the forest.

After a short period, the Caladri around the table began murmuring to themselves. Belwynn sensed an intensification in the atmosphere throughout the building.

'It's started,' said Soren. 'The forces of Ishari must have decided to try to break open the barrier and let their soldiers in. I suspect that they have gathered a large group of their own wizards together somewhere in order to do so.'

The Caladri were now fully focused. Odon sat still, palms flat on the table and eyes open, staring forward at the tree in front of him. Other magicians held a different pose. Some had eyes closed, some leaned forward, and some muttered chains of words under their breath. Belwynn felt goose pimples on her skin as the magic being deployed in the building rose to new heights. Her companions sensed it, too. Their expressions ranged from disapproval on Rabigar's face to exhilaration on the face of her brother.

Somebody began shouting on one of the floors below. It didn't stop, a lone Caladri voice wailing and crying out.

'What's going on?' demanded Herin, his voice on edge.

'They will soon begin to suffer,' said Soren. 'The longer this goes on, the more casualties will be taken on each side. Clarin, have a look below, will you?'

Clarin stomped off down the stairs. Belwynn studied the faces of the Caladri magicians around the table and could see the strain starting to show. Sweat ran down the side of Agoston's head. Others frowned in concentration or clenched their teeth. A number looked like they were in pain. As time went by, other noises from below added to the wailing. Shouts of pain, muffled grunts, and bangs. But the magic battle did not seem to relent.

There was a sudden bang on their floor. Belwynn looked for the source of the noise and saw that it was the head of a wizard, cracking onto the table. He sat, unmoving.

'What happened to him?' asked Moneva, fear plain in her voice.

'Most likely dead,' said Soren, a strange tone in his voice. 'They're getting drained of all they have. I think they should stop. I'm not sure that they can keep Ishari out.'

Clarin re-emerged from downstairs. 'It's worse down there.'

Soren stood up. 'Stop!' he shouted in Odon's direction. 'You are taking too many casualties.'

For a few moments, the Caladri elder seemed too involved to reply. But then his voice rasped out, 'Then so are they!'

It was impossible for Belwynn to know whether Odon was right about the Isharites, but she could tell that the pressure on the Caladri did not seem to relent. Individual wizards continued to fall, now on the top floor as well as below. One of them suddenly started screaming, her hands gripping the sides of her head and her eyes bulging out. Another jerked backwards as if physically pushed. He fell back in his chair to collapse in a heap on the floor. Yet another simply crumpled down, head resting on arms as if he had suddenly gone to sleep.

Belwynn and the others were now standing up, the deaths around them becoming unbearable.

'Let's get out of here now,' advised Gyrmund. 'They're losing and there's nothing we can do to help.'

Belwynn felt he was right. Up to a quarter of the Caladri magicians on their floor were dead or broken. She sensed the situation was even worse on the floors below. As each magician fell, their ability to resist Ishari must surely be diminishing.

Then there was a sudden burst of power. The building was rocked by it. Some of the Caladri were thrown backwards from the table. Others shouted at each other or screamed in terror. Agoston, the white-haired elder who had led them upstairs, stood up.

Bolts of magic shot out from his outstretched hands, striking the ceiling and the walls of the room. His face was stuck in a grimace as he staggered around the room, with no control over his movements. Those Caladri who could, were standing up and moving away from the table.

It looked like they had lost. Ishari had broken through the defences and had killed at least half of the Grand Caladri's best wizards in the process.

Then Soren leapt forward. Agoston's magic was still draining out of him in an uncontrolled way, fortunately not striking anyone since his hands were in the air. Soren rushed over and seized them.

Belwynn looked on in dread. Soren cried out in pain as the magic entered his body. His body shook. But after a moment, his expression gradually changed, until it was one of exultation.

'Yes!' he cried out, 'oh, yes!'

Agoston's magic continued to pump into him. Soren must have been able, somehow, to control and direct the magic into restoring his own powers.

He shouted out again, a wordless cry of delight as his eyes shone with ecstasy. Belwynn was a swirl of emotions, deeply disturbed by what she was witnessing and aware that the others were watching it too. She felt like she no longer recognised her own brother: his facial expression, his voice, were different. At the same time, she knew how much this meant to Soren, and a part of her could be happy for him.

Agoston's body fell to the floor, a discarded husk that her brother had sucked dry.

Belwynn looked around. The others were staring at her brother, fear and even loathing in their faces at what they had seen. Even Clarin looked at Soren with something approaching disgust.

Elsewhere, those Caladri magicians who had kept their sanity and their lives were rushing down the stairs to evacuate the building. Others lay dead, or twitching, or still sat in their chairs, screaming out their madness.

'Let's go,' Belwynn shouted desperately.

The others reacted to her voice, and they all made their way to the stairs. Belwynn went over to grab Soren and pulled him along.

The defeat of the Grand Caladri had engendered a sense of panic in the building. Surviving wizards scrambled down the stairs in a hurry, tripping over each other to leave. The feeling spread to Belwynn and her companions as well. Herin and Clarin barged ahead at the front, while Belwynn and Soren brought up the rear. It was silly, really, thought Belwynn. The defences had been broken and the Ishari army of Drobax could now invade. But that army was miles to the north. On the fourth floor, she looked for Ignac, but couldn't see him. Perhaps he had left with Kelemen. Then a thought struck her.

Soren, she said.

Yes, he replied. His mind still seemed foggy with euphoria.

The forces of Ishari can now enter the forest. Does that mean that they can teleport into Edeleny like we did?

Soren paused while he thought about it. When he replied, the fogginess had left his thoughts, as if he had been suddenly sobered up from too much drink.

Yes. They have more magic users than the Grand Caladri. Although the battle will have been draining, some of them may still be strong enough to teleport. They may even have kept a fresh force of them ready for such a purpose.

Nexodore knew we had the dagger, said Belwynn. *They might know that the staff is here.*

You're right, said Soren. *We need to get it and get out of here as soon as possible.*

The twins reached the ground floor of the Temenos and ran for the exit. Caladri wizards lay dead or broken on the floor.

They rushed through the front doors of the building, still guarded by the eight Caladri pikemen, before nearly crashing into the others who had come to an abrupt stop.

Belwynn's worst fears were already realised. In the distance, on the far side of the city square, a small force from Ishari was gathering. Perhaps forty of them. They would soon head their way. The Grand Caladri wizards were running in the opposite direction. Their clawed feet allowed them to sprint away at an incredible speed. All of them ran, except for Odon the elder, who faced the invaders alone.

He turned around to look at them. 'Flee. Everyone must flee. We cannot win this battle now. You cannot be captured with the dagger in your possession.'

'Onella's Staff,' said Soren. 'It must be made safe.'

Odon nodded. 'Dorottya has gone to get it. She will take it away from here.'

Only Odon and the eight pikemen remained to defend Edeleny. Those who still could were running into the forest. These survivors would be needed to defend their people. But Belwynn was in no doubt that the forces of Ishari would hunt them down and the Drobax would come. Whatever makeshift army Kelemen could raise wouldn't be able to stop them.

'To the Temple,' Soren said to the group.

For a moment, they hesitated. Soren's performance in the Temenos had lost him the unquestioning trust of the group. But Belwynn followed her brother, as did Elana and Dirk, until the entire group followed the path around to the left, where the Temple stood.

Soren looked across the square behind them and took a sharp inhale of breath.

'It's Arioc himself,' he said.

ONELLA'S TEMPLE

XXVI

Everyone stopped in their tracks and looked in the same direction. Striding ahead of the group of Isharites who had been transported into Edeleny was Arioc: King of Haskany, member of the Council of Seven, second in command to Erkindrix himself. Tall and powerful, he wore gleaming black armour. Black shoulder-length hair framed his features. Even at this distance, he exuded power like no one Belwynn had seen before. More even than Pentas or Nexodore. It was an alien power, as if he did not truly belong among mortals, and it struck Belwynn with fear.

Arioc was marching his troop directly towards Odon. The sword he carried did not have the glint of metal but was black like his armour. He reached the path which took a route around the central square of Edeleny. The grassed recreation area in the middle was desolate, save for the solitary figure of Odon.

But then Belwynn felt something stir from behind her. She spun around. The eight Caladri soldiers. They stood so much like statues that Belwynn had forgotten about them. The presence of the Isharites on the path had seemed to trigger a reaction. Moving in perfect unison, the eight soldiers lifted up their pikes and marched to join Odon in the defence of their city.

'Come on,' said Soren, as the pikemen crossed past them. 'We don't have much time. We can expect a number of them to be wizards, not just Arioc.'

Soren sprinted towards the Temple, and everyone else followed at the same pace. Clarin and Herin barged open the white wooden doors.

A scream echoed around the square behind them. Belwynn turned back to look. Odon was hanging in the sky, suspended four feet from the ground with an orange light surrounding him. Belwynn traced the light back in a line to Arioc's outstretched hand. Another burst of power, and Odon's body turned black and the screaming stopped. Arioc withdrew his hand and the body fell to the ground.

A few Isharites looked in their direction. The Caladri pikemen had formed a line on the grass of the central square and were taking most of their attention. Their long pikes whirled around them, making a ghostly whirring noise as they cut through the air. The main group of Isharites looked at the pikes warily, unsure how to tackle them. The smaller group detached itself and headed towards the Temple.

'What do we do?' asked Belwynn. She wanted to run.

'Some of us are going to go inside and get the staff,' said Soren. 'Some of us are going to hold out here for as long as possible. I am staying here. Belwynn, you go in so that I can communicate with you. Dirk, you go in because you have the dagger. Everyone else, do what you think is best.'

Separate? Belwynn didn't want that. 'But—'

'Hurry up, now. Just do it, Belwynn. And take this. Just in case.'

Soren reached into his cloak and handed her Edgar's bag of money.

Belwynn knew she shouldn't argue. She entered the building. Dirk and Elana went with her. Everyone else drew a weapon and waited with Soren.

'Rabigar,' said Soren. 'Will you go with them? They might need protection.'

Rabigar looked at Soren for a moment. Belwynn thought he might argue, but he nodded and followed them in.

The entrance chamber to the Temple was large but poorly lit. Before Belwynn had time to look around, Elana had opened a door at the far end of the room and was beckoning everybody through.

Belwynn took one last look behind her. Moneva and Gyrmund were talking to each other hurriedly. They kissed once. Gyrmund and Herin knocked arrows to their bows. Soren and Clarin turned to look at her. Soren looked at peace. Clarin lifted a hand in farewell.

Belwynn turned around and left them behind.

* * *

THERE WERE FOUR OF THEM. Gyrmund noticed their swords. They weren't made of metal, but he couldn't put his finger on what they *were* made of. In fact, they were different colours. Two of them had swords which looked more like clear glass. Another was yellowish, another light blue. Crystal. They were made out of some kind of crystal.

The Isharites advanced further.

'Now!' shouted Herin.

They drew back their strings and let fire. Both hit their mark. One of them went down and did not get up. The three that remained ran at them. Gyrmund discarded his bow and drew his sword.

Clarin charged at them, supported by Moneva. Gyrmund and Herin followed close behind. They backed away from Clarin's lunge, but two then moved in on him, lashing in simultaneous blows. He blocked them both, on sword and shield, but was forced to back away.

The third took on Moneva. He avoided her first blow and met her second with his yellow crystal sword. He smashed her sword out of her hand and moved in for the kill.

Gyrmund arrived just in time. The Isharite had to back off, and now faced both Gyrmund and Moneva, still grasping her second sword. He feinted towards Moneva and then launched a savage blow at Gyrmund. Gyrmund blocked it and they held for a while. The Isharite seemed stronger. He suddenly raked his sword down the length of Gyrmund's blade towards his hands. Gyrmund pulled away.

Moneva lashed in with her sword held in both hands, but her blow was sidestepped. The Isharite moved straight into the path of a blow from Clarin. It was too late for him to change his momentum, and Clarin's sword entered his chest and came out the other side. The big man yanked his weapon free. He and Herin had dealt with the other two. They backed up towards the door of the Temple.

Gyrmund looked up at the fight in the central square. There were only three Caladri soldiers left. They were being pressed backwards and were moving towards the Temenos, backing up one pace at a time while trying to keep in touch with each other.

The pikes were swung wickedly around their heads. The length of the pole and speed and power they generated kept the Isharites at a distance. One of the Isharite attackers got too close and the passing blade sliced open his neck. Gyrmund saw him stagger back and put his hand to the wound. Then he collapsed to the ground.

Ultimately, however, the fight was not even. One of the Isharites blocked a swinging pike and three others pounced in, making quick work of the soldier once inside the pike's arc. Another Isharite launched a blast of magic at a soldier's feet at the same moment he swung his pike. He toppled over forwards and was quickly finished. One soldier remained. He backed up closer and closer towards the Temenos. Arioc and his men drew closer, crystal swords in hand. Gyrmund dropped his sword to the floor and picked up his bow. Moneva handed him an arrow. He notched it onto the string.

* * *

BELWYNN and the others put their faith in Elana, hoping that she knew where she was going. She raced along the corridor from the entrance chamber. The Temple was deserted and eerily quiet. When they got to the end of the corridor they passed through another door. They found themselves in what must have been the central place of worship. It was a circular room with seats, capable of holding about two hundred people, facing the centre. Here there was a dais, from where ceremonies could be conducted. The treated wood with which the Caladri had built the Temple shimmered brightly, illuminated by the sun shining in through glass skylights in the roof.

They stopped. Elana stood by the dais, still and silent. Belwynn wanted to ask her how she knew where she was going, but the priestess seemed to be concentrating. She swung to her right and moved to the far end of the chamber. Another door was opened, and Belwynn found herself chasing Elana down a second corridor.

The end of the corridor opened up into a small circular antechamber. Inside, a woman's body lay face down on the floor. Rabigar knelt down and gently rolled it onto its back. It was Dorottya, the elder who had greeted them at the Temenos. There were no obvious signs of physical injury. Rabigar put a hand to her neck, checking for a pulse.

'She's dead.'

Belwynn looked around nervously. Wooden shelves, from floor to ceiling, lined the wall. Most were filled with objects: metal chalices stood next to wooden bowls; jewelled rings and decorated knives shone out in greeting.

'It's here somewhere?' hissed Belwynn.

Elana nodded, but seemed unsure.

'Looking for something?'

A voice behind them.

Belwynn whirled round. Standing in the corridor was Pentas, the wizard who had joined them on the Great Road and who had fought with Nexodore.

In one hand he held a staff.

His red eyes surveyed them, inscrutable.

Belwynn looked from Pentas to the body of Dorottya on the floor.

'We had an argument,' he explained. 'Unfortunate,' he added.

Rabigar took a step to stand between Pentas and the others, sword in hand. Pentas took a step back and held out one hand.

'I'm not here to kill you or take the dagger you have in your possession. You must know I could if I wanted to,' he added, studying them again with a light smile. 'I am wondering, in fact, whether I owe any of you a word of gratitude. Last time we met, you will recall, I ended up in a fight with the dread Nexodore. I came off second best in the end, found myself trapped underground by one of his spells. Thought I might live out my days buried alive. Then, all of a sudden, I was able to break free. I assumed, at first, that I would be too late, that Nexodore would have found you and killed you. But he didn't?'

'Dirk killed him,' said Elana after a pause.

'Then thank you for saving my life. I will now return the favour. Arioc is outside. We can't let him get his hands on either of these weapons. I'm going to teleport you away. If you help me rather than resist, the easier it will be for all of us.'

A riot of thoughts swirled around Belwynn's head all at once. Could they trust this wizard? Did they have a choice? Who was he? But one thought shone through clearest of all.

'Soren and the others. They are at the Temple entrance. They need your help.'

'Very well. I will do what needs to be done. The quicker we do this, the sooner I can get to the others. Here,' he said, passing Belwynn the staff, which she reluctantly took. It was an ordinary enough piece of wood to her, with some runes carved into the side that were similar to those on Toric's Dagger. 'You can look after this for now.'

Belwynn nodded in compliance.

We've found it, she said to Soren.

Good. Don't come back this way, came her brother's quick reply. *Find another way out.*

Pentas got them to link hands. Then it happened again. A swirling feeling in the pit of her stomach, the senses dissolving away, and Belwynn was moving.

* * *

GYRMUND WITNESSED the fall of the last Caladri defender of Edeleny, surrounded and brought down by the Isharite attackers. Herin told everyone to retreat into the Temple. If they took their stand inside, the Isharites couldn't surround them and would have to force their way in through the small opening.

Of course, that was without adding magic into the equation. The Isharites approached. Gyrmund could see them gather outside. Then one of the wizards sent a blast of magic towards the door. Gyrmund grabbed at Moneva to shield her, but a sudden burst of white light in front of the door blocked the attack.

Soren. Gyrmund had no idea what had happened up in the Temenos. He hadn't liked it one bit. But obviously the result was that Soren had his powers back.

Soren put a shield up in front of the door, made up of the same bright white light.

'Get into the Temple and find the others,' he said. 'They've got the staff. I'll hold this for as long as I can.'

But it was no longer. The white shield was exploded away. Then Soren buckled over, crying out in pain. He seemed to be gripped by some magic. He whined in pain and sank to his knees, head on the floor. A couple of figures approached the doorway. A wizard was concentrating on Soren, holding him down. Next to him stood Arioc, sword in hand. He peered in.

'Well, well,' he said, looking from the dead bodies of his soldiers lying on the floor to the group huddled in the doorway. 'I didn't expect to find this. I have strict instructions from Lord Erkindrix to kill every Caladri I find. But he didn't say anything about humans.'

He put on a puzzled face, in mock consideration of the situation. Herin was standing on one side of the door. Gyrmund saw him gripping the hilt tight as if ready to take a swing. If he did, Gyrmund was sure they would all be dead in an instant.

'I'll tell you what,' said Arioc, apparently enjoying the confrontation so much that he gave a smile. 'You surrender now, lay down your arms and I will spare your lives. And his,' he said, gesturing towards Soren who was still pinned to the floor.

They weren't going to win this fight. But did they really want to be captured? Gyrmund's thoughts went back to Coldeberg, the cell in the dungeon, the feeling of helplessness. He looked at Herin, who was no doubt thinking the same way.

Arioc looked around at them, a smile still playing on his face. His eyes finally rested on Herin's.

'Well? What's it to be?'

Herin stood, still gripping his sword. *My life is in his hands,* thought Gyrmund. *There's a very good chance I'm about to die.*

He felt strangely calm.

Herin dropped the sword onto the floor with a clang. Clarin and Moneva followed his lead.

'Surrender,' said Herin.

* * *

Belwynn opened her eyes. She was in a rocky clearing. Nearby, Elana and Rabigar muttered to one another as they knelt over Dirk's prone form.

She forced herself to her feet, legs wobbly, stomach churning, using the wooden staff for support. So, Pentas had done what he'd promised. She looked around her: the clearing was surrounded by grassy vegetation and trees. Where he'd teleported them to, she had no idea.

Belwynn waited, as Elana and Rabigar got Dirk awake and alert enough to drink something. She waited for her brother to come. She waited for Clarin, Herin, Gyrmund and Moneva.

Soren, she said, waiting for him to respond.

But Soren and her friends didn't come. Eventually, Belwynn realised they never would.

Soren, she said. *If you're alive, I'll find you. Wherever you are, I'll find you.*

BOLIVAR'S SWORD

BOOK TWO OF THE WEAPON TAKERS SAGA

For Mum

PROLOGUE

Siavash paused outside the private chambers of Lord Erkindrix, a thrill of anticipation coursing through his body.

To be invited here was a rare honour, even for him. Ordinarily, Erkindrix only held meetings in his Throne Room, or the Council Chamber. The private chambers were only accessed by those servants who tended to his physical needs. They were nameless, nugatory creatures, who no doubt saw him at his most vulnerable and repulsive. Siavash didn't dwell on that.

No. Siavash, High Priest of the Order of Diis, member of the Council of Seven, didn't thrill at the thought of sharing an enclosed space with Erkindrix and his decaying, putrid body. He craved proximity with a God. For Diis himself, the mightiest deity of all, inhabited the body of Erkindrix. His eyes rolled beneath the Lord of Ishari's. His words could, at times, be heard through the reedy voice of his vessel.

Siavash entered the room. The stink of Erkindrix knifed through the cloying perfumes which were used to mask it. The Lord of Ishari lay prone on his bed. He had yet to regain strength enough to stand since the attack on Edeleny. Ishari had won a great victory against the Grand Caladri, but at a price. Scores of their magi lay dead, scores more had been pushed into madness by the confrontation.

'What news?' asked Erkindrix through a gargle of saliva.

Siavash approached the bed. He felt the presence of Diis—powerful, malevolent. It was as if his God, crushed inside the tiny, wizened frame of an old man, cast a shadow the size of a mountain. Siavash felt the primeval fear of encountering such a being; he felt the ecstasy of proximity to such power. Instinctively, he dropped to his knees.

'Most of the lands of the Caladri are being taken with no resistance. The only exception is to the south, where a faction has organised a military defence, supported by some surviving magi. It is not a significant threat, but they are using the terrain to their advantage.'

'Good.'

Siavash prepared to deliver the bad news. He would enjoy the telling, but he had to be careful not to let Erkindrix see it. The Lord of Ishari's relationship with Arioc was a close one, and Siavash knew that he always had to tread carefully on such territory.

'Unfortunately, when our forces reached Onella's Temple, Her Staff was missing.'

'Missing?' Erkindrix spluttered.

'I should say, taken. It is unclear by whom, or where. But King Arioc has captured some prisoners whom he believes can reveal that information.'

'Inept,' Erkindrix barked, 'to allow such a thing.'

Siavash smiled inwardly.

'What other news?'

'Queen Shira's force has crossed into the Empire. Given her victory over the Rotelegen army, she should not take long to complete the conquest.'

Calling Arioc's bitch a Queen never fails to stick in my throat, he added to himself.

Erkindrix grunted. With what looked like some effort, he pushed himself up into a sitting position. 'The weapons,' he hissed. 'The threat from these weapons should not be underestimated. Nexodore has failed to deliver them. Now Arioc fails me.'

Siavash almost volunteered. To gain these weapons would be a trifling task and yet give him success where the dread Nexodore and Arioc had both failed. But to leave Samir Durg, to leave his Master and his God, when he enjoyed such unrivalled proximity; that could be a dangerous mistake.

'Send Pentas,' said Erkindrix. 'He must retrieve them.'

Siavash's lip curled up into a sneer at the mention of the name.

'What?' demanded Erkindrix.

'A human? He can't be trusted with such a task,' he replied with distaste.

'Then who?'

Me? No. I must play a cautious game. My place is here, at the centre; at the very heart of power.

'You are right, My Lord. I will instruct Pentas. I will make sure that he understands the importance of these weapons.'

STRANGERS

I

The light of morning forced Belwynn to open her eyes. Her mind gradually returned the events of yesterday to her consciousness. Splitting up from her brother Soren and the others, Belwynn had joined Elana, Dirk and Rabigar in a search for Onella's Staff. They had found it in the Temple, Elana seemingly guided to its location. The wizard Pentas had then teleported them away from danger. They had travelled a long distance under his spell, and once they had stopped, felt exhausted and ill. They had fallen asleep pretty much where Pentas' magic had dropped them, too tired to prepare a fire or even to eat a cold supper.

Belwynn pushed herself up into a sitting position, rubbing her head, which banged with pain. She looked around. Pentas had dropped them halfway up a hill. The trees which had surrounded them in the forest of the Grand Caladri were sparser here, while the ground beneath them was rocky; large chunks of stone littered the landscape about them.

Elana and Dirk were still asleep a few yards away. Rabigar wasn't there. Belwynn supposed he had gone to collect firewood or search for food. Her stomach grumbled at the thought.

So, Soren and the others had not made it. Perhaps Pentas had failed to reach them in time? They could be dead. A feeling of dread stabbed at Belwynn's insides. She tried to reach her brother.

Soren. Soren?

A few moments of silence passed, but then there was a response.

Belwynn? Is that you?

It was Soren, and he was alive. It was difficult to pick up what he was saying, though. There was some kind of interference—more than the distance that separated them.

Yes, it's me, Belwynn replied. *Where are you?*

Captured...must be careful. We defended the entrance to the Temple, but Arioc himself came for us. We're all alive, but they caught us. They're taking us north, to Ishari or Haskany. They've got wizards monitoring me...must be careful.

There was a pause. Soren's voice was thin, and Belwynn's ability to pick up what he was saying varied, as if he were putting his hand over his mouth and taking it away again. Belwynn had experienced something similar once before, when her brother was with Delyth, the marsh witch.

Where are you? Soren continued. *Did you get the staff?*

Yes, we've got it. Pentas, the wizard with the red eyes, found us in the Temple. He told us we had to escape. He teleported us away. I don't know where we are, but we're safe. He said he would look for you.

Thank Toric you're safe. It must have been too late for him to get to us. You must get the weapons to safety. Contact me again tomorrow when you've found out where you are. But we'll have to keep it brief. It's dangerous. Goodbye Belwynn.

Bye Soren, Belwynn answered.

She wanted to cry. Her brother and the others had been captured by Arioc and the Isharites. There was no way of knowing what would happen to them and she had no way to help—she didn't even know where she was. She suddenly felt tired and alone. Gripping her head in her hands, she wiped away a tear with her palm. She had to control herself. *She* was in charge now. She would have to be strong.

A noise to her left made her turn sharply. It was Rabigar. He marched over and opened his arms, a pile of tree branches dropping on to the floor. He yanked at his belt and held up a brace of squirrels.

'Breakfast,' he declared.

Belwynn forced a smile. 'Thank you, Rabigar. I've just spoken to Soren. He and the others were captured by Arioc. He said that they're all alive and being transported northwards.'

Rabigar nodded. 'I think that's about the best we could hope for. If they're being transported north, it means that Arioc wants them alive. He would have killed them otherwise. I'm sorry if that's not much comfort.'

'No, it's fine. I know it could have been much worse. It's just that the prospect of rescuing them is so daunting—we don't even know where we are!'

'Not entirely true,' replied Rabigar. 'I got a clear look at the stars last night.

Pentas sent us in a north-westerly direction. I reckon we're on the border between the Grand Caladri and Kalinth. Now, we'll have to be careful. By all accounts, the King of Kalinth is nothing more than a puppet of Erkindrix these days. But we're not far from my homeland. If we make it there, the weapons will be safe. Then we can work out what to do about your brother and the others.'

That Rabigar had a plan, even if somewhat vague, was something for Belwynn to hang on to for now. He was taking the initiative, and Belwynn was grateful for that.

'First things first, though,' Rabigar continued. 'We'll get breakfast ready and try to wake those two up.'

THEY DID NOT GET FAR that day. The exhaustion caused by the events in Edeleny had not left their bodies. Dirk, in particular, was not well. He walked on in grim silence, as if all his concentration and energy were needed just to put one foot in front of the other. Belwynn gave him Onella's Staff to lean on across the difficult terrain. Although Rabigar seemed to think that they were in Kalinth, the landscape in this region seemed to be a combination of the forests of the Grand Caladri and the hilly country of the Krykkers. When Belwynn complained about this, Rabigar would point to the distant mountains to the south-west and claim that *they* were real hills, not these. Occasionally, when they crested a hill, they would get a glimpse of the Plain of Kalinth stretching away to the north, and though Belwynn disagreed with the Krykker that such a view made the climb worthwhile, she had to admit that it was a fine sight.

What they really missed were horses. On various mounts, they had travelled over half the length of Dalriya in the past two weeks. By comparison, walking pace seemed slow and laborious. Belwynn suspected they had barely covered ten miles when they stopped to make their camp for the night.

When she woke the next morning, Rabigar had again been the first up. A small fire was already burning and chestnuts were cooking.

'Are those edible?' asked Belwynn suspiciously.

'Yes. Sweet chestnuts. Horse chestnuts are the poisonous ones. Here,' he said, pointing at them. 'They have a little tail on the bottom. That's how you tell you've got the right kind.'

He sounded more than a little pleased with himself.

'I've been thinking about our position,' Rabigar informed her as she sat up. 'There is a trading town called Korkis. It should be about five miles west of here. I know it well. It sees trade between Kalinth, the Krykkers, and the Grand Caladri. We could do with picking up some supplies and utensils. If I'm right, we should get there by lunchtime.'

Belwynn nodded. She was happy for Rabigar to make the decisions for now. Last night, she and Soren had a very brief conversation, partly because he was worried they would be caught; partly because neither had anything new to say. Her brother and her friends were still being transported north. Part of her wanted to turn around and follow, but Soren insisted she find a secure place for the two weapons before she did anything else.

'Then what?' she asked Rabigar, leaning over to the fire to inspect breakfast.

He pointed out a couple. 'When the shell splits, they're ready.'

Belwynn grabbed one. It was hot, too hot for her fingers, and she juggled it around in the air before letting it drop into her lap. She sucked on her fingers to cool them down. Rabigar looked on with a disappointed expression on his face.

'Then we head south-west for my homeland. I don't know what kind of reception I will get. But at the very least, they will keep the Dagger and Staff safe. They may do more to help.'

He paused, studying her face, as if unsure whether to continue. 'I've mentioned this to Elana already. The Krykkers have another of these weapons. In our Great Meeting Chamber, in the mountain of Kerejus. Bolivar's Great Sword, which he used in the Battle of Alta.'

Belwynn nodded. She wondered why Rabigar hadn't mentioned this before. She could tell that a part of him still had a loyalty towards his people, despite his years of exile. No doubt this sword was a great treasure.

'How many years is it since you left?' she asked.

Rabigar seemed to think about it.

'Thirty. And then some.'

'Do you ever miss it?'

'I will always miss my home.'

It was said with such feeling that it stopped Belwynn from asking her next question. *Why* was he exiled? But Rabigar knew her thoughts.

'You're curious to know what happened?' he asked her.

She shrugged. 'A little.'

'I will not tell you, Belwynn. It is no disrespect to you: it is a question of honour to me. It is a matter for my people only—not a story to be discussed by others. I have kept it to myself for all these thirty and more years. That is a long time. But I would have you understand one thing. I was a very different man then than I am now.'

His gaze drifted to the mountains of his homeland and a faraway look came to his face.

WHEN ELANA and Dirk were ready, they set off for the town of Korkis. They walked mostly in silence, everyone in their own thoughts. For Belwynn, though, the morning walk made her feel lonely. She missed her brother. But she also missed the sharp asides of Herin, and Clarin's calm, protective presence. She had come to value her three current companions, but was not close to any one of them. Belwynn dwelt on her captured friends. She wanted to talk with Soren again, but since it could be dangerous for him, she resisted.

It was a long morning, made worse by grey clouds that blew in and deposited a constant drizzle; but by midday they were on a path heading towards Korkis. The town had been built on top of a hill, and as they got closer, they could make out a wooden palisade encircling it. As they made their way up, Belwynn could make out the individual wooden stakes, buried into the ground and sharpened at the tip to make an effective barrier against an attacking force. The entrance to the town was through a formidable looking wooden gate, perhaps fifteen feet high, from where defenders could fire down at the enemy.

Today, the gate was wide open and there was a single guard on duty, who looked out at their approach with a lazy expression.

'We're here to buy some basic provisions,' Rabigar shouted up.

The guard simply waved a hand to let them through, seemingly more than used to strangers arriving.

Once through the gate, there was an open plaza. A log built road led straight ahead towards the centre of town. Wooden built shops and stalls were positioned on either side. A statue of a knight on horseback marked the central square. It was midday and the town was busy.

'The number of people here makes it safer for us,' said Rabigar, speaking under his breath as the four of them mingled with the crowd. 'But there's no point in staying any longer than we have to. I'll get the cooking utensils, clothes and any other extras we need if you three get the food. We'll meet up by the statue.'

Belwynn, Elana and Dirk soon found that oats were the most plentiful crop in this region. However, prices were still high, and Belwynn noticed that several shoppers in Korkis looked hungry, prepared to buy damp bags of oats or old, shrivelled looking vegetables that in happier times wouldn't have been sold in the first place. As they moved from stall to stall, Belwynn picked up on the problems the merchants were encountering: trade from Haskany and Persala had all but dried up since Ishari had taken control; the produce which did arrive was mostly smuggled out. Very little arrived over the mountain routes from the Krykkers, while nothing came in from the Grand Caladri at all. There were even problems within Kalinth. A dispute between King Jonas and the Knights of Kalinth, along with rumours of Drobax raids, discouraged people from travelling too far.

After surveying the choice that was available, they agreed on what to buy. Oats could form the basis of a gruel, quick to prepare and full of energy, if rather dull to eat. They were able to supplement this with beans and vegetables, especially cabbage. Several stalls sold pickled cabbage in clay jars, which would stay edible for weeks.

They found themselves fully supplied with food and waiting by the statue for Rabigar to return with the more complicated items. Armed guards walked about in twos and threes, dressed in brown leather with a spear and shield motif sewn on to their front jackets. Belwynn noticed how the people in the town shuffled out of the way at their approach and tried to avoid eye contact. The guards would sometimes stop off at a stall to help themselves to some of the food, while the stallholders looked away as if they hadn't noticed. All in all, there was an unsettling atmosphere in the town. It seemed to Belwynn that with less to go round, the bullies of the community were making sure that they didn't go hungry. Elana and Dirk seemed to sense it, too. They were both silent and huddled down by the statue, as if the smaller they made themselves, the less they would be noticed.

Suddenly there was a disturbance a few stalls away from where Belwynn was standing. A young child was struggling in the grasp of a stall-holder. Peering over, Belwynn could see that it was a girl with close-cropped hair, perhaps about the age of seven. She was thin and hungry looking, but still seemed to think that she had a chance of escaping from her captor.

'Caught her trying to nick a loaf,' the stall-holder was saying to the surrounding crowd.

A couple of guardsmen appeared at the scene. One of them held out a hand. The baker wordlessly passed the child over. The guard gripped her wrist hard. She continued to struggle, but the guard struck her across the face with the outside of a gloved hand. The girl stopped struggling and now had tears in her eyes, looking around with a fearful expression.

'We know how to deal with thieves,' said the guard in a voice designed to carry across the crowd, which had now stopped what it was doing to look.

Belwynn had seen and heard enough. She didn't think through her actions. Some part of her mind propelled her body towards the confrontation in the street. As she approached their space, the group turned to look at her. The baker frowned at her. The young girl looked up nervously. The two guards stared, stony-faced.

'I will pay for her bread,' suggested Belwynn reasonably. 'I don't think she's a thief. Just a hungry child.'

Almost as the last syllable left her mouth, the rest of Belwynn's brain caught up with her actions. This was not clever. The second guard hefted a long spear, pointing the metal end in her direction.

'We don't have strangers coming here telling us what to do. We have town laws to respect.'

Some in the crowd murmured their agreement. The guard, perhaps emboldened by this, gestured at Belwynn's waist where her sword was belted. 'Drop your sword to the ground. You're under arrest.'

Belwynn expected no justice from these men.

'No,' she said. Instead, she drew it out, stepping back slightly to give herself room for a swing.

At this gesture, there was a sudden rush of movement and noise. The stall-holders and shoppers moved away from the confrontation, some gasping in shock at the turn of events. At the same time, two groups moved to join them. Three guards who had also been patrolling the centre of town moved over to support the first two. Meanwhile, Dirk and Elana moved over to join Belwynn. Dirk looked ill, but at least he carried a short sword. Elana had no weapon at all.

'Back off,' said Dirk in a cool voice.

The guardsmen smiled, their dirty teeth bared in delight at the sudden sport they were being given. All five now had weapons out, two of them holding spears with a reach far greater than the swords held by Elana and Dirk. They moved towards Belwynn.

'Kill them,' shouted one guard, his eyes staring at Belwynn.

'Try to leave the women alive!' suggested another, to the laughs of his comrades.

They did not take the threat from Belwynn and Dirk seriously, and why should they? Belwynn might show them she knew how to fight. Dirk could probably draw on his last reserves of strength if he had to. But they were outnumbered by bigger and stronger men. Belwynn wished that Elana and

Dirk hadn't come over to help. They would have been more use staying out of the fight. At least, she thought to herself, the little girl had been forgotten. Belwynn could not see her anywhere. No doubt she had slipped away by now.

Belwynn held her sword out in front of her and edged backwards. Behind her, Dirk and Elana also retreated. The guardsmen fanned out so that they could attack from the sides. Someone came at her from behind and to the right—another guardsman sneaking up on them?

'Rabigar is here,' said Elana.

Belwynn was glad she did, because she had just begun to take a swing at the Krykker.

'Don't worry,' he whispered as he walked by.

Rabigar put himself in-between Belwynn and the guardsmen. His sword was in one hand.

'We're leaving,' he informed them in a matter-of-fact voice. 'Let us go and there will be no bloodshed.'

The guardsmen sniggered.

'We want bloodshed,' said one of them. 'Yours.'

To the guards, Rabigar's arrival didn't change their superiority and control of the situation. Rabigar's eye patch perhaps seemed to suggest he was no real threat to these soldiers. But Belwynn knew better. They might have a chance now.

Rabigar was moving at some speed towards the guardsman who had shouted out.

'You want my blood?' he shouted, almost roaring a challenge.

Rabigar reached the guard before the others could react. Once in range, the guard let out a roar of his own and swung a club in a descending arc towards the Krykker's chest. Rabigar blocked the strike up high and then spun into the remaining space. In the same motion, he swung his blade up into the undefended neck of the guard, the sharpened point slicing through the jugular vein. As Rabigar retreated, he was sprayed by a squirt of blood, the guard sinking to his knees before toppling over. Screams erupted all around them, as the crowds which had been watching the confrontation turned and fled. The four remaining guardsmen suddenly looked worried. Rabigar turned around.

'Dirk, you lead us towards the far end of town. I know a way out. Belwynn, we're walking backwards to put off anyone from following. Elana, you're guiding our steps. Let's go, as quick as we can.'

PURSUIT

II

Belwynn knew how lucky she was that Rabigar knew an alternative exit from Korkis. The trading town was in chaos after the confrontation she had started in the central square, but its soldiers were organised enough to close the gates to prevent an escape.

Rabigar led Belwynn, Elana and Dirk through a maze of side streets. Following them all the way were two of the town guards. They were wary enough of Rabigar not to challenge them directly, but they made sure not to let them out of their sight. Doubtless, they planned to corner them until reinforcements arrived.

The guards hadn't bargained on Rabigar's knowledge of the town.

They arrived in an alley. Rabigar led them on, but they soon stopped at a dead end. Ahead of them were the wooden stakes of the town walls, driven in too deep to lift out with any ease. The two guards stood at the top of the alley, holding their prey in, but reluctant to move any further. One of them began shouting out their location to anyone who would listen. It wouldn't be long before they attracted the right attention.

Rabigar approached the wall. He kicked at it. A section swung open. It was attached with hinges to the rest of the wall, effectively opening as a gate with a space large enough for one person to fit through. It had been constructed well, invisible except to those who knew to look for it.

Rabigar stepped one foot over onto the grassy hill outside the town wall. 'I'm glad that's still there,' he grinned. He turned around and climbed right through. Belwynn, Elana and Dirk quickly followed, and they were all outside by the time the two guards reached the gate themselves.

Rabigar led them away from the town, making for a wooded area about a mile to the north. For a moment Belwynn thought they were safe, but the guards were not giving up so easily. Korkis seemed to be an independent and military minded town. The soldiers were not about to let them escape unpunished. The two guards had soon attracted the attention of their colleagues manning the northern gate tower, to the west of the postern gate. By the time Belwynn and the others had reached the outskirts of the wooded cover, Rabigar was leading them to, a force of about a dozen soldiers had set out from the town to chase them down. There was no doubt that the men of Korkis could see them.

When they entered the tree line, Belwynn glanced back once more. A single rider had now joined the men on foot. He could eat up the distance between them and ensure that the soldiers wouldn't lose their quarry. She shared a glance with Rabigar.

'I think they've got a couple of dogs as well,' he said, his head cocked upwards, suggesting he had heard rather than seen their presence.

They pressed on into the wood. It felt a little safer once they were out of sight from the soldiers, but Belwynn knew that their pursuers would have no problems following their trail.

Rabigar looked upwards. 'Less than two hours until it gets dark. Then they'll have to stop. A night out in the cold might persuade them to give up the chase. We've got to keep going.'

Dirk and Elana nodded in agreement at his words, but they didn't seem reassured by them.

Belwynn felt terrible that they were in this position because of her actions. 'I'm sorry,' she said. 'If I had just kept out of it, we wouldn't be in this mess. It was stupid.'

'No-one blames you,' said Elana, gripping her shoulder. 'You acted bravely, for that young girl.'

'Maybe, but there are more important things. I should have been thinking about the weapons, about Soren—'

'No,' said Elana. 'You did the right thing.'

Elana sounded like she meant what she said. It made Belwynn feel better.

It wasn't long afterwards that they heard the barking of dogs behind them, indicating that their trail was discovered, and their pursuers had entered the woods. They were travelling as fast as they could, but Dirk was still unwell and they had been walking almost all day. The soldiers would be stronger and faster. They had to make it to nightfall.

They marched on, Rabigar trying to find a passable route through the trees. The sound of the soldiers and the dogs behind spurred them on. Rather than following directly behind them, they seemed to have fanned out to the left.

'Cutting us off from the deeper part of the wood,' said Rabigar grimly in explanation.

Belwynn gave him a worried look.

He shrugged his shoulders as if it didn't matter. 'They want to push us out into open ground. If they want to waste time doing that, it's fine by me.'

Gradually, but inevitably, they were getting closer. An hour passed in this way, Belwynn and the others trying to maintain the ever-diminishing gap which would keep them safe. Meanwhile, the Korkis soldiers continued to herd them in a north-easterly direction. The sun moved lower and lower in the sky and the light began to go. Soon it would disappear altogether and they would have to stop.

Belwynn heard a horse's hooves behind them. She turned around, grabbing the hilt of her sword. The horseman from Korkis was a hundred yards behind them. He had moved ahead of his other comrades and was alone. Rabigar moved towards him, sword in hand, to stand in front of the others.

The horseman moved closer and then stopped, eyeing up his opposition. He was a young man, perhaps just into his twenties. He drew a sword from his belt.

'I've found you,' he said, smiling at the idea. 'The others aren't far behind. Turn yourselves in now.'

'Why?' asked Rabigar. 'Scared of spending the night out in the woods?'

'You're the one who should be scared,' the soldier retorted hotly. 'Give up now, or I'll finish you off myself!'

'Go ahead and try,' replied Rabigar calmly. 'I could do with that horse after I slit your throat.'

Rabigar's bravado seemed to pay off. The soldier looked at him uneasily. He did not seem entirely comfortable on the horse and may have heard that Rabigar was a dangerous opponent.

'Maybe I'll just wait here for the others,' said the soldier. He cupped his hands to his mouth. 'Over here,' he shouted.

A surge of panic ran through Belwynn's body.

'We're going,' said Rabigar, maintaining his steady voice. 'Belwynn, you lead the way. I'll stay behind in case he tries anything,' he said.

Belwynn nodded. She led them off in the same direction they had been going. Elana and Dirk followed behind while Rabigar brought up the rear, his one eye on the mounted soldier. After a while, the soldier urged his horse on and followed behind, all the time keeping a safe distance from Rabigar. Every now and again, he would shout out to the other soldiers, who would shout back. These new tactics were certainly scaring her, but Belwynn realised they were using them in desperation. There was little light left and the other soldiers were too far away to reach them tonight.

Another half an hour passed. Then Rabigar suddenly turned and ran at the soldier who had been following them, his sword ready to strike. For a moment, the soldier seemed unsure whether to take on the Krykker or retreat. He decided on the latter, turning his horse around and giving it a hurried kick, urging it away. Rabigar stopped and let him go. Once a safe distance away again, the soldier turned around in his saddle.

'See you in the morning,' he crowed, before continuing until out of sight.

Rabigar made them carry on walking until he was sure that their pursuers had stopped for the night. He threw his bag down on the floor, making a jingling sound as his new cookery items hit the ground.

'Well, I'm not going to cook *now*,' said Rabigar. 'I don't know whether to leave these things behind in the morning. How did you three get on with food?' he asked.

'We have little that tastes good raw,' replied Dirk. 'Dried oats, vegetables...'

'Get that pickled cabbage out,' suggested Belwynn. 'It will taste alright and then we can leave the jars behind.'

Belwynn forced herself to eat the food so that she would have enough energy for tomorrow. She could hear noise from the other camp, less than a mile away, and it set her on edge. For all they knew, there could be soldiers out in the trees right now, watching them.

Rabigar insisted that the other three get to sleep and that he would keep watch all night.

Belwynn was too tired to argue. She considered contacting Soren. But what could she say, except to blurt out the danger they were in? That wouldn't help them one bit, and it would only add to her brother's worries.

She lay down, desperate for rest. But her mind was reeling and couldn't switch off, and the hard ground was uncomfortable. She wept then, silent tears of frustration at the events of the last few days.

Elana appeared next to her. Without saying a word, the priestess put her hands to her shoulders, then to her neck, and on to the top of her head. Belwynn lay still. She felt her body let go of some of its tension.

'Is this magic?' she asked drowsily. She had witnessed Elana's healing abilities more than once over the last few weeks; not least on Dirk, as he lay close to death in the lands of the Blood Caladri. He had killed the dread sorcerer Nexodore with Toric's Dagger, though had paid a heavy price for it with internal damage that not even Elana could fully heal. But Belwynn had never seen Elana use her powers for something as trivial as this. 'I have no injury that needs to be healed,' she added.

Her question went unanswered, and she drifted into sleep.

Rabigar woke them while it was still dark. Belwynn still felt exhausted, and her muscles ached, but within minutes she was ready to go. They agreed to leave their non-essential items at the camp, so that they did not have to carry them.

Rabigar left his new pots and pans. 'Maybe they'll be happy when they pick this lot up and forget about us.'

Belwynn doubted that. They were only a matter of minutes behind them, and the mounted soldier knew exactly where they were.

They headed north, scraping their way through the trees in the dark. By sunrise, the force from Korkis was after them again. They soon heard the barking of the dogs to the west, and again Rabigar was forced to head eastwards to evade them. Belwynn couldn't help wondering whether Gyrmund would have been able to get them out of this situation. The tracker had led them through the Wilderness, with its dangerous vossi inhabitants. Rabigar was doing the best he could, but the men from Korkis were gaining on them.

As they moved further east, the trees became more and more sparse. They had reached the plain of Kalinth. No more woodland to hide in, just rolling open countryside.

They had no choice but to press on, despite feeling more exposed. It seemed to be mainly sheep country in this area. They marched uphill through a field covered in sheep dung. They reached a thick hedge which stretched away in either direction as far as the eye could see. Rabigar heaved himself over a gate into the next field. The sound of shouting reached them from the direction of the woodland. They had been spotted. There were still about a dozen soldiers, just emerging from the trees. One of them had two hounds held on leashes. His arm was out in front as they pulled. The horseman who had found them the previous evening accompanied them. They waved their weapons in the air in triumph at seeing their quarry.

Belwynn bolted over the gate. Elana and Dirk quickly followed. Rabigar looked around. There was nowhere to hide. He took them in the same direction, gently rising uphill in an easterly direction, perhaps hoping there would be some rescue for them on the other side.

They reached the crest of the hill, which gave them something of a vantage point. The woodland lay to the west of them. To the south and east was more grassland, divided up by the local farmers with hedges or stone walls. Some had sheep in, most lay empty. Some distance to the east, Belwynn could make out a set of buildings which was probably a farmstead, but it was too far to reach in time. To the north, the plains briefly dipped low, before rising again to a point slightly higher than their own. Behind them, the soldiers from Korkis had almost reached the gate into their field. They were close now.

Rabigar pointed north. 'This way,' he said.

Belwynn almost refused. She was tired and scared, and Rabigar was dragging them onwards with no hope of escape. Elana and Dirk wordlessly followed him, and Belwynn found herself doing the same.

They jogged, taking advantage of the downward slope and trying to put some distance between themselves and the soldiers. A series of shouts and whoops rose behind them. As she ran, Belwynn could now make out some of the words shouted at them. She heard the phrase 'slit your throat,' more than once, but most frightening was the excited barking of the two dogs.

They reached the bottom of the hill and began moving uphill again, slowing to a tired walk. Belwynn used the staff she carried to push herself along. She heard a noise behind her and knew it must be the horseman again. She turned around to see him approach them at a gentle canter. She drew her sword but kept on walking.

'Where are you going?' he laughed at them cruelly. 'There's nowhere to hide here.'

The only answer he got was the panting of breath as Belwynn and the others tried to push themselves up the hill. Dirk was slowing alarmingly. He stopped to cough. It wracked his body, and he gasped for breath which would not come. Belwynn thought he was going to collapse there and then, but Elana supported an elbow and the attack eventually passed. Dirk leaned over and whispered something to Elana, but she angrily refused and dragged him onwards.

The horseman came in close behind Belwynn, sword drawn. She was forced to stop and hold her sword in front of her to protect herself. A cheer went up from the soldiers behind them. Rabigar came back to stand next to her.

'Carry on, Belwynn,' he said, 'I'll keep them busy here for a while.'

'I may as well stay with you,' she answered.

'No,' said Rabigar, pushing her away.

Belwynn turned away, tears in her eyes. She looked up to where Elana and Dirk were still struggling. She saw something strange. Belwynn wiped the tears away from her eyes on her sleeve so that she could see more clearly. At the top of the hill sat two men. One was clearly a knight of Kalinth. He wore gleaming armour which sparkled in the sun and was dressed lavishly in sea blue with a gold trim. He rode a huge warhorse, decorated in the same colours. Next to him sat what must be his squire, riding a palfrey and dressed in simple brown leather. He was carrying two huge lances. Their presence somehow didn't seem real, like an out of place and bizarre addition to a nightmare that lets you know you are dreaming.

Belwynn gathered her senses. 'Help!' she cried up towards the knight in desperation, stumbling up towards him as she called out. 'We are being attacked! Please help us!'

The knight turned to his companion and said something, holding out his hand. The squire passed him a lance. It had a blue and gold flag attached, which snapped in the breeze. The knight kneaded his mount forwards, down the hill. He reached Elana and Dirk.

'Move on up, there,' Belwynn heard him say in a clear voice. 'My squire will look after you.'

The knight reached Belwynn. He wore no helmet, and looked at her with dark brown eyes, framed with mid-length, chestnut brown hair.

'Please help us!' implored Belwynn. He nodded to her. 'Please carry on up the hill, My Lady,' he said.

The knight rode on. Belwynn turned around. The horseman from Korkis sat open mouthed as the knight descended the hill, stopping next to Rabigar. But the soldiers from Korkis now arrived on the spot. They looked at the new intruder fiercely, in no mood to let him interrupt their sport.

'My name is Theron, Count of Erisina. What business goes on here?'

'These men are trying to kill us!' shouted Belwynn down the hill, knowing that she sounded hysterical, but unable to control herself.

'These four killed a man yesterday in Korkis,' one of the soldiers spoke up. 'We're placing them under arrest.'

'I killed a man in self-defence,' stated Rabigar calmly. 'There is no law or justice in Korkis,' he added.

'Liar! You're gonna pay, Krykker! And this dandy ain't gonna help you.'

The soldiers laughed roughly at the comment and began to edge forward.

'These are the lands of my uncle, Sebastian of Melion,' said Theron, his voice rising in anger. 'Not the lands of Korkis. He directs the law here. These four will face justice at *his* court. I am prepared to escort some of you there to put forward your case.'

'Put forward our case?' said a soldier in disbelief. 'We've tracked these for a day. They're gonna get their justice now. I suggest you get out of our fucking way!'

Theron wheeled his horse around. 'So be it,' he said over his shoulder and pushed his horse back up the hill.

Belwynn felt as if she had been physically struck. This knight had given her hope of an escape and had then ridden away. Rabigar backed up the hill towards her as the soldiers moved forwards, spreading out in a row with grins splitting their faces. There was less than a hundred meters between the group of soldiers and Rabigar and Belwynn, who were now standing side by side again.

The soldiers approached, but then stopped and looked past Belwynn and Rabigar up the hill. Belwynn heard a rumbling noise and turned to look behind her. Count Theron had not departed the scene, but had moved back up the hill in order to charge back down it at the enemy. He had gathered considerable pace and was heading directly for them, with one hand on the reins and the other gripping his lance, held up at ear level.

The soldiers from Korkis were unsure what to do. If Theron and his horse struck one of them, it would most likely be deadly, but surely then the rest of them could finish the knight off. They waved their weapons ahead of them, hoping to ward off the charging knight. Theron rode past Belwynn and Rabigar, now at some speed. His horse thundered forwards, and he locked onto an enemy. His aim was accurate, and the lance went straight for the chest of one of the soldiers. The target saw it coming, but was unable to get away in time. He twisted his body to one side, but the lance struck just below the armpit and embedded deep into his body. The momentum of the charge delivered a huge amount of power into the strike and sent the soldier spinning into the air as Theron let go of the lance.

Theron veered his mount to the right, avoiding the line of soldiers. He drew his sword and headed toward the mounted soldier who had followed and tormented Belwynn and the others. He was sitting positioned slightly apart from the rest of his comrades. Theron's mount sidestepped around the young soldier, who had gone pale with fear. Theron made several quick feints towards the soldier with his sword. He eventually got a response when the soldier swung his own sword out to block one of the feints. Theron pulled out of the way and then swung his sword back again, smacking the flat of the blade across the soldier's chest. The shock and impact of Theron's strike caused the soldier to lose his balance, and he toppled backwards off the horse, which bolted away.

The other soldiers of Korkis caught up with the combat. Theron dug his heels in and pushed his mount away with seconds to spare. Two soldiers tried to chase after him, but they soon looked absurd as Theron's horse pranced away from them, seemingly able to move in any direction. Theron moved back towards the top of the slope. The soldiers looked unsure about how they should cope with the manoeuvrability of this new enemy. Belwynn could hear them discussing what they should do about the knight. They had all but ignored Rabigar and herself, as they backed away up the slope to join Elana and Dirk.

Theron claimed the second lance from his squire. Meanwhile, the Korkis soldiers had decided on their approach. They marched up towards Theron in a closely packed line. The two soldiers who had been attacked by the knight remained sprawled on the ground behind them. As they drew closer, the dog handler released his two hounds, which both headed straight for Theron. They soon reached the knight and his mount. One of them kept a safe distance and barked at them, but the other moved in closer, trying to nip at the horse. Theron's mount leapt up on its hind legs and kicked out in front of it. The kick connected soundly with the hound, which went flying up in the air and landed in a heap. The second dog continued to bark, but did not seem willing to get any closer.

Theron made a second charge down the slope, his lance tucked under his right armpit. He charged straight at the centre of the group of soldiers, who stopped their march to defend themselves. Theron veered away at the last minute, to the left. He passed by the line of soldiers and buried his lance in the midriff of the soldier at the end of the line. There was a loud cracking sound at the moment of impact, and Theron rode on.

Dirk appeared at Belwynn's shoulder, accompanied by Theron's squire. He was just a boy, perhaps fifteen years old. But he had his sword drawn. The young squire motioned down the hill with his weapon.

'Let's give them something else to think about,' he suggested.

Belwynn turned her head to look at Rabigar. He shrugged and marched towards the enemy. The other three marched alongside him. Theron pulled his horse around to Belwynn's left, threatening to attack from a different angle.

The odds of the confrontation had been evened up. It was originally ten soldiers and two dogs against four tired runaways, only one of whom was a real fighter. It was now seven versus five, but the five included a deadly horseman and the seven had lost three comrades already. The morale of the soldiers broke. They weren't prepared to shed more blood.

'I'm out of here,' one of them was saying.

Another tried to rally the others, arguing that they could still win.

'You're free to go,' Theron called over. 'We won't pursue you. Enough lives have been taken here.'

That was it. The soldiers walked away at speed, desperate to get away from the encounter. The horseman had recovered enough from his fall to go with them. With only the occasional look over the shoulder to check they weren't being followed, the men from Korkis disappeared from view. Belwynn realised she had been standing still for some time, as the mixture of physical exhaustion and drop in adrenaline left her in a torpor.

Elana had joined them and was seeing to Dirk, who was sitting on the floor, looking deathly pale. Theron was seeing to his horse, making sure that the stallion had received no injuries. He looked up from his inspection.

''Vander, check the bodies, see if they live. If not, see if they have anything useful on them. Then we'll have to bury them.'

Theron's squire nodded and did as he was told, moving from one body to the next, closely inspecting the items he found but discarding most. 'They're dead,' he declared in a steady voice.

Theron looked up. 'Right. Better get this over with,' he sighed.

This man has killed many times before, Belwynn thought to herself, as she watched the knight and squire work. Still, they were going to give the soldiers from Korkis a proper burial.

'I'll help,' she said, walking over to where the corpses lay.

Theron turned to look at her and frowned. 'This is no job for a lady.'

'It's no job for anyone,' replied Belwynn. 'But it's a job that needs to be done.'

TO PROTECT AND SERVE

III

Farred looked around the hall of his new house, somewhat bewildered. He wondered whose home it had been. A wealthy family, judging by its size and location. They had taken virtually everything with them, leaving the place bare and sad looking. His weapons, armour and saddle bags lay in a pile next to the hearth—on a warm summer evening such as this there was no need for a fire, though he was tempted to light one just to bring some life to the room. He wasn't quite sure what to do with himself, so that when the knock came on the door, he felt a sense of relief.

He opened the door to find a prince and a war chief standing outside. The chieftain, Brock, had the rich, brown skin colour of the Middian people, while the prince's skin was lighter in tone, reflecting his mixed Middian-Magnian parentage.

Ashere, styled prince, though in fact the younger brother of Cerdda, the ruler of North Magnia, gave a sly grin. 'What's it like?' he asked.

Wordlessly, Farred waved them in so they could inspect it for themselves.

'Nice,' commented the Prince.

'I don't like them,' growled Brock, folding his arms.

Brock was the leader of a tribe on the Midder Steppe, a people whose Farred's own family were descended from, though they had long ago given their allegiance to the Magnian crown. His family had become settled farmers and landowners, whereas the Middian tribes of the Steppe still followed their traditional nomadic way of life. And they didn't live in houses. 'What if these houses fall down on top of us in the middle of the night?' he demanded, staring up at the ceiling suspiciously.

'Do you have this to yourself?' asked Ashere, avoiding returning to a topic of conversation with Brock that they had already endured several times.

'Yes.'

'Are your men well quartered?'

'I've left that to Burstan,' Farred said.

Ashere raised an eyebrow.

Farred smiled. 'He can be a pain in the arse. But he's a good organiser. More suited to barking out orders than me.'

Ashere nodded. 'Shall we go?'

They exited into a street in Guslar, the capital of the northern duchy of Rotelegen. It was a grim city, empty of life and full of ghosts since the defeat of Duke Ellard's army four days prior. Most of the citizens had now fled south, fearing the approach of the Isharite army, which had crossed into the Empire.

The exodus meant that it had not been difficult to find enough space in the city to house the Southern army they had led here. Farred had been given command of two thousand South Magnians by Prince Edgar. Brock led another two thousand from his own tribe, funded by King Glanna of Cordence. Finally, Ashere had brought the same number of North Magnians, and had assumed overall leadership of the combined force.

The street was full of the sounds of soldiers shouting and carrying on, but as the three men made their way into the centre of Guslar, that noise soon faded and the city became eerily quiet. The street they followed ran dead straight, bisected at regular intervals by crossroads.

'I've never seen a city built like this before,' Farred murmured, thinking of the disorganised warrens of streets usually found in the towns of Magnia.

'The Persaleians founded Guslar,' said Ashere. 'All their cities are built to the same layout. Which means that if we follow this street, we'll arrive at the central plaza.'

Brock shook his head and muttered something to himself, making clear his aversion to the urban environment.

Farred, however, admired the precision. Sure enough, ahead of them the street opened onto a huge open space. Spaced regularly around this plaza were other streets leading off in all directions. Inside the plaza was common land, which Farred supposed was used for markets and public gatherings. A few buildings were located here, the largest being a cathedral and castle, the latter of which belonged to the dukes of Rotelegen. It was

Brasingian in style, with high stone walls and towers. And it was to the castle they headed.

Much of the city of Guslar lay abandoned, but its castle was still occupied. As they approached the gates they were waved through, expected guests of the Duchess. Farred met eyes with some of the soldiers on guard duty as he entered the castle bailey. They stared coldly back. *Hardly a warm welcome,* he considered, *for foreigners come to fight on your behalf.*

THEY WERE WINED and dined at Guslar Castle, given prominent places at the top table. Ordinarily, Farred would have relished the role of honoured guest. But the mood was sombre, and the food basic. These were people making ready to leave their home.

The new duke, Jeremias, was still a boy. He did his best to play the host, but it was a role he had clearly never attempted before, and he had no conversation. He sat, white-faced and barely eating, clearly wishing he were somewhere else. He had lost his father and brothers only a few days ago, and his new responsibility weighed heavily on his young shoulders.

His mother, the Duchess Adalheid, still lived, and she was a stern woman. Her hair, dark but greying, was pulled back from a face heavy with lines. Her eyes, small and brown, regarded them without warmth. Farred wondered how stern she had been before her husband led an army of men, including her sons, to their destruction. Maybe she had smiled and laughed a lot before that. Now, it looked like she would never smile again.

Adalheid explained, exhaustively, how she had sent most of the people of Guslar south, along the Great Road to Essenberg. She was keen to give them every detail. It seemed to Farred that it was partly to demonstrate her ability to fill her late husband's shoes; partly to share the burden of leadership with strangers.

'Those who can fight and ride still serve the duchy,' she said. 'I am sending them into the countryside, where the people are often ignorant of the threat which faces them, or too stubborn to leave. The message they carry is stark. Everyone in Rotelegen must evacuate. The duchy has been given up to the enemy. Emperor Baldwin's point of defence is Burkhard Castle. No help is going to come.'

The Duchess made only a token effort to hide her bitterness regarding Baldwin's perceived lack of action, and the other diners clearly agreed with her assessment.

Prince Ashere made a sympathetic face. In truth, Farred knew full well that Ashere agreed with Baldwin's decisions. Moreover, the suggestion that no help was forthcoming was offensive. Hadn't all three of them led thousands of men here? And hadn't they been asked to fight the Isharite army, to cover the Rotelegen retreat?

'I wanted to ask a favour,' Farred began after a pause. 'None of us know the territory here and it would be an immense help if you could assign some local men to us, to act as guides.'

Adalheid raised an eyebrow at the request, turning her eyes to the men at the table. One of them gave a brief nod.

'I will send a man over to you tonight,' she said.

'Thank you.'

The meal continued, and not once did Adalheid ask after their men, offer them any further aid, or express a single word of gratitude.

FARRED FELT a sense of relief when Ashere had excused them soon after the end of the meal, citing the need to supervise their soldiers. The Rotelegen looked equally relieved to see them go.

'Thank Toric that's over,' Farred exhaled as they retraced their steps through Guslar back to their new quarters.

'It's a sorry mess to have a woman and young boy lead this tribe,' commented Brock.

'It's a shame,' said Ashere. 'Duke Ellard was perhaps the most respected soldier in the Empire. Baldwin needs all the experience he can get.'

'You have to give Adalheid her due, though,' Farred argued. 'Who would envy her position?'

'Agreed,' said Ashere. 'Well, here we are back at your new abode, Farred. Have a good night.'

Farred said his farewells and once more found himself alone in the hall of his new house. The same feeling of not knowing what to do with himself came over him. The room was just as bare as before, except someone had been in and left a small pile of firewood by the hearth.

'It could get chilly tonight,' Farred said out loud, and knelt by the hearth to arrange a fire.

He stood back to admire his work, but then hesitated before lighting it. There was a knock at the door.

Upon opening it, he found Ashere waiting there, a half smile playing on the Prince's lips.

'Come in,' said Farred.

'Up to much?'

'No. I was debating whether I should light a fire,' he said, gesturing at the hearth.

'Hmm,' said Ashere, examining it.

There was a silence. Farred turned to meet his eyes.

The Prince held his gaze. 'I could keep you warm tonight.'

THEY LED four thousand soldiers north west from Guslar on their first mission. They had left when it was still dark. After two hours, the sun had risen and they were in position, a few miles to the west of where they expected the Isharite army to be.

They had acquired the services of Veit, a local man who knew the land well enough to act as a scout. While the main force waited, Veit led Farred, Ashere and Brock eastwards. The general of the Isharite army was Shira, Queen of Haskany. Ashere expected her to send out small war bands from her main army, to raid the surrounding territory and look out for enemy forces. He was hoping to find and intercept one of these bands.

It did not take them long.

Veit led them up a hill to a vantage point overlooking the Great Road. It looked like it was alive, a giant worm wriggling across the landscape. The numbers moving south along the road were mind numbing, and they stretched back as far as the eye could see—the soldiers at the front were miles ahead of those at the rear.

They looked to see if any smaller units were heading in their direction. From their position, they could see three units all heading westward, to separate destinations.

'They move across the land in a brazen manner,' growled Brock. 'As if they own it.'

'This army has seen no opposition since it broke through the defences on the northern border,' said Ashere. 'And they act as if they don't expect to see any more. It is time to change that.'

Farred looked at the nearest unit. He estimated its size at no less than two hundred soldiers. 'Where are they headed?' he asked Veit, pointing at the group.

'There is a village in that direction,' he replied.

'How far from here?'

'Three miles.'

'Could we get there before them?'

Veit considered the question. 'They're much closer than our forces. Even though they're on foot, they're probably going to get there first.'

'A shame,' said Farred, frustrated.

'But we won't be far behind?' asked Ashere, interested.

'Nope,' Veit replied.

Ashere nodded. 'Instead of intercepting them on the way, we will have to get to the village as soon as possible.'

He looked at Farred and Brock for confirmation and they both nodded, a fierce grin emerging on the Middian's face, which spread to the rest of the group.

'I will take the main force,' Ashere continued, 'and head directly for the village. Farred, you take your men and circle around, entering from the same direction as the enemy and blocking off a retreat. Brock will hold on to five hundred of his Middians and act as a reserve force, looking out for trouble.'

ON THE OUTSKIRTS of the village, Farred and his men waited in silence, their breath visible in the cold morning air. The anticipation of battle throbbed in Farred's chest. The sensation moved outward from there to his gut and throat, threatening to make him physically sick. He could see the same tension in the faces of the men around him. They had to wait a while longer yet.

When they could hear Ashere's attack, they would move in. Not before, because the enemy force in the village was too large for his men to handle alone.

Then they heard voices in the wind. Everyone looked at each other, but especially at Farred. Farred waited. More voices. They sounded like shouts. Then the clang of metal on metal.

'We go!' shouted Farred.

Farred slowly led his force along the dirt road. At first, they passed open fields on both sides, but then they found the odd hut. Each building they passed, and any other cover, had to be inspected carefully. However small, there was the chance of an ambush. The enemy could be armed with bows and arrows. Farred had no intention of getting caught out on his first military engagement.

The sound of fighting drew closer, yet they could see nothing. He could see the tension on the faces of his soldiers. Farred knew his troops wanted to release it and go charging in, because that was how he felt.

'Steady,' he said in a loud voice. 'We're nearly there.'

They rode on, approaching a row of mud and wood built dwellings on the right-hand side which marked the beginning of the village proper. Then they saw it. Standing outside the door of the second hut, staring back at them. These raiders weren't Haskan troops. They were Drobax.

It was like a monster from a children's story. Half-naked, with grey skin, spindly limbs, sharp nails and teeth and black, beady eyes. The eyes of the Drobax bulged with fear as it realised how many mounted soldiers were heading its way. It dived back into the house, shouting something unintelligible, presumably in its own language. There were likely more of them inside.

That was when Farred lost control.

He shouted something out aloud and then he was riding straight for the house, many of his men with him. Realising that they couldn't ride inside, Farred and those with him began to dismount. It soon became a disorganised mess, as soldiers handed the reins of their mounts over to comrades to hold.

Any kind of counter-attack would have caught them out. The Drobax, however, had stayed inside.

Farred approached. He peered through a crack between the door and the wall and could make out a few figures inside, weapons held at the ready. They favoured their chances inside rather than out.

One of his soldiers shouted a war cry and ran for the door. Farred and many others followed behind. One of the Drobax thrust out a spear into the doorway, but Farred's men were half expecting it and blocked the weapon down.

Then they were in. Farred had to squeeze into the small house as the Magnians crammed in, eager to meet the enemy. It was dark and cramped inside the hut—difficult to make out the enemy and all but impossible to swing a sword properly. Shouts and screams filled Farred's ears. A figure leapt out of the shadows to his left. It struck at the soldier standing next to Farred. The soldier, though surprised, was able to block the attack. Farred used his sword to punch the Drobax, smashing his hilt into its face. The force of the strike sent it over backwards and it was then pounced on as his men jumped in to deliver a death strike.

Taking a breath, Farred looked around. The fight was over already. About a dozen bodies lay on the floor. Some were Drobax, others dead villagers. None of his men seemed injured.

'Sir!' said a soldier, part of a group huddled over a body in the far corner.

Farred walked over and the group parted to let him see.

It was a woman. She was naked but alive. She stared up at him with wild eyes. Suddenly Farred realised what had happened here. The Drobax had killed the men but stayed in the hut to rape the woman. He felt sick at the thought. He couldn't begin to think what this woman had gone through. His men were standing around, unsure what to do.

'Get some bloody clothes on her!' shouted Farred. 'Anulf, Morlin. You're assigned to protect her until I get back.'

Farred marched out of the house to see what was happening. His soldiers were entering the other houses on the row, but they seemed to be re-emerging without having found anything.

Farred needed to restore discipline. He barked out orders. Leaving a hundred of his troops at the huts with the horses, he led the rest ahead on foot.

They half walked and half jogged into the village, the road slowly rising uphill where they could see the church spire, in the centre of the village.

The noise of fighting got closer. Then the chaos began again.

More Drobax were found. They were in isolated groups, and they dived into buildings when encountered. Farred sent groups of soldiers to deal with them while he continued to march towards the centre of the village, making sure that each building was fully searched along the way.

They crested the top of the slope and looked down at the scene below. Ashere's larger force was mopping up the last of the opposition. The last point of resistance was at the village inn on the left, where a large group of North Magnians were forcing their way in. Despite already having huge numerical superiority, many of Farred's soldiers couldn't be prevented from running over to join in.

As Farred walked down the road, Ashere rode up to meet him. He dismounted, and they clasped hands.

'What happened to your horse?' asked the Prince.

'Oh...we left them behind,' said Farred, smiling ruefully. 'We met little resistance. What about you?'

'When we got here, the villagers had locked themselves inside the church. Most of the Drobax were out in the open, trying to force their way in. They fought back viciously, didn't run away. Once the main group was dealt with, we had to search everywhere else.'

'Good. I'm glad there are some survivors,' said Farred, his mind going back to the poor woman they had found.

Ashere nodded.

'What are we going to do with them?' Farred asked.

Ashere shrugged. 'Nothing.'

'But some will be wounded. They should be taken back to Guslar. More Drobax might come—'

'Farred. It's not our job to take these people to safety. That's what the Rotelegen soldiers are doing. We'll tell them what happened here when we get the chance. But our job is to take on this army—try to buy a little time for Baldwin and Jeremias to get ready. We need to make another strike now. I can't afford to have part of our forces wandering about escorting civilians all over the place. We need to stay united.'

Farred could see the sense of what Ashere said from a military perspective. But he still found it difficult. They had just rescued these villagers, and now the Prince proposed to abandon them to their fate again?

'Very well,' he replied. 'But I'm sending some of my troops back with a woman we found.'

Farred could feel his jaw sticking out, daring Ashere to disagree.

The Prince of North Magnia grimaced. 'So be it, Farred,' he said. 'They're your soldiers, after all. You're a stubborn man,' he said, shaking his head.

Farred couldn't tell whether he was annoyed or amused. Perhaps both.

'Right,' said Ashere, 'gather your men. We need to meet up with Brock. We're moving out.'

THE WAVES AT THE SHORE

IV

Belwynn was in a bed. She sat up with a start. Where was she?

As her muddled brain tried to think, the chase through the woods came back to jolt her. She felt sick at the memory. They had been chased out of the woods, across some fields—she had thought they would all be killed. Then Count Theron had arrived.

After that it was a bit of a blur, as if a part of Belwynn's mind had turned off in order to recover from the trauma. Theron and his squire, Evander, had escorted them to the home of his uncle, Sebastian of Melion. Belwynn had felt safe in the knight's company, a feeling she hadn't had since their stay with the Blood Caladri. Theron offered his mount for Belwynn to ride, but she knew that though he might protest, Dirk could walk no farther. He was bundled on top of the warhorse and soon fell asleep.

Theron had asked them why they had been chased from Korkis. Belwynn was able to answer this truthfully, telling him about the encounter with the soldiers and her intervention to help the little girl. The knight seemed to admire Belwynn's actions and muttered darkly of developments in Korkis and elsewhere in Kalinth. When his questions ranged further, Belwynn's answers became much vaguer. The fear of revealing too much information, along with her general tiredness, left her virtually monosyllabic.

Theron had been too polite to press the matter, but Belwynn knew that this morning she would have to give a better performance. Uncle Sebastian would doubtless be present as well, she thought sourly. They had arrived so late and so exhausted last night that Theron had ensured they were found rooms immediately—she had yet to meet her host.

Belwynn pushed away the bed covers, and swung her legs over the side of the bed, where they landed on a soft rug. They had all been given well-appointed rooms in Sebastian's house, which Theron had called Sernea. It was a fortified structure with strong stone walls that served as the headquarters of the estate. The steward had originally arranged for Elana and Belwynn to share the same room, but the priestess had insisted on looking after Dirk during the night, giving Belwynn the luxury of a room to herself.

Opposite her was an empty bed, where new clothes had been laid out for her. She dressed quickly, since it was chilly without the covers.

Her room was sparsely decorated, designed for defence as much as for comfort. The two outside walls each had an arrow loop, where archers could be positioned. These wedge-shaped openings allowed the archer to target a wide angle, while the slit in the wall gave good protection. Belwynn peered out of the loop which faced the front of the house. An archer stationed here could cover the track which led up to the main gate. There was no gatehouse, and the house could not withstand a sustained attack from an armed force. It was designed to afford protection from minor threats, such as anything Korkis might offer. And that was good enough for Belwynn.

Her thoughts turned to her brother.

Soren? Can you hear me?

Belwynn? How are you?

Soren's voice sounded unclear once more, as if distorted by some barrier.

Fine.

She paused to think. Was it worth the trouble of telling Soren about the events in Korkis when she was now safe? She decided not.

We're still in Kalinth. We're at the home of a knight. How are you?

No change here. I don't want to talk for too long. Contact me tomorrow, Belwynn. And stay safe.

That was it? She desperately wanted to talk to her brother, and had to stop herself from replying. She stood in the room, fighting to control her emotions. She was suddenly struck by an overwhelming sense of loss. Her parents were dead, both taken from her too soon. She had always leaned on her brother for support, for purpose. His goals had become her goals. And now he was gone, too. She was in the middle of a strange country. And she didn't know what to do.

'Deal with it, Belwynn,' she told herself out loud.

She gave herself some time, taking some deep breaths. She stretched, forcing her body to wake up. *What should I do first?* she asked herself.

She suddenly realised how hungry she was. She felt like she hadn't eaten in days. Leaving her tower room, she took the stairs down, looking for the kitchen where she expected to find breakfast.

It did not take her long to find it, the smell drawing her to the right place. The kitchen was warm and inviting. A huge pot hung in the fireplace and several people stood around it, chatting quietly while they had their breakfast, no doubt after their early morning chores. Belwynn didn't recognise anyone and entered a bit hesitantly.

'Porridge, love?' asked an older woman, perhaps a cook, with an encouraging smile.

'Yes please,' Belwynn replied, her stomach rumbling.

She was handed a bowl and spoon and the cook ladled the steaming breakfast into it.

'Honey?' asked a younger woman, maybe a maid at the house. A pot of honey was being passed around the group, and Belwynn took the dipper and let the honey drip into the bowl. Wasting no more time, she tucked in, blowing on the hot porridge to stop it burning her mouth.

The staff at the house were pleasant enough, but Belwynn was glad when Rabigar wandered into the kitchen and took a bowl of porridge for himself. They found a corner to stand in out of the way while they ate.

'How are you?' he asked.

'Fine. I slept well enough and this food should sort me out. Thank you for taking charge back there. I didn't think we were going to make it—' she began, getting a lump in her throat and leaving the statement there.

'We weren't; not until the knight showed up. We owe him our lives, but we need to be careful. We don't know who they are.'

Belwynn thought they needed all the help they could get, but she nodded along.

A familiar face entered the kitchen and approached them.

'Evander, isn't it?' asked Belwynn, recognising Theron's squire.

The lad smiled, seemingly pleased that she had remembered his name.

'Yes, that's right. My lords would like to speak with you now. I've been asked to fetch you.'

'I see. Have our friends come down, yet?' asked Belwynn.

Evander looked over at the servants, who shook their heads.

'Would it be possible to bring their breakfast up to their room?' she enquired.

'Of course,' said the woman who had served her.

Evander led Belwynn and Rabigar back upstairs to a small room that appeared to be Sebastian's private study. He had a shelf of books, a desk and a few chairs. Theron and Sebastian were seated, deep in conversation, but stood up to greet them.

Theron walked over with a warm smile.

'Ah, how are you?' he said. The knight gripped Rabigar in a handshake and gave him a slap on the shoulder. 'My lady,' he said to Belwynn, taking her by the hand and lightly touching his lips to it.

'We're much better, thank you,' answered Rabigar. 'But Elana and Dirk are tired. We suggested they stay in their room.'

'Of course,' said Sebastian. 'From hearing Theron's account, I assume that you both must be tired, too. Theron and I are going hunting shortly, but I insist you stay and get some rest today. My people will see to you.'

Sebastian of Melion was a tall and handsome man, his hair still dark despite middle age. His face was welcoming if care worn.

'This is the Lady Belwynn,' said Theron, 'and Rabigar, a skilled Krykker warrior by my reckoning.'

'Good to meet you, please take a seat,' said Sebastian, gesturing to the chairs.

They all sat down.

'Welcome to Sernea, my house,' began Sebastian. 'Please, anything you need, just ask someone and it will be provided. Now. Here in Kalinth, we are rather cut off from events elsewhere in Dalriya. This is something which I deeply regret and is largely because of difficulties within our kingdom. So, when foreigners arrive out of the blue, I hope you will understand I am eager to share news. Theron has told me what happened to you in Korkis, and there is no need to explain that episode to me. You are quite safe here. Unfortunately, Kalinth has become a rather dangerous place for travellers recently. And you are a rather—can I say, out of the ordinary group of travellers?'

Belwynn smiled and nodded at the comment. It was all very polite, but Sebastian had got straight to the point, nonetheless.

'Now, now, uncle,' said Theron, smiling at Belwynn in a conspiratorial way, 'before you subject your guests to an interrogation, it is perhaps incumbent upon us to explain *why* our kingdom is a dangerous place for travellers. It is a disgrace for which we should apologise a thousand times over in shame before we ask whats and wherefores to visitors in our land.'

Theron said the words in good humour, but Belwynn could clearly see the passion that lay behind them.

Sebastian smiled thinly at his nephew's outburst. 'Theron, this is not the moment to discuss politics.'

'Politics? That is a strange word to use when our country and its people are on the brink of ruin and subjugation!'

It was now Sebastian's turn to bristle with passion. 'Are you saying that I don't care?'

Theron reached a hand over to rest on the older man's forearm. 'No. I apologise uncle. I know that isn't true. I just get so...frustrated.'

Sebastian grunted and turned his attention back to Belwynn and Rabigar. He looked embarrassed that he had argued with his nephew in front of them, but set his jaw firmly and continued. 'It is incumbent upon me to ask strangers in my lands what their business is.'

'We have travelled from the Empire,' began Rabigar.

'Up the Great Road?' demanded Sebastian, sounding astonished.

A Drobax army had passed down the Great Road. The idea of the four of them travelling up it sounded ludicrous.

'Not quite,' explained Belwynn. 'We came via the Grand Caladri.'

'The Grand Caladri?' responded Sebastian, sounding no less surprised. 'I've never heard of humans entering their lands before.'

The count looked at them, eager for an explanation. Rabigar and Belwynn shared a look. Making up a story seemed pointless.

'I'm afraid we have grave news for you,' said Rabigar. 'We were in Edeleny four days ago. It was invaded by Arioc and his forces. I fear the entire realm is taken.'

'Invaded?' gasped Theron. 'How?'

'They used magic.'

'I haven't heard of this,' said Sebastian, seemingly in disbelief.

'Why would you have?' asked Theron.

'We saw it with our own eyes,' said Rabigar firmly, in a voice that left no doubt.

'How did you escape?' asked Theron.

'Magic, again,' replied Rabigar. 'A wizard, by the name of Pentas, teleported us out.'

'He got some of us out,' added Belwynn. 'But the rest of our group was captured. Arioc has taken them prisoner...' Suddenly, Belwynn felt herself breaking down. Her voice wobbled and tears streamed down her face.

Pull yourself together, she demanded.

'My brother, Soren, is one of them...'

Again, she couldn't finish speaking, her voice sounding hysterical. It was like listening to some other person in the room talking, rather than herself. She looked at the sympathetic faces of the two counts looking at her and she felt totally embarrassed. She wiped her nose on the back of her hand, imagining what a state she must look like.

'I'm sorry,' she blubbered, and decided to stop talking.

'Not at all,' said Sebastian, somewhat awkwardly. 'You have experienced an awful few days. There is no need to apologise. Excuse me if I am a little shocked by what you are telling me.'

'And please,' said Theron, reaching over and holding her hand lightly, 'understand that as knights we will do whatever we can to get your brother back.'

'Thank you,' whispered Belwynn.

'You haven't explained, I have to say,' Sebastian added, 'what exactly you were doing in Edeleny.'

There was a silence. Rabigar looked over to Belwynn with a raised eyebrow, as if seeking permission to tell more. She nodded her acquiescence.

'I suppose,' said Rabigar, 'we were there to get a staff.'

'A staff?' said Theron. 'The staff Belwynn was carrying yesterday? Why is that so important?'

Rabigar puffed out his cheeks. 'This isn't a short story. It begins in Magnia, about three weeks ago...'

* * *

AT LAST, Shira could see the outskirts of Guslar for herself.

Despite the resounding success over Duke Ellard and his forces, the progress of her army had been frustratingly slow. This was primarily because she had agreed that a large force of Drobax should make up the army's van to deal with any resistance. They were far less effective than the well drilled Haskan soldiers, but were totally expendable. Indeed, despite considerable deaths, she had been advised that there had been no significant depreciation in the numbers of Drobax in her army. No-one knew exactly how many there were, not even to the nearest tens of thousands. Such calculations were complicated, she had learned, by the Drobax army repopulating as it went along; so that while many died every day, more infants would be born. Only a small proportion of these might be expected to live, but that left hundreds who would.

All of which meant that, while Shira's army had begun its march south days before Arioc's forces had even assembled, he had now successfully conquered the lands of the Grand Caladri, while she had only made a small inroad into Imperial territory. The resistance offered by the enemy had been tiny, but had succeeded in slowing her army down. Still, it was a totally futile gesture. The Drobax she commanded were like the waves lapping at the shore. Endless. Infinite. Relentless. You could wade into the sea, slash and hack at it with all your might if you wished, but it would avail you none.

Shira beckoned over her Uncle Koren, the man who had taught her how to fight and who she trusted the most. She pointed toward Guslar. 'How far?'

'Apparently, a couple of miles to the city walls.'

'I want to lead the force in. We'll take Haskans only.'

Koren furrowed his brow. He was a logical thinker, a tough realist, carefully weighing up the possible and ignoring the impossible. Shira had huge respect for him, though found him humourless and dull company.

'You shouldn't go. There may be some resistance, enough to put you in danger, but not enough to justify your presence.'

'I'm bored, uncle. That's my justification. And it's an order.'

Koren turned away and began organising a force, though Shira knew full well that every time she disagreed with him it rankled. She called over Roshanak, the Isharite who oversaw the Drobax forces.

'I'm going to lead the force into Guslar. I will billet all the Haskan forces in the city, but I don't want a single Drobax there. Can you organise a suitable overnight location elsewhere?'

'Of course. Anything else?'

'When you've done what you need to, come to Guslar yourself and we'll meet there tonight.'

Roshanak nodded courteously and began giving out orders. It was not long before the huge army began going its separate ways. The Haskan forces, relatively small in number, began heading towards the capital of Rotelegen, with Shira and Koren in charge of the mounted regiment who would attack the town. The Drobax were herded west of Guslar where they would spend another night in the open. Shira felt a flush of relief that she would be free of their stink and repugnant presence for a night. Excited, she called out the order to advance before all her soldiers were fully lined up, and pressed on at the head of her forces.

As they rode, the countryside of Rotelegen merged into the city of Guslar. At first, they passed unremarkable looking dwellings, but the walls of the city soon took shape ahead of them. The main gates, guarding the northern entrance to the city, were closed; but there was no sign of any guards on the walls.

Shira and Koren pulled up at a safe distance. Her mounted soldiers milled about ahead of the gates, gradually daring to get closer and closer, but there was still no sign of defenders. Eventually, a couple of more daring individuals dismounted and gave the gates a good push, but they were locked in place.

'Up there!' a soldier cried, pointing up at the battlements above the gate.

Shira, along with everyone else, strained to see movement, but she couldn't make anything out.

'I'm sure I saw something move,' argued the soldier defensively, as his comrades began to question the sighting.

A wagon pulled up and Koren began barking out orders, as the contents of the vehicle were unloaded and assembled. A battering ram, that most straightforward of siege weapons, was soon made ready and volunteers quickly emerged to grab a hand grip.

'I've not seen them so quick to put themselves forward before,' Shira said to her uncle with a smile. Taking hold of the ram usually made you a target for the enemy. This time, however, there did not seem to be an enemy.

'Swing!' commanded Koren.

The ram, made of an oak log but encased with metal at the tip, was attached by ropes to an overhead beam. The men raised it backwards before swinging it at the target, using the energy created to make a stronger impact. A dull thud echoed around the walls, but the gates remained solid. However, after a few more strikes, and with the men starting to find a rhythm, the splintering and cracking of wood could be heard.

Suddenly, a missile came down from overhead. A soldier working the ram was sent to the ground.

'Arrows!' was the fearful shout, and the soldiers looked up at the walls. Those who had bows began firing upwards until Koren shouted at them to desist. No enemy was visible. The unfortunate victim of the attack was dragged over for Shira to inspect. It had actually been a short spear which had been hurled from the battlements, hitting the man in the chest and killing him.

'Restart the ram!' demanded Koren, shouting at the top of his voice.

The men quickly returned to their task, but now some of the other soldiers had their sights trained on the walls in case of a repeat attack. None came, and the gates made a horrible ripping noise. The ram had twisted the left gate in on itself. The right gate was pushed ajar, and Guslar was open to the invaders at the loss of only one life.

Shira nudged her horse forward and peered into the city, but it seemed completely deserted. While the spear thrower on the wall was a warning that this was not entirely true, it seemed there was no longer any genuine military presence left in Guslar. Still, Shira would take nothing for granted.

'We're taking the city! Keep discipline and stick with your unit at all times. Anyone who disobeys will be fed to the Drobax!' Shira raised her sword in the air. 'For Haskany!'

With that, she manoeuvred her horse past the gates and led her force towards the centre of town. The central square was dominated by two buildings—the castle of the duke, and the cathedral of the bishop. But each road leading in was lined with the tall, well-built houses of the nobility and merchant class—men who had grown rich on the trade coming up and down the Great Road.

Shira led her forces to the two targets. As they approached down the main street, missiles came in from the houses on either side. Shira reacted to the first signs of organised resistance by waving units of her men into the houses to clear them out. She continued herself, taking half of the remaining force towards the doors of the cathedral while her uncle took on the castle. The doors were locked shut, and arrows were fired down at them from the thin windows of the building. The Haskan soldiers were quick to overwhelm the defenders, though, firing arrows and stones at the windows to push them back. Then, the ram was quickly brought back into operation.

This time, the going was slower than at the city walls. There were clearly a significant number of people taking refuge inside the building, and they had barricaded the doors. Time went by and the ram seemed to be having little impact.

Shira took some time to look over at the castle. Koren's forces had got into the building, but the fighting was still ongoing.

She ordered fire arrows to be shot into the cathedral, hoping it would cause a distraction for the defenders. The tactic seemed to have some effect, as the battering ram rattled the doors. Then, one door fell over towards the attackers, the hinges and locks shattered by the ram. With whoops of excitement, the Haskans headed for the opening, ripping out the tables and benches blocking their way into the cathedral. The defenders stabbed out with their spears and threw whatever missiles they had to hand. Several Haskans were struck, and had to be dragged away from the fight by their comrades. But the blood lust was up, and more soldiers took their place.

Shira was one of them, and the presence of their queen gave even more impetus to the Haskan attackers. Their superior weight of numbers began to tell, and they slowly pushed themselves forwards. Shira, in the middle of a scrum, made sure she held onto her sword and shield, kept relaxed, and kept her breathing even. The movement forwards gathered pace, and suddenly Shira found herself heaved into the central part of the cathedral. She peered around her, letting her eyes get accustomed to the darker environment. She picked out the enemy. They were not so many as she had expected. Many were women and children. It confirmed her earlier suspicions that the Emperor had given up Guslar and pulled his forces out.

Ready, Shira led her men into the attack. She feinted at a defender armed with a spear, drawing in the thrust which she sidestepped, and then flicked her blade along the shaft of the spear, cutting the fingers off the hand of her enemy and forcing him to drop his weapon. He retreated to the far wall, and already, it had moved from a fight to a slaughter. Shira led the work, not shirking to cut down her share of victims. It was the women who disgusted her the most. Crying out for mercy, or asking for their children to be spared. Grown women who still thought some tears would save them, who hadn't armed themselves to fight for what they wanted. Shira felt no remorse at ending their lives: useless, overgrown children who had no chance of survival in this world.

The work was soon over. The blood of the defenders was splattered up the walls of the cathedral. Shira's soldiers checked to see if anyone survived, perhaps playing dead. They then took anything they valued from the corpses.

Shira called over one of her men. 'Find my captains, ask them to meet me in here as soon as possible.'

She raised her voice so that those in the cathedral could hear. 'Fan out from here in your units. Check the remaining parts of the city for any survivors. Then find somewhere to sleep for the night, but stay together. We must be vigilant. The Imperial forces are still at large. They may counter-attack.'

She made a point of watching the soldiers go, so that they reconnected with their units under her stern gaze. After they had left, she looked about her. Wandering over to the far side of the cathedral, she found some chairs and busied herself with setting them up, one for her and three for her captains. She took a seat and waited.

Koren was first. She gestured to a seat, and he sat down in that stiff, formal way she associated with all old soldiers.

'Any news?' she asked.

'The castle is taken,' Koren looked around the cathedral dispassionately. 'Probably more in here than there.'

'Really?' replied Shira, surprised. 'Trusting their gods more than their rulers?'

Koren shook his head. 'Baldwin must have organised a full evacuation days ago. The people left here are those who refused to go. Those in the castle weren't his servants, they were...squatters. Oh, and before Baldwin's forces left, they poisoned the water supply. I've sent orders round for the men not to drink or eat anything they find.'

'Poisoned the water?' came a voice from the doors. 'What a dirty trick.'

Shira's other captains entered the cathedral, both of them Isharites. While Koren was in charge of the Haskan troops, Roshanak was in charge of the Drobax—or, at least, in charge of the Isharites who controlled the Drobax. When Shira had been assigned control of the army, she had some initial curiosity about how this was done, but as time had gone on, she decided she did not want or need to know. The Drobax seemed to behave like mindless animals in a lot of ways, but the Isharites had somehow trained them to follow strict orders, so that they could behave like a military force of sorts.

Mehrab, meanwhile, led the magi assigned by Erkindrix to Shira's army. While they had contributed absolutely nothing so far, he still managed to take a superior tone, as if he were actually in charge. The thought that he might be made Shira dislike him even more.

'Well, you've chosen a lovely venue,' he continued, waving his arms around the cathedral interior, the walls smeared in red blood. There was something rather comical in the way he did it, but Shira kept her lips tight and gestured to the chairs she had prepared for them. Both took a seat.

'So, I take it there's little of value left?' asked Mehrab.

'No,' replied Shira. 'I was hoping for some treats for our soldiers. Loot. Even some nice food. It's good for morale. But I don't think we'll find anything.'

'We caught them by surprise, and got lucky when Ellard over-committed himself and attacked us the second time,' commented Koren. 'But since then, to give him credit, Baldwin has done well. Slowed us down long enough to strip out the duchy and deny us any sustenance. I don't think we'll find anything 'til we get to Burkhard Castle.'

'How will that affect supplies?' asked Mehrab.

'We're still getting enough provisions to feed the Haskans,' answered Shira, 'but it means no spare food for the Drobax. How are things with them?' she asked Roshanak.

'We've settled them. Their camp begins about a mile away from the city. As for the food issue, I still don't see any major depletion in our numbers. I will tell you if that changes.'

'In which case, our objective is still secure,' commented Mehrab.

And that is it, thought Shira. When she had been given this command, she had seen it as her chance to shine. But the nature of the task didn't allow it. There were no genuine strategic decisions to take. She was just taking the Drobax to the Empire, whereupon they would destroy it. While Arioc would win praise and support for his daring invasion of the Grand Caladri, Shira was simply expected to succeed. Indeed, it was unthinkable that she wouldn't.

Koren was looking at her, perhaps reading her mind. Shira had seen a chance to escape Arioc, but even hundreds of miles away, she was still in his clutches.

OF WIVES AND WAR

V

In the courtyard of Sernea, Belwynn sat on her horse and waited. Her friends Rabigar, Dirk and Elana were also seated and ready to go. They looked healthier and happier from having spent three nights at Sebastian's home. Some colour had returned to their faces, though Dirk still had his racking cough, and was clearly in need of more permanent rest.

Belwynn suddenly felt a wave of sadness flow over her and she gripped the reins of her mount as she fought it away. Dirk had lost his health. Rabigar an eye. Belwynn's twin brother Soren, and her closest friends Clarin and Herin, were captured by the Isharites, facing only Toric knew what torments over the coming days. What price had already been paid, and was yet to be paid, for getting involved in this? The only thing keeping her going was a feeling that they were making progress. *A journey somewhere always feels like progress*, Belwynn considered—*assuming, that is, that you do eventually leave.*

Also seated on their mounts in the courtyard were the Counts Sebastian, Theron, and twenty of Sebastian's retainers. They had been trying to set off on the road to the High Tower, the seat of the Knights of Kalinth, for some time. So far, they had failed. Just as they seemed ready, a servant would rush out from the house and load up some forgotten provisions. Or one of Sebastian's soldiers would clamber off their horse and sheepishly run back in on some unnamed errand, returning to the sound of gibes and curses from his comrades. Even Sebastian himself was at it, remembering some gift to be presented to someone or other, but he couldn't quite remember where he had placed it for safekeeping. Belwynn and her friends looked on somewhat bemused—they had so few possessions, that they were hardly going to forget anything.

Sebastian seemed a little ill at ease, anxious even, and it appeared to be rubbing off on those around him. Not Theron, however, who seemed to take great delight in the proceedings and laughing heartily at each delay. It made Belwynn wonder whether Sebastian had ever had a wife. She thought things might run more smoothly if he did.

When, at last, they did get going, Theron fell in with Belwynn and began chatting in his easy way, pointing out local landmarks. In truth, Belwynn found the area around Sernea to be quite monotonous; a hard and dry landscape, very different to the lush farmland of home. She listened politely, enjoying his company, but turned the conversation to matters of more interest to her.

'I was wondering, Theron, about Sebastian. I was thinking this morning that he does not have a wife—has he ever?'

'No, never. The Knights of Kalinth do not take wives.'

'Oh, I didn't know that.' Belwynn was taken aback by the news. 'So, you are sworn to be chaste?'

'Well, I didn't say that, did I?' responded Theron, giving Belwynn a look. She wasn't sure if he was trying to make her blush, but having spent so much time in the company of Herin and Clarin, it took a lot to make Belwynn blush.

'So why can't you take wives?'

'It makes us better soldiers. Men with wives have their heads cluttered with other things. Usually money.'

Belwynn made a face at him, but let him continue.

'Men with children have other priorities, are wary of risking their lives—rightly, of course. When you become a knight, you join the Order. Your brothers in the Order are your family. You must be prepared to give your life for it.'

'I can understand that. But to never have children?'

'Not never. Not for most men. Most knights serve for a limited time only, often ten years. Then, if you want to leave, you are given some land, and you can find a wife. And raise some boys to be knights!'

This prospect seemed to please Theron. He had a big, beaming smile on his face.

'But Sebastian has served for over ten years, hasn't he?'

'Yes. Those who choose to rise high, the commanders and officers, must stay in the Order. Those are the men who devote their whole lives to the Knights. By doing so, they win the respect of the soldiers.'

'So how important is Sebastian in the Order?'

Theron shifted in his seat, suddenly looking more serious about things. 'In influence, my uncle is second only to the Grand Master, Galenos. But more popular than he is.'

'Why?'

'Galenos continues to follow a policy of absolute loyalty to King Jonas. The King has made a peace with the Isharites and has forbidden any military action against them. The most cowardly, cynical act I've ever witnessed.'

'You disagree with Galenos?'

'Of course I do. The Knights of Kalinth are sworn to protect the people, but most of them are standing by while raiding parties from Kharovia pillage, burn and rape with impunity. The king's own soldiers do nothing, but sit whimpering behind their walls.'

'I see,' said Belwynn. 'And you?'

Theron looked around him, in case anyone was listening. 'Can I trust you, Belwynn?'

'Of course.'

'I and others of my comrades have been forced to take action. We go by the name of the Kalinthian Defence League. We ride out and intercept the war bands when possible. But we are few. And we must keep our identities secret. People suspect the League is comprised of knights, but if our identities were discovered, we would be expelled from the Order.'

'Does Sebastian know?'

'He knows alright. We've had plenty of arguments over it. But he's the one who can change things, not me. And I think what you told us yesterday about the power of Ishari, the weapons, what's happened to the Caladri—all of that—that might have done more to persuade him than all the arguments I've tried. That we're all going to the High Tower today is a start. We need to be prepared for a confrontation.'

Oh Gods, thought Belwynn. *As if we are not in enough trouble. I seem to have started a civil war.*

* * *

FARRED WAS EXHAUSTED. But equally, he felt lucky to be alive, as he always did after a raid.

Ashere liked to vary the time when they attacked the army of Ishari, to maintain the element of surprise. This last time, he had chosen sunrise. They had never done this before, mainly because it meant travelling through the night from their base to reach the enemy, a manoeuvre with so many difficulties it was usually avoided. However, Ashere's forces, made up of his own North Magnians, Farred's South Magnians, and the Middians under the leadership of Brock, had united into an effective and disciplined force under his leadership. They were also much more confident about the terrain, having traversed the borderlands of Kelland and Rotelegen many times now.

This time, Ashere had taken Farred and about seven hundred men to the enemy camp. Farred, like most, had got no sleep before they set out, nerves getting the better of him. They then had a protracted journey north in the dark, trying to locate the enemy camp without being identified themselves. Usually, Ashere targeted the Haskan soldiers in these raids. This was because they had things worth destroying: supplies, horses, transport. This time, however, they approached the Drobax.

The sun had risen enough for them to be seen as they approached. But, unlike the Haskan positions, the Isharites rarely set up watches over the Drobax. They didn't seem to see the point, and had a general disregard for the well-being of these monsters. So, as Ashere led the charge, there were no warning calls, and the Drobax were still asleep, mostly lying on the cold floor with no protection from the elements.

Farred felt the usual surge of excitement as they swept in on horseback. The attack provoked chaos as the Drobax, waking from their stupor, ran in all directions, slow to organise an ordered resistance. They killed freely, until Ashere ordered the retreat. He was wary of his small force getting caught, and so they sped away again.

Turning round in his saddle, Farred could see the bodies and the blood left behind. But the Drobax who remained seemed unconcerned. They would march as normal today, and inch their way closer to the imperial forces in Burkhard Castle. It made him wonder what they were doing. The futility of it. The other soldiers seemed to share his mood, and it was a quiet and sombre journey back to the base.

When they got there, Ashere ordered an evacuation. The enemy was getting too close, he judged. Time to relocate to Burkhard Castle.

ASHERE MADE sure that he rested his forces, rarely taking the same man on two raids in a row. He was scrupulously fair about this. The only exception was himself. He had led every single attack. If Farred was exhausted, he wondered how the Prince kept going. The effects on his body were clear to see. He had always been a striking figure, with jet black hair and light brown skin, that seemed to glow with health. But now he seemed permanently drained of colour, with hollowed eye sockets. Like a ghost. The men liked this. They admired him but also feared him, whispering about supernatural powers. They liked to think that this dark prince brought fear to the enemy.

The emotions Farred felt as he came within sight of the Empire's mightiest fortress, he knew, were shared by the rest of the soldiers. They were tired, but more united than they had been before they left. They felt overwhelmed at the numbers of their enemies, but proud of what they had achieved.

The two giant outcrops that formed Burkhard Castle loomed ever larger until they reached the small settlement at the foot of the castle. It was noticeably busier since they had left for Rotelegen, with soldiers from different parts of the Empire now stationed in separate camps. Tradespeople had arrived to set up shop, since wherever there are soldiers, there are goods needed, and money to spend. They even rode past what appeared to be a makeshift brothel, a wooden hut outside of which two women called out to the men as they passed, offering a night to remember.

But the space set aside for the Magnian forces when they had first arrived had been kept for them, and the men returned to their old tents. Plenty of food and drink had been provided, much more than the sparse rations they had been living off over the last few days. Ashere was informed by an official that the castle had been told of their arrival, and that someone would come down to meet them. Farred looked up at the battlements on top of the nearest outcrop. It looked like a tiny toy castle had been placed there, precariously, by a giant child; and that it might, at any moment, slide off the edge.

As the soldiers prepared their camp fires, and the smell of roasting meat filled the air, Farred and Brock waited with the Prince for a messenger to arrive. Eventually, Brock gave a whistle. He had caught sight of a group of half a dozen men making their way down the path. Farred looked over at the group and got something of a shock.

'It's Baldwin himself.'

Wearing a chain mail vest, the Emperor came marching over towards them, flanked by his most powerful allies. Walter, his younger brother and Marshal of the Empire, whose job it was to organise the defence of the fortress. Arne, his father-in-law, and Duke of Luderia, who had brought his own contingent of soldiers with him to the castle, second only to Baldwin's in size. Rainer the Chamberlain, chief administrator, and the man entrusted with the Emperor's money. And finally, Gustav the Archmage, known as 'the

Hawk', who seemed, to Farred, to walk as if he were the one who was really in charge.

Ashere walked over to meet them and gestured for Farred and Brock to follow.

Baldwin beamed as the two groups met and grasped Ashere on each arm, in a kind of half-hug. 'Prince Ashere, my Empire owes you a debt of gratitude I hope one day to repay. You have done far more than I could have hoped for,' Baldwin said earnestly, nodding at Farred and Brock as he delivered the words. 'I trust your men are settled well?'

'Yes, thank you, Your Majesty. You have been most generous with your supplies.'

'Please, Baldwin will do. I will need to catch you up on some developments. You and your two lieutenants have got rooms in the castle. Eventually we'll get your men up there as well.' Baldwin clasped Ashere on the shoulder and began leading him up the path.

'I hope you will notice that we have been using the time you have bought us well. Our defences are now much improved.'

As they began heading up the path, Farred fell in with Walter. The Marshal pointed out the improvements he had made to the fortress, no doubt picking out the same features Baldwin was explaining to Ashere. Since this was the only path up either of the two huge rocks that constituted the fortress, it was the obvious point of attack.

Walter had built a series of wooden gates along the path, each a foot thick and bound with metal, to stop attackers. In addition, ledges had been constructed along the path which wound its way around the rock above them. This allowed defenders to rain down missiles directly over the heads of attackers, and yet remain safe. The combination of the gates, and the height advantage provided by the ledge, was murderous. Attacking them seemed suicidal. Despite being well aware of the size of the force that Ishari was about to deploy here, Farred felt a little more confident that they could be stopped.

Although Rainer had taken them up when they had first arrived at Burkhard a week ago, Farred was no less impressed by the defences the second time round. They took the left-hand path as they approached the summit, Farred recalling that the middle and right paths led nowhere—just another way to bottle up the enemy. As they reached the top of the crag, Farred could see that the walls and five towers of the Duke's Keep had been heightened and strengthened. Baldwin led them across the stone bridge to the larger castle atop the other rock, known as the Emperor's Keep.

In the main hall, the Emperor and Prince sat down in a corner, intent on their own conversation, ignoring everyone else. Farred got a sense, perhaps, of why Baldwin was so keen to talk with Ashere. The weight of leadership and responsibility must have lain heavily on him. Ashere was one of the few men who could talk to him as something of an equal.

Walter gestured for Farred and Brock to follow him. He led them to the far tower and up the stairs until they were at the top of the battlements. 'This is the best view from the castle,' said the Marshal, resting his elbows on the wall and leaning out. He pointed to the east. 'You can see the Great Road for miles in either direction. To the south, the lands of the Empire. Mostly undefended. To the north, the horde will head down this road. They could go on past. But they won't.' Walter turned to look at them. 'You've seen their army. And you've seen this castle.' He looked at them, his eyes asking an unsaid question.

Farred and Brock looked at each other.

'We'll kill many,' said Brock.

A flicker of pain crossed the Marshal's face. He looked at Farred, who tried to choose the right words.

'You've done well, Walter. I think you'll hold out for a long time.'

He nodded, a resigned look now on his face. 'I see. Thanks for your honesty. Then we'll kill as many as we can and hold out for as long as we can.'

A brief silence fell on them, since there was nothing much more that could be said on that topic. Walter turned back to look out from the battlements. He pointed again, this time south down the Great Road. 'That's why I brought you both up here,' he said, allowing himself a small smile.

Farred looked out over the battlements into the distance. At first, he saw nothing. Then, as his eyes focused on the monotonous terrain, he saw movement. The Great Road was moving.

'An army,' he said.

Brock moved over to the wall and peered over. 'Who is it?' asked the Middian.

'The army of Gotbeck,' replied Walter. 'Archbishop Godfrey is leading them himself. There's at least another ten thousand men on top of what we've already got.'

'That's more Drobax we'll kill then,' remarked Brock with a serious expression.

'I think we'll hold out for a while longer now,' added Farred, keeping a straight face.

'Well, you two are delightful company,' responded Walter, frowning balefully. 'We'll have to do this again sometime. I can't wait to tell my brother the good news.'

. . .

WALTER INVITED Farred and Brock to Baldwin's war council. In the Emperor's Hall, a table had been laid out with food. To either side of Baldwin, who was positioned at the head of the table, sat the dukes, the men who controlled one of the seven duchies of the Empire: Arne, Duke of Luderia; Godfrey, Archbishop of Gotbeck; Jeremias, the new Duke of Rotelegen, who was accompanied by his mother, Adalheid, the widow of Duke Ellard. Prince Ashere and Walter were positioned after them. Farred and Brock were at the opposite end of the table to Baldwin, seated with his advisers, Rainer and Gustav the Hawk.

'The spread of these foul ideas has been like a fire in dry woods,' intoned Godfrey, his voice deep and compelling. 'A contagion of the soul which will not lose hold. Even when I arrived with my forces to restore order, men and women, often of the labouring class, whom I have always felt to have been the most sensible and level headed of our peoples, chose to die in futile resistance; leaving their children orphaned, rather than submit to my authority. And I have been far more forgiving, far more ready to accept false recantations and weak compromises, than I would ordinarily have done, because I was only too aware of my duties here, to defend the Empire from another, far greater threat. I hope you understand, Baldwin, that for me to have left Gotbeck in such a chaotic state, taking my forces with me, would have done far more harm than this delay in reaching Burkhard.'

Farred was just about following the Archbishop's story, which centred on a religious revolt he had felt forced to put down before leaving his duchy. However, he had a tendency not only to speak in long sentences but also to deliver them in what Farred supposed to be his sermon voice: loud, booming, and talking to his audience as if they were stupid. Most of the others at the table had polite faces on, but Farred also detected a certain amount of discomfort with the subject matter.

'I quite understand the predicament you have been in, Godfrey,' began Baldwin. 'Do you have any suspicions about the origins of these teachings?'

'More than suspicions, Your Majesty. It is quite clear that preachers from the Confederacy have been behind it. What is more, they have clearly been allowed to come and go across the border without the authorities there interfering. In my opinion, they have even encouraged it. They have certainly been as difficult and unhelpful as they could have been, when they know very well about the great enemy that threatens Brasingia. I understand in present circumstances there is little that we can do, but if the situation were different, I would be advocating an aggressive response against them.'

'I see. Well, the Confederacy has ever been a thorn in our side. I don't need to remind you of the endless problems they caused my late father, the gods rest his soul. But, as you say, that will have to wait for another time. I am keen to hear everything you know about our southern duchies. Emeric in Barissia is in open revolt. Coen in Thesse claims that he cannot spare any troops because of this.'

'Well, Your Majesty,' began Godfrey, 'all my sources, which, of course, are principally from trusted men in the Church, tell me that everything Coen is telling us is the truth. Emeric seems to have access to huge wealth, presumably via Ishari, and has used it to amass a large army. Coen's forces are significantly smaller, but are able to shadow his movements, and so far, the Barissians seem unwilling to make a move. Of course, now that my own army has left Gotbeck, the situation in the south has changed. The Barissians don't have to worry about a second front any longer. I would think it only a matter of time until Emeric moves against Coen. He will plan to neutralise Thesse and then turn against our sparsely defended duchies.'

Although Godfrey liked the sound of his own voice, his face looked suitably grim, and he did not appear to be enjoying what he said. 'In truth, Baldwin, he must surely intend to move on Essenberg when he can, and claim your imperial throne for himself.'

'Well, Godfrey,' said Duke Arne, 'no doubt you're right, but the man is a fool. Surely he must see that it will only be at the whim of Ishari that he holds it.'

'Ambition can easily cloud a man's judgement,' interjected Duchess Adalheid. 'When Baldwin was elected emperor, my husband accepted the decision and gave him his full support.'

Baldwin bent his head in acknowledgement.

'But most men can't do that,' Adalheid continued. 'Emeric will have been festering over it ever since, believe me.'

'Well,' said Baldwin, 'I have as much to fear as any man from Emeric, since I have left my family in Essenberg. That said, we cannot afford to worry about it now. A threat of far greater proportions will be with us soon. Prince Ashere, what was your estimate of the arrival of the Isharite army?'

'Your Majesty, the full army will arrive in three to four days' time. It is slow moving due to the Drobax. It is possible that they will send Haskan units faster than that.'

'Who leads it?' asked Godfrey.

'Gustav?' asked Baldwin, indicating that the mage should field the question.

'Shira, Queen of Haskany,' began the wizard.

'Arioc's slut?' interrupted the Archbishop.

Gustav inclined his head towards the Archbishop, presumably in confirmation of the statement. 'She has with her an uncle,' he continued, 'who is an experienced general, and a coterie of Isharite sorcerers. So, although she herself lacks experience, and Arioc is not with them, I think we need to expect strong leadership.'

'Walter,' said Baldwin, 'what needs to be done?'

'The defences are almost ready. Now that Your Grace's soldiers have arrived,' continued the Marshal, nodding to Archbishop Godfrey, 'they will need to be accommodated in the castle, along with all the other fighting men still outside. We also need to ensure that any non-combatants leave for the South.'

'We can lead one more sortie out,' said Ashere. It was half statement but also half question, since he turned to Farred and Brock for confirmation. Farred and Brock looked at each other and then nodded their consent.

'I don't expect you to do that,' replied Baldwin. 'You and your soldiers have already done us a great service. Now that you are here, I intend to keep you in reserve. It is time for others to risk their lives. My own men can go if you need more time, Walter.'

'I would request one final sortie, Your Majesty,' said Ashere. 'Then I would feel that I have done my job to the best of my ability. After that, I would be happy to be deployed as you see fit.'

Baldwin looked at the Prince and nodded. 'Very well. If you put it like that, I must grant you your request. Please ask my brother to provide you with whatever resources you need, Prince Ashere.'

Farred felt a shudder go down his spine at the exchange. For some reason, he wished Ashere had not volunteered them. But it was done.

TWO TOWERS

VI

The High Tower of the Knights of Kalinth was not what Belwynn had expected. The knights seemed to be a sober, disciplined group of men. They dedicated themselves to a military life, forgoing a family. They lived in a tough landscape of hills and moorland. So, to find that their Tower was an elegant folly, with its thin walls and slim, tall spires, totally useless as a defensive structure, was a surprise.

'It's very pretty,' said Belwynn as they crested a hill and she got her first full look at it.

'Yes, it is,' said Theron, smiling sweetly at it like you might smile at your favourite aunt or uncle.

'It's not very formidable looking, though. It's not going to intimidate your enemies.'

Theron kept smiling. 'True enough, but we have the Fortress of Chalios as our defensive bastion, should the need arise. The High Tower is a much more pleasant place for the Order to meet. Most everywhere else in Kalinth is bleak and imposing,' he said and looked Belwynn in the eyes. 'So when you have something delicate and beautiful, you treasure it all the more.'

Belwynn looked away. They rode on in silence, eating up the distance to the Tower, until they were dismounting and organising the stabling of the horses. Theron boasted that the stables at the High Tower were the largest in Dalriya, and several grooms descended on them, ensuring that all the horses were marked up with Sebastian's coat of arms, a simple blue shield with one red chevron, before leading them off to what looked like a maze of buildings.

The importance of the High Tower to the knights had led to the growth of a town around it, with shops and guest houses providing services to the knights and their entourages. Apart from the horses, accommodation for humans in the Tower was confined to knights only, so Evander was sent off to book lodgings for himself, Belwynn and the others, while Sebastian's retainers and servants organised themselves separately.

'Come, now the boring arrangements have been made, let me show you the Tower,' said Theron, gesturing all four of them to the grand entrance.

Again, no real effort had been made to make the entrance defensible. It was approached by a set of polished, grey marble steps, with a six-pillared portico above it. The entrance itself was wide enough for the five of them to walk through side by side. Ahead of them was a wall, dominated by a huge embroidery depicting a battle scene, where knights on horseback were charging at an army of Drobax. Theron took them to the right, then a right-angle turn to the left brought them into a large hallway. Various people were milling about here, while others leaned against walls chatting. Some were dressed in all their knightly finery; others were servants who worked in the Tower.

'In there,' said Theron, pointing to the room on the right, 'is the chapel. Only knights may enter; that is where we are inducted into the Order. Opposite,' he said, waving to the left, 'are the kitchens and stairs leading up to the sleeping quarters. But I wanted to show you the Great Hall.'

Theron led them ahead to the formidable oak doors of the hall. Each was flanked by a giant marble statue. On the right, a white mounted knight, his horse risen on its hind legs, was thrusting his lance ahead of him. On the left, a fearsome green dragon, on its hind legs in a similar pose to the horse, reached out with its clawed and scaled front legs.

Theron pushed at one of the doors, already slightly ajar, and with a bit of a creak it opened wide enough for them to slip through. Belwynn was first struck by the height of the room; the ceiling was a good twenty feet high, and was decorated with painted murals. Servants were coming and going through a door which connected into the kitchens, preparing for the evening meal. At the other end of the room was a raised dais.

The rest of the room was taken up with round tables. In front of the dais was the largest and grandest, and the other tables radiated out from it, like the spokes of a wheel. Belwynn had never seen a set up like it. The halls she had been in were almost always set up in a horseshoe shape, with most people sitting on benches. The nearer you were to the top of the horseshoe, the more honoured you were by the host.

'The round tables denote equality?' she asked.

'Yes,' replied Theron, 'of a sort. The idea is that all the knights are brothers, and therefore equals. But everyone wants to be seated as near to the main table as possible. You can't avoid human nature.'

On their way out, heading down the hallway, a huge shout rang out, and another knight came bounding over towards them. Theron let out a similar cry and the two men embraced in a big bear hug.

Theron turned to the others.

'This is Tycho, my best friend. Tycho, these are new friends I have made. It's rather a long story. Belwynn, Elana, Rabigar and Dirk.'

Tycho was of a similar age to Theron, but of a darker complexion. Even standing next to Theron, Belwynn could see that he was heavily muscled, with a broad chest, huge shoulders, and a thick neck. He had a friendly, open face, and he shook each of them by the hand, Belwynn's hand disappearing into his when it was her turn.

'Well, sometime soon you'll have to tell me the story. Is it true that your cousin is here?'

'Yes...' Theron began, but his attention was diverted. 'Evander! Over here!' he shouted, interrupting himself.

The young squire, who was making his way over to them anyway, hurried faster.

'Lord Tycho,' he said in greeting to the other knight.

Tycho gave him a whack on the shoulder, which sent a shudder down the young man's body, but he seemed to expect it, and continued unfazed.

'I have secured our accommodation, my lord,' he said to Theron. 'Good rooms at the Green Dragon.'

'Excellent. Well done, 'Vander.'

'Well, I think we should go there now,' said Belwynn, sensing that Theron needed to get away and discuss politics with his friend. 'Thank you for showing us the Tower, Lord Theron.'

They said their goodbyes and followed Evander away from the Tower and into the town. The town had clearly grown up next to the Tower in a completely disorganised fashion, and Belwynn found herself concentrating hard on remembering the route, as Evander navigated the twists and turns. Solid stone buildings stood next to temporary shacks built of untreated wood, and the paths narrowed and widened at random, so that at one minute they would all be walking side by side, the next in single file, as they squeezed their way past people coming in the opposite direction.

As well as grocers feeding the knights and their entourages, they walked past farriers and blacksmiths, who seemed to be making a good living.

A bellow of pain erupted from one of the smithies, followed by a scream. They hurried over. Outside, they found a smith on his knees with a splinter of metal sticking out of his neck. Blood was pouring from the wound. A small crowd had already gathered around him.

'Careful!' cautioned one of them, as the smith fumbled at his neck with big, grimy fingers. 'You might make it worse!'

'Let me deal with this!' said Elana, making her way over to the man.

Belwynn and the others followed her.

'It might have hit his jugular,' murmured Rabigar as he inspected the damage.

Belwynn looked around at the crowd for resistance, but they seemed willing enough for Elana to tend to the man.

'Who are you?' demanded the smith, wild eyed with fear.

'Calm down and let me have a look,' replied Elana, going down onto her knees so that she was at the same height as her patient. She had a look at the injury, and then used one finger to put some light pressure on the neck below the wound, which reduced the flow of blood.

'My name's Elana,' she said calmly. 'What's yours?'

'Nestor. Can you get it out? I was hammering iron, and a bit flew off. Is it bad?'

'Don't worry, I'll get it out.'

Elana placed the fingers of her other hand around the injury and closed her eyes in concentration. Nothing seemed to happen at first, but the blood flow reduced further. Then she carefully placed a thumb and forefinger on Nestor's neck where the piece of metal had entered. She gripped the end of the metal with her other hand and slowly pulled it out. The crowd, which was growing in size, gasped as she removed it and placed it on the ground beside her. She kept her hand over his neck for a while longer and then removed it. The injury was still visible, but it had stopped bleeding, as if the internal damage had been healed.

'There,' Elana said. 'It should be fine now, but you need to take the rest of the day off and rest—no physical activity. Protect the wound from any damage.'

'Thank you,' said the smith, getting gingerly to his feet and then pulling up Elana with him. 'Thank you,' he repeated, enfolding her in a hug. 'You saved my life. Please, let me pay you.'

'No,' responded Elana, frowning, 'I don't need payment.'

'Then take something from my store, please, anything you want.'

But other members of the crowd were now moving in, asking Elana what she had done, and how. Rabigar approached Nestor and took him to one side, no doubt discussing their shared trade, if not the accident itself. Belwynn shared a look with the young Evander, who was staring open mouthed at what he had just witnessed. She gave him a brief smile and shrugged. Something told her that this story was going to get retold. A lot.

* * *

It had been a hellish journey since they had been captured in the lands of the Grand Caladri. Moneva had been kept away from the others. She had her hands tied the whole time, and had to ride on the same horse as an Isharite. They had taken it in turns to ride with her, their arms wrapped around her from behind as they held the reins of the horse, squeezing her more than necessary, gripping her with their knees. Their breath was heavy on the back of her neck. Sometimes they would hold the reins one handed and rest the other on her thigh. It was all Moneva could do to stop herself from screaming out and fighting. But she knew that was what they wanted. So instead she kept quiet, didn't react, and gave them as little pleasure as she could.

The treatment handed out to Herin, Clarin and Gyrmund was no better. They would get kicked and slapped about regularly. Some days they would eat, others not. They sat on a cart most of the time, but at other times, the Isharites might decide that one of them should walk. They would tie their hands to a rope connected to the cart. If they tripped, they would get dragged along until they regained their feet. Their captors laughed a little when this happened, but most of the time showed no interest in them.

Soren, meanwhile, was kept in his box. A special group of Isharites watched over him and his box, which had been placed on a second cart away from the others. Moneva had never seen them open it to let some air in, or give him anything to drink.

When they stopped for rests, they would manhandle her off the horse and dump her on the ground. But they made sure that she got enough food and water. She would always sit away from the others, but sometimes near enough that she could take surreptitious glances to see how they looked. She knew better than to do more than that. Gyrmund didn't. The first time he had called over to her. Herin quickly shoved an elbow into his ribs so that it came out as a meaningless yell. The Isharites walked over and kicked him. Moneva stared at the floor, a lump in her throat, praying that he wouldn't be so stupid again. He wasn't.

Most often she sat alone while a group of them would eat and stare at her, talking amongst themselves with their leery faces trained on her. One would say something and the others would all laugh, staring at her all the more fiercely. She repeatedly asked herself why they didn't rape her, why they stopped short of any direct sexual contact. She assumed Arioc had given the order, and that they were too scared to break it. But she didn't know that. He wasn't with them, and she hadn't seen him since the day of their capture. So, she said nothing, didn't react, or draw any kind of attention to herself. She behaved the same way day after day, hoping that if she did, they would leave her alone again; and surely, eventually, they would get where they were going, and the journey would end. She deliberately didn't think about what would happen then.

It had been obvious to Moneva that they had been travelling northwards, and that the lands of Ishari were the most likely destination. But her geography was pretty poor, and anyway, those lands were steeped in mystery, since few people had been there and returned to tell the tale.

There were signs of permanent habitation. They travelled on proper roads, and she saw grazing animals in the distance. But no buildings, and no other travellers.

Then a vast fortress emerged on the horizon, growing bigger as they approached. Moneva had seen nothing like it before. It hadn't been sited on any significant geographical position. The surrounding land was flat and featureless. It was as if it had been dropped in this location from the skies. Its walls were three times as high as any she had ever seen before, with huge circular towers in the corners. A wall extended out in either direction from the fortress proper as far as the eye could see, presumably enclosing a vast complex. The most remarkable thing was the colour. It was not just the dark jet colour of the stone; but that the walls, when touched by the pale sun above, glimmered and sparkled, as if infused with some dark magic, which, thought Moneva, was entirely possible. The effect was to suggest that crossing to the other side of the immense wall would take you into a new, unknown world, somehow separate from the rest of Dalriya.

As Moneva wondered what they would find behind that wall, her rider steered the horse away from the rest of the convoy. One other rider joined them. It was all done in seconds, with no talking or farewells to their comrades. They were making their way directly towards the fortress, along a gravel road, while the rest of the convoy headed in a more north easterly direction, presumably to some other part of the complex. She turned back in her seat. She made eye contact with Gyrmund and Herin, who were staring in her direction. Clarin seemed to be slumped asleep on the cart. She then turned around again.

The two riders seemed to be in a hurry. They trotted their mounts over towards the huge metal plated gates which were the main entrance to the fortress. As they neared, Moneva realised that the glimmer of the walls came from crystals which had somehow been embedded amongst the black stone of the wall. When opened, the gates would be big enough for ten cavalrymen to ride through abreast. Above them, about ten feet up, a small, square section of the metal gate swung open with a squeak, large enough for a head to pop through.

The head belonged to an Isharite soldier, and a brief conversation ensued. Moneva still found the language incomprehensible, and they talked fast, but she noticed both her captors and the fortress guard use the word 'Arioc'. It was impossible to tell how the conversation went, since their faces showed no emotion that she could read. After a short time, the head poked back inside, and the metal window was slammed shut.

They waited outside. Moneva's body gave an involuntary shudder. Her rider noticed and said something to his comrade on the other horse, before putting his arms around her chest and giving her a hug. Both of them laughed. Moneva stared straight ahead at the gates, trying to keep her breathing steady.

Shortly, another squeaking and grating noise preceded a door being opened. Like last time, it wasn't either of the main gates. Instead, someone had opened a smaller door that had been built into the main gate. Moneva had not noticed it before.

Once opened, the two riders manoeuvred through the gate. Six feet ahead of them was another length of wall. Any attackers who made it through the gate would, at this point, find themselves trapped between the two walls which ran parallel to each other. She got a brief glimpse of the inside of the outer wall, which was a complex of stairs and platforms leading all the way to the top. It seemed lightly manned at the moment, but could clearly hold many fighters if necessary. Before she could take in more, they were off, turning left and moving between the two walls until they headed through a gap in the wall on their right. They continued straight ahead for a while before some more zigzagging brought them to the entrance to one of the huge towers that

Moneva had seen from a distance. One guard stood sentry. The two riders dismounted and one of them lifted Moneva from the horse. After a brief conversation with the guard, they were admitted inside.

The entrance room was sparsely furnished. A closed wooden door faced them. Instead, the soldiers gripped Moneva's upper arms and guided her towards the set of stone steps. They were steep, twisting stairs, winding their way up to the next floor of the tower. Moneva's legs felt stiff from all the horse riding, and she had trouble with her balance on the first few steps with her hands still tied. But the two men then gripped each arm and part shoved, part lifted her up the stairs, so that she had to move her feet quickly to avoid being dragged up.

They arrived at a wooden door leading to the rooms on the second floor. One of the soldiers banged on the door roughly. Then, without waiting very long, banged again. The door was unlocked and opened from the inside. Another Isharite stood in the doorway. He glared sternly at each of them, showing no surprise that Moneva was standing in front of him. He began questioning the two men. He seemed older, or at least superior, to the other two. But it was hard to tell. He had the same dark colouring as the rest of the Isharites and his face showed no obvious signs of age.

Making a strange clicking noise with his mouth, he waved his hands at the two men to bring her in. Moneva was propelled into the room. Even though she knew how big the tower was, the room seemed huge. It was expensively furnished with handcrafted bookshelves, soft Haskan rugs, a wardrobe, and scattered with other strange objects she had never seen before. Three doors led off from this room, all closed. There didn't seem to be anyone else in.

'Welcome to Lord Arioc's chambers,' said the man easily. 'I am Babak.'

Moneva made an involuntary gasp, both because she had heard no one speak Dalriyan for days, and because of where she was.

He paced over to one of the doors and opened it. 'You will stay in here until he returns,' Babak informed Moneva casually, his accent thick, emphasising the consonants.

Making the same clicking noise at the two soldiers who had brought Moneva here, he waved an arm at the room. Grabbing Moneva by the arms once more, they propelled her into the room, which was much smaller, and dominated by a four-poster bed. The men didn't stop, and before she realised what was happening, they had thrown her unceremoniously onto the bed. She picked herself up to the sound of their laughter. Both men were staring at her, one of them licking his lips. But, to her relief, they turned around and sauntered out of the room.

Babak appeared in the doorway. He looked at her but said nothing and closed the door, staying on the other side. She heard the click of the door being locked. Moneva was alone for the first time in a week. And she began to cry—big, heaving sobs, which she hid by pressing her face into the mattress of the bed.

FRIENDS AND ENEMIES

VII

The warm spell they had been enjoying in Magnia showed no signs of stopping, though there was enough of a breeze to make travelling comfortable. Edgar, accompanied by a small entourage, approached Wincandon, the lair of his enemy. Cerdda, Prince of North Magnia.

At least, that's what Magnian history recorded: two families, bitter rivals who ruled a divided country. But recent events had questioned that old narrative. South and North had united against a much more serious enemy. They had come together to form an army, led by Cerdda's brother, Ashere. This army would now be active, helping to defend the Brasingian Empire from Ishari. And here, in Wincandon, they might achieve even more.

Wincandon was a small agricultural estate, surrounded by the lush Magnian countryside. But it was owned by the royal family of North Magnia and here, in Cerdda's hall, a Conference of the South was to be held.

Edgar nudged his horse onwards into the village. Orderly, well-maintained houses sat either side of a dirt track that led to the hall, visible in the distance. To his right, just beyond the houses, the gentle tinkling of a stream provided some background noise. Looking across, he saw a large, vertical waterwheel that dominated the skyline. The watermill provided the villagers with the power to grind their grains into flour.

When they reached the hall, Cerdda was waiting for him outside. Edgar dismounted as servants arrived to take away the horses. Cerdda approached, and they embraced.

'You found us, then?' he asked.

Edgar nodded. 'We made good time. Some hall you have here,' he added, taking in the building's size before them. It was larger, by a distance, than any hall in South Magnia.

'Yes. This is where we spent our childhood—I have fond memories of the place. I have enlarged it since. It's a place to get away. For family time. Talking of which, you must come in and meet them.'

Edgar followed Cerdda into the hall. It was light and airy inside. Groups of armed men had claimed different parts of the hall for their own, talking amongst themselves while servants brought them food and drink. They made their way towards the back of the hall. Edgar noticed some familiar faces on the way. He nodded to Frayne, the Middian chieftain who had participated in the Conference that Edgar had hosted some two weeks past. His presence was a good sign that the Middians might supply more soldiers.

A set of wooden stairs zigzagged its way up one wall to a second floor. The two princes took the stairs. Half way up, Edgar could hear female voices talking above them. The stairs opened into a large reception room. An unlit fireplace dominated the opposite wall. In between, there was a table, with trays of food and wine glasses atop it. Half a dozen chairs were positioned around it, with rugs and cushions scattered on the floor. To the right, three doors led off from the room, presumably bedrooms.

Three women were in the room, all working with needle and thread, which they put down when the two of them entered.

Now that he was here, Edgar felt hesitant. He wasn't used to female company. He had grown up an only child, and his relationship with his mother had always been distant, more so since the death of his father and his inheritance of the throne. More than that, however, the people in this room had been enemies of his family in the civil war. He wasn't at all sure how they would react to him.

'Edgar, may I introduce the three most important people in my life. My mother, Lady Mette,' Cerdda began.

'*Please*, Cerdda,' said Mette, standing. 'Mette will do. It is a pleasure to meet you, Edgar.'

More than once, Edgar's father had emphasised how beautiful Mette was, and he could now see for himself. She had a deep brown skin tone with large, almond-shaped eyes, framed by straight, jet black hair. Edgar moved to take her hand. Instead, Mette opened her arms and embraced him.

Releasing him, she took over the introductions.

'This is my lovely daughter-in-law, Irmgard,' she said.

Irmgard, Cerdda's wife, was a handsome woman with more typical Magnian looks. She was tall and slender, brown hair hanging loose to her swan-like neck. She seemed more reserved than her mother-in-law, allowing Edgar to take her hand and plant a kiss.

'And Elfled, my daughter,' finished Mette.

Turning to Cerdda's sister, Edgar found himself looking at the most attractive woman he had seen in his life. Elfled had inherited her mother's dark brown eyes and dark hair. Her hair was curly, however, falling in ringlets about her face. Her skin, like her brother's, was a golden-brown colour.

'Hello Edgar,' said Elfled, embracing him just like her mother had.

Edgar froze. The closeness of her, the smell of her, threatened to overwhelm his senses. His mind went blank and refused to work properly. When she withdrew, he became conscious that he had been speaking, but had no idea what he had said. He looked around at the faces in the room. No-one was making a face as if he had said anything stupid, but he suspected they might all be too polite to let him know if he had.

'Is your mother well?' enquired Mette.

'Yes,' Edgar replied, recovering. 'I visited with her a few weeks ago. She is very content.'

'I am so happy that we have got the chance to meet you at last,' said Mette. 'You will both be very busy today, and it is not a time to dwell on the past. But I wanted to let you know, Edgar. I have never felt any resentment towards you. My husband and your father ended up on different sides in the civil war. Bradda could no longer support King Alfrith. Your father decided he must. But there was never any personal animosity between them. Your father acted with honour in everything he did. So have you. I am proud that you and Cerdda have built bridges. It is time to put the past behind us.'

'Do you two have time to stay awhile and have a drink with us?' asked Elfled. 'We have some Cordentine red. It might help you get through the evening.'

'I don't know,' said Cerdda. 'We have more guests arriving, and—'

'Yes,' said Edgar, interrupting. He found himself a seat. The only way he was leaving, he had decided, was if a demon dragged him out.

EDGAR RUBBED HIS EYES. He was struggling to stay focused on the discussion at hand. He had, perhaps, had one glass of wine too many. Lord Rosmont, representing King Glanna of Cordence, was demanding chapter and verse on what he would get for his master's money. As with the earlier force sent to the

Empire under the leadership of Prince Ashere and Farred, the Cordentines had not been persuaded to supply their own soldiers, but were prepared to bankroll others. Edgar accepted it was necessary for them to make sure that nobody ran off with their money. But since most of Glanna's money would be going elsewhere, Edgar found it hard to stay interested.

Instead, his mind kept returning to Elfled, Cerdda's sister. There was something about her. He couldn't keep his eyes off her when she was in the room, and kept thinking about her when she left.

Making his excuses, Edgar left the negotiating table. The conversation continued without him. He headed out of Cerdda's hall and took a few deep breaths of fresh air. It was a warm summer evening, and he felt a fleeting sense of disappointment that he wasn't getting to enjoy it.

Still, he had to take pleasure in the fact that they were close to achieving something very important. Wincandon was an ordinary estate in North Magnia but, in Edgar's view, it was the setting for something extraordinary. No one he had talked to could recall a treaty with signatories from so many nations. As well as South and North Magnia, led by himself and Cerdda, there was Frayne, a chieftain from the Midder Steppe, who had offered to recruit soldiers so long as someone else would pay their wages; Russell, representing Duke Bastien of Morbaine, who could not formally commit soldiers without the authority of King Nicolas of Guivergne, but was negotiating on other sources of aid; Lord Emmett, representing Duke Coen of Thesse, who, with the backing of Emperor Baldwin, was requesting aid against the traitor, Emeric of Barissia; and finally, Lord Rosmont, who had authority to commit Cordence to the war. They were close to signing a full treaty and declaration of war, on both Ishari and Barissia—and, crucially, to committing to another army, even larger than the one they had sent to Brasingia.

Edgar wandered away from the hall towards the southern end of the village. He stopped at the mill pond, a pleasant spot dominated by a large willow tree. Some of the yellow catkins had fallen onto the surface, and were twirling around in the breeze. Beneath the surface, sinewy eels patrolled their underwater kingdom, wriggling into view and away again.

'Penny for your thoughts?' said a female voice.

Edgar turned around sharply. He had assumed that he was alone and his heart beat fast as he peered at the shaded end of the pond. Emerging from under the willow tree, Elfled, Cerdda's sister, walked towards him. He met her half way, keen to take the chance to spend some time with her alone.

'Well?' she asked him.

'It was getting a bit boring in there,' replied Edgar.

'Going that well, then?'

'No, it's not going badly. Just slowly,' said Edgar, looking around them. 'Sometimes I crave a bit of peace.'

'Oh. Well, I can't share that sentiment. I get more than my share of peace and quiet.'

Edgar looked at her quizzically.

'That's the life of a princess,' she explained. 'Over protected, spending your days sewing and reading. Excluded from important meetings,' she said pointedly, making Edgar feel a little embarrassed. 'Until you get married off to some stranger twice your age.'

'Right. I'd never really thought about it before. No sister, you see.'

Elfled laughed.

'And what's so funny?'

'I was thinking to myself, what a shame for you, being an only child. It's the strangest thing. When I was growing up, you were the devil. Sitting on my family's throne, dripping in the blood of innocents. I happily hated you: a childish, unthinking kind of hate. But now I've met you, I can't hate you anymore. You're so fair and...*reasonable*.'

'I'm not always that reasonable.'

'Come on Edgar, you were emoting with a spoilt princess about her not having any work to do!'

Edgar laughed. 'I suppose so. Anyway, it's made me very happy to have befriended you and Cerdda.'

'I think it's a really important thing that you are both doing today.'

'Yes. Although we're hardly going to make an impact on the Isharite forces.'

'Maybe. I didn't mean just the war, though. Nobody would have predicted North and South Magnia working so closely together, even a year ago. It's an important step towards uniting our country again.'

'Union? That's a long way off.'

'Is it? Cerdda and Irmgard love each other very much. But they haven't had children after years of marriage.'

'Ashere?'

Elfled's mouth gave a twitch of a smile. 'I doubt that my brother Ashere will have any children.'

Of course, that left Elfled herself, but Edgar knew that if he pursued that avenue he would end up going bright red and tongue tied. 'Well then, maybe it is possible,' he murmured.

'It is. Don't you think Magnia should be one country again?'

'Yes. Of course I do.'

Elfled seemed pleased with that response. 'So, what's left to sort out in there?' she asked, nodding toward Cerdda's hall.

'Well, we're yet to agree on the objective of intervention in the Empire. We want to keep Essenberg out of Emeric's hands. Anything more than that would be over-stretching our resources, in my opinion. The other main sticking points are money, as usual, and leadership of the force we send.'

Elfled sighed. 'Hardly sticking points. Sometimes I think you should let the women sort these things out, it'd be done in half an hour. The money is just like buying something from the market: you haggle and meet in the middle. As for who is in charge, it should be the complete opposite. No compromises. Who would you trust the most to do the job? Make sure it's them.'

Edgar smiled. 'Maybe you should go back in there instead of me and sort them all out.'

'Who *would* you be happiest with in charge?' Elfled persisted.

'Well, it would be unfair to ask Cerdda to go when his brother led the first force.'

Elfled nodded. 'So?'

'Me.'

'I agree,' said Elfled with a shy smile.

Edgar let out a big breath as he came to terms with the idea. It would mean being absent from South Magnia for a long time, a move not without its dangers. He had no military experience to speak of, either. But it felt right. The force they would raise needed someone with his status to take overall command. It also meant that he would keep control of things. 'Well. Looks like I might be going to Brasingia.'

Elfled looked at him solemnly. 'Good luck, Edgar.'

* * *

Soren? Soren!?

Nothing. Belwynn had been trying to contact him for a day now. She knew that something was wrong.

She didn't know what to do. Opening the door of her room at the Green Dragon, she stumbled out into the corridor. She crashed into someone coming the other way. Elana.

'Belwynn, what's the matter? Is it Soren?'

Belwynn tried to say something, but instead burst into tears.

Elana put her arm around her and directed her back into the room.

'Sorry, Elana. I'm embarrassing myself all the time at the moment.'

'No, you're not. Don't be silly. You still can't talk to him?'

'No. I don't know why,' said Belwynn, then paused for breath. 'Well, there's one obvious reason. He's dead.'

'You don't know that, Belwynn. Why have they kept him alive for a week, transporting him somewhere, only to kill him? How do you feel? Do you feel he is dead or alive?'

'I don't know, Elana! I can't speak to him; I can't sense his presence.'

'So we don't know what's happened, Belwynn. Don't give in to despair yet.'

Belwynn took a steadying breath. 'You're right. But I need to do something about it. I can't just sit around here anymore being useless.'

'We will do something, Belwynn. We'll do something here, in Kalinth, first. I know that we're supposed to be here, and that what we do will be important. Can you have patience a while longer?'

Belwynn wiped her eyes. 'I don't have a choice, do I?'

Elana shook her head. 'Not that I can see. Look, why don't we go to the Tower, and see if there's any news?'

Belwynn nodded. 'Alright.'

'First, I need to check on the other two.'

Belwynn went with Elana to the room across the corridor which Rabigar and Dirk shared. Belwynn looked away as Elana lifted Rabigar's patch and inspected his eye; or, at least, where his eye used to be. Taken from him by Emeric's jailers in Coldeberg Castle, it was a wound that could have killed him had Elana not been there to treat it.

'It's still looking good,' she told him.

She then moved on to Dirk. He didn't look well. Placing her hands at various places, she moved around his body, murmuring prayers to her goddess, Madria. When she had finished, he seemed to Belwynn to look visibly better, his skin losing the grey tinge it had before.

'We're going to go to the Tower. Either of you fancy a walk?'

'No thanks,' said Dirk. 'I think I'll rest up here.'

'I'll take you there,' said Rabigar. 'I've a mind to visit with our new friend, Nestor the smith. I think he could do with an extra pair of hands.'

Belwynn smiled to herself. It looked like Nestor was going to get some extra help, whether he needed it or not. They said their goodbyes to Dirk and left. The visit made Belwynn realise how much Elana had been doing in recent days, looking after the victims of two serious attacks. She felt guilty about leaving it all to the priestess while she remained absorbed with her own troubles. She had even heaped those on to Elana, as well as everything else.

'How is Dirk doing?' she asked Elana.

'He's not recovering. The injuries are too severe. I'm keeping him alive, but...' Elana trailed off, perhaps struggling with her own emotions.

The news made Belwynn go cold. She had assumed that Dirk would make a recovery in the end. But if even Elana couldn't properly heal him, what hope was there? 'I'm sorry,' she said, feeling like she should say something else, but knowing that whatever she said would be inadequate.

'Thank you,' said Elana. 'I am trying to help him find peace with his situation. Madria helps him.'

They headed down into the main lounge of the Green Dragon. Its dark interior and smell of ale, familiar to virtually every inn Belwynn had visited, was not appealing this morning, and she felt much better once they got out into sunlight and fresh air.

They began making their way through the maze of streets towards the High Tower. They had not gone far when they heard a shout.

'There she is!'

Swinging round, Belwynn saw a group of half a dozen women gesturing towards Elana. Elana waited as the group headed towards them. As they got closer, one of their number held out a small bundle of blankets towards Elana. It was a small girl.

'My child, she is sick,' pleaded the woman, her eyes raw with emotion. 'We don't know what to do.'

Elana looked at Belwynn, as if to say sorry.

'Don't worry. I'll be fine on my own,' said Belwynn.

'Are you sure?'

'Of course.'

'I'll stay with Elana,' said Rabigar. 'Just in case.'

Belwynn watched the women lead Elana and Rabigar off down a side street. At that moment, she envied Elana her talent, God-given or not. It allowed her to be useful.

Belwynn continued alone. The atmosphere in the town felt safe enough for her not to worry. A palace full of armed knights no doubt had something to do with it. As she approached the Tower, she noted the complete absence of security. It seemed that anybody could walk in, yet nobody who was unwelcome tried to.

Belwynn walked up the colonnaded steps leading to the Tower entrance, and she noticed someone looking in her direction. It was Tycho, the friend

Theron had introduced to her when they had first arrived. He was in conversation with two other knights, both about the same age as him. He said his goodbyes to them and they headed off together, away from the Tower. Tycho smiled and walked over.

'Lady Belwynn, a pleasure to meet you again.' He gestured at the two departing knights. 'Just sending for reinforcements,' he said and then looked at her with a frown, as if he wasn't sure whether that was information he should have revealed.

Belwynn pretended she hadn't heard. 'I was hoping to see Theron or Sebastian?'

'Right, I'll take you up. They're in a meeting together.'

'Oh. I've come at a bad time?'

'No, no, just a small meeting—an *unofficial* meeting,' he said mysteriously.

Belwynn wasn't convinced that Tycho was cut out for cloak and dagger politics.

He led Belwynn through the Tower entrance and into the main hallway. Instead of going straight on towards the Great Hall, they veered off to the left and through a doorway. Straight ahead, Belwynn could hear the sounds and smell the aromas of the kitchens. Tycho led her to a set of stairs that took them to the next floor.

'These are the chambers of the knights,' he commented as he led her down a corridor. 'They are allocated to us when we visit the Tower,' he added.

They passed door after door. Compared to the splendour of the Tower elsewhere, the living quarters seemed sparse and cramped.

'The rooms are small,' she commented.

'Yes, but big enough for one man to store his possessions and to sleep.'

They moved further up the corridor, and Tycho rapped on one of the doors. There was a shout from inside and he opened the door. Sebastian, Theron and a third man whom Belwynn did not recognise were seated inside, on a bed and two chairs.

'Hello, Belwynn,' said Sebastian, standing up. 'This is my good friend, Remi.'

Remi looked to be of a similar age to Sebastian. He was a big man with a big black beard which was flecked with grey. Remi gestured at them. 'Come in, come in,' he said.

'I'm not intruding?' checked Belwynn, squeezing in but finding nowhere suitable to sit.

'No,' said Sebastian. 'We need to talk to you, anyway. I should have come to see you before, but I've only recently come out of my meeting with Galenos.'

Sebastian's tone of voice suggested that the meeting had not gone well. They shuffled onto the bed to make room for Belwynn and Tycho on the two chairs.

'I explained to him that I had changed my position on King Jonas,' Sebastian continued. 'That I thought it was our duty as an Order to intervene. I used some of the information you have given us, about Ishari aggression,' he said, looking at Belwynn, 'and all the other arguments, including our responsibilities to the people.

'I thought I could persuade him. But he wasn't interested in persuasion or debate. He just repeated his position, that the Order should remain loyal to the King of Kalinth. In every situation. He didn't engage with me at all.' Sebastian shook his head, evidently still bemused by his lack of success. 'I didn't get anywhere.'

It seemed as if the energy and drive had all been sapped out of the knight by the setback.

'The man's an idiot, that's the problem,' said Remi darkly.

Sebastian shook his head as if to stop his friend's tirade, but the other knight raised his hand and pressed on.

'And he's surrounded himself with idiots. Men like Euthymius. He listens to them more than the rest of us now. They spend too much time in this Tower, and not enough in the real world.'

'I think he felt like I was challenging him,' said Sebastian dolefully. 'That I was being disloyal. I'm afraid that he now sees me as an enemy.'

'I'm sorry for you, uncle,' said Theron, 'but I'm not surprised. This is how our Order has been run for years now. Anyone with a different opinion to the leadership is cast as a traitor. It is weakness. Galenos is old and weak and doesn't want to confront the truth. In fact, he would rather turn on his own brothers than do that. And it is our country and our people who have been suffering for it. Weak leadership from the knights and from the royal court. It is killing our land.'

They were stark words and delivered without Theron's usual good humour. It left the room quiet and still as the words were digested and their implications, which had been left unsaid, hovered in the air.

'I think we need to think ahead carefully from now on,' said Remi. 'Starting with the feast tonight. We can't afford to be naïve: if Euthymius and his allies now see some of us as enemies, they may be on the attack.'

Belwynn swallowed, and after a moment's hesitation, piped up. 'I was thinking. I would like to go to the celebrations tonight. I would like to sing.'

The four knights in the room all looked at her with the same expression.

'You want to sing?' asked Theron after an uncomfortable pause.

She smiled reassuringly, her first proper smile of the day. 'Let me sing tonight, Theron. It will help. Trust me.'

Belwynn was done with feeling useless. It was time for her to do something.

* * *

IT WAS a strange day for the middle of summer. It felt more like one of those winter days, grey and wet, when the sun never really appears, and the day never gets going, offering a half-hearted interruption to the night before retreating again. A non-event of a day.

The weather doesn't help things, Farred thought to himself, *but we have other problems.* The force led by Prince Ashere had been unable to locate the Isharite army since setting out from Burkhard Castle over six hours ago. A big bank of fog to the west slowed down the scouting parties who struck off in that direction, so that long after the other groups had returned to report their findings, the army had to sit and wait for the western party. The most recent group had yet to return at all.

He sensed the mood of the soldiers, much more negative and frustrated than they had ever been before, and he understood it. Upon arriving at Burkhard, they had received a warm welcome. They had all felt satisfied at a job well done, and they had mentally prepared for the next stage of the conflict. Leaving again so soon, and heading back out against the huge and seemingly invincible enemy army, left them feeling flat and fed up. The prince had asked Farred and Brock to bring only half of their men, but even those more willing amongst them didn't really want to be here.

Ashere sat astride his horse a few feet in front of his army, gazing into the distance. He seemed not to notice or care about the morale of his soldiers. Farred wasn't sure whether it was an act or not. His aloofness and intensity had been a strength until now, but today it didn't seem to be working so well.

Farred nudged his horse forwards. His eyes met with Brock's, and the Middian pulled in alongside him, before they walked their horses up to Ashere's.

'They're still not fucking back yet,' said Ashere by way of greeting, still looking into the far distance.

'When they do get back,' replied Farred, 'I think we should call it a day. We can always go out again tomorrow.'

'Maybe,' said Ashere.

'Definitely,' responded Brock. 'Even if we find the bastards, we have to engage, withdraw, and make it back to the castle. We've run out of time.'

'Yes,' said Ashere in an absent-minded way.

Silence.

'Ashere?' demanded Farred, getting exasperated.

Ashere finally looked at them both. 'I'm sorry. I just don't get it. They should be here. We should have found them by now. I'm missing something.' Ashere's voice trailed off. He then cocked his head slightly to one side. 'What's that noise?'

Farred heard nothing. But Ashere obviously had, so he concentrated harder. Then his ears tuned in. A rumbling sound. Farred realised it had been going on for a while now, in the background. It seemed to come from the west. Then suddenly, in a flash, it came to him.

'Form up!' he yelled at the top of his voice, stretching his arm out to the west.

The South Magnians he commanded stared back in shock at the sudden explosion of volume. But Ashere and Brock, coming to the same realisation as him, shouted the same command, and so their small, mounted army wheeled in the direction of the noise.

It was the fog. The Isharites had been here all along, hidden by the mists, no doubt engineered by their magicians. Farred cursed himself. They had got so used to attacking the unsuspecting Drobax that they had got casual about the threat posed by the magic wielding Isharites. This time, the Isharites had set their trap, waiting for Ashere's approach, eager to get their revenge.

The rumbling noise got louder, and Farred began to make out fast approaching figures on horseback coming through the mist. The Haskan cavalry. His adrenaline kicked in, his mouth went dry. They had no idea how many they were up against. He turned to look at Ashere for guidance.

The Prince was standing up in his stirrups. He raised his sword in the air. 'Charge!' he bellowed.

Shouts rang out all around as the soldiers dug their heels into the sides of their stallions, trying to build up acceleration as fast as possible to meet the oncoming attack. Ashere's mount sprinted ahead and Farred urged his horse after it, trying to keep pace and not lose sight of him in the enveloping fog.

In a matter of seconds, they had engaged with the enemy, who came hurtling through the mists towards them, shouting their own war cries. These were Haskan soldiers, disciplined and well-armed fighters, not the Drobax they had got used to. Some of them held lances tucked under their armpits, which they waved in his direction, trying to unseat him before continuing past to get at the ranks behind. They were like ghosts, flitting into view and then disappearing into the mist again. Farred knew they would carve right through his force, and then wheel around and approach from the rear, surrounding them.

A mounted Haskan soldier came at him with a sword. Farred pulled at his mount's reins so that the beast sidestepped away, and he twisted in the saddle to avoid the blow. But the Haskan wasn't giving up and returned for another go. This time Farred met the blow with his own sword. They held position for a while, each trying to push the other back while their stallions buffeted each other. The Haskan twisted his wrist and scraped his sword down the length of Farred's blade, aiming to chop off his fingers.

But Farred was prepared for that. In one fluid motion, he pulled his sword away and then swung it back with all his strength towards his opponent's neck. The Haskan put his sword in the way just in time, but the sudden movement and the strength of Farred's stroke caused him to lose his balance in the saddle and he tumbled backwards. One foot came out of its stirrup and he spiralled onto the floor.

Farred saw movement out of the corner of his eye, and he turned just in time to see Ashere's mount going down. The Prince was surrounded by three Isharites, their crystal swords still glinting in amongst the tendrils of mist.

Farred looked around, but no support was in sight. They had got separated from Brock and the rest of their comrades, and the fog made it impossible to see where they were. He knew he had to act fast and urged his mount straight at the group.

Ashere was on his feet, sword still in hand. The three Isharites circled warily, not least because the prince's horse was still alive and writhing on the floor, kicking out with its legs. They realised Farred was bearing down on them just in time and turned to meet him. He couldn't slow the pace of his charge, and the nearest soldier evaded him and swung out his sword. Farred sensed his mount take the impact, and he slid his feet out of the stirrups just before it collapsed under him. Their momentum carried them into one of the Isharites and they became a swirling mass of bodies, until Farred was thrown off to the side. He landed badly and was too winded at first to move.

Forcing himself up, Farred grabbed his sword and looked around. The Isharite he had crashed into was trapped under his horse, not moving. Farred stabbed down to make sure he was dead.

He turned around, looking for Ashere. He forced his body to return to the location where Ashere had been brought down.

Peering through the mist, he saw the familiar figure of the Prince. Ashere was staring ahead, a vacant, far away expression on his face. At his feet lay the bodies of his two assailants. Ashere made eye contact with Farred. Something broke. He dropped his sword to the floor, and his legs buckled underneath him. Farred rushed over and knelt over him. Turning him gently onto his back, he saw a large wound where a blow had pierced his armour. The prince had fallen unconscious but was still breathing.

Farred stood up and looked around. The sound of fighting came but it was some distance away. He presumed that they had ended up behind the enemy's lines. He tried to fight down the panic and think clearly, but his predicament seemed hopeless.

He heard the rider approaching before he saw him. Brandishing his sword, he stood in front of Ashere's prone body and waited.

It was Burstan.

Quickly taking in the situation, his captain dismounted. 'Let's get him on the horse,' he said gruffly.

Farred had never been so pleased to see anyone in his life, but couldn't find any words. In silence, they grabbed Ashere's limbs and, with Burstan murmuring soothingly to his horse, hoisted him up and laid him on his front ahead of the saddle, with his legs and arms dangling over the sides. Farred wasn't sure if it was the best position, but hoped that it might put pressure on the wound and stop the blood loss.

'Get him out of here,' said Burstan, gesturing at the horse.

Farred looked at him in disbelief. 'I'm not getting on there. You get him out of here.'

The captain shook his head.

'Burstan, that's an order.'

Burstan turned his back on Farred. 'I'm going back to be with the men,' he said over his shoulder. 'He's your responsibility, Farred.' His captain walked away.

'Burstan, get back here!' hissed Farred at the departing figure, but it ignored him and disappeared into the mist, so that he was alone with Ashere again.

Swearing, Farred clambered into the saddle. A sharp pain in his back told him that his fall had done some damage, but his immediate concern was escape. Assuming that they had charged to the west, and that Burstan and the sound of fighting were over to the east, Farred turned his new mount to the south and hurried away.

Once he had escaped the sound of fighting Farred relaxed a little. He thought of his men back there—those who were still alive would be surrounded by the enemy. He thought of Burstan returning to the fight. But it did no good to dwell on it, and he pushed those thoughts away.

As the nervous minutes ticked by and became first one hour, then two, Farred accepted that he had escaped. He checked Ashere's pulse every now and again. He was still alive but showed no signs of consciousness. He had to get him back to the castle as soon as possible.

He thought that anyone else who had escaped would be well ahead of him, since his mount was slowed down with two riders, but after a while he caught up with other escapees. Two Middians shared a horse, and explained that they had both escaped, but one of their mounts had pulled up lame. A North Magnian gave a huge smile of relief to learn that his prince was still alive. Later on, they caught up with an injured South Magnian who looked almost as grateful to see Farred. More had got away than Farred had feared. He supposed that the fog might have helped. But despite that, they all knew that many of their friends were dead. They travelled in silence, all nursing the same soldier's guilt that their comrades were dead and dying on the battlefield, while they were running away.

By the time they reached the outskirts of Burkhard Castle, the sun was going down, officially giving up on the most miserable day Farred had ever experienced. A party of Brasingian soldiers found them as they approached. They took Ashere away and led Farred, now totally exhausted, up to the Duke's Keep, where the other survivors had gathered in the main hall. They were bedding down for the night but got up again to greet Farred and the other latecomers. It was a strained greeting, sombre in mood, and yet with genuine pleasure to see others who had escaped.

Farred was grabbed in a big bear hug, and there was Brock standing before him. 'I heard about Ashere. At least you got him out of there.'

'It was Burstan. He gave me his horse—'

'You look terrible. Try to get some sleep.'

Farred nodded. His body was desperate to lie down. Brock guided him over to some bedding and a blanket. Farred turned to him. 'Burstan? I don't suppose...'

Brock shook his head.

No. It was a stupid question. Burstan, like so many others, was dead.

DOGS AND DRAGONS

VIII

Blood welled inside the glove of Gyrmund's right hand. He tucked it under his armpit in what he knew was a vain attempt to stop the flow. But he had no way to bandage it up, and he could not stop working. He continued to hack at the walls of the mine with the axe, now held in his left hand. His muscles ached each time he raised his arm, and each time he smashed it into the wall. But the Isharites who controlled the mine had made it quite clear that whoever gathered the smallest amount of diatine crystals would be executed at the end of the shift.

Gyrmund excavated the patch of crystals he had exposed further, chipping away the rock that encased it. The crystal itself, he knew, was incredibly strong. If he missed a stroke and the blade hit the crystal, it wouldn't chip or crack: the danger was to the axe blade.

One further blow and the crystals came free. He breathed a sigh of relief. That, surely, put him in the clear. He looked up and down the underground tunnel. Torches placed along the walls cast enough light to see what was in front of him, but not beyond his little area of light. He could not see any of the guards, so he rested while he could.

Time was impossible to measure down in the mine. It was his first day, but it felt like he had been down there for a week. *The end of the shift must surely come soon,* he persuaded himself. He'd had nothing to eat or drink since breakfast. The oxygen down in the tunnel wasn't sufficient to fill his lungs, and with the heat, cramped conditions, and hard physical work, he had felt like he was going to faint more than once. He held his right hand up in the air to slow the bleeding.

After a while, he heard footsteps from down the tunnel. A guard. As he came into sight, Gyrmund bent down and carefully picked up the chunk of crystals, placing it in the wheeled metal box which he would take back up to the surface. The guard kept watching, so Gyrmund began hammering at a fresh patch of wall, making sure he put enough effort in to keep his observer happy. Bored, the guard moved on. After he was sure he had gone out of earshot, Gyrmund stopped again.

Eventually, the sound of whistles blew throughout the mine. The other miners began heading to the exit tunnel, and so Gyrmund fell in with them, dragging along his box, and making sure that none of the others filched any of his crystals. He looked at what they had collected. Some had more than him, but some had less. He knew that he would have a physical edge over many of the miners, because the conditions would take their toll on those who had been here longest. But he had worried that they would have the advantage of experience. In the end, he had done enough.

As they reached the exit tunnel, the miners had to crawl on their hands and knees to get out, hauling their precious cargo with them. The walls pressed in on Gyrmund. He tried to keep his breathing steady. The truth was he couldn't stand the confined space, but if he thought about where he was, he would lose control.

After Moneva had been led away towards the fortress at Samir Durg, their Isharite captors had led them further along the wall until they approached one of the many towers that were spaced along it. They had reached their destination, and unpleasant thoughts had entered Gyrmund's mind. His sense of foreboding had risen further when Soren, still enclosed in his box, had been led away elsewhere. Gyrmund had exchanged nervous glances with Herin and Clarin. They didn't need to say it, but they were all thinking the same thing: was this the time when their captors killed them? And if not, what did they intend to do with them?

In the end, it was nothing much. They had been shoved in a room on the ground floor of the tower and left. All day and all night they had sat in the cold, with nothing to do but wonder about their fate. Even Herin and Clarin had been quiet. There was, in truth, little to say. They had dozed away the time, lacking the energy to exercise. It had felt terrible, but it had been easier than being trapped underground all day. Gyrmund would now have grabbed the chance to be allowed to go back to that room in the tower.

It was not until this morning that, still with no explanation, they had been led to the crystal mines, and turned over to the guards who ran them with slave labour. One reason they had been kept alive had at least become clear. Strong bodies were needed to man the mines, especially since the attrition rate was so high. In a brief welcoming speech, it had been made clear to them that at least one miner was killed at the end of each shift to ensure that they all worked as hard as possible. As Gyrmund made it to the last stage of the journey up to the surface, he was about to find out if that was true.

The route up to ground level was the same as the route down he had taken this morning. The miners crammed into a rickety metal lift and a pulley system was used to raise it to the surface. At the entrance, a pack of mules were taking the weight, and by walking from one end of the yard to the other, they pulled up the ropes attached to the lift. The ropes strained and squeaked as Gyrmund and the other miners shuddered and jolted their way to the surface. When Gyrmund shoved himself out of the lift and took a proper, full breath of air into his lungs, a wave of emotion came over him and he had to stop himself from crying.

He noticed that the other miners were handing in their specially made protective gloves to one of the guards. He waited his turn and handed his over. The guard looked at the ripped gloves and at Gyrmund's bleeding hand. With no warning, the guard struck him hard across the face, muttering angrily in words that Gyrmund didn't understand. Gyrmund turned away quickly, fighting to control himself so that he didn't strike back.

He noticed Herin and Clarin standing next to each other a few feet away, and walked over to them. They must have come out on an earlier lift. They had placed their boxes of crystals in front of them and had joined a loose semicircle of miners that was forming opposite a group of Isharite guards, who were observing the activities with apparent boredom at the far end of the yard. Gyrmund joined in the line next to Clarin. Both brothers had mean looks on their faces, and Gyrmund felt grateful that he was in with them rather than on his own.

'What the hell did you do to your hand?' asked Herin, leaning over to look at him with a disgusted expression on his face.

Gyrmund assumed it was meant as a rhetorical question.

Clarin peered into his box. 'I got more than you,' he said, looking inordinately pleased with himself.

They waited for a while and then, gradually, the atmosphere changed and there was a quiet hush. The guards were walking along the semi-circle, looking at how much each miner had brought out. One miner was pulled out into the middle of the yard. He was grinning and laughing to himself hysterically. It was horrible to watch.

The guards emptied his box onto the ground. There was next to nothing in there. It was as if he had slept all day. But Gyrmund thought he understood. He had just given up.

He was pulled over to a tall wooden post with a horizontal bar at the top. A piece of rope was fetched over and a noose placed around his neck. He was still grinning manically. Gyrmund looked at the expressions on the faces of the other miners. They suggested that what they were seeing was the normal procedure. Herin and Clarin looked on impassively. The rope was fed through a metal hook attached to the bar, and then three guards pulled on it, dragging the unfortunate victim up by the neck. He hardly fought it. By the time they had finished and were winding the rope around some hooks half way up the post to keep him hanging there, he was already dead.

The guards began shouting and Gyrmund and the other two followed the lead of the other miners. The individual boxes of diatine crystals were emptied into larger containers, and then the boxes were carefully stacked along the wall of the yard for the next day. They were then led out of the mine yard along a path, presumably towards their sleeping quarters.

They walked through open, unused land, but they were still behind the main walled enclosure, which was visible in the gloom ahead of them.

The path took them to a large fenced area. They were led through a flimsy looking gate. There were no buildings, suggesting that they were supposed to sleep in the open air. The idea was bearable in this weather, but would surely see them all off in the winter.

The guards stayed inside with them. Herin and Clarin marched over to the far side and Gyrmund kept close to them, looking at the height of the fencing and imagining escape. They stopped and stared out through the fence toward the main fortress, too far away to be visible.

'I'm surprised they don't get escape attempts over this fence,' said Gyrmund. 'I know we're still behind the wall, but—'

Herin frowned at him and nodded over to their left, the section of the area closest to the wall.

And Gyrmund saw them. Pits. Big metal grates at ground level covered the entrance, which was why he had missed them. Only the handles stuck up slightly. They were kept underground during the night. He looked around at the guards and the miners who were pacing up and down. They were being given a bit of time above ground before being sent down.

Gyrmund shook his head, panic rising in him. 'No,' he hissed, 'I can't do it. I can't do this.'

Herin turned on him angrily. 'You'll have to do it. We do it until we get the chance to escape.'

'How do we do that?'

'I don't know yet. But I'm not going to die in this shithole. I'm going to get out of here. So, Gyrmund, you're gonna go down into that pit, you're gonna work in the mine tomorrow, and you're gonna keep on doing it until the day comes when we get out of here.'

Gyrmund nodded. He hated Herin at that moment. He hated him because he was being so much stronger than he was. Lost in the wild somewhere he would have coped with: no, he would have been in his element. But this was not something he was coping with. He needed Herin and Clarin to get through it. He didn't like it, but there it was.

A group of guards made for the pit grates. They unlocked them and pulled them open, the metal landing on the floor with a clang. The other guards began shouting at the miners and rounding them up. Herin and Clarin made straight for the pit entrance, and Gyrmund followed them.

It was a six-foot drop into the pit. The walls had sconces attached, and the guards lit them, shedding a dim, flickering glow along the straight lines of the pit, and creating shadows which danced along the walls. One end of the pit stank of faeces and urine, so they made their way towards the other end.

Herin chose a position for them at the far end of the pit, and all three leaned against the wall and watched as the pit filled up with the other miners. The men who found themselves in this stinking pit were from all over Dalriya.

The greatest number were humans from the east of Dalriya, commonly referred to as Barbarians. Gyrmund had visited there himself, and learned that they did not refer to themselves by that name. There were, in fact, over fifty different tribes, each with their own name and traditions, all independent of each other. They had never been united and had no wish to be, but lived out a tough existence, farming and foraging on difficult land. Over the past year, the forces of Ishari had been gradually subduing these tribes, and many of the men folk had clearly ended up here.

Gyrmund had learned that this campaign had been successful, and that Ishari had moved south into the lands of the Bear-men. This was confirmed by the presence of one of them at the opposite end of the pit, where the prisoners made their toilet. It was crouched down against a wall, seemingly oblivious to the smell. Although he was well travelled, Gyrmund had never seen one before. In most respects, it was human like, but larger in every way, with huge, powerful shoulders. Bigger than Clarin or any human Gyrmund had met. A huge mop of dirty hair and a scruffy beard covered most of its face. But they didn't completely disguise the huge, powerful jaws that protruded out from its face. Certainly, nobody was getting too close to it.

Gyrmund had spoken to fellow travellers about the Bear-men, and knew that they avoided all contact with other races. If humans entered their territory, they would usually disappear. They had their own language, impossible to understand. Gyrmund wondered how they had persuaded it to go down the mine in the first place.

In addition, there were a few prisoners from other lands. Gyrmund could identify some Persaleians, who had likely been captured defending against the recent invasion; and Gyrmund studied two men in quiet conversation who had taken up position on the opposite wall to them. They had Brasingian moustaches, though how they came to be here wasn't obvious.

As Gyrmund was considering going over to introduce himself, the dungeon fell silent.

'Who are they?' asked Clarin, glancing over to the other end of the pit.

Gyrmund took a quick look. Five creatures were heading in their direction. 'Dog-men,' he replied, recognising them as a race who lived in the north, and who had long ago come under the control of Ishari. They were known as fearsome fighters, built like humans but taller and stronger, their bodies covered in fur, and with a muzzle full of sharp teeth.

'Don't know what they're doing down here,' Gyrmund added. 'They usually fight for Ishari.'

'Punishment. For ill-discipline of some kind,' said Herin. 'Be very careful with them,' he advised, emphasising each word.

The five Dog-men walked slowly up the centre of the pit, eyeing the other prisoners, who all looked away and avoided eye contact. The one in front was the biggest, a great beast of a creature, whose muscles rippled as it walked along, and whose black eyes stared out with hatred and aggression. The other four flanked it, walking slightly to the side and behind, signifying it as the leader. Inevitably, it led the group to the three newcomers. It walked up to Clarin, who happened to be standing in the middle of the three of them, perhaps because it saw him as the primary threat. The others stood two to each side, so that they stood in a straight line of five facing Gyrmund and the others, black eyes staring and muzzles twisted into snarls. Gyrmund took a quick glance at Clarin and Herin, and was impressed at how relaxed and unflustered they looked; he did his best to do the same.

'Where are you from?' demanded the leader, its voice incredibly loud so that it rang out around the pit. It was shoving its muzzle into Clarin's face, but the rank smell still carried over to Gyrmund.

'Got caught in Brasingia,' said Clarin casually, as if it happened to him all the time.

'Well, you're in your worst nightmare now,' said the Dog-man, pulling back his lips into what Gyrmund guessed must be a smile, but looked like a snarl. The other four pulled the same face as if a great joke had been made.

Clarin nodded in agreement. 'It's a shithole alright.'

The comment displeased the Dog-man, who clearly wanted to see fear on Clarin's face.

'And I'm Vamak, the tormentor in chief,' he added, turning around to look at his four allies, 'we're in charge down here. If we don't like someone, we make their existence so miserable they beg to go back down the mines.'

'I understand,' said Clarin.

Gyrmund could not help but be impressed by Clarin. He answered the Dog-man politely enough, and did nothing to provoke him, but at the same time his body language suggested that he was unaffected by the intimidation. Vamak clearly found this unsatisfactory, and felt the need to assert his authority further, but didn't seem sure how to deal with it. Then, suddenly, he raised a hand, revealing a vicious looking set of claws at the end of his fingers with which he gestured at Clarin.

'You'd better understand or you won't live long. Here, this will help your memory,' he said, and, with a quick flick, scraped one claw along Clarin's cheek. Blood instantly welled along the wound. Clarin started forward, but Herin quickly put one arm across his chest, shoving him back against the wall. Vamak looked at Herin, then Clarin, before throwing his head into the air and laughing—a sadistic bark of a laugh. The others followed suit and Vamak took a long look around the pit, making sure that everyone in it had learned the lesson.

'I'm in charge down here,' he shouted loudly, so that the whole pit could hear him. 'The Isharites don't let me kill new ones,' he said, speaking now just to Gyrmund, Herin and Clarin. 'They like to get their full use out of you first. But in a few days' time I'll be free to do what I want with you.'

They then moved away, taking up position at the end of the pit farthest away from the toilet. This area had been left free for them by the other prisoners, and this was clearly part of establishing a pecking order.

Gyrmund looked over at the other two. Clarin stared straight ahead, still struggling to stop himself from going straight after Vamak. Herin turned around to face his brother and Gyrmund, putting his back to the Dog-men.

'Well, now we have our first objective to work on,' he murmured. 'How to take down that son of a bitch.'

* * *

'LADY BELWYNN? They are ready for you now.'

Belwynn felt a fresh burst of nerves.

While the Knights of Kalinth had been celebrating their feast of Saint Stephen in the Great Hall of the High Tower, she had been waiting in the kitchens until they were ready to hear her sing. She had spoken a little to the kitchen maids at first, but they were clearly very busy catering for so many knights at once, and so she had sat there with little to do but watch them, go over the song in her head, worry about it, and wonder why she had ever suggested it in the first place.

Now that it was time to go, she had to see it through. Evander led her out of the kitchen to the Great Hall. Most halls in Dalriya had a harp to provide music in the evenings, but the harp she had been given to play by the Order was the most beautiful she had ever seen, made from alder wood, and with golden strings. When she had given it a test, it played as good as it looked. That gave her a bit of confidence.

The room went quieter as the assembled knights watched her being led to the dais. It felt like a very long walk. She got herself settled on a chair while Evander positioned the harp for her. He then departed the dais and left her alone. All eyes were now fixed on her, and the room had gone completely quiet.

Theron stood up from his position at one of the tables near the middle of the room, though not at the large, central table where the highest ranked knights were seated.

'Introducing the Lady Belwynn of Magnia,' he boomed into the silence. Belwynn thought he slightly slurred the words, and noticed that a lot of wine had been flowing during the feast. Maybe that was no bad thing.

Belwynn located Sebastian at the central table. Two seats to his left, Theron had told her, would be Galenos. She checked that the man sitting there fitted the description she had been given. Yes. Straight back, closely cropped grey hair, clean-shaven, and an aquiline nose.

'Grand Master Galenos,' began Belwynn, making eye contact with him before looking around the room, her voice ringing out clearly around the hall. 'Knights of Kalinth. I am honoured to be given the chance to perform for you tonight. I intend to perform a song which I learned when I was very young, but instantly fell in love with. It was a song about a place called Kalinth. At the time, I fancied it was a pretend, fairy tale land. When I was older, and knew better, I used to dream of visiting Kalinth to see its knights for myself. And, finally, here I am. The song I will sing is called Stephen and the Green Dragon.'

There was polite applause and mild cheering from the audience once Belwynn had finished speaking. She had hoped for something more when she introduced the song, Stephen and the Dragon being the best loved story of the knights. It was a different atmosphere than any other hall she had been to. She had to hope that she could have the same effect on this audience as she usually did.

'In Chalios there dwelt the beast
That wrecked our land from west to east
No king nor duke nor count had fay
To seek the dragon out to slay

No spells nor rich man's wealth had he
But Stephen had his bravery
No men to fight for him had he
But Stephen had his chivalry'

Belwynn looked over at her audience, many mouthing the familiar words themselves. Some stared at her, already captivated by her voice. She knew the lyrics of the song had a crucial role to play in their plan. She glanced at Galenos, watching on with a frown. Did he suspect?

'So long the people of the land cried out
For saviour with no fear or doubt
'Til one young knight swore, 'It shall be me
To end this monster's tyranny'

. . .

No spells nor rich man's wealth had he
But Stephen had his bravery
No men to fight for him had he
But Stephen had his chivalry'

Some of her audience were now entering the trance like state Belwynn could induce with her voice. Galenos and his entourage were looking around the hall, suspicion on their faces. But it was too late to stop her now.

When Belwynn finished the song, with the dragon slain, many of the knights jumped to their feet to applaud. Theron, Tycho and their allies were prominent at first, but others in the room followed their lead. After the applause ended, some sat back down again but others stayed on their feet.

'A lesson for the Order,' shouted Tycho, gesturing with one arm at Belwynn. 'The Knights of Kalinth were founded to confront and fight evil. Ishari is our dragon. Yet here we are cowering in the High Tower, while they grow in strength and infect our kingdom with their poison.'

Tycho moved his arm along until it pointed directly at Galenos. If he felt fear, he showed none.

Belwynn suspected he wasn't the kind of man who did.

'Our Grand Master has failed us!' he declared.

An intake of breath followed this statement and then there was shouting from all over the room, some for and others against, but nobody could properly be heard, until Euthymius pushed his chair out and stood up to confront Tycho. He pointed straight back at the young knight.

'Treason!' he shouted, his voice slightly hysterical. 'Tycho attacks our Grand Master and our King! Does your oath of loyalty mean nothing to you, Tycho? We are the Knights of Kalinth, and we are sworn to obey! But you and your allies have made a habit of defying orders!'

'No!' shouted Theron, who was already on his feet. 'We are speaking for our Order. We are sworn to protect our kingdom and our people! They must come before loyalty to any one man.'

Theron's argument seemed to take everyone assembled by surprise. Belwynn could see many of the knights frowning as they tried to grapple with the contradictory statements offered by Euthymius and Theron.

Into the moment of silence, Remi struck home. 'Sebastian! Lord Sebastian must speak!' he demanded.

Other knights, prepared by Theron in advance, joined in the call. 'Sebastian! Sebastian!'

All eyes turned to him, even those of Euthymius and Galenos. The Grand Master seemed uncertain, almost in shock at the unexpected attack he was facing. Sebastian looked at him for a moment. Then, slowly and deliberately, he stood up and looked out at the room. He took his time before he spoke, to make sure that everyone was listening.

'I have come to the conclusion that our Order can no longer ignore the threat to our kingdom. It is with regret that I say Grand Master Galenos has failed to show proper leadership in recent months. I am therefore submitting myself to replace him as Grand Master.'

The Great Hall erupted in uproar. Belwynn surveyed the scene. Theron and his allies, plus those knights who had been persuaded by her song and who agreed with what they had done, were certainly making the most noise, cheering Sebastian's name. A smaller group was hostile and shouting back, calling Sebastian a traitor. The majority of the knights, those not on either side, were looking around in bewilderment.

Overall, Belwynn believed it had worked. It had certainly gone to plan, though she feared it had been a bit too slick. It must have been obvious to some that it was a deliberate ambush, as well organised and thoroughly planned as a military campaign. Those knights caught in the middle might blame Theron and Sebastian for dividing their Order. But Belwynn believed that most of them would support Sebastian in the end.

Evander appeared at her side to lead her away. The Great Hall was chaotic and, fearing it might even erupt into violence, Belwynn was quick to leave the dais. Turning around, she took one last look at the central table. She saw Galenos, white as a sheet, and suddenly looking much older. She saw Sebastian, sombre and serious looking, with his head slightly bowed. While all around them both, younger men jostled and shouted and jeered.

Belwynn had made her impact in Kalinth. But at that moment, she did not feel proud.

IN ARIOC'S CHAMBERS

IX

Moneva had now spent a day and two nights in the bedroom in Arioc's chambers. The only contact she had was with Babak, the man whose job seemed to be looking after the rooms. He brought her meals. He was polite enough. He showed her another tiny room off the main chamber, which was a toilet with a hole in the floor. Other than that, he left her alone.

During the day, he left the chambers to run unspecified errands for a few hours. He locked the door behind him with a key. Moneva considered trying to escape. When he returned, she considered attacking him and taking the key. That would have been easy enough. But she knew that trying to escape from the tower, and then the fortress, would be next to impossible, so she didn't try. That was why she had been given the relative freedom she had, rather than being locked in a dungeon somewhere.

Deep down, she knew why she had been taken here.

Moneva felt like she understood men. She had inhabited the world of men for as long as she could remember. She had no memory of her mother, who had died when Moneva was two. Her father was a kind enough man, but not an attentive parent. When he died from a fever, she was still only ten, an only child with no income. She was not completely alone, but led a transitory existence, staying with various family, friends and neighbours. She spent increasing amounts of time on the streets of Essenberg, getting involved in petty crime. That was how she came to meet Max.

Max, it turned out, was a ruthless crime lord. But to Moneva, he was kind, complimentary, and, above all, interested in her. A father figure. He was like that with all the children, always having time for them. It wasn't an act. Not completely. But he showed a special interest in Moneva. She was better than the other kids: quicker to learn, sharp witted, and more hardworking. Also, she was a girl, and that gave her a special edge. He could send her to spy on people, run special errands for him, and people wouldn't suspect her.

Moneva left her old ties and immersed herself in Max's world. She devoted herself to learning the trade, just as if she had been apprenticed to a cloth maker or a dyer. She wanted to please Max, and any small praise or acknowledgement from him was enough—was all she wanted. As she got older and stronger, she was taught to fight and to kill, just like the boys. Max insisted she be given equal treatment, not spared anything because she was a girl. She never asked to be. Despite her age and her gender, she became a respected member of the unit. People knew she was completely loyal to Max, and that he trusted her completely. More than anyone else. That made her powerful—even feared.

But things changed when Moneva stopped being a girl and became a woman. Max began to flirt with her. It was innocent enough at first, but gradually got more serious, and Moneva was very flattered by it. She was young and naïve and thrilled when Max paid her any kind of attention. Eventually, they became lovers. Looking back, older and wiser, Moneva realised she had never wanted that. She had wanted a father. But she had wanted to please Max and had felt grateful for what he had done.

Their relationship lasted a few more years. Max became increasingly controlling and possessive of her. But, in a strange way, by making Moneva his lover, he had lost her. Their relationship became more equal. Whereas before Moneva had idolised Max, she now began to challenge what he did or said; she began to stick up for herself. He wanted her to remain unquestioningly loyal and compliant. In the end, she walked out on him and on his business. But she couldn't entirely regret that part of her life. She had been given the skills to make a living, and to look after herself in a dangerous world.

Alone in Arioc's bedchamber, Moneva found herself returning again and again to that period of her life. A part of her knew she was preparing herself for what was to come.

Despite that, when Arioc arrived she still went into shock. One moment he was not there, the next he was. He was shouting at Babak in the rough language of the Isharites, apparently issuing one angry demand or order after the other. Moneva sat in the bedchamber, looking at the door which stood between her and the King of Haskany, trying to keep calm. Eventually, the shouting stopped and was replaced with more subdued murmurs, though she could not make out what was being said.

The door swung open and Arioc was standing there, looking at her. To Moneva, he had the sort of expression someone has when they have put aside a treat for later, forgotten about it, and then rediscovered it. He had a very expressive face, and did not try to hide his thoughts, but then, Moneva acknowledged to herself, why would he?

Arioc held out one hand in a formal way, almost like he was asking her to dance. Steeling herself, Moneva stood up and took his hand.

'Your name?' he asked.

'Moneva.'

'I am Arioc.'

'I know.'

He smiled briefly at that and led her into the main room and directed her to sit at the table. 'I am very hungry, Moneva. You will join me for supper,' he said, sitting opposite her.

It wasn't phrased as a request, but then Moneva got the feeling that this was a man who didn't need to make requests very often. He was being polite, though, which was something. A small thing ordinarily, but in this situation, Moneva took some reassurance from it.

Arioc was an impressive figure, emanating authority more than anyone she had ever met—and Moneva had met several of Dalriya's rulers in the last few weeks. His presence filled the room, and Moneva felt like his chambers had reduced in size now that he was here. He had the build and physique of a warrior, and, much like Clarin, didn't seem at ease sitting down, as if his body struggled with the inactivity. But in addition, he had the intellect and aura of a sorcerer: like Soren, but more powerful. His dark eyes seemed to possess the power to see everything. Moneva felt like his gaze was a weapon whose full power she had been spared from for now, but that could be turned on her at any moment.

As Babak prepared food for them in the background, Arioc made idle conversation. He asked her where she was born, and into what kind of family. Moneva answered with the truth. Even before Arioc had arrived, she had concluded that this was the best strategy; but now, she was even surer that she should be totally honest. Arioc could find out what he wanted from her, one way or another. If she gave him what he wanted freely, she might live. If she lived, there was a chance that Gyrmund and the others might live, too.

Babak served the food and then left the chambers. It was a bird, heavily spiced, with a range of vegetables. Arioc poured a bottle of Cordentine red into two glasses. Despite her predicament, it was the tastiest meal Moneva had eaten in a long time. Arioc didn't seem to want to talk much while he ate. The silence might have been unbearable, but Moneva had barely been fed during the last few days, and this made it easier for her to focus on the food.

When they had finished, Arioc walked over to his desk and poured out two more glasses of a rich looking, amber coloured liquid. He handed one over to Moneva. 'Would you like to move into my bedroom, now?' he asked. Arioc's dark eyes focused on her own, studying her reaction.

Moneva didn't trust herself to speak, but nodded her assent.

In the bedroom, Arioc gestured for Moneva to sit on the bed before joining her. He took a drink and indicated that she should do the same. Moneva took a sip and rolled her eyes at the strength of it. She swallowed it down and felt it move down her chest into her stomach. Her tongue felt pickled from it.

Arioc watched her with some amusement. 'You've never had arak before?' he asked needlessly.

She shook her head.

Arioc's face turned more serious. 'You are not stupid, Moneva, so you must know why you are here. It was a great surprise to find you and your friends in Edeleny. I found you in the Temple. I went there looking for something. A staff. It wasn't there. I need you to tell me everything you know. Miss nothing out.'

There were no threats and, again, Moneva was grateful for that. But that didn't mean that Moneva was unaware of the consequences if Arioc decided she was lying or holding something back. So she told him everything. She began with the attack on the Temple of Toric in South Magnia and explained what happened from there. She left out no names or major events along the way. Occasionally, Arioc would stop and question her when he wanted more information. When she described the fight between Pentas and Nexodore on the Great Road, he got rather childish, and wanted her to recount every tiniest aspect of it. He actually giggled at the ending. When she was trying to explain their run in with Duke Emeric in Coldeberg, he grunted and made a face.

'What did you think of him?' he asked.

'I never actually met him, Your Majesty.'

'Oh,' he replied, disappointed. 'Call me Arioc, for fuck's sake.'

When she recounted her rescue of her friends from Coldeberg prison, he didn't hide his respect. His expression and manner towards her changed, as if he suddenly realised he was talking to a different person than he had previously thought.

He whistled when she told him about the death of Nexodore in the lands of the Blood Caladri, but let her carry on with her retelling. He listened intently when she described what went on in Edeleny.

'Well,' he began when she had finished, 'that was more than I could have possibly expected. But at the Temple,' he said, following up on the issue that he most wanted solved, 'your friends disappeared. With the Staff. Teleported away somewhere. Where, and by whom?'

Moneva thought about it. She was worried now, that he would insist she answer a question she couldn't.

'Soren was the only sorcerer. He was with us—'

'It wasn't him,' interrupted Arioc. 'The woman, Elana. She is also a magic user.'

'Well,' said Moneva, considering the possibility. 'I suppose she is, but not in the same way as Soren. Maybe she could have done it.'

'But highly unlikely,' conceded Arioc.

He looked at Moneva, measuring her with those dark eyes for a while. He then nodded, as if accepting that she was telling the truth as she knew it.

'Then the most likely agent of their escape was Pentas. With Nexodore's death, he escaped and made his own way to Edeleny. But why would he do that?'

Arioc was speaking to himself now, lost in his own musings. 'I have no proof of his involvement,' he continued, then looked at Moneva. 'Nor any idea where your friends are. But at least I know exactly who I'm looking for now,' he added.

The last comment made Moneva feel even worse than she already did. She wondered what the others would think of her, revealing their secrets at the earliest opportunity? What torments were Gyrmund, Soren and the others already suffering now, while she sat on this comfy bed, well fed with a drink in her hand?

She looked up at Arioc to see that he was staring at her now, a new, hungry look on his face. This was the moment, she knew. She had to finish through with her strategy. Give Arioc everything he wanted. He was interested in her more now, she knew. Interested in her as a person, to some extent. She also knew that he had taken a liking to the Haskan woman, Shira, who, like Moneva, had been taught how to fight. He had even made Shira his queen. Moneva had to make sure that he was interested enough in her to want to keep her alive.

Arioc took Moneva's drink from her. He reached down to the floor, putting both glasses down with a clink.

'I've never met anyone quite like you before, Moneva,' he said, moving towards her.

Wanting desperately to recoil away, Moneva instead made up the distance between them. At any moment, Arioc could decide he didn't want her, and might make her a prize for his soldiers to enjoy. She had to be strong. Wanting to hit out and run away, she instead let Arioc put his hands on her body. As he leaned over to kiss her, she wanted to scream out for help, but she let him touch his lips to hers. Wanting to cry and to sob and to beg him to stop, Moneva parted her lips and let his tongue into her mouth, let it find her own, as the smell of the arak on his breath filled her nostrils.

ATOP BURKHARD CASTLE

X

Sitting by Ashere's bed in his small convalescing room in the Emperor's Hall, it was almost possible for Farred to forget there was an army, thousands strong, on its way to kill them all. The myriad sounds of a castle garrison barely penetrated this room: rowdy soldier banter became faint whispers, while the clang and scrape of armour and weaponry might have been a bird walking on the roof.

Instead, the sound that dominated the room was Ashere's breathing. It was unnaturally loud—the sound you make when you are struggling to suck in air after heavy exercise. Except that Ashere had been laid up in bed since Farred brought him back to the castle two days ago. His face, once a healthy golden brown, now seemed drained of colour. His black hair hung lank at his sides, and sweat gathered on his brow.

But it was the smell that dominated Farred's senses. Someone had tried their best to mask it by littering the room with rushes, fennel, and other herbs. But the cloying smell of fever, and of the prince's rotting flesh, would not be denied. Farred had spent as much time in the room as anyone, but it was not a smell that you could get used to. Staying in the room was an ordeal, and everyone, Farred included, would soon find a reason to leave.

It was the wizard, Gustav, who had identified that there was poison in Ashere's wound. It was, apparently, common practice amongst the Isharites to lace their crystal swords with a poison. Gustav had also declared that there was no cure that he was aware of. The wizard had done his best to treat the

Prince. His apprentice, a slight young woman called Inge, had taken on most of the care. She had cleaned the wound and applied a salve of fennel, mugwort, and various other herbs. But both had made it clear that their magic could not help.

There were mutterings from several quarters, North Magnians and Brasingians, about the role played by the two wizards. But when one of Archbishop Godfrey's priests had barged in to the room insisting that Ashere should be bled, Brock had threatened to gut the man on the spot, and there had been no further attempts to wrest control of the patient away.

'I thought I would hate you, you know?' said Ashere, his voice breathy and weak. It was perfectly audible in this room, but would have got lost in the noise of the castle outside it.

'What do you mean?'

'Before I met you. South Magnians were the enemy, as far as I was concerned. How stupid. How stupid that seems now after the horrors that we've seen.'

'Yes, pretty stupid,' answered Farred, pleased to see that this got a smile out of the Prince, 'but understandable.'

'Well, if we've done anything, Farred, you and I, we've proven what a load of horse shit that is. We've proven that North and South can work together. *Should* work together.'

'Agreed.'

There was a brief knock at the door before Walter entered. 'Your Highness,' he said, nodding at Ashere.

'Walter. How are the preparations going?'

'I now have to hope they've gone well enough,' Walter responded.

Farred and Ashere looked at one another and then back to the Marshal.

'You both asked me to let you know when it happened. Well, the army's now in sight, heading this way.'

There was a silence for a moment, simply because there was nothing to say. Farred made eye contact with Ashere.

'Go on, you two,' said the Prince. 'Let me know what happens.'

'You're not coming to skewer a few more Drobax, Your Highness?' enquired Walter with mock solemnity.

Ashere smiled at that. 'I can't be bothered. Maybe tomorrow.'

Farred turned and left the room, hiding a lump in the throat he didn't want Ashere to see. He took a few breaths of fresh air to steady himself.

Walter joined him. 'That's a brave man,' commented the Marshal.

Farred nodded. He thought of two or three replies, but none of them seemed right.

Walter sensed his mood and gestured forwards. 'Come on, there's a viewpoint along here where some of us will watch what happens. We'll witness some more bravery.'

Walter led Farred along the flying bridge that connected the Emperor's Keep on one crag with the Duke's Keep on the other. While Walter must have crossed this bridge countless times by now, and didn't give doing so a second thought, Farred still found it daunting, trying to resist looking at the huge drop to the ground below. Once he was safely across, Farred realised he could hear the thud of the Drobax army marching towards them.

They arrived at the viewing point, which overlooked the winding path leading up the first crag to the Duke's Keep. A few other spectators had already assembled here. Adalheid, the Duchess of Rotelegen, with a small group from her duchy, peered down with a grim expression. The soldiers who had been asked to defend the path were all in place. Adalheid's son, Jeremias, was down at the bottom of the crag with the Rotelegen soldiers, awaiting the onslaught.

Farred wondered at the decision to send him down there. If he was killed, the last son of Ellard would be dead, and the morale amongst the men of Rotelegen would plummet. But he understood why she did it. Her son had escaped the duchy and left it in the hands of the enemy. If he was to keep the support of his people, and ever return, he had to prove himself worthy.

In addition to the Rotelegen group, several other high-ranking figures were gathered there, including Godfrey, the Archbishop of Gotbeck, with some of his priests.

'No Baldwin?' Farred asked Walter.

The Marshal shook his head. 'Gustav advised him against it. The Isharites might target him. The Kellish are all on the other side,' he said, gesturing back towards the Emperor's Keep. 'Who knows, they might attack both crags simultaneously.'

It made sense for Baldwin to stay protected. Farred recalled the trap the Isharite wizards had laid for the Magnian forces two days ago, the bank of fog which had hidden their whereabouts. It wouldn't be a surprise if they had similar plans for taking Burkhard Castle.

Walter walked over to talk with Godfrey, leaving Farred to have a good look down at the forces lined up to receive the initial strike from the Drobax. He could make out the slight figure of Jeremias, still a boy really, surrounded by men, presumably the best warriors the Rotelegen had left, whose job would be to protect him at all costs. The Red Rooster standard of his duchy flew at his side, almost an invitation to the horde heading his way.

Farred looked out into the distance, his eyes straining to detect movement. He could hear the army of Drobax coming, knew well enough what to look for. His brain began to fill the hole, telling him he could see something when he couldn't. At some point in time, when exactly he couldn't be sure, the vision his mind created became reality. He could see them. Farred looked at those around him, but no-one else seemed to have noticed. He looked back. Yes, they were definitely in sight.

'There they are!' he shouted, pointing into the distance.

The words seemed to burst from his mouth without being told to, and he had shouted so loud he startled himself. The soldiers on the ramparts looked up at him and then out to where he indicated. Suddenly the whole crag was alive with conversation as the soldiers began to spot the approaching army, or complained that they couldn't. Weapons and shields were readied, buckles tightened, last prayers or swear words muttered under the breath. The nervous energy seemed to make the crag come alive, the air almost crackling around them.

The movement that Farred had detected on the horizon became a full army. The noise of thousands upon thousands of feet, clanking weapons and armour, grunts and shouts, wheeled carts and mules to pull them, all mingled with the steady thud of drums banging out a beat to announce the presence of a fearsome horde; maybe the largest army Dalriya had ever seen. The tactic of hiding their presence, which had worked so effectively against the Magnians two days ago, had now changed. Now the Isharites were intimidating the defenders with the sheer size of their army.

Before long, Farred could distinguish individual shapes marching towards them. He was not surprised that he saw no Haskans or Isharites. Instead, row upon row of Drobax headed their way, stretching as far along the horizon and as far back as one could see. Still they came, a plague of Drobax, as if there were enough of them to fill the whole of Dalriya. They intended to overcome the defenders by force of numbers.

The first lines of Drobax stormed into the remains of the settlement, which Walter had finally cleared out yesterday. He had done a good job but, mused Farred, some people just won't be helped. Sure enough, a young woman, flushed out by the Drobax, emerged from the jumble of wooden walls and rafters and came running towards the castle. Farred presumed she was a prostitute, desperate enough and stupid enough to ignore the warnings, and instead staying close by the castle to ply her trade.

The reaction of some soldiers seemed to confirm it. Some men cheered her on as if she had entered a bizarre sporting event. Others laughed hysterically, pointing at the sight and gripping their sides.

Farred didn't share in the humour of the spectacle. But he understood it. The soldiers of the Empire were tense, fearful, and, having seen the enemy army for the first time, doubtless in shock. The sight of the fleeing prostitute allowed some of them to break the tension. However, before long she was run down and speared by the Drobax, who continued their advance on Burkhard Castle.

When the first of the Drobax got within distance of the imperial lines, they faltered, waiting for greater numbers to advance. But the Drobax didn't operate in formations or any similar tactics. Once there were enough of them, they moved forwards again, relying on their greater weight of numbers. They approached in a disorganised mess of shouts and roars, intending to force their way up the castle. But the narrowness of the path meant they were funnelled into lines of only half a dozen wide, unable to make their superior numbers count by getting around and behind their enemy.

Farred watched the initial clash from his vantage point atop the crag. The Rotelegen soldiers moved down to meet the Drobax with their spears levelled and a horrendous crunch echoed upwards. There was little to see for a while as the two armies pushed against each other, the great force of the Drobax horde pushing against the Brasingians who had the height advantage. Spears wouldn't be much use down there now: smaller weapons, which could be used in the crush of bodies to stab and rip at the enemy, would be more effective.

The standard of Jeremias, the young Duke of Rotelegen, held firm. After a while, his men got the upper hand. Their superior armour and weapons, along with the height advantage, began to tell. The bodies of Drobax piled up at the bottom of the crag and got in the way of the next line, trying to move forward. In the end, they pulled back about fifty metres. The men on the castle cheered, but the Drobax leered back, inviting them to come and fight out in the open.

A flurry of activity at the bottom of the castle ensued, as soldiers from the front lines either made their own way or were helped up the path: presumably those injured in the fighting. Farred quickly noticed the standard of Jeremias was among them. He couldn't help looking over at Adalheid, but she observed stony faced. It would be a disaster for them if the young duke had been killed in the first of the fighting.

Time passed and the two armies remained separated by a few feet of ground in front of the castle. As they got closer, Farred could see that amongst the group of men climbing the path was Jeremias, alive but being speedily manhandled up by his bodyguards. The small group arrived at the top. Jeremias yanked off his helmet, his face red with exertion, his hair dripping wet with sweat, but he didn't look injured.

'Mother, how dare you order that I be dragged up here? I should be down there with my men,' he demanded, genuinely fuming.

'You've done your job, Jeremias,' Adalheid replied matter-of-factly. 'There's nothing to be gained by risking your life more than is necessary. Are you hurt?' she asked, the mother's concern for her child slipping out at the end despite herself.

Jeremias pulled a face. 'Of course not—' he began, but was interrupted by Walter.

'Well done, Your Grace,' he effused. 'You and your men fought well and hard. It was vital we stopped their momentum at the beginning.'

Everyone else joined in with their own congratulations, which succeeded in mollifying the young duke enough for him to drop his complaints. Of course, the Drobax had hardly been defeated, and they were already readying for another assault. Many Rotelegen still occupied the bottom of the castle path, apparently unwilling to give up their position at the front, but they were also being supplemented by the men of Gotbeck, proudly watched over by their Archbishop a few feet from Farred's position. The Drobax charged on in a second assault, a cacophony of drumming, shouts, and the clanging of metal rising to the top of the crag.

As he watched on, Farred had to admit that he had underestimated the Brasingians. He had been all too aware of the terrifying effect the Drobax could have, but had not fully considered the point of view of his allies. They had been waiting for weeks to engage the enemy, their frustration and anger building as the Drobax destroyed their homes, and Baldwin's orders had been to retreat and concede ground. They had witnessed Farred and the other Magnians ride off to take on the enemy, while they could only watch them go. And they had endured weeks of gruesome stories about the ferocious creatures who had invaded the Empire, so that when they finally appeared, the Drobax may even have been an anti-climax.

Because as Farred watched the carnage, he recognised that it was the Brasingians who were the more ferocious. They were desperate to spill blood, snarling with rage and fear, releasing the pent-up adrenaline of all the waiting they had endured. They didn't seem to tire or want to stop. They fought with the desperation of the cornered animal—of the outnumbered.

The Drobax had been force marched all the way to the castle: they tired more quickly and had less to fight for. They attacked a third time, in just the same way as they had done, and with just as little success. After the third attack, the Drobax, presumably receiving an order, perhaps via the booming drums, made a full retreat. They marched away from the castle, and kept on marching until they were completely out of sight. It might even have been possible for the defenders of Burkhard Castle to wonder if they had imagined the attack, were it not for the pile of bodies that lay at the bottom of the crag.

EVERY MORNING, after breakfast, Emperor Baldwin met with his war council. He was joined by the leaders of the armies stationed at Burkhard Castle. Duke Arne of Luderia, father of the Empress Hannelore, sat on his right. On his left was Godfrey, the vigorous Archbishop of Gotbeck. The young Duke Jeremias of Rotelegen attended with his mother, Adalheid. Due to the sickness of Prince Cerdda, Farred attended, representing the Magnians and Middians. Walter the Marshal, Baldwin's brother, always began the meeting with an account of the defences, supplies, and any other information on the current situation. Finally, Gustav the Hawk, Archmage of the Empire, was usually there. This morning he wasn't. It was never clear to Farred what his role was, though he would occasionally provide information about the enemy forces. No one ever asked how he obtained this information.

After Walter gave his briefing, talk naturally turned to the attack on the castle the night before.

'I must start,' announced Baldwin, 'with my congratulations on the way Duke Jeremias fought and led his troops yesterday. Your father would have been proud.'

The other dukes banged their fists on the table in appreciation, and so Farred joined in.

Jeremias nodded sombrely. Whatever emotion he felt he kept to himself. 'Thank you, Your Majesty,' Jeremias acknowledged. 'The people of my duchy will be ready to fight whenever you ask.'

'Nobly said,' commented Duke Arne.

'Bearing the attack in mind,' continued Baldwin, 'now is a good time to review the disposition of our forces. I don't want people to gain the impression that myself and the Kellish have been put in a safer location than the other imperial forces.'

'Oh,' said Arne, puffing out his cheeks, 'I don't think anyone has that impression at all.'

'We are perfectly content where we are,' added Godfrey.

'I think,' began Walter, 'that the soldiers will not like to be moved about unnecessarily. We don't yet know whether the enemy will always target the Duke's Crag. If the situation arises where one group has done much more of the fighting, then we can think about moving things about.'

Everyone seemed happy with this judgement. The meeting lasted a little longer. It was agreed that Arne's Luderians would defend the bottom of the crag for the next attack. But in truth, they were ready, and there was very little to do. They just had to wait for the next attack to come.

The meeting broke up and Farred made his way to the Emperor's Crag where the Magnian forces had been barracked. He dropped in on Brock and the Middians to pass on the details of the meeting. Farred had now taken over the leadership of the Southern troops and felt responsible for these men, cooped up in some castle miles from their homelands. He spent as much time with them as possible, chatting or playing dice, finding out about their families and lives back home. He was especially careful to spend time with the North Magnians, who had effectively lost their prince. Farred took his lunch with them, and in the afternoon, he and Brock went up to the walls of the keep, from where there was an excellent view of the lands surrounding the castle, including the Great Road. He knew he was avoiding Ashere, but tried to put the thought out of his mind.

'I wonder what they're doing,' Farred said as they gazed out into the distance. 'I've heard some people suggest that the entire army is marching south to Essenberg.'

Brock considered this, screwing up his face in thought.'If you were them,' said the Middian eventually, in his deep voice, 'would you do that?'

'No—I wouldn't. If I had an army that large, I wouldn't run away from a fight.'

Brock grunted, nodding. 'I agree. They'll be back soon enough.'

There was a pause as the two of them looked out over the landscape.

'When it's time,' Brock said, 'will you ride out with me?'

'What?'

'I can't die on this rock like a cornered animal. When it's time, I'm going to ride out against them. Walter says I can have a horse. He'll give you one.'

It was a heroic image, and Farred couldn't help but like the idea of it. 'Very well, Brock. I'll ride out with you.'

They stood in silence for a while, and they were amongst the first to see the return of the Drobax army. From every direction they appeared, a mass of tiny figures closing in on the castle. From mid-afternoon until the evening they came, surrounding the castle, but stopping short of missile range.

The numbers were incredible to see. Men kept shaking their heads in disbelief until it became a general source of humour. They chuckled at the sight and made dark jests about the victory they would enjoy tomorrow. Everyone now realised what Farred and Brock had known for days. This wasn't an army that could be defeated in battle. It wasn't an army at all in the sense that people had understood the word up to now. It was a migration.

The Drobax made their camps. As the sun went down, the light from their fires shone out around the castle. It was a terrifying sight, yet somehow beautiful, as if all the night sprites had gathered together for a midnight party. The soldiers in the castle got their supper. The mood seemed to drop. There was no escape now—Ishari had demonstrated that they were all doomed. Few of them would get a good sleep tonight.

Farred rose and said good night to Brock. He took in a deep breath. It was time to see Ashere.

When he entered Ashere's room, the smell was worse, and he couldn't help covering his nose. The Prince was lying on his back, and his eyes had been closed, but he opened them when he heard Farred enter.

'Hello,' Farred said quietly, 'How are you?'

What a stupid question, he thought to himself. He looked worse than ever; didn't look like himself any more. His body seemed to have shrunk, except for his bones, which threatened to burst out of his skin.

Ashere made a facial gesture which may have been intended as a smile, but was just a grimace.

'How do I look?' he croaked, as if there was no water left in his mouth.

Farred moved over to the bed, propped him up and put a drink of water to his lips. Ashere gulped some down, but it looked like it pained him to swallow. Farred let him back down. 'Have you heard that the army is back again today?'

'Yes, Inge has been in. She told me.'

There was a pause.

'Farred. I'm dying. I'm in agony,' Ashere's voice cracked with emotion when he said these words, as if he was going to break down, but he pulled himself together. He took a deep breath. 'Please end it for me.'

'No!' said Farred in horror. But was he really surprised? Was this why he had avoided visiting Ashere all day?

'I'm sorry, my friend. I thought I would be much stronger than this. But I can't take it anymore—' Again, his emotions got the better of him. A tear rolled down his cheek.

Farred's heart felt like it would break. 'I don't think I can do it,' Farred said, now struggling to get his own words out.

'It has to be you, Farred. I can't ask anybody else. Please.'

Farred nodded. He knew it had to be him. 'Is there any...message for anyone?'

'If you get out of here alive, tell my brother and sister I love them. I—I hope you *do* get out of here, Farred.'

There was nothing else to say now. More words would only make the job harder.

Farred gently lifted Ashere's head, pulled out his pillow, and lowered his head back onto the bed. He placed the pillow firmly over Ashere's face and pressed down.

To the Prince's credit, it was only at the very end that his arms shot upwards. His hands found Farred's arms, but they had no strength in them. Then the struggling stopped.

Farred waited a while longer. He carefully replaced the pillow.

He bent down and kissed him on the lips.

'Farewell, Prince Ashere,' he murmured. 'Be at peace.'

PRISONS

XI

It felt good to get away from the High Tower and its claustrophobic atmosphere.

Looking at her riding companions, Belwynn got the impression that they felt the same way. Theron, more than anyone else, had taken responsibility for confronting Galenos: organising his supporters, persuading others that the cause was just. Tomorrow he would achieve his goal, and his uncle, Sebastian, would be sworn in as the new Grand Master of the Order of the Knights of Kalinth.

Sebastian was spending the day fasting and praying to prepare for the ceremony. Theron would have no special role to play, and so could afford an excursion today. His squire, Evander, accompanied them as always.

Rabigar also seemed a changed person today. He had gained a new sense of purpose for the first time since the sickening attack in Coldeberg prison, which had left him blind in one eye. Now that he had resolved to return to his homeland, he seemed to be more alive, more in charge of his own destiny.

The four of them rode along at a steady pace, being as kind as they could to their horses on a hot summer's day. The grassland they rode through was scorched dry, with few trees to offer shade. No one felt the need to talk much, but they travelled in an easy, companionable silence.

It was still before midday when they reached the crossroads. Rabigar's journey would take him south, to the mountainous lands of the Krykkers, where humans were forbidden. They all dismounted. Rabigar and Theron gave each other a rough embrace.

'Look after her,' Rabigar growled.

'I will,' said Theron obediently.

Rabigar gave Evander a big slap on the back before turning to Belwynn. She suddenly burst into tears, surprising herself as much as anyone else.

'Don't worry, I'll be fine,' said Rabigar.

Belwynn understood that Rabigar was an exile, and that it was therefore dangerous to return home. But that wasn't why she was crying. 'I'll miss you,' she explained, sobbing, and feeling like a silly little girl.

Rabigar nodded. 'I'll miss you too. But if everything works out the way I want it to, I will see you again soon.'

He climbed back onto his mount, a gift from Sebastian, and continued his journey alone. They waited until Rabigar was out of sight before heading east.

'I'm looking forward to showing you the fortress,' said Theron, smiling like a goofy boy. He had remembered their conversation about the High Tower, and had decided that he had to show Belwynn the fortress at Chalios before they left for the north, and missed the chance. Belwynn had been happy to go along and, though she kept it to herself, pleased that the knight was taking such an interest in her.

It was another hour's ride until they drew within sight. The path Theron led them on grew steeper and rockier; not quite the mountainous terrain that Rabigar was heading for, but part of the same chain. The surrounding area was largely heathland, and while the path towards Chalios was well maintained, the view it afforded was of a sparsely settled landscape, relatively untouched by human habitation.

Chalios was certainly impressive. Not in the same way as the castles of the Empire Belwynn had recently visited, with their carefully designed geometric shapes and thick walls imposing themselves onto their surroundings. Neither was it like the Knights' High Tower, designed with beauty in mind. This fortress was a huge rock cliff jutting out of the ground with steep sides. As they rode closer, Belwynn could see that it had been cleverly augmented by human engineers. The path up to the entrance was flanked by huge rock walls and towers, allowing defenders to resist an approaching army from almost every angle. The top of the cliff had battlements and some other indefinable structures, too far up for Belwynn to make out. But in essence, it was a natural defensive structure rather than man made. It would be a strong place of defence even with none of the modifications. Belwynn felt it had a sense of ancient history to it, as if peoples had been using it for the same purpose centuries past, before the Knights of Kalinth existed; and would continue to use it long after they disappeared. The thought was a little melancholy but somehow reassuring.

They left Evander with the horses on the path; Theron explained that there was stabling for horses inside, but that it wasn't worth risking injuries to them by leading them in today. As they approached the open gates, Belwynn turned around to wave at Evander. He waved back.

'He looks so tiny sitting there, surrounded by those enormous towers,' she said.

'Mmm,' said Theron, attempting to sound interested in the size of his squire. 'The gates are solid, but they have to be quite wide to bring horses in and out. That makes them the weakest point of the fortress. That's why we've constructed such a heavily fortified approach to them. Any army would suffer huge losses before they got here.'

'Are his parents alive?' Belwynn asked.

'What?'

'Evander's parents.'

'Yes. They have estates in the north-east. I know his father very well,' answered Theron. He made a face.

'What is it?'

'You're not that interested, are you?'

'Sorry, Theron, I am. Please tell me more.'

'This is the very place where Stephen fought the Green Dragon, you know?'

Belwynn wasn't sure whether Theron really believed the story, but thought it best not to ask. 'Yes, I know. It's in the song.'

He smiled. 'Come on. I'll take you to the top.'

The inside of the fortress couldn't have been a greater contrast to the High Tower. The whole place was deserted. There were no separate rooms, just one huge open space. It was the middle of a bright summer's day, but it was still dark and gloomy inside. Much of the inside space had been carved out by hand, and the walls were rough and unfinished. Its purpose as a last place of refuge could hardly have been lost on even the most casual visitor. To Belwynn, it felt like a place to die. She mused to herself that, if ghosts truly came out of their graves on certain nights to revisit the lands where they once lived, this must surely be a popular haunt.

Theron led her up a twisting stone stairway to the top of the cliff, and they emerged back into the sunshine. The cliff top was also well fortified. Battlements faced out towards the path while at the rear of the cliff, more stonework protected the area from enemies who had discovered alternative routes to the top.

Belwynn peered over the edge. 'Evander!' she bellowed out.

The squire, now an even tinier figure than before, dutifully waved up towards them.

'Well? What do you think?' asked Theron.

'It's very impressive. I was wondering when was the last time it was used?'

Theron puffed out his cheeks. 'Not for generations. Not since the great wars with the Kharovians.'

Belwynn nodded. 'Because it is a strange place for the Knights of Kalinth to hold.'

'Yes, I understand what you mean. Our strength is as a cavalry force, which is useless here. But this place isn't meant to be just for the Knights. It's for all the people of Kalinth. We maintain it on their behalf.'

'I see.'

'Belwynn,' began Theron, and she immediately caught the change in tone. Butterflies flew about her stomach even before he continued speaking.

'I enjoy spending time with you. I—' he began, but seemed at a loss for words, and walked towards her. Belwynn let him take her hand. He looked into her eyes and shook his head. 'Why can't I get my words out?'

Belwynn felt a sudden, mad urge to kiss him. It felt like, atop this cliff, they were free to do whatever they liked, with no consequences. She took a breath and controlled herself. They weren't free. And she wasn't a wilful child.

'I understand what you are trying to say, Theron,' Belwynn said. 'But you are a Knight of Kalinth and have taken your oaths. You are about to lead a Knights' army against your king. I need to find my brother. If we both get to the other side of all of that—then we can speak about this.'

Theron nodded. He clasped her hand in both of his as if he didn't want to let it go. 'Very well, Belwynn. But I promise you. After I restore my country, I will find and rescue your brother.'

Don't make promises you can't keep, she thought, but didn't say it. Instead she moved forwards and they embraced, not letting go of each other until it was time to leave.

* * *

HE SWAM from unconsciousness towards consciousness, sliding through the membranes in his path, but being careful not to go too far. A queasy feeling in his stomach made him stop. He peered ahead tentatively, fighting down the natural urge to re-join his body. Pain and fear. That was why he was hesitating. That was his waking life now. Fighting down panic, he tried to force his cloudy thoughts to think clearly, without waking him up.

Who am I?

It sounded like a stupid question, but he had to start somewhere.

Soren.

Yes, that was it. Soren the wizard. Not a very clever wizard, though, because he had let himself be captured. He had been captured in Edeleny, by the Isharites. He had been part of a group. Some of them had been captured, but...

Something made Soren wake up. He couldn't see or hear anything. Since being separated from Herin, Clarin, and the others, they had somehow removed his senses. He didn't know what kind of room he was in, or whether there were other people in it. He didn't know if he was lying down, sitting, or standing. He didn't know how long he had been there.

He knew about the pain. The excruciating, agonising pain that He had inflicted on him. It wasn't happening right now, but his nerve endings were so raw it felt like it was. The pain overload would have caused most people to have gone mad or die by now. He hadn't, because his magic powers helped to keep him alive; and, because He still wanted something from him.

Who 'He' was, Soren couldn't be sure. He was a powerful wizard and so could have been Arioc, or even Erkindrix himself. Or some other. He had done this many times before. Using the pain, He had gained entry into Soren's mind, finding out all about his life; his magical gifts and knowledge had been forced out of him; all the details of his journey from Magnia to the Grand Caladri. Soren had fought him all the way, protecting and separating information, with the aim of keeping any small secret; but the pain was unbearable, and his torturer already knew all the tricks, shoving a clawed hand around in Soren's brain, scratching and picking out the pieces until his job was done.

And yet his job wasn't done. Because Soren was still alive. There was one thing his torturer didn't know, hadn't fully found out, that he was still looking for. Soren's link with his sister, Belwynn.

Soren had closed this off early on, knowing that if the link was found, it could be used to locate and kill Belwynn. His interrogator knew there was something Soren wasn't telling him; that there was something unusual about him. But He didn't know what it was: as far as Soren knew the link was unique, so his interrogator didn't know exactly what he was looking for. The pain had forced Soren to give everything else up—he would have given his life for it to stop a long time ago. But because this involved the life of his sister, he had found the strength to resist. It had surprised and shocked his torturer at first. Soren had got some small sense of satisfaction from that. But he soon realised that it had also sparked an interest, and that He wouldn't let go until he knew everything.

'Soren.'

It was Him. The voice of his tormentor. Smooth and confident, it was the voice of a God, and Soren was an insect squirming on the sole of His shoe. Had He just arrived or had He been there all along? Was He speaking inside Soren's head or was He there in the room?

'Soren, I'm glad you've returned. Because you know we have unfinished business, don't you?'

'Please,' whimpered Soren. His pathetic and purposeless begging made Soren disgust himself, but he pleaded and begged anyway, every single time.

'I've been thinking, since last time. This thing you are hiding from me, and can't tell me about. I've been thinking that maybe you don't know what it is yourself. That maybe someone else has hidden it. That would explain why you haven't been able to tell me so far. Do you think I'm on to something, Soren?'

'Yes,' said Soren. 'Yes, that must be right.'

'Right. Well, let's focus on that this time then. Are you ready?'

'But—but doesn't that mean you don't have to hurt me?'

'Oh, no. The pain still has to be there.'

'Please. If I don't know where it is, maybe there's no need for the pain—'

But the pain came. It coursed through Soren's body, his nerve receptors flaring until there was nothing but pain, unbearable pain that somehow didn't stop. Soren screamed and screamed. I'm screaming, he thought to himself. I'm screaming, but am I screaming out loud, or just in my head?

* * *

Cyprian would always be much faster than him, Gyrmund admitted to himself.

Another day in the mines, and Gyrmund's back was aching, his knees were creaking, and his head felt dizzy. His work partner, on the other hand, seemed to be built for this kind of work. Cyprian was small and wiry, able to bend down and stretch back up all day long without getting noticeably tired. It might have been demoralising if they had not got along with each other. Occasionally, the Persaleian would shake his head in bemusement at

Gyrmund's efforts, and chuck some of the crystals he had excavated himself into Gyrmund's box.

Cyprian was from the busy port of Lumberco in Persala, and the two of them had first hit it off when Gyrmund recounted a visit he had once made to the city, being careful to emphasise his admiration for the place. Cyprian had now taken over the conversation, and was running through all the jobs he had worked in Lumberco since childhood.

'You can get dock work all the time, once you know who's who and you've got a reputation for doing a full day's graft. You just turn up with your hook early in the morning, and you can work through 'til evening. Tough work that, mind. By the end of the day, you're starving and gasping for a drink. I'd end up spending half my wages in the pub on an evening.'

At that moment, the thought of spending all day working outside, and all evening in the pub, sounded like heaven to Gyrmund. 'And did you get any work on ship, Cyprian?' he asked.

'Yes, I did that several times. Local routes, usually up the rivers, to sell on the goods that had arrived in port.'

'And the longer routes—they're all controlled by the Sea Caladri?'

'Yes, that's right,' said Cyprian, hacking away at one side of a clump of crystal he was excavating.

It was said as if it was something he wasn't happy about, but wasn't going to complain about either, so Gyrmund didn't probe any further. He knew the Caladri control of sea trade was a sore point in many kingdoms, and that one reason the Persaleians had originally constructed the Great Road was to open up an alternative, inland route, which they could control.

Anyway, Gyrmund thought, *I've done enough skirting around the issue.* 'We need to get out of here,' he said in a quiet, low voice.

Cyprian looked over. 'That we do,' said the Persaleian, before resuming his work. Just as Gyrmund thought that might be it, he looked over again, with a slight twinkle in his eyes.

'And you and your two friends are the ones that can do it. I can feel it.'

'Well—the other two, maybe.'

Cyprian shrugged. 'Maybe more them. But if they can lead, there's plenty of us who can follow. I've been here as long as most. I know who could be persuaded to help.'

This was exactly what Gyrmund wanted to hear. 'That's great. How many do you think?'

'First, though,' said Cyprian, apparently ignoring the question, 'you'll have to deal with Vamak. He has a good relationship with the guards, and if he gets a whiff, he'll tell 'em about any escape plan. Plus, he's feared enough to stop people siding with you. So, like I say, that's your job. In the meantime, I'll be quietly sounding out some of the other miners. But don't worry 'bout that. I'm not going to blab anything to the wrong person. So, to answer your question about numbers, we won't know exactly how many. We'll have a few on side. And we'll have the rest, who we just won't know about for sure until it happens.'

Gyrmund nodded. 'I'll let Herin and Clarin know. When you have some information, you can tell any one of us.'

'Fine. Now, help me along with this, will you?'

Gyrmund hefted his axe and resumed his back-breaking work in the mines, but now with a little more hope that he might make it out alive.

A BLESSING

XII

The Knights of Kalinth were on the move.

Belwynn had mixed emotions as the High Tower of the Knights receded into the distance behind them, and then disappeared. But most of all, she was glad to be moving on.

The sun was out as the mounted force made a good pace along a narrow but well-used road. They had left the seat of the Knights of Kalinth for Heractus, the seat of its kings. The road was mostly mud, and looked like it got wet and boggy in the winter months, but after several weeks of warm weather it had now been baked dry, leaving cracks on the surface. There was little shade on the route, the landscape dominated by low-lying vegetation like heather and gorse, which allowed the scouts to get a good view of the surrounding area, in all directions. Nesting birds, disturbed by the armed force passing their homes, would fly or run away, causing the few dogs with them to bark, the handlers to curse, and the horses to get jittery. But apart from the wildlife, there seemed little else to worry about, and the mood was relaxed.

The momentous events at the High Tower had culminated yesterday in the formal removal of Galenos as Grand Master of the Order, and the adoption of Sebastian as his replacement. It had been a bloodless revolution, and Galenos was now being held in comfortable conditions in a room in the Tower. But Sebastian and his advisers knew that news of their actions would already be spreading across the country to their enemies. They had to move fast and retain the initiative.

Sebastian already had the makings of an army at his disposal. Almost all the Knights had been in attendance at the High Tower, and most of those who supported Sebastian, who were in the clear majority, now joined him in the march south. Remi, Sebastian's long-time friend, had been left in charge at the Tower, to run things in the new Grand Master's absence, and to coordinate communications and supplies.

Many of the knights had brought with them a sizeable entourage of squires, men at arms, and other followers. In addition, Sebastian now had charge of the Order's servants, which included craftsmen whose expertise lay in working with metal, leather, or wood. These groups swelled the force at Sebastian's disposal to something like three thousand fighters in all. But, as Theron explained to Belwynn, as they rode together near the head of the army, many other knights had not brought their soldiers with them. Theron himself only had Evander, his squire.

'My largest estates, in Erisina, are to the west. I've written some letters and given them to messengers to take to that part of the country. Other messengers are heading to the estates of our supporters all over Kalinth. Enough should get through in time to add to our army by the time we reach Heractus.'

'How many soldiers might come from your estates?' asked Belwynn.

Theron thought about it. 'Probably about fifty men who know how to fight. Not all of them are trained soldiers, though. More of them are farmers, or other workers. Blacksmiths are usually pretty good in a fight.'

'How many more might we get altogether?'

'If you include the force that Remi will bring over from the High Tower, we might reach five thousand.'

Belwynn thought about that. It wasn't very many, even though the Knights were the best warriors in Kalinth. If they were to enter the capital, Heractus, they would need a superior force, and it didn't seem like they had one.

'And what do we do when we reach Heractus?'

'That depends on the reaction we get. The city is well defended. There is a city guard who patrol the walls, and a royal guard of well-trained soldiers who serve the king. Jonas has many wealthy supporters who can raise soldiers of their own. We can't rule out resistance.'

In the early afternoon, they made a stop by a fast-flowing river. Theron identified it as the Pineos, that travelled west and emptied into the Lantinen Sea.

The squires and other servants quickly got to work giving the horses a drink and a feed. The riders dismounted so that their animals could get a proper rest, and their own legs could get a stretch after hours in the saddle.

Theron went off to speak to Sebastian and the other leaders, and so Belwynn led Elana and Dirk away from the busy atmosphere somewhere quieter. They found a flat piece of rock by the river that was big enough for all three of them to sit on. It had been nicely warmed by a full morning's sunshine. Belwynn leaned back, enjoying the warm rays of the sun on her skin. Looking over at Dirk, she saw the ride had done his health little good. His skin still had a white pallor to it, and his hair and face were wet with sweat. Elana began attending to him, working her healing magic by holding his hands inside hers and then pressing her hands onto the back of his neck and his forehead.

It was a routine they had both got used to, but it still made Belwynn feel awkward, as if she were intruding on a private moment. She looked around them, thinking she might go for a short walk by herself, when she saw a group of half a dozen knights making their way towards them. She got to her feet. Elana noticed and stopped attending to Dirk, a quizzical look on her face.

As the knights got nearer, Belwynn recognised a couple of faces as younger knights she had seen here and there at the High Tower, but she didn't think she had been introduced to any of them.

They seemed unsure of themselves and glanced nervously at one another. One knight eventually stepped forward. He was a sandy-haired young man, whom Belwynn judged had not yet reached twenty years.

'Lady Belwynn, I am Philon, a Knight of Kalinth as are my friends here,' he said, gesturing at the others. His friends nodded, one or two staring sheepishly at the ground. 'We apologise for disturbing you all at your rest.' He paused, waiting for a response.

Belwynn wasn't sure how to proceed, but the group of knights seemed harmless enough. 'Please, there is no need to apologise. What is it you have come for?'

'Well, we all listened to your song—your singing, in the Great Hall, and we all got talking about how inspiring it was for each of us. All of us have said it was a very moving experience, each in our own way...'

Philon's voice drifted off, unable to continue the sentence any further. He turned around to his friends and flapped his hands a little, as if to appeal for help.

The nearest knight cleared his throat and stepped forwards. He suddenly went down on one knee. 'Lady Belwynn,' he began—large brown eyes framed in long, wavy brown hair looked up at her, 'we are all going to war for our first time, and we have a request that—would it be possible for you to bless our swords?'

Belwynn was taken aback and looked at Elana for help. The priestess nodded. She could hardly refuse such a request.

'Yes, of course,' she said, having no idea what was involved in blessing a sword.

The other five knights, including Philon, adopted the same position as the brown eyed knight. They all drew their swords and, gripping the hilt in both hands, placed the sharp end into the ground. When this was done, they bowed their heads, ready to receive the blessing.

Belwynn turned to look at Elana again, who to her surprise had put one hand to her mouth, and was trying not to giggle out loud.

She approached the first knight. 'May I ask your name?'

'Leontios.'

'And where are you from, Leontios?'

'From Fyllo, my lady.'

'Leontios of Fyllo, I bless your sword. May it serve its master well in battle.'

She studied the down-turned faces of the knights to see their reaction, but there was no sign that they were disappointed with the choice of words. So, Belwynn moved from Leontios to Philon, and on to the rest of the knights, giving the same blessing to each of them.

Half way through, Theron came striding over, the initial look of concern on his face quickly turning to bemusement as he took in the spectacle. Once Belwynn had finished, the knights returned to their feet, evidently pleased with what had passed. They offered their thanks, and giving a final bow, made their way back to the road.

Theron's eyes followed the knights and then turned back to Belwynn, as if studying her closely.

'What, Theron? Was I wrong to do that?'

'No, not at all. I think it was good,' he said, his voice light and breezy.

But he continued to look at Belwynn, as if in some way he were now truly seeing her for the first time.

* * *

MONEVA WAS FINALLY out of Arioc's apartments. After two more nights with the King of Haskany, she was now allowed the freedom of the fortress. He had held her chin in one hand, and agreed to her request as if he were an indulgent father. The memory of it made her stomach twist, but Moneva ruthlessly pushed it aside. She had to learn to banish those memories. She had to use the little time she had to achieve something.

Moneva knew that this meant that Arioc had started to trust her, but that if she did anything to lose his trust, there would be no second chances. So, she couldn't stay out for too long. Neither could she ask him about the whereabouts of her friends. This left the chances of her finding out anything of use dismally low, but at least she could get her bearings.

Babak had given her a brooch with Arioc's sigil on it: a serpent, coiled around into a circle and eating its own tail. This allowed her free passage around his tower.

Since virtually all the people she came across in the tower also displayed the same sigil somewhere about their person, on uniforms, or necklaces, or brooches just like hers, Moneva concluded that the whole tower was Arioc's domain and everyone in it a follower of his. She therefore acted on the assumption that since Gyrmund and the others had been captured by Arioc, they would most likely be here too. But after a couple of hours of fruitless searching, she gave up on that idea. Presumably, most of the other towers of the fortress were occupied by great Lords of Ishari, just like Arioc. But there were likely to be other areas where prisoners were kept, and it was these she must locate.

Knowing that she had little time left before raising suspicions, Moneva made her way to the eastern exit of the tower. Two guards stood on duty at the door, mean looking men like the ones who had held her captive on the way here.

Moneva approached them, making sure that the brooch was visible. The guards saw her coming. One of them said a few words to the other, and they both laughed in her direction, lips curling in contempt. Steeling herself, Moneva approached the exit, trying to make her expression and body language look as confident as possible.

One of them put out an arm, his hand grasping a spear that blocked her from leaving. 'Where are you going?' he asked, speaking Dalriyan in a much more heavily accented voice than Arioc did.

Moneva nodded ahead of her. 'Out there,' she said.

'No, not allowed.'

'Arioc says I *am* allowed.'

Moneva sensed some doubt in them now. These men didn't want to make a mistake and displease their master. Arioc's last lover, Shira, was now on the Council of Seven, after all. It wouldn't be wise to insult Moneva if she was going to become his new favourite.

'You can tell him where I went,' she said, looking impassively at both guards.

The guard with the spear looked at his partner, who gave a small nod. The arm was withdrawn. The second guard opened the wooden door for Moneva, who wasted no time in passing through it.

The corridor she entered was just the same as the one she had left, rough stone walls on either side, and a wooden ceiling above her, which served as a walkway for the castle defenders above. Torches in the wall made just enough light to see ahead.

But the feeling of this corridor was totally different. Everywhere she had been on the other side of the door—every inch of every room—had resonated with Arioc's presence, as if he were aware of everything that happened there. But once Moneva had passed through the door, beyond his part of the fortress, the feeling vanished. It was powerful magic, admitted Moneva, but even Arioc's magic had boundaries. That thought gave her hope.

Passing through an unguarded door at the end of the new corridor, Moneva found herself in a small courtyard. The wooden walkway above her continued its route around the fortress wall. As she passed under it, she found the courtyard was open to the elements, and she could breathe fresh air for the first time in days. The yard narrowed sharply ahead of her, making it a wedge shape. The left of the courtyard was being used as a dumping ground for materials: a pile of stones, neatly stacked lengths of timber, and several large canvas sacks tied with rope.

Servants were carrying more of these sacks into the courtyard and dumping them against the wall with a clatter. A couple of soldiers entered the courtyard from an opening in this wall and passed through to a similar opening on the other side. Servants and soldiers alike gave Moneva a brief look, but were too busy, or perhaps too disinterested, to do more than that.

A stone bench ran along the far end of the courtyard, the thin end of the wedge. A lone figure seated on the bench gestured to Moneva to come over. Moneva looked around uncertainly, but no-one else was watching. She moved over warily. The figure gestured with his arm again, as if she should hurry. He was wearing a cowl that partially hid his face, but as Moneva moved a step closer, she could see a pair of red eyes staring out at her. She stopped with a start. It was Pentas.

Pentas beckoned a third time, looking frustrated. Moneva moved over more quickly, taking a seat next to the sorcerer and trying not to look suspicious.

'Moneva,' he began, turning towards her, his red eyes drawing her in. 'We don't have long. Don't draw attention to our conversation. We don't want anyone to remember us. I am under surveillance and so will you be.'

Moneva nodded. 'How did you find me here?'

'I've known where you were all along. I've been waiting for you to get out of Arioc's Tower.'

Moneva felt anger flare to the surface. 'You knew what was happening to me, and you did nothing?' she let out, trying to stop her whisper from becoming a scream. She felt tears in her eyes.

Pentas stared straight back at her. 'Yes. I hoped you would survive it.'

'You hoped?' said Moneva incredulously, and lashed out, aiming to slap Pentas in the face; but his hand shot out, grabbing her wrist.

'I told you not to draw attention,' he said sternly, pushing her arm down before letting go. He looked around the courtyard before continuing. 'I am sorry for what has happened to you, Moneva. But there are many lives at stake right now.'

It was said with some feeling, but hardly made Moneva feel better. She tried to control her emotions, surprised at how quickly they had come flooding out.

'I have to be very careful,' continued Pentas. 'You are strong, and you have survived. But now I need you to help me. I know where your friends have been taken.'

'Where?' demanded Moneva.

'I will give you full directions. Gyrmund, Herin and Clarin have been sent to a slave mine attached to the fortress, and Soren is being held in one of the towers here. There is only so much help I can give you all. Soon Herin and the others must be ready, somehow, to escape the mines. I want you to find them and give them warning of this. You, too, will have to be ready. But I can't risk seeing you again, Moneva, unless there's an emergency. I won't be here in the fortress all the time, either. I must give you all your instructions now. Do you understand?'

Moneva understood that she was putting herself completely in the hands of this sorcerer, whom she had no reason to trust. But at least he was offering her a plan and giving her purpose, when she had been hopelessly lost before.

'Yes.'

'Good. And there's one other thing you can do. You don't like it, I know, but you are now in a position to influence Arioc. That makes you powerful. There are certain things I would like you to talk about with him. But I need to know now whether you agree to all of it? You will be risking your life if you do.'

Moneva sighed. Did she have any choice? 'I agree, sorcerer. Now tell me where my friends are.'

* * *

FROM WHERE THEY STOOD, Burkhard Castle looked like the model castle her Uncle Koren owned back home and had, on special occasions, let her play with. The Drobax, on the other hand, didn't resemble the toy soldiers that went with it: Koren just owned brave knights and men at arms, not deformed creatures like these. Shira was only too aware of the irony that the brave soldiers she had imagined in her childhood games were the ones defending the castle from *her* army.

Shira's own people, the Haskans, were stationed two miles away, and weren't being used in the attack. Joined by Koren and Mehrab, she had located a rocky outcrop from where they could observe the attack. But she had no real role to play herself. It was Roshanak and his team of Isharite wizards who were in charge, driving the Drobax forwards and giving them their instructions.

The drums pounded out the beat for an all-out attack, and the creatures charged at the castle like rabid animals. As much as Shira and Koren despised the Drobax for not being true soldiers—and Mehrab despised Roshanak and his associates for not being true magi—the reality was that this army of Drobax was the most powerful force in the land.

As she looked on, they swarmed towards the two outcrops of rock, which represented one of the best natural defensive positions in Dalriya. On the left of the scene stood the larger of the two crags, with the Emperor's Keep on top. The Drobax approached it from all sides and climbed. No path had ever been constructed by the Brasingians on this crag, and the Drobax had to negotiate their way up the steep rock surface. They used roughly made wooden ladders, propping them up against the side, but the going was slow.

The crag on the right was the obvious target for the Drobax, and was heavily defended by the castle's soldiers, who had stationed a force right at the bottom where the path began. The narrow path neutralised the numerical superiority of the Drobax and gave the defenders a height advantage. The Drobax launched their attack at this part of the castle, but the defenders held firm. Although she was too far away to see the individual weapons, Shira knew that there would be a wall of shields bristling with spears and pikes waiting for the Drobax. As she watched, a pile of dead bodies grew at the bottom of the path.

'Whose banner is that?' asked Mehrab, pointing at the device of the green tree which was being flown over the heads of the defenders who were engaging the Drobax.

'The duchy of Luderia,' replied Shira. 'Arne is their leader; the Emperor's father-in-law. A fat waste of space, so I am told.'

'Well, his men are doing alright,' said Koren sharply. 'I'm going for a piss,' he added, heading off back down the outcrop.

'Your uncle isn't enjoying this?' asked Mehrab when Koren was out of earshot.

'Not his idea of how wars should be fought,' said Shira. 'Nor mine, but I guess I'm more philosophical about it.'

'You mean that you understand that this is the last war humans will ever fight.'

Shira shrugged. She didn't like the comment. But then, she didn't like Mehrab.

The hours went by and little changed. Koren never reappeared, and Shira didn't blame him.

The Luderians retreated up the path. Not far, but it represented some progress. They moved behind a gate which blocked the path up the crag. The Drobax attacked, hacking and ripping at the gate. From a ledge above them, the defenders threw missiles down. It was hard to make out what, but there would be rocks, spears, arrows. Maybe hot oil, which was commonly used by castle defenders in Haskany. It would be carnage, and the Drobax retreated under the onslaught.

At the same time, the Drobax on the other crag were finally encountering the defenders. About half way up, a small wall had been built which encircled the whole crag. The Brasingians manned this wall so that they had a common point of defence, and as the Drobax struggled up towards it, the imperial soldiers could thrust with their spears or fire missiles down, with the wall to protect them. It was easy work for the defenders. The Drobax arrived at the wall in small, irregular numbers rather than all at once, and could be picked off at will. Shira had no faith that any of them would get through.

The attack continued for the rest of the day. Towards the end, the Drobax on the path managed to rip down the gate, but were then counter-attacked by the Luderians who had been able to conserve their strength. The Drobax were driven right down to the bottom of the path. Finally, the drums ordered a retreat, and the Drobax made their way back to the pathetic camps that encircled the castle. Thousands of them were dead, and Shira knew that some of the bodies would be collected and cannibalised tonight.

She sighed. 'We're not getting anywhere like this.'

Mehrab nodded. 'We might as well not bother, and just starve them into surrender. Can't your Haskans do a better job?'

'I'm not sending them into this death trap! No, it's time for you to contribute something now. Arioc sent you Isharites to overcome problems like this.'

Mehrab grunted. But he didn't disagree. 'Like what? There's no point getting ourselves killed in the fighting. We're not expendable like the Drobax.'

Shira thought about it. 'The leaders,' she said finally. 'The soldiers up there fight for their leaders. If we can kill Baldwin and the others, their morale will collapse. But Baldwin most of all.'

'That's easier said than done, Shira.'

Shira stared at him. 'You don't address a member of the Council of the Seven by their first name.'

Mehrab looked a little disconcerted. 'Apologies, Lord,' he muttered.

'I didn't say it would be easy, but that's your job. I want the Emperor dead, Mehrab. Find a way. Find a way, and then we can smash Burkhard and finish the Empire.'

A GREAT MOOT

XIII

Rabigar urged his horse on, guiding it along the uphill track. They were now entering the impenetrable mountainous terrain that was the heartland of the Krykker realm. He had made decent time since leaving Belwynn behind in Kalinth four days ago, and it had been good to spend a few days on his own, travelling in the open air. Since his exile from his homeland, when he had still been a young man, he had been forced to spend a lot of time in his own company. He had settled in various places and made acquaintances, but had always moved on, eventually. Whereas in his youth he had been surrounded by family and friends, Rabigar had now grown used to being alone.

The few days of light travelling had done his health good. It had given him time to think, too, especially about the injury he had received in the dungeons of Coldeberg Castle. With only one eye left, he knew his sight would never again be what it was. But he also had reason to be thankful that it hadn't been worse: that Moneva and the others had rescued him before more damage was done. He had survived his exile with no kin to support him, and he had lived to an age that most people never saw.

As he had crossed from the borderlands of Kalinth into the lands of his people, a sense of peace had fallen on Rabigar. He was coming home. His life had come full circle. If his homecoming wasn't accepted and he was to die—well, then so be it.

Rabigar decided it was time to dismount and walk the rest of the way. He gave the mare a pat and some food and water. Sebastian had given him a good mount. When she was ready, he led the beast along, studying the rocky terrain closely with his one good eye for familiar features.

After a while, Rabigar found what he was looking for. To his left was a cave entrance, mostly hidden by scrub, a few metres away from the path. Gently encouraging the horse, he got it to climb up the rocks and into the darkness of the cave. The roof of the cave was only a foot higher than the horse. It wasn't very deep either, but there was enough space for Rabigar to walk in his mount. He tied it up on a hook carved into the cave. He unloaded his carrying bag, took off the saddle, and laid out the remainder of the fodder and water.

'Here you go,' he murmured reassuringly. 'You'll be safe here until someone collects you.'

Rabigar moved over to the wall of the cave, touching the rock for the first time in over twenty years. Tears came to his eyes as he did so. This rock could not be found elsewhere in Dalriya. It belonged only to the Krykker, and the Krykker belonged to it. It would last forever. And so would the Krykker, the first people of Dalriya. Before the Isharites, Humans, Caladri, before even the Lippers had come, the Krykkers had been in Dalriya. They would outlast them all, too.

He concentrated now, focusing on his hands and on the rock, emptying his mind of any other thoughts. He stood like that for a while, he was not sure for how long, as he entered a trance like state. It had, after all, been a long time since he had last done this. Then, slowly, his hands began to disperse the particles of rock. Pushing forwards, they submerged into the rock as if he was sticking them into a vat of butter. As they did so, the rock shifted around him to make room. Rabigar pushed further, using his thighs to force his arms into the rock. The mare whinnied nervously as his limbs disappeared.

The critical moment came as Rabigar's face and shoulders met the wall. The temptation, especially when a Krykker was learning this technique at first, was to panic as the face entered the rock, due to the natural fear of asphyxiation. Krykker rock walkers had to train themselves to ignore this natural reaction, and have faith in their ability. Rabigar pushed head first, holding his breath as if he were diving through water rather than rock. Gathering speed, he pushed until his whole body was inside the rock, and he had left the cave behind. He kept moving, secure in the knowledge that this was a safe area to pass through. Nevertheless, when Rabigar's head emerged on the other side of the rock, he took a relieved breath of air.

He had passed into an underground tunnel. It was pitch black. Rabigar knew where he was going, but he gave himself some time to let his eyes adjust to the lack of light. Turning right, he began walking towards the nearest Krykker settlement.

Rabigar's plan was to keep walking until challenged, arrested, and taken before the local chieftain. The clan in these parts were the Dramsen. Rabigar remembered the local Dramsen chieftain as being young and fair minded. He hoped he was still alive, and that age hadn't soured him.

It didn't turn out quite as Rabigar had foreseen it. Instead of being challenged while making his way along the tunnel, he caught up with a young Dramsen. The youth had a flat, open wheeled cart attached around his shoulders with rope, and was steadily pulling it up the tunnel. It was filled with timber. Rabigar remembered being given the same job many times when he was the same age, no longer a child but not yet an adult warrior. The Krykker blacksmiths had an insatiable appetite for timber, and young men were sent out with these carts and an axe to cut down and strip trees. They would not be allowed to return until their carts were full.

The rumble of the wheels on the floor of the tunnel meant that the young man didn't hear Rabigar catching up to him, and so in the end he had to holler out for him to stop. The young man turned and peered at Rabigar, trying to place him; his puzzled expression indicated that he couldn't.

Rabigar approached steadily and held out a hand. 'My name is Din.'

'Stenk,' came the reply.

The young man was friendly enough and willingly shook hands. However, his puzzled expression returned as he stood looking Rabigar up and down. 'Din?' he repeated, eyeing Rabigar carefully. 'But—you're not—Rabigar Din? Are you?'

Rabigar held up his hands. 'Yes, I am. But I'm not here to harm you.'

Stenk looked back with a strange mix of awe, fear and uncertainty.

'I will surrender to you, and you can take me to your chieftain. Is Torinac still in charge here?'

'Wow—' said Stenk, ignoring the question. 'I never thought I would meet Rabigar Din. I thought you would be dead by now. Everyone knows about you,' he informed Rabigar.

Rabigar wasn't sure how to respond. 'Torinac?'

'Oh, yes, sorry. I'll take you to him.'

'You had better take my sword from me,' said Rabigar.

'Right. Yes.'

Rabigar unbuckled his sword from his belt and passed it over.

Stenk took a good grip and gave it a couple of swishes. 'That's a good weapon,' he commented, before carefully placing it into his cart.

They set off up the tunnel to find Torinac. Rabigar was under arrest. Though the process hadn't been as formal as he had expected.

'ARE you sure you want to do this?' asked Torinac. 'This is your last chance. I could say you escaped in the night.'

It was the next day. Rabigar had been treated with great respect by the chieftain of the Dramsen. Stenk had led him up a series of tunnels to the outside, where Torinac had his stone hall. Rabigar had been given pride of place by the fire as if he were a guest, and there was no guard set over him.

Torinac had sent out messengers to the other chieftains of the Krykker clans, advising them of Rabigar's presence and calling for a Great Moot, a meeting of the clans. This is what Rabigar had wanted, for it would give him a chance to explain his presence and warn his people of the threat posed by Ishari.

'No. I need to address the Great Moot about something very important. More important than my life.'

Torinac shrugged. He looked interested in what Rabigar had said, but didn't pursue it. He was a powerful looking warrior. His great grey fur coat, made from raccoon, made him look twice as big as he really was. He turned around to the score of other fur clad warriors who had gathered in the hall.

'On!' he bellowed, in a booming voice which was used to being obeyed. 'Clan Dramsen has called a Great Moot!'

A cheer rose up, and before Rabigar knew it, the group was barging its way to the doors of the hall. He readied himself to follow, when he caught sight of Stenk watching on from the side.

'Torinac?' he said.

'What is it, Rabigar Din?'

'You may think it highly presumptuous. I would request your man Stenk to be my man for the duration of the moot.'

'Stenk!' bellowed Torinac.

Stenk sidled over.

'You will serve Rabigar Din.'

'Yes, lord!' replied Stenk, nodding excitedly. He hurried off in the opposite direction.

'Stenk! Where are you going?'

'To get a weapon, lord.'

'Hurry up!'

Rabigar waited for Stenk to fetch an axe, and then they hurried after the Dramsen warriors. It all felt rather madcap and disorganised to Rabigar. He sighed. He had been away from his homeland for so long that his people seemed strange to him. It was an uncomfortable feeling.

Torinac's men scrambled down the mountainside at pace. What would be considered a dangerous climb down to most humans was a daily journey for them. Rabigar and Stenk caught up with them half way down, where the group had stopped in front of a sheer drop to a rocky area below. Two of the warriors were pulling on a rope, which seemed to operate a pulley system below. Rabigar peered over the edge. He could see two sets of metal rails running down a smooth slope into the shadows. It wasn't possible to see how far they went.

Torinac came over, grinning. 'You're about to see that times have moved on since you were last here, Rabigar Din.'

His grin became rather manic looking, and Rabigar looked down the slope again with alarm. He could hear a scraping sound of metal on metal, which didn't make him feel any better.

Eventually the item which the two warriors were pulling up the slope came into view. It was a very large, open, rectangular shaped metal box. The scraping sound was the metal wheels at the bottom of the box, which were passing between the two sets of metal rails on the floor.

'Well, what do you think?' asked Torinac, as the closest edge of the box was attached to the rock face with a giant metal hook. 'I call it a rail way.'

One of his warriors clambered into the box.

'You don't expect me to get in that?' asked Rabigar, as the other warriors began jumping in.

'I'm ordering you to get into it. You're my prisoner, remember?' said Torinac, pleasantly enough.

'We'll all die.'

Torinac seemed very disappointed. 'Don't worry. We've tested it plenty of times.'

'How many?'

'Just get in.'

Rabigar got in, heading for one side of the box, which he gripped tightly.

Torinac and Stenk followed him in. It was now a tight squeeze inside the box. The final warrior joined them. Using the handle of his axe, the warrior knocked the hook out of the rock.

Rabigar watched him, aghast. One moment they were being held in place, next, over twenty Krykkers inside a giant metal box began rolling down a mountain slope.

As the box gathered pace, the warriors began screaming and whooping in delight. The noise nearly masked the scraping of the metal wheels on the rails. Rabigar closed his eyes. He could hear Torinac laughing hysterically. He felt the box getting faster and faster. The shouting got louder and then, suddenly, with no warning or reduction of speed, the box hit the bottom. Rabigar fell onto his back from the impact, and some of the Krykkers fell on top of him. The box had become a mass of flailing arms and legs. The box lurched forwards back up the rails a few feet, causing everyone to roll over to the other end of the box. It then slid back down to the bottom again, causing further mayhem as elbows and knees struck people in the face, where at last it came to a rest.

Dizzily, Rabigar made his way to the end of the box and hauled himself out, moving away a few feet. His head was spinning, and he sank down to his knees. Torinac appeared.

'What do you think?' asked the chieftain.

Rabigar felt like he was going to vomit. 'Very good. I guess that's saved us a lot of time.'

'Certainly has. It's a very popular invention. A lot of the other clans are building their own. We haven't quite perfected the landing yet, though.'

THOUSANDS OF YEARS AGO, the Great Meeting Chamber of the Krykkers was carved out of the mountain Kerejus. Only accessible via underground tunnels, it represented neutral ground, where all the clans could meet on equal terms.

It was a dramatic setting. Great pillars, made of the original mountain rock, had been left in place, supporting the rough ceiling of the cavern. They had been intricately carved, some in arresting patterns, others depicting the collective stories and heroes of the Krykkers' past. These heroes were also depicted in over-sized statues that lined the walls of the hall. Warriors abounded, but also justice givers, like Chief Huderam the Righteous, who dispensed justice on behalf of the oppressed against the mighty.

In the middle of the chamber stood the circular arena. Tiered stone seats looked down on the central stage, where the chief speakers of a Great Moot would address their audience. The representatives of each clan could be seated and heard, and the circular shape meant that no clan was given more status than another.

It was here that Rabigar had been tried and sentenced to exile. He had been a different man, then. Young and arrogant, he had revelled in his status as one of the best warriors of the Grendal clan, and as a rock walker. Popular and respected amongst his peers, he was talked of as a future clan leader.

But that had all ended one night. Rabigar and his friends had drunk far too much, feasting in the hall of their chieftain, Lidimas. Rabigar had long held a fancy for the chieftain's daughter, Maragin. He couldn't remember exactly what he had done to upset Lidimas that night. It was more than the usual flirting, certainly. He had not behaved with respect. Lidimas had come storming over, demanding an apology. Ordinarily, Rabigar would have backed down, understanding the rules that governed clan life, and recognising the danger of the situation. But the drink made him behave differently. Maybe the presence of his friends, or of Maragin, affected his behaviour too. But in failing to back away from Lidimas, he was challenging his chieftain's authority.

Before Rabigar knew what was happening, both men had weapons in their hands. It was over quickly. Narrowly avoiding a swing from Lidimas, Rabigar had lashed out violently, all of his angry, beer-fuelled strength in the strike. His sword connected with the side of Lidimas's neck. His chieftain collapsed to the floor. He didn't die immediately; but in the last few days of his life, he never regained consciousness.

Rabigar had suddenly sobered up. Then came the screams. It was the screams that stayed with Rabigar, visiting him even now when he slept. Maragin's screams as she knelt by Lidimas, looking accusingly up at Rabigar, and back to her father.

Rabigar's memory of the trial was hazy, as if he had been asleep at key moments. Many favoured death, but some, like Torinac, had accepted that Rabigar struck in self-defence. Still, he had killed his own chieftain. The sentence was reduced to exile for life.

Many Krykkers in Rabigar's position would have preferred death to such a punishment. But, guilt ridden, he accepted the verdict as his penance. One final judgement was made. Rabigar was a noble warrior's name among the Krykker. He was no longer entitled to it. He would thereafter be referred to as Din, a low born name. Rabigar who was, now no longer existed.

Torinac and his men filed into the chamber, quietly taking their places. Rabigar sat next to the Dramsen chieftain on the front row of seats. Some of the other clans had already arrived and taken their seats in the arena. Their chieftains also took positions at the front, so that if needed, they could enter the circle and speak for their clan. There were murmurs from some of the other clans, but they respected the rules of the Great Moot, and did not challenge Torinac or Rabigar before proceedings had formally started. They had to wait for the remaining clans to arrive first.

Rabigar kept his eyes fixed on the floor, not talking, aware that he was the centre of attention. Time went by slowly. Stenk had to empty his bladder against the far wall of the chamber. Finally, the last clan to arrive settled into position.

Torinac stood. He strolled into the centre of the space in the middle of the arena, turning around in a full circle so that he was addressing everyone gathered. Rabigar lifted his head up, looking out at the faces, his eyes naturally searching out his own clan, the Grendals. When he found them, he got a shock that twisted his insides. Staring back at him was Maragin, seated as the chieftain of the Grendals. They made eye contact briefly. Her face was expressionless and composed. It was Rabigar who turned away, unable to hold the gaze. As Torinac spoke, Rabigar could barely concentrate on what he was saying. A feeling of desperation came over him. Things had gone well to this point. But with the daughter of the murdered Lidimas speaking for the Grendals, it would surely be impossible to persuade the Moot of his case.

'I am Torinac, chieftain of the Dramsen and I have called this Moot,' began Torinac in a booming voice. 'Yesterday, unknown to me and uninvited, the exile, Din, came into the lands of the Dramsen clan. It is fair to say, that we all know who Din is, and that we all know the penalty for breaking his exile is death?'

Shouts of 'agreed', 'yes', and other affirmatives met this question.

'Din explained to me that he had come back to warn our people of a dire threat, to the peoples of Dalriya, including our own. He argued that instead of killing him, I should allow him to pass on this warning. This is what I bring before the Great Moot today.'

Torinac fell silent, waiting for a response. After a pause, chieftain Guremar of clan Plengas raised an arm.

'Guremar,' said Torinac, indicating that he gave way to the chieftain.

Torinac returned to his seat, and Guremar made his way to the central stage. He was one of the oldest chieftains, stern-faced, with grey, bushy eyebrows, that seemed to be set in a permanent frown.

'I understand why Torinac has brought this matter before the Moot. But my verdict is clear. When Din murdered his own chieftain over twenty years ago, my clan demanded the death penalty. Others, such as Torinac, disagreed. Now that Din has returned, I propose that the sentence be carried out.'

Guremar now fell silent. Rabigar sneaked a look over towards Maragin, but she remained still. Instead, another chieftain, of clan Swarten, had raised an arm.

'Hakonin.'

Rabigar did not recognise the name Hakonin, and so didn't know what to expect from the next speaker. When he walked to the centre of the stage, Rabigar saw why. He was a young man, and must have been a child on the day of Rabigar's exile.

'No one can disagree that our laws say that Din's punishment should be death. But I propose that first we hear what he has to say. It would be foolish of us not to listen to him in case his warning is genuine. I would add that Din has not attempted to return since his exile, and so something serious may have motivated his arrival now.'

Two more chieftains stood to agree that Rabigar should be heard. Heads turned towards Maragin, wondering what she had to say, but still she sat unmoved, stony faced.

'Din.'

He had been called. This had been his objective, to speak to the Moot. He had prepared himself to accept whatever came afterwards. Rabigar stood and walked to the circle. He took a last glance at his old clan. He detected a mixture of expressions. Some, naturally, were hostile. Others, those who had been his close friends, nodded solemnly; some even smiled. At the front Maragin remained expressionless; unreadable.

'I, Din, have spent these last years living as an exile in the lands of men. I accepted my punishment, but I have returned to speak these words, and I swear they are true. In the service of Prince Edgar of Magnia, I was ordered, with other warriors, to retrieve a dagger that had been stolen from his lands by agents of Ishari. Here,' he said, gesturing to the patch that covered the hole where his eye had been, 'is where the agents of Ishari took my eye.'

He hoped, not for sympathy, but for a sense that he had received a suitable punishment for his former crime. 'I am now sure that this dagger which we retrieved is one of the seven sacred weapons from the Battle of Alta, when our greatest hero, Bolivar the Bold, defeated the dread lord of Ishari.'

Rabigar paused here, stretching his arm out and gesturing to the statue of Bolivar in the Meeting Chamber, who held his great sword across his chest. He waited until his audience had turned to look at Bolivar before continuing. 'Not only this, but we entered the lands of the Grand Caladri moments before their destruction by the forces of Arioc, retrieving a wizard's staff, which I am sure is a second sacred weapon.'

There were gasps at this statement, but Rabigar continued. 'Both weapons are now in Kalinth. As I speak, the Knights of Kalinth are moving to take control of their kingdom. I must tell you that an army of Drobax entered the Empire about two weeks past. Torinac said I came to warn you, and there is some truth to this. The Krykkers are in danger from Ishari, just like everyone else in Dalriya. But you already know that. No, I come, humbly, to summon the clans to war. A second great battle is coming. Bolivar's Sword is needed to fight Ishari again. The Krykkers are needed to fight for Dalriya once more.'

Rabigar nodded to indicate that he had finished speaking.

Whispering broke out amongst the Krykkers seated in the chamber. The chieftains turned around in their seats, glaring at their followers to keep quiet. Several hands shot into the air. Rabigar looked around. Maragin's hand was not one of them. By custom, he chose a chieftain who was likely to present a counter argument.

'Guremar.'

'Clan Plengas observes the arrogance of Din who dares to come here, a criminal and exile, and call the Krykkers to war. The Krykkers are under no threat and this is not our war. As for Din's stories of sacred weapons, does he bring us any proof of this? No. Just the word of a murderer,' finished Guremar, pointing directly at Rabigar.

'Hakonin.'

'We cannot close our eyes to the threat posed by Ishari. Who amongst us would have thought that the Grand Caladri could have been destroyed in a matter of days? Do not forget the conquest of Persala, or the invasion of the Empire. We Krykkers do not have such short memories as the other peoples of Dalriya. We know we are not safe from Ishari, even here in our mountains. The return of the sacred weapons cannot be ignored. That the messenger we hear this from is Din is irrelevant; it is the message itself that we must all heed.'

Hakonin looked around the chamber.

'Porimin.'

Next to stand was not a chieftain but an old man, seated on one of the stone benches half way up the arena. Porimin made his way slowly down to the floor. He was well known as a historian of the Krykker people.

'Hundreds of years ago,' he began, his voice more fragile than those who had gone before, but still strong enough to carry to those listening. 'Our ancestors helped to defeat Ishari at the battle of Alta. But they knew the enemy wasn't vanquished, and they recorded for us their accounts, and their warnings that the threat would need to be faced once more. We have kept these safe for generations, as we have kept Bolivar's Sword, knowing that it would need to be used again. Given what we now know, it is hard to do anything but conclude that we are facing the very same threat they faced. The Krykkers must face it with courage, just as we did once before.'

The old man looked around the arena.

'Torinac.'

Torinac took the floor. 'I would like to remind those gathered of a messenger I received, sent from a Lord of the Grand Caladri, named Kelemen. He wanted to request safe haven in our lands for his people. If we agree to act, we should also consider our response to him. My clan has always defended the northern border of our lands. My view is that we should stand shoulder to shoulder with the Kalinthians and the Caladri in this war. I also believe that Din has shown bravery in coming here, and that his life should be spared.'

Torinac looked about the arena. His eyes widened somewhat. Rabigar followed his gaze. Maragin's hand was raised.

'Maragin,' said Torinac softly.

Maragin stood slowly and walked to the centre of the arena. A hush fell over the moot. She looked around, looking the men about her in the eye. She was a formidable figure, and the longer she waited to speak, the more the tension in the chamber rose.

'Din killed my chieftain and my father,' she began. 'He was rightly exiled from our lands, but has returned, nonetheless. On the other hand, we as a people must respond swiftly to a vicious enemy that would kill us, kill our children, stop our children's children from coming into the world. To do this, we must be united. I propose we raise an army, just as Din has suggested. Further, Din's punishment for breaking his exile is death: and this punishment must be carried out.'

Murmurs of agreement could be heard. There was little sign of dissent, such was Maragin's moral authority on the issue. 'However, to maintain unity, I propose a solution. Din will lead us north to Kalinth and serve the Krykkers one last time. His punishment of death will be postponed until he has done this.'

Rabigar looked around the assembly. Everywhere, from chieftains to followers, from one clan to the next, the Krykkers nodded in agreement.

Hakonin raised his sword in the air. 'War!' he cried.

Guremar and Torinac raised their swords. Maragin, still in the centre of the arena, did the same. The other chieftains followed suit. The warriors of every clan raised their weapons.

'War!' they cried.

Rabigar breathed a sigh of relief. He had achieved his purpose in returning home. And, for a while at least, he had kept his life.

A CLOTH OF GOLD

XIV

There were strong winds on the steppe, hurrying the clouds across the sky, but the sun still shone down. Edgar's army, four thousand strong, and made up equally of men from South and North Magnia, was making good progress; but there was no shade to be found. The soil underfoot was bone dry, and the long grass was being blown about by the wind. It had been a couple of days since they had passed a stream safe enough to drink from, and the soldiers had been given strict orders to conserve the water in their skins.

The Middian Steppes were good land for husbandry. The tribes who lived here were used to roaming the landscape with their animals, mainly cattle and sheep, locating good pasture before moving on to a fresh area when the land had been used up. They had lived this way for hundreds of years, and the presence of their big herds prevented trees and bushes from growing in most places. Edgar could look in every direction and see grassland for miles and miles.

The nomadic lifestyle of the Middians meant they were in the saddle all day, and they were known for being amongst the best horsemen in Dalriya. It also meant that they were not rich, with far fewer towns than in Magnia, and no great cities such as they had in Brasingia or Persala. This combination meant that they were often recruited as mercenaries by merchants or warlords. On this occasion, the men of Frayne's tribe had been recruited by the kingdom of Cordence, and would join with the Magnians under Edgar's command. The rendezvous was supposed to be happening today, but so far there had been no sign of them.

'Where are we?' asked Edgar irritably.

Wilchard, Edgar's chief steward, made a sighing sound, and pulled out a piece of parchment from a leather bag he carried around his shoulder. As he continued to ride, he laid the parchment down on his mount's withers and studied his map of the area. The wind frustrated his efforts, flapping at the edges of the parchment. He persevered, squinting his eyes at the lines and spidery writing which denoted the internal and external borders of the Steppe. He looked about him in a vain search for landmarks that might help his task, before turning back to Edgar. 'I don't know where we are,' he said, equally irritated.

Edgar kept his face straight as he watched Wilchard fold up the parchment and put it back in his bag. It was about a week ago, in a treaty signed at Wincandon in North Magnia, that Edgar had volunteered to lead a Southern army to Brasingia to support Emperor Baldwin. Initially, he had thought to leave Wilchard behind in South Magnia to act as his regent, since he was Edgar's most trusted and most able adviser. However, once the preparations for the army got under way, he changed his mind. The logistical complexities of raising an army, and keeping it fed and properly equipped, were a full-time job, and he needed Wilchard with him. The maintenance of this army had to be Edgar's priority.

He turned to his left, where his chancellor, the wizard Ealdnoth, rode to one side of them, seemingly oblivious to the conversation. Edgar had noticed that it was a trait of wizards to spend a lot of time in their own private world. His cousin Soren was just the same. His thoughts turned to Soren and Belwynn, who had retrieved Toric's Dagger from the Empire; only to head north into the lands of the Blood Caladri and disappear. Another situation he had no control over. He had to focus on the here and now.

'Ealdnoth?'

'Yes, Your Highness?'

'We've just been wondering where we are?'

Ealdnoth frowned and looked around, as if such a troublesome question had never occurred to him before. 'Well, I would think we hardly have to worry about finding the Middians, Your Highness. Surely they will find us?'

It was not an entirely satisfactory answer and yet sufficed to end the conversation.

In the end, Ealdnoth was proved correct. It was two hours later when a small group of riders could be seen heading towards them, coming from the northwest. As they approached, Edgar could see that it was a group of six men. They wore leather boots, and wraps around their waists, and little else. They were bare-chested, with the dark-skinned bodies and the long hair of the Middians pulled back and tied behind them. Most carried spears. They came at quite a pace and pulled up when they reached the front of the army. Frayne was not amongst them, but Edgar nudged his horse forwards, expecting there to be a message or discussion.

Instead, one of the riders raised his spear. 'Follow!' he shouted, before turning his horse around with one hand on the reins and kicking it forwards.

Edgar looked back and forth amongst his advisers. 'I guess we follow them,' he said, slightly bemused, and no one disagreed.

Two of the riders went back in the direction they had come at some pace. The other four continued at a slower pace, but still too fast for Edgar's army to keep up with, which had to travel at the speed of the carts which carried their supplies. Big strong horses pulled their carts, but they had heavy loads and had been walking all day. Their four guides turned around and rode back to the front of the Magnian forces, muttering and shaking their heads, before riding on at the same pace. This happened several times, on each occasion the Middians incapable of adjusting to the speed of Edgar's army.

Eventually, they came to the site where Frayne's forces had made camp. Dotted around were the tents of the Middians, conical shaped and covered with animal skins. Soldiers lounged around in the grass and the smell of cooking meat made Edgar feel suddenly hungry. He was satisfied that the size of the Middian army looked equal to Edgar's force of Magnians, which had been the original agreement made in Wincandon. To the south side of the camp, Edgar could see and hear a vast number of sheep and cattle which had been paddocked, giving it the feel of an outdoor market as much as a military camp.

One of the Middians had moved over to Edgar. 'Frayne!' he stated, jutting his spear toward a large tent close by.

Edgar dismounted. Wilchard ordered the officers of the army to make camp, leaving an appropriate space between the Magnians and Middians to reduce the chances of conflict between the two groups. Together with Ealdnoth and Edgar's ever-present bodyguards, Leofwin and Brictwin, they walked over towards the tent to meet with Frayne, the chieftain. As they approached, Frayne saw them coming—he bounded out to greet Edgar, giving him a great hug.

'You remember Ealdnoth, Wilchard—' Edgar began.

'Of course, of course,' said Frayne, patting them all on the shoulder and gesturing that they should enter the tent. He clapped his hands and two girls ran off. Edgar hoped they would bring food.

Two men stood up to greet Edgar as he entered the tent. Lord Emmett was a Thessian nobleman, representing Duke Coen. Lord Rosmont performed the same role for King Glanna of Cordence. Both men had signed the Treaty of Wincandon on behalf of their leaders and had now been sent to accompany the army.

Edgar took a seat on the floor where cushions had been laid out. The other men did the same. There was not much room, so Leofwin and Brictwin remained outside the tent, keeping watch.

'So, how have things gone since we last met?' asked Edgar, primarily addressing Emmett, since he had been back to the Empire.

'Things are more serious,' began Emmett, and the grim faces of Rosmont and Frayne confirmed it.

'Emeric has become more aggressive: our local forces on the border have fought several skirmishes. The Barissians have been coming off better. Emeric has committed more troops than Coen, and he's taken several of our castles. Duke Coen has been waiting for you to arrive before pushing his main army north. But the Barissians are getting bolder, and look likely to invade in force any day now.

'Duke Coen asks that we change our earlier meeting point of Lindhafen. Instead, he requests you head north east, and he will rendezvous with his army. Our joint forces will then be able to intercept Emeric's army before it does further damage.'

Edgar shared a glance with Wilchard and Ealdnoth. Emmett made it sound like they would be in battle any day now.

'How long do you think it will take us to reach the new rendezvous point?' asked Wilchard.

'Two days,' said Frayne.

Emmett nodded in agreement.

Two days. Edgar felt his stomach tighten with anxiety. He let out a deep breath. He could be leading his troops into battle in two days' time.

The serving girls returned to the tent, carrying dishes of spiced lamb. Edgar looked at the food. His appetite had disappeared.

* * *

Arioc was in a talkative mood this night. Some nights he would return to his chambers in a foul mood and he would use Moneva's body, barely talking to her, before falling asleep. Those nights she feared for her life all over again. Other nights he was all charm and smiles, taking an interest in her, holding her close in the night.

'What is Erkindrix like?' began Moneva, feeling her way into the conversation. Pentas had asked her to use her position to influence Arioc. She knew she had to try.

Arioc was lying next to her on the bed, leaning back on his elbows. He laughed; it was a short, humourless sound. 'I'll have to introduce you to him. It's an experience, believe me.'

'Well?'

Arioc considered it. 'The closest thing you can get to raw power. It both attracts and repels you at the same time...it's hard to explain.'

Moneva studied Arioc carefully. He seemed partly in awe of his leader, partly greedy for that kind of power himself.

'How old is he?'

'He's ancient. Centuries old. The magic has kept him alive.'

'That's not natural.'

Arioc smiled. 'It's not natural. Not natural at all. But then I can't complain about my father living a long life, can I?'

'Your father?' asked Moneva, genuinely shocked.

'So they say. No-one knows for sure. You've never heard the rumour?'

Moneva shook her head. 'Why don't you know? Has he never spoken to you about it?'

'No. There is no reason to. I doubt whether he would remember.'

'But—he's never been a father to you?'

'Ah, well now you are learning about the differences between Isharites and humans, Moneva. Your father cared for you as a child, but that's not how we do things. I have several sons, but I don't owe them anything. I've brought them into the world; that is enough.'

'Your mother?'

Arioc gave Moneva a strange look. 'Do you know why I only have sons, Moneva?'

Moneva shook her head again.

'It still amazes me how little your people know about us. In Ishari, we have a saying, 'know your enemy'. But you humans like to forget we exist. If you close your eyes for long enough, we will disappear. Like a bad dream.'

Moneva felt troubled by the conversation. There was some truth on the edge of her understanding. 'You don't have...' she began, uncertainly. 'There are no women, are there?'

'You've got it,' said Arioc, condescension clear in his voice. 'Isharites are aliens here, in Dalriya. We should not be here. In your own words: it is not natural. One side effect of this is that when the first Isharites arrived in Dalriya, our women conceived no girls, only boys. Our womenfolk died out a long time ago. So, we now breed with humans like you. Human women make our babies, but still, they don't conceive girls, only more boys.

'My mother was a human slave. Erkindrix could have been the father. People gossip about it, but it doesn't matter. He is one of the last of the pure blood Isharites. The rest of us are half-castes, or worse. That is one of the reasons he has been kept alive for so long.'

'But even he must die sometime?'

Arioc shrugged. 'Yes—he is half dead now.'

'So what happens when he dies? Who will be the leader then? You?'

Arioc's dry laugh returned. 'It should be me—don't you think? I'm the son. That's how it works in your kingdoms, isn't it?'

'But not in Ishari?'

'In Ishari, the next person to sit on the throne will be the one who takes it.'

'So, who will take it?'

It was Arioc's turn to look troubled by the conversation now. 'Erkindrix will not die. He is too powerful.'

Arioc rolled on to his side away from Moneva. She felt a sense of relief. Moneva knew Pentas would want her to pursue the subject. But she had learned more than enough for one night.

* * *

Belwynn and Theron sat contentedly outside his tent, sharing a quiet moment after breakfast.

On previous mornings, they would be packing up by now, orders passed around to make ready to march. But today, Sebastian and Theron had agreed to wait awhile. They were in striking distance of the capital of Kalinth, Heractus—and they were sure that King Jonas and his court were still there. What they weren't so sure of was the kind of response they were going to get.

Sebastian's army had swollen to about five thousand fighting men, half of whom were fully trained knights. The rest were squires, men-at-arms, armed labourers and the like.

'Will they know we are here?' asked Belwynn.

'Yes. Jonas will know about Sebastian replacing Galenos, and he'll have been told by his scouts exactly where we are.'

'What do you think he'll do?'

'Well,' answered Theron, 'if I were king and the Grand Master of the Knights led a rebellion against me, I would fight. But then I would also have fought if Ishari had threatened my kingdom. So who knows what a coward like Jonas will do?'

'A rebellion? Is that what this is?'

Theron shrugged. 'That depends on your point of view. We can sweeten the words we use, and we will when we speak to him. But essentially, we are trying to take over his government and give it to Sebastian. I don't think we're rebels—I think we're trying to free our country.'

Tycho strolled over towards them, winding his way around the tents and campfires, which were crammed together on the large expanse of moorland.

'Morning,' he called.

Theron and Belwynn got to their feet. Theron and Tycho hugged each other.

'My lady,' Tycho addressed Belwynn.

'Lord Tycho,' she greeted him.

'Sebastian wants to see you. Seems like a royal army has left Heractus and is heading our way.'

'How big?'

'The scout's in with Sebastian. He'll tell you what he's seen.'

Belwynn turned to return to the tent she shared with Elana and Dirk.

'Come,' said Theron.

She followed the two knights, who strode the short distance to their leader's tent. Sebastian hurried all three of them inside, eager to get on with it.

There was no-one else inside except for the scout, a young knight who stood nervously in the far corner of the tent. Belwynn recognised him as Philon, the young, sandy haired knight who had asked for her blessing a few days before. With all eyes on him, the young man went a little red.

'Right,' began Sebastian, looking at Philon. 'Take us through what you have seen.'

'We were keeping a lookout on a ridge that overlooks the city. We had seen two different groups of soldiers already this morning. Both seemed like scouts for the king. Then the gates of the city opened, and a royal army passed through them. We waited until we thought the entire army was through the gates, then I set off to report it. The others are still there and will send a message with more news when it is clear where the army is headed.'

'How many?' asked Theron.

'We reckoned about the same size as ours, five thousand. Mostly foot soldiers, but some horsemen.'

'Well, I say we get going and head straight for them. That gives us the most options,' suggested Theron.

Sebastian was frowning. 'Why send out a force that seems to be inferior to ours? They could have just stayed in the city.'

'Could be a trap?' suggested Tycho.

'Could be,' said Theron, but he didn't sound convinced. 'Could just be a poor decision. They can't have gathered many more than five thousand in the time we've given them. Once we get closer, we can decide what to do. I'd like to go ahead now with Philon, and take a look for myself.'

'I'll come with you,' offered Tycho.

The three knights made a quick exit from the tent.

'Excuse me, Belwynn,' said Sebastian. 'I'll have to get this army moving.'

Sebastian left the tent and Belwynn could hear him barking out orders. The new Grand Master was getting ready for battle.

IT TOOK over an hour before the army was ready to go. Horses' hooves were checked and rechecked; the giant warhorses bred by the knights were the crucial component of their army and gave them a clear advantage over the king's forces. Weapons were sharpened; squires helped knights into their mail armour, tightening and adjusting straps until everything was perfect. Once they were on the move, battle might come at any time, and they needed to be ready.

In contrast, it had taken Belwynn, Elana and Dirk only a few minutes to get ready. They were used, now, to packing up their possessions into a sack and moving on. At last, the army got going. It was organised into several fighting units, each one made up of knights, squires, and usually some men-at-arms or other infantry. All combatants travelled on horseback. Belwynn and the others travelled with the baggage towards the back of the army, along with any other hangers on who were not preparing to fight. Evander had offered to accompany them, but Belwynn knew he belonged with Theron, so she declined.

They headed in an easterly direction. After an hour, Theron came trotting down the line to find her. 'The army's heading in our direction. Philon was right, they've got about the same numbers as us.'

'But are they as good fighters?'

'Few of them are as well trained or equipped as a Knight of Kalinth. But some of them will be from noble households and will be our equals. Of course, we have a lot of untrained fighters with us as well as knights; but then I suspect that will be the same for them as well.'

'What's the plan?'

'I've told Sebastian I think we should keep going as fast as possible. We're all mounted, and it's not far. The terrain around the city is flat. If we catch them quickly, they will not have time to find a defensive position that could cause our horses problems.'

'They'll have less time to retreat to the city too?'

'Yes, exactly. We need to capitalise on this. I think it's an opportunity for a quick victory over Jonas. That's what we need. Not a civil war.'

Theron was excited and spoke fast. His nervous energy was contagious. But Belwynn also noted how focused he was on his objectives. It reminded her more of her brother Soren, than most of the soldiers she had met before. Men like Clarin, who in her experience was typical, tended to be easy going, almost childlike in their approach. Theron was different—more of a general than a soldier.

Theron returned to the front of the army and the pace picked up noticeably for the rest of the morning. The baggage train fell behind, unable to keep up with the mounted soldiers.

Approaching midday, they caught up with the soldiers. Word passed down that the enemy was in sight.

Belwynn pulled to the side of the column and looked ahead, but she couldn't see the royal army from her position. She shared the nervous anticipation of everyone else as they waited. Then more orders came. The soldiers were being lined up in formation. From being a long column on the march, Belwynn watched as the army slowly transformed itself into battle formation. They faced the enemy in a semi-circular or arc shape, the cavalry on each end of the formation pushed furthest forwards, as if they were the pincers of a crab ready to snap.

The baggage train, made up of horse-drawn carriages that carried the supplies, was positioned behind the army. Belwynn, Elana and Dirk were asked to carry water bottles over to the soldiers. Belwynn took hers to a group of mounted knights on the left wing of the army.

'Thank you, my lady,' the first knight said graciously, taking a glug of water, and then passing it on to a comrade. Belwynn still found it rather strange that she had become so well known—most of these knights had been in the Great Hall of the High Tower on the night when she had sung of Stephen and the Green Dragon.

'Can you see the enemy?' she asked.

'Over there, my lady,' said one of the knights, pointing eastwards in the direction they were facing. 'If your eyesight is good, you can make them out.'

Belwynn looked in that direction. Seeing nothing, she moved forward a few feet. She was nearly ready to give up when she finally saw a smudge on the horizon. It was moving slightly, and she realised it was a long row of infantry assembling. To each side, she could see smaller groups of soldiers—presumably cavalry forces positioned on the wings. It was the first time she had been on a battlefield, and it held a grim fascination. So much so that she didn't realise her name was being called until Theron was nearly on top of her.

'Lady Belwynn!' he shouted again, sounding exasperated.

He pulled up. Behind him came Evander, also mounted, who was leading a spare mount. 'What are you doing here?' he asked. 'I've been looking for you everywhere. I thought you would be with the baggage.'

'I was, but they asked us to give out water.'

'Who did?' demanded Theron, sounding angry.

'Oh, Theron! No one in particular. What is it?'

'Sorry. I just got worried,' he said, dismounting. 'We're going to talk with the leaders of the royal army under a truce flag. I would like you to come with us.'

'Me?' asked Belwynn. 'What good will I be? You don't want me to sing again, do you?'

Theron forced a smile out. 'Well, that would be lovely, but no.'

He helped Belwynn into the saddle of the spare horse. Evander then had to clamber off his horse and help Theron get back up, because of the weight of mail the knight was wearing. Belwynn shook her head in disbelief, wondering what the rest of the army made of the spectacle; they were surely all staring at them by now.

'You've become very popular with the knights, Belwynn,' said Theron. 'We need that because, after all, we're asking them to fight against the king they've sworn oaths to defend. You can help to persuade them they're doing the right thing. Evander, do you have it?'

'Yes, my lord,' answered the young man brightly. From his saddlebag, he drew out a lavish cloth of gold. Theron took it from him before presenting it to Belwynn.

Taking it, she could see that it was a robe made of silk, with the yarn wrapped in strips of gold. It was a magnificent piece of clothing. 'You can't be serious? You want me to wear this? Now?'

'It's one of the most precious items belonging to the Order. I know you think it's ridiculous and in one sense, you're right. But it would mean a lot to the men to see you wear it. Things like this matter when you're about to go into battle.'

'Well, I can hardly say 'no' to that, can I?'

Belwynn put her arms into the robe. The right side of the robe was wider than the other and Theron and Evander helped her to wrap it around her chest, pulling it tight before tying it up at the back. A cheer could be heard on the battlefield. Theron looked her up and down, a big smile appearing on his face.

'You look amazing,' said Evander, going a little red but grinning, nonetheless.

'Come on then,' said Theron. 'Let's try to talk some sense into these people.'

Theron trotted forwards and Belwynn and Evander followed on. Waiting for them were Sebastian and his squire, Alpin, who held a white flag of truce on a long pole. Sebastian stared at Belwynn for a moment, then nodded, but said nothing.

'Are you ready, uncle?' asked Theron.

'Yes. Let's just hope they've got someone sensible in charge.'

'Will Jonas not be there?' Belwynn asked.

'Very doubtful,' said Theron, 'but not impossible.'

Sebastian led them on. As they got closer, Belwynn could make out the royal forces ranged against them more clearly. 'Who are they?' she asked Theron, indicating a group wearing red cloaks who had been positioned near the centre of the infantry line.

'They're the city guard of Heractus, used to defend the walls and the castle. They're reasonably well equipped, but not trained for pitched battles. Most of the rest of them are individual noblemen and their retinues. A bit like us, they'll be a mix of soldiers and extra men pressed into service. The best fighters will probably be mounted.'

'To counter your cavalry?'

'Yes, but they simply don't have the numbers for it. We *are* the cavalry of Kalinth, after all.'

Sebastian raised his arm, and they stopped, approximately half way between the two armies. Then they waited. It was unnerving for Belwynn, but she supposed that if the enemy ignored the flag of truce and tried to attack, they should be able to turn around and ride back to their own lines without fear of being caught.

'There,' said Evander, pointing.

A small group of riders could be seen making their way towards them. As they got closer, Belwynn could count four in all.

'Can you see who's there?' asked Sebastian.

'Not quite,' answered Theron, waiting. 'I think that's—yes, it's Diodorus. Count of Korenandi. Looks like he's in charge. He's not an idiot.'

'It could have been a lot worse,' agreed Sebastian.

The four riders continued to approach before one of them raised a hand, indicating that the other three should wait where they were. It was a gesture which emphasised his authority and lack of fear in approaching the knights alone. He moved his horse on a few paces before stopping in front of them.

'Diodorus,' acknowledged Sebastian.

'Sebastian. Theron.'

Diodorus looked at Belwynn and appeared to be about to say something, but then seemed to think better of it. He was a big man, with huge shoulders, a thick neck and a large head. His hair was shaved short and Belwynn thought he had something of a sad, or at least world weary, expression.

'I presume King Jonas has made you general of this army?' asked Sebastian.

'That's right. And I understand that you have taken control of the Order of the Knights of Kalinth. But what is your army doing here?'

'The Order has come to restore strength to our country. Kalinth must stand up to Ishari. I am here to make sure it does.'

'By starting a war with your king?'

'Come on, Diodorus,' interjected Theron. 'We could go on like this all day, but it isn't the time or place. We've come to speak to you to avoid bloodshed.'

Diodorus shrugged. 'I'm listening.'

'You must have had an idea about what you were trying to achieve with this force of yours—but you've ended up in the open, facing our army which has a cavalry force far superior to yours, and is capable of inflicting heavy losses. You must also know that it was never our intention to spill Kalinthian blood.'

Diodorus turned behind him to look at the other three riders before turning back. When he spoke again, it was in a low, quiet voice.

'Jonas ordered me to destroy your army. Of course, we tried to reason with him, but he got hysterical, wouldn't listen. Started throwing wild accusations at everyone. So, I obeyed his orders. But I'm not stupid, Theron. I know I'm in a heavily compromised position. And I would be happy to avoid a battle if possible.'

'If possible?' repeated Sebastian.

'I've been asked to defend my king. If I don't fight you, what will you do with him?'

'I swear a knight's oath,' began Sebastian, 'that if you surrender now, no-one in your army will be harmed, no-one in Heractus will be harmed, I will not harm Jonas, and he will remain king. What I *will* do is wrest control over the government of his kingdom, and restore some direction and dignity to it. I admire your loyalty to your king, Diodorus. Believe me—I have tried my best to be loyal to him, too. But that must be weighed against loyalty to Kalinth and its people.'

'Alright, Sebastian,' Diodorus said quietly. 'I regard you as an honourable man. I will take your word.'

'However,' added Theron, 'if you surrender you must ensure that everyone in your army disperses immediately, that none of them will return to the city, and if any try to return, our offer of protection will be withdrawn and they will be killed.'

Diodorus seemed taken aback at first, but then nodded. His gaze turned to Belwynn again, a puzzled look, as if he wondered who she was and what she was doing here. She looked away, embarrassed by her presence and her golden robe.

'There's one more thing,' said Diodorus. 'If I surrender, you must also make an oath to protect me. Many men will call me traitor and want me dead after today.'

'I offer you my protection,' confirmed Sebastian.

'Then it is agreed,' said Diodorus. 'I will order my army to disperse.'

He turned his horse around and began to return to his three companions.

'But don't disappear,' called Theron. 'We'll need your help to get into the city.'

Diodorus looked back, a pained expression on his face. 'Very well,' he said finally.

'No battle after all,' commented Sebastian as they made their way back to their own lines. 'So far, so good.'

Belwynn turned around to look at the retreating figure of Count Diodorus and wondered how many lives the melancholy looking man had saved today.

IN THE PRESENCE OF ROYALTY

XV

The men of Kelland manned the Emperor's Keep for another day.

From its walls, Farred watched the Drobax climb the steep sides of the crag—tiny figures inching their way up to meet the spears of Baldwin's men. On the other crag, he could see the Mace flying, as the men of Gotbeck took their turn to defend the path up to the Duke's Keep.

Prince Ashere's death lay heavy on him. They had buried him yesterday, deep inside the bowels of the Emperor's Crag, where dark caverns seemed to stretch on interminably. Walter had stored all sorts down there—barrels of drink and food, even horses, that had somehow been winched down. It seemed to Farred a desolate sort of resting place, and he feared that Ashere's soul might be unhappy. But at least the prince was far from the monsters who were tormenting the living.

Despite the fighting going on around him, Farred couldn't shake off a strange feeling of disinterest. Maybe, he wondered, this is what all of us will be like by the end. Maybe when they finish us off, we won't care very much anymore.

'Farred!' a voice interrupted his thoughts, and he was glad of it.

'Thought I'd find you up here,' said Walter.

They clasped hands. Walter looked at Farred for a while, perhaps judging whether further words on the Prince were required, and instead slapped Farred on the shoulder. 'We've found something very interesting up in the keep, Farred. And I know you'll want to be one of the first to see it.'

Walter had the face of a child torn between blurting out some exciting news and keeping it to themselves.

'Well, I'm in suspense already. Lead on, Lord Walter.'

Walter led Farred to the top floor of the Emperor's Keep, and into the corridor off which Baldwin, Walter, and the other key members of the imperial entourage had their rooms. 'Notice anything unusual?' asked Walter, that childish expression still on his face.

Farred looked. There was nothing in the corridor to see. Castle corridors were dark by nature, but this one had plenty of wall sconces on each side, with torches throwing up light. There. Towards the far end of the corridor, shadows flickered off an irregular shape. He looked over at Walter. Walter made a 'what could that be?' facial expression.

Farred walked over to investigate. At first, he didn't quite believe what his eyes were telling him. Poking out of the wall was half a forearm, a wrist, and a hand flopping downwards at the end. Farred gave it a long, hard look. He gave it a touch. It was a human hand. A man's hand. He turned around to Walter with a quizzical expression.

'Quite,' came the reply. 'How does one respond to that? I decided to tour the keep, checking the walls, floors, ceilings. I won't drag you down there to see, but in the granary, behind a sack of flour, one of my men found the edge of a shoe. I cut into it and sure enough, there was an inch of someone's foot poking out.'

'So—you think it's Ishari?'

'Who else? Haskan soldiers. Their sorcerers beamed them up here, presumably in the night. Almost certainly more than these two. Who knows where the others ended up? Mid-air, presumably, some of them. And there's more.' Walter reached under his cloak and retrieved a dagger. 'This is what our friend here was holding when he got beamed up. It was on the floor. That's what I saw first, actually.'

'Assassins, then.'

'Yes. Sent to kill my brother.'

Farred nodded. All things considered, it wasn't so much of a surprise. 'You've told Gustav?' he asked, thinking it was something a wizard might protect against.

'Yes. He knows. He says he's working on a response, and Inge has been added to Baldwin's bodyguard.'

'Can I do anything?'

Walter smiled. He clearly hadn't confided in him just for the sake of it.

'Oh, I see.'

The Marshal put his hands up. 'It's not a big deal, Farred, really. Baldwin's pretty set on not ordering your men into battle for the foreseeable future.'

Farred nodded. He wasn't about to disagree with the Emperor—the Magnians and Middians had given a lot already.

'But I haven't got many spare men to reassign. If you could give me some trusted men to stand guard at certain points around the keep? It would need to be day and night, in shifts. I'm thinking thirty at a time, eight hours on?'

'That's not a problem. I'll get them for you. Starting tonight?'

'If you can do it.'

'We can do it. Anything else?'

Walter hesitated.

Farred raised an eyebrow.

'Something else just for you, Farred. But completely optional. I am led to believe that, in Magnia, people are often...less bothered by sorcerers than they are in our country?'

Walter seemed surprisingly uncomfortable with this topic. 'In Brasingia,' he continued, 'there is a great deal of animosity. Especially from the Church. Baldwin can get away with having them: he's the Emperor. But that's the exception.'

'Well, I suppose it's more accepted in Magnia. My prince, Edgar, has a wizard. His relative is a wizard too.'

'What about you, Farred?'

Farred thought about it. 'I know little about it. I guess I'm not particularly bothered.'

'The reason I ask. Inge is with Baldwin now, and no longer assisting Gustav. But the Archmage needs some help. I don't know what it involves. Frankly, I don't want to. You're trustworthy, discrete; not too involved elsewhere. If you can do it, it would be a big help. If not, that's fine too.'

'I'll think about it, Walter. How about that?'

'That's as much as I hoped for.'

* * *

THE ISHARITE JAILERS ushered them over to the pits. Another day in the mines, another man hanged at the end of it, and now another night spent underground.

Gyrmund took in his last breaths of fresh air. He gulped it in, as if that would help him last until morning. He felt the now familiar sense of panic as they approached the pits. His breathing grew more rapid, his heart beat fast, his palms began to sweat. His feet stopped, refusing to get any closer.

He felt a hand grasp him tightly round the arm. He turned his head around. It was Clarin. The big man held him in an iron grip and, without words, forced him towards the edge of the pit, then forced him down into it.

'There,' said the warrior, 'you did it.'

Gyrmund nodded.

But he knew that one day soon Clarin wouldn't be able to get him down here.

He moved over to the far wall and stood for a while, letting his eyes adjust to the darkness, hoping that his nose might adjust to the fetid smell. He began to pick out the other figures in the pit. He noticed Cyprian, the small Persaleian he had befriended, signalling him over. He was standing with some other prisoners, and as Gyrmund approached them, Cyprian gathered him into a small huddle of half a dozen men.

'Gyrmund, meet Zared,' Cyprian whispered, indicating the youngest member of the group.

He was strong looking, wearing what once must have been fine clothes. He was already losing his hair, but still had boyish looking facial features. Zared offered his hand and Gyrmund took it.

'I wanted to meet,' said Zared, his voice confident but tired sounding. 'Cyprian has told me you plan to escape. I speak for the Persaleians in here. We are ready to support you when the time is right.'

'Thank you,' said Gyrmund. 'I will pass that on to my two friends.'

'There are others, too,' continued Zared. 'This is Tamir.'

Before he knew it, Gyrmund was shaking hands with the tallest and oldest man in the group, who had an iron grip.

'I am a chieftain,' said Tamir, with a strong eastern accent. 'My people, whom you know as Barbarians, have suffered more than anyone from the Isharites and have been in this hell for the longest time. I can speak for them. We too are ready to give our lives.'

Gyrmund nodded his appreciation.

'Rudy.'

'I'm Jurgen.'

The last two men had Brasingian accents. They looked similar, both slight of build and smaller than average height.

'We're cousins, from Rotelegen. Both of us were at the battle in Grienna where our army was butchered,' Rudy explained. 'We were among the few to survive, and they brought us back here. We haven't been here much longer than yourself—still got enough energy to fight.'

'I can't stand it no more,' added Jurgen. 'I'll do anything you ask.'

'I met Duke Ellard, briefly,' replied Gyrmund, remembering the journey they had taken with the Duke and his men, north from Essenberg. Messengers from Rotelegen had found them and informed Ellard that the Haskan army had arrived on his northern border. He had rushed ahead to meet the threat. 'I'm sorry to hear about what happened to your people.'

Rudy gave him a piercing look. 'We'd like a chance for revenge.'

'Do you have a plan?' asked Zared.

'Not a complete one,' Gyrmund answered uncomfortably, mindful of the needy stares of the other men. 'We need to get rid of Vamak first,' he said, looking around for the Dog-men, but they were in their usual place at the far end of the pit. 'Then we will be free to organise as many of us as we can. We get over the fence outside. But after that—'

'After that, there's the biggest fortress in Dalriya, full of Isharite soldiers and magi, in the middle of nowhere,' Zared finished for him.

They were in a desperate position, it was true. But what did these men want him to say?

'Will your friends be able to get us out?' asked Jurgen hopefully.

Gyrmund looked over to Herin and Clarin, stood not far away from the Dog-men, murmuring together. There was something about them, a sense of confidence they exuded in the middle of this horror, that these men looked to. Just like Gyrmund, they were desperate and needed hope. He understood what they wanted from him.

'Yes, give them a few more days,' he said, doing his best to look and sound confident. 'Hold on a while longer. Then we're getting out of here.'

Gyrmund made his farewells and shuffled over to stand next to Clarin. He hoped that he had done enough to keep up the spirits of the other men in the pit. They would need their support if they were going to make a successful escape bid.

Exhausted, Gyrmund dropped to the floor, his back resting against the wall behind him. He felt like offering hope to the other men in the pit had somehow drained it from him. He put his head in his hands, experiencing a sudden certainty that they weren't going to escape from this alive. None of them—not even Moneva, wherever she was. If she wasn't dead already. From out of nowhere, he felt the urge to cry. He hadn't cried since he was a kid.

He turned at movement to his right. Clarin had sat down next to him.

'Want to tell me about it?' asked the big man.

'About what?'

Clarin gave a half shrug. 'About whatever is making you suffer in here, and in the mine. You're not the same man you were in the Wilderness. Tell me. It might make you feel better.'

Gyrmund looked Clarin in the eyes. There was an intelligence, an empathy there, that he hadn't seen before. Perhaps he'd just ignored it, assumed that he was all brute strength, no brains. And perhaps Clarin played up to that.

'I've never told anyone before.'

'Then perhaps it's time you did.'

Perhaps so, Gyrmund considered. *And in all honesty, what is there to lose now?*

'It's from my childhood. We got ill. My entire family, my parents and sisters and me. One of the things I found hardest to accept, for a long time, was that my father was the one who brought it into the home. I idolised him when I was a child. He was strong, resourceful—I thought he was invincible. Do you understand that?'

'Yes. My father was a tough man, too. A soldier. He trained me and Herin as fighters from when we were mere lads through to adults. Every lesson I had worth learning was down to him. Ain't that right, Herin?'

'Yes, that's right. If I've done anything well in this life, it's down to him.'

So, Herin has elected to stay standing, but he is listening in too. So be it.

'No-one knew where he got it from. He was a huntsman, so perhaps he picked it up from the forest—a poisonous plant, or diseased animal. He came home and fell sick. In a few hours, we all had it. His landlord—his friend—decided it best to quarantine us, to stop the disease from spreading. We had to stay in our tiny little house, with no fresh air or sunlight, and they posted food and water under our door.

'We lay there, too ill to move, for days. Dying. My mother and sisters passed away. Then my father died. I had thought he would last the longest, but it was me who was left alone at the end. Then, I started to get better. For some reason, I fought off the illness. They made me stay in there, with my family, 'til they were sure I was better. My father's landlord raised me as part of his family afterwards.

'Since then, I've had a dread of enclosed spaces. Cowardly, I know.'

'Not a bit,' said Clarin quietly. 'Understandable.'

'No,' Gyrmund replied firmly. 'I'm a coward. I was the one who lived, and what have I done with my life? I've been running away from that memory, like a scared child, ever since.'

* * *

When the army had reached the outskirts of Heractus, Theron went to the gates of the city. With him went Count Diodorus, the general of the king's disbanded army. Evander accompanied them with the white flag of truce. Theron's role at the gates was to speak for Sebastian and the Order—to calm fears about their objectives in taking the city, but also to demand peaceful entry. Diodorus was there to make it plain that there was no longer a royal army, and that no help would be forthcoming.

Belwynn wasn't required to appear in her golden robe on this occasion, for which she was grateful. Sebastian wasn't required either, so they stood around and waited while the army made camp.

She was a bit underwhelmed by the city of Heractus from this distance. There was no extravagance like the Knights' High Tower. No defensive structures that came close to the fortress of Chalios. It didn't seem to be half the size of Essenberg in the Empire. What it did have was a lot of grey. There were grey stone walls defending the city, and she could make out more grey walls inside, presumably the royal castle. The walls looked strong enough, but there was nothing to give the Knights much cause to have doubts, and, she thought, nothing to give those inside the city much hope.

'Do you think they'll open the gates?' she asked Sebastian, impatient for Theron to return. She feared the Kalinthians inside the city would turn on him while he was negotiating.

'It would be best if they did. Jonas won't want to do it, and his eldest son, Straton, is a bit of a hothead. But we must hope that other voices in the city put their foot down. A siege would lead to misery for everyone concerned.'

Eventually, they spied Theron and the others returning at a leisurely pace, which suggested that at least they weren't in any danger. In fact, Belwynn became frustrated at their speed, desperate as she was to hear their news.

When they made it to the camp, Evander had to help Theron from his horse before he was ready to share his news.

'They're opening the gates for us,' Theron declared with a grin. 'Diodorus played his part in persuading them that was the better option.'

'Thank you both,' said Sebastian.

Diodorus nodded in acknowledgement, but still had the slightly sad expression Belwynn noticed when they had first met him.

'What do you think our approach should be now?' asked Sebastian.

'I still think we need to be careful,' replied Theron. 'Tycho and I will bring some troops in first, I reckon about two thousand. Take some into the castle, find quarters for the rest, and set up a new city guard. When I'm happy the whole place is secure, we'll send for you. The rest of the army will have to stay out here for the night, unless you want them all in. But that would mean turfing people out of their homes.'

'No, that's fine,' said Sebastian. 'We want to get people on our side as soon as possible, not upset them.'

'I'll get started straight away,' said Theron. 'We want to get control before nightfall.'

THERON AND TYCHO rounded up the units they needed and marched them to the city gates. There was a pause of some minutes before they slowly opened and the Knights of Kalinth entered Heractus, to the cheers of the men left behind.

Sebastian's tent was erected for him. Belwynn, Elana and Dirk sat inside with the new Grand Master, while his squire Alpin came and went on errands. Sebastian suddenly seemed very alone, with only the three of them for company. Time crept slowly as they waited for the news that Theron had the city under enough control for him to enter.

'Waiting is hard,' Sebastian commented, perhaps noticing Belwynn's tension. 'But such is war. Endless waiting, interrupted by brief moments of terror. Theron will have the city secured soon,' he said reassuringly.

'How does being a Grand Master suit you?' asked Elana.

Sebastian thought about it. 'Not so well. I'd rather be in Theron's position. Doing something instead of sitting here like a precious relic that needs protection. But that's the way it has to be, so there's no point in moaning about it.'

Indeed, Theron was playing the role of the villain in the capital, using force to exert his authority over Heractus. This allowed Sebastian to be disassociated from any unpleasant measures and, hopefully, to retain his popularity.

'But you're still the one in charge, in control of the situation,' said Belwynn. 'Theron and the knights are only doing what you want them to.'

'True enough,' Sebastian replied, 'to a point. You would think I should feel in control of things. Leader of the Order, in charge of an army. But I don't—not fully. I wonder if that's how Jonas has had it all these years. King of Kalinth, but not even in control of his own country.'

Belwynn thought it was a gloomy reply in the circumstances, and she wondered why. Sebastian was perhaps looking ahead to his meeting with Jonas, and the daunting tasks ahead of him now that he had secured power. Standing up to Ishari, being first among them. Indeed, she considered, taking power away from Jonas was all very well. But it didn't, by itself, solve the problems that the Kalinthians faced.

Sebastian was studying her. 'Of course, here I am dwelling on my position when your own situation regarding the fate of your brother is far worse. But rest assured, Belwynn. Once we get inside the capital, we are another step on the road to rescuing him. And I should take this chance to thank you all. In your own ways, you have strengthened the faith of my supporters. It doesn't feel like chance that our paths crossed at this very moment.'

'Indeed,' agreed Elana, 'it is not.'

The priestess said no more, but everyone understood what she meant.

A RAP AT THE DOOR. Theron.

'Come in,' said Belwynn, seated on her bed in her room in Heractus Castle. Though really, she didn't want him to. She wanted to be left out of this.

Theron entered with an expression grim enough to match her own. They looked at each other for a while.

'This is going to be the worst dinner of my life,' said Belwynn eventually. 'Why are you making *me* go?'

Theron shrugged without much sympathy. 'They invited you.'

'But they don't know me!'

'The Lady of the Knights. That's who they asked for. That's what people are calling you now.'

'Ridiculous,' said Belwynn, standing up and smoothing down the white linen tunic that had been put out for her to wear.

Theron, who was wearing a man's version of the tunic, put out his arm and when Belwynn took it, led her out into the castle corridor.

She suddenly wondered who Theron had forced out of the room for her to have it. They were making a lot of enemies in Heractus, and top of the list was the royal family, who had invited them to what was surely going to be an excruciating dinner. It summed up the uneasy situation they were now in. Jonas was still king; but Sebastian had taken over the capital and the government. No-one in Heractus quite knew what was going to happen next.

Theron knocked at Sebastian's door and they waited outside for him to come out. Alpin opened it and Sebastian walked briskly out before getting straight to business.

'Right. Jonas's queen is Irina,' he began, speaking to Belwynn. 'It is tradition here that she hosts the dinner. The only other guests at the table will be their two sons. Straton is the eldest. He tends to speak before he thinks. The younger, Dorian, is quieter and brighter. Now,' he continued, turning his attention to Theron. 'They are all going to be upset. That is understandable and we shall let them be. Belwynn and I will control ourselves, so you must as well, Theron. Now is not the time to throw our weight around or argue, so save it for another time, even if Straton gets in your face. The fact that they are being civil, and invited us to a meal, is a good sign for the future. So let's not spoil it.'

'I will be cool as ice, uncle. Don't worry.'

With a sinking feeling in her stomach, Belwynn let them lead her down to the king's hall. A small table on the dais was being laid by servants, while at the fire stood the royal family, just as Sebastian had described them.

Jonas had long, iron grey hair that matched the colour of his capital city. He had a strong looking physique, but nonetheless looked like a man past his best years, his skin pallid looking and wrinkled. His wife, too, had gone grey, and to Belwynn the pair of them looked like someone's grandparents rather than a king and queen. Straton, a big looking ox of a man, looked kinglier, with brown, shaggy hair on his head and his face. Dorian was slimmer and clean-shaven.

As they approached, the family turned to look at them, a mix of emotions playing on their faces. Jonas himself looked at them impassively enough, but his wife Irina didn't disguise her hatred. Straton's face flushed red with anger.

'Sebastian,' said the king, 'welcome, it's been too long.'

The two men crossed the distance between them and embraced.

'Your Majesty,' responded Sebastian.

He turned to Irina, who gave him a filthy look. But, after a glare from her husband, she held out her hand and allowed Sebastian to kiss it. Sebastian moved on to speak to the two princes while Theron led Belwynn over.

'Count Theron,' Jonas got out through gritted teeth, his dislike overcoming his manners.

'Your Majesty,' replied Theron neutrally.

The king turned to Belwynn.

'This is the Lady Belwynn, Your Majesty,' introduced Theron.

Jonas stared at her until it became uncomfortable. Belwynn looked at Theron, who nodded that she should offer her hand. She did so, but the staring continued.

'Jonas,' whispered his wife.

The king seemed to come out of his reverie and took her hand, briefly putting it to his lips. The skin of his hand and lips felt rough to the touch, and Belwynn was relieved when it was over.

'So,' said Irina, an icy expression on her face, 'you are the one who calls herself the Lady of the Knights?'

'I—no, I don't call myself that,' answered Belwynn, feeling herself blush.

'I see. Your idea, was it, Theron? I should have known. Clever.'

'No, not me, Your Majesty,' replied Theron smoothly. 'That is the name the people have given her.'

'The people? Ha!' snorted Irina. 'And I hear,' she continued, 'that you have the gift of healing?'

'No,' said Belwynn, startled by the question. 'That's not me—'

'I see. What *have* you done to earn this name then, I wonder?'

Belwynn didn't know what to say. She saw Sebastian looking at her with concern and knew that she had to keep control. 'Nothing, I'm sure.'

'Oh, not nothing,' persisted Irina, her voice full of sarcasm. 'You sang to the Knights, didn't you?'

Belwynn looked at Theron and Sebastian. This had started just as badly as she thought it was going to.

'Come,' said Jonas, rescuing her. 'Let's dine.'

The group of seven walked over to the dais, Irina smiling at her as if she had won a victory.

Once seated, they were served with vegetable barley soup, a hearty dish that Belwynn enjoyed after what already felt like a long day. She noted that they were all served from the same tureen, which reassured her. She didn't know how paranoid she was being, but she wondered if it wouldn't be in the interests of the king to have the three of them poisoned. Then again, it wouldn't have surprised her if Theron had installed his own people in the kitchens. His occupation of the city had been nothing if not thorough.

The king sat with his wife on one side and Sebastian on the other, while opposite them were Belwynn and the three younger men. She felt as if she was a member of a dysfunctional family, with three parents sternly staring over at their unruly offspring.

'What are your plans for the government, Grand Master?' asked Jonas mildly, looking at his spoon as he brought it to his lips. 'I understand you are not happy with current policies.'

To her left, Belwynn heard Straton snort, though she couldn't tell if it was with humour or anger. She didn't turn to look, but kept her attention on her soup, waiting for Sebastian to reply.

'Well, I thank you for the opportunity to discuss this so soon, Your Majesty,' replied Sebastian. 'I am not sure how familiar you are with recent developments abroad. Ishari has not only invaded the Empire, but conquered the lands of the Grand Caladri.'

Belwynn took a peak at the king. He looked upset enough and nodded along. Whether he already knew about Ishari's aggression or not, she couldn't tell.

'In these circumstances,' continued Sebastian, 'I believe the current policy of...peace,' he cleared his throat, 'while well intentioned, must now change.'

'Ah,' said Jonas, nodding along. 'And a king's duty is to defend his people, am I right, Sebastian?'

'Agreed.'

'Then I ask you this,' began the king, his voice getting slightly more animated. 'If the Isharites have destroyed Persala, the Grand Caladri, and the Brasingian Empire, what makes you think Kalinth can stop them? And if we try and fail, what will happen to my people?'

'It is the duty of Kalinth to fight in such a war,' responded Sebastian. 'Not to stand by and do nothing.'

'Answer my question!' demanded Jonas, his voice suddenly full of aggression. 'What will happen to my people if you fail!'

'You talk as if Kalinth has escaped the war,' interjected Theron, coming to the rescue of his uncle. 'But war has come already. Raids in the east from Haskany, in the west from Kharovia. Your people have suffered murder, seen their property destroyed and stolen, and countless other crimes. And your government did nothing!'

'Not your noble League, though, Theron.' Now it was Straton's turn to get involved, his voice dripping with sarcasm. 'Riding about with your friends, undermining royal policy, so that you can play the hero. You've broken every oath to your Order and betrayed your king, but you're still as self-righteous as you've ever been. This crusade against Ishari is going to drag the whole country to hell!'

'We've been sleepwalking into hell these past years,' said Theron, his voice measured despite Straton's taunts. 'Now it's time to make a stand. The honour of the country demands it.'

'Don't talk to me of honour,' Straton shouted back down the table, the two men wisely positioned at opposite ends. 'Not you.'

'Then join us,' Theron asked, his voice almost pleading. 'You can be the one to rouse the country to defend itself!'

Belwynn looked at Straton, seething with anger. But did his face show some doubt; was he tempted to take up Theron's challenge? She looked over at the king and queen, concern visible on their faces lest their son should join up with the Knights; Sebastian, equally keen that he did.

'What's more,' began Straton, 'I demand the release of Count Ampelios, who is at this moment languishing in the dungeons of this very castle! You have no authority to imprison the man, who has been a faithful servant of the crown for years!'

'I warned him several times that if he tried to impede the Knights' business, I would have to arrest him. It was his own foolish actions that got him there.'

The moment had gone. Theron and Straton continued to argue across the table as the servants came to take away the soup bowls and brought in hot, steaming pies. Belwynn could smell spiced mutton and pear but couldn't help a small sigh, as her appetite had now disappeared.

'Are you alright, my lady?' Prince Dorian whispered to her while the raised voices to either side continued, his face looking genuinely concerned.

Belwynn looked around the table, but no-one was looking in her direction. 'I was wondering,' she replied, keeping her voice down. 'How many more courses are there likely to be?'

GUSTAV THE HAWK

XVI

Duke Coen was a vigorous man, and had set off at quite a pace. Lord Emmett and Frayne followed close behind, while Edgar brought up the rear, unfamiliar with the Thessian terrain. Prematurely bald, Coen's head glinted in the sunshine. Otherwise Edgar would have lost sight of him altogether.

Coen's route took them uphill, allowing Edgar to fall in behind Emmett as their mounts slowed down a touch. As they made their way up Herne's Hill, Edgar got glimpses of more of the Thessian countryside, stretching out in all directions. Looking behind them, he could see the army camp, where a sea of tents had been erected.

Emmett stopped ahead and dismounted, so Edgar did the same. Coen had already left his horse chewing at a clump of grass and was marching up the final few feet to the top of the rise.

Edgar followed on. It was windy up here, and the breeze cooled him down after the brisk ride.

Coen had asked that just the four of them should come to Herne's Hill alone. He had decided that they were to be the four commanders of the army, and should come and look at the terrain for themselves. Perhaps, also, to bond, since apart from Coen and Emmett, they hardly knew each other.

Coen pointed off in a north-easterly direction as they gathered round. 'The Thessian-Barissian border is mostly a porous one. Walk a mile or so from one village to the next and you've crossed it. The Barissians have been in my territory for a few days now. It's been hard, letting them destroy homes, take castles, kill our people. Hard not to go right after the bastards. Instead we've been harrying, making life difficult, without committing to a fight we'd likely lose. But the numbers you've brought can tip the balance, and I thank you. Sincerely thank you.'

Coen certainly looked sincere as he looked Edgar and then Frayne straight in the eye. The duke paused briefly, the first time Edgar had seen him stop. It suddenly hit Edgar how much this campaign meant to the Thessians. Their lives, and those of their families, hung in the balance.

'You're welcome, of course,' replied Edgar. 'Can we see potential battle sites from here?'

Coen nodded. 'I've got a good idea where the battle will be, though in truth my duchy is as flat as your hand; this hill we're on is as high as it gets.' The duke pointed off into the distance again. 'Salvinus has been pushing south, trying to draw us into a pitched battle.'

'Salvinus?' Edgar blurted out. 'That's the man who attacked our temple.'

'Well, sounds like your men might have even more reason to fight,' commented Emmett.

Edgar nodded. He would be happy to take some revenge. He remembered them studying each other in the temple complex at Ecgworth, before Salvinus had retreated, with Toric's Dagger in his possession. Brictwin had lurched out and knocked one of his riders off his horse. Ealdnoth and Soren had interrogated the man, and that was how they'd been able to put a name to the face.

'He's Emeric's general,' Coen informed him. 'I assume Emeric allows him to make most of the military decisions. Either way, he's forced me to give ground and head west, so that we could meet up with your forces. The Barissians have driven further south, cutting off the road to Lindhafen. They're now free to march on my capital. Tactically sound on their part, but of course they didn't know I was getting reinforcements!'

At this, Coen's eyes sparkled a little. 'If we march straight on them now, they'll be keen for a battle. Defeat us and they can take Lindhafen quickly, before heading north for Essenberg, which is Emeric's real goal. I can't delay engaging any longer, even if I wanted to. I would lose too much, and my soldiers are fed up with retreating as it is. Are you ready?' he asked pointedly.

'Yes,' replied Edgar, hoping he sounded surer than he felt. 'How do you envisage deploying the forces?'

'Three main divisions,' said Coen. 'Myself in the centre with most of the Thessians, the rest under Emmett on the right. You and the Magnians on the left. The Middians are the best horsemen, so Frayne, I would ask your men to act as the reserve.'

Frayne nodded, his face impassive. 'We will fight wherever you put us.'

It all sounded so simple. Edgar, still unsure of the geography, looked out over Thesse to where he guessed the road to Lindhafen was. Two armies, now roughly equal in numbers, fighting it out in the open.

'How long will it take us to get there?' he asked.

'Two days.'

* * *

Why do I agree to things? Farred lectured himself as he slowly made his way up the steps to the top room of the tallest tower in the Emperor's Keep. *What am I, a child?* he berated himself, *as if walking slowly will somehow prevent it from happening?*

Despite the telling off, he found his legs moved just as slowly as before. In the end, though, they took him to the room of Gustav, Emperor Baldwin's Archmage.

He rapped on the door.

'Enter,' came the reply.

Taking a deep breath, Farred swung the door open.

The room was one of the biggest in the keep, but it was less alien than his imagination had led him to believe. No magic potions bubbling away; no body parts kept in jars. A long table dominated the central part of the room, and it was completely bare. A window let in the fresh air from outside. Gustav stepped forwards and offered his hand, which Farred took.

'Farred, I'm much obliged that you've agreed to help me out,' said the wizard, ushering him into the room.

'You're welcome.'

Gustav, Farred had to admit, wasn't much like the wizards from the stories that had been told around the fire back home. He didn't have a large scraggly beard, didn't display unconventional behaviour, didn't have a wild animal sharing his living quarters. He was business-like, broad shouldered, and healthy looking for a man of older years.

'I'm not going to ask you to do much at all, you'll be relieved to hear,' Gustav began. 'Walter has explained to you about the Isharites teleporting killers into the keep?'

'Yes. He showed me.'

'Mmm. Well, I have agreed that my apprentice, Inge, should stay with the

Emperor for the time being, until we can be more relaxed about his safety. Not that we can ever guarantee it, of course. Baldwin has asked me to respond to the attacks. So, I'm asking you to fill in for her when I need some help. Right. I'm about to turn into a hawk,' the wizard explained.

Farred's jaw dropped open. Had he just heard Gustav correctly?

'I could just do it myself, but to be on the safe side, I need to be restrained while the transformation occurs,' continued Gustav matter-of-factly. 'When I become a bird physically, my mind doesn't change; I can still think perfectly clearly. So, I will just want to be moved over to the window so that I can fly off.'

He opened a box by the window and pulled out three lengths of rope. 'It's best if I lie down on my chest. Tie me to the table, as tight as you can. You'll need to hold me down as well. And take care of my head, I don't want to bash it too much.'

Gustav handed Farred the ropes, undressed himself, and proceeded to climb onto the table.

I take it back, Farred thought to himself. *I'm tying up a grown man—naked, by the way—onto a table.*

Farred looped the rope around the wizard and the table, pulling hard on each before tying them off.

Gustav didn't waste any time. He began muttering to himself, and then his whole body shook, seemingly uncontrollably. Farred turned Gustav's head to one side, and with one hand held it down onto the table so that he didn't bang himself. He used his other hand to put weight onto the wizard's back.

Gustav then let out a loud, throaty cry of pain, and Farred could see the change happen right before his eyes.

The wizard's legs sprouted talons where his toes had been. Feathers sprouted all over his body, countless shades of brown, grey and cream, including a tail that reached out beyond his legs. A sharp beak extended out of his face where his nose had been, pushing his eyes out to the sides. All the while this was happening, his body shrunk in size, so that the ropes, which had been tight moments before, loosened until they weren't holding him at all.

Farred released his hold and backed away a couple of paces, alarmed at what he had witnessed. Gustav the Hawk—for now his nickname made perfect, dreadful sense—stood up and looked at Farred. The bird's eyes that stared at him were the same colour as the man's had been before the transformation. For some reason, that was the thing that disturbed him most, and it would be those hawk eyes that haunted his dreams over the next few nights.

Farred remembered Gustav had wanted him to help him to the window. He looked cautiously at the wicked, curved talons of the hawk, sharp enough to slash through clothes and skin, strong enough to mangle his arm. Gustav had said his mind would be intact. But still...

Tentatively, Farred held out his arm. Slowly, Gustav walked towards it and climbed on, holding onto Farred with only the gentlest pressure. Carefully, Farred turned around and took him to the window. Gustav stared at him again with those large, brown eyes. Farred leaned his arm out of the window and the hawk was gone in an instant, its powerful wings beating fast as it developed the speed required to fly. Farred followed its flight until he lost sight of it.

He turned and looked around at the empty room. What was he supposed to do now? He decided quickly. Gustav had said nothing about waiting for him, and Farred made straight for the door.

* * *

'HOW MANY DAYS have we been here now?' asked Shira, her bored tone an attempt to hide her increasing frustration and anger.

Every day seemed to be identical to the last. She watched as the Kellish defended their wall on the large crag. The flags of Gotbeck and Rotelegen, the Mace and the Rooster, flew on the opposite crag. Hadn't the Gotbeckers manned the path yesterday? Maybe it had been the Luderians—she couldn't remember and didn't care.

'It's been a week,' replied her uncle, Koren, to what Shira had largely meant as a rhetorical question.

A week. Arioc had conquered the Grand Caladri in a day, and she couldn't take one fortress in a week. Like every other day, Shira, Koren, and the Isharite wizard, Mehrab, had travelled from their camp to the castle, to observe the siege. Not that they had intervened once. Roshanak and his wizards were in control, sending the Drobax against the Brasingian defences in one mindless attack after another.

'What about Baldwin?' she demanded of Mehrab. She had ordered him to use his Isharite wizards to kill the Emperor, and thereby crush the morale of the enemy.

She heard Koren sigh, letting her know his displeasure at the idea, but ignored him.

'We have sent soldiers into the Emperor's Keep two nights running,' replied the Isharite.

'And?'

'Well, I can't confirm any success, Your Majesty.'

'Huh,' sneered Shira. 'I think we would know if it had been a success.'

'Maybe so,' the Isharite replied.

'What we know,' interjected Koren, 'is that brave soldiers have been sent up there to their death in a pointless exercise.'

'Pointless?' Shira retorted, turning to face her uncle. She'd had enough of his patronising attitude. '*This* is pointless!' she shouted, waving her arms at the gory spectacle of Burkhard Castle.

Koren reached over and grabbed the front of her coat. Her uncle had never manhandled her before, and it shocked Shira that he would do so now. She tried to twist away to the side, but Koren pulled at her with all his weight and they both stumbled over to the ground. As they did, Shira felt a searing pain along the side of her head.

Koren released her and pointed up at the sky. 'Get it!' he shouted.

Shira looked up and saw a hawk wheeling away from them. An orange coloured blast of magic flew into the sky after it, as Mehrab tried to down the bird. But the hawk soared away from the path of the bolt, and was gone.

Shira staggered to her feet.

'Their wizard, Gustav,' said Mehrab bitterly, looking up at the sky.

Shira followed his gaze, but the hawk was out of sight, and was unlikely to return now that the element of surprise had gone.

'Let that be an end to it,' demanded Koren harshly, looking from Shira to Mehrab and back again. 'No more magic tricks and quick fixes. We have brought the Drobax all the way here to take the fortress. Let them do it.'

Shira put a hand to her head. It came back wet and sticky with blood where the talons of the bird had raked along her scalp. If her uncle hadn't yanked her out of the way, it could have been much worse.

Mehrab was looking at her for confirmation.

'Very well,' Shira said, giving in. 'No more attacks on the Emperor.'

She gazed over at the Drobax slithering up Baldwin's crag like a swarm of insects. 'He can live and watch us destroy his Empire.'

* * *

THE WAITING TIED her stomach into knots. Each moment that passed, Arioc or his servant, Babak, were more likely to notice that Moneva had been gone longer than usual, raising their suspicions. At the best, her movements would be restricted. She needed the freedom of movement Arioc had granted her, or her hopes of escape would be over.

Moneva crouched behind some bushes. She hoped the evening darkness would conceal her position. She had spied on the prison camp at Samir Durg at the same time last night. She had seen Gyrmund and the others with her own eyes. When the guards released them into the open area, they had made straight for the stretch of fence she was now hiding near. It seemed like this might be a routine they had developed, looking out towards the fortress and talking amongst themselves before they were herded, along with the other prisoners, into the underground pits where they were kept overnight.

It was risky, but she had to make an attempt to talk to them. She was sure they had been out of the mines by this time last night. Perhaps they had been brought in early, and were already in those miserable looking pits.

A noise on the other side of the site interrupted her thoughts. Gates were being opened. Orders shouted. Then, she could make out the tired looking figures of the prisoners entering the fenced area. Gyrmund, Herin and Clarin made their way over to the same part of the fence they had occupied last night. Gyrmund put his hands onto it, as if he needed to hold himself up. He looked awful. Moneva hadn't been close enough to make out their faces last night. Gyrmund looked tired and lined, big bags under his eyes. He was a lot thinner. Herin and Clarin didn't look quite so bad, though they too had lost weight.

She couldn't waste time. 'Hey!' she whispered. 'It's Moneva!'

Herin's eyes narrowed, and he looked over in her direction.

'Did you hear that?' he asked the other two.

'What?' asked Clarin.

'Shush.'

'It's Moneva,' she repeated.

'I see you,' replied Herin, looking around to make sure that no-one else was in earshot.

Clarin and Gyrmund also seemed to pick her out from behind the bush. Gyrmund's eyes filled with tears, but he said nothing.

'I've got to be quick,' began Moneva. 'I'm going to free you one night soon. Not tonight and not tomorrow. But from then on, you need to be ready each night. I'll let you out of the pits. You need to be as ready as possible. We've got to go back to the fortress to free Soren.'

'Is he alright?' whispered Clarin.

'I haven't seen him. But I think he's still alive. How are you?'

'Well, we've just come back from a double hanging, but otherwise we're doing fine,' said Herin drily.

Gyrmund looked like he was about to say something, but he couldn't get any words out. Now wasn't the time, anyway.

'I've got to go,' said Moneva. She didn't wait for a reply and didn't give them a final look. She turned around and headed back to Arioc's chambers.

THE BATTLE OF LINDHAFEN

XVII

'Edgar!'

It was Wilchard, looking excited as he hurried over. 'Coen's scouts have located Emeric's army. Only a mile away.'

Edgar's heart hammered in his chest. He felt his hands go clammy. This was what they had been hoping for, and yet the news made his guts twist with anxiety. He found himself following Wilchard to the front of the camp.

Coen was already there, talking hurriedly with Lord Emmett and a group of Thessian noblemen. A mood of anticipation hung in the air. Coen was one of the smaller men in the group, but his bald pate made him stand out, and he had an air of authority which Edgar found reassuring. The duke noticed him and welcomed him over. Edgar offered his hand, and Coen grasped it wordlessly. They would need to work closely together today and so would their soldiers. It was important for them to be seen to be united.

'The Barissians are more or less where I expected them to be. My scouts are sure that Emeric's entire force is there. They're on the road to Lindhafen, but haven't gone too far east; no doubt suspecting that I would double back on them. It means that we can approach them from the south.'

'Why do you want to do that, Your Grace?' asked Wilchard. 'Is the terrain better on this side of the road?'

'Not particularly, Lord Wilchard. No, it's nothing to do with that—this whole region is mostly flat and featureless. I'd prefer to approach from the south because I don't want his soldiers to feel trapped when we engage them. A large proportion of his army is comprised of mercenaries. When the going gets tough, I want them to feel free to retreat north. Our numbers are going to be similar. I'm relying on the fact that our men will be stauncher today.'

Edgar had never fought in a proper battle. He had trained for it plenty enough, since he was a young boy. Hours of physical exercise and weapon training, every day. He had even read up on tactics. But Coen's description of what was going to happen this morning suddenly sounded very real, and not very appealing. Two sides hacking at each other until one couldn't stand it anymore, and vacated the field. The Thessians were fighting to defend their homeland. He had to make sure that the Magnians, with less to lose, also stood firm.

'I say we march towards them now, and when we're within sight, get into formation. Are we still agreed on deployment?' Coen asked.

'Yes,' replied Edgar.

On tactics, at least, he was clear. The Magnians would form the left division and mostly fight on foot. Edgar would stand with his men on the left, the North Magnians to his right. A small detachment of cavalry, led by Wilchard, would protect the left flank.

'And Frayne?' asked the Duke.

'He's fine.'

Frayne and the Middians would act as the main cavalry force and stay in reserve, to intervene where and when needed. The middle and right divisions would be commanded by Coen and Emmett, respectively. Everyone understood their roles.

'Then let's crush the bastards!' declared Coen, with real malice.

Leofwin and Brictwin finished tightening off Edgar's straps. The chain mail was heavy, but it was a weight he was used to, his father stressing more than once the importance of accustoming oneself to movement in armour. Uncle and nephew then checked each other, while all about them men did the same.

Ulf the smith, who until a week ago had worked under Rabigar the Krykker, was bright red in the face, as he ran from one emergency to the next, making small adjustments to armour and weaponry.

Edgar had a sword strapped to his waist and a dagger in his belt. It had been agreed with his advisers that he would not stand in the very front row. There he would be too much of a target for the enemy. But he had insisted that he wouldn't position himself so far away as to be considered a coward.

Supporting the front lines, he knew he would see his fair share of the battle once it started.

He looked around. The men of Magnia were ready to fight. He would lead them, and he prayed to Toric that he wouldn't let them down.

The combined army of Magnia and Thesse was soon moving into position. Coen placed them in open grassland, which ran gently down to the Lindhafen Road. Emeric's full army wasn't in sight, but the Barissians knew they were there. Their scouts came and went on the north side of the road, reporting their numbers and deployment back to Emeric and his commanders.

Once he was happy with the arrangement, Coen had his soldiers place caltrops on each side of the army. These metal spikes were particularly good at defending areas from cavalry advances. Coen was keen to constrict the space on the battlefield and to protect the infantry from the Barissian cavalry.

Edgar began organising the Magnian forces, nearly four thousand men, subdivided into smaller units who would fight together. They were formed into a rectangle, with the long end facing the road. He angled it away from the road slightly, making it harder for the Barissians to force their way around. Here, at the front, the most experienced and ablest soldiers were placed. Quite a few of them were older men who had fought in the Magnian Civil War—on both sides. All Magnians now fought together, and Edgar was proud of that.

He walked down the line, exchanging words with the men under his command. Some were eager to talk, boasting to their Prince about what they would do in the upcoming battle. Others preferred to nod and greet their Prince but keep their thoughts private. Some drank, using it to stiffen their courage before the fight. Others prayed to Toric or other gods. Edgar showed equal respect to all.

The front row was heavily armoured, and all carried shields which they would hold together to form a defensive wall. The second row stood a few feet back, spears driven into the ground point first beside them. When the Barissians came, the spearmen would poke their spears over or under the shields of the first row, trying to find gaps in the enemy's shield wall.

The ranks at the back were taken by those who were less experienced and less well armed. If they had been placed at the front, they were likely to break and allow the enemy through. Here they could play a support role, and fill in at the front when required. Some had bows. These archers could move through the ranks to get the best shot at the enemy. Edgar's job with the rear ranks was to reassure and encourage, reminding them of what was expected of them. It wasn't complicated, and Edgar found himself repeating the same two words.

Stand firm.

Ealdnoth approached. 'Do they look ready?' asked the wizard.

'Yes, they do. I feel like I want it to start now.'

Ealdnoth harrumphed at that idea in displeasure.

'Where will you be during the battle?' Edgar asked him.

'Everywhere,' replied Ealdnoth. 'In her letter, Belwynn made it clear that Emeric has an Isharite wizard as an adviser. He will be here. My job will be to nullify anything he tries.'

'Well, be careful.'

'Oh, it can be done quite safely. I won't be in any danger. It's you who are putting your life on the line.' Ealdnoth was far from happy with Edgar's decision to fight near the front. 'Listen to me. No heroics, Edgar. Just get through the day alive, that's your job.'

'Right,' Edgar agreed. Getting through this alive sounded like very sensible advice.

Finally, the Prince met up with Wilchard. The steward was already mounted, along with two hundred of the best Magnian cavalry to the left of Edgar's infantry. Wilchard knew his job was to protect the flank of Edgar's infantry and, if possible, to outmanoeuvre the enemy.

'Any news?' Edgar asked.

'No. Still can't see the Barissians. Do you think they'll come to us?'

'Coen seems to think so. Be careful, Wilchard. There aren't many of you. Don't get caught up in a fight you can't win.'

Wilchard nodded. 'I will do my best not to get anyone killed, Your Highness.'

They clasped hands, and Wilchard then turned his horse around to join up with his cavalry. It was time. Edgar moved into his position in the third rank of his infantry. His bodyguards stood either side of him. On Leofwin's left stood Ragulf, a young nobleman who had the honour of holding the Prince's standard. The flag of the Sun in Glory stood tall, symbol for all Magnians.

The Magnians were ready. The Thessians were ready also. Their flag, a six-spoked wheel above two crossed ears of corn, could be seen in the central division, indicating Coen's presence there. The army was ready, but the Barissians did not come.

Soldiers sat down and rested. Those with the stomach for it had their lunch, making sure that they had enough energy to last as long as required.

'Will we have to go and meet them?' murmured Brictwin, as the initial excitement of the preparations turned to boredom.

'Coen seems pretty convinced Emeric wants to bring him to a fight,' replied Edgar, who had been starting to think the same thing as the younger man. 'He's been trying to for days, apparently.'

'Maybe they don't like the odds any more,' said Leofwin.

There was that. Coen was about eight thousand fighting men stronger with the Magnian and Middian forces. The outcome was far from a foregone conclusion for either side.

Then, noise spread back from the front ranks in a wave. Edgar made his way forwards. There they were. Coming over a rise and into view were rank upon rank of Barissian soldiers.

The noise became shouts of anger and howls of derision from the Thessians. The Thessians had suffered their homeland being ravaged for the last few days. They weren't about to forget or forgive. They sounded ready for the fight. The Magnians joined in, letting out tension by shouting at the approaching army. Some hurled abuse, some just let out wordless, animal noises.

The Barissians stopped just before the road, only a few hundred feet away. Edgar got a good view of them.

'About the same numbers of infantry as we have,' suggested Leofwin, peering over Edgar's shoulder.

Edgar nodded. 'More cavalry than we do, though. And they'll be holding a force in reserve, too.'

The enemy were organised into three divisions in the same way as Coen had done with their forces. The boar of Barissia was held aloft in the central division. A second flag was displayed there too, a golden crown on a red background.

'Of course,' Edgar murmured to himself. 'He's a king now.'

Would Emeric himself be there? If so, the two dukes would fight in the centre of the battlefield. However, Edgar thought it more likely that Emeric was sat on a horse some distance from the front line.

They watched on as the Barissians organised themselves into their formations. It was tempting to order a charge now. But the plan they had all agreed to was for the Barissians to come to them.

It seemed, however, like they would be disappointed. The Barissians got themselves ready and then waited. The battlefield went quiet. Neither side seemed willing to make the first move.

'Gods, let's just get this done,' Edgar heard one of his soldiers say, almost in despair.

The waiting was excruciating. But no doubt better than what was to come.

Then, finally, sound and movement. Brass instruments were blown. Drums were pounded.

The Barissians shuffled forwards.

Edgar moved back into position. In amongst his men, he lost his unobstructed view of the whole battlefield, but he could still see down to the road. The infantry division opposite his own, the Barissian right wing, was now crossing it. The Barissian drums beat out a steady rhythm, so that the ranks could march at the same pace and keep their order.

All the Magnian soldiers were now on their feet, weapons ready. The front rank locked their shields together, presenting an intimidating wall to the enemy. Shouts began to roar out again as the moment of impact drew close.

They heard the clash over to their right as the Barissians engaged with the Thessian units. Shouts and grunts filled the air, followed by screams.

A roar erupted from the Barissian infantry ahead of them, and they charged the remaining distance towards the Magnian shields, intent on smashing their way through. A few feet to go and the Magnians responded, running to meet them. An enormous thud filled the air as shield after shield smacked against each other in a long line.

In some places along the line Magnians were pushed over, in others Barissians had fallen backwards. As the two sides heaved against each other, those in the front rank who had a free hand stabbed with short swords, or hacked with hand axes. The spearmen in the row in front of Edgar began their deadly work. One of them leaped high into the air, thrusting his spear downwards over the shoulder of the man in front, trying to find an undefended spot. Again and again he did it, the wicked iron tip thrusting down at different angles. Next to him, a second spearman used a different technique. He crouched down on one knee and he thrust his spear in between the legs of the men ahead of him, hoping to connect with the shin or ankle of the enemy, either to wound or to knock them off balance.

Meanwhile, the Barissians were doing the same. Ear splitting screams rang out from both sides as metal plunged into limbs, weapons of all kinds found exposed faces, necks and groins.

The ranks ahead of Edgar had stabbed and maimed several enemy soldiers. It looked like there might be potential to open a gap in the enemy line. Edgar and Leofwin shared a look and nodded in agreement.

'Push!' shouted Edgar at the top of his voice, though he wasn't optimistic about how many of his men heard the instruction above the shouts and screams around them. He had to lead by example. Edgar, Leofwin and Brictwin moved forwards together, adding their weight to the front rank. At the same time, Edgar had to beware Barissian thrusts coming over from their side of the wall. He bent his legs somewhat so that the top of his head wasn't too exposed. The rest of the Magnians, to the side and behind, joined in, so that Edgar was now himself being pushed forwards by those in the ranks behind him.

He stuck his head up to grab a quick look at the enemy. The Barissians had been quick to react and were now pushing back, the two armies involved in a massive scrum. The Magnians had gained a little ground at first, but the contest had become even. He looked along the line in both directions. The same pushing match was taking place wherever the two armies had met. But the Magnians had made better progress in some places than others, so that while Edgar's section of the line was ahead, off to the sides, the line bent back behind him.

A Barissian short sword jabbed down, inches from Edgar's head. Its owner had leaned over the shoulder of the man in front of Edgar and was driving down with the blade. Edgar tried to move out of the way, but he was so squashed in now he didn't have much wriggle room. He knew he needed to act.

Edgar struggled to release his right arm, which still gripped his own sword. He did so by pushing himself backwards with his left hand, allowing enough of a gap for him to jerk his right arm free. The Barissian sword came down again. This time the tip of the blade hit the back of the soldier in front of Edgar, but didn't come down with enough force to puncture his armour. Edgar reacted quickly, chopping at the wrist of the Barissian with quick, brutal hacks. The enemy was forced to release his sword and drew his arm away before Edgar could do serious damage.

Edgar followed the retreating arm, standing up tall to take a good look at his enemy. He took in a sea of squashed soldiers, red faces groaning amid the crush of bodies. Ahead and slightly to the left was the man he had clashed with, shouting in his direction, spittle erupting from his mouth. Edgar crouched down a little, pulled his arm back, then launched up and forwards, thrusting his sword towards the Barissian's face. The man reacted, gripping Edgar's forearm just in time to stop the blow. Edgar didn't stop, though. He yanked his arm backwards and forwards until it broke free. He shoved his sword into the neck of his enemy, drew it out, shoved it in again. Again, and again. Making sure that he was dead. When he was sure, he looked. The man was dead alright, his head lolling to one side. But the crush of bodies meant that his body was still upright, with no room for it to fall to the ground.

Then, something gave. Edgar found himself stumbling forwards as the resistance of the Barissians collapsed. He just managed to keep his feet and looked around him. The clear lines of the two armies had disappeared and Edgar was unsure which direction he was facing. The shield walls had collapsed into a chaotic melee. Leofwin and Brictwin were soon by his side.

'Back off!' Leofwin shouted in his ear.

But Edgar didn't want to back away from the fight now, not when they had broken through the enemy's line.

Leofwin grabbed him by the arm.

'We need you alive!' he demanded.

Edgar nodded. He had to control himself. He let Leofwin lead him back a few yards, to where young Ragulf held the Magnian flag.

He took the opportunity to look around the battlefield. While the Barissian shield wall had given way at this point, it had stood firm elsewhere along the line, and the Magnians hadn't been able to take advantage of it, getting caught up in hand to hand fighting with the rear ranks of the Barissians who had moved to block the hole. Even now, Barissians and Magnians were backing away from each other as the first few frantic minutes of battle led to a pause. The Barissians continued to retreat, leaving a space between the two sides, and allowing everyone to catch their breath.

Edgar could hear the sound of fighting from his right, suggesting that the Thessians and Barissians in the centre were still going at it, but he was too far away to see. Ahead, though, he could quite clearly see the bodies of the dead littering the ground between the two armies. It hadn't taken long for the two sides to have killed so many. Some of the badly wounded took the chance to leave the front line, helped along by their comrades. Their fight was over already.

The Barissians were on the move again, but instead of renewing the attack they retreated further backwards. Edgar looked down after them. He was about to ask Leofwin whether they should order an attack, then he closed his mouth again. The infantry was withdrawing to allow the Barissian cavalry to advance.

'Spearmen!' Edgar shouted, and others joined in the call, as the Magnians reorganised themselves. The long spears were the best defence against cavalry, a bristling line of wood and iron that deterred a charge. The Magnian spearmen readied themselves, some of them planting the shaft against the ground to give the weapon greater resistance.

The Barissian cavalry also carried spears. They had now organised themselves into a straight line and advanced towards the waiting Magnians. Not a charge, but intimidating nonetheless. Their warhorses were bred for the battlefield and could reach sixteen hands in height.

The Barissian cavalry came at the Magnian position. Some of them hurled spears, standing in the stirrups to give them extra force. But all had to be mindful of the Magnian spearmen, who could cripple their horses if they got too close. Unlike the brutal shoving and thrusting of the infantry clash, this was more a test of discipline. The horsemen started to approach the Magnian line, looking for any weaknesses, before retreating away. Some of the Magnian spearmen gave chase but those who went too far found that the horses could quickly be turned around and were cut off, isolated, and brought down. Meanwhile, those spearmen who worked together could approach an isolated horseman from several angles and get in a strike on a horse, bringing the rider to the ground and skewering them.

This game of cat and mouse went on for some time, before the Barissian cavalry retreated down to the road. They had made little impact in terms of casualties, but had tied up the Magnian spearmen, forcing them to concentrate while their own infantry could rest. The Barissian infantry, though, now returned for a second time—the drums behind them beating out a marching rhythm.

Once more, the Magnian shield wall set itself in place to meet the attack. Once more, Edgar placed himself in the third rank. His army needed him to stay alive. Even at the best of times it was common for soldiers' morale to break if their leader died. Here, in a battle that Edgar knew not all his men thought necessary, that was even more likely.

Those archers who still had arrows left fired them at the enemy. Those with shields raised them in defence. Then, the Barissians came at them again, the shield walls clashing against each other. The Magnian spearmen in front of Edgar resumed their deadly work, reaching out to strike the enemy where they could. The Barissians forced the Magnians a few paces backwards. The spearmen, unable to use their weapons effectively in the more confined space, gave way for Edgar's rank to move in, pushing back against the Barissians and chopping and thrusting with their shorter weapons.

The grunts and screams of pain returned as men on both sides suffered injuries. The stink of sweat and piss assailed Edgar as he supported the man in front, while looking to attack the Barissian wall. Their shields were packed tight. He thought about crouching down to look for an opening, but with the press of bodies feared that he might lose his footing. He found that he was shouting: mindless, animal roars. *Madness,* he thought to himself. *Why do men do this? Utter madness.*

Eventually the two walls broke apart, nothing gained by either side. Again, it was the Barissians who withdrew. Were their efforts getting more half-hearted, Edgar wondered? He remembered Duke Coen's thoughts about Emeric's army. Many of them were mercenaries, and mercenaries weren't keen on getting themselves killed or maimed. But that was what everyone faced here. Neither side was gaining an advantage, and the longer it went on, the more the casualties would pile up.

The front rank was battered and bruised. Some had huge gashes inflicted on them. Others had broken ribs. Fresher soldiers came in to replace those who couldn't remain. But the new arrivals were generally younger and less experienced. Edgar was getting increasingly keen for this to end, but Coen's tactics were to hold their position, and so that was what they must do.

There followed a lull in the battle as the Barissians seemed in no hurry to renew their attack. Some of the soldiers sat down to rest. From somewhere Brictwin had been given a flask of ale which he passed on to Edgar. Edgar took a swig before passing it on to Leofwin.

'Your Highness!' came a shout.

Edgar walked to the front of his army, and looked into the distance, where some of his soldiers were pointing. Onto the road came a new cavalry force. It took Edgar a while to register what it was. The Barissian reserves. A large force of mounted men was heading their way. Emeric had played his last card. The intention was clear. His reserves had been sent to drive the Magnians from the battlefield, and then turn on the Thessians.

'Ready yourselves!' shouted Edgar. 'Get a message to our cavalry!'

He wanted to make sure that Wilchard had seen the danger—though in truth, his steward's small force could have little impact on the numbers heading their way.

The Barissian reserves joined up with the cavalry of their right division and swung around, aiming for the far corner of the Magnian line. They were constrained from manoeuvring much farther to their right by the caltrops laid by Coen's men.

They were coming at speed, much faster than the first cavalry attack of the day. His men had their line of spears ready for impact. Edgar got a glimpse of Wilchard's force making a feint towards the Barissians, before turning their mounts around and retreating. A good portion of the Barissian cavalry chased after them.

Well, considered Edgar, *that was all Wilchard could have done. If he had tried to engage he would have been swept aside.*

Meanwhile, the main part of the Barissian cavalry came crashing into Edgar's infantry, only a few yards from where the Prince himself was standing. Some of the horses were speared and came crashing down to the ground, thrashing in agony. The Magnian line was disrupted, with more horsemen riding through and engaging the defenders. The far corner of Edgar's division started to bend out of shape, as the impact of the attack pushed people out of place.

Edgar was quick to see the danger. If he didn't shore up the Magnian position it could quickly be overrun.

'Come on!' he instructed his two bodyguards and, for once, Leofwin didn't argue.

'The Prince! The Prince!' Leofwin shouted, letting those in front know that Edgar was coming.

Men saw Edgar arrive and redoubled their efforts, organising a line around him. Edgar pressed onwards, taking the fight to the Barissians. The battle line was now a mess of bodies, both man and horse. The Magnians could move in and out of the obstacles more easily than the mounted Barissians, who had to take care where they took their horses.

Edgar knocked away a lunged spear with his sword and then slashed it across the face of the rider's horse. The beast backed away, its rider struggling to stay on. Edgar then moved to support Brictwin, who was being pushed back by two riders. He drew one of the riders towards him.

Looking up, Edgar got a shock. It was a face he recognised. It took a split second for him to work out why he would recognise one of the Barissians. It was Gervase Salvinus, the man who had led the attack on Toric's Temple. Edgar remembered their eyes meeting across the yard of the temple complex, before Salvinus had led his men away. This time, they were a lot closer. They locked eyes again. Recognition flared on Salvinus's face. Maybe only now did he realise that the man he had encountered at Ecgworth was the Prince of South Magnia.

'To me!' shouted Salvinus, his voice carrying across the battlefield. 'Kill their Prince!'

Salvinus trotted forwards, raising his spear above his head as if Edgar were a fish he was about to skewer. Leofwin appeared to Edgar's left, threatening the mercenary leader. Outnumbered, Salvinus was in a dangerous position. If he made a lunge at Edgar, he would expose himself to an attack from Leofwin. Instead, he backed away from them.

'To the Prince!' shouted Leofwin.

Magnian soldiers began to congregate around them. Ragulf arrived with the standard. At the same time, Edgar could see Salvinus organising his mercenaries for another attack. These were the men who had served under him for years. Experienced, ruthless men. No doubt many of the soldiers who had raided Toric's Temple were here. So be it. It seemed to Edgar that the next few minutes would decide the outcome of the battle.

After being protected back in the third rank for most of the battle, Edgar now stood in the centre of his front line. Leofwin had found him a shield to use. If the Barissians were in any doubt, Ragulf's flag flew above him, indicating exactly where he was. But he needed to be there. His men needed to see him fighting for them, if they were to fight for him.

Salvinus and the Barissians came for them. Their objective was clear: kill Edgar, force the Magnians off the battlefield, and then encircle Coen and the Thessians.

Salvinus wanted the kill for himself. He shoved his spear straight at Edgar. Edgar blocked it with his shield. The force of the strike made him stagger backwards, but someone behind propped him up and kept him on his feet. Someone sent a spear in Salvinus's direction, but he casually swerved out of the way. He sent his spear back towards Edgar, but somehow Leofwin was waiting for the move. Edgar's bodyguard lashed out with his sword, and cut the wooden shaft in two. Salvinus let out a roar of frustration, throwing the useless half of the weapon in Leofwin's direction, and drawing his sword.

A few of Salvinus's men came for them, trying to take Leofwin down as much as Edgar. Edgar fought with desperation. For the first time, he felt the battle rage that men talked about around the fire, as adrenaline pumped through his body. He shoved forward with his shield arm, blocking strikes, aiming for the nose of any horse that got too close. He swung his right arm down, raining down blows with his sword, forcing the enemy to keep their distance. Again, and again, he hammered his weapon down, his fury seemingly giving him limitless energy. Beside him, Brictwin was doing the same. As Brictwin moved forwards so too did the soldiers to his right, so that the whole Magnian line shifted around.

Salvinus was now out of sight, the to and fro of battle pulling him one way, and Edgar another.

The Magnian aggression had seen off the Barissian attacks for now. Cavalry were used for speed and manoeuvrability, for chasing down enemies. They could be used for a mass charge. But against an organised shield wall equipped with spears and swords, they were less effective.

Edgar could see some of them circling around, trying to get behind the Magnian line. This was dangerous. If they got into the softer rear of the Magnian forces, the Barissians could break up his division and isolate his men. Edgar looked over to where Frayne's Middian reserves had been kept for such an eventuality, but there was no sign of them. If they didn't come and help soon, his division might be lost.

Shouting from behind grabbed his attention. Turning to look, Edgar could see his worst fears being realised. A large group of Barissian cavalry were engaging with the rear of his force.

'Shit,' he said out loud.

'It's the force that chased off Wilchard's cavalry,' commented Leofwin, who had turned to look in the same direction. 'They've double backed on us.'

'We'll have to deal with them,' said Edgar. It was part statement, part question.

Leofwin nodded grimly. 'I think so.'

Ordering some of his men to hold the front line, Edgar led another group towards the new threat. Again, Leofwin and Brictwin shouted and pushed men out of the way, so that Edgar could march straight towards the enemy. Ragulf followed on, bringing a stream of soldiers who would fight under the Magnian flag. Edgar wasted no time in getting stuck into the enemy, reinforcing the resolve of the more inexperienced and poorly equipped soldiers in his army. Brictwin leapt into the air, crashing his sword against a mounted Barissian with the full force of his bodyweight and armour behind the blow. The Barissian toppled off the back of his horse which turned and bolted, straight into a group of riders, causing their horses to fret and dance away. A cheer rose from the Magnians who ran at the enemy while they were still disoriented, grabbing at reins and pulling more men from their horses.

Any attempt at creating a shield wall now seemed hopeless. Instead Edgar and his band of men began to roam the battlefield, looking for the most dangerous looking Barissians. They intercepted a group of Barissian infantry who had marched into the melee with some degree of discipline, and had begun to pick off stranded Magnians. Edgar attacked, swinging his sword at the tallest of them, who blocked it with a shield, the impact sending a vibration up Edgar's arm. The man returned the favour, launching a massive axe in his direction. Edgar got his shield in front of it just in time, but was still stunned by the force of the blow, which sent him down to one knee. It also gave him a dead shield arm, making him unable to clench his left hand. Still on one knee, Edgar swung his sword at the axeman, hoping to catch his legs. But the Barissian jumped back to avoid the stroke.

The battle fury of a few minutes before was now dissipating. Edgar was getting tired from his exertions in full armour, and every muscle in his body seemed to ache.

The Barissian infantry came at them, but Leofwin was at his most dangerous when he could counterattack. He avoided a wild spear thrust and lunged forwards, smashing his shield into the face of the spearman with a massive crack that floored the Barissian. With lightning speed, he crashed the hilt of his sword into the face of another soldier, before thrusting it into the side of the axeman who had tangled with Edgar, penetrating his armour. He struggled to pull it free, but by then Edgar and Brictwin were falling on the enemy, forcing them on the defensive until those that could, turned and ran back the way they had come.

Suddenly, Edgar couldn't move.

It was the strangest feeling. His feet couldn't lift from the floor, his fingers were stuck in place, holding his sword and shield. He couldn't turn his head to look around. Then, he heard and felt horsemen approaching.

Something clattered into him, dragging him to the floor. He felt, rather than saw, riders whistle past him. He found that he could move freely once more.

Brictwin quickly helped him to his feet. Edgar looked around to get his bearings.

The disintegration of the Magnian shield wall was allowing the Barissian cavalry to manoeuvre around the battlefield at will, and this group had come at Edgar from behind, while he had been pinned in place by some force. Brictwin had pushed him out of the way just in time. Others hadn't been so fortunate. Ragulf, his standard bearer, lay dead on the floor, the Magnian banner of the Sun in Glory trampled into the ground.

'Get them!' shouted Leofwin off to the side, keen to engage the Barissians before they could wheel away and do it again. They had ridden into a second group of Magnians, and were trying to extricate themselves.

Edgar, suspecting magic, looked about the battlefield, but couldn't see any signs of a wizard. He had to assume that Ealdnoth was protecting him.

Edgar wasn't sure if he had the energy to move anymore, but when Leofwin ran after the Barissians he made himself follow. His lungs burned with the effort, and his legs felt like jelly. How could he swing his sword when he was this exhausted? At that moment, he wished that he had fought on horseback instead of on foot. But when he got to the enemy he somehow found the strength to raise his sword and fight once more.

One of the horsemen had dismounted and came for Edgar, perhaps keen to win the glory of taking down the Magnian Prince. Edgar had lost his shield, probably when Brictwin had bundled him over. When the Barissian swung his sword at him, Edgar blocked it in a two-handed stroke. The clash of steel rang out and Edgar's arms shuddered with the impact.

He was tiring, he knew. He could no longer raise his arms up high enough anymore, his shoulders aching with each effort. He blocked another swing. Self-preservation was the only reason he could keep doing it. If his life wasn't in immediate danger, he would have collapsed onto the floor by now. The Barissian came at him again. This time, Edgar used footwork to avoid the swinging sword. There was an opening in his opponent's defence, but Edgar was too tired to take it, preferring to circle around. Just gripping the hilt of his sword and moving was hard enough now. His opponent smiled at him, sensing his weakness. Then, Brictwin approached from behind, striking down on the top of his head like he was cracking a nut. The skull caved in and the body collapsed to the floor.

Edgar put the tip of his sword into the ground to keep himself standing. His head was spinning. He vomited, too tired to lean over, instead letting the fluid dribble down his chest. He looked around the battlefield but struggled to make much sense of it. For the moment, there weren't any Barissians in the immediate vicinity.

Another group of horsemen approached them. But they were wearing Magnian colours. The lead rider removed his helmet. It was Wilchard.

'We've done it!' he crowed, a big beaming smile on his face.

Could it be true? Edgar took a second look over the battlefield, trying to focus. The Barissian cavalry had mostly departed. A few skirmishes continued, but the fighting had almost stopped. He looked down towards the road. Barissian infantry could be seen heading north the way they had come. His Magnians stood or slumped all over the battlefield. Any sense of organisation had all but gone. But they had won.

He looked at Brictwin and Leofwin, both wearing grins of their own. For some reason, Edgar couldn't bring himself to smile back.

'What happened?' he asked Wilchard, his voice coming out as an unrecognisable croak. His throat was parched dry.

'Emeric threw his reserves at you,' said Wilchard.

This, Edgar already knew.

'When Frayne saw that you were withstanding them, he took the Middians around and attacked the Barissian left. He fought off their cavalry and then got into their infantry. The Barissian left collapsed, and then their central division was hit.

'Meanwhile, the reserves who chased us off the battlefield came back and hit you hard. But we came back to hit them from behind. When they realised what was happening on the rest of the battlefield, they knew they had lost.'

'So,' said Edgar, 'the Magnians took the brunt of the damage when Salvinus brought his reserves against us.'

'True,' said Leofwin, 'it sounds like we suffered the most. But we won, Edgar! And you led us to victory. I know that your father would have been very proud to see you today. Today you became a different kind of leader to the one you were yesterday. The men who fought here won't forget it.'

Edgar had rarely seen Leofwin get so emotional. It brought a lump to his own throat, and he reached out to grab the older man's shoulder, who hugged him back.

'Thank you both,' he said to Leofwin and Brictwin. 'Brictwin? Would you mind recovering our standard?'

'Of course, Your Highness.'

Brictwin carefully picked up the standard, still cradled by Ragulf's broken body. He took it to Edgar who passed it up to Wilchard. When his steward held it aloft, it elicited a cheer from those men gathered about. It was dirty and damaged in places. But it had survived.

THE SECOND DISCIPLE

XVIII

Belwynn was looking forward to getting out of Heractus Castle. The atmosphere remained awkward, with a King and a Grand Master occupying the same building, and nobody sure who was in charge of what.

Yesterday's news made her even more eager to leave. A Krykker army was marching to Heractus to ally with the Knights. Belwynn could only assume that Rabigar had worked some miracle there, and persuaded those who had exiled him to join in the fight against Ishari. But the result was that the castle had become a hive of manic activity as Theron and Sebastian worked day and night to prepare for another military expedition—this time into Haskany. Food and other supplies had to be found. Maps of enemy territory needed to be carefully studied. Belwynn was delighted that things were suddenly moving so fast, but she knew she wasn't needed.

Prince Dorian had offered to take her down into the city. Unlike the rest of his family, he seemed to bear her no ill will. As they left the castle gatehouse, Belwynn wondered whether it was all an elaborate sham, and she was about to be killed and dumped somewhere. But she doubted it.

As Dorian pointed out the sights in Heractus, Belwynn warmed to the city a little. The morning sunshine helped to dispel the poor first impression she had received. There was still a lot of grey, it was true. But she realised that Heractus wasn't trying to impress her. The Kalinthian people seemed reserved, yet dignified; and Belwynn didn't mind that.

'The building where your friends are staying is just up here,' said Dorian, taking them along one of the central city streets.

'I have to ask,' said Belwynn. 'You've been very welcoming, Dorian, under the circumstances. Is there a reason you don't hate me, like the rest of your family?'

'Hate you?' Dorian responded. 'I'm not sure that anyone in my family hates *you*. Count Theron is another story, maybe,' he said with a grin. 'The way I see things is, Grand Master Sebastian wants the best for the country. So does my father.' He shrugged. 'I'm hopeful that they can work things out. Here we are.'

It was a large town house, built from grey stone and wood. It suggested that some of Elana's supporters had been willing to spend a considerable amount of money.

The door was open, and she knocked before entering. Several people were sitting or standing in the front room, mostly women and children. Elana was there, talking with a middle-aged woman. She looked around to see Belwynn come in and smiled at her. Belwynn and Dorian waited near the door. With a few words, Elana extricated herself and came over to greet them. 'Belwynn, it's good to see you. How are things?'

'Fine. It's busy up at the castle. We've got word that a Krykker army is coming. I'm hoping that Rabigar will be with them. This is Prince Dorian, the son of King Jonas.'

Dorian took Elana's hand and pressed his lips to it. 'You are a healer?' asked the Prince.

'Yes. Word's got around a bit,' Elana said wryly, indicating the group of people congregating in the room.

'Thank you for ministering to our citizens. Please let me know how I can help. Any provisions you need, or anything else—'

Elana smiled. 'Well, there are a few things.'

'Write me a list before we leave. I will see to it.'

'Thank you, Your Highness. Was there anything in particular you wanted, Belwynn?'

'Yes, I wanted to speak to you and Dirk. Is he in?'

'Yes, he's upstairs resting. Come up.'

Dorian waited downstairs while Elana led Belwynn up to the next storey.

'Are there many people staying here?'

'Oh, yes. Theron has filled the house with his knights. I think the whole city is full to bursting. The Prince seems nice.'

'Yes. The rest of his family are a bit of a nightmare, but he seems different.'

'How are Sebastian and Theron?'

'Fine. Just busy with army stuff.'

Elana stopped and knocked on the door of one of the upstairs rooms. After a pause, Belwynn heard Dirk's voice.

'Come in.'

Belwynn followed in behind Elana, to the sound of Dirk coughing. He was sitting up in bed, looking no better than the last time Belwynn had seen him.

'How are you feeling?' she asked.

Dirk pulled a face. 'The honest version is, not great. I think the last week has taken a lot out of me.'

'I wanted to talk to you both,' Belwynn began nervously. Now that she was here and ready to talk, she felt a bit foolish.

'Go on,' said Elana encouragingly.

'I've been doing a lot of thinking lately. About all kinds of things. Not just Soren, but what we've all been through—what we still must do. I've changed my mind about a lot of things.' Belwynn was still struggling to get her words out. 'Elana. I would like to become a disciple of Madria. If you think it's not a good idea, I totally understand—'

'Oh, Belwynn!' Elana interrupted her, smiling. 'Of course! It feels perfect!'

The two women embraced. Dirk struggled out of his bed and gave Belwynn a hug.

'It just feels like the right thing to do,' said Belwynn, wiping her eyes which had become wet with tears. 'Thank you for saying yes.'

'I know that you've made the right decision,' said Dirk, settling back onto his bed. 'I've been doing a lot of thinking myself. For some reason, this feels like the right place for Elana to settle and work. I'm so grateful that you've made this decision now. Because it helps me with my own. I've asked Elana to stop healing me. She's kept me alive for this long, but she can't do any more.'

'No, Dirk!' said Belwynn.

Dirk raised a hand, asking her to let him finish. 'I'm in a lot of pain, and I feel like my work is done, now.'

'You can't mean that.'

Belwynn looked to Elana, but the priestess had a resigned look on her face, as if Dirk had already discussed this with her.

'I am at peace with the decision, Belwynn,' Dirk explained. 'I protected Elana from Nexodore. I travelled with her to safety here. My responsibility as first disciple is complete. I now pass it on to you. But first, let me witness the moment.'

At first, Belwynn didn't understand what Dirk meant by 'the moment'. Then she recalled how he had become Elana's first disciple back in Vitugia.

The image of it was burned into Belwynn's memory. She went down onto her knees.

'Elana, I submit my soul to Madria's keeping, and ask that I become your disciple.'

'This is what Madria wishes,' replied Elana. 'Belwynn of Beckford, you shall be my second disciple.'

Elana reached over to touch Belwynn's forehead. Belwynn stood. She felt like something very important had just happened—maybe the most important moment of her life. At the same time, she had the feeling that a great weight had been lifted from her.

* * *

'We'll need your support,' Gyrmund said to Zared, the young man who seemed to be the leader of the Persaleian prisoners.

'It's tonight?' Zared asked.

The poor light inside the pit flickered on his features, emphasising the look of manic excitement that briefly flitted across his face.

'Phase one,' replied Gyrmund, before moving on to his usual position with Herin and Clarin towards the far end of the pit.

They looked as calm as ever, but their insides had to be churning as much as Gyrmund's. They were taking their first step towards escape.

Vamak and the other four Dog-men began their nightly tour of the pit.

'Mind where you tread,' demanded Clarin as they walked past. The Dog-men turned their heads to look at him, disbelief showing on all their faces. Clarin's challenge had come from nothing, and Gyrmund could see that, for a moment, it had put them on the back foot.

Vamak slowly approached, his muzzle widening into an unpleasant grin. 'So, it's time for us to play, is it?' he asked, his eyes lighting up in anticipation.

The other Dog-men backed him up. One of them stared straight at Gyrmund, as if he was challenging him to their own, separate fight.

Herin moved forwards. Gyrmund did the same.

'This is between the two of them,' Herin demanded, indicating Clarin and Vamak. 'You four can back off,' he added.

'Is that right?' asked Vamak.

'Yes,' said Zared, moving towards the confrontation with Cyprian and about another dozen Persaleians. Rudy and Jurgen were there too, the cousins from Rotelegen who had fought with Ellard. They formed a circle around

Clarin and Vamak. Gyrmund and Herin joined it, Herin pointing to the Dog-men, to indicate that they should do the same.

They looked to Vamak for leadership, who angrily shoved a clawed hand in their direction, directing them to join the circle. He clearly wasn't happy at this show of strength against him, but he was trying to look in control.

Now that the circle was complete, Vamak and Clarin paced around it, eyeing each other up. Vamak's dark eyes glittered in the half-light of the pit, and his muscles rippled as he moved. Some of the others in the pit scurried over to watch.

Vamak came for Clarin, clawed hands going for his neck. Clarin met him, grabbing Vamak's arms around the biceps. The Dog-man snapped his jaws, but Clarin kept him at arm's length. Vamak lifted one leg and aimed a kick, but Clarin blocked it with his knee. Each now had a firm grip on the other's arms and they pushed and pulled at each other, twisting one way and then another. Neither gained an advantage. Gyrmund could see blood where the Dog-man's claws gripped Clarin's arms. Clarin let go, banged Vamak's arms away and punched him hard in the stomach. Vamak let out a bark of pain and jumped backwards.

'Finish him!' shouted Herin in a bloodthirsty voice.

The Dog-men barked across the circle, baring their fangs.

Clarin moved towards Vamak, but the Dog-man sprang out of the way, then unleashed a vicious swing, his claws scraping down Clarin's forearm, drawing more blood. Clarin grabbed his arm in pain and Vamak was on him, claws flashing. The big man tried to move out of the way, but Vamak launched himself at him, sinking his teeth into Clarin's shoulder. Now Clarin cried out in pain, smashing his elbow onto Vamak's head to dislodge him. Vamak kicked out and sent Clarin sprawling backwards towards Gyrmund.

Gyrmund quickly reached down and picked him up before Vamak could do more damage. Clarin fumbled around with one hand behind him. Gyrmund looked down just in time to see Herin passing something into his hand. He caught a glimpse of something glinting in the darkness before Clarin staggered off to the side.

His movements looked tired and clumsy. A cruel smile spread over Vamak's face as the Dog-man took his time to move in for the kill.

Gyrmund looked at Herin in concern.

Herin winked at him.

Vamak leapt towards his prey. Clarin sidestepped the attack and brought one hand down on top of Vamak's head, holding him still in an iron grip. With the other hand, he punched hard into Vamak's neck. From his place in the circle, Gyrmund could see a piece of crystal, with a strip of leather wrapped around it to make a grip, poking out of Clarin's fist as he punctured a blood vessel.

Clarin punched again, tearing into Vamak's neck. Blood gushed out, soaking Clarin, and spilling onto the floor of the pit. Clarin let Vamak drop to the floor, blood still pumping out of the lifeless body.

A cheer rose around the circle.

'We're in charge now!' shouted Herin, striding into the circle to stand with his brother. He pointed at the Dog-men. 'Either you accept that or you die.'

Gyrmund looked at the men of Persala, blood lust showing on their faces. They seemed more than ready to finish the job, and the Dog-men saw it too. They scurried over to Clarin and Herin, heads down in submission, tails tucked between their legs.

'You do what we tell you, now,' Herin informed them.

The Dog-man on the far end was grabbed by a couple of Persaleians and dragged away. One of them punched him to the floor, the creature yelping in pain. Others then joined in, punching and kicking at their victim. Gyrmund moved to intervene, but Herin put an arm to his chest, shaking his head. They made short work of it, leaving a bloody corpse. Emboldened, a group of them came back for another one. It whined in fear.

'No,' said Herin, holding out an arm. 'They might be useful.'

'That's enough,' said Zared, coming over to add his authority. 'Back to your places.'

The men shuffled off, obedient enough.

'You do what we tell you or die,' said Herin to the remaining Dog-men.

Their eyes already filled with terror, they nodded at him. 'Yes, sir,' one of them said.

'Go to your old places for now,' said Herin. 'It's the safest place for you.'

They backed away to the far end of the pit.

'Well done,' said Zared, shaking Clarin by the hand. 'Are you badly hurt?'

'I don't think so,' said Clarin with a little grin. 'I was faking the injury. He gave me a good bite on the shoulder, mind.'

Herin took a look. 'I don't think it's too bad. I'll do my best to clean it.'

'What now?' asked Zared.

'We need to be ready to escape any night from now,' said Herin. 'But we can't give anything away to the guards. What do you think they'll make of them?' he asked Zared, nodding at the two corpses.

'They're not going to care about two dead prisoners. Fights happen all the time in this place. So long as there are enough of us for the mines, they don't give a shit about anything else. My concern is over them,' he said, gesturing at the Dog-men who had been spared.

'Let us deal with that,' said Herin. 'They don't know anything about the escape plan, after all. But when it comes to it, they might just be useful. We're going to need all the fighters we can get if we're going to break out of here.'

Zared nodded, conceding the point. 'I can't believe we're going to do it.'

'It won't be easy,' warned Gyrmund.

Zared looked at him. 'We're all ready to get out of this hell or die trying. Don't worry about that.'

* * *

RABIGAR LOOKED about him as thousands of Krykkers shouted at each other in the fields outside Heractus.

There was already a camp owned by the Knights of Kalinth outside the city—Heractus itself was too full to house all the Knights, never mind being able to find room for the biggest Krykker army that had been raised in generations. It looked like a logistical nightmare. But it wasn't Rabigar's problem. Three clan chiefs—Torinac, Maragin, and Guremar, had joint control of the army. No. Rabigar was quite happy to leave things to them, and wandered over towards the Kalinthian camp, leaving the noise and aggravation behind him.

He wasn't used to being with so many people for so long. Torinac had allowed him to serve with the soldiers of clan Dramsen—it wouldn't be possible to fight with his old clan, the Grendals. To many of them, he would always be a chieftain killer. Rabigar was extremely grateful to the Dramsens for accepting him, and was keen to pull his weight. But as the days passed, his patience wore thin. Long days marching in the heat of summer; inane conversations and pointless banter; shouting, snoring and farting; boasting, posturing and bullying. It all got too much after a while. His younger self would have loved the experience. But Din the exile was too used to his own company. In other words, he had become a miserable old git.

'Rabigar!' called a voice.

Looking up, he saw Belwynn, half running towards him from the direction of the Kalinthian camp. Rabigar smiled. He had missed the girl; he hadn't realised how much until now. She looked as beautiful as ever—though there was sadness in her eyes, too.

'I can't believe it was that easy!' she said in greeting, slightly out of breath. 'I thought I was going to have to search through the whole army to find you.'

They gave each other a hug.

'Well, it's good to see you,' said Rabigar. 'How is everyone else?'

'That's why I came to find you. Dirk is dying.'

THEY TALKED little on the way to Elana's house. Belwynn spoke of her decision to become Elana's disciple, a move that surprised Rabigar. But it didn't feel right to discuss other things before seeing Dirk.

'Here it is,' said Belwynn.

The front door of the house was open, and she led Rabigar in, then up the stairs to Dirk's room. He was sitting up in bed, but his eyes were closed. Rabigar had only once seen him look so ill, in the immediate aftermath of the attack by Nexodore, in the lands of the Blood Caladri. At that time, they had all assumed he would die, but Elana had somehow kept him alive all this time. He was emaciated, his skin thin and translucent looking, his bones more pronounced. Elana sat in a chair by his bed. She rose to greet Rabigar. He gave her a hug.

'How is the patient?' he asked.

Dirk opened his eyes. 'Rabigar?' he said. 'It's good to see you again.'

'You too, my friend,' said Rabigar, gripping his hand.

'And you've brought an army with you?'

'Yes. The Krykkers and the Knights of Kalinth fighting together. Things should get interesting over the next few days.'

Rabigar took a couple of paces back to stand next to Belwynn.

'I'm sorry I'll miss it,' Dirk said quietly.

'Me too. Is there nothing Elana can do?'

'Yes. She could keep me alive a while longer, I'm sure. But I don't want that any more, Rabigar. I'm at peace with it.'

Dirk turned awkwardly on the bed. 'Belwynn has become Elana's disciple. I won't be leaving her alone, now.'

'Yes,' said Rabigar. 'So I've heard.'

'I'm glad you're all here,' Dirk continued. 'Elana?'

'Yes,' replied the priestess. She opened a chest located in the corner of the room, taking out Toric's Dagger. She silently passed it on to him. They had obviously discussed the weapon between themselves before.

'I will no longer be the keeper of Toric's Dagger,' said Dirk. 'I used it once, to kill Nexodore. Now someone else may have need of it. I think it should be you, Belwynn. In this also, you are my successor.'

'Are you sure?' asked Belwynn, hesitant to accept the weapon. 'I already look after Onella's Staff.'

'True,' replied Dirk. 'But the staff will be Soren's eventually.'

Belwynn smiled. 'I hadn't thought of that. I hope you are right.'

'I have a sense that he will take ownership of the Staff. As for the Dagger, I feel it still has more work to do. Will you accept it, Belwynn?'

'Of course.'

Belwynn moved to Dirk's bed. He handed her the weapon, and they held hands for a while.

Dirk closed his eyes and leaned back in the bed. It looked like he had been freed of the responsibility and could finally rest. They stayed with him for his last moments until he passed away. Rabigar and Belwynn left the room so that Elana could have some time alone. Wordlessly, they both headed downstairs, keen to get outside and take some fresh air.

'So, in the end, Nexodore *did* kill him,' commented Rabigar, unable to avoid a feeling of bitterness.

'He died at peace, Rabigar,' said Belwynn. 'Most people don't get that.'

'True. And I can understand the timing.'

'You mean my becoming a disciple? It makes me feel a little like I killed him.'

'I wasn't thinking about that, though I expect it helped him to make his decision. I mean, the war ahead of us. Elana's powers will be needed when the fighting starts. Who knows how much it cost her to keep Dirk alive all this time?'

'I hadn't considered that,' said Belwynn. 'I'm not even sure that Elana's powers work like that—in the same way as Soren's magic.'

'It's exactly the same,' said Rabigar.

He seemed so sure that Belwynn didn't see the point of discussing it further.

'Have you heard from Soren?' Rabigar asked.

'No, not in the whole time since you left. I fear for him, and for Clarin and the others too, of course. But I sense that he still lives. Maybe you don't understand, Rabigar, but finding my faith in Madria has helped me to deal with it. I feel like their fate is in Her hands. It's a comfort.'

'I understand well,' replied Rabigar. *After all, I know much about loss.* 'I take Elana's message from Madria seriously. I mentioned to you before, after we left Edeleny, that the Krykkers have one of Madria's weapons. Bolivar's Great Sword, that he used to defeat the Isharites at the Battle of Alta. It is here. We have brought it with us. So, we now have three of the seven weapons in the same place. Maybe that is enough to destroy Ishari.'

'Elana believes we need all seven to do that.'

The Krykker legends implied Bolivar won his victory single-handed. But Rabigar had learned enough of the world to think that Elana's version was probably correct.

'Then maybe it is enough for us to win a victory. A victory big enough to see your brother go free.'

'I pray that it will be.'

SIEGE

XIX

The walls of Coldeberg loomed large. Edgar could see the southern wall ahead of him, but also the far northern wall, which rose higher. The city was situated on a hill, on the summit of which the dukes of Barissia had built their mighty castle. *Nothing in Magnia comes close to being so well defended,* Edgar reflected. None of this deterred Duke Coen, however. Along with his troops, he had carted huge siege engines to the capital city of his enemy, Emeric.

Inside somewhere was Emeric and the remnants of his army. It had been defeated at the Battle of Lindhafen, but not destroyed. Frayne's Middian cavalry force had given chase to the Barissians, but a substantial part of Emeric's army had been on horseback, and they had successfully fought a rearguard action, allowing his soldiers to make an orderly retreat, and thereby avoiding a massacre.

Edgar's Magnians had seen the worst of the fighting. Many had died. Many more had serious injuries, and Coen had sent them to his capital, Lindhafen, for treatment. The rest of the Magnians, who could be described as the walking wounded, had travelled on to Coldeberg to see the campaign to the end.

Edgar put himself firmly in the camp of the walking wounded. After the battle was over, he noticed injuries he hadn't even known he'd sustained. They had celebrated with barrels of Thessian wine, which did a good job of keeping the pain at bay. But it came back with a vengeance the next morning.

He felt like he had been thrown from a castle's battlements onto the ground below. His shoulders, arms and legs were a constant dull ache, muscles too stiff to move after his exertions the day before. His back and neck were agony, the slightest movement flaring sharp jolts of pain up and down his spine. He had a headache that wouldn't go away, and a ringing in his ears.

Leofwin and Brictwin had picked him up and forced him to walk around while they supported him on each side. They insisted it did him good to loosen up his muscles, though all they received from him for their help was a string of curse words. Edgar was by no means the only one in such bad shape, and the Magnians had been excused any physical duties since the battle. Edgar still had aches and pains today. He was quite happy to take an observer's role in the siege, while the Thessians prepared camp defences and began constructing siege equipment.

Edgar had one job to do, however. Coen insisted on the formality of offering the besieged army terms. To Edgar's mind, Emeric's association with Erkindrix of Ishari made such an approach unnecessary and dangerous. But Coen saw it as important, and Edgar had agreed to go with him as the representative of the Southern Alliance. Though he had insisted that Ealdnoth accompany them. Emeric had his own wizard within the walls, and Edgar had no doubt that he would love to see Edgar and Coen dead.

Edgar and Ealdnoth rode ahead to meet Coen, who had come with only one man, holding up a white flag of parley. They made their way to the main gate of the city.

It was a still summer's day, and the flags on the battlements hung limply. The Boar of Barissia could be seen, along with Emeric's newest banner, the Golden Crown. Emeric's decision to claim a crown for himself was starting to cost him dear. Edgar had no sympathy.

The walls were heavily manned by soldiers, confirming their intelligence that Emeric retained a large portion of his army within the city.

Coen looked over at Ealdnoth with poorly concealed distaste. 'This wizard of Emeric's. He was at the battle, then?'

'He was, Your Grace,' replied Ealdnoth. 'He was working against the Magnian division and targeted Prince Edgar.'

'Hmm. Is he likely to pose us problems during the siege?'

'He is a powerful wizard. He could pose several threats. Setting fire to siege weapons, targeting individuals on our side. I will need to be vigilant.'

Coen nodded, seemingly willing to let Ealdnoth deal with that issue. He held a hand up, indicating that they should stop. They were still some distance from the walls, and Edgar noted that some of his own suspicions about Barissian honour had rubbed off a little on the duke.

They waited a while for someone in authority to arrive. Eventually, a man's head appeared atop the main gate. 'You are safe to approach,' he shouted at them, noting the distance at which they had stopped.

Coen looked at Edgar, who nodded his acceptance. They moved a few feet closer.

'This is Coen of Thesse, and Edgar of Magnia. With whom do we speak?'

'I am Curtis, an officer in the king's army. I recognise a truce for parley and will take your words direct to the king.'

'Nobly said, Curtis. Our message is simple. After our victory at Lindhafen, and with a superior force, we intend to take this city and to arrest the traitor, Emeric. If Duke Emeric surrenders his person to us and the city is opened to us, everyone else here will be free to leave with their possessions and will be unharmed. If there is no surrender, we will take the city by siege, and the lives of those inside will be forfeit. Is that message clear, Curtis?'

'It is, Your Grace. I will pass your terms on to the king.'

'Thank you. Then we are done.'

Edgar turned his horse around, keen to be on his way. The others came with him. 'Do you have any hope of a surrender?' asked Edgar.

'We will see,' replied Coen. 'But never underestimate the willingness of men to save their own skins.'

* * *

WHILST ASHERE'S death still haunted him, especially at night, Farred found that his days had become busy enough for him to put it to the back of his mind.

He would, at any odd time of the day, be summoned to Gustav's room. Almost always, it was to help with the wizard's transformation into a hawk. The strangeness of it didn't disappear, but each time it happened, he got more used to it. Brock had noticed these comings and goings, but Farred had made it clear it wasn't something he wanted to discuss. After his first experience, he had made the decision that it would be much easier to keep it to himself.

In addition, he supervised the watch in the Emperor's Keep. All the Kellish soldiers were deployed in the defence of the Crag, and so Walter had asked Farred to use his Magnians to keep a permanent guard, especially outside the imperial bedchamber. He made sure that his men did their duty, and rotated them regularly. But since Walter had first made him aware of the Isharite attempt to send assassins into the keep with magic, it had not happened again.

Farred was carrying out one of his checks with his men when the door to Baldwin's room slowly opened. Turning towards it, he saw a figure emerge.

It was Inge, Gustav's young apprentice. She had been given the job of staying at Baldwin's side, in case there was another attempt on his life. She looked straight at Farred, as if expecting him to be here. 'Will you come in?' she asked.

Farred crossed the few feet of floor space and arrived at the door. 'Is everything alright?'

'Yes,' she replied, smiling at him. He wasn't sure that he liked this witch's smile. 'Will you come in?' she repeated.

'Isn't His Majesty inside?'

'Yes.'

She tugged at his arm, pulling him inside the room before closing the door behind him. 'There,' she said, pointing at the bed.

Farred got a glimpse of Baldwin and quickly looked away. The Emperor was spread-eagled on the bed, completely naked. Concerned, Farred took a second glance, but could see his chest rising and falling. He was asleep. He looked at Inge.

She was studying his face, enjoying his reaction. 'I'm afraid I've tired him out,' she said.

Farred could feel his cheeks go red despite himself. There was Inge's smile again. She was smiling at him, not with him.

Farred took a second look at the witch. He had not paid her much mind, until now. When they had first met, he had been too concerned about Prince Ashere's injuries to notice her very much.

There was no doubt she was pretty. Very slim, with more of a girl's body than a woman's. Her face, too, was thin and young-looking, framed by braided, long blonde hair. Her bright blue eyes were fixed on his: sparkling at him, and mocking him at the same time. He could understand why some men might find her attractive. She was making it perfectly plain that Baldwin did.

Why had she brought him in here? To toy with him? Because she wanted to show off that she had bedded the Emperor?

'You seem surprised,' she whispered at him, her voice sounding huskier. 'What would you do if you shared a room with me day and night?'

Again, that mocking smile.

Farred felt a burst of anger. He grabbed the door handle. 'What the Emperor does is his business.'

At the same time as he said it, a contrary train of thought ran through his mind. Should he tell someone? Should he tell Walter that his brother, the Emperor, was fornicating with a witch? While his men fought for him outside on the Crag?

He pulled open the door and left the room, closing it behind him to the sound of tinkling laughter.

In the corridor, he was met with knowing smiles and winks from his men.

His mind raced with paranoia. *What, exactly, are they smiling about? Does the sound of Baldwin and Inge screwing carry through the walls?*

'Not a word,' he said, keeping the warning suitably vague.

Turning, he stomped off down the corridor.

More secrets, he said to himself. *More secrets I don't want.*

* * *

Until Theron had shown her a map, Belwynn hadn't fully appreciated how precarious Kalinth's position was.

To the north lay three enemies: Kharovia, the lands of the Drobax, and Haskany. All were under the control of Ishari. To the east lay conquered Persala. To the south, the newly conquered lands of the Grand Caladri. The only friendly border the kingdom had left was with the Krykkers. Thanks to Rabigar's intervention, they had now provided a formidable army to bolster the Kalinthian forces. But the odds seemed stacked against them, nonetheless. It made her wonder to herself whether King Jonas's policy of peace was so wrong after all. But she wasn't about to express that thought out loud. Not when Sebastian, Theron, and the rest of the Knights were risking so much on this venture.

Sebastian's close friend, Remigius, had come down with his force of knights from the High Tower, where the old Grand Master, Galenos, was still held captive. Sebastian added these knights to his army, but appointed Remi to take control of Heractus until they returned.

Prince Dorian had agreed to join the army, bringing with him a few hundred Kalinthians willing to fight for wages or advancement. When Belwynn had asked him about it, he admitted his father was unhappy with the decision—a comment which she was sure must be a massive understatement. Even if the force under Dorian's control was small, his presence lent a legitimacy to the army, for which Sebastian was extremely grateful.

After a Council of War with the Krykker chieftains, Theron had got agreement for his invasion of Haskany. There were various strategic reasons behind the decision, which Theron had explained to her, and which Belwynn only half understood. Of course, the fact that the main Haskan army was besieging Burkhard Castle in the Empire, and had therefore left the country only lightly defended, was easy enough to comprehend. But it was also felt that the move would put the greatest pressure on Ishari, and for Belwynn, that was all that really mattered. It meant that it held the greatest chance of a rescue of Soren, Clarin and the others. However remote that chance might be.

They marched at a slower pace than the army of the Knights had done on its way to Heractus. While the Krykkers kept up a mean walking pace, they travelled on foot rather than horseback. The Knights of Kalinth scouted the route ahead, but otherwise were restricted to the pace set by the Krykker infantry.

In addition, both the Knights and the Krykkers had brought many carts filled with siege equipment and other supplies. These carts trundled along at the rear of the army and acted as another brake on the pace they could set. The Kalinthians used draft horses, specially bred for their size and strength. They were larger but slower than the horses used for war. The Krykkers, meanwhile, pulled their carts with buffalo. The biggest of these reached the height of a horse. They had wicked looking curved horns that sprouted from a solid bone base which covered the top of their heads. This bone shield made them even more formidable looking, and Rabigar had warned Belwynn not to get too close to any of them.

The weather was fine. Belwynn rode next to Elana, with Dorian on the other side of the priestess. The Prince's force of Kalinthians followed behind them, positioned between the Knights and the Krykkers.

To the east, the Dardelles mountain range knifed out of the ground, serving as a natural boundary between the lands of Kalinth, Persala and Haskany. Their route took them to the far north of Kalinth, from where they could cross east into Haskany. It was rough, hilly land. The Krykkers, however, referred to it dismissively as flatlands, and it proved no obstacle either to them or to their buffalo drawn carts.

A feeling of exhilaration swept over the force as they crossed from Kalinth into Haskany. Belwynn was no exception. It felt daring to be in the lands controlled by Erkindrix of Ishari. There was also a sense of relief that they were no longer cowering in fear from the threat, but acting to deal with it. Belwynn was sure that nobody present doubted that the odds were stacked against them. For now, though, they could almost feel like they were winning.

It wasn't long afterwards that the Kalinthians came to a halt. Dorian ordered his men to wait, too. Behind them, the stragglers from Dorian's unit and the Krykkers would take a while to catch up. Belwynn and Elana dismounted to stretch their legs.

A group of riders came down the line from the front. One of them was Evander, Theron's squire, and he stopped when he saw them.

'The Grand Master asks that you attend the War Council,' he said, addressing Dorian. 'He also invites you to come too,' he said, turning to Belwynn and Elana.

'You two go,' said Elana. 'If we're stopping for a while, it's a good time for me to attend to the soldiers.'

'Are you sure you don't want me to accompany you?' asked Belwynn.

'No, I'll be fine.'

'Moris, please accompany the Lady Elana while I'm away,' Dorian asked one of his men.

'Of course, Your Highness.'

The soldier immediately dismounted and attended on Elana.

'Thank you,' said Elana.

Belwynn remounted her horse, and she followed Evander and Dorian up the line to the front of the army. Evander turned to the left and took them off the track. A flock of sheep moved out of their way as the squire led them up a slope to the top of a rise. Here, Sebastian, Theron and Tycho were waiting for them. Evander helped Belwynn to dismount, and she and Dorian joined the three knights. Theron pointed ahead of them. The terrain sloped downhill and then back up. On the far rise lay a large Haskan fortress. It was a square shape and had good views over the surrounding area.

'Masada,' said Theron. 'Built to control this route into Haskany. Our two countries have been at peace for a century, but nonetheless it's been upgraded recently.'

It looked a formidable structure to Belwynn, with thick walls all the way around.

'I believe that we still have the element of surprise,' Theron continued, 'and that there will only be a skeleton garrison inside. But that doesn't mean it's easy to break in.'

'What about ignoring it and carrying on past?' asked Dorian.

'It's an option,' agreed Theron. 'But at some point, if he has not already, Erkindrix will get news of our army. If that fortress gets reinforced, and we find ourselves wanting to retreat, we could get trapped.'

Dorian nodded, acknowledging the dilemma.

'What's up?' demanded a gruff voice, as Sebastian's squire, Alpin, led four Krykkers up the slope to join them.

The voice belonged to Torinac, one of the Krykker chieftains. He carried Madria's weapon, Bolivar's Great Sword, tucked into his belt wherever he went, and acted like he was in charge of the Krykker army. But, in fact, the other two chieftains held equal weight. Maragin, a female chief, was much quieter, but Belwynn suspected had a sharper mind. Guremar was the third. He scowled a lot, especially at Rabigar, who had accompanied them. He clearly didn't like the fact that Rabigar attended these meetings, but Sebastian always made a point of inviting Belwynn's friend along, and Guremar had stopped short of directly complaining about it.

'Greetings,' said Sebastian, shaking each of them by the hand. 'We have a good view of the fort of Masada from here,' he explained. 'We were just saying it's an impressive structure, but probably lightly defended. We need to decide what to do about it.'

'Take it,' said Torinac immediately. 'Between us we have all the necessary siege equipment.'

'The trouble is,' said Tycho, 'a conventional siege may last days. That would give the Haskans and any other Isharite forces time to get an army together and attempt to raise the siege. We may end up facing superior forces here with very little achieved.'

'I take your point,' said Torinac. 'But we can't leave it in enemy hands behind our lines either. That could lead to disaster. We'll have to leave a force here to carry out the siege while the main part of the army moves on.'

'That might be the most sensible move,' agreed Theron. 'I was thinking of trying a ruse of some sort. Moving our army past the fort as if we are gone, but staying hidden. Then allowing a small force to get close to their gates, see if we can draw them out into the open.'

Torinac shrugged. 'It's worth a try, Count Theron. Why not? I would say the chances of them opening the gates are small, though. They must know that their best chance of survival is to hold tight and wait for support.'

'You're sure there's only a small force inside?' asked Rabigar.

'I can't be completely certain,' said Theron. 'But we know that the main Haskan army is in Brasingia under Queen Shira. Until a few days ago, Kalinth was a neutral neighbour. There would be no reason to leave a significant force here. Why do you ask?'

'I have an idea of a ruse that may work and save us some time. I would have to put it to the three chieftains first, in private. They may well disregard it.'

The three Krykker chieftains looked at him, their faces showing varying amounts of interest and suspicion. The four of them walked down the slope for their private conversation, dispersing the flock of sheep who had dared to venture half way up.

Belwynn looked over at the fortress. In a matter of minutes, this war had become very real, and rather complicated.

* * *

IT WAS PITCH BLACK. Even with his superior eyesight, Kaved had to tread carefully. One false move and the whole Magnian army might wake. The Magnians had the same tents as the Middians, which made it hard to determine if he was in the right spot.

Every tent had soldiers inside, with guy ropes pegged into the ground. They were invisible in the darkness, and Kaved had to move cautiously to avoid tripping over them. Despite his care, more than once he walked into a rope, some down at his ankles, others at chest or waist height.

He positioned himself in what seemed to be the right spot and waited. Out there in the darkness somewhere were Salvinus and Tirano. The tent they were all aiming for belonged to Prince Edgar's wizard. Tirano had insisted that they had to kill him first, if their assassination of the prince was to be a success. The wizard had frustrated Tirano's attempts to kill Edgar at the Battle of Lindhafen. That had probably been enough to turn the tide of the battle from victory to defeat.

Well. Now it was time for revenge.

An owl hooted. That was the signal. Tirano must have somehow determined that the wizard was in the tent.

Kaved moved towards their victim, treading carefully once more. He took his hand axe from his belt, the perfect weapon for close quarter butchering. To his left, his eyes just made out the form of someone else heading for the tent. Tirano. So, he was in the right place.

'Go.'

The wizard's voice, drifting through the night, was so quiet you could make yourself believe you had imagined it.

Kaved got to the tent. A last-minute change of mind. He swapped his axe for his sword, since it would be easier to get in with the piercing blade. Holding the canvas taut, he punctured it with the sharp tip of his sword blade, then sliced down, making an opening big enough to get through. He dived in, keen to be as quick as possible.

Someone entered from the opposite side of the tent. Salvinus. Kaved looked around. There. The wizard was sitting up, but held immobile by Tirano's magic. He had one arm outstretched towards the front of the tent as if he were trying to combat the spell. Kaved moved in for the kill. The wizard caught the movement, his eyes turning in his head to look at Kaved. But the rest of his body still couldn't move. Kaved plunged his sword into the wizard's chest from the side. Salvinus had now caught up with the action, and he finished the job, repeatedly stabbing the wizard, to make sure that he was really dead.

Kaved gave a shudder. He relived the eyes of the wizard turning towards him, looking at his killer but unable to move. Not a good way to die.

'Come on, let's go,' whispered Salvinus in the dark. 'We need to kill the prince as quickly as possible.'

THE ROCK WALKERS

XX

It was still night-time. What had woken him?

It took a moment for Edgar's mind to break through the fog of sleep. He was in a tent outside the city of Coldeberg. He always slept lightly in a new place. Maybe that was all it was. Still, some instinct made him sit up and reach over for his sword.

His movement stirred his ever-watchful bodyguards, Leofwin and Brictwin. Then, black forms could be seen: out in the darkness, outside the tent. Edgar tried to call out a warning, but he found that his voice didn't work. His muscles couldn't move. The same thing that had happened to him in the Battle of Lindhafen. He pushed against the restriction, trying to move his body, but it was no good.

From three different directions, the tent was suddenly invaded by the black forms. Edgar could see Leofwin and Brictwin stumble to their feet. To Edgar's right, a Krykker, heavy-set and carrying a sword and axe, burst in. Brictwin reacted first. As the Krykker spotted Edgar, Brictwin slashed at the creature with his sword, forcing it to block the strike.

To Edgar's left, the second figure to enter the tent was familiar. Gervase Salvinus. So—they had come to kill him. Perhaps he should have expected this. Salvinus walked towards him, but Leofwin blocked his path.

From the front of the tent a third figure emerged, the whites of its eyes focused on Edgar in the darkness. Edgar instantly knew that this was the Ishari wizard who served Emeric, and that his immobility was caused by the wizard's magic. With the wizard's focus fully fixed on him, he had no chance of escaping the spell.

Where was Ealdnoth?

Leofwin feinted towards Salvinus, who blocked at a strike that never came. Instead, Leofwin launched himself towards the wizard.

'Stop him!' the wizard screamed, turning his attention from Edgar to Leofwin.

Edgar struggled to move, but the wizard's spell still kept him pinned down.

The Ishari put out a hand towards Leofwin, and a bolt of magic leapt from his outstretched hand towards Edgar's bodyguard.

Leofwin cried out in pain, but forced himself to push through the bolt at the wizard. Salvinus had now caught up with Leofwin, and ran him through from behind.

Edgar let out a silent scream as he watched his enemy slay the man who had been by his side since youth.

Somehow, with whatever strength he had left, Leofwin kept his momentum going forwards. Edgar could see the wizard's eyes open in fear, as Leofwin plunged his blade into the man's chest, before collapsing to the ground.

Suddenly, Edgar was freed. Rising, he raised the sword still clutched in his hand, and charged at Salvinus, who leapt out of the way.

'It's lost,' shouted the mercenary leader, backing out of the tent.

The Krykker, who had been contained by Brictwin, followed suit, exiting through the slit he had cut in the tent's side. Brictwin rushed over to his uncle, stabbing down into the neck of the wizard to make sure he was dead.

Edgar glanced down at Leofwin's prone body before following Salvinus out of the tent. He could just see the mercenary ahead, making his way in between two tents.

'Awake! Awake!' shouted Edgar at the top of his voice. 'Enemies!'

He chased after Salvinus, determined not to let him out of his sight. Suddenly, his face had slammed into the dirt floor.

'Shit!'

He'd tripped over a damned tent rope. Pushing himself up, he looked for Salvinus. But he was out of sight, swallowed by the darkness.

His warriors were emerging from their tents.

'Two of them,' Edgar yelled at them. 'One of them was Salvinus, the other a Krykker.'

Bleary eyed, the Magnian soldiers began their search, but Edgar knew he had lost his best chance of catching Salvinus.

With a heavy heart, he returned to his tent. Brictwin was kneeling next to his uncle's body. He had turned Leofwin over onto his back, but there was no life left in him.

'I'm sorry,' said Edgar, sinking down to his knees on Leofwin's other side.

'Don't be, Your Highness,' said Brictwin. The younger man's face was grave, but there were no tears. 'He died to save your life. He wouldn't have wanted it any other way.'

A rustle of noise made Edgar look up.

Wilchard entered the tent, blanching at the sight of Leofwin's corpse. He locked eyes with Edgar. 'I'm sorry, Your Highness. It's Ealdnoth. They killed him first.'

'No,' Edgar moaned.

Too much. The price he'd paid for this war. Too much.

* * *

Shira walked gingerly towards the great doors of the Council Chamber of Samir Durg. She had been forced to endure a teleportation from the siege of Burkhard Castle all the way to the Isharite fortress. Her stomach roiled as if she was going to be sick.

Waiting for her outside the room, as was his custom, was her husband. With Arioc stood Rostam, one of his lieutenants. Shira was surprised to see him here. As she neared, she noticed a strange expression on Arioc's face. She couldn't quite identify what it was, but decided it was probably bad news.

'Husband,' she said to Arioc, nodding at Rostam as well.

'Wife,' said Arioc, with equal irony.

Rostam had his usual smirk on his face. He was favoured by Arioc, useful as both a military commander and as a magus, though Shira was unsure how powerful his magic was. He was certainly an intimidating man, who wore only black and carried a black crystal sword, matching his dark hair and eyes. There were also the rumours that he was Arioc's son. It was nothing Arioc had ever commented on, but it added to Rostam's sense of self-importance, that was for sure.

What a twisted little family we are, thought Shira.

'Well, we have *some* good news,' said Arioc. 'Rostam has been promoted to the Council.'

Shira couldn't hide her surprise. Rostam's smirk grew bigger.

'Congratulations. But how?'

'Nexodore is dead,' replied Arioc. 'I informed Erkindrix of this some time ago, but it took him this long to believe me. Rostam was appointed in a small meeting of the Council yesterday.'

Arioc openly voicing frustration with Erkindrix was unusual. There was a strange tension in the air, something Shira couldn't quite put her finger on. Arioc should have been happy. He now had both herself and Rostam, essentially two puppets, on the Council. Nexodore, one of his biggest rivals, had been removed. Yet he still looked troubled.

There was no time to find out more. Without further comment, Arioc moved to the doors of the Council Chamber and pushed them open.

Everyone else was waiting for them. At the head of the table sat Erkindrix. Shira tried to avoid looking directly at him. To his left was Siavash, High Priest of Ishari, Erkindrix's shadow. Next to Siavash sat Pentas, the haughty red-eyed wizard. To the right of Erkindrix was Ardashir, an Isharite said to equal Erkindrix in age, and who had been a loyalist for centuries. Sat next to him was a strange-looking creature Shira had never met before. Logic said it must be Dorjan, King of the Shadow Caladri. He was a thin, wizened man—his limbs looked like they might snap if put to too much use. Yet he carried an aura of power that matched the others at the table.

The full Council was here, for the first time since Shira had been made a member.

Shira, Arioc and Rostam took their places at the opposite end of the table to Erkindrix. Shira was glad to be as far away from him as possible.

'We *should* have had a victory by now,' said Erkindrix with no preamble, his voice wet with saliva. 'Diis is not pleased.'

Diis, Arioc had once explained to Shira, was the being that inhabited Erkindrix. She hadn't wanted to know more than that, and the mention of its name put her on edge.

'Shira,' continued Erkindrix, his grey eyes turning to her and the black eyes beneath burning like hot coals in her direction. 'Why have you failed to conquer the Brasingians?'

Shira swallowed. She was to feel the wrath of the dread lord, and neither Arioc nor anyone else on the Council would offer her the tiniest amount of support.

'They have put up a stern resistance at Burkhard Castle,' she explained, only too aware of how pathetic she sounded. 'Even the Drobax have not yet been able to break through. When we take Burkhard, the rest of the Empire will fall.'

'The Empire is proving tougher than we expected, Arioc?' continued Erkindrix, his voice full of sarcasm.

'Indeed. We have a setback to report. The forces of Duke Emeric have been defeated by a mixed force of Thessians, Magnians and Middians. I had not anticipated the intervention of the Southerners, for which I apologise. However, Rostam and I have completed clearing the Grand Caladri from their lands. The remnants of their race have been given sanctuary by the Krykkers. I am now free to deal with the Empire.'

Shira went hot with anger, struggling to hold it in. Rather than backing her, Arioc had implied that he should take over the invasion of Brasingia.

'*I* will decide who goes where,' said Erkindrix, letting vent to his own anger. He pointed a finger at Pentas. 'The weapons of Madria are still at large. They have found their way to Kalinth.'

'Then he spirited them there himself,' accused Arioc.

'That is a lie,' responded Pentas, remaining calm but defending himself. 'Arioc had the chance to get the dagger and staff in Edeleny and bungled it. I have only just traced them to Kalinth. It would now seem that the Krykkers have raised an army and joined the Knights of Kalinth. I suspect they have their sword with them. They intend to go on the offensive.'

'How could you have let this happen?' demanded Siavash, looking around the table. Shira had never heard him speak before. He had a quiet but deadly sounding voice. 'We have committed our forces to gain a quick victory. The longer the enemy resists, the more they could become a threat to us. The weapons should have been taken by now.'

'Don't forget,' said Pentas, 'that it was Nexodore who was tasked with finding Madria's weapons, something he singularly failed to do. But this turn of events should be seen as an opportunity, rather than something to fear. Now that I know where they are, I can put my hands on three of the weapons at once. That will end the threat from Madria for good.'

'I'll get the weapons,' snarled Arioc.

'You just said you would deal with the Empire,' Pentas pointed out smugly.

'Enough,' said Erkindrix. 'Siavash is correct. We must deal with these threats quickly. A new army must be raised to confront the Kalinthians and Krykkers. All remaining forces in the north, including the Drobax, will be deployed. Rostam, you will raise this army and defeat the enemy. You will take some of the forces based here, and supplement them as best you can. Pentas, you will liaise with him, but your focus will be on bringing me the three weapons, as soon as possible. Arioc and Shira, you will destroy the Brasingians. Use Emeric's forces or ignore them, but either way, I must see this done. No more excuses. Ardashir and Dorjan, your campaigns have stalled. I need to see them concluded so that your armies can be redeployed. Anyone who fails me will be killed and replaced.' Erkindrix looked around the table. '*Anyone.*'

They left the Council Chamber. Arioc was quiet, but Shira could tell that he was fuming.

Rostam's smirk had gone. 'I'd better get straight to it,' said the younger man.

Shira knew what he was feeling. The exhilaration of commanding his own army for the first time, mixed with the responsibility. 'Good luck in Brasingia,' he added.

Arioc and Shira nodded at him and he marched off.

'How *dare* he threaten me?' whispered Arioc hoarsely.

Shira hadn't seen him this angry before. She was unsure what to say. Caught between the hostility of Erkindrix and Arioc, she felt out of her depth.

'*I* should have been put in charge of dealing with the Krykkers,' he continued. 'My record is flawless.'

'Well, for what it's worth, I agree.'

And she did. Arioc's presence could offer little to speed up the siege of Burkhard Castle. While Rostam and Pentas hardly inspired confidence as a team.

'Greetings,' said a smooth voice. Pentas, a sardonic smile playing on his lips. Shira got a creepy feeling, as if he had been reading her thoughts.

'What do you want?' snapped Arioc, full of hostility.

'I will get the weapons,' said Pentas confidently. 'But still, all is not well. Erkindrix is getting weaker; his decision making less sound. This whole campaign has been poorly managed.'

Arioc's eyes opened wide. 'Disloyalty. You play a dangerous game, Pentas. I should kill you where you stand.'

'I could be an ally, Arioc,' replied Pentas, sounding serious for once, looking him in the eye, doing the same to Shira. Those red eyes, repulsive and inscrutable. His gaze turned back to Arioc. 'How long can we let this go on for?'

With that, he turned and walked away.

Shira raised her eyebrows, waiting for some comment from Arioc. But there was none. Instead, that unfamiliar expression had returned to his face. Then she realised what it was. A state of mind she had never witnessed in him before. Indecision.

* * *

The Dramsen clan were a hive of activity: assembling, testing, and then firing their great siege weapons toward the Haskan fortress of Masada. Making his voice heard above all the noise was their chief, Torinac. Instructions, advice, admonitions—all were hurled in a torrent of words at his hard-working soldiers. Whether he was any help; whether his men were actually paying any attention to him, Belwynn couldn't be sure. But she admired his energy nonetheless.

She watched, fascinated, as the Krykkers working on the machines made their modifications. Each time, they got a bit closer to their target.

Rabigar's plan had asked for a lot. He wanted the biggest boulders that the Krykkers had carted with them from their homeland to be fired, not at the walls of Masada, but over them. That required such a huge amount of force that only their largest weapons, the trebuchets, could be used. The Knights had nothing as large as this, and so had been deployed to defend the army's position, preventing any attempt by the defenders to destroy the great weapons.

The Krykker machinists had to move slowly and carefully. The pressure on the wooden frame was immense, and if the beam holding the ammunition were to snap, those standing close by could be seriously injured. In addition, a massive counterweight had to be deployed to create enough force to send the boulders over the walls, and there was a danger that this could pull the whole contraption over.

By the end of the day, the Krykkers had built two trebuchets that could successfully and reliably fire the required weight over the walls. Rabigar had wanted the boulders fired at night time, and so, in the gathering darkness, they were laboriously and carefully nestled into the trebuchet's sling.

The first weight was released, and everyone's hearts were in their mouths as the boulder soared high into the sky. Once it reached the top of its arc, the boulder descended quickly, but Belwynn could clearly see it come down on the other side of the wall. A thud could be heard as it hit, suggesting that it had landed on the ground within the fort's walls.

Everyone looked at each other for a while. They had done exactly what Rabigar had requested. Only time would tell whether his plan would work. Torinac gave the command, and the next boulder was loaded on.

* * *

RABIGAR WAITED. It had been a long time since he had stayed in rock for this long. He had to rely on the training from his youth, to make his mind ignore the feelings of claustrophobia and suffocation. If he let himself panic, he would die.

Suddenly there was a massive crack above him, and Rabigar felt the impact as another boulder landed on top of his. He heard it roll off onto the floor. *That's a good sign*, he told himself. *It shows the targeting of the trebuchets is accurate.* He waited until the noise of boulders thudding into the fort had stopped, and then he waited some more, just in case.

It was time to move. He began to push his way out of the boulder. It wasn't easy to get started from his position: fully encased in stone, lying all ends up. He pushed hard with his legs, pulled with his arms, until he forced his head out of the rock. He took a long, deep breath of air. The dirt floor of the fort was just a few inches beneath him. He wriggled free of the massive boulder, taking great care with his movements. He had the cover of darkness in his favour, but the fort's defenders could be close by.

Once Rabigar was out, he lay prone for a while, avoiding any further suspicious movement. He scanned the area. It was difficult in the darkness, in an unknown environment, to get his bearings. He could see the outline of half a dozen other boulders around him. At one, then a second, he saw Krykkers slithering out. But he still wasn't sure about their location. Slowly, he crawled around to the other side of the boulder. Here, he could see the outline of two walls. Where they met, at one corner of the fort, he could see a tower. So, they had made it, then. They had been thrown inside the fort.

How many had survived? He crawled back around his boulder. He could see a group of Krykker meeting up in the darkness and joined them. He was relieved to see that one of them was Maragin. When he had first come up with the idea of using Krykker rock walkers to get into the fort, he'd known it was Maragin who would have to be convinced. Guremar had been against the idea, of course, because it was Rabigar's. Torinac was easy enough to persuade. It was Maragin, as a rock walker herself, and as the leader of the best trained rock walkers from the Grendal clan, who would have the decisive say.

Krykkers couldn't move through just any rock, or they could have pushed their way through the fort walls. They could only move through Krykker rock, from their homeland. The fact that they had brought with them four carts full of massive boulders had given Rabigar the idea in the first place. But the only way for the plan to work was for them to enter the boulders and get catapulted over the walls while inside them. Rabigar had thought they would be relatively safe inside the rock, but he couldn't be sure. Maragin had thought about it for some time before agreeing.

'How many?' Rabigar whispered to her.

'Seven of us here,' Maragin replied. 'Seven still out there somewhere. It's too dark to see where all the boulders landed. We'll have to look for them.'

Rabigar hadn't fully thought through this part of the plan. In his mind's eye, they would quickly leave the boulders and head for the fort's gate. It wasn't as easy as that.

'We can't afford to be seen,' he warned Maragin. 'We'd be better off going straight for the gate.'

'Give me two minutes,' she said.

'Alright,' Rabigar acquiesced.

It had been more of an order than a request, anyway. The other rock walkers were *her* soldiers, and would do what she said. They were all younger than Rabigar, and still had two eyes each, so he let them head off around the courtyard of Masada to locate their comrades. It didn't take long. As he watched them move about, other figures emerged from the darkness to join up with them. The only delay occurred around one boulder. Rabigar could see two Krykkers push into it and drag out a body. They left it on the ground. So, one of them hadn't made it: killed by the initial impact as they had landed on the ground, or perhaps by suffocation inside.

Maragin led her soldiers back to Rabigar's position.

'Thirteen,' she whispered.

Thirteen of the fourteen rock walkers were here. They had suffered the first casualty of the war. War, when lives suddenly became assets which leaders traded for advantage. If they lost just the one life in exchange for opening the gates of the fort, it would be considered a good trade.

'Are we ready to go then?' he asked her.

'Ready.'

They moved off, the plan of attack agreed before they had climbed into the boulders. They all headed to the left, away from the tower, before moving ahead. Rabigar, along with most of the Krykkers, aimed straight for the main gate.

'Who goes there?' came a call from the walkway along the wall above them.

It was quickly followed by warning shouts.

'Invaders!' went the cry.

They had been seen. No great surprise, but they had to act fast. Rabigar ran faster, hoping to make the gate before he was shot down in the open. He sensed an object flash past him in the darkness, but kept on moving.

Two other groups, each made up of three rock walkers, had peeled off to the sides: heading for two rooms located either side of the gate. Beyond the gate was a portcullis. One room would contain the lever mechanism that raised it. The gate and portcullis had been built a few feet apart, creating an area known as a killing field. The two rooms would have murder holes facing this area, used to kill an enemy that got trapped between the gate and portcullis. The two smaller groups had to neutralise these rooms. It was risky, because they didn't know whether Haskan soldiers would be stationed there; and if they were, how many there would be.

Rabigar and the main group of Krykkers got to the main gate. It was made of solid wood, shod with iron. Their first job was to lift off the heavy iron locking bar that ran horizontally across the full width of the gate. They heaved together, lifting it up from the hooks it rested on. They walked back with it a few steps before dumping it on the ground. The other Krykkers got to work on the locks on the gate, fumbling in the dark.

Rabigar got to his knees and took out the torch he had brought with him on his belt. Holding it between his knees, he reached inside his pockets for flint and steel. Scraping the steel along the flint, Rabigar got a spark to land on his char cloth. He carefully coaxed it into a flame until the tinder of his torch caught alight.

Without warning, a blow on his chest nearly knocked him over. He put one hand out to break his fall, only just holding on to his newly lit torch. Quickly getting to his feet, he saw an arrow lying on the floor. Luckily, it had deflected off the tough scales on his chest, and he was unharmed.

The other Krykkers had got the gate open. Rabigar rushed forwards. Ahead, he could see the portcullis being raised. That meant that the other rock walkers had successfully cleared at least one of the rooms. There could still be Haskan soldiers in the other room, plus there were the soldiers manning the walls. But he had to risk it.

Rabigar sprinted through the gate and kept going. Before he knew it, he was ducking under the portcullis, still only half way up, and then outside the fort. He waved his torch from side to side and hoped that he could be seen.

PENTAS THE WIZARD

XXI

After the excitement of the trebuchets, Belwynn rushed over to the forward position of the assault squads. They were located as close to the fort as they could get, without the risk of being seen. Here, a jut of rock emerged from the ground that provided sufficient cover. If Rabigar and the rest of his Krykkers managed to open the gate, it was a relatively short dash to get inside the fort. Sebastian wanted both the Knights and the Krykkers to gain credit for a victory, so there were two units. On the right side of the rock, Guremar led a force of Krykkers. On the left, Theron led a force of Knights, all on foot. Both units were fully armoured, to give them maximum protection when they approached the walls.

There was a nervous tension in the air as the soldiers waited in silence. It began to affect Belwynn. She worried about Rabigar—had his gamble worked or not? It had taken her aback when she had first heard his plan. The idea that some Krykkers could immerse themselves inside rock was something she had never heard of. Moreover, the news that Rabigar was one of those with the power surprised her further. It wasn't just that he had never mentioned it before. She remembered, more than once, the Krykker expressing a hostile attitude towards magic. If walking through rock wasn't magic, she didn't know what was. But it appeared that the Krykkers didn't see it that way.

Excited murmurs rose amongst the Krykkers, suggesting that they had seen something. Belwynn peered in the fort's direction, but couldn't make anything out in the darkness. The Knights hadn't reacted either—perhaps the Krykkers had better eyesight in the dark.

Guremar moved his forces out, around the jut of rock, towards the fort.

'It's open,' he shouted gruffly across to Theron and his knights.

Belwynn could see Theron's Knights hesitate, before they too moved out from their hiding place. She peered towards the fort a second time. Yes—perhaps she did see a flicker of light at the bottom of the fort, where the gate would be.

Once they were out in the open, the Krykkers and Knights picked up speed, running for the fort as fast as they could in their heavy armour. The Krykkers moved faster, since they only required armour for their limbs and heads; the thick scales on their torsos negating the need for the heavy coats of mail that weighed down the Knights. There was no time to waste. Rabigar's team may have got the gate open, but the fort's defenders would be desperate to get it closed again as soon as possible.

Belwynn watched on anxiously as the assault squads disappeared into the night. Part of her wanted to chase after them, but she stayed where she was. She peered into the darkness, and listened out for the sounds of fighting.

THE RISING sun shed its light over the newly captured fortress of Masada. The generals of the army, led by Sebastian and Prince Dorian, made their way through the gate that Rabigar's team had forced open. Sebastian's knights now manned it, as they did the high walls of the fort, which had been left undamaged by the trebuchet attack.

Belwynn had spent the night inside the fort. She had helped Elana tend to the injured. There were mercifully few of them: only four fatalities in all, and the priestess had carried out her healing on those with serious wounds. Elana was confident that there would be no more deaths, though some soldiers would survive with permanent disabilities. The priestess had healed the injured Haskan soldiers with equal attention. There had been some grumbling at this, but they had been allowed to complete their work.

Sebastian and Dorian inspected the courtyard of the fort. While the walls of the fort had been avoided, the same could not be said for this area. Great boulders, that had once contained Krykkers, still lay scattered about where they had landed the night before. It was a strange sight, and Belwynn had to smile at Sebastian's slightly baffled expression. He noticed Belwynn at the far side of the courtyard, and he and Dorian walked over to join her.

'Lady Belwynn,' Dorian said, formally.

'Your Highness,' she replied. 'Theron is in the main hall. I can take you both there, if you wish.'

'Yes,' said Sebastian. 'We need to be on our way this morning.'

Belwynn led them to the far end of the courtyard, where the fort buildings were located. She passed the barracks, where some soldiers still slept, and led them to the hall of the fort commander. It was a simple affair, with an open space for public meeting, and some private quarters. Inside, Theron was alone, standing over a table. On it was a map he was carefully studying, but he stopped when he noticed his visitors.

'Congratulations!' said Dorian as they entered.

'I can hardly take much credit, Your Highness,' said Theron, moving over to shake the Prince and then his uncle by the hand. 'That should go to Rabigar and the Krykkers, for getting inside and opening the gate. Once we got inside, the Haskans couldn't put up much resistance, they were too few. When we forced our way onto the walls, it was over.'

'Well,' said Dorian, 'I shall make sure that I find Rabigar and offer my thanks.'

'We have about fifty of them altogether as prisoners,' continued Theron. 'I wasn't sure whether we should keep them alive—'

'Theron!' said Belwynn, shocked.

'I should think so,' said Dorian. 'The Haskans aren't our real enemy, after all. They are following the orders of Arioc and Erkindrix.'

Theron shrugged. 'If we keep them alive here, it will mean leaving a larger force behind to guard them. Otherwise we should just let them go.'

Sebastian nodded. 'Letting them go may be the best option. Have you any thoughts about today?'

'It gets difficult from here. We need to head north east so that we threaten the Ishari fortress of Samir Durg. That is likely to have the biggest impact. But we need to scout carefully about us. The Dardelles mountains become a forest to our east, and it's a perfect place to hide an army. To the west lie the lands of the Drobax. If he doesn't know already, Erkindrix will soon learn about our invasion. We're in very dangerous territory from now on.'

'At least we have the fort here to fall back on,' commented Dorian.

Theron looked at him. 'I've been thinking about that. We need to leave a garrison behind here, and I think your Kalinthian force is the perfect size. It would also mean we don't lose any Knights or Krykkers from the army. We'll need every one of them should we come to battle. Would you be willing to stay as the commander?'

Dorian looked taken aback by Theron's suggestion, glancing first at Sebastian, then at Belwynn.

'It makes sense,' Sebastian added. 'We need a firm presence here. It's strategically vital.'

'Then, of course, I will stay at the fort,' said Dorian, regaining some composure. 'I will organise my men at once. If you will excuse me?'

Sebastian nodded and Dorian turned about, leaving the hall at a pace.

'Was that necessary?' Belwynn asked Theron when the Prince had left.

'His force is perfect for the job,' said Theron. 'Able enough to defend the fort, but not so big a loss from the army.'

'Yes, but someone else could have stayed behind to lead them,' Belwynn pointed out.

'Well, I don't trust him,' Theron admitted. 'He's only here to gain the glory from the campaign for himself.'

'That's unfair,' said Belwynn, angry that Dorian was being done a disservice.

'Maybe so,' said Sebastian. 'But this way, at least he stands a better chance of living through it. I don't particularly want to get an heir to the throne killed. Those of us who carry on need to be aware that their chances aren't good.' He paused, looking her in the eyes. 'I think you should stay here too, Belwynn. I know you want to get your brother freed. But there's no point in getting killed in the process.'

'No way,' she insisted immediately.

'It will be dangerous,' commented Theron. 'But the Knights...many of them will fight better if she comes. They've come to see her as a fortune bringer.'

A fortune bringer. It was a stupid idea, and Theron had played it for all it was worth. But Belwynn wanted to go, so she kept her thoughts to herself.

Sebastian sighed. 'I've noticed. Warriors are superstitious by nature. We have no king to inspire them, and now we are leaving our Prince behind. But if you come with us, Belwynn, you can't expect any special protection. We can't spare a single soldier.'

'I understand that. And should there be a battle, I hope I will be of some help to Elana.'

The Grand Master of the Knights nodded, his expression grim. 'So be it.'

AFTER DAYS OF SUNSHINE, grey clouds covered the skies above Haskany and the temperature cooled. On the ground, the combined army of Krykkers and

Knights left the fortress of Masada far behind, heading out into the featureless landscape of the far north.

Dry scrub dominated the terrain, making it seem, to Belwynn's eyes, an inhospitable land. It certainly wasn't farming land, and they didn't pass near a single settlement as they trudged along. Despite the cloud cover above, it didn't rain, and the land looked like it rarely got watered. Instead, Belwynn could see evidence of fire damage on the tinder dry landscape, as the army marched along a dirt track that would take them to the lands of the Ishari. The Dardelles mountain range receded behind them, but nothing of interest replaced it. As the hours dragged by, it felt like the scrubland would stretch on forever. It reminded Belwynn of their visit to the forests of the Caladri. The Grand Caladri had used magic to make it seem like they were making progress, when, in fact, they were walking in circles, getting nowhere. Was it possible that the Isharites were doing the same thing?

The army's march came to a mid-morning halt. Evander and Alpin, the squires to Theron and Sebastian, came riding down the line. Evander stopped when he found Belwynn and Elana, while Alpin continued going; presumably on his way to find Rabigar and the Krykker chieftains. Something was going on.

'What is it?' she asked the squire, as she and Elana nudged their horses over to join him.

'A man...a magus has arrived,' replied Evander, sounding slightly troubled. 'He says he knows you. Count Theron asked me to fetch you.'

For a moment Belwynn's heart leapt, imagining that Soren had somehow escaped and met them. Then her logic kicked in and told her she was being ridiculous.

'What does he look like?' asked Elana.

'He—' Evander paused, frowning. 'He has red eyes.'

Belwynn and Elana shared a look.

'You'd better take us to see him,' said the priestess.

'He was just standing in the road. Waiting for us,' Theron whispered to her.

Belwynn allowed herself a grim smile. Pentas was just as Belwynn remembered him. Friendly; seemingly oblivious to the reaction his sudden arrival had caused. But Belwynn knew it was all an act. She recalled his magical fight with Nexodore on the Great Road. She recalled too their brief meeting in Onella's Temple in Edeleny, before he had spirited them away. The corpse of

Dorottya, the Caladri elder, had lain dead on the floor. *We had an argument,* he had said. She knew they were dealing with a powerful and ruthless individual.

They were standing in a patch of scrub by the side of the road. There was Belwynn, Elana and Rabigar, who had all confirmed the identity of the wizard; Sebastian and Theron, representing the Knights of Kalinth; Torinac and Maragin, representing the Krykkers.

'Your brother lives,' said Pentas casually, as if it were something he had almost forgotten to mention.

The information provoked a flood of emotions and questions in Belwynn. All she could get out, though, was a brief question in a croaky voice. 'Where?'

'In Samir Durg.'

'And the others? Clarin, Herin...'

'All alive for now.'

'For now? What do you mean?'

Pentas looked at her with his unreadable red eyes. 'None of them are *safe,*' he replied, as if it were such an obvious point it shouldn't have needed saying. 'You've done well getting this far, the three of you. Much better than I had hoped. Though I was hoping the fourth member of your party would be here. The dagger wielder.'

'Dirk died a few days ago,' said Elana. 'He didn't recover from his injuries.'

'I see,' said Pentas, sounding disappointed. 'I am genuinely sorry. I owed him my life.'

'Why are you here?' asked Belwynn.

Pentas looked around the group. 'As I say, you have done well; enough to create some doubts on the Council of Seven. Erkindrix has ordered an army to be raised to defeat you. As we speak, Isharite magi, Haskan soldiers, and Drobax, are being gathered just south of the Ishari border. The army is under the command of Rostam, Nexodore's successor on the Council. It is a hastily assembled force. Militarily, you stand a chance. But Rostam will also command magic users. You will need my help.'

'Who are you?' asked Elana, in her direct manner.

Pentas looked at her thoughtfully, as if weighing up what to say. He nodded, whether to himself or at Elana, Belwynn couldn't tell. 'I am a servant of Madria, Elana. Just like you. Unlike you, I was born into it. My job has been to halt the rise of Ishari—as much as possible. To undermine them, I have served Erkindrix. More accurately, I have served Diis: the being who sent the Isharites to Dalriya, to take control of our world from Madria. Most of the peoples of Dalriya have let themselves forget about this foul creature. But he hungers for control as much as he ever did.'

Maragin spat on the floor. 'You're a member of the Council of Seven; no doubt responsible for countless atrocities. Are we supposed to believe that all this time you've really been on our side?'

'You may doubt what I say,' responded Pentas, 'but twice in the last few weeks I have stopped Madria's weapons from falling into their hands and you three,' he said, pointing at Belwynn, Elana and Rabigar, 'have witnessed that. Some in Ishari have their suspicions of me, but I have evaded them so far. Now, if your army does meet theirs, I must again ensure that the three weapons you carry are not lost.'

Torinac put his hand to the hilt of Bolivar's Sword, frowning at the idea.

'What of my brother?' asked Belwynn, desperate to know more. 'Is he well?'

'I have not seen him personally. But no, he will be far from well.'

Belwynn put a hand to her mouth.

The wizard watched her impassively. 'I have a plan that will give your brother and his friends a chance of escape. A chance, mind you—and a small one at that. But that is the best you can hope for. To give them the best chance possible, we must hurt Erkindrix. Even if we don't win, we need to land a blow. We need to hurt the Isharites and shake their confidence.'

'That's why we're here,' said Sebastian.

'You said,' began Theron, 'that, militarily, we had a chance. Can you tell us anything about the forces this Rostam will have? What kind of man is he?'

The two Knights and the three Krykkers began to talk tactics with Pentas.

Elana put a reassuring arm around Belwynn. 'Are you alright?' asked the priestess.

'Yes,' she replied. 'It is the best news I could have expected.'

'We can do this, you know,' said Elana, with the easy confidence that had become familiar to Belwynn—the confidence she had come to rely on.

'Yes,' Belwynn replied. 'I believe we can.'

* * *

THE FUNERAL PYRES for Ealdnoth and Leofwin were still smoking when the gates of Coldeberg were opened.

The men of Thesse, Magnia, and of the Midder Steppe, were armed, just in case. Edgar, standing at the head of his men, looked across as the Barissian army filed out of the city. Next to him were Wilchard, his steward, and his surviving bodyguard, Brictwin. Few men jeered, or even talked much. The

Barissians were largely met with silence as they approached the besieging army.

Most of the Barissians left on foot, but a group at the front were on horseback. Edgar recognised Gervase Salvinus, leading his mercenaries. He had a smirk on his face as he approached the waiting army.

'It's him,' Edgar hissed.

'Control yourself,' said Wilchard. 'Don't give him the satisfaction of seeing you hurt. That goes for you too, Brictwin,' he added, trying to dissuade the young warrior from doing anything rash in revenge for the death of his uncle.

Salvinus's troop passed them and stopped in front of Duke Coen. Salvinus reached into a cloth sack that was tied to his saddle. Holding it by the hair, he pulled out a decapitated head. Emeric. No doubt Salvinus had ordered the killing himself, so that he and the rest of his men could escape unharmed. It was no more than Emeric deserved. But it made Edgar sick to his stomach that Salvinus would get away completely free. Free to sell his services to some other lord.

Coen nodded. 'You have met the terms I offered,' he shouted, loud enough to carry to most of the men present outside Coldeberg. 'You are therefore free to go. But I warn you against raising a sword against the Emperor ever again. He would not be as lenient as I.'

Salvinus gave Emeric's hair a swing and let go, so that the head landed on the floor a few feet from Coen. He then led his men away. The rest followed, many probably ordinary Barissians recruited into a false king's army, and glad to be going home alive.

'No sign of the Krykker you fought with, Brictwin?' Edgar asked.

'No, Your Highness. I can't see him.'

'He's no doubt found his way out of the city by now,' Edgar said. 'By Toric, how I want those two dead.'

'We defeated Emeric,' said Wilchard, trying to lift Edgar's spirits. 'The Empire can be united again. We achieved what we set out to do.'

'Yes. I know. At too high a price, though.'

'You've heard,' said Wilchard, 'that Coen is talking about taking his army to Essenberg next? Baldwin had to leave it virtually undefended when he took the Kellish army north.'

'I've heard,' Edgar replied. 'But we've shed enough blood here. It's time to go home.'

* * *

THE PRISONERS in the pits started to wake up. Men shared whispers in the darkness. There it was again. A scrabbling sound on the metal grates above them.

Dare I believe, thought Gyrmund. *Dare I believe that Moneva has come to rescue us all?*

Then, one of the grates swung open. Gyrmund stood and peered out to see the night sky above them. A figure loomed above the pit opening.

'Well? Let's get a move on, then!'

Moneva's voice drifted down, incongruous sounding in the circumstances.

Some of the prisoners rushed to the opening.

'Wait!' demanded Herin.

It seemed strangely cruel to Gyrmund, to make these desperate prisoners wait a moment longer. He felt his own desperation to escape so keenly. But Herin wanted to assert his authority, and Gyrmund understood why. If any of them were going to make it out alive, they had to work together, not go charging off in all directions.

Herin ushered Clarin, the hero of the pit fight with Vamak, over to the opening. He was to be the first to leave. Clarin reached up to the edge of the pit with one hand, while Moneva grasped the other. Between them, they pulled his body up and over the edge. Herin was next, then Gyrmund. He gave Moneva a brief embrace, holding her tight, because he had thought he would never get to hold her again.

Then, it was back to work. Working in pairs, they hauled the rest of the prisoners out of the pit, keeping as quiet as they could. First out were the Persaleians: Zared helped up by his men; Cyprian so light and wiry that Gyrmund hardly felt any weight. Once out, the Persaleians took over, giving Gyrmund and the others a rest. Out came Rudy and Jurgen, the two cousins from Rotelegen; Tamir and his Barbarians, the biggest group, were next. Zared looked to Clarin when it was the turn of the three Dog-men; but when Clarin gave the nod, he told his men to lift them out as well. Finally, the great Bear-man staggered over to the pit entrance, sniffing the air. Clarin and Herin took a huge clawed hand each and, bracing themselves, heaved backwards, dragging it up and out.

Moneva took Gyrmund, Cyprian, and a few other Persaleians to a small pile of bodies she had dumped to one side; the guards she had killed to get inside the camp. The pile was invisible in the darkness, but would be all too revealing when the sun came up. Gyrmund and the others took a body each, holding them under the armpits. They dragged them over to the pit opening and dropped them inside. Rudy and Jurgen took great pleasure in closing the metal grate with a soft clang.

For a few moments, everyone stood around, looking at each other. Gyrmund studied the faces. Some had looks of exhilaration, some fear. Many looked tired and bemused. He disliked the way some men stared at Moneva, but understood it. These were men who had not seen a woman in months, and perhaps never expected to again.

'Well?' asked Herin, as the four of them stood to one side. 'What's the plan?'

'I've been told where they are keeping Soren,' Moneva replied. 'It will involve getting into the fortress.'

'Told by whom?'

Moneva made a face. 'By Pentas.'

'The wizard?' exclaimed Gyrmund. 'What's he doing here?'

'I don't know exactly. He told me where to find you three. I have to assume he's telling me the truth about Soren.' She looked at them. 'So, what do we do?'

Gyrmund understood the question well enough. Moneva was asking whether, having rescued them, they really wanted her to lead them back into danger. A big part of Gyrmund wanted very much to turn around and get as far away from Samir Durg, as quickly as possible.

'We go and get him,' said Clarin decisively.

Gyrmund accepted the decision. Soren had helped to rescue him from Coldeberg prison—he owed the wizard.

'What about them?' Herin asked, indicating the thirty or so men waiting to one side. There was no doubt that some of them would be very useful if it came to a fight.

'Would they come with us?' asked Moneva.

'Yes; some of them will.'

'Then I think we should take them.'

Clarin moved back to speak to the prisoners, who gathered round. 'We are going to the fortress to rescue our friend,' he said plainly. 'We will have most success if we all stay together.'

Some, such as Rudy and Jurgen, nodded along enthusiastically. Others looked less convinced.

'Breaking into that fortress is virtual suicide,' said Zared, the leader of the Persaleian group.

Gyrmund could see that he was mentally weighing up the options for himself and his men. Going it alone might be safer for them. But although they had escaped their prison, they were still behind the massive walls of Samir Durg, with no obvious way of escape. Gyrmund knew the Persaleians saw something special in Clarin and Herin. Trying to get out of Ishari territory by themselves wasn't going to be easy. Despite his youth, Zared was a shrewd man, and would follow the option with the best chance of success.

'Our friend is a wizard,' said Herin. 'He's going to be our best chance of getting out of here alive.'

That seemed to be enough to swing it, and Zared nodded his acceptance.

'I will come with you,' said Tamir, the tall leader of the Barbarians. 'But some of my people want to stay, to free the men kept in the other pits here. They have family.'

'That is understandable,' conceded Clarin.

'How many?' asked Herin.

The Barbarians briefly talked amongst themselves.

'Five to stay,' said Tamir.

'If they do,' said Gyrmund, keeping his voice quiet, 'it could be a useful distraction for us.'

Herin nodded. 'Agreed. But ask them to wait for one hour to give us time to get to the fortress.'

Tamir relayed the order.

'What about him?' Gyrmund asked, gesturing at the Bear-man.

The Bear-man stood, looking around as if confused by what he saw. Down in the pit he had been a sad looking creature, kept in the corner. But out here, as he stretched his limbs, it was possible to see the sheer physical strength he possessed.

'I think he will come with us,' said Tamir.

'As will you,' said Clarin, addressing the three Dog-men.

'Yes, master,' one of them agreed, bowing its head. The other two copied the motion.

Everyone looked about again until all eyes fell on Moneva.

'Follow me.'

She had collected a small pile of weapons from the guards she had killed, mainly short spears and knives. Gyrmund grabbed a knife and shoved it into his belt. There weren't enough weapons to go around yet, and they would have to rectify that as soon as possible.

Moneva led them away from the pits and out through the fence gates, which she had already contrived to open. The path to the crystal mine led off to the right, and Gyrmund felt a powerful sense of relief that he would not have to travel that way ever again. He promised himself that he would not be captured this time. If he was to die in the next few hours, then so be it.

Instead, Moneva took them in the opposite direction, through a no-man's-land that led to the eastern walls of the main fortress. Huge towers stood at regular intervals along its length, and Moneva made for one of these before stopping a few hundred feet away.

'That's where I came out,' she explained, indicating a wooden door. 'I had to kill some guards to make sure I wasn't seen. I think a few of us need to go first to make sure it's still safe.'

Clarin told the other prisoners to wait, while the four of them crept over to the tower. It was an unnerving feeling for Gyrmund, knowing that soldiers patrolled the wall walks above them, with only the darkness of night to hide their approach. He wondered at Moneva's ability to do all this on her own.

They reached the door, weapons at the ready. With one hand, Moneva slowly reached out to it.

Behind her, Gyrmund tensed, ready to fight or run depending on what waited for them. It was so quiet that he could hear the others breathing.

Slowly, slowly, she pulled on the door with her fingertips, peering inside for any signs of movement. The door opened wider and wider, giving her a full look inside.

Then she was in. Gyrmund moved to the door, holding it open as he looked inside. It was dark, and it took a moment for his eyes to take in the salient features. The ground floor room of the tower was a rough, semi-circular shape. There were no other exits except for a set of winding steps to the right that led up to the next floor. To the left was a table and chairs, but other than that, it was bare. It reminded Gyrmund of the room that he, Herin and Clarin had been kept in on their first night at Samir Durg.

Moneva was already creeping up the steps to look at the next floor. Gyrmund entered the room, followed in by Herin and Clarin. He spotted something in the shadows under the stairs. Three bodies had been dumped there, no doubt by Moneva.

'Good,' whispered Herin next to him, peering at them. 'More weapons.'

Moneva had now gone out of sight, but Gyrmund didn't think it was wise to follow her up, in case she had to retreat down the narrow steps.

'How come,' Herin whispered, 'she has been given the run of the fortress?'

It was a question that had also been in the back of Gyrmund's mind. She seemed able to move around Samir Durg at will: two visits to the pits; a conversation with Pentas. Clearly, there was something she wasn't telling them. He sensed that now wasn't the right time to ask, however.

Moneva returned down the steps, fast yet silent. 'We're fine for now,' she whispered. 'The tower's empty.'

'I'll get the others,' said Clarin, exiting via the door they had come in through.

'What next?' asked Herin.

'I'm not sure,' replied Moneva. 'I wasn't convinced that we'd get this far,' she added, a tense half-smile playing on her lips.

Gyrmund could see her hands shaking. She looked pale and drawn. No doubt he looked worse; but she had doubtless been through a lot since Arioc's Isharite soldiers had separated them.

'Pentas told you where Soren is being held?' asked Herin.

Moneva nodded. 'The Tower of Diis. It's on the north side of the fortress.'

'To my mind,' Herin began, casting a quick glance outside to where his brother was rounding up the rest of the escaped prisoners, 'we have two objectives. One, get Soren. Two, get the hell out of here. Objective one requires as few people as possible. We don't want all thirty of us wandering about this fortress. We won't last five minutes. Objective two is where the numbers are needed, to break out. Any idea how we do that?'

'When it's time to leave,' said Moneva, 'we need to head south to the external towers. The wall walk links every tower. We'll reach another tower just like this one to the south,' she said, indicating the direction with a hand. 'Keep going, and the next tower along is an external one: a corner tower much bigger and better defended than this one. But it has a southern exit. That's our best hope of getting out.'

'So,' replied Herin. 'I think it's best if you two go for Soren. Clarin and I will control things here. We'll hold on until you get back.'

An idea occurred to Gyrmund. 'I could put on a guard's uniform, and act as if I'm taking Moneva to this Tower of Diis. It worked for us back in Coldeberg Castle.'

Moneva nodded. She didn't look enthusiastic. The truth was, there was little hope of success. Moneva and Gyrmund were more than likely to get stopped. The force here was bound to be discovered soon—when new guards arrived, or the dead ones were noticed missing.

'Look,' said Gyrmund, speaking to Herin. 'We need to be honest. We're not likely to get back. You can't wait here for us forever. What if you give us two hours before you go?'

Gyrmund looked at Moneva for agreement. She shrugged her acceptance.

'I understand what you're saying,' said Herin. 'But I think we'd be better playing it by ear than fixing a time. If we're going to be brutally honest, the chances are that we'll get discovered here well before two hours are up. We'll wait for you for as long as we can. Who knows, if there is a disturbance here, maybe it will help you three to escape.'

Gyrmund nodded. He and Herin had never got along. But he admired the man's courage. He offered his hand and Herin took it. Gyrmund got a strange feeling—some would call it a premonition—that they would not meet again.

BOLIVAR'S SWORD

XXII

Clarin insisted on accompanying Gyrmund and Moneva to the third floor of the tower, where they would exit onto Samir Durg's battlements. He had helped Gyrmund put on the armour of one of the dead tower guards. It would not bear close scrutiny, but it might work at a distance.

Moneva opened the northern door, and they peered out. A walkway led along the walls to the next tower along. Clarin looked down into the inner courtyard. A maze of further walls led off towards a central structure with a domed roof. Everything seemed still in the dark of the night, but it was clear that the fortress, with its walls that stretched off as far as the eye could see, and its many towers, would barrack hundreds of soldiers. It was perhaps best not to dwell too long on that.

He said his farewells and watched as the two figures crept off into the night. Both were quiet and agile—they were the right people for the task. He hoped they could get Soren out of here and back to Belwynn. He hoped he would see them again.

Clarin looked out to the east, where the mine and the pits lay. It had been a place of horror and hardship, of course. But it was also a place where he had stayed strong and become a leader. He felt different. Responsible. More clear-minded.

On the horizon, he detected the first light of sunrise. A new morning. That, probably, would mean a change of guard, as those on night watch would be relieved by a new set of soldiers. There wasn't much time left. They had to be ready.

* * *

BELWYNN WORE the cloth of gold and played her role as Lady of the Knights. Her outfit caught the light of dawn and drew all men to her. Knight after knight came for their weapons to be blessed before the battle. The younger knights: Philon, Leontios, and their friends came first. But so too did the older knights—so too did knights she had never met before. The biggest surprise came at the end of the queue, when Theron appeared with his friend, Tycho.

'Are you serious?' she demanded, raising an eyebrow.

'I would receive your blessing before the fight, my lady,' said Tycho plainly.

Belwynn understood a soldier's need for magic charms before they went into battle, and didn't argue further. She gave her blessing to Tycho and then turned to Theron. She felt a lump in her throat but said the words despite it.

'Theron of Erisina, I bless your sword, may it serve its master well in battle.'

She embraced them both. No more words were spoken, and the two knights left to make their way to the field of battle.

Belwynn walked a little way towards the lines of soldiers forming up into position. Just visible in the distance was the enemy. Rostam of Ishari had gathered an army of tens of thousands to block their path to Samir Durg, and then drive them from Haskany.

His force, so the Kalinthian scouts had reported, was predominantly made up of Drobax. Thousands upon thousands had left their northern homeland and travelled south down the Great Road to invade the Brasingian Empire. But there had still been plenty available to fill the ranks of the Isharite army here.

They weren't the only ones fighting under Rostam's command, however. Some Haskan soldiers remained to defend their homeland. A Kharovian force had been spotted too—the dread rovers of the sea were more used to raiding than fighting pitched battles, but they had heeded the call of their masters, nonetheless. The barks of the Dog-men, also loyal to Ishari, could be heard from time to time, the wicked sound crossing the distance between the two armies and making Belwynn's blood run cold. Finally, of course, there were the Isharites themselves. They were few, but a good proportion of them would be wizards, and this made them the most dangerous enemy of all.

In contrast, their own army had only one wizard, and not one that Belwynn totally trusted, either. As if reading her thoughts, Pentas strolled over towards her.

'I see that the Knights have made you their mystic,' he commented.

Belwynn shrugged. She saw no reason to feel any embarrassment about it in front of him.

'Not necessarily a bad thing,' he added, perhaps aware that she had taken it as a criticism.

'What can be gained today?' she asked him, changing the subject.

'Win or lose, you are making those on the Council feel very uncomfortable right now,' he replied. 'After the destruction of Edeleny, the Isharites thought they had won Dalriya. Now there is an enemy army not so very far from Samir Durg itself.'

'And what chance that we might do more than make them feel uncomfortable?' Belwynn asked him.

She tried to keep bitterness from her voice, but it would be a sorry waste of lives if that was all they achieved.

It was Pentas's turn to shrug. 'We shall see.'

Belwynn returned her gaze to the battlefield. Between the two armies was a few hundred yards of flat scrubland, nothing to offer protection to either side. Although it had been a chill night, the sun had risen in a cloudless sky, and Belwynn knew the conditions would be hot and dry. In front of her was a simple formation. The Krykkers stood in the middle, all on foot, a few ranks deep. They fought in their clan groups, and their job was to hold position against the enemy. Some distance behind them, to each side of the Krykkers, were two units of Kalinthian Knights. Theron commanded one and Sebastian the other. They would have an offensive role, threatening to outflank and encircle the enemy. Whilst it was vital that the Krykkers withstand the enemy, the Knights had to find a way to win.

Trumpet calls blasted out ahead of her. The Krykkers and the Knights were signalling their readiness for battle. It was about to start.

'Time for me to get ready,' murmured Pentas.

Belwynn turned to him. 'There are people here very important to me,' she said. 'I don't want to lose them.'

Pentas nodded, his red eyes gleaming. 'There are people here who are very important to Madria, too. There is a priestess of hers. A Krykker man wielding her sword. A human woman carrying her dagger and her staff. In the bigger picture, all others are expendable.'

He turned and left. Belwynn turned her back on the battlefield and made her way to the camp, about a mile behind the front line. There she would find Elana, whose healing skills would be needed today more than they ever had before.

* * *

TRUMPETS RANG out from the infantry ranks of the Krykkers, answered by the massed cavalry of the Knights.

Rabigar hefted his polearm, readying himself. He stood in the middle of the front line, with Torinac and the Dramsen clan. The other clans were positioned in separate rectangular units to either side. These units were known as buffalos amongst the Krykkers, since they shared the defensive strength and offensive reach of the horned creatures. On the left, Maragin led the Grendals; Guremar and the Plengas clan were on the right. Next to Rabigar stood Stenk, holding a great, long, two handed pike. Rabigar was keen to keep his eye on the lad in his first battle.

A few feet away, Torinac held aloft Bolivar's Great Sword, symbol of their people's defiance against the forces of Ishari. He pointed it ahead, towards the enemy. The Krykker army began to move.

The first two ranks of their army all held pole-arms of various descriptions. Those fighters situated on the two short edges of their rectangle also carried the same weapons, so that they could engage with any enemy who tried to attack from the side. Most common were the long, straight pikes that Stenk carried. But other warriors had variations on this basic design, often crafting their own weapons. Some had added an axe head to the long blade of the pike, so that their weapons could be used for chopping as well as thrusting. Rabigar himself favoured a weapon with a crossbar across the end of the pike. It prevented the blade from sliding too far into an enemy and getting stuck, and he anticipated his blade would see a lot of action today.

Despite these minor variations, the Krykkers could still present a long line of bristling metal points to the enemy. Holding the deadly points of their weapons up in the air in front of them, they picked up the pace of their march.

The knights who had scouted out the Ishari position had done a good job. They identified that forces had been arriving at the enemy camp from various directions. But they were not yet well organised, and Rostam was most likely waiting for more to arrive before moving against them. His location had been chosen as a place for his forces to meet up, rather than as a location for a battle. But if he had been expecting the Krykkers to sit and wait for him, he had made a serious mistake. Now was the time to fight, before the superior forces of Ishari were ready.

Drums pounded as the enemy realised that the Krykkers were on the march. Rabigar could see enemy units moving in their direction. Unsurprisingly, the Drobax were being sent to intercept them. Rostam's plan would be for his most expendable troops to soften them up before sending in his elite soldiers.

Rabigar looked along the line with pride. Despite marching at pace, the Krykkers held their positions, presenting a long, impenetrable forest of steel-tipped wooden shafts. The Krykkers didn't have horsemen like the Knights. They didn't have archers like the Caladri. They lacked the sheer numbers that the Brasingian Empire could field. But Rabigar knew they had the best infantry in Dalriya. They were the best equipped and the best drilled, learning iron discipline from youth. They fought, not as individuals, but as one whole. It had not been witnessed by the rest of Dalriya for generations. But here and now, it would be.

The Drobax were now close enough to pick out individually. Most went semi-naked, their hairy grey bodies rarely protected by anything resembling armour. Their weapons were rudimentary, made from wood or stone. They had been sent to fight in rough units, but they were already disintegrating. Some of the creatures came at a faster pace than others. The different units began to merge, so that the Krykkers faced an undulating sea of creatures bearing down on them.

Torinac called a halt. The first two rows gathered themselves, making sure that there was the correct space between each other. Rabigar's front row put their left knees to the ground, bracing their weapons for impact. The Drobax charged. When they came into missile range, stones and spears were hurled at them from the rear rows. Many of the Drobax went down. Others tripped over the fallen bodies. Still more had stopped, in an effort to avoid the flying missiles. The Drobax advance stuttered.

'Charge!' bellowed Torinac.

Rising to their feet, pikes now pointing straight ahead, Rabigar's line went for the enemy. He could see the fear on the faces of the Drobax as the wall of pikes bore down on them. Some of them carried spears and held them out in front of themselves, but they were barely half the length of the pikes, and no real competition. Still others carried short clubs. They would have to avoid the pikes and get in close to do any damage.

Rabigar fixed his weapon on a Drobax spearman. As he approached, he saw the whites of its eyes. It lurched to its left at the last moment to avoid his strike. But Rabigar simply pulled his arms into his body and then thrust forwards, going down on one knee, skewering it through the chest. He checked on Stenk, who had also struck his target through the thigh. Rabigar pulled his pike free and sent it into the chest of Stenk's Drobax, to make sure that it was killed. With a shout, the second rank of Krykkers levelled their pikes over the heads of Rabigar's rank and thrust forwards, finding more targets in some cases; in others, dissuading the Drobax from counterattacking.

Rabigar's line moved forwards and thrust again, killing the next rank. A Drobax holding a club ran in between Rabigar and Stenk's pikes, making for the younger man. Rabigar let go of his pike and moved to intercept it, but a pike emerged from the rank behind, and skewered the creature before it got close.

Again, the Krykkers moved forwards to strike at the Drobax, and once more. Rabigar found himself having to kneel on a corpse as he kept his position in the line. Pools of dark blood lay across the parched ground.

In the end, the inevitable happened, and the Drobax broke. Unable to halt the Krykker war machine's progress and facing certain death, self-preservation took over, and the horde of Drobax turned and fled back the way they had come.

The Dramsen clan paused briefly to draw breath. A few injured soldiers were being guided through to the back of the unit, but Rabigar couldn't see any fatalities. He looked to his left and right. The Drobax had been broken right across the battlefield, meaning that the other two buffalos were also free. Seeing this, Torinac wasted no more time and ordered an advance.

They followed the retreating Drobax across the dusty ground. Rabigar could now make out the beginnings of the Isharite camp, where tents had been pitched, and wagons parked. Moving out to challenge them were a dozen smaller units of Haskan infantry. The Drobax ran through the gaps between the Haskan units and on into their camp. Hopefully, they would keep on running.

Rabigar could see that they were now dealing with a different, superior threat. The Haskan soldiers were well armed and their smaller units were fast —faster than the Krykker buffalos, with their long pole-arms that had to be held aloft as they moved.

Some of the Haskan units were moving to the sides, outflanking the buffalos of the Grendal and Plengas clans without getting too close. Looking across to his left, Rabigar could see Maragin's dilemma. If she moved her unit across to deal with the threat, the Grendals would become detached from the

Dramsens and potentially encircled. If she kept moving ahead, the Haskans would be able to attack from the rear. Both the Grendal and Plengas buffalos came to a halt, pikes facing outwards at all angles. Still, the Haskans manoeuvred around them without engaging.

Rabigar could see Torinac looking around nervously. Their advance had come to a halt. If the Isharites were able to regroup the Drobax, they could be in real trouble.

Rabigar felt the ground tremble. Everyone turned around to look.

'The Knights!' declared Stenk enthusiastically.

Two streams of cavalry were arriving on the battlefield in a wide arc. As Rabigar watched, they quickly outflanked the Haskan units and turned around to face them from the sides. In a matter of minutes, the dynamic on the battlefield had changed. The Haskans found themselves caught between the Krykkers and the Kalinthian cavalry with no means of escape—the Knights were too fast. Sebastian and Theron had arrived at just the right time.

Trumpets sounded from both groups of cavalry. They formed into a long line, levelling their lances so that they pointed ahead. Another blast from the trumpets gave the order to charge. It was an imposing sight, watching the armoured horses gathering pace. The Haskan soldiers would be terrified. Meanwhile, Maragin had taken advantage of the situation to order the Grendals to attack. The Haskans would be crushed between the two forces.

Rabigar looked at Torinac. He saw the chieftain peering ahead. Rabigar could make out Haskan cavalry forces leaving the enemy camp and heading to engage the Kalinthians. But surely, they would be no match for the Knights? Ahead of the Dramsens were two of the Haskan units. They had kept a safe distance from the Krykkers, but now seemed unsure of what to do. Rabigar knew what Torinac's order would be before it was given. Torinac wanted to win the battle right now. He raised Bolivar's Sword again and gave the order to attack.

Pole-arms raised, the Dramsen clan marched forwards, leaving the rest of the battle to their allies. The two units of Haskan soldiers reacted, looking to trap them in a pincer. Torinac ordered an attack on the Haskan unit to their right. The Krykkers turned in that direction, held their pikes aloft, and ran towards them. The Krykkers could be surprisingly fast when they picked up speed. The Haskans dithered, and that was their downfall. They seemed to be unsure whether they should retreat, or attack the Krykkers in order to implement their pincer. In the end, they did neither, merely holding their ground.

As the Dramsens approached, the Haskan front line locked shields together. They wore mail armour and presented a formidable defence. Rabigar's rank dove to their knees and thrust their pikes at the legs of the shield men. The second rank thrust forwards at head level. No shield was big enough to defend against pikes at both ankle and face level, and many Haskans fell. Those that survived counterattacked with shield and spear. Rabigar was quick to drop his pike, drawing the sword that he favoured in close combat.

With neither the wall of shields or pikes intact any more, it quickly became a vicious melee. Rabigar hacked and sliced with his sword. He swung at a Haskan spearman who took the blow on his shield, and then thrust forwards with his spear. Rabigar stepped back out of range. The spearman poked at him, creeping forwards. He then launched his attack, thrusting forwards. Rabigar sidestepped and grabbed the wooden shaft of the spear. He yanked at it, pulling the spearman off balance, before thrusting with his sword into the neck area, between hauberk and helmet. He pulled his sword free with a gush of blood.

Rabigar looked around for Stenk and spotted him, keeping an enemy at bay with his pike. Rabigar joined him but didn't press the attack. The longer line of the Krykker buffalo was now curling around the Haskans, who found themselves being attacked from the sides. Rabigar waited until the odds were fully in his favour before joining in with the slaughter. The red mist rose as he strode around, looking for enemies to kill. Assailed from all sides, the Haskans had no chance. Many begged for mercy, but the Krykkers cut them all down.

When the job was done, it was time to turn around to deal with the second Haskan unit. As they had been drilled countless times, the pikemen at the rear end of the Dramsen buffalo had formed a defensive line to stop the oncoming Haskans. This kind of defensive formation was three ranks deep, with pikes facing the enemy from three different heights, like the quills of a porcupine. Rabigar and the other Krykkers moved around it to face the enemy, who had been unable to break through. Without waiting for an order, the Krykkers now charged the second Haskan unit. The pikemen who had been on the defence now thrust forwards. Rabigar and the men with him outflanked the Haskans and attacked from the side. The Haskans put up a stout resistance, but their defences were inevitably breached, and a second slaughter, just like the first, ensued.

When it was done, the Dramsen clan paused to take breath. Soldiers looked at each other, grim smiles for comrades covered in blood and gore. The stench of it was overpowering. Rabigar wiped his sword clean on a corpse.

He looked at the rest of the battle. Things were still in flux. The Haskan cavalry had engaged with the Kalinthians, and some of their infantry units were still active. None were close to the Dramsen's position, however, and the way was now clear to the enemy camp.

'Forwards!' bellowed Torinac, Bolivar's Sword now dripping red.

They marched for the camp where Rostam and the other leaders were based. If they could drive them off now, there was little chance of the Isharites regrouping from such a defeat any time soon. Those who still had their pole-arms moved to the front ranks. Rabigar found Stenk and persuaded him to stand with him in the third rank. Stenk passed his pike over to another soldier and took an axe from his belt.

No-one was there to prevent them from entering the outskirts of the camp. They looked around. Tents lay empty. Horse-pulled wagons and carts with food and other supplies sat undefended. Rabigar spied a forge wagon, fitted up to carry the furnace, bellows and other tools required by a black-smith to make running repairs to weapons and armour. But the craftworkers to go with it were nowhere to be seen. The camp was deserted.

Torinac led his clan into the centre of the camp, a feeling of slight unease spreading amongst them. Something didn't feel right.

Then, from out of nowhere, words were being shouted in an alien tongue. The Krykkers turned to look for the source in all directions, but there was nothing to see. Suddenly, an enemy force appeared in front of them. It was the strangest sensation. Part of Rabigar realised they had been there all along, but they had somehow been hidden from sight. By magic.

But there was no more time to think about it. Charging straight at them, howling and barking, were the most fearsome creatures in the Isharite army. Dog-men. The Krykkers turned to face the threat, quickly trying to get their pikes ready to face the attack. A force buffeted them, like a powerful gust of wind. It caused men to stumble and lose their footing. Polearms were blown about, difficult to hold on to; more than one soldier got a crack on the head or arm from their neighbour's weapon.

Then, the Dog-men were on them. They bounded up to the row of pikes and leapt high in the air. Some were caught before they landed. In front of Rabigar, a Dog-man failed to avoid a pike and was skewered, the force of its descent making its body slide all the way down the length of the pole. But others leapt powerfully over the pikes and crashed into the ranks behind. More of them came, recklessly throwing themselves into the Dramsen buffalo.

Before he knew it, a Dog-man was descending on top of Rabigar. He braced his sword arm, ready to thrust through its middle. But the creature somehow pushed his blade aside with its hind leg and crashed on top of him. Rabigar went down like a sack of oats, the wind knocked out of him. On top of him, the Dog-man grabbed his forearms with its sharp claws and pushed itself up into a seated position, its weight on his chest keeping him pinned to the ground. It opened its muzzle, revealing two rows of vicious teeth, and aimed for Rabigar's jugular, which he knew it could rip out in one go. Before it got the chance, however, Rabigar could see Stenk's axe coming down from behind the creature. The blow was true, the blade of the axe smacking down straight into the back of the Dog-man's skull, killing it instantly. It collapsed on top of Rabigar, who shoved the creature off.

Stenk had his axe blade stuck, and planted his foot on the creature's head to help him yank it free. Just as he did so, the whole rank of soldiers in front of them collapsed backwards as more Dog-men leapt into the fray. Stenk collapsed under a mound of kicking arms, legs and claws.

Rabigar snatched for his sword, which was lying on the ground next to him and forced himself up. He knew he had to act quickly. The wicked claws and powerful jaws of the Dog-men gave them a distinct advantage in a scrum like this. Meanwhile, the pole-arms carried by the Krykker soldiers were now useless, and they had to be given time to get their hands on their shorter weapons.

He thrust down into the sprawling mass in front of him, being careful to avoid his comrades, and finding the exposed flesh of the poorly armoured Dog-men.

Reaching down with his left hand, he grabbed Stenk around the chest and pulled him out, all the while keeping his sword in front of him to deflect any attack. Stenk picked himself up, looking none the worse: he had even kept hold of his axe. They both returned to the fray, helping the surviving Krykkers up and fending off the Dog-men, who backed off.

Then, Rabigar saw him. Torinac lay dead amongst the bodies, his arms spread wide and his eyes staring up at the sky. His throat had been torn out. Rabigar looked around the body of the fallen chieftain. Much as he regretted Torinac's death, far more important was the whereabouts of Bolivar's Sword.

He turned bodies over, getting more desperate by the second. Stenk helped him. There! Buried in the body of a Dog-man, perhaps the same creature that had killed Torinac, was the Sword. Rabigar grasped the hilt and pulled the blade free. He could feel the power of the weapon coursing through him, from his grip, along his arm, and into his chest. He held the sword aloft, marvelling at it. Now it belonged to him.

A blast hit them again, this time accompanied by a blinding light. It seemed to strike the Dog-men as much as the Krykkers. Rabigar sank to one knee, holding Bolivar's Sword close to his body in an effort not to lose his grip on it. He looked down at the ground to avoid looking at the light. Just as he thought he would be forced to close his eye and topple over, the magic stopped. Looking up, patches of light still obscuring his vision, he saw just in time that a new enemy had appeared. Striding past the sprawled Dog-men came the Isharites themselves.

They made straight for Rabigar, since he was the only Krykker nearby who had not collapsed from the blast of magic. A crystal sword came swinging down at him. Still on one knee, Rabigar blocked it. The Isharite pushed down on him with all of his weight, his thin, dark features snarling with hatred; but Rabigar resisted, matching his strength. Pulling back, the Isharite took a quick swing at Rabigar from the side but he was ready for it, blocking the strike again, and then regaining his feet. Another blow came for him, but he managed to block it, as if the Sword he held guided his hands.

He danced backwards, out of the reach of the Isharites who outnumbered him. Now he felt the presence of the other Krykkers, who joined him to face down the new threat.

The Isharites and the remaining Dog-men stood for a moment, staring at the Krykkers. *No,* thought Rabigar, *they are staring behind us.* Then suddenly, without warning, all of them turned and ran. They ran as fast as they could, to the far side of the camp, and kept running.

Looking behind him, Rabigar could see a group of Kalinthian Knights heading in their direction. It took the Knights seconds to reach them, and Rabigar just got a glimpse of Theron in the lead of the mounted force before they shot past, chasing down the enemy.

This was when a cavalry force such as this really came into their own. The Knights could chase down and harass the departing Isharite army for miles if they needed to. There would be no chance for the Drobax forces to regroup and come back at them now. They had won.

The others felt it too, and a wave of relief came over them all. Stenk appeared next to Rabigar, and he gave the young man a great hug.

Some shouting ahead of them caused them to break their embrace. The Dramsens had found their fallen chieftain. Rabigar turned in the direction where the noise was coming from and strode over.

The clan gathered around in shock at the sight of Torinac lying lifeless on the ground. A strange feeling came over Rabigar.

'Your chieftain died as a hero today,' he intoned. 'Now the duty and honour of wielding Bolivar's Sword falls to me.'

The Krykkers of the Dramsen clan looked at Rabigar with blank expressions. But no-one challenged him. And that was as it should be. For this sword sang to Rabigar and told him that he was meant to have it.

SAMIR DURG

XXIII

Moneva led Gyrmund along the walls of Samir Durg, always on the lookout for sentries. She kept a fast pace, keen to make as much progress as possible while the last hour or so of night afforded them protection. When she spotted a guard, she would indicate for Gyrmund to wait while she investigated. Sometimes they could detour around them, or wait until they moved. Invariably, the safest and quickest way to deal with them was a knife through the base of the skull; before moving on as fast as possible.

Gyrmund needed minimal attention; he knew how to conceal himself and was content to leave the decisions to her. What did concern Moneva, however, was his pale, drawn face, and lack of energy. It was only after they had been going for a while that she realised he must be half starved and dehydrated. While she had been eating Arioc's rich, spiced food since she had arrived in his chambers, Gyrmund must have been on the meanest of rations, while working all day.

Moneva took more care to secure food and drink on the way. She then led Gyrmund to the top room of a tower. She had learned that these rooms were mostly deserted, sometimes serving as storage. Occasionally, Isharite soldiers used them as places to rest up or sleep.

She handed Gyrmund a pile of dry crackers, which seemed to be the staple rations of the Isharite soldiers. She also pulled out a pot of something strong smelling. She thought it might be similar to the arak that she had drunk in Arioc's chambers. She took a sip and scrunched up her face. The alcohol in it wasn't as strong as the arak, but it tasted of sour milk. Gyrmund took it to go with his crackers. He didn't seem to mind the taste, and a bit of colour returned to his face once he had finished it.

They sat for a moment, looking at each other.

'If we get out of here—' whispered Gyrmund.

'If we get out of here, we can talk then,' said Moneva.

She hadn't meant to be so abrupt. It was the stress she was under. But she couldn't do emotions—not now. It was a distraction, and Gyrmund should have known better.

It looked like he was about to reply, and then he stopped, perhaps thinking better of it. He cocked his head, as if listening to something. Moneva tuned in. It was the sound of soldiers moving.

She got to her feet, drawing a knife. Gyrmund's eyes widened, and he grabbed his weapon too.

She could hear footsteps, getting louder. If they tried to leave the room now, they were likely to run straight into the soldiers. She surveyed the room quickly, imagining a soldier coming up the stairs and looking in. Pointing at a straw mattress, she gestured that Gyrmund should lie on it. He didn't argue, again trusting her judgement, which she was grateful for. She draped a blanket over him. Perhaps, just perhaps, they might mistake him for a lazy soldier and not investigate further. She chose the corner of the room that lay in shadow for herself. She draped her hair over her face and put her hands behind her back, so that her skin could not be seen. Then they waited.

Moneva heard the soldiers entering their tower, arriving from the north of the fortress. *Have we been spotted?* She fingered the blade of the knife. If the soldiers were after them, they would be in the room in seconds. She knew that a fight in this chamber wouldn't last very long. But a part of her still hoped that the soldiers were heading somewhere else.

They were moving fast. She could now hear them directly underneath the room. She listened to the hurried conversation that drifted up the stairs, but while she had got somewhat used to the Isharite language during her time at the fortress, picking up a few words, she couldn't process anything she heard now. And then they were gone, heading south along the fortress walls. She stayed still for a while longer, not yet daring to believe it. The sound of footsteps disappeared. Then, just as Moneva began to relax a little, a second group came past, passing directly underneath them and heading in the same direction. She detected a slight movement in the room and looked to see Gyrmund's head poking out of his blanket.

Moneva indicated that he should remain where he was. She forced herself forwards, willing her muscles to move and peel her body away from the wall against which she had flattened herself. She was used to operating with fear swirling around her body, and steadily, if jerkily, her limbs did as she commanded. She approached the stairs down to the third floor of the tower on her belly and, edging over the gap, peered down to have a look. The room below seemed empty. Pulling herself up into a crouching position, she made herself creep down to make sure.

It was empty. She could smell the sweat and the leather of the soldiers who had passed through. She glanced outside. A new day's dawn was throwing its light on the walls of Samir Durg. She quickly made her way back up to the top chamber.

Gyrmund had come out from under the blanket.

'It's empty now,' Moneva whispered.

'They're going for Clarin and Herin, aren't they?' he asked.

Moneva shrugged. 'I don't know for sure, but...'

But it was the most obvious explanation.

Gyrmund nodded. 'What now?'

Moneva sighed. 'The sun's up. No more night to hide us. I think we need to take a risk now. Leave this tower and head into the centre of the fortress. Go straight for the Tower of Diis. I'll lead us, but you need to act as if you're taking me there. Look people in the eye, but don't stare at anyone. Everyone in the fortress may be preoccupied with taking Herin and Clarin's tower, and we can slip past unnoticed.'

For Gyrmund's sake, she sounded as confident as she could. He nodded his acceptance of the plan.

'What about getting in?' he asked.

'Here,' she said, producing the brooch with Arioc's sigil on it. 'It's the symbol of Arioc and his men. Tell them he's sent me to the prisons there. He's the King of Haskany—he has humans working for him.'

Wordlessly, Gyrmund took the brooch and studied it, tracing a finger along the circular shape of the serpent. She knew he wanted to ask how she had got it; about her time with Arioc. Instead, he did as she had asked, and pinned it to his cloak.

They slipped down the tower stairs unchallenged, all the way to the ground floor. Moneva nodded at the door that opened into the central part of the fortress. Gyrmund moved over and opened it, taking one step outside. He then reached inside and grabbed her arm, pulling her with him.

* * *

THEY HAD TAKEN care of the change of guard when it came.

Six soldiers had arrived as the sun rose in the sky. Clarin asked Zared and a few of his men to help with the ambush. The Isharite soldiers were surprised as they entered the tower from the walkway. They were attacked from all angles: Herin cutting off their retreat; the agile Cyprian even jumping down on top of them from the chamber above. None of them could escape, and Clarin and his men avoided injury. But killing six men isn't easy. During the desperate fighting in the enclosed space, there was many a shout and scream, and Clarin knew it was now only a matter of time before more soldiers came. Next time, there would be more of them, and the element of surprise would be gone.

The Persaleians busied themselves stripping the Isharite bodies of their armour and taking it for themselves. All the Persaleians, and most of the Barbarians, were now armed with a weapon.

'What now?' asked Zared.

Clarin was still getting used to the fact that he was in charge. Even more strangely, Herin looked at him, as if waiting for orders. He considered their situation. There was little more they could do for Gyrmund and Moneva now. He had to think of their own predicament, and the last thing he wanted was to get everyone trapped in this little tower. The Isharites could approach from both directions and take their time digging them out. They could use fire and smoke, and Toric only knew what else. That was no way to die.

'We'll close off the northern door with whatever we can find,' he decided. He looked south along the wall. The next tower was identical to the one they were in and would be lightly defended.

He pointed. 'Then head for the next tower.'

Clarin looked at the Persaleians in their Isharite armour. 'Those of you who can pass off as Isharites should go first. If they shut the door on us, we'll be trapped. Get as close as you can until they realise something's up and then charge it. We'll be right behind you.'

Apart from a table and chairs, there was little else but dead bodies to prop against the north door of the tower. The young Rotelegen cousins, Rudy and Jurgen, each armed with short spears, insisted on staying back to defend the position while the rest of them went ahead.

'Don't hesitate to retreat when the position is lost,' instructed Clarin, and they nodded obediently.

As Clarin watched from the doorway of their tower, armed with a spear of his own, Zared and four of his best men left the tower and moved along the walkway. To their left, crenellations had been constructed to protect the defenders of the fortress, while to the right was a sheer drop to the inner courtyard. Two Isharites manned the wall on the far side of the walkway and turned at Zared's approach. They shouted over, unintelligible words in the Isharite tongue.

'Shit,' commented Herin, crouched next to Clarin in the shadows. His brother gripped a knife, ready to charge down the walkway.

Zared called back. Clarin couldn't tell if the Persaleian had picked up a bit of the Isharite language, or was simply bluffing. But it seemed to work. The two Isharite soldiers waited and let Zared and his men approach. Then, suddenly, they began shouting. Herin didn't waste any time, shooting off down the walkway. Clarin followed close behind.

Ahead, the Persaleians ran at the two Isharite soldiers. It was a narrow walkway, and for a moment, the Persaleians found their path blocked. The two Isharites continued to shout out their warning. The impasse continued until they contrived to throw one of the Isharites from the wall down to the courtyard below. The second Isharite was bundled to the floor, while Zared and two of his men sidestepped past and ran for the tower door.

Clarin edged carefully past the prone, struggling figures on the walkway, wary of falling off into the courtyard below. Then, picking up some speed, he made it through the door of the next tower. His brother was already grappling with an Isharite on the floor, while Zared and one of his men were fighting two more soldiers in the confined space of the chamber. Unable to use his spear effectively, Clarin dropped it and grabbed a soldier around the head, twisting his neck until it broke. The two Persaleians finished off the other soldier. Clarin stamped on the head of Herin's adversary, allowing Herin to pull his knife hand free, and stab into the Isharite's exposed neck. One of Zared's men was seated on the floor, his lifeblood ebbing away from a stab wound in his chest. But he was the only casualty.

Clarin helped Herin up. Wordlessly, his brother headed down the stairs to make sure that the rest of the tower was empty. Looking behind him, Clarin could see that the second Isharite soldier on the walkway had been disposed of, and that Tamir was leading the Barbarians across towards them.

Shouts came from the courtyard below. It was no surprise that their assault had been witnessed. Clarin moved over to the southern door of the chamber and looked out. As Moneva had described, beyond the next stretch of walkway was a huge corner tower. It guarded the southern wall of Samir Durg, and was a massive piece of construction, the size of a castle keep. It would have many rooms inside it, with more soldiers posted there. Indeed, as

Clarin thought about it, it was quite likely that it represented the living quarters of a substantial number of Isharite soldiers.

He moved back from the door as the rest of the escaped prisoners began filing into the tower. Herin was telling them to head down into the lower floors. A few feet away, Zared was kneeling by his dying friend's side, whose face had gone deathly white, but whose eyes continued to stare forwards.

Zared looked up at him. 'What now?'

* * *

IT WAS impossible for Shira to deny that they were making better progress than before. To be fair to herself, Arioc hadn't changed the basic strategy. He had just added an extra layer of ruthlessness to the tactics.

They were standing a mile or so away from the looming presence of Burkhard Castle. Ahead was the path up the nearest crag. The Drobax were hurling themselves up this steep track, pushing the Brasingian defenders back. They had already smashed their way through three of the wooden gates that had been constructed to stop their ascent. The Brasingians continued to enjoy a height advantage, and the losses were still far heavier on the Drobax side. But any Brasingian slow enough to get caught by the monsters was immediately overwhelmed and torn apart; or else simply thrown off the crag to meet the same fate down below.

At the bottom of the path was Arioc's innovation. A group of armed Drobax waited for any of their kind to descend from the crag. Here, retreating Drobax would be butchered. They had been given a stark choice: force your way up to the top of the crag and live; fail, and die. It had provided the extra motivation needed for the progress to be made.

Arioc stood watching the attack impassively. Shira's uncle, Koren, always deferential to her husband, waited on him attentively. The Isharite wizard, Mehrab, was also present. Since Arioc's success, he wore a permanent smirk on his smug face.

An arrival from further behind them interrupted the silence. An Isharite strode forwards and sank to one knee in front of Arioc. His long black hair was plastered with sweat, and he looked pale and ill. He physically shook as he spoke.

'Your Majesty, I have come from Lord Rostam with haste. Our army engaged with the Krykkers and Kalinthians. We were driven from the field by their forces, and our own soldiers are in full retreat.'

A wordless shout of fury erupted from Arioc's mouth. Shira felt something close to relief. Her own lack of success in Brasingia suddenly didn't seem so bad compared to such an utter disaster.

'I need to get to Samir Durg immediately,' said Arioc, fighting to control his anger. 'Mehrab, get your men ready.'

With that, Arioc marched off, accompanied by Mehrab. As an afterthought, he turned back to Shira.

'You're in charge here,' he said curtly, before departing for good.

Shira met eyes with her uncle. 'That's one Council meeting I might have enjoyed attending.'

THE TOWER OF DIIS

XXIV

Gyrmund held Moneva as if she was a captured prisoner, while she led him through a maze of corridors and courtyards towards the Tower of Diis. On their left, a domed central building loomed over them; on their right were the high walls and towers of Samir Durg, the diatine crystals within them glinting in the morning sun.

Moneva had been right. The whole fortress seemed to be alive with energy and tension, soldiers and servants rushing in every direction. It was hard to believe that Herin and Clarin's small force, in one small tower, could have caused such disruption. Of course, Gyrmund considered, some of the Barbarians had chosen to stay behind and release their kin from the other slave pits. Maybe they had succeeded in raising a second force which had been discovered? Whatever the reason, everyone they passed seemed to have an urgent job to do, and few gave them a second glance.

Ahead of them, the Tower of Diis came into view. It was by far the largest of the towers Gyrmund had seen, situated in the central section of the northern wall of the fortress, and dominating its surroundings. He could see two guards on duty outside the main entrance. This was it. Ignoring the tightening in his gut and chest, he steered Moneva towards the entrance, doing his best to look nonchalant.

The Isharite guards were tall and well built, each holding a spear that crossed each other to bar entrance to the Tower. As Gyrmund approached, they caught sight of the brooch with Arioc's sigil and pulled their spears in. Even here, Arioc's power counted.

'She's for the prisons,' said Gyrmund. He did his best to put on a Haskan accent, just in case the guards could notice the difference.

The guards nodded disinterestedly. 'Why's Arioc got a human running his errands?' asked one of them pointedly.

'*King* Arioc,' said Gyrmund, as if taking offence, 'rates me very highly. My family is very important in Haskany.'

The guards laughed at him, pulling open the doors.

'Very important in Haskany,' repeated the second guard, imitating Gyrmund's accent. 'That don't mean shit in Samir Durg. You're just an errand boy, here.'

Gyrmund guided Moneva through the doors. 'Where do I go?' he asked.

'Down,' said the guard unhelpfully, before they closed the doors on them.

The entrance corridor was only dimly lit, and they took care as they walked. Neither spoke. They had to assume they could be heard; someone might even be watching them. It was therefore vital that they keep up the pretence of prisoner and soldier.

After a short distance, the corridor branched off to the left and right. It looked like the left path led to a guard room, so they headed to the right, into the main part of the Tower. They arrived in a large, slightly better lit, irregular shaped ground-floor chamber. It was empty of people. Various dimly lit passages led off it, at all angles. On the far wall, a set of stairs led upwards to the next floor—but the guards had said 'down'.

Turning to the left, they began circling the chamber, looking for a route down. It didn't take long. The second passage they came to was very short and ended with a set of stone steps heading down into the dungeons. Gyrmund could smell the damp coming from the underground rooms below.

Warily, Gyrmund began the journey down, still holding Moneva by the arm. Below ground level, the Tower of Diis was even more poorly lit. Gyrmund, his eyes not yet fully adjusted to the gloom, could barely make out the next step in front of him as he slowly negotiated his way, his footsteps sounding heavy in the silent and oppressive atmosphere. Gingerly stretching his front foot forwards, he finally found himself on the dungeon floor, and helped Moneva down to join him.

Their descent must have alerted someone. Gyrmund could hear quick footsteps coming in their direction. As they got nearer, he made out a cowled figure approaching them. The figure looked Gyrmund up and down, taking in the brooch still attached to his cloak. As he did so, Gyrmund got a glimpse of the face under the hood: a man with a thin, mottled face, surrounded with lank, greasy hair.

'You have someone for us?' he asked in a croaky voice.

'King Arioc has sent his prisoner here. She's to go with the wizard he captured.'

The cowled jailer, if jailer he was, turned his attention to Moneva. 'Ah,' he said with an unpleasant grin. 'Arioc's whore. Had enough of you, has he?'

Gyrmund went cold. *Arioc's whore?* His eyes flicked to Moneva, but she had turned her face away to the side. So, that was how she had been allowed to move around the fortress so freely. He knew he shouldn't have been surprised. He knew she had done it to save herself, and had risked her life to save him and the others. Nonetheless, emotions swirled around his head—anger, hatred, jealousy, and every other kind of pain threatened to overwhelm him.

The jailer was watching them both.

'Didn't think I'd know about the goings on up there, did you?' he asked, misreading both of their reactions. 'I know plenty.'

Gyrmund didn't reply. He took a deep breath, trying to regain a sense of control.

'Well, anyway, I'll take her from here,' said the jailer coldly, perhaps offended by Gyrmund's lack of response.

Gyrmund was reminded of his own journey to the dungeons of Coldeberg Castle. He remembered being accompanied by Salvinus's soldier, who had taken him all the way to the cell, making sure that Gyrmund was in chains before he left. Curtis was his name. Gyrmund wasn't likely to forget it. 'Have fun' were the last words Curtis had said to him before leaving.

'I need to see her to the cell,' he said to the jailer.

The jailer frowned with displeasure, looking at Gyrmund with suspicion. Gyrmund stared back, and something in his expression dissuaded the jailer from making an argument of it.

'Very well,' he conceded, retreating up the corridor.

Gyrmund led Moneva after him. They followed the jailer down the dark corridor. Gyrmund's eyes adjusted somewhat to the light. The walls of the corridor were made from rough stone. They passed through a wooden door. Now Gyrmund could see doors leading off the corridor, regularly spaced along each wall. These must be the prison cells. He looked about. No other jailers or guards could be seen. Was Soren in one of these cells?

The jailer stopped at a door, fumbling at his side for a set of keys.

Gyrmund tried to remain relaxed. It hadn't crossed his mind before, but he wondered what kind of state Soren would be in after all this time.

The jailer unlocked the door and swung it inwards. The door shuddered along the floor as he did so, making a loud scraping noise. Gyrmund peered inside. At first, he thought it was a trick, and eyed the jailer nervously. Then he returned his gaze to the inside of the cell. There was nothing in there but a large wooden box. But now he recognised it as the box in which the Isharites had transported Soren from Edeleny to Samir Durg. Had he been kept in there all this time?

He swung his gaze to the jailer, his mouth open in mute shock.

The jailer gave him a toothy grin. Then, before either of them could react, Moneva was shoving the blade of her dagger into the base of the jailer's skull. He shuddered—a throaty breath escaped from his mouth—and then Moneva caught his limp body, carefully lying it down on the floor of the cell.

As he watched her, Gyrmund wondered how many people she had killed in her short life.

'Can we just lift it off?' she asked him, nodding at the box as she wiped the blade clean on the jailer's robes and sheathed it.

Gyrmund moved over to the box to examine it. It had a heavy lid, but no locks or chains on it. 'Yes. Come on.'

Standing on each side of the box, they lifted the handles and heaved the lid off. An appalling smell assaulted Gyrmund's nostrils as they did so.

'Get him out,' said Moneva, gagging at the smell.

Gyrmund peered in. Soren was in the box, sitting with his knees hunched up and his head resting against the side. His eyes were closed, and he looked dead. He had soiled himself many times, and the stench inside the box was horrendous.

Gyrmund reached in carefully, trying not to injure him. He grasped the wizard under the arms and lifted him up into a standing position. He had lost a lot of weight, and his thin limbs dangled in the air.

Soren groaned; he was alive. But he seemed unable to put any weight on his legs as Gyrmund held him. Moneva grabbed his legs, and they lifted him gently out of the box onto the stone floor of the cell.

'Strip him,' said Moneva.

Gyrmund pulled at Soren's trousers as Moneva moved over to remove the jailer's clothes. He looked worriedly at the cell's open door, dreading it slamming shut on them. But so far, no-one else had come to interfere with their rescue.

Soren lay with his eyes closed, barely moving as they did their best to wipe him clean, then dressed him in the robes of the dead jailer. Gyrmund sat him up, holding onto him, while Moneva got out her pot of fermented mare's milk.

'Soren, I'm going to give you a drink,' she said gently, putting the pot to his lips. 'Don't drink too much.'

His lips were cracked and bloody, but he took a sip and swallowed. He took some more. Gyrmund felt his body relax somewhat.

'Where am I?' he said.

'You're in the Tower of Diis, in Samir Durg. This is Moneva. I've come with Gyrmund to rescue you, so you need to keep quiet. Your eyes are closed. Can you try to open them?'

Soren scrunched up his eyes and forced them open, blinking in the paltry light of his prison cell.

'We need to go, Soren,' said Moneva.

Gyrmund lifted him up, but Soren couldn't make his legs stand.

'Put him down,' whispered Moneva. 'Rub his legs.'

They worked on a leg each, rubbing the wizard's muscles back into life. As the blood flowed back into his legs, Soren screwed his face up in pain, but resisted crying out.

Again, Gyrmund pulled him up. This time, Soren was able to stay on his feet. But his back was bent double, and he looked to be in considerable pain. If he had spent the last three weeks constricted in that box, it was no surprise. He had clearly been starved in that time too, but his captors must have been feeding him something, or he would be dead by now.

'I can't see,' said Soren, his voice croaky, as if he had been doing a lot of shouting.

'What?' asked Gyrmund.

'It's all a blur,' added the wizard, waving a hand in front of his eyes.

Moneva and Gyrmund shared a look. This was proving to be far more difficult than they had anticipated.

'Rest on me,' said Gyrmund, putting Soren's hand on his arm. 'I'm sorry, but we have no more time. We have to go.'

They exited the cell. Gyrmund was relieved to be leading them back up the dungeon corridor without having been noticed by anyone else. He took the stone steps up to the ground floor slowly and carefully, guiding the frail wizard, reaching the large, irregular chamber of the Tower of Diis. It was still empty.

Gyrmund and Moneva looked around uncertainly. They didn't have an escape plan. The two guards outside the main entrance would be virtually impossible to remove in broad daylight. Gyrmund could see Moneva looking around for alternative exits. Maybe she could somehow sneak her way out of the Tower, but not with Soren in tow.

'What is it?' asked the wizard, frowning at them.

'There are two guards outside the main door of the Tower,' explained Gyrmund.

'Take me,' Soren commanded.

Shrugging at each other, they led him down the corridor to the entrance. Gyrmund was uneasy. Soren sounded sure of himself—but he wasn't convinced that the wizard was in full control of his faculties after his prolonged confinement.

'Go on,' said Soren, his voice sounding irritable.

After exchanging glances with Moneva, who seemed willing to trust Soren, Gyrmund rapped on the door. It was opened and the two guards raised their eyebrows at the sight of Gyrmund, not only still accompanied by Moneva, but also by a strange third figure in a hooded robe.

Soren walked slowly forward, looking toward the guards. There was something about the wizard's eyes, as they stared, unseeing, at the two Isharites, that disturbed Gyrmund.

'I will need an escort,' Soren said, in a voice that was both his and not his.

Nodding in agreement, the two guards turned around and walked forward a few paces, each holding their spear out in front of them.

Gyrmund understood that magic was being used. He had seen it used often enough over the last few weeks, both by Soren and other wizards. But he had seen nothing quite like this. He cast his mind back to the events in Edeleny. Soren, who had lost his magical powers when using them in the Wilderness, had regained them in the Temenos in Edeleny. Gyrmund had witnessed with his own eyes Soren draining the magic from a Caladri wizard, Agoston—and restoring his own. He recognised that, somehow, in ways he didn't understand, Soren was a different wizard than the one he had been before.

Soren put a hand on Gyrmund's shoulder to steady himself, and they followed the two guards out into the daylight. Soren took a deep breath of fresh air, closing his eyes and smiling with pleasure. Gyrmund understood the feeling.

'We escaped with Herin and Clarin,' he informed Soren, only just realising that they had yet to explain this to him. 'They have a small force of escaped prisoners in a tower in the south-east corner of the fortress,' he added, pointing in the approximate direction, before realising that Soren probably couldn't see this gesture.

Soren nodded. 'I am glad they're alive,' he said. 'But we need to go there.' He pointed instead to the domed structure in the centre of the fortress. 'What is that?' the wizard asked the two guards.

'That is the Great Hall of Lord Erkindrix,' one of them replied.

Soren nodded. 'Take us there.'

'We can't go there!' said Moneva in a shocked voice. 'We need to escape!'

'Herin and Clarin need us,' Gyrmund added. 'You need to help them.'

Soren looked from Moneva to Gyrmund. 'Herin and Clarin don't stand a chance. Not unless we strike at Erkindrix now. We need to finish this.'

He shuffled off after the two Isharite guards.

'Wait!' said Gyrmund angrily, grabbing Soren and spinning him around. 'What makes you think we stand a chance of defeating Erkindrix? What makes you think Erkindrix is even there?'

Soren looked at him. He had changed again: the powerful wizard was gone, and all Gyrmund could see was a frail and vulnerable looking man.

'Belwynn told me.'

* * *

'CAN YOU TELL HIM,' Clarin murmured to Tamir, 'that is the way out of here.'

Tamir pointed to the large corner tower of Samir Durg and made a series of gestures and grunts at the Bear-man. The Bear-man waved his hands in the air, vicious claws threatening to cut those around him. He roared. Clarin sighed. There seemed to be no way of telling the creature to keep quiet. Meanwhile, time was running out.

'Well?' he asked, trying to keep the frustration out of his voice.

'I think he understands,' replied Tamir.

'That will have to do,' Clarin replied. 'Can you tell your men it's time to go?'

The longer they lingered, the worse their situation got.

Clarin was gambling that they had persuaded the Bear-man to lead a charge on the entrance to the corner tower. Clarin and Herin would lead Tamir's Barbarians and follow up the charge in an attempt to secure the tower for themselves. If they did, they would have a much stronger tower to defend. They would also, according to Moneva at least, control an exit out of the fortress. If they didn't—well, the gamble will have failed.

'We've got to go,' came Herin's voice, who had been monitoring the tower. 'They're coming.'

Clarin rushed over to see. A group of spear-wielding Isharite soldiers were walking in double file towards them, along the walkway that connected the corner tower with their own. It was now or never.

He signalled the Bear-man over and they looked into each other's eyes. They made a connection—an understanding, of sorts. Beneath the fur and the protruding jaw, this creature was probably no less intelligent than he was. Clarin was asking it, almost certainly, to go to its death. But then, they were all likely to die, anyway.

The Isharite soldiers marched along the walkway, looking confident. Then, they set eyes upon a great beast emerging from the tower. The Bear-man roared its defiance at them, and Clarin could see them quail, momentarily, before they regained their composure. Then, it charged. Clarin ran behind, gripping a spear, ready to assist with the attack.

No doubt, Clarin considered to himself as he ran, being charged by a Bear-man would be terrifying. Commendably, the two Isharites who found themselves at the front of their line held their ground, spears at the ready. But, as the creature hurtled towards them, jaws open and teeth out, they thrust their spears forwards too soon. Understandable. Understandable, but a fatal mistake.

The Bear-man stopped in time. It grabbed hold of the top of each spear and pushed them to the side. Then, before the Isharites could react, it was in amongst them. Its clawed hands struck at armour, grabbed at weapons. When the claws found purchase, they pulled the Isharites off their feet, throwing them from the wall. Even if the claws didn't connect, the Bear-man's powerful limbs battered them to the ground. The Isharites still thrust their spears forwards to defend themselves. One of them found their target, the blade skewering the flesh of the creature's thigh.

The Bear-man was so big that there was no room for Clarin to fight alongside it; but, by leaning against the crenellations, he could thrust his own spear forwards. He found the groin of a soldier who had been focused on the wild swings of the monster.

Despite its injury, the Bear-man continued to slice and crush, until the neat line of soldiers had disintegrated. Not stopping, it charged forwards once more.

Clarin followed, leaving the sprawled Isharites on the walkway for those behind him to deal with.

A small group of soldiers stood by the door and hurriedly tried to close it before the Bear-man arrived. All too late. The first through tried to shut it on those still on the walkway, who shoved it open, trying to escape. The creature hurled itself at them before they could defend themselves. It crashed into the door, trapping a soldier against the wall, who screamed in agony.

The Bear-man had pushed the door wide open. The Isharites stabbed at him with spears and swords. The Bear-man fell on them, swinging its arms and snapping its jaws.

Clarin followed it through, thrusting overarm with his spear into the midriff of a swordsman. The blade of the spear didn't get through the soldier's chain mail, but the force of the blow caused the Isharite to double over in pain.

Dropping his spear, Clarin knelt and grabbed the sword out of his enemy's hands. It was made from crystal—the very crystal he had been mining this time yesterday. He felt a certain sense of justice as he chopped into the Isharite's neck, driving him to the ground—chopping twice more to make sure he was dead. The sword seemed like a decent weapon—surprisingly light, and easy to use in the confines of the tower.

Clarin got a quick view of the interior of the tower. As elsewhere in the fortress, the third floor connected one section of walkway to the next. This room was open plan like the others they had been in, but much larger. The Isharites were arriving from all directions: from the walkway opposite, and from the floors both below and above them.

Herin and Tamir joined them, along with the rest of the Barbarians. A desperate struggle ensued as they tried to force their way into the tower, and the Isharites tried to force them out.

The Isharite soldiers were well fed and stronger. They were better armed. The Barbarians, however, knew that they were fighting for their lives. A wild fury overtook them, as they sought revenge for the weeks of captivity and brutality. Clarin joined in with it, glorying in having a sword in his hands; revelling in the chance to fight one last time, when it had looked like his life would be snuffed out in a slave pit.

Several Barbarians fell to Isharite crystal in those brutal minutes of hacking and thrusting. The Bear-man, whose path of destruction had given them the momentum they needed, was finally driven to the ground from multiple wounds, the Isharites desperately spearing its exhausted corpse to make sure it was dead.

But more Barbarians took the place of their fallen kin. Behind them were the Persaleians and the Dog-men. And it seemed to Clarin that it was the Dog-men who finally turned things decisively in their favour. He had been wary of them, unsure whether they would fight with the other prisoners or betray them. But they seemed to understand that if the Isharites won, they would be killed too. Their agility and strength were superior to anyone else's, as they leapt at the enemy. Their barks, and the vicious snaps of their jaws, more terrifying than spears and swords.

The Isharite soldiers, who had seen many of their comrades killed, now decided that they had suffered enough. They didn't turn and run, though. It was an orderly retreat, and Clarin and Herin were obliged to continue to harry them, as they turned the corner and made for the walkway at the front of the fortress.

'Secure the ground floor,' Clarin shouted at Zared, turning his neck and shouting as loud as he could. With relief, he saw the Persaleians following the command, heading down the steps to the lower rooms, where there would be other entrances into the tower.

The Isharites ahead of Clarin backed off further until Herin could shut the door on them. Clarin slammed home the wrought iron bolt. It would hold for a while, but they would have to shore it up further. For now, though, the priority was securing all the other entrances into the tower.

As fast as he could, his legs now trembling from the exertion, he made his way back to the third-floor room. He hadn't seen such a bloody massacre before in his life. The walls were painted with blood. Some Barbarians were lying or sitting in the gore, too injured or exhausted to move. Wordlessly, he moved through them to the stairs, and headed down to the next floor. Here, he found himself in a small hallway with doors to three separate rooms off it. It seemed deserted, and he moved to head down the next flight of stairs to the ground floor.

Hurrying back up the stairs was Cyprian, the small Persaleian that Gyrmund had befriended.

'Ah, Clarin. The ground floor is secure,' he said seriously, as if he was reporting to a general in an army. 'Just in time, though. Soldiers are gathering down in the courtyard. We've also located a small larder and a small armoury.'

A wave of relief crashed over Clarin. No more soldiers, for a while at least. Food and weapons as well. 'Well done,' he said, giving Cyprian an embrace.

There was one more entrance to secure: the door which they had entered from. Forcing his tired body to move again, Clarin slogged his way back up the stairs to the third floor. He moved gingerly to the door of the tower, the floor slick with blood.

'Wait!' came a shout.

Ahead of him, running at full speed along the walkway, came Jurgen and

Rudy. Not far behind them was a group of Isharite soldiers. Clarin had forgotten about the two cousins and had come close to locking them out. They skidded into the room, slipping over on the wet floor, eyes wide at the sight of the carnage that had taken place there. Clarin slammed the door shut and locked the bolt, breathing a sigh of relief.

'We held them off for as long as we could,' said Jurgen, his breathing ragged from his exertions.

'Well done,' said Clarin.

Herin emerged from the top floor, followed by the Dog-men.

'The Persaleians have secured everything on the ground floor,' Clarin told his brother. 'What's up there?'

'Two bedrooms on the next floor,' said Herin. 'One of them has a set of stairs leading up to the tower roof. You get quite a view from up there. Not a bad place for a last stand.'

THE KILL

XXV

'Put him here,' Belwynn said to two Krykker soldiers, who had walked a third man into camp, his arms wrapped around their shoulders.

They laid him down gently, looking exhausted from the effort it had taken to get him there. They showed her where the injury was: a heavy weapon had hit the top of their friend's thigh, leaving a massive dent in his armour. There was very little to see without removing the armour, and a broken bone was unlikely: but Belwynn understood it could be a serious injury nonetheless. She would get Elana to see to him sooner rather than later.

Belwynn's job, in the battle's aftermath, was to organise the injured: directing where they should be lain, providing water and other necessities. She made the initial assessment of their injuries. She would then explain this to Belwynn and help the priestess prioritise who she should see.

The injured were, mercifully, far fewer than she had feared. The battle had gone as well as anyone could have expected, with Rostam's forces chased from the field. Groups of Krykkers were already making their way back to camp, whereas the Knights were still out there somewhere, harrying the enemy to ensure that it was as complete a victory as possible. She was yet to see the return of any familiar faces, but one of the Krykkers had assured her that Rabigar was alive and well.

Pentas appeared. Belwynn and Elana stopped what they were doing as he approached, his red eyes drifting over the injured soldiers, wearing his laconic smile. 'Victory!' he declared, his smile getting broader, though Belwynn was still unsure of its sincerity.

'What happens next?' Belwynn demanded, keen to get some straight answers. 'Can we reach Samir Durg from here?'

Pentas raised one eyebrow. 'This army cannot reach Samir Durg. It barely has enough supplies to get there, never mind to conduct a siege. Meanwhile, the Isharites will simply raise another army against it. I would say that you have achieved all you could have hoped for.'

'What, then?' asked Elana, sounding angry. 'What of Belwynn's brother and friends?'

'This army cannot reach Samir Durg,' Pentas replied, 'but I can. I will be going back presently. It will be an interesting visit, if nothing else.' He looked at Belwynn. 'Although it will tax my powers, I can take you there if you wish. Who knows? That staff, or the dagger you carry, may come in handy. Of course, I would be taking you into a highly dangerous environment, one that I myself may not escape from alive. I can't guarantee your safety.'

'Will we be able to rescue Soren?' she asked.

Pentas made a face. 'That, I cannot promise. With a lot of luck, your friends may rescue him. Have you tried speaking to him recently?'

She hadn't. She tried, opening that channel of communication that had been so natural since childhood, but that she'd barely used in the past weeks.

Soren?

She was met with silence again. But then, was she? This time felt different, as if her brother was there, even if he wasn't speaking.

Soren?

Belwynn?

He sounded distant; confused. But this was the first time that he had answered her in two weeks.

'What is it?' interrupted Pentas, who was studying her closely.

'He's there. He replied,' Belwynn said, her voice shaking.

Where are you? she asked Soren.

I don't know...

His voice had that same groggy quality to it.

I'm in a prison.

How are you? Are you well? Belwynn asked, trying to keep the sound of panic from her voice.

Gyrmund is here. Gyrmund and Moneva. They're helping me.

'He says that Gyrmund and Moneva are with him.'

Elana beamed at the news.

Pentas pursed his lips thoughtfully. 'What about the other two?' the wizard asked.

What about Herin and Clarin? Belwynn asked Soren.

No. Not here.

Belwynn shook her head.

'Listen, Belwynn,' said Pentas. 'You need to tell him to make his way to the Great Hall. It's the large building, right in the centre of the complex, with a domed roof.'

Belwynn passed on the instructions.

'I need to leave as soon as possible,' said Pentas.

'I'm coming,' said Belwynn.

She ran over to her small pile of possessions to grab Onella's Staff. Toric's Dagger was already tucked inside her belt.

'Are you sure that's wise?' asked Elana, as Belwynn returned. 'What if the weapons fall into the hands of Erkindrix?'

Belwynn looked to Pentas. He didn't seem sure himself.

'What do you think?' the wizard asked Elana, returning the question.

Elana considered it. Was she having a private conversation with Madria? Was it all intuition? Belwynn wished she knew. The priestess sighed. 'Take them,' she said.

'I don't see any gain in bringing you,' Pentas said to Elana. 'You are more use here,' he said, gesturing at the wounded soldiers she still had to treat.

Elana nodded. 'Agreed. Good luck to you both. Madria goes with you.'

Pentas offered Belwynn his hand. When she took it, he placed his other hand onto Onella's Staff. He began the spell of teleportation immediately. As before, when the wizard had transported her out of Edeleny, into Kalinth, Belwynn felt her stomach drop. Her mouth filled with the taste of bile. Then came the sensation of moving, the air on her face and arms; but her vision was too blurred and indistinct to make sense of where she was going.

For a while they travelled in this way, though it was hard to say how long the journey took. When they stopped, they were inside a building. Belwynn stood bent double, waiting for the room to stop spinning as she slowly regained her senses.

She looked at her surroundings. The room was expensively furnished and lightly scented. Belwynn presumed they were in Pentas's personal chambers. A stone fireplace was the centrepiece. It had a wooden surround that had been decorated in swirling red and green colours. Tapestries hung on the walls, and rugs adorned the floor. Wooden chests lined the room. In the middle was a table, with red velvet covered chairs adding yet more luxury.

'Very nice,' she commented, standing up straight as her body recovered from the journey.

'Yes, well. I have to keep up appearances.'

'So, your appearance is that of a mighty sorcerer of Ishari. But in reality, you are a humble servant of Madria?'

Pentas smiled his enigmatic smile. 'Yes, in essence. I've never claimed to be an Isharite, though. I was born in Persala, as I believe I mentioned when we first met.'

He had, Belwynn recalled. 'The Isharites don't mind?'

'Oh, they mind. Many of them mind very much. But I am a very powerful wizard, you see. And power matters the most to Erkindrix—and to Diis. So, while I have never been fully trusted, I have made myself very useful to them over the years. My behaviour has raised some suspicions from time to time, but never enough to see me removed.'

'And what dark deeds have you done to make yourself useful?' Belwynn asked him.

'What choice did I have?' Pentas answered passionately. His cool demeanour slipped, at last. 'When the stakes are so high, how else should I have dealt with such a threat to Dalriya? A heroic stand, destroyed by the combined wizardry of the Isharites? What good would that have done? No, I have swallowed my pride—ignored my conscience. For this moment. To engineer a situation where maybe, just maybe, Erkindrix is vulnerable.'

He looked at her with those inscrutable red eyes. Was he looking for praise? Waiting for her to condemn him further? Belwynn had nothing else to say. Right now, she just wanted to find her brother.

'If you are ready,' he said, 'it is time to act.'

Pentas's apartments were in a tower in the north-west corner of the fortress of Samir Durg. From here, he led Belwynn out to the massive compound that lay inside the high walls of the fortress. She hadn't really known what to expect of the place: her mind had pictured, in a vague way, some dark lair where the Isharites hid and plotted their conquests. She hadn't expected this. The walls were crenelated, and sparkled with crystals that had been embedded amongst the stone. They were punctuated by countless towers of different shapes and sizes: some large and military looking; some with turrets; some slim ones ending in tall spires. In the middle of the space stood an impressive stone building, topped with a golden dome.

'It's beautiful,' she said. 'Why would anyone who owned this need to conquer more?'

Pentas looked around him, as if examining the site for the first time. 'No,' he said. 'If there is beauty here, I can't see it.'

They walked to the stone building in the middle of the fortress, passing some soldiers and other officials who seemed busy with their own business. Some of them took surreptitious, interested glances at Belwynn. Clearly, however, none had the authority to ask questions of Pentas, who strode to his destination with authority. The guards stationed by the entrance respectfully gave way, and he led Belwynn into the building. They walked down a stone corridor, Belwynn's fear growing as they did.

Pentas stopped. 'Around this corner,' he said, 'are the doors to Erkindrix's Throne Room.' He studied her face, his own becoming almost gentle. 'Once we're inside, I cannot control what will happen, Belwynn. You must follow my lead. I want you to talk to Soren now. I need you to explain to him what he needs to do.'

* * *

'Down here,' muttered Soren, his mouth nearly too dry for words to escape.

Starved of food and water, his body was giving up. Gyrmund was having to half carry him along the corridor, Soren's legs no longer willing to move. All he wanted to do was lie down to rest. But the reason he had stayed alive was the same reason he kept going now. Belwynn. Somehow, she had found her way to Samir Durg—to rescue him. He couldn't let her down.

They stopped at a door. Soren had to take a few breaths before he could speak again. 'I think this is it,' he gasped. 'But there may be servants in there.'

'Leave it to me.' Moneva's voice.

'You're not going in there by yourself,' said Gyrmund.

'You'll just get in the way,' she replied. 'Here, give him some of this.'

Gyrmund didn't argue further. He lowered Soren down against a wall. Soren felt Gyrmund putting the clay jug of kumis to his lips, and he took a sip. His dehydrated body wanted him to gulp it down, but he knew that would make things worse. He took a second drink and then a third. He felt the liquid fire up and revive his body. The desperate need for sleep was banished, but instead, he became more aware of the sharp pain in his back.

He looked up as the door opened. A figure emerged. He still couldn't see clearly, but he somehow knew it was Moneva.

'Well?' asked Gyrmund.

'There were three of them. All clear now. Looks like the right place,' she added.

Belwynn had told Soren to find the rear entrance to the Throne Room, accessed via the private rooms of Erkindrix. If they had found it, they were only a few feet away from Erkindrix and his Council. And Belwynn.

Gyrmund and Moneva both bent down to lift Soren back up to his feet. He bit hard on his lower lip to stop himself from shouting out as pain lanced down his spine. They guided him through the door into the room.

It was small and dimly lit, with a musty smell. One of Erkindrix's servants lay sprawled dead on the floor opposite them. Soren could make out items, probably wooden chests, dotted around the room; but he had no interest in his surroundings. He made out an open door to the right and gestured for Gyrmund to take him there. A soft rug underfoot muffled the sound of their footsteps. As they approached the door, he could hear raised voices.

Gyrmund guided him into a second, larger room, with the paraphernalia of living quarters. But now Soren took even less interest in his surroundings. Directly ahead was a stone archway. Beyond it, he could hear the voices as if they were in the room with him.

'They hit us hard,' someone was saying. 'The Drobax broke like a pack of cowardly animals. After that, it was impossible to regroup.'

Soren dropped to his hands and knees as he approached the archway, moving carefully to avoid being seen. Gyrmund and Moneva joined him, dropping to their haunches. Soren peered through.

They were behind the throne—on which, presumably, Erkindrix was seated. Two figures stood on either side of him. Above, the vaulted walls of the Throne Room rose impossibly high. With his limited vision, Soren couldn't properly make out the ceiling, though he could see a golden shimmer at the very top.

A palpable sense of tension filled the atmosphere. In front of the throne, Soren could make out four figures, stood in pairs. He heard Moneva gasp to his right.

'Belwynn!' she whispered.

A chill ran through Soren's body. What was his sister doing here? He focused on the four figures and picked out the one that was smaller and slimmer than the others. He had thought he would never see Belwynn again. Here she was, so close, yet he could not see her clearly, never mind go to her.

Perhaps seeing Soren squinting into the room, Gyrmund leaned over and quietly filled in the details that Soren couldn't make out.

'She's standing next to Pentas. She's holding Onella's Staff. Across from them is Arioc, with one of his men.'

Soren struggled to take in the information. Arioc? It was Arioc who had ordered Soren's transportation in a box to Samir Durg. Was it also Arioc who had tortured him here? Delving into his brain, picking out all his secrets? All but one: his special bond with Belwynn. His torturer had been unable to unlock that puzzle. That was why, Soren was sure, he had been kept alive. But now Belwynn was standing only a few feet away from him, with Madria's weapons. Why had she brought them here, of all places?

Soren felt his mind reeling. Starved and tortured, he couldn't think clearly. He couldn't see what was happening in the throne room, and even after Gyrmund had told him, he couldn't understand it.

He recognised the voice of the next to speak. Smooth and self-controlled, despite the tension in the air. Pentas, the red-eyed wizard they had first encountered on the road to Coldeberg. According to Belwynn, he had rescued her from Edeleny, spiriting her and Madria's weapons away from Arioc. Why do that, and then bring them here, to Erkindrix?

'I have recovered two of Madria's weapons,' he was saying, as if defending himself from some accusation. 'That was the priority. It means that we are now safe from Madria's threat. The fate of one army is inconsequential compared to this. We can simply raise another one to deal with the Krykkers.'

'True enough,' came a voice, a voice that grabbed at Soren's throat and nearly made him choke. The voice of his tormentor. It was coming from the throne, so close to him that Soren could almost reach out and touch its owner. So, not Arioc after all. Some other.

'The weapons are more important to Diis than a defeat,' the voice continued. It wasn't coming from the throne itself, Soren realised, but from a cowled figure, all in black, who seemed to stand in shadow even where there should be none. Soren's mind, assaulted by a slew of emotions, slowly worked it out. Siavash, the leader of the Order of Diis. Arioc had passed him on to this man for interrogation.

'Nevertheless,' Siavash continued, the sound of his voice grating on Soren's nerve endings, reminding him of the agony he had suffered at his hands. 'A defeat such as this is unacceptable.'

Soren's first instinct was to escape. He wanted nothing more than to run and hide from his tormentor. But other instincts prevented him. Anger came to the fore. A savage desire for revenge. Ambition, still there despite the weeks of torture. And a brother's love for his sister. These instincts won out over fear, and Soren took to his feet. Gyrmund laid a restraining arm on him, but he shook it off and took a step through the arch into the Throne Room.

'Indeed,' replied Pentas, as Soren emerged behind the throne.

He must be able to see me, Soren considered. *Did those red eyes flicker,* he wondered, *and give me away? Or did Pentas keep his composure?*

'It would have been much sounder,' Pentas continued, his voice giving no indication that anything had changed, 'to have given the command of the army to Arioc.'

'Treason!' said the figure on the other side of the throne to Siavash.

Soren considered what he knew of the leaders of Ishari. This one must be Ardashir, long-time ally of Erkindrix. His voice sounded like the dry crackle of parchment paper, but it was alive with surprise and pleasure at having caught Pentas out. 'Those were the orders of Lord Erkindrix!'

Ardashir stopped, puzzled perhaps by the reactions of those who stood before the throne. Ignoring him, their eyes had drifted to Soren who now emerged, shuffling onto the scene. It took what felt like an age to manoeuvre his broken body around the throne, as the eyes of the greatest wizards of Dalriya studied him. They could have destroyed him in an instant. But they didn't. No-one seemed quite sure how to react.

This gave him a chance. Ignoring everyone, even Erkindrix himself, even his own sister—Soren moved in front of the throne until he could look Siavash in the face. The stink of rotting flesh from the throne assailed him, but he stared into the dark eyes of his torturer. Siavash looked back, but there was no sign of recognition.

'What—' began Ardashir, but Soren suddenly unleashed a bolt of magic at Siavash. In his mind's eye, his attack would blast Siavash into pieces, but the High Priest casually negated the bolt as if it were nothing. He smiled then, a thin smile of wicked pleasure.

'Soren!' shouted Belwynn.

Then, things suddenly happened very fast.

Belwynn threw Onella's Staff towards him. He reached out, using his magic to draw the weapon into his grip. On contact, he felt the magic within the stave funnel into him. He understood—instantly, instinctively—its power to enhance and channel his magic.

Immediately, he used its help to address his greatest weakness: his vision. He constructed a picture of the room and the people in it. This was a picture that his mind, and his magic, told his eyes they could see. His eyes returned an image, wonderfully clear and detailed, of his surroundings. The crystal throne sparkled in a range of red hues. The crumpled figure of Erkindrix who sat there had a grey tinge to his skin, interrupted by crusty, yellow scabs. Eyes like black coals stared out from behind the face of the Lord of Ishari. The whole throne room was bathed in a golden light that came streaming through the dome above. It was a version of reality that he could see and react to.

Just in time.

Siavash launched a counterattack at him, blasting a scorching flame in his direction. Holding the staff out in front of him, Soren put up a shield to resist the High Priest's magic. The flames were diverted either side of him, though he only just stayed on his feet from the force of the blast.

Belwynn continued to move forwards, Toric's Dagger now in her hand. But the Isharite next to Arioc reacted quickly, throwing a punch which connected with the side of her head, sending her to the ground like a sack of potatoes. The Dagger dropped from her limp hand as she hit the floor, skittering a few feet away. She lay unmoving—unconscious, or worse.

From behind Soren, Gyrmund came storming out from their hiding place. He launched himself at the Isharite, a flash of steel in his hand as he stabbed at him. His opponent, however, was quick. He grabbed Gyrmund's wrist, stopping the blow. They struggled for control of the weapon.

'No you don't!' shouted Pentas, launching an attack on Ardashir.

Soren turned to see the old wizard's outstretched palm facing him, ready to fire a surprise blast. Instead, Ardashir had to quickly change direction, hurling a bolt of magic towards Pentas. The room crackled with energy as the two attacks met. Both wizards visibly strained against each other, but neither seemed able to get the upper hand.

Soren had no time to watch further as a second attack from Siavash came his way. He blocked it, redirecting the blast of magic to the side where it hit the wall of the Throne Room, scorching the stone black. Using Onella's Staff to strengthen his wasted muscles, he backed away, recognising the trouble that they were in. He and Pentas were both fully engaged in defending themselves, while Arioc and Erkindrix remained free to act.

From the corner of his eye he saw Erkindrix slowly rise from his throne. He walked forwards. His was a frail body, centuries old—it looked like it was held together by sheer force of will. Then, Arioc finally moved too, to meet his master. He was the opposite: strong and powerful looking, full of vigour.

'Finish them,' Erkindrix commanded Arioc.

Arioc raised a hand, but to Soren's utter astonishment, instead of turning on himself or Pentas, Arioc fired at Erkindrix. The blast sent Erkindrix flying backwards until he crashed into his throne.

Siavash, rage spread across his face, prepared to strike at Arioc, but Soren got in an attack first. Siavash saw it coming and blocked it easily enough. But Soren knew he had to keep the High Priest pinned down, so that he couldn't come to the aid of his master. For whatever reason, Arioc had turned on Erkindrix, and this gave them all a chance of survival.

'You are too old now, Erkindrix,' said Arioc matter-of-factly. 'No-one can live forever. It is time for new leadership.'

A bitter laugh escaped from the old wizard. Despite looking like a crumpled bag of bones, Erkindrix regained his feet, seemingly unharmed. 'You think to replace me, Arioc? For so many years you have served me, and yet, it seems you have learned nothing.'

Erkindrix shrieked and bolts of white light emerged from his outstretched fingers to shoot at Arioc.

Drawing a sword, Arioc swatted them aside and marched forwards, an implacable look on his face.

Soren, trying to concentrate on his own task, fired another bolt at Siavash. But he was growing tired, and his attack was predictable. Siavash had been waiting for it, and somehow turned it back on him. Soren dived out of the way, narrowly avoiding being hit by his own magic. As he fell to the floor, he lost his grip on the staff. His recently regained eyesight vanished. His back spasmed in agony. He would have been killed there and then, if Siavash had not had another priority.

Scrabbling on the floor, his fingers clutched around the staff. A burst of light erupted as his eyesight was restored.

Looking up, he saw that Siavash was using his magic to tug on Arioc's crystal sword. Arioc was concentrating on pulling it back. The interruption allowed Erkindrix to fire his bolts of white light a second time. This time, they hit home, enveloping Arioc's body in white light, forcing it into spasms, and finally driving him to the floor.

Using Onella's Staff, Soren fired a shot at Erkindrix, but Siavash was ready for him. The thin smile had returned to the High Priest's face, and he easily blocked Soren's attempt, before forcing him back onto the defensive with a blast of his own. Soren blocked it, but he was now running on empty. Without the Staff, he couldn't have kept going this long. He had failed to keep Siavash occupied, and despair crept into his thoughts, as he saw the fight going the wrong way.

Then, Erkindrix screamed out—a deafening, unnatural sound unlike anything that had gone before.

Soren looked over, and there was Moneva.

She was holding Toric's Dagger, and had plunged it through Erkindrix's chest, into his heart. She withdrew the weapon. Erkindrix howled once more in agony. No blood could be seen where the Dagger had punctured his body. Instead, Soren could make out dark vapours escaping. Erkindrix's howling stopped. His body collapsed and sank to the floor—a dried-out husk that could no longer be kept alive.

Everyone in the Throne Room stopped and stared for a moment, in shock. None of them, it seemed, had quite thought it possible. But the evidence was there for them all to see. Erkindrix had been killed.

Ardashir was the first to react. With a snarl, he raised his hand in Moneva's direction. A shield of magic appeared in front of her.

'I think not,' said Arioc from a kneeling position, his voice calm. 'Moneva has done me a service, today. I am the new Lord of Ishari. Your allegiance now goes to me.'

Ardashir sneered at him. 'You think this makes you Lord of Ishari? Your treachery today has sealed your doom, Arioc.'

The two wizards faced off, ignoring everyone else. Soren quickly looked around. The remaining threat was from Siavash. The High Priest and Pentas had turned to each other, ready to fight.

Soren limped towards Siavash, Onella's Staff raised. It was a bluff—a desperate bluff. He didn't think he had anything left to give now. But Siavash didn't know that.

The High Priest looked from Pentas to Soren. He was outnumbered. It seemed that it was a risk he wasn't prepared to take. He turned and ran a few steps before leaping into the air. One moment, there was a man. The next, a crow was flapping its wings in his place. It flew around the empty throne and headed for the arch from where Soren had entered the room moments ago. Pentas unleashed a blast of magic in Siavash's direction, but the crow flew to the side, avoiding it. Then, it was gone, through the arch and away.

The duel between Arioc and Ardashir had begun. Ignoring them, Soren made for the prone form of Belwynn, but two figures blocked his path.

Rostam and Gyrmund's fight was over now. They had separated, neither seriously injured by the other. The Isharite backed away from them warily, drawing a crystal sword from his scabbard.

'I serve Arioc,' he said.

'Go serve your master, then,' said Pentas.

Rostam's withdrawal allowed Soren to reach his sister. He crouched down by her side.

Moneva arrived. Her hands were shaking, but she still gripped Toric's Dagger tightly. She leaned over Belwynn, as did Gyrmund and Pentas.

Soren wanted to check his sister, but suddenly, an enormous fatigue descended on him, and he fell to his hands and knees. He felt like he was going to faint and had to fight to stay conscious. He watched Gyrmund put a hand to Belwynn's neck.

'There is still a pulse,' he said.

An immense feeling of relief flooded Soren. Was it possible that they would all escape with their lives?

'We need to get them out of here,' said Moneva, looking at Belwynn and Soren, who was still too tired to get up from his hands and knees. He gripped Onella's Staff tightly, using its power to keep his senses working.

'Indeed,' said Pentas. 'Siavash will return with his followers soon. I can't let these weapons fall into his hands. I think I have enough energy to teleport us away to relative safety. If I can get us to her, your friend Elana can treat them.'

'What about Herin and Clarin?' asked Gyrmund.

Pentas shook his head. 'If we try to get to them, Siavash will track us down. If not him, Arioc or Ardashir,' he said, looking over at the struggle between the two wizards which continued unabated. 'If your friends are still alive, they will have to make their own escape.'

Soren wanted to protest. He wanted to get Herin and Clarin out of this place, too.

A crashing sound behind him made him turn to see Ardashir pinned against the wall of the room by Arioc's magic. Rostam closed in on the old wizard, sword in hand.

'Alright,' he said, accepting the reality of their situation.

He reached over and took one of Belwynn's hands.

Gyrmund looked at him for a moment, before conceding, and reaching out for Moneva's hand. Pentas put a hand on the staff. Once they had formed a circle, Pentas began his spell.

Soren took a last look at the Throne Room of Samir Durg.

The dried husk that had been the body of the dreaded Erkindrix lay, ignored, by his throne.

They had killed the Lord of Ishari. Soren was reunited with Belwynn. And they might just escape with their lives. It was almost too much to comprehend.

And then Soren's vision left him. His mind gave out, and his body began to move.

LAST STAND

XXVI

The small armoury in the tower turned out to be a treasure trove. Clarin did his best to supervise the distribution of weapons and armour, to ensure that everyone was at least adequately armed. The last thing he wanted was a dispute between the Persaleians and Barbarians over who got what.

He was helped in his task by their different sizes. The Barbarians were taller, and claimed the largest pieces of armour, because they were the only ones that would fit. The Persaleians, many of whom were already well armed, favoured the smaller weapons. For himself, Clarin claimed a quilted linen jacket, on top of which he had shrugged on a riveted chain mail hauberk big enough to fit him. He decided to keep the crystal sword he had acquired in the fight earlier, enjoying the feel and weight of it.

Cyprian had organised the distribution of food and drink from the larder, ensuring that everyone, even the Dog-men, received an equal share.

With everybody fed and getting a chance to rest, Clarin got to work on planning the defence of their position.

He began by exploring the ground floor of the tower. A door to the west led out into the courtyard of the fortress beyond. It was here that the largest group of Isharites were being readied for an assault. Clarin ensured that any spare item was shoved against it, to hold them off for as long as possible. A second door, cleverly built into the curved south wall of the tower, was an exit from the fortress. If they attempted to use it now, they would be cut down by Isharite horsemen in a matter of minutes. Nonetheless, it still represented a chance that they might somehow escape. Even if any realistic assessment of their situation would suggest that wasn't going to happen.

Clarin decided he would take charge of the defence of the ground floor, along with Zared and the Persaleians, the three Dog-men, and the two Rotelegen cousins, Rudy and Jurgen. Up on the third floor, which the Isharites could access from both the southern and eastern walls, Herin led the defence, along with Tamir and the Barbarians. Herin had taken a liking to the open roof on top of the tower. He had acquired a bow and a quiver of arrows from the armoury, and was keen to make use of the height that the position afforded.

When the Isharite assault came, it hadn't been what Clarin had expected. With all his military planning, he had forgotten that Samir Durg would be crawling with wizards. Not that he could have done anything about it, anyway.

The door to the courtyard suddenly engulfed in flames. The Dog-men yipped in panic as the fire took hold immediately. Clarin sent them into the armoury so that they were out of the way. With a whoosh of air, the flames spread onto the furniture that Clarin had ordered should be stacked against the door. Smoke blew at the defenders, forcing the Persaleians back a few paces. Clarin could feel the heat from the fire on his face as the smell of wood smoke hit his nostrils.

There was a crack, and the door crashed down into the tower, resting precariously on the burning furniture underneath. Clarin could just about see through the smoke to the courtyard outside. A mass of Isharite spearmen stood waiting for the order to attack. In front of them, he could make out what must be the wizards. They raised their hands and another blast of air surged into the tower, scattering hot ash at the defenders. Clarin covered his mouth, his eyes watering from the black smoke that roiled around them, making the Persaleians cough and splutter. The courtyard outside was no longer visible, but Clarin could hear the sudden shouting that told him the soldiers had been ordered to attack.

He found Rudy and Jurgen. 'Go and tell Herin what's happening,' he shouted at them, grabbing them and pushing them away when they hesitated. They headed for the stairs up to the next floor, which were now barely visible as the thick smoke continued to spread.

Zared had found him. 'What do we do?' asked the young man, his voice dry and strained.

'Retreat slowly to the second floor,' Clarin ordered. 'Don't make it easy for them, but give ground when you have to.'

Clarin moved into the armoury with the Dog-men. There was more air here, and he took a chance to get his breath back.

'Fight with me,' he told them.

'Yes, master,' said one of the creatures, bowing its head. They had eschewed the weapons that had been available to them, and were instead ready to fight with tooth and claw.

Clarin peered out of the room, waiting. He heard the shouts of battle and, slowly, the sounds grew louder as the melee drew closer. The Isharites would have had to get through the flames, negotiate the debris in their path, and then fight in a very enclosed space. The Persaleians were in a good position to hold them off, but he knew that the superior numbers would tell in the end.

Eventually, he could see them being pushed back, and he ducked back into the room, out of sight. He nodded at the Dog-men to be ready, and then waited for a while longer. Finally, gripping his sword, he ran out of the room.

Clarin got to the Isharites before they knew what was happening. Concentrating on the Persaleians ahead of them, they had ignored the rooms on the ground floor. He raised his sword above his head and slashed down with it, doing as much damage as he could while he had the advantage. The Dog-men joined him, slashing out with their sharp claws in all directions, as the Isharite progress came to an abrupt halt. The Isharites were heavily armoured, but the claws of the Dog-men could still find exposed throats and faces.

Clarin took a weighty blow on the shoulder that nearly knocked him over. He tottered backwards, but managed to stay on his feet. One of the Dog-men was hit with the full force of a spear thrust, the weapon sinking into its belly. It scrabbled at the shaft of the weapon, but there was nothing it could do.

'Back!' Clarin shouted, recognising that they were in trouble. Fortunately, the Persaleians had supported his attack, giving him a retreat route. He took it, the two remaining Dog-men following close behind.

The Isharite advance paused and the two groups backed away from each other. The floor between them was covered with mangled corpses and injured soldiers. The Isharites were being ordered into the rooms on the ground floor to make sure there were no more defenders hiding there.

'Defenders,' shouted Clarin, his eyes kept firmly ahead of him on the Isharites. 'Back up to the stairs.'

They took advantage of the pause in the fighting to make it to the stairs that led to the second floor. Here, they not only had a height advantage, but the narrow, twisting stone steps negated the superior numbers of the Isharites. If done properly, it was a position that could be held for a long time.

'Zared!' Clarin shouted.

'Out of the way!' came the Persaleian's voice, as he tried to reach Clarin through the bodies on the stairs.

'You need to defend this position,' Clarin told him when he got there. 'Two men with spears or other long weapons are needed to keep them back. They need to be given space behind them to retreat into: don't get too bunched up. Rotate the men at the front so that they don't get too tired. I'm going to check on what's happening upstairs.'

'Understood,' agreed Zared. 'Pass me a spear,' he yelled to his men, and began to relay Clarin's orders.

'You two,' Clarin said to the two remaining Dog-men, 'with me. Cyprian, you too.'

Clarin marched up to the second floor. It was deserted, but he could already hear fighting on the third floor above them. This came as no surprise; he had expected the Isharites to coordinate their attacks. His worry was that his group of defenders could get trapped between the two Isharite forces coming from below and above.

Taking the stairs up to the third floor, a quick glance confirmed his fears. Rudy and Jurgen were struggling to fend off the attackers from the east wall, the defences that had been placed there still holding. The Isharites from the south wall, however, had broken into the room, leaving the Barbarians dangerously divided. Half a dozen of them had their backs to Clarin, trying to stop the Isharites from getting further into the room. The rest had been pushed back to the stairs that led up to the tower roof.

Clarin turned around to Cyprian. 'Go back and get the rest of them up here as soon as possible,' he told him. 'There's no time to waste.'

Cyprian immediately disappeared back down the stairs.

'Clarin!' said Jurgen, relief in his voice. 'Can you help?'

Clarin could see that Jurgen had a nasty wound across his calf where a spear had sliced into his leg, gouging out muscle and probably cutting tendons. Blood was pooling in his shoe, and he could barely stand. Clarin quickly moved over and took his weight, manoeuvring him out of the way. The Dog-men replaced him, standing next to Rudy, and snapping menacingly at the Isharites who were trying to force their way in.

Clarin then moved over to help the Barbarians, who were hard pressed to keep their positions against the Isharites who had poured into the room.

'Have you seen Herin?' he shouted at the Barbarians.

One of them nodded a head toward the stairs. Herin was probably using his bow and arrow up on the roof while he still had the chance.

When the Persaleians arrived, he moved back to meet them. Their faces had dropped at the situation.

'We're going to force our way up to the roof,' he told them. 'Zared, you will lead the attack. Join up with the Barbarians. Then start feeding your men up to the roof. I'll hold things here.'

Zared nodded, though it was the dull agreement of a man who couldn't think of anything better. To their credit, though, the Persaleians wasted no time and ran at the Isharites.

'Rudy,' said Clarin, moving over to the far side of the room. 'Take Jurgen up to the roof. I'll replace you here.'

The young Rotelegen man looked like he was going to argue, but nodded his assent and put his arm around the back of his cousin. Together, they hobbled towards the steps that led up to the roof.

Clarin took a glance nervously down the steps to the second floor, checking to see if the Isharites from below had followed the Persaleians up yet. It was still clear, so he joined the two remaining Dog-men. Although they lacked the reach of the Isharite spearmen, their snarling presence seemed to have done enough to keep them at bay.

A spearman jabbed at him through the door, going for his legs. Clarin knocked the strike away with his sword. He waited to see if he would try the same thing again. He did. This time, Clarin stamped down on the shaft of the spear. Before the Isharite could withdraw it, Clarin reached down and pulled at it with all his strength. He won the tug of war, pulling the Isharite along before wrenching it out of his hands. One of the Dog-men leaned over and sunk its claws into the head of the Isharite and somehow pulled him out further, before sinking its teeth into his neck, its face coming up bloody and triumphant.

Gripping his newly won spear, Clarin moved back over to the steps leading down to the second floor. There they were. The Isharites were marching quickly up the stairs. In a matter of moments, they would find themselves stuck between the two forces. He launched his spear down the steps. The soldier in front tried to move out of the way, but there was nowhere for him to go, and the spear lodged in his shoulder, sending him tumbling over.

Clarin looked across. The momentum of the Persaleian attack had now stalled. They had to move. He went back to get his sword.

'Come,' said Clarin to the two Dog-men.

Leaving the entrance to the east wall undefended, they rushed for the set of steps leading upwards.

'Go!' Clarin thundered as he arrived.

The Barbarians went first, running up the steps after Rudy and Jurgen, who had only just hobbled their way to the roof above. Next went the Persaleians, fighting a desperate rearguard action as the Isharites swelled around them.

That left Clarin and the Dog-men. They backed up to the steps. Clarin held his sword out in front of him, daring the Isharites to attack. The two Dog-men snarled, crouching down low, ready to leap at the enemy.

The Isharites now seemed reluctant to make a move. Clarin, moving backwards, put a foot on the first step and then his other foot on the second. Still, the Isharites didn't come, content to let them take the stairs. There were shouts from amongst them, and he could see that some of them now looked confused, as if they had been ordered to hold their position.

Glancing behind him, Clarin could see empty stairs, and he quickly made his way up before the Isharites changed their mind. He took in the scene. Jurgen and Rudy sat together a few feet away, leaning against the circular wall of the tower roof. Rudy was wrapping a rag around his cousin's calf. Persaleians and Barbarians alike lay or sat on the tower roof, utterly spent. Only a few still stood around the stairwell exit with weapons in hand, ready to continue the fight when the Isharites arrived.

The two Dog-men appeared on the roof, but still the Isharites waited below.

'Clarin!' called Cyprian. He was looking over the edge of the roof at the courtyard below. Smoke from the fire on the ground below swirled past him.

Ordering the Dog-men to defend the stairs, Clarin went to see what he wanted. Cyprian pointed down. The Isharite soldiers were now leaving the tower and heading away. For a while Clarin watched in disbelief as they kept moving—heading, it seemed, for the circular building in the centre of the fortress. He tried to understand what was happening. They had been all but defeated, with nowhere else to run; and yet the Isharites had left without finishing the job.

He frowned, thinking. 'Soren?' he croaked to himself.

'What?' asked Cyprian.

Clarin shook his head. 'Gyrmund and Moneva went to rescue Soren. Maybe they found him...'

Cyprian looked far from convinced. 'I hope so.'

Clarin turned away.

Zared approached him, offering his hand. 'Thank you,' said the young Persaleian.

Clarin took his hand, though he didn't feel like self-congratulation. 'Have you seen Herin?' he asked.

Zared shook his head.

'Herin?' shouted Clarin, staggering into the middle of the roof. His shoulder had gone numb and his sword hand ached. He had to concentrate on opening his fingers, they were gripping the hilt so tightly. As he did, the sword dropped to the ground with a clatter.

What was left of their sorry group had all collapsed onto the ground. None of them had escaped without injury. He spied Tamir, the Barbarian chieftain, who was sitting down in the centre of the roof, nursing one of his hands. As Clarin approached, he saw that he had lost two of his fingers from the hand, and a third was barely attached.

'Where's Herin?' he asked him.

Tamir frowned and turned around. With his good hand, he pointed to the far wall of the tower. 'He was fighting over there.'

He wasn't there now. Then something made Clarin's heart quicken with fear. A bow and a quiver of arrows lay where Tamir had gestured. He moved over to look. Herin had perhaps used the position to fire on the Isharites approaching from the south wall. Clarin peered down. You could get an excellent shot in from here, and stay well protected by the wall that ran around the roof. But then what had happened? Maybe Herin had drawn his sword and left the roof to fight the Isharites? That would make sense.

Clarin scanned the roof once more. He then peered down at the walls below: all the way to the courtyard, though it was hard to see clearly down there. He walked right around the roof, looking to see if Herin had fallen off, and landed over on the other side of the fortress. There was no sign of him.

Wearily, he headed for the stairs.

'Where are you going?' asked Zared, as Clarin walked past him.

'I have to find my brother.'

* * *

'WHAT DO YOU MAKE OF IT?' asked Walter.

Farred looked out from their vantage point atop Burkhard Castle. 'It's like our prayers have been answered,' he said.

Beyond them, the horde of Drobax had turned around and were marching away from the castle. They left a trail of devastation behind them.

The last few days had taken their toll. The Drobax had attacked the Duke's

Crag night and day, and had nearly reached the summit. All but two of Walter's wooden gates were torn down.

It was a scene from a nightmare. They'd been prevented from removing the bodies that littered the path up the crag. The crumpled bodies of Drobax had lain rotting in the sun for days. The stench was unbearable, and many of the men had come down with maladies: vomiting and diarrhoea were rife, and they spread yet more disease. Even the bodies of the Brasingians lay where they had fallen: some of them defiled by the Drobax, who had gnawed on the corpses of men who had died defending their country.

Footsteps behind them made Farred turn around. Emperor Baldwin had arrived to see for himself. 'We did it,' he said, so quietly that Farred wasn't sure whether he was speaking to himself or to them.

'It could be a ruse,' warned his brother.

'I think not,' Baldwin replied, pointing out to the east of the castle, toward the Great Road. Here too, the Drobax, who had surrounded the castle for the last two weeks, in numbers so overwhelming that it had made any chance of survival seem impossible, had disappeared.

'What kind of ruse would it be?' continued Baldwin. 'To make us believe they had left, only to return and crush our spirits? We were fighting for our lives, anyway.'

'Maybe so,' acknowledged Walter warily, seemingly unwilling to accept what he was seeing at face value. 'But why leave now? It makes no sense.'

'Because they failed,' replied Baldwin. 'They failed to take this castle.'

Hardly, thought Farred. He doubted it had much to do with the siege. Hour by hour, the Drobax had been gaining the upper hand.

'Whatever the reason,' he said, 'the Isharites didn't lose this war. I fear they will return.'

THE JALAKH BOW

BOOK THREE OF THE WEAPON TAKERS SAGA

For Dad

PROLOGUE

Erkindrix is dead,' Shira said, keeping her voice steady. 'Arioc and the other members of the Council are at each other's throats. Now is the perfect time.'

The men in the hall didn't look convinced. Many of the most powerful noblemen in Haskany had made the journey to Shira's estate. She had fed them all, and plied them with arak to drink. But evidently, none of that meant they were going to commit to her cause.

These were hard looking men. Wrapped in furs that made them look twice as big as they were, they had agreed to come despite a cold snap that signalled late autumn was turning to winter.

They had served Arioc since he had become king. They would continue to serve him if necessary. But Shira knew that their country's servitude to Ishari chafed at each and every one of them. They were proud Haskans, who would see their country become independent. But they were careful. A failed rebellion could see them and their families destroyed.

'Together we could raise a reasonably strong and well-provisioned army,' suggested Etan, a widely respected figure. 'I have no doubts over your leadership of it, or that of your uncle,' he said, nodding at Koren, who was standing to one side of Shira, arms folded. 'But the Isharites have magi. They have the Drobax. While that remains the case, we are not in a position to act against them.'

'*They* are not in a position to act against *us*,' she retorted, not willing to give in. 'Arioc, Ardashir and Siavash all fight each other to succeed Erkindrix. Not one of them has the resources to take on a united Haskany, and who knows how long their conflict may take? Even if one of them should emerge victorious, how likely is it they will have the same power and reach as Erkindrix did? Would you cower in your halls, year after year, waiting until the Isharites return to claim our throne?'

There was anger at that—murmurs and whispers filled the hall. Maybe she had pushed them too far. But she knew she needed to win these men over *now*. Should they drift aimlessly into the spring and summer months, divided and purposeless, a year would go by and they would have done nothing.

She looked at the faces before her. As many were against her as with her. And most weren't in either camp, unpersuaded and reluctant to commit to any path.

A knock at the door to the hall. Koren walked over to investigate. A whispered conversation followed. The attention of Shira's guests shifted in that direction. Uncertain, Shira turned to look.

Koren pulled the door wide open. 'Lord Pentas,' he announced in a firm voice, that gripped the attention of those in the hall.

Pentas sauntered in. It was the first time that Shira had ever been pleased to see him. He surveyed the hall, his red eyes fixing on the key figures in the room, making eye contact, a half-smile playing on his lips.

The atmosphere in the hall switched instantly. Pentas possessed powers that none of these men could understand or measure. Shira was their Queen, a member of the Council of Seven, yet Pentas exuded an authority she could never possess. It galled her, and yet she knew it might make the difference between success and failure.

'So,' Pentas said, drawing out the syllable, and raising his arms to encompass everyone who had gathered in the hall. 'Here are the new rulers of Haskany.'

And that, Shira knew, as she observed her countrymen, *is that.*

COLD COMFORT

I

Winter had smothered the north of Dalriya.

Belwynn, raised in the temperate south, had never seen anything like it.

She thought that the city of Heractus, capital of Kalinth, was made for winter. Here the snow that fell in the streets turned to a dirty slush, complementing the grey walls of the city and its castle. The citizens of Heractus stoically endured the freezing conditions.

These people love being miserable, Belwynn told her brother. *Cold days and winter rations make them happy as pigs in shit.*

It was a slow time of the year. The Kalinthians had worked hard from spring to autumn, brought in their harvest, and most people had full enough larders to see them through comfortably enough. They flocked to the inns of the city, drank strong beer, told tall stories and sang old songs. For all she tried to resist it, Belwynn found herself liking the people here a little more each day.

Travel seemed to be virtually non-existent. On the occasions she ventured out beyond the city limits, accompanied by Theron, or sometimes Gyrmund, she never tired of the spectacle of a land blanketed in white. Thick snow crunched underfoot. Streams and lakes were frozen, some hard enough to walk across, others dangerous, with quick flowing, icy water beneath a thin top layer.

Otherwise, she spent her time in Heractus. She helped Elana with her work. She slept; she ate; she drank. She talked with her brother and her friends. It was a slow time of the year, and that was exactly what they all needed.

Belwynn and Gyrmund stood before Dirk's grave.

It was easy to find, since it was the only plot in a brand-new cemetery in Heractus. It was connected to the new Church of Madria, where Elana performed her healing. The land had been paid for by Elana's many supporters. The rich and powerful men of Heractus had contributed: Theron and Sebastian, and many other Knights of Kalinth—even Prince Dorian, second son of King Jonas, had supported the project. But so too had the ordinary men and women of the city. Elana's reputation had followed her from the High Tower, the seat of the Knights of Kalinth, where her earliest miracles had been witnessed. She had accompanied the Kalinthian army into Haskany, and there, word of her powers grew further.

Now everyone knew about her. She was visited daily, with ailments from the most serious to the most petty, to the purely imaginary. The Church of Madria had become the most visited in the city, and a source of envy from the other temples who had seen their congregations diminish. But with powerful protectors like Sebastian, the new Grand Master of the Knights, whose army still occupied Heractus, there was little they could do.

'I am sorry I wasn't able to speak with him before he died,' Gyrmund murmured, staring down at the tombstone. 'He helped to rescue me from Coldeberg prison. I never thanked him properly for that.'

'He died at peace, Gyrmund,' Belwynn said. 'With no regrets. You should have none too.'

Gyrmund nodded, looking up at her. 'And how are you and Soren?'

Both twins had been in a bad way for a while, not that Belwynn herself had known much about it. The wizard, Pentas, had spirited them out of Samir Durg, all the way to the Kalinthian army and Elana. Belwynn had been knocked unconscious by Rostam in the Throne Room of Samir Durg, shortly before the assassination of Erkindrix and their miraculous escape. She had remained in and out of consciousness for some time.

'I'm fully recovered,' she assured him. 'Soren isn't, though.'

Her brother had been tortured in Samir Durg, in ways she did not fully understand. The Isharites had kept him in a box, never letting him out until Gyrmund and Moneva had found him. Never physically strong, his body seemed irreparably damaged from the ordeal.

'His back still troubles him, and he tires easily from physical exertion. His eyesight hasn't recovered, either. Elana thinks it never will. He clutches that staff all the time now. It's the only way he can see properly—he's virtually blind without it.'

'I'm sorry.'

'Well, don't be too sorry. I thought I would never see him again. And you and Moneva rescued him. So, for the thousandth time, thank you. And I remind myself of how desperate I was to see him again, every time he moans at me, which is at least half a dozen times a day.'

Gyrmund smiled at that, something he rarely did these days.

'How is Moneva?' she asked, already knowing the answer, but knowing that it was a subject that Gyrmund needed to talk about. Moneva had been remote and uncommunicative ever since their return from Samir Durg, and it was Gyrmund who suffered the most from it.

'No change,' he said. 'She won't speak to me properly. I know she suffers, but she won't share it with me. I was wondering if you could try talking with her?'

Yet again? thought Belwynn. She and Moneva had built a friendship during their weeks together. But since Moneva, Soren and the others had been captured in Edeleny, and taken to Samir Durg, while Belwynn had escaped to Kalinth, their paths had been very different. There didn't seem to be much of that friendship left.

'Yes. I'll try,' Belwynn found herself saying. She knew she should.

'I've been thinking,' Gyrmund said, 'of what I should do once this snow melts. I've been treated well here, and I get on with Theron. He has asked me to stay for a while, help to train new soldiers, that kind of thing. But I don't think that's me. I can't stop thinking of Herin and Clarin. I bear a tremendous guilt that I left them to their fate. I feel like I should go back.'

Belwynn nodded. She had spoken with Gyrmund several times about the two brothers. Once they had broken out of the slave pits in Samir Durg, Gyrmund and Moneva had gone to find Soren, while Herin and Clarin had remained behind, occupying a tower of the fortress along with a ragtag band of escaped prisoners. Anything could have happened. Clearly, the most likely outcome was that they had all been slaughtered. But the chaos engendered by Erkindrix's assassination may have given them a chance of escape. She knew that the two of them weren't easy to kill and there was a chance, however slim, that they lived.

'I will talk with Soren about Herin and Clarin. Though I'm not sure what we can achieve without Pentas. And I will talk with Moneva, too.'

'Thank you,' said Gyrmund, and he smiled ruefully. 'I'm sorry I've passed on all my problems to you.'

Eudora's Tavern was a small place, centrally located in Heractus; not too rough and not too expensive, either. It was where Moneva had chosen to spend her time.

The brief hours of daylight were already disappearing, and the inside of the establishment was dim, meaning Belwynn had to search before she saw her, sitting at a table by herself. A plate of food sat in the middle of the table, seemingly untouched, while Moneva had clearly begun drinking. As Belwynn sat down next to her, Moneva gripped both handles of her cup and tipped it back, guzzling it down.

'Hello, Belwynn,' she said when she was done, her breath strong with alcohol.

'Hello. How are you?'

Belwynn refused to play the role of mother, asking Moneva how much she had drunk, or similar interrogation. That was her business.

'Fairly bored. But there will be music later.'

Moneva gestured over a serving girl. 'Same again for both of us,' she said, indicating herself and Belwynn. Turning to her side, she said, 'I'm still sober if it's something important you've come to discuss. It's taking me longer to get drunk now I'm doing it regularly.'

'Why are you doing it so regularly?'

Moneva shrugged. 'It's fun. And what else is there to do around here?'

Belwynn studied her friend, the woman who had killed the dread Lord Erkindrix. She knew if it had been someone like Theron, he would have become a legend by now. It would have been all too easy for him to capitalise on it, turn himself into a hero. And to be fair, everyone had been perfectly ready to treat Moneva in the same way at first. The Knights; the citizens of Heractus; even the royal family had acclaimed her in their own ways. When they first got back from Haskany, Moneva couldn't walk the streets without people buying her drinks, asking her about the events in Samir Durg. But she wasn't interested in that. She was tight-lipped, suspicious—almost contemptuous of the accolades. And so, people had backed off. Moneva had built a wall around herself that no-one, not even Gyrmund, was allowed to get through.

The serving girl brought them their drinks. Belwynn took a sip. The wine was watered down. Someone had put some food on Moneva's table. Maybe people hadn't completely backed off after all.

'Gyrmund asked me to talk to you,' Belwynn said tentatively.

Moneva sighed. 'Can't he just leave me alone?'

'No. He cares about you too much to do that.'

Moneva sneered at that, taking a swig of drink, before looking Belwynn in the eye. 'Do you know what happened to me in Samir Durg, Belwynn?'

Belwynn didn't know, not for sure. But she could guess. 'What happened?'

'He raped me. Not just once. Over and over again.'

Belwynn knew that *he* was Arioc, King of Haskany—the man who had captured Moneva and Soren in Edeleny. Their escape from Samir Durg felt miraculous and had depended on the intervention of the wizard, Pentas. What would have become of them if they hadn't been rescued, she wondered? As it was, Soren and Moneva were still suffering.

'I'm sorry,' she said. 'Have you told anyone else?'

'No. And I don't want you to tell anyone. Especially not Gyrmund.'

'Whatever you say. Though I would suggest that you speak with Elana about it.'

'Why? What's *she* going to do?'

'I don't know, but you won't know either until you talk to her.'

Moneva shrugged. She turned her attention back to her drink, knocking it back, her need for it all too clear.

Belwynn knew about that well enough. She had watched her father descend into the same addiction after the death of her mother. The alcohol had taken the edge off the raw emotions. But it had made him less of a man in the end. She didn't want to see Moneva do the same thing to herself.

'You know we're all here for you,' she persevered. 'We all care for you. Gyrmund most of all.'

Moneva curled her lips into a cruel smile. 'He cares about getting into my pants.'

'That's not fair.'

Moneva turned to her, face red, eyes red. 'I know, Belwynn,' she said, her voice raised, struggling to keep her emotions in check. 'I know I'm not being fair. That's why I don't want to see him.'

Belwynn nodded. She actually felt pleased. She had got more out of Moneva than their previous conversations. 'I have something for you,' she said, producing an intricately made leather scabbard and belt, the cross-guard and hilt of a dagger exposed.

Moneva took the weapon, pulling it free from the scabbard. 'Toric's Dagger?'

'When Dirk died, he entrusted it to me. I think you should have it.'

'I thought we were supposed to return it to Magnia?'

'I think things have changed since then. Theron had the scabbard and belt made for you.'

Moneva twisted the weapon around in her hand, staring into the blade, seemingly lost in thought.

'Thank you,' she said at last, as if awakening from a stupor. She reached for her drink, hesitated, then pushed it away, before grabbing her plate of food.

BELWYNN LEFT the tavern and took the street that led up to Heractus Castle. Evening had arrived. The sun had departed the scene, and the temperature had dropped, Belwynn's breath hanging mistily in the air. Most people out and about were heading in the opposite direction to her, small groups going down to the taverns and inns in the city centre, where there would be a welcoming fire, plenty of ale and wine, and the stories and songs would continue deep into the night.

For a city that seemed so peaceful and happy, there were still plenty of soldiers on duty at the gatehouse and on the walls. That was Theron's doing, since he always insisted on strict routines and discipline.

But Belwynn also knew that beneath the surface, all was not so calm in Heractus. Sebastian and Theron had occupied the capital with their army in the summer, drawn from those Knights of Kalinth who had switched their loyalty to Sebastian as the new Grand Master of the Order. But King Jonas of Kalinth also resided here—not imprisoned by Sebastian, but kept under close watch. His wife, the Queen Irina, and his sons Straton and Dorian, were here also. All of them, except perhaps Dorian, wanted the Knights gone and their freedom to rule restored. In the city and out in the wider kingdom, their supporters would be plotting just such a restoration. This winter, with its harmony and its merriment, would not last forever.

Not that Belwynn had any trouble with gaining access to the castle.

The Lady of the Knights, they called her. Since her performance at the High Tower, she had become a figurehead of sorts for the movement, much to her own embarrassment. All of them now believed that she brought luck, confirmed by their victory in the Battle of Masada, the culmination of the Kalinthian invasion of Haskany. Outnumbered by the Drobax, Haskans and other forces of Ishari, she had blessed the swords of each knight before the battle. And, with no small help from their Krykker allies, they had won a seemingly miraculous victory. If any had doubts before, they had now evaporated. And so it was that if Moneva had become the mysterious, enigmatic killer of Erkindrix, Belwynn had become the angelic saviour of the Knights of Kalinth. It was bullshit, but nonetheless, it was a role that now felt impossible to escape.

The guards waved Belwynn through into the castle, and she took the winding steps up to her tower room, that she now shared with Soren. Inside, she found her brother lying face down on the floor, with Elana knelt by his side. She had her hands on his back, doing her best to heal his twisted spine and torn muscles.

'How is it going?' she asked them.

'His muscles are getting more relaxed,' commented Elana, a look of concentration on her face. Belwynn had some small experience of receiving Elana's healing powers, the warm sensation that repaired damaged tissue. It didn't always completely heal an injury, but she had already noticed Soren's movement improving.

'They tense up again by morning,' Soren complained, his voice muffled by the floor.

'You need rest,' reprimanded Elana, in the authoritarian voice she had developed to use with her patients. 'You can't expect an immediate recovery, even with my powers. And you must continue to exercise during the day.'

'I can't be bothered with all that,' he grumbled.

You really should listen to her, said Belwynn to her brother, using the telepathic link they shared.

'He just sits around and reads,' she added out loud, keen to tell tales on her brother.

'Too much sitting will tighten your back,' said Elana strictly. 'You should be stretching out on the hard floor and going for short walks.'

An indecipherable noise emerged from the floor where Soren lay, while Elana got to her feet.

'I should go,' she said to Belwynn. 'It grows dark. How are you?'

'Good. I had a productive talk with Moneva just now. I suggested she speak with you about something.'

'Of course. Well, I shall see you tomorrow.'

Elana left them to it.

'Well? Are you going to take her advice, or end up a cripple?' Belwynn demanded of her brother.

'I know. Still, I'm getting better. If I don't move from this position, it doesn't really hurt that much.'

'Well, at least Elana's treatment is working. She has truly been blessed by Madria.'

'Please,' said Soren. 'Don't start with that nonsense.'

The words were so rude, Belwynn was taken aback, even if the fact that they came from someone lying prone on the floor lessened their impact somewhat.

'What do you mean?' she said at last. 'Have some respect for my choices.'

'I can't respect it,' countered Soren. 'You were vulnerable when I was in Samir Durg. That's how they take advantage of you. There's no doubting Elana's powers, but all this religious hogwash that she's sucked you into is ridiculous.'

Soren's arrogance galled her, and it was getting worse. It wasn't just that he had to be right and, therefore, she was wrong. It wasn't simply that her decision to follow Madria was, in his estimation, all about his absence from her side. It was also the disrespect he showed to Elana, who had just gone out of her way to come here to treat him. Yes, she knew Soren was in pain, and was short tempered as a result. But her patience with him was wearing thin.

She was just formulating an appropriate response when there was a knock on their door.

'Can I come in?'

It was Theron.

'Yes,' she said automatically, before thinking Soren might prefer to be on his feet before Theron entered the room.

'Hi Soren,' Theron said, cheerfully enough. 'Everything alright?'

'Yes,' replied Soren gruffly. 'Are you two going to help me up?'

Theron grabbed Soren around the chest and Belwynn took his hands, and the three of them somehow got him to his feet, Soren grimacing the whole time and letting out a cry of pain as he straightened up. Belwynn passed him Onella's Staff, and he instantly looked better: his eyes focused on them, the grimace and frown disappeared.

'We've got a visitor,' Theron said, 'and he's asking after you both. You especially Soren. A mage by the name of Gustav.'

THERON LED them to Sebastian's private room in the castle. It wasn't any bigger than the room she shared with Soren, which was typical of Sebastian. He had attained the highest position in the Order of the Knights of Kalinth, was now de facto ruler of the kingdom, but would always be frugal in his tastes.

Sebastian and Gustav the Hawk were waiting for them. As she took a seat offered to her by Theron, she looked at their visitor. He was pale and tired looking. He had been given a woollen blanket, which he clutched around him, but she could see that he still shivered from time to time. Next to him on a table was a cup of spiced milk, still steaming, which he would occasionally blow on before taking a sip.

'Well,' Sebastian began, 'thank you for coming. You have both met Gustav before, at the Brasingian Court. We both felt it only right that you should be included in this conversation. His visit here should remain a secret, so please think carefully about to whom you repeat what you hear here.'

'Of course,' said Soren. 'It is good to see you again, Gustav.'

'Likewise,' said the Archmage of the Empire, his voice deep and confident, but Belwynn could hear the exhaustion in it too. 'We parted as you and your friends undertook what seemed like an important quest, to the lands of the Blood Caladri. I have heard nothing substantial of you since, so it is good to see you both alive. I have heard rumours of significant events in the north, however, and based on these my master, Emperor Baldwin, has had me travel here to find out the truth of them.'

Soren smiled. 'It has been so eventful that it is hard to know where to start. Our visit to the Blood Caladri was brief and led us to journey into the lands of the Grand Caladri. There I was lucky enough to resolve the—,' he paused, 'personal issue we discussed.'

This, Belwynn knew, was the loss of magic that Soren had suffered, only restored when he had formed a connection with the broken Caladri wizard, Agoston.

'Our time in the lands of the Caladri confirmed the importance of Toric's Dagger and revealed that it is one of seven weapons that can protect us from the Isharites. In Edeleny, we found a second such weapon, the Staff of Onella which I now hold.'

'Truly?' asked Gustav, leaning forward in his seat and reaching out a hand for the staff.

Soren hesitated. No doubt, Belwynn supposed, Onella's Staff would be a great boon to Gustav's considerable powers. If her brother handed it over, would he get it back?

Soren gave up the staff, and as soon as he did so, he slumped back in his chair, weakened.

Gustav, meanwhile, intently studied it, looking along its length from all angles, touching it in various ways and whispering under his breath. Eventually, and with a similar look of reluctance to Soren's, the Archmage returned it.

'That was where our luck ended,' said Soren, restored. 'Half of our number, including myself, were captured when Arioc's forces invaded the lands of the Grand Caladri.'

'I heard of this event,' said Gustav. 'Such an utter calamity. It is hard to put into words the loss to the world of magic that Ishari inflicted in that one episode. The Empire has carried out various reconnaissance missions in the region recently. So far, they all suggest that Ishari has abandoned the area.'

Soren nodded. 'My sister escaped with both the dagger and the staff,' indicating that Belwynn could take up the story.

'How?' asked Gustav.

'Through the intervention of the wizard, Pentas,' she replied.

Gustav raised his eyebrows in recognition of the name, but said nothing.

'He sent us here, to Kalinth, where we were lucky enough to be taken in by Sebastian.'

'And Kalinth has seen its own share of excitement?' Gustav asked, looking from Theron to Sebastian.

'Indeed,' Sebastian replied, 'much of it necessary, but regrettable. Our former Grand Master, Galenos, has been deposed, and I have taken over the position. Acting in what I believe to be the interests of the kingdom, Theron and I have secured control over the government here in Heractus. In alliance with the Krykkers, we led an army into Haskany last summer.'

'Incredible,' said Gustav, impressed. 'Kalinth has been asleep for a long time. Thank you for waking your nation, just in time.'

'That's not the half of it,' said Theron. 'While we scored a victory over Ishari, the wizard, Pentas, and Belwynn here, broke into Samir Durg itself, rescuing Soren—and one of their friends, Moneva, killed Erkindrix himself.'

As Theron told the climax of their story, he looked at Belwynn, and his words were said with such pride that she found tears in her eyes and a lump in her throat, which she swallowed away.

'Then the rumours I had heard are true? I hadn't dared to believe them. Erkindrix dead? Then, let me tell you all the news from the Empire. A great army of Drobax and Haskans was sent to the Empire. They first struck in Rotelegen, killing its duke, Ellard, and taking over the whole duchy. We were forced to evacuate the entire area.'

Gustav paused, noting the reactions of Belwynn and Soren, who had shared shocked looks.

'Of course, I forget, you left Essenberg with Ellard. I am sorry to bring you these tidings. Emperor Baldwin then defended our greatest fortress, Burkhard Castle. It became a scene of great slaughter, but we were able to hold out until this great army departed. We didn't understand why they left at the time, but I presume that the death of Erkindrix left Ishari without clear leadership and the army was recalled. I should add that we were aided by a force of Magnians, led by Prince Ashere of the North, who was killed by the enemy, and a man from the South by the name of Farred.'

'Did Farred survive?' Belwynn asked quickly.

'He did.'

'His friend is here in Heractus. He will be pleased to know.'

'There is more regarding your home kingdom. I won't need to remind you of the treachery of Duke Emeric of Barissia.'

The name struck Belwynn cold. She was immediately transported back in time to Coldeberg, where she had given a private performance in front of the duke, distracting him while they attempted a rescue of their friends. She remembered Kaved, who had betrayed them to Emeric's forces, wandering in while she played, and the desperate struggle and escape that ensued. Most of all, she remembered Rabigar, blinded in one eye by the savage jailers of the castle.

Soren glanced her way, checking on her reaction. 'Go on,' he said.

While we were besieged in Burkhard, Emeric was attacked by Duke Coen of Thesse, fighting alongside a Southern force led by your own ruler, Prince Edgar.

'Our cousin,' said Belwynn, wonderingly. 'Really? Edgar fighting in the Empire? It doesn't seem real.'

'It happened,' said Gustav, 'and by all accounts, Edgar and the South Magnians played a crucial role in the Battle of Witmar. Emeric escaped, but was killed by his own men.'

Belwynn laughed, covering her mouth as she did. It felt inappropriate, but the thought of Emeric defeated, by Edgar no less, had made her feel incredibly happy. It had been such a dark year. That it had all ended like this was truly the work of Madria.

'And so, to the ultimate purpose of my visit,' said Gustav. 'Baldwin has appointed his brother, Walter, as the new Duke of Barissia. There will be a formal ceremony and celebration in the spring. Baldwin would like to extend an invitation, both to Kalinth, and to the heroes of Samir Durg. He wants to meet with you and discuss the future of Dalriya. When the snows have gone, you are all cordially invited to Coldeberg.'

THE HANDMAID, THE DUCHESS AND THE QUEEN

II

'My place is here,' said Elana, her gesture taking in the newly built Church of Madria. Her patience, Belwynn could tell, was wearing thin.

Belwynn had tried several times to persuade the priestess to accompany them on the journey to the Empire. Elana had stood firm, however, insisting that her role was to serve her new flock in Heractus. She had even, to prepare for Belwynn's absence, already appointed a new disciple from among those who regularly attended on her. Belwynn couldn't help but feel like she was being replaced.

'That's settled then,' said Moneva with finality. Moneva, in turn, had declared that if Elana were to stay, she would too, since the priestess would need someone to look out for her. 'Success breeds enemies,' she said darkly, and Belwynn wondered what kind of conversations Moneva had overheard whilst deep in her cups in the city's taverns.

'Then I will need the Dagger,' responded Belwynn. 'Edgar and the others deserve to see it,' she added, when Moneva looked like she was about to argue.

'You've only just given it to me and now you're taking it away,' complained Moneva, who nonetheless unbuckled her belt before slapping the weapon into Belwynn's palm and stalking off.

It was, no doubt, a self-indulgent emotion, but Belwynn felt a loss at their decisions. She had always tried hard to keep their group together. Now it was to become more divided than ever. Rabigar had returned to his homeland, his exile seemingly at an end. Herin and Clarin were lost, left behind in Samir Durg. Now Elana and Moneva were staying behind, while she would travel with Soren and Gyrmund to Coldeberg.

So be it. She wouldn't beg them to come. She said her farewells and returned to her room in the castle to get her pack. Soren and Gyrmund were there, waiting for her, and she soon found herself in the courtyard of Heractus Castle, mounted on a beautiful mare and ready to go.

Also staying behind was Sebastian, the position in Kalinth too precarious for him to take an extended absence. Theron would represent Kalinth in the Empire. His absence was enough of a loss, since while Sebastian was the leader of the new regime—respected and diplomatic—Theron had provided much of the energy and organisation.

Sebastian saw them off. He shared some last private words with Theron before wishing them all good luck. Accompanying him was Prince Dorian, younger son of the king, who had formed a friendship with Belwynn despite her role in his family's diminution.

'Don't worry about your friends,' he said, coming over to give her horse a pat. 'I'll keep an eye on them.'

THERE WAS little talk as the four horses clip-clopped their way along the city streets, making for the East Gate. Gyrmund was subdued, upset at leaving Moneva behind, their relationship still not fully repaired. Soren was focused on the physical requirements of riding while clutching his staff in one hand. His condition had continued to improve, but he would now be without Elana's help. Belwynn rode next to Theron, who seemed to have a contented expression on his face.

'Looking forward to the trip?' she asked him.

'To be honest, yes. I've felt the responsibility of the last eight months. It's unrelenting. It will be a pleasure not to worry about everyone else for a while. And to spend so much time with you,' he added.

Soren snorted behind them, but they both chose to ignore it.

Evander was waiting for them at the gate, already opened, and as they nudged their horses through he fell in on the other side of Theron.

'Have you spoken with Tycho?' Theron asked his squire.

'Yes my lord, his force is ready, they are waiting on the road up ahead.'

'Very good. It's not like him to be so organised,' commented Theron. 'When we were young knights, I used to have to wake him up every morning, or he would sleep in 'til noon. I suppose we've all grown up since those days,' he said wistfully.

They soon joined with Tycho's force of fifty knights. They were too disciplined to shout out, but to a man, they all smiled and grinned as soon as they saw her. It was the strangest thing, but in truth, she was getting used to it. She knew all their faces now, and could name all but a handful. She recognised the handsome face of Leontios, big brown eyes framed by shoulder-length brown hair. He always beamed when he saw her, puffing up in importance, since he was the first knight whose sword she had blessed, on the road from the High Tower to Heractus, and he was ever keen to remind his peers of that fact.

Tycho trotted over to greet them, shaking hands, kissing Belwynn's, and giving Evander a big slap on the back. It used to be that a slap on the back from Tycho would send a shudder through the boy, but not so now. Not only had Evander grown as tall as Belwynn, he had filled out as well, after spending the autumn and winter months on the exercise yard, training to become a knight.

'How far will you be travelling with us, Lord Tycho?' asked Soren.

'As far as Korkis,' Tycho replied. 'I have my orders,' he added, with a sly grin at Theron, 'to ensure the town is fully—what word did you use, Theron?'

'Integrated.'

'Yes. Fully integrated into the kingdom.'

Quite right too, Belwynn said to Soren.

Of all the dangers they had faced, the flight from Korkis somehow felt the most terrifying. It was perhaps because as a group, they had been so vulnerable. Dirk had been ill, Elana and Belwynn helping him along, Rabigar was the only fighter with them, and he had recently lost an eye. If Theron hadn't intervened at the last minute, they would likely all be dead.

That moment would forever be emblazoned on her memory, Belwynn thought. Theron, a lone knight, charging down the hill at the men who had been chasing them. She knew that regaining control over Korkis was politics. But she thought that a part of it might be to punish them for what they did.

THEY MADE SURPRISINGLY GOOD PROGRESS. Belwynn wasn't at all convinced that spring had come yet. It was cold, and snow still lay on the hills of Kalinth. But Theron had argued that of all those invited, they would have the longest journey to Coldeberg, and would need to set off earlier than Baldwin's other guests. Although the ground was wet, they were amongst the first to journey on the roads since the snow had melted, and they weren't as torn up as they were likely to get in a few weeks. Their horses, kept indoors and fed on hay for the winter, also seemed enthusiastic about stretching their legs. The stark but beautiful Kalinthian countryside rolled by and as the evening of the second day drew in, they had reached Sebastian's house, Sernea, where Soren and Belwynn were allocated a room for the night.

The next morning, they began the short journey to Korkis. As they neared the town, Belwynn recognised the countryside they passed through. Rolling hills with grazing animals, which today on horseback seemed gentle and innocuous, but last time she was here, escaping from their pursuers on foot, seemed impossibly steep and forbidding. To her right was the woodland where they had spent the night, and where the horseman from Korkis had followed them, taunting them, as his companions and their hunting dogs closed the gap to their prey.

The wooden palisade of the town came into view, Belwynn recalling how Rabigar had known about an exit in the north of the wall, a section swinging open that allowed passage in and out for those who didn't want to be seen. She thought about mentioning it to Theron or Tycho, but decided she liked the thought of it remaining there.

Anyway, the Knights had arrived with a far superior force to anything the town could muster. They were content to wait patiently outside until the authorities inside reacted.

More and more heads bobbed into view along the wall, staring out at the force that had arrived unannounced outside their town, until the gates opened, and half a dozen men walked out to greet them. Belwynn stared at their faces but didn't recognise any of them.

'I am Peros, Mayor of Korkis,' said one of them, trying to sound confident but looking more than a little intimidated.

'Unfortunately for you,' said Tycho, pitching his voice so all could hear, 'you are mayor no longer.'

He produced a roll of parchment from his saddle bag. 'By order of the king, I have been appointed the new mayor of Korkis.'

He moved his horse slowly towards Peros before holding out the document. Peros took it and began reading.

I wonder how they persuaded Jonas to sign that, Belwynn said to Soren.

Assuming they didn't forge his signature, said Soren.

'Under our constitution,' said Peros, looking up from the parchment, eyes wide and anxious, 'the townspeople choose their own mayor.'

'This is an emergency royal writ agreed by the Council,' said Theron.

'Have I done something wrong?' asked Peros.

'I don't know,' said Tycho. 'But if you have, you can be sure I'll find out about it. Now, let's get moving. I need to garrison my knights.'

Belwynn knew Tycho as a light-hearted, friendly man. But he could clearly be intimidating when needed, and Peros and the rest of the men turned around and began leading them into town.

'Come,' said Theron to the others. 'We will be leaving soon but we might as well get an early lunch here to send us on our way.'

Tycho had the knights' horses stabled and food brought out, while the people of Korkis organised how they were going to quarter fifty knights. He had already gone a long way towards asserting his authority over the place, and Belwynn felt sure he would soon identify the corrupt members of the town guard and remove them.

Belwynn, Theron, Evander, Gyrmund and Soren had found a place to sit and eat in the central plaza, giving their horses a chance to rest before it was time to move out.

'Are you not itching to get involved yourself?' asked Belwynn with a smile, knowing that Theron usually couldn't help man-managing.

'No. I trust Tycho. My problem is there aren't many others I trust. With Tycho here, I hope Sebastian has enough help in Heractus.'

'Belwynn,' said Gyrmund quietly, nodding to a location over her shoulder. 'Looks like you have a visitor.'

Belwynn turned around, wondering what he meant. A young girl was standing awkwardly nearby, and she startled somewhat when Belwynn looked at her. She looked familiar. Belwynn suddenly let out a gasp when she recognised who it was. She had tried to defend this girl when she was accused of stealing bread. It was that intervention that had prompted the Korkis soldiers to try to arrest them. The girl had obviously survived the winter, but she looked pale and malnourished.

'Come here,' said Belwynn, holding up a hand.

The girl looked warily at the men sitting with Belwynn, weapons lying by their sides. Belwynn kept her hand up, smiled, and waited patiently. Hesitantly, the girl came over, then flopped down next to Belwynn.

'I'm so pleased to see you,' said Belwynn, handing her some bread and cheese. Theron passed over a drink and the others donated some food, until the girl had a mini-feast in front of her, which she tucked into with vigour.

'This is the girl I tried to help last time I was here,' she explained to the others, all of whom had heard the story, but hadn't been with Belwynn at the time.

The girl nodded seriously in confirmation, her mouth full of food.

'What is your name, child?' Belwynn asked.

'Alyssa.'

'And where are your parents?'

'My mam died when I was seven,' said the girl matter-of-factly.

Belwynn guessed that was about two years ago. 'So who looks after you now?'

'No-one.'

That explained why the poor thing was taking the bread. She would ask Tycho to make sure she was looked after.

Alyssa looked at her. 'You can look after me if you want.'

Belwynn's heart broke. She found herself thinking of how to explain why she couldn't look after her. But *why* couldn't she? No-one else in this town had done so in two years. And Belwynn was in a far better position to care for this child than most people were.

'She could come with us,' she found herself saying.

Don't be ridiculous, said Soren, but she ignored him.

She looked at Theron. 'You have a squire attending you on this journey,' she said to him. 'Why shouldn't I have a handmaid?'

Gyrmund chuckled, Soren scowled, and Evander looked expectantly at Theron.

'Should I fetch a horse for her, my lord?' asked the squire.

Theron looked at them all, keeping a neutral expression, before his eyes settled on the girl. 'Go on then, Vander,' he conceded.

Evander grinned, leapt to his feet, and ran off to find Tycho.

THE ROUTE from Korkis to the Brasingian Empire wasn't straightforward. The fastest way was to head due east into Persala, and then south down the Great Road. But that involved heading into territory that was, they suspected, still controlled by Ishari. While Gustav had suggested that Ishari had withdrawn from their more southerly conquests, no-one was really sure what the situation was, and so it was deemed safer to avoid that option. The alternative was to head south-east, to the border with the Grand Caladri, and follow it east all the way to Trevenza, avoiding population centres. It was a more difficult route to navigate, but Gyrmund was confident of leading them, and they were in no rush. Borderlands could be dangerous places, but Soren's powers seemed enhanced, especially with Onella's Staff, and Belwynn had few concerns that they would face a threat that this company couldn't handle.

More of a problem was Alyssa. Belwynn's spur-of-the-moment decision to bring the girl immediately looked foolish when they discovered she had never ridden a horse before. She therefore had to ride with Belwynn, gripping her tightly around the waist and screaming with alarm when they went too fast. As soon as she got used to the sensation of riding, she developed saddle sores, and spent two days crying, both on and off the horse, until she toughened up.

After a miserable few days with her, they had a go at teaching her to ride, short stints at first. Theron spent a lot of time with her, since Gyrmund was often way ahead of them, scouting the route. But she liked Evander best, would listen intently to everything the squire said and never moaned, which she did with the adults. Like most children, she was a fast learner. The short rides gradually got longer, until Belwynn found herself riding alone again, and much to everyone's relief, the crying and whining stopped.

Perhaps because of Alyssa's presence among them, everyone made an effort to entertain when it came time to sit around the fire. Soren would tell stories of the past, Gyrmund would tell stories of his travels to strange places, and Belwynn would sing for them. If there was enough light, Theron and Gyrmund would give Evander weapon training. At such times, it was up to Belwynn to keep Alyssa occupied, especially after Soren's attempt to teach her how to read ended badly. The girl liked having her hair plaited, and so one night Belwynn let her practice on her hair, Alyssa sitting behind her by the fire, quietly working away. It was a peaceful, contented moment.

'How is it going, Alyssa?' asked Belwynn, not able to turn to face her because the girl had her hair in both hands.

There was a pause before the girl replied. 'My mam used to call me Lyssa. You can call me that if you want.'

Belwynn swallowed, and decided it best not to turn around. 'Thank you, Lyssa. I will.'

She shared a look with Soren across the fire, his expression unreadable, before he returned to his book.

IN THIS WAY, they spent their days and nights, until Gyrmund announced they had left the borderlands and had entered the province of Trevenza. Along with Grienna, Trevenza had declared independence from Persala so that they could join the Brasingian Empire, only to find themselves conquered by an army of Haskans and Drobax. They were likely to find a ravaged country, and Gyrmund felt more comfortable riding straight for the Great Road. They had sufficient provisions, and the horses remained in good condition, so there was no need to stop.

As soon as they set foot on the road, Belwynn felt more relaxed, since all they now had to do was follow it due south to Grienna and then to Rotelegen, the most northerly of the seven duchies of Brasingia. The temperature was milder than when they had set off, and it was easy travelling compared to the first part of the journey. Their horses ate up the miles. Despite the warmer weather, there was very little traffic on the road. The people they did meet were groups of travellers heading south like them, but at a slower pace, with wagons full of possessions and sometimes livestock accompanying them. When Gyrmund asked, they explained they were heading to Rotelegen to start a new life in a safer part of the world. Belwynn wondered whether they would be welcomed in the Empire, but they all seemed convinced they would be.

In Grienna Belwynn was reminded of their journey from the lands of the Blood Caladri to those of the Grand Caladri. When crossing the Great Road, they had encountered the corpses of the Drobax who had died on their march south to invade the Empire. Presumably, similar casualties were suffered on their retreat north. But there was no sign of either now. Belwynn speculated that the birds and other creatures of the forest that ran either side of the Road had feasted on the remains.

There had once been a sizeable settlement on the Brasingian side of the border with Grienna, giving the dukes of Rotelegen the opportunity to inspect and monitor the people and goods leaving and arriving in their duchy. But there was little left of the buildings and it was empty of people. Gyrmund had planned to spend the night there, and so that was what they did, making a small camp amongst the unclaimed debris. Their mood was sombre, as if they were sharing the land with the ghosts of the settlement.

Next morning, they were quick to pack up and leave, heading for Guslar, the capital of Rotelegen. After the devastation at the border, Belwynn was unsure what to expect from the city, but as they approached, she could see that the defences were intact. Soldiers manned the walls and waved them through an open gate. It looked like a city open for business.

The straight roads of Guslar took them to the central plaza. Belwynn enjoyed sharing Theron's interest in the city, the layout and building designs all a novelty to him. Lyssa showed little interest, wondering instead when they would stop for lunch.

It was agreed that Belwynn would accompany Theron as envoys of Kalinth and present themselves at the castle, while the others sourced supplies for the journey south. A brief meeting was organised with Adalheid, mother of the young Duke of Rotelegen, and with little ceremony they found themselves waiting in what looked like one of her private rooms. After a couple of minutes, the door swung open and Adalheid entered, accompanied by only one minister and a bodyguard, who stood by the door and looked straight ahead, avoiding eye contact with those in the room.

'Lady Adalheid,' said the minister, making the introductions, 'Count Theron and Lady Belwynn.'

'You're on your way to the festivities in Coldeberg,' said Adalheid with a note of sarcasm.

'Yes indeed,' replied Theron. 'Will you or the Duke be attending?'

Adalheid snorted. 'We don't have time for that. The rebuilding task here is enormous; never ending. Jeremias needs to be seen to be leading it, not trying to curry favour with the Emperor who will never lift a finger to help us here. He'd rather spend the Empire's money on a party in Coldeberg.' She shook her head in distaste. 'Giving Barissia to his own brother...'

At least, thought Belwynn, Theron and I are used to the awkwardness of the royal court in Heractus. It's been good preparation for this.

'The people of Kalinth offer their support to Rotelegen. If there's anything we can do to help, please ask,' said Theron.

Adalheid studied him. 'You in Kalinth know what it is to share a border with Haskany and the Drobax. When the time comes, fight them. You may buy us some time here. Should they come for us first, we will do the same for you. I think that is all we can do for each other.'

'We noticed immigrants heading here from Trevenza and Grienna,' said Belwynn.

Adalheid turned to her. She looked prematurely aged to Belwynn, who thought she could just make out the features of a younger, carefree Adalheid. If she had really existed, that Adalheid must have disappeared on hearing the news of her husband and sons.

'Yes. We're depopulated. Many died in the fighting. Others, who were evacuated, have decided to stay where they are rather than return here to their homeland. So there are opportunities in Rotelegen for those from the north, and for those from across the Empire. Where else could you be given your own plot of land to farm for free? Unfortunately, it means that we have become a magnet for the indolent and the criminal. But that is what the Gods have given us to work with. We must do our best. Anyway, it was a delight to have met you both.'

With that, Adalheid was on her feet, and as soon as Theron and Belwynn muttered their pleasantries, she was gone.

'I feel sorry for her son,' commented Theron once they were out of the castle, 'such a dragon for a mother.'

'I disagree,' said Belwynn. 'Surely it's better to have a dragon on his side than to have been left alone.'

Theron nodded. 'Alright, you win.'

We've finished early, Belwynn said to Soren. *Where are you?*

I'll give you directions, Soren replied instantly. *I think you'll be surprised who we've bumped into.*

Intrigued, Belwynn led Theron a few streets away towards the market area of the city. Evander saw them and waved. He was standing with Soren and Lyssa, next to a carriage which had been parked up on the other side of the street. Attached to the carriage were four gaurs.

'It can't be,' said Belwynn out loud, a stupid grin appearing on her face.

Theron frowned at the spectacle, but followed on as Belwynn practically skipped over to the carriage. As she neared, Gyrmund came into view from behind the carriage, talking animatedly with two Caladri women. She recognised them immediately as Marika and Dora, the carriage attendants they had met when they had entered the lands of the Blood Caladri the previous summer. When they saw her, they both let out a little scream and rushed over to give her a hug.

Belwynn introduced them to Theron, and in their excitement, they hugged him as well, making her giggle.

She peered into the carriage, but it was empty. 'They can't be here on their own?' she asked Gyrmund.

'From what I can understand, the men are out buying provisions and left them here for a short while.'

Sure enough, it wasn't long before the Caladri returned. Amongst them was Hajna, Princess of the Blood Caladri. She walked over, poised and elegant, all the more noticeable when her attendants were so excitable and over-familiar.

'How nice to see you all again,' said Hajna once the various introductions were made. With her were Gyuri, the same carriage driver who had driven them before, and two of the male Caladri attendants, Vida and Joska. The three of them were carrying sacks of items they must have purchased at the market. In addition, Szabolcs, the wise man they had met during their visit, was with them. Soren immediately gravitated towards Szabolcs and drew him away for a private conversation.

'I presume you are also on your way to Coldeberg?' Belwynn asked.

'You are correct. We were invited to attend by Gustav the Hawk. It is very important that Szabolcs and I meet with the leaders of Dalriya.'

'Prince Lorant is not with you? Is he well?'

A look of grief passed over Hajna's face. 'Lorant is well. We faced very serious fighting soon after you left, the worst I have ever known. My husband's father, King Tibor, was killed in the fighting. So Lorant is not a prince anymore, but a king.'

'And you are a queen?'

'You are correct. We agreed to a truce with the Shadow Caladri not long after our king's death, and it has held over the autumn and winter seasons. But Lorant dare not leave our lands and so I have come without him.'

'Are you about to leave now?' Belwynn asked.

'Yes. We thought it wise to replenish our supplies here first.'

'Can we accompany them?' Belwynn asked, looking at her companions.

'Of course we will,' said Soren.

'That is so kind of you,' said Hajna.

Gyuri climbed up to his seat, while Hajna and her four attendants took their places inside the carriage. Giving a shout and a pull on the reins, Gyuri got his gaur moving.

Belwynn and the others looked at each other with a mixture of expressions.

'So we just bumped into the Queen of the Caladri?' asked Theron, disbelievingly.

'I liked the cows,' said Lyssa.

COLDEBERG

III

Spring rainfall hit them on the road from Guslar to Essenberg. It was incessant, and Belwynn soon gave up on trying to keep dry, reconciling herself to travelling while soaked through. Her inner thighs got sore from the constant rubbing of riding. The Caladri kept out of the rain inside the carriage; the men taking turns driving the gaur. But their slow pace became a source of frustration. In the end, Belwynn bundled Lyssa into the carriage with Hajna and the rest of them rode on ahead: the sooner they reached Essenberg, the sooner they could get warm.

The Great Road took them to the northern Castle Quarter of Essenberg and they went straight to the royal castle. Baldwin and his court were probably already in Coldeberg, but someone would have been left in charge of things, and both the Kalinthians and the Caladri were invited guests of the Emperor. After explaining who they were, Belwynn and the others were admitted to the castle, but had to wait awhile before someone arrived to greet them. That someone was a priest.

'His Grace is on his way to meet you. I can take you to your rooms first.'

Belwynn shared a little smirk with Gyrmund as they both recalled the pace at which the Archbishop moved.

'Is Decker in charge in the absence of Baldwin?' asked Soren.

'That's right.'

'Well, you might want to mention to him that the Queen of the Caladri is on her way here too.'

The priest's eyes widened at the news, but he otherwise kept his composure. 'I will certainly tell him. Please, follow me.'

IT WAS a few hours until the Caladri were settled into the castle and ready to meet with the Archbishop. Outside, the sun was setting, and a chill descended, much to Belwynn's disappointment, since she had only just got herself warm again. Hajna and Szabolcs attended, leaving the rest of the Caladri in their rooms. Theron left Evander to look after Lyssa, adding babysitting to the list of duties expected of a squire.

Decker was alone. He had found them a cosy room to meet in, with a roaring fire, and while the Archbishop was best positioned to take full advantage of it, the heat spread nicely through the room. Belwynn wasn't the only one whose eyes looked droopy, as the heat, a generous helping of Cordentine red wine, and a long day of travelling combined to make everyone feel sleepy.

Decker was naturally eager to hear their news and mostly listened at first. But Belwynn soon had questions for the Archbishop.

'You did not want to go to Coldeberg, Your Grace?'

'Well, I might have enjoyed it when I got there, but I don't enjoy travelling so much these days. And a city this size needs to know that someone is in charge. Otherwise people get to thinking they might be the ones in charge.'

'Wouldn't you have been involved in the coronation?'

'Dukes do not get crowned,' explained Decker. 'That's what went wrong with the last one,' he added mischievously.

'Oh,' said Belwynn, slightly confused by the politics. 'They are just appointed by the Emperor?'

'No, not that either. The duchies choose their own rulers, usually in line with the laws of inheritance. Emeric had no direct heir. In the situation they are in, the wise people of Barissia would want their ruler to be an able ruler and, most of all, loyal to the Emperor. I think you will agree that Walter is the perfect candidate.'

'Of course,' said Belwynn, not wishing to appear that she was suggesting otherwise.

'And the not so wise people of Barissia?' asked Soren.

'Well, they are the ones who brought the duchy to its knees. Baldwin has been merciful with Barissia, placing all the blame for their treachery on Emeric's shoulders. But neither he nor Walter will tolerate any further opposition. The Barissian rebellion nearly led to the fall of the Empire, let's not forget. Emeric was in alliance with Erkindrix himself. And how would Emeric and his minions have treated us if Burkhard Castle had fallen and the Emperor had been slain?'

'That would have been a disaster,' suggested Hajna softly.

'I agree, Your Highness,' said Decker. 'None of us have forgotten what Barissia did. This meeting of the rulers of Dalriya has many purposes, of course. But one of them is to affirm, for all to see, who is in charge of the duchy now.'

EVERYONE WAS UP EARLY for the final leg of their journey. The sky was overcast, but the rain was holding off for now.

Theron had a brief opportunity to see the sights of Essenberg, all of which held memories for Belwynn of their time in the city last year. On their left, Decker's cathedral dominated the skyline. Ahead of them lay the River Cousel, swelled by the recent rain. They used Albert's Bridge to cross the river. Downstream of them was the First Bridge, that used Margaret Island to cross the river. Belwynn pointed it out to Theron and Evander, explaining that they had spent a night on that island, hiding from their enemies.

Far to their left, out of sight, was the Imps, the headquarters of the Imperial Army. It had been Walter's to command; perhaps would be still, though surely he would be spending less time in Essenberg now that he had become a duke. It was to Walter's duchy that they now headed, riding straight on through the Coldeberg Gate, from where a road took them directly to the capital of Barissia.

The rain that had threatened them never came, and so they were content to ride along at the same pace as the Caladri carriage. Just as the light was fading, Coldeberg came into view. They saw its distinctive slope, descending from the high point where the castle adjoined the city walls, down to the southern end at the bottom of the hill. The sight made Belwynn's insides twist. Her memories told her that Coldeberg was a place of evil, but she knew it didn't have to be, now that Emeric's regime was gone.

The gate into Coldeberg was closed for the night, so they had to request entry from the night watch. That would involve the soldiers finding someone with enough authority to give permission, so Belwynn expected a long wait.

She was surprised when the gates opened after a few minutes. Waving them into the city was Rainer, Baldwin's chamberlain, who had assembled a team of officials to expedite their arrival. As she entered the city, a stable-boy ran up to grab the reins of her mare and take her away. Another boy jumped up beside Gyuri and guided him away to a suitable place to leave the carriage.

'Lord Rainer,' Belwynn greeted him.

'Lady Belwynn,' the chamberlain replied.

She was impressed that he remembered her, but he had always seemed a man in control of the details. 'May I present our travelling guests? Queen Hajna of the Blood Caladri and Count Theron of Erisina, representing King Jonas of Kalinth.'

Rainer took their hands. 'On behalf of Emperor Baldwin and Duke Walter, may I extend you all a warm welcome. You are expected, and I have already organised your accommodation. Queen Hajna, Gustav insisted on taking charge of your rooms, so I will personally take you and your attendants to see him right away. As for the rest of you, I have a town house picked out for you by Duke Walter. I hoped you could share it with Prince Edgar and his entourage?'

Belwynn briefly checked with Theron, who nodded his approval. 'Is Edgar here already?' she asked.

'Yes, you are the last of our guests to arrive. Everyone else who accepted our invitation is here.'

'We are very grateful,' said Theron. 'I can only imagine the amount of work such an operation has given you.'

'Yes indeed, but once I accepted the inevitability of the odd mistake here and there, I have been able to embrace the challenge. Werner!' Rainer said, calling over a member of his staff. 'Please take our guests to their house.'

They said their farewells to Rainer and to the Caladri, before the six of them followed Werner on foot through the dark streets of Coldeberg. Belwynn had never felt safe in this city, and made Lyssa hold her hand as she peered down dark alleys suspiciously. In truth, however, Werner was leading them to the wealthy part of the city, where the houses were sheltered by the looming presence of the Duke's castle. Whereas before the castle had been crawling with Emeric's mercenaries, she knew that now it was Walter's soldiers who kept an eye on things, and her fears subsided.

When Werner approached the door of the building and gave a knock, she almost gasped in surprise, for he had led them to one of the most expensive looking buildings she had seen. It was brick built, and no expense seemed to have been spared in the choice of materials, with glass windows and clay tiles on the roof.

The door was opened by a young woman who Werner introduced as Heike, before explaining to Heike who they were.

'You will have a staff to attend to you here during your stay,' Werner explained. 'Any concerns, please ask for me—I am more likely to be available than Lord Rainer himself,' he said with a smile.

With that said, Werner hurried off down the street and Heike took them all in to the hall of the house.

As they gathered there, looking about them, the far door opened, and Edgar suddenly appeared in the room, flanked by Gyrmund's friend Farred. Farred and Gyrmund embraced; Edgar shook hands with Soren, then found Belwynn for a hug; Belwynn introduced him to Theron; and soon the hall was filled with so much talk that Belwynn couldn't really follow any of it.

In the end, the travellers discarded their cloaks and entered the kitchen, where they sat at the table. Heike piled the table with a cold supper and Belwynn, realising that she was famished, didn't hesitate to tuck in. Soren and the others, even little Lyssa, all did the same, and so it fell to Edgar and Farred to relate their news first.

And what tales they had to tell.

Edgar went first. He began with the worst of it, recounting how Gervase Salvinus, Emeric's Isharite wizard, Tirano, and their former friend turned traitor, Kaved, had broken into his camp. They had killed Soren's mentor, Ealdnoth, before attempting to kill Edgar himself. His bodyguard, Leofwin, had died in the desperate fight, but not before killing Tirano. Belwynn looked at Soren on hearing the news, who had bowed his head in grief. She indicated that Edgar should carry on with his account and let her brother be. Edgar then filled in the bare bones of the campaign in Barissia, which had ended with the surrender of the very city they were now in, and Salvinus emerging free from Coldeberg in return for the head of his former master.

'This was Salvinus's house,' added Edgar with a wry smile. 'Walter thought it apt that we should be the ones to enjoy it.'

Next it was Farred's turn, whose story was no less dramatic. He had taken a force of South Magnians to the Brasingian Empire where, led by Ashere of North Magnia, they had engaged with the invading Isharite army. The idea of this small force taking on an impossibly large army sounded like it should be made into a song. Farred's story had its own share of tragedy, when Prince Ashere died of the wounds inflicted on him. Farred then found himself, along with Emperor Baldwin and the imperial army, under siege in Burkhard Castle. They had been surrounded by the huge Drobax army that had descended the Great Road, having to defend their position from daily onslaughts. When Farred explained that the Isharites had suddenly and unexpectedly retreated north, he and Edgar looked at them quizzically, and it was time to tell their story.

Before that, Belwynn insisted on putting Lyssa to bed, whose eyes had glazed over, despite her best attempts to stay awake. Gyrmund ended up carrying her to her bed, where she was too tired to resist, and went straight to sleep. When they returned to the kitchen, they had a glass of wine waiting for them. Heike had cleared the table.

'Please, Heike, there's no need to stay up,' said Belwynn. 'We can sort ourselves out.'

'If you don't mind,' replied the young woman, 'I asked if I could stay and hear your story.'

Soren and the others gave a smile, and so Belwynn took a seat and helped her brother and the others relate their adventures since leaving Edgar's court at Bidcote in Magnia. It was less than a year ago, but seemed so much longer, and during the telling it felt like the events had happened to someone else and not to her at all. The chase through the Wilderness; Kaved's betrayal in Coldeberg; Arioc's invasion of the Grand Caladri; Belwynn's escape to Kalinth; Soren and Gyrmund's imprisonment in Samir Durg. When Gyrmund finally told how Erkindrix had died, betrayed by Arioc in his own throne room, the hour had grown late, the wine was gone, and everyone looked eager for sleep.

At the end, Belwynn produced Toric's Dagger and handed it to her cousin, who drew it from its new scabbard and studied it carefully.

'So this blade killed Erkindrix?' he asked wonderingly.

'We brought it back,' said Belwynn. 'It just took a little longer than expected.'

'I had total faith,' said Edgar, grinning. 'But what to do with it now? From what you say, returning it to Toric's Temple isn't the wisest move.'

'I hope we will gain some answers tomorrow,' said Soren. 'Szabolcs has been researching the history of the weapons. He tells me he has more substantial information than he did in the summer.'

Edgar nodded, returning the weapon into Belwynn's keeping. 'Then I, for one, am looking forward to what tomorrow brings, a day that was already threatening to be very busy. But now my bed is calling me.'

THE EARLY MORNING event of the day was a service celebrating Walter's elevation to the duchy. After a quick breakfast, they left the house to walk the short distance to the cathedral, leaving Evander and Lyssa behind.

Mingling outside Coldeberg Cathedral was a veritable who's who of the Brasingian aristocracy, not to mention representatives of states beyond the Empire's borders. Between Edgar and Farred, there were few individuals their group was not familiar with, and they found themselves greeted by a bewildering array of powerful figures, Theron struggling to keep up with so many new faces.

Baldwin himself was there, accompanied by his queen, Hannelore. It was the first time Belwynn had ever seen Hannelore. She was tall and full-figured, her brunette hair elaborately piled on top of her head, making her appear even taller. Their children accompanied them: two daughters about to enter adolescence and a younger boy. The children seemed somewhat shy and stood to one side of the gathering until someone familiar approached them and engaged them in conversation.

Hannelore's father was Arne, Duke of Luderia, and his son and heir was Tobias. The whole family had the same large framed look to them, but whereas the men, Belwynn felt, ended up looking corpulent, Hannelore looked shapely, turning the heads of those present. Arne had been a defender at Burkhard Castle, and came over to talk with Farred and to introduce himself and his son to everyone else. He was friendly, down to earth, and proud of his family.

Most of the other great men of the Empire were also here with their entourages. Duke Coen of Thesse, energetic and bald, spoke at length with Edgar. Archbishop Godfrey, ruler of Gotbeck, had a voice that could be heard wherever he happened to be standing. And, of course, Walter himself came over to see them, enquiring about the house he had chosen for them. There was a touch of humour in his eyes as he asked, all of them recalling the first time when they had met, on the road from Coldeberg to Essenberg, when he and his soldiers had intervened at the last minute and saved them from Gervase Salvinus.

'Any news of him?' asked Edgar, a hungry look in his eyes, as if he could not wait to hear that the man was dead.

'Possibly in Cordence, last I heard,' said Walter. His humour had disappeared. 'Unfortunately, men like him can always find new work.'

From beyond the Empire had come a collection of chieftains from the Midder Steppe. They strolled around in their flowing kaftans, with their distinctive long hair tied behind them. There was a delegation from Guivergnais, and one from Cordence. Queen Hajna was there, along with Szabolcs, talking quietly with Gustav, the Archmage of the Empire. They, of course, attracted the most stares. For the vast majority of guests, this was the first time they had lain eyes on a Caladri, and their clawed feet, bird-like head swivels, and delicate frames marked them out as something alien and other.

The last group of guests to emerge onto the cathedral precincts, guided by

Rainer the chamberlain, were three Krykkers. They came striding over towards Belwynn's group, swords strapped to their belts, as if they were marching to war rather than attending a church service.

Belwynn smiled, for the Krykker in the middle wore an eye patch: Rabigar. He smiled too, giving her a rough hug when he reached them. Flanking him were Maragin, chief of Rabigar's clan, the Grendals, and Guremar, the stern faced chief of clan Plengas. They made a bee line for Theron, each clasping his arm in greeting, a mark of their respect for him as a warrior who had fought by their side. Belwynn could tell that he was pleased: finally, Theron was the one with connections. Meanwhile, many of the other guests were staring at the Krykkers as a curiosity. With the armour-like skin covering their torsos; Rabigar's eye patch; the fact that Maragin was carrying a sword as large as the men's; and the confident, bordering on superior way in which the Krykkers stared back at the humans, there was something slightly menacing about them.

Now that everyone had assembled in one place, Rainer was keen to press on with the programme, and began politely coercing people into the cathedral. Belwynn's group filed through two sets of doors into the nave, which stretched before them, a vast space both length-ways and in height. The vaulted ceiling of the cathedral must have been thirty metres high, and the myriad conversations taking place echoed around the vast space.

Wooden pews filled out the space, with a clear path down the centre. Ushers were on hand to take the guests to their seats. The Magnians were allocated to a pew in the middle of the nave. Belwynn looked about, watching as the seats quickly filled. She didn't envy Rainer the headache of organising such an event. Not only did he have to decide who made the guest list in the first place, but then where they should sit. Not everyone would end up where they felt they deserved to be. Did a count from Kalinth outrank a chief from the Midder Steppe, for example? There was surely no definitive answer, but somehow everyone was seated without incident and the ceremony could begin.

The bishop of Coldeberg ascended his podium and welcomed his unusual congregation. There was something familiar about him, but she couldn't quite place her finger on it.

Do we know him? she asked Soren.

Soren already had the bored expression he used in churches, but perked up when he heard the question. He placed one hand onto the staff that had become his sight aid and focused on the man who, though young looking, was talking in a rich, smooth voice.

Ancel, he said definitively. *The priest who found us in Essenberg and took us to see Decker.*

He was right. They had been caught in two minds about where to go, fearing that Emeric's agents in the city were waiting for them. Ancel had led them to a side door in Essenberg Cathedral, and Decker had then taken them underground, via the Crypt of the Dukes of Kelland, to Baldwin's Castle.

You're right, she agreed. *But how is it that he is now the Bishop of Coldeberg?*

I don't fully know the politics of it, Soren said. *But presumably, the previous Bishop of Coldeberg was the one who crowned Emeric as a king. Baldwin will have wasted no time in ejecting him and needed a replacement. No doubt Decker recommended Ancel, who I suppose is someone they can trust.*

Yes, said Belwynn. *But that means they have replaced both duke and bishop with Kellishmen. That surely can't be popular.*

Well, they defeated the Barissian rebels in battle. I think Baldwin is more concerned with asserting his authority than being popular.

That said, and with Ancel moving from his introduction to his sermon, Soren placed his staff on the floor in front of him, adjusted his position to get more comfortable, and closed his eyes.

Since the Brasingian Church worshipped many gods, Ancel's sermon was theologically vague and, Belwynn believed, had nothing in it to offend the ears of most of the guests, be they Middians, Cordentines, or even Caladri. Compared to Elana's ideas, it lacked a singleness of purpose. Belwynn was interested in the references to Lady Alexia, however, who protected the people. She remembered something Hajna had said once, that she had taken little notice of at the time. Hajna had equated her goddess, Onella, with Elana's Madria, and also with Alexia. Were they one and the same, worshipped by different peoples under different names?

After expounding on the duties that Walter owed to the Barissian people, and on the obligations they had to him in return, Ancel and his audience seemed satisfied with the ceremony and stood up before filing out of the building.

Their next destination was Coldeberg Castle, as the guests of Walter and Baldwin. It was a short walk to the castle, where Walter's hall was already set up with tables of food and drink. The Magnians sat around a table with the three Krykkers. Belwynn took something, but it was so soon after breakfast that she wasn't hungry, and anyway, she hadn't come all this way to eat, drink and be merry. She wasn't the only one who felt this way and the tension in the hall grew, conversations became muted or stopped altogether, and the gathering waited for someone to speak.

Into the void came a bang from the top table, and everyone turned to face Walter, who had read the mood.

'Thank you all for being here. I am not a man for ceremony, so I would like to turn our collective attention away from myself and my new responsibilities, and to the real reason why most of you have been invited here. Everyone attending today, in different ways, to a larger or smaller degree, has experienced the threat posed by Ishari. Only recently have we started to unite together to face it. Late, but I hope not too late. There is much we can do here. There are individual alliances to be made. If I know my brother at all, I know the Emperor is itching to speak with the leaders, or their representatives, of the other nations who have graciously agreed to his invitation.'

Heads turned to Baldwin, seated next to the new duke. He looked older than Belwynn remembered, more grey in his hair now, but he was still a formidable presence in the room. He held his hands in the air. 'He knows me,' he conceded grudgingly, with a smile, before gesturing to his brother to continue.

'But,' continued Walter, 'we have agreed that first, we must grasp the thorniest issue, or at least the issue that the Emperor and I find the most difficult. Magic. Whatever anyone's personal feelings on this issue, it cannot be ignored. Last year, Ishari used magic to destroy the Grand Caladri. They used magic to aid their invasion of the Empire, and it has been used in many other ways. In turn, magic had a role to play in the death of Erkindrix, the event that arguably spared many of us from further disaster. Anyone who is not comfortable with the topic is not required to stay and hear this. But magic will play a role in the future, too, and if we pretend otherwise, we are giving the enemy an advantage.'

There was a pause between Walter taking his seat and Gustav getting to his feet. It allowed some to leave the room. Queen Hannelore quietly vacated her seat, along with her children. Archbishop Godfrey left much more loudly, not able to resist uttering dire warnings about the use of magic. But most people stayed.

'Amid the battles, sieges and other acts of war,' Gustav started, calmly and clearly, 'a second conflict raged last summer. It revolved around weapons, and this conflict was started by none other than Duke Emeric, in alliance with Erkindrix. Emeric's servants attempted to steal a holy weapon, Toric's Dagger, from Magnia. Not only was this attempt foiled by the Magnians, but a small group of them went further, to Edeleny itself, where they took a second weapon, Onella's Staff, before Arioc could get his hands on it. The Krykkers, sensing the threat, raised an army and took their own weapon,

Bolivar's Sword, deep into Haskany, where together with the Kalinthians, they inflicted a defeat on the Isharites. Finally, this group of Magnians went one step further, getting into Samir Durg itself, where the staff and dagger were used to kill Erkindrix.'

Gustav then gestured at their table. Not everyone in the room knew of these events, and many turned to look at Belwynn and the others with curiosity. Rabigar did not hesitate, getting to his feet and drawing Bolivar's Sword from its scabbard, before holding it in the air for all to see. Somewhat more self-consciously, Belwynn and Soren also rose, revealing the weapons they carried.

'So,' continued Gustav, 'events would have turned out rather worse without these weapons. It turns out, however, that there may be seven of them altogether. As I have said, the Isharites were keen to get their hands on these weapons for themselves, or at least to prevent us from using them. It would be logical to presume, therefore, that it would be in our interests to find the remaining four. To do so, we need to know two things. What they are, and where they are. Master Szabolcs of the Blood Caladri has spent the winter consulting the ancient texts of his people and has found that these histories will help us in this respect. So, I invite him now to address us.'

The aged Szabolcs stood up and turned to address the room. 'I have been instructed by my Queen to keep this simple,' he said with a self-deprecating smile. 'She believes there may be little general interest in the sources I have used to ascertain my information. So here it is. Many years ago, when the Isharites first invaded Dalriya, they were resisted by the peoples of our world, who fought together. Lady Onella, known in the Empire as Lady Alexia, provided us with the seven weapons that Gustav has mentioned. These weapons were used to fight a war with the Isharites, a war that ended with an event known as the Cracking of the World. The texts say that this is when the continents of Dalriya and Halvia split apart.'

Murmurs greeted this assertion, but Szabolcs continued.

'Each of the seven weapons was then taken home by a champion, to be kept safe should it be needed again. Time has passed and much of this story has since been forgotten, or corrupted into stories and songs.'

'Not by us,' Belwynn heard Guremar say under his breath.

'And so, to the weapons themselves. The Caladri took away the staff. The Krykkers, the sword. The Lippers had the dagger, later taken from them by the Magnians.'

Belwynn knew all this. Now, it was going to get very interesting.

'The humans took back a shield. It was not easy to find where they took it.

Our texts gave them a different name, but I am now sure that they were referring to the Persaleians.'

Mutterings of dissension could be heard in the room, at the idea that the great enemy and conqueror of Brasingia, the Persaleians, were the heroes of this story.

The Empire grows arrogant, said Soren darkly, as he observed the response from the Brasingian nobility.

'To the north,' Szabolcs continued, 'the Jalakh people took a bow. To the west, in Halvia, a people known to the Caladri as the Orias, but commonly known as the Giants, took a spear.'

Now the mutterings in the hall got louder, and there was laughter at the idea of Giants.

Giants? Belwynn asked Soren.

I have read of their existence, her brother replied. *But they must have died out years ago.*

Szabolcs persevered, though his voice now struggled to be heard. 'Finally, a people referred to as the Asrai. They are the most obscure by far. The weapon is referred to as a cloak, or coat. The location given appears to be somewhere in the Lantinen Sea. I could speculate that their lands were submerged when the Cracking caused a great flood, but—I can't be sure.'

Belwynn could see that this had not gone well. There were those—the Caladri, the Krykkers—who believed everything Szabolcs had said. There were others—the Cordentines, Guivergnais, most of the Brasingians—who now thought the entire subject ridiculous.

Baldwin stood. Walter angrily banged a cup on the table for silence. 'At this point I will pass this matter on to my Archmage, who will discuss it further with those who wish to make a contribution.'

He's washing his hands of it, said Belwynn.

Don't be surprised, Soren replied. *His head is full of supply requests, military affairs. He has no understanding of this. We should feel lucky he agreed to raise it in the first place.*

'As my brother said, I am now holding talks with the other leaders of Dalriya or their representatives. I will not bring advisers—no Dukes of Brasingia, not even my brother. I hope the other leaders can do the same, to keep the numbers small and the meeting efficient. Please, step this way to my apartments.'

The Krykkers looked at one another.

'He's not coming,' said Guremar, jabbing a thumb at Rabigar.

Rabigar held his hands in the air to signify his acceptance, and Maragin nodded. The two Krykker chieftains stood and made their way to the exit from the hall, followed by Edgar.

'I'll see you later,' said Theron, before following them.

Once Baldwin and the other rulers had left, most of the assembled guests drifted out of the hall, their participation in the day's events over. Those who remained in the hall were those with an interest in the subject matter raised by Szabolcs. Belwynn was a little surprised to see that Walter had remained. He called everyone over to the top table and Belwynn and the other Magnians joined him there, along with Gustav, Szabolcs and Rabigar.

'So, we have an idea what we are looking for,' said Soren. 'Can we come up with a plan?'

'Szabolcs mentioned the Orias, in Halvia,' began Rabigar tentatively. 'It might be possible to contact our Krykker cousins in Halvia, and ask them what they know of this people, where they lived. The problem we have is the crossing of the Lantinen Sea. The Kharovians control the waters now. They sink any ship that is not theirs.'

'The Jalakhs had a bow?' Soren asked Szabolcs, who nodded in confirmation. 'That is perhaps the most precisely identified location. It makes sense for those of us based in Kalinth to travel to the Jalakh Steppe. But it won't be easy, we would have to travel through Haskany. Gyrmund?'

'There is no easy route. It would be impossible to sail past Kharovia. Overland, it may be possible for a small group to travel unnoticed, through the Dardelles mountain range, where few people live. But it would be time consuming and dangerous.'

'If myself and a group of companions were to go for the bow,' said Soren, 'the Empire can focus on the shield, in Persala. This is the perfect time to send a force there, while the Isharites remain leaderless. The Blood Caladri are also positioned well to help with that.'

Walter and Gustav looked at each other. 'Don't count on my brother sending a force north of Rotelegen.'

'Why not?' demanded Soren. 'Now is the perfect time for Brasingia to assert itself to the north—you are unchallenged. The Drobax are gone; the Haskans have thrown off Ishari's dominion; Arioc is fighting his rivals. Why not?' he repeated.

'I will ask him for resources here in Barissia. Adalheid will do the same, more shrilly, for Rotelegen. Our soldiers, who sacrificed so much at Burkhard Castle, have still not been fully paid. Farred knows what it was like there, what they went through. It is too much to expect him to invade Persala.'

'If he doesn't strike at Ishari now,' countered Soren, 'he is merely waiting for them to regain their strength. And when they do so, they will return to Burkhard Castle. If he liberates Persala, he can create a buffer state between them. Maybe then form an alliance with Haskany against Ishari. Surely, you both see that?' Soren asked them, looking from Gustav to Walter.

'If Baldwin and I tried to raise an army to invade Persala, no-one would go. Our people have had enough of war, and your arguments won't work.' Walter looked at them all and sighed. 'Look, Baldwin's meeting with the other leaders will decide the extent of his participation. But I am warning you. Don't expect too much from him.'

'Theron will persuade him of the need for more,' said Belwynn.

'What about you?' Soren asked Gustav.

Gustav spread his hands open. 'I serve Baldwin. But I will do what I can.'

'And the Caladri?' Soren persisted, turning to Szabolcs.

'We do not have the power to invade Persala, with our enemies pinning us down. Further, we cannot easily enter the country unnoticed. But my queen will decide what our contribution is to be.'

Leave it for now, Belwynn warned her brother. She knew he was angry, but if he kept pushing for more, it could do more harm than good.

'Then there is the cloak,' Farred reminded them all.

'Yes,' said Szabolcs. 'Owned by the Asrai people. I am afraid I don't know who they are.'

'What is said of them?' Soren asked.

'Virtually nothing. They are mentioned by name by two different writers, neither of whom takes the time to explain who they are. By all means, Soren, I can show you my texts. But what I have told you is all that they reveal, and I have exhausted all my sources. It is possible the Grand Caladri had other books, but those are now gone.'

So that was it. Soren had volunteered to lead a perilous mission to the Jalakh Steppe. Beyond that, nothing much, except to hope that more would come from the Emperor's negotiations than his brother expected.

IT TAKES AN ASSASSIN

IV

Moneva let the sharp tip of the knife slide along her neck. She had come close to shoving it in since her time in Samir Durg.

She should have been happy to have escaped. That was the part of it she didn't get. Why was she feeling so low all the time, so tired of it all?

Maybe it was just as well that she'd found an enemy in Heractus. It had given her something to focus on.

She had noticed the same faces on three separate occasions, watching Elana. Moneva had been trained to kill people, and she knew exactly what to look for. *But even when I was thirteen, I wasn't as inept as these fools.*

She shifted her position on the warehouse roof, stretching her legs and then giving them a good rub to make sure they didn't go to sleep. She then turned back to the alleyway that Elana took when she walked from her house to the church.

She heard them first, talking to each other, then saw them. It was Elana with one of her new disciples: the big, dopey man called Bemus. He was the size of a warrior, but instead spent all his time praying. They might try it now, even with him there.

Yes, behind them, at the top of the alleyway, Moneva made out a third figure, trailing them. Elana and Bemus were too busy talking to each other to have noticed, exiting the alleyway into the courtyard. Then, to her left, Moneva saw two more figures emerge from the direction of the Church of

Madria, walking towards Elana. It was a simple trap, but it had worked, and Moneva knew she had to act fast.

Jumping to her feet, she leapt off the warehouse roof, over a wall, and landed on all fours in the courtyard. Grabbing the knife from her boot, she stood and looked around. The two figures, a man and a woman, had drawn wicked looking long knives of their own, and were staring at her. Bemus had put himself between them and Elana. The third assailant had remained in the alleyway, ready to cut off their escape.

'Moneva?' said Elana.

The man lurched towards Moneva. 'Kill them!' he shouted to his partner.

Moneva made a feint towards him, making him thrust forward with his weapon, before, in one fluid motion, jumping sideways and throwing her knife at the woman. It hit her in the chest and she fell over from the force of it, dropping her knife. Moneva then drew her short sword from her hip and spun around to face the man. She sensed behind her the third assailant coming at her from the alley and knew she had to act quickly. The man was wary of her now, backing away, and she used that to her advantage. She ran at him and instead of thrusting his knife at her, he tried to sidestep out of her way. But his footwork was clumsy, and she hacked the length of her sword into his neck with considerable force, knocking him to the ground.

She whirled around to see the third assailant stop in his tracks, turn around, and run for the alleyway.

'Pick up her knife!' she shouted at Bemus, pointing at the dropped weapon. But where he was slow to respond, Elana was fast, darting forwards to grab it.

Moneva saw no more as she gave chase. She approached the alleyway with some care, in case he tried something, but when she looked around, he was already at the far end, running at top speed. She sprinted down the alleyway, looked in both directions, and saw that he had turned right and was running down one of the main city streets.

'Stop him!' she shouted, before saving the rest of her energy for the chase. The bystanders in the street backed away from them, avoiding the blades they both carried.

A few months ago, she might have lost him—spending her time sitting and drinking in the taverns of Heractus had left her slow and weak. But she had stopped all that nonsense now; had made herself stick to a rigorous training schedule, easy enough to follow when she had nothing else to do. So it was that she began to run him down, sticking to an even pace that she could keep up for a while if necessary. The man she was following, however, had been fast at first, but was now slowing, looking more and more ragged.

She was gaining on him, and he must have known he couldn't outrun her, because he turned around, red in the face, holding out a long knife of the same type his accomplices had. Moneva wasn't sure, but she may have killed both of the other assailants, and so she wanted this one taken alive. She didn't make a rash move, but stood opposite him, controlling her breathing, taking her time.

'I would advise you to drop that,' she told him.

He said nothing, his breathing still heavy from his exertion.

Footsteps came from the left. Two men were running over. Young knights, she was fairly sure she recognised their faces from somewhere or other, but had made a conscious decision not to bother learning any of their names. There were so many of them, and they all acted the same.

'Moneva?' said one of them, obviously perfectly aware of who she was. 'What's happening here?'

'This man tried to kill Elana,' she said.

The eyes of the knights grew wide, and they both drew swords, turning to the accused.

Now facing three opponents, he knew he had no chance, and threw his knife to the ground.

MONEVA HAD ONLY KILLED one of them. As well as the man she had chased, the woman was alive, and they were both being interrogated. Two adjoining cells had been found for them in the castle dungeon, so that when one screamed, the other could hear.

Moneva had to admit that this Sebastian, Grand Master of the Order of Who Cares, had a much more robust approach than she had imagined he would take. She had been worried that it might all be polite requests, but he was quite willing to use threats and violence, attested to by the row of sharp instruments he had deployed. Yes, much of it was for show; they had barely used them. No, it wasn't anything close to the savagery inflicted on Rabigar by the jailers at Coldeberg. But it was getting quick results, and that was what Moneva was concerned with. The people who wanted Elana dead were still out there, after all.

They had ascertained from the woman, the more talkative of the pair, that they had been hired by a representative of the temples of Heractus. When they had put this to her colleague, he had confirmed it. These were the people whose flock, and funding, had largely been taken from them by the success of the Church of Madria, and their motive was clear. Neither was Moneva surprised; she had picked up on this source of animosity herself. But neither she nor Sebastian were convinced that this was the full story, and so the questions continued.

'You know that I will happily use this,' Moneva said to the woman, holding a scalpel just close enough to her face to be uncomfortable. Arms and legs bound, and strapped to her chair, there was little the woman could do to avoid it. 'These knights wouldn't do it to a woman, but you know I would. As a fair punishment for trying to kill my friend. It would require a lot of work, however. You're so ugly in the first place I'd have to make quite a few changes so that people would really notice. Cut the ears off for a start,' she said, walking slowly around to the side and then behind the woman, so that she couldn't see her any more. 'Give you a big sad smile,' she continued, walking back around to the front and miming cutting either side of the woman's mouth.

'Gods, what do you want?' said the woman.

'Your accomplice has told us who else was involved,' came in Sebastian, voice hard. 'Confirm it and we're done.'

'He wasn't involved with us, with our orders. But I saw him speaking with my elders.'

'Him? Who?'

'Straton.'

Even Moneva knew who Straton was, the king's oldest son. Sebastian's expression went cold. He jerked open the door of the cell. Moneva saw him speak with one of the young knights who had helped her to apprehend the man. When he was done, the young man turned and ran off down the corridor.

Sebastian gestured to her. She left the woman in the cell and shut the door.

'Let's check with him,' said Sebastian quietly.

He opened the door to the second cell, and they entered, staring at the man. He had said little, even when under torture, but it had been enough.

Moneva smiled at him. 'We know,' she crowed. 'Straton.'

'What about him?'

'We know he's a part of this.'

'He wasn't involved.'

'But?' asked Sebastian, his voice loud, full of authority.

'I don't know. I don't know what his role is. But he wasn't involved with us. I never spoke with him.'

But you're not denying he was there. In the background, Moneva said to herself.

'We'll find out if you're holding something back,' she said.

'That's it. They don't tell me anything.'

Sebastian nodded, and they left the cell, waiting in the corridor.

It wasn't long before the young knight returned, his face flushed.

'Well, Philon?'

'Straton's not in his chambers. He's not been seen by anyone since yesterday evening. He may have left the castle last night.'

Sebastian banged his hand against the wall.

'Damn it. If he's out there recruiting an army, we could be in serious trouble.'

* * *

Farred clasped hands with Edgar.

'I hope to see you before too long,' said the Prince.

Farred smiled, a little nervous about his new mission. 'I hope so.'

Edgar said his farewells to the others, giving his cousin Belwynn a hug, before climbing onto his horse. Brictwin was waiting for him, and without further ado, they trotted away to meet up with the Middians. They would travel with them through the Steppe before returning to Magnia.

They left behind a sombre looking group. The decisions taken at Baldwin's meeting had not been to the liking of Gyrmund and his new friends.

'What now for you?' Gyrmund asked him.

'Rainer says he will bring the Queen here, then we will set off.'

Gyrmund nodded, unhappy about it. He had hoped that Farred would accompany him back north, but that wasn't to be.

'Visiting with the Sea Caladri may be very helpful,' said Soren, the wizard, a tone of complaint in his voice. 'But we're leaving with too many things unresolved. Most of all, no-one is taking responsibility for the shield, in Persala. I'm in two minds about what we should do.'

'Well, Edgar is doing his part, don't blame him,' Belwynn reprimanded her brother.

'I don't enjoy saying so about your cousin, but he was on Baldwin's side in everything,' said Theron, the Kalinthian knight, nodding in the direction Edgar had departed to. 'All he could say was how much sacrifice his people had already made.'

Farred bridled at the arrogance of the knight, who had won a single victory with the help of the Krykkers and thought himself superior to everyone else. Magnians had spilt blood fighting the Isharites and the Barissians—fighting other people's wars.

'And what would you have Edgar do?' he demanded. 'Send an army across the Lantinen to go looking for giants?'

'It's the Brasingians,' said Theron. 'They have the resources of an Empire at their disposal, the largest army of all of us, and what was decided yesterday? That they would do nothing. My people are surrounded by enemies and all we have received from anyone here is good luck wishes. Why call this meeting in the first place? It has been a waste of time.'

'The last time they sent an army north,' countered Farred, 'it was destroyed to a man, leaving the whole of Rotelegen defenceless. The only reason the Empire still stands is because they threw everything into defending Burkhard Castle. It's unreasonable to expect them to change that strategy.'

'Unreasonable?' repeated Theron.

'Stop it!' said Belwynn. 'This isn't helping. Look, the Caladri are here.'

Farred turned to look. The Caladri carriage, pulled by the strange horned creatures, was ambling down one side of the street. On the other, Queen Hajna and two of her companions were riding horses, accompanied by Rainer. They seemed ready to go. It was time to leave. Gyrmund was already offering his hand.

'I wish we could have had longer,' said Farred.

'The times won't allow it, it seems. I wish you all the luck in your mission.'

'Thank you. I wish the same for you, whatever you decide to do.'

The squire, Evander, was already leading his mount over. They had these boys well trained, the Kalinthians.

'Thank you, young man,' he said as he climbed into the saddle.

'I appreciate your offer to ride with the carriage,' Hajna said.

'You're welcome,' Belwynn replied for her party.

'Take care of Onella's Staff,' the Queen said to Soren. 'My husband, Lorant, asked me to bring it home with me. It does, after all, belong to the Caladri. But you will be putting yourselves in danger if you are heading for the Jalakh Steppe. I will explain to him that you need to keep it a while longer.'

'You should perhaps explain to him,' Soren replied, 'that I will be keeping it permanently. I have suffered for this weapon, and it is now mine, whatever its history.'

It was an unnecessarily rude response and, to Farred, seemed typical of Gyrmund's new acquaintances. But in the end, that was his friend's lookout, not his.

'I will pass on your words,' said Hajna. 'I do not keep anything from him.'

She nodded at the rest of them and turned her horse around. Rainer followed her lead and led them off, heading for the eastern gate.

Farred followed on before turning around. He took one last look at Gyrmund, wondering as he always did whether he would ever see him again, and then turned back to his present task. He had a job to do, and it was important. Control of the Lantinen Sea had been lost to the Kharovians. The Sea Caladri were apparently the only people with a strong enough fleet to take them on. If Hajna could persuade them to act, the harbours of South Magnia would be the ideal location for them to base their fleet, and that was the reason Farred was getting involved with the mission.

Rainer, as organised as ever, led them to the east gate where Archbishop Godfrey's small entourage was waiting for them. Baldwin had asked Godfrey to ensure they had safe passage through his duchy of Gotbeck. The Archbishop approached them. His horse was lively, and he had to give it a good slap on the neck to calm the beast down. Farred couldn't help thinking that the forthright churchman and the enigmatic queen had very little in common, but the Archbishop was meticulously polite.

'Your Majesty,' he greeted her. 'The weather looks set fair for our journey.'

'Good. I am most grateful to you for offering to escort me.'

'Not at all. We certainly can't have you navigating the swamps of South Gotbeck by yourselves. It's not just the risk of getting lost. Lizardmen still inhabit the marshland. I have done much to cull their numbers in recent years, especially since the death of the evil witch who protected them. But it's nigh on impossible to eradicate them completely, especially since the Caladri won't lift a finger to help.'

Extraordinary, Farred thought to himself. *In one little speech he has insulted magic users, the Caladri, and expressed his regret at not being able to commit genocide.*

'Well, I will leave you to it,' said Rainer. 'I wish you all the best of luck.'

The chamberlain gave Farred a brief look, suggesting that he might need a good share of luck, before leaving them for the castle.

'Lord Farred,' said Godfrey, acknowledging him. They had got to know each other pretty well, having spent the summer stuck in Burkhard Castle together.

'Your Grace.'

'I think we may have an interesting few days ahead of us,' muttered the Archbishop.

'I couldn't have put it better myself, Your Grace.'

THE BATTLE OF SIMALEK

V

Shira studied the army arrayed before them.

Pentas had been right. The forces facing them were deadly, yes. Isharites with their crystal swords, no doubt laced with poison, that left you paralysed when it entered the bloodstream. She heard the barks of the Dogmen rather than saw them—kept in reserve, perhaps, as a weapon to shatter her own lines. But no Drobax. And as for numbers, Arioc had raised no more than they had. Maybe less. Arioc hadn't won complete control in Ishari, then. He was taking a risk bringing this army into Haskany. That gave her Haskans a chance. And that was all she had asked for.

The plain on which the two armies met was flat, with a tree-line to the rear of Arioc's position, from which his force had arrived, hoping to surprise them. But Pentas had given them good warning of the enemy's approach. The flat terrain meant that the cavalry contest would be decisive, and so Shira had chosen to lead the Haskan cavalry herself. The infantry divisions were under the command of her uncle, Koren. As she thought of him, she heard the Haskan trumpets blaring, and ahead of her cavalry position, the infantry started to march. This was a battle she wanted, and so she couldn't wait for the Isharites to attack. If she did, Arioc might choose to stay where he was and slink away in the night to fight some other time.

Behind her lines lay the watchtower of Simalek. That was where Pentas would observe the battle and help when needed. He had the task of neutralising Arioc and any other magi her husband had brought with him. Could he hold them off long enough for her to win a victory? She knew nothing of magic, and so had to put her faith in the red-eyed magus. He had his role, and she had hers.

The waiting before a battle was the worst part. The battle itself was horrible, but at least then time rushed by, as the mind and body were fully occupied. But as Shira's infantry slowly marched forwards, she experienced the gut-wrenching anticipation with none of the physical release.

The Haskan infantry marched farther and farther away, individuals disappearing into units, units disappearing into a line on the horizon. The Isharites didn't move, waiting for the Haskans to come to their position. But Shira and her generals had expected as much.

Eventually, the sound of trumpets blared; the clash of wood on wood and steel on steel; the shouts and the screams of men killing and men dying; all the noises of war came to them on the air. Moneva's cavalry waited. They were too far away to see which side had the advantage, except that there was little movement. The sounds continued unabated, telling her that the fighting was fierce.

Shira's stallion raised its head, and she patted his neck as gently as she could with steel gauntlets. 'Easy, Shadow,' she whispered in his ear, 'not our turn yet.'

He relaxed, putting his head back down. She loved this one. He was black as night, muscled, and savage in combat.

And then the infantry sent them the signal. First one, then two riders could be seen, detaching themselves from the infantry units, riding hard in their direction, and waving red flags as they did.

Her force readied themselves to go. Shira stood up in her stirrups and twisted around to look at her main cavalry force, and the smaller reserve force who would stay put for now. She pulled her visor down, limiting her vision to a narrow strip. She raised one arm.

'For Haskany!' she shouted, and her soldiers repeated the war cry.

Shira turned back, picking up the lance she had skewered into the ground. She leaned forward, saying 'Now, my friend.'

He didn't need much encouragement, springing ahead, leading the other horses who followed him, as she led her subjects.

'You can be my new king,' she told him, exulting in her freedom, in the moment. 'We don't need the old one anymore.'

The signallers waved their flags to the right, and so they swung around in that direction. When they straightened out, on the flank of the infantry battle, they could see the Isharites up ahead. The enemy didn't carry lances, instead they already had their swords drawn. The Haskans would have the initial advantage on impact, but would then have to be wary of the Isharite weapons. Shira and Koren, knowing full well the threat of poison, had insisted on covering all their soldiers head to toe in metal armour, to give them the best protection possible.

As they gained speed, the distance between the two forces rapidly diminished. Shira could now see the individual riders who were coming at her, identifying one with a bluish coloured sword as her target. The clash of cavalry could be terrifying, but she knew that neither she nor her mount would pull up.

She levelled her lance at her target, and then the two lines crashed together. As the Isharites tried to avoid the lances aimed at them, they crashed into one another. Shira's target was buffeted to the side at the last second and her lance missed, but connected with someone else; she couldn't see who. Her mount was kicking and biting, turning around in a circle, and it was hard for Shira to get her bearings. She drew her sword and pulled on the reins, wresting control back over the beast.

She looked around her, trying to focus as the noise of battle engulfed her—men's shouts combined with the screams of horses, some of which were writhing and kicking on the ground; others were riderless, their riders now fighting on foot if they had survived the fall. She could see her soldiers slashing a path towards her. She waited for them to arrive before striking out with them, working as a unit to gain the advantage over the Isharites. One of her men lost the point of his sword, shattered by the hard crystal of an Isharite blade.

Nonetheless, they were forcing the enemy back. Until they came upon a line of Isharite cavalrymen. They had the biggest horses, the most expensive armour. And in the middle of the line sat Rostam, newly appointed member of the Council of Seven, and Arioc's chief henchman. Until recently, they had been on the same side, both working to further Arioc's ambitions. Now Shira had chosen her own side, but Rostam had remained loyal.

She raised her visor, making sure that he had seen her. He held his sword vertically in front of him, in a kind of salute. Instinctively, the soldiers around them left a space. Shira would fight with Rostam, and the outcome, she knew, was likely to swing the course of the battle.

She pushed her visor down, kneeing her horse so that it circled to the left. Rostam copied her movement.

There are many ways to win a fight, Shira knew, and one of them is to know your enemy. Predict what they will do. She knew Rostam well enough, knew that he would consider himself superior to her in every way: strength, skill, stamina. He believed he could win any number of ways: beat her down with strength, or kill her with a thousand cuts, especially if he had applied poison to his blade. Shira knew that her enemy might have one weakness: over-confidence in himself, and an underestimation of her.

Shira suddenly kneed her horse forwards into a charge. She pulled her sword back and put everything into a massive strike. If Rostam had evaded her, she may have toppled off her horse. But he chose to block. He blocked, thinking he could parry and counter-attack; demonstrate his superiority. He hadn't realised quite how strong she was. He hadn't anticipated she would take such a huge risk. Rostam's block was too weak—Shira's strike forced through it, her hips, core and arms working together to push him back. The power of her blow pushed his blade back against his body, pushed his body back in his seat so that he lost his balance. Shadow bit at the face of Rostam's mount, causing it to skitter away.

For a moment, that seemed to linger longer than it really lasted, Rostam tottered back in his seat, arms windmilling to regain his balance. Shira brought back her sword over her left shoulder, then struck down. Her strike was true, connecting with Rostam's neck and virtually severing his head from his shoulders. His body sprawled to one side, feet still caught in the stirrups.

There was a moment of shock on both sides, at the speed of the outcome as much as anything else. Then the fight resumed.

That one incident changed the course of the contest. Rostam was just one man, but his death boosted the confidence of the Haskans, just as it put doubt in the minds of the Isharites. Slowly at first, then faster, Shira's soldiers gained the upper hand, pushing the enemy back, until one turned around and fled, then others, then all of them. The Isharite cavalry escaped back the way they had come. The Haskans gave chase, hoping to run them back to their camp and into the woods, making sure they didn't regroup.

Shira was with them, a grim smile on her face. Then something, an intuition maybe, made her slow down and stop. Some of her soldiers saw and stopped the chase too, started calling to those ahead. Shira raised a hand for silence.

To her left, she could see that the infantry had stopped fighting. The two sides stood a few feet apart, and an eerie silence had descended over them. And they weren't looking in her direction. They weren't reacting to her victory.

They were looking in the opposite direction. To the south.

* * *

PENTAS STOOD on the roof of the watchtower of Simalek, which rose almost one hundred feet into the air, a marvel of Persaleian engineering. Here the wind battered him, but the position allowed him a unique view of the plain around the tower. He observed the clash of cavalry on the battlefield. He had found two Haskan magi, an older man and his younger and more gifted protege. The younger of the two, Rimmon, could also ride a horse, and so Pentas had sent him with Shira.

Rimmon helped him to see Shira and Rostam circling each other, and when Shira attacked, Pentas and Rimmon suppressed the use of magic. He could see Shira strike Rostam down, see the battle turn in the favour of the Haskans.

But he didn't see the black kite gliding towards the tower until it was too late. The bird landed on the parapet and only then did Pentas give it his full attention. The bird transformed before him, taking the form of Arioc.

They looked at one another for a short while. Pentas felt a brief feeling of despair. He hadn't wanted to die, and now that the time had come, he regretted it. And yet, he told himself, this was always going to be the likely outcome.

'What's happening?' Arioc asked him, gesturing at the battle down below.

'Rostam has fallen.'

'That's a shame.'

'He was your son, was he not?'

'I believe so. But I can always raise another army. It is you I have come for.'

'I feel honoured that this is all for me,' Pentas waved his hand at the spectacle before them ironically.

'Don't be surprised, Pentas. I have killed Ardashir. Now I will kill you. That only leaves me Siavash, and all my rivals will be gone. Then Diis will join with me.'

'He has not done so already?' Pentas asked.

He genuinely wanted to know. He had wanted this Haskan rebellion to be an inconvenience for the Isharites. But their failure to crush it in its early stages had surprised him. If Diis had not intervened, leaving the Isharite leaders to their own devices, that would explain their weakness.

A look of annoyance, maybe even insecurity, flickered across Arioc's face.

'He will not join with me until I have proven myself. I would expect nothing less. But the time draws near. And so it is your time, Pentas. I have wasted some of my own time wondering why you engaged in this foolishness. Surely you knew it couldn't last long.'

'I am Madria's servant, Arioc. I always have been.'

A look of surprise now crossed Arioc's face. He smiled then, and looked at Pentas with a new expression, almost one of respect. 'Well, I admit it had occurred to me. It certainly explains your regular incompetence. Your failures regarding her weapons, of course. You were in Edeleny, then?'

'Yes. That was me.'

'And you were behind the attack on Erkindrix?'

'I helped them,' said Pentas. 'But then, so did you.'

'Indeed. We just had very different motives. Well, you have played a good game Pentas, I will give you that.'

Pentas looked past Arioc. 'You may think this one last game,' he said, 'but perhaps you should look behind you.'

'Really. Now you disappoint me. This is more like the Pentas I thought I knew.'

'This is no joke, Arioc.'

Arioc turned and saw what Pentas could see. Seven crows, flying in a V-shape towards them.

'Not your magi?' Pentas asked him, already knowing the answer.

'No.' Arioc seemed to tear his attention from the birds to the battle below them. 'See there,' he said.

Pentas looked where Arioc pointed, to the south of the fighting, and saw nothing. Then he realised what he was seeing. The Isharite fog, creeping towards the two groups of infantry. A third force had arrived, concealing its presence, and was now close to the two armies.

Pentas could see on the battlefield, but he had no way of communicating over such a distance. The twins, Soren and Belwynn, were surely the only ones with that power. But maybe he could send a kind of warning; encourage Shira to notice the trap. He tried but would not know whether he had succeeded.

'Siavash,' he said to Arioc. 'And I think now we know who Diis has chosen. And perhaps has chosen for some time.'

'I have been fooling myself,' Arioc admitted. 'Diis has not forgiven my role in Erkindrix's death.'

'Maybe you are altogether too human for him, Arioc.'

'Enough of your silver tongue, Pentas. What do we do?'

'It's 'we' now, is it?'

'Of course it is. That's the only chance we have of survival.' Arioc looked him in the eyes. 'My assumption is we can't beat them, even working together.'

'I would agree,' Pentas replied cautiously.

'Then we flee,' determined Arioc. 'Then they must decide whether they chase one or both of us. It may give one of us a chance to escape.'

'Agreed,' said Pentas. He paused, not quite believing he was saying it. 'Good luck.'

But Arioc had already transformed into his kite. The bird took one last look at him, then flew away, heading north.

Pentas looked at the approaching crows. No doubt seven masters of magic. Maybe even Siavash himself was amongst them. The truth was, Pentas had never learned to transform into animal form. It was a highly complex piece of magic, generally only mastered by the Isharites.

But he had mastered an alternative means of travel: the teleport. It was equally difficult, and perhaps more dangerous, requiring him to focus on a precise location to send his body. If he got it wrong, he could send himself to his death. He concentrated, focusing on a location he had identified before the battle. It was, after all, always prudent to be prepared. As he felt himself move, as the sensations of blurred vision and stomach churning took hold, he spared a brief thought for Arioc.

Good luck escaping from all seven of them, you bastard. You're going to need it.

* * *

SHIRA TROTTED her horse back the way they had come, then stopped again, listening.

This time, she knew she heard it. It was a sound she was all too familiar with. Drobax. Thousands upon thousands of Drobax, marching in their direction. She could hear them and, she now thought, even smell them. But she couldn't see them.

It was magic. Arioc had brought the Drobax with him, somehow circled around their position without them noticing. He had concealed them with magic, the same trick her magi had used in Rotelegen.

Pentas had missed it. Had failed.

But if it was Arioc, she asked herself, why had his soldiers stopped fighting too? She smiled, a mirthless smile, when she understood what was happening. Siavash. He had outwitted the pair of them.

One of Pentas's pet magi, the one with the red hair, rode up to her. 'We must flee,' he said urgently.

But Shira knew deep in her bones that she wasn't fleeing from this. 'You go,' she told him. 'And rescue my uncle if you can.'

She raised a hand and the Haskan cavalry rallied to her. She took them south, in the direction of the enemy, and the Haskan reserves joined them. They peered ahead, listening to the noise of the Drobax getting closer. She remembered the fears of the Haskans when she had called for this rebellion. They had warned her of the Ishari magi; of the Drobax. And she had not listened, and Pentas had sweet-talked them into doing his bidding.

Shira never hid from the truth. She knew this was her doing. But she would ride against the enemy and show them what free Haskans could do. And maybe the rest of her soldiers could make their escape, return to their homes, and live to fight another day, when the odds weren't so stacked against her country.

The fog was slowly dissipating. The work of Siavash's magi was done, and now his Drobax could be seen, emerging through the tendrils of smoke like the monsters they were. And not just Drobax, but other creatures, too. Shira could see a unit of Isharite infantry, men who had chosen Siavash over Arioc. And small groups of spindly legged creatures had been positioned in between the Drobax, creatures Shira did not recognise at first until she realised she had met one of them before. Dorjan, King of the Shadow Caladri. He had led his people here, too. Well done, she silently acknowledged. You chose well. You chose the winner.

Shira raised her arm one last time. Her cavalry gave a shout. Those who still held lances held them to the sky. Most, like her, now had to make do with swords. She pointed hers at the enemy.

'For Haskany!'

They rode hard, gaining speed, the lancers moving to the front, Shira and the rest positioned behind.

The Drobax came, relentless and unthinking. The Shadow Caladri raised bows.

No, Shira thought, but it was too late now.

A hail of missiles rose high into the air, before dropping from the sky towards them, as if they were sentient creatures that could target their victims. They rained down on the Haskans. Shira had insisted that her cavalry were equipped with the strongest metal armour, many of them covered head to toe in plate, their horses protected with scales. The casualties weren't therefore as bad as they might have been, but they were bad enough. Horses went down in front of her, to the sides. The riders following behind crashed into them, causing more devastation. The Haskan line was now uneven. But it hardly mattered.

Twenty yards out. Ten. And now they were into the enemy and Shira could swing her sword, Shadow could kick, and the Drobax fell under her fury. Her arm tired from swinging her sword and still she swung it, in a fierce desperation to kill as many of the creatures who had invaded her land as she could.

She mistook it at first for another Drobax. She swung down to her right dismissively, but it blocked her stroke with a shield, then casually stepped inside and shoved a short sword into Shadow's throat, finding a gap in his armour. The sword came out with a gush of blood, and Shira barely had time to get her feet out from the stirrups before her mount collapsed.

She landed on the ground heavily, her armour making it difficult to move well, but she had kept her grip on her sword. A blow landed on her back, nearly knocking her over, but it felt like it skidded off her armour rather than penetrating through.

She struggled to her feet and turned to find a Drobax coming in for a second attempt. She backed off just in time to avoid the thrust, then lunged forward and thrust her own sword into the creature with both hands, skewering through flesh and bone, before tugging the blade out again.

It collapsed, dead.

Shira walked around Shadow, assessing her situation. Fighting raged all about, and she could see more and more Haskans being pulled from horses as her force became overwhelmed. She reached his head, where the soil was drenched in his blood, and there it was, waiting for her.

It was fighting bare-chested, but appeared to have a naturally armoured torso. Then she knew it as a Krykker, but what it was doing here, in this fight, she had no idea.

A couple of Drobax approached her, but the Krykker shouted at them, waving his sword, and they retreated to find some other victim.

The Krykker discarded his shield and took a hand-axe, readying himself to fight with a weapon in each hand. He gave her a smile before walking towards her.

She let him approach, before launching a two-handed strike. But, not weighed down by armour, he seemed to move so much faster than she did. He blocked her sword with his own, before going down on one knee and bringing in his axe in a long horizontal slash. The axe blade connected with her knee and her leg was taken from under her, causing her to collapse to the ground.

Excruciating pain erupted from where the blow had landed. She tried to stand, but screamed out loud in agony when she tried to put her weight on the injured leg, and had to give up. So she knelt, putting her good foot on the ground in front of her.

The Krykker came, in no rush. She fished her sword in front of her and quick sharp he flicked his sword at her wrist, trying to disarm her. She pulled back just in time, then swung for his legs, trying to repay him in kind, but he skipped away just in time.

She knew his game now. He knew who she was, and he would get a nice reward for capturing her alive. She held her sword out in front of her in one hand, before grabbing a dagger from her belt in the other. She smiled at him now, and he smiled back, pleasantly enough.

She flung her sword at him.

His natural reaction was to move out of the way.

Shira went down on both knees. She grabbed her dagger in both hands and put the sharp point of the blade to her throat.

'No!' he shouted.

Shira held the dagger in place, elbows spread out wide, and let herself fall to the ground.

BROKEN VOWS

VI

They retraced their journey back to Heractus.

Once they were through the Empire, Szabolcs and the other Caladri said their farewells and returned to their home. Belwynn and the others continued on, through the disputed lands of Grienna and Trevenza, then west, skirting the southern border of Persala.

Slowly, their spirits rose. Most of them had things to look forward to in Kalinth. Belwynn could resume her work with Elana. Gyrmund would see Moneva again. Theron, she could tell, was keen to get back to work. His mind had moved on from the disappointments of diplomacy in Coldeberg. He started talking to her about the Kalinthian army, mainly about the need to develop an infantry force to complement the Knights. She understood the basic problem he had. It had been the Krykker infantry and the Kalinthian cavalry that together had defeated the Isharites. Neither could have done it alone.

Soren, while not exactly a force of optimism, had also come to terms with the meeting in Coldeberg. He still smouldered with anger at what he saw as a lack of action from others. But he had learned from Szabolcs the locations of the remaining weapons. That had helped him to focus on what he needed to do.

'Yes,' he said to her out loud, as their horses clipped along, the deep forest of the Grand Caladri on their left, the ancient kingdom of Persala to their right. 'The shield is on our doorstep, somewhere there,' he continued, indicating Persala. 'But who else is going to travel to the Jalakh Steppe but us?'

That was a question that did not require an answer. And though Belwynn took issue with the word 'us', she kept that to herself for now.

When they entered Korkis, they found a town in some turmoil. The central plaza was a mess of wagons, horses and soldiers. In amidst it stood Tycho, normally so relaxed, red-faced and barking out orders.

'Thank Madria you are back,' he declared when he saw Theron, with little humour.

'What is going on?' Theron asked.

'Straton is raising an army,' Tycho replied. 'Sebastian has ordered me to bring a force back to Heractus.' He looked at Belwynn. 'Elana was attacked—she's fine, don't worry,' he assured her. 'But Straton seems to be making alliances with our enemies.'

'What are Sebastian's orders?' Theron asked him.

'Bring back most of the knights and recruit infantry. I have enlisted fifty townsfolk. It means leaving a skeleton force here. I've put Leontios in charge.'

Theron nodded his approval.

'It's not as simple as you might think, Theron. I've had reports of armies marching up and down Persala, of war in Haskany. The Isharites are on the move again. If they strike at our eastern border now, there's nothing to stop them.'

'Then we need to deal with Straton as soon as possible.'

They rode to Heractus with all speed, leaving behind the soldiers who had to travel on foot. As they approached the capital, they saw that a tented camp had been established on the fields to the south of the city. They could see some soldiers there, being drilled on spear work. But there were not many.

When they were admitted past the city walls, the others went straight to find Sebastian, but Belwynn had a job to do first. Little Lyssa, tired out from the ride, needed a place to stay. Belwynn took her to the room in the castle that she shared with Soren.

'This is where you will stay now,' Belwynn explained to her. 'That is Soren's bed, and this is mine.'

'I don't have a bed,' observed Lyssa.

'You can sleep with me for now,' said Belwynn. 'And soon Soren will be leaving. Then you can have his bed.'

Lyssa nodded sleepily.

'I will fetch you something to eat and drink. Then I need to speak with Soren and the others. But I will come back here when I am done.'

WHEN BELWYNN FOUND them in Sebastian's office, they had already talked much of it out. Who the enemy was, where they were, what they should do. Belwynn found she wasn't as desperate to know all the details as she once would have been.

Sebastian, Theron and Tycho had a map before them and a pile of letters, no doubt reports from their supporters on the situation in the different parts of the country. Gyrmund and Moneva were sitting, not far apart, both of them looking more contented than she had seen them in a long while. Soren sat with his arms folded, one hand resting on his staff. Finally, Elana was there too. She looked perfectly well despite her scare. Belwynn slipped in while Sebastian was talking and sat next to the priestess, placing a hand on her shoulder.

'You are well?' she whispered.

'Of course,' Elana whispered back. 'Soren tells me you know the whereabouts of the rest of the weapons?'

Belwynn nodded.

Elana smiled and returned her attention to the conversation.

'So,' said Soren, 'you are suggesting it won't be a week until your army can leave Heractus?'

'I would say so,' replied Sebastian. The Grand Master looked disappointed in the delay. In fact, Belwynn thought, he looked older, more careworn.

'And you are sure you won't need my help?'

The Knights all looked at each other.

'We need to match their infantry force,' Theron said eventually. 'Once we do that, I am convinced of our superiority. So, thank you Soren, but I don't think that will be necessary.'

'Then it is decided,' said Soren. 'I don't think we should waste any time. Gyrmund, Moneva, Belwynn and I will make plans to head to the Jalakh Steppe. If tomorrow is too early, then the day after.'

I'm not going, Belwynn told him.

Soren turned to her, looking unsettled, and she felt a rush of guilt at not discussing this before. He opened his mouth to say something else to the group, then closed it again. 'Belwynn,' he said. 'Can I talk to you?'

While the rest of them looked on, Belwynn got up from her chair and followed her brother out of the room.

Soren walked on a bit farther, and then turned to face her in the corridor.

'I'm sorry,' she said. 'I should have said something to you. But you did kind of assume I was going without asking me.'

'Why?' he asked, looking genuinely baffled. He was hurt too; he couldn't hide it from her.

'I have people here who need me, Soren. I have left Elana for too long. You know that Theron—' she paused, embarrassed. 'However foolish it might be, the Knights find strength when I am there.'

'Yes, but I need you too, Belwynn. I'm your brother. No-one else is doing anything to find these weapons. I need your support. I always have. You know that.'

'Soren,' she chided. 'Gyrmund and Moneva will be with you. Besides, what real use am I going to be to you? I'm more use here. And, although I don't like us being apart, our abilities may be useful this way. We can keep in touch with each other.'

Belwynn thought better of mentioning one other factor. Lyssa. She really didn't like the idea of leaving her, even though she knew Elana would look after her.

'Belwynn,' he said. 'I'm asking you to come with me.'

She smiled. He knew he always got her to do what he wanted. That had been at the heart of their relationship for years.

She took his hands. 'And I'm telling you no.'

It was time for that to change.

They stood for a while, his hands still in hers, looking into each other's eyes. Something important and unspoken passed between them.

I understand, said Soren.

When they returned, everyone was standing, ready to go. The hour was getting late and everyone looked tired.

Belwynn undid the belt that held Toric's Dagger and held the weapon out to Moneva.

Moneva took it and then embraced Belwynn. 'Thank you,' she said quietly in Belwynn's ear. 'Not just for the Dagger.'

Belwynn smiled as Moneva released her. 'Thank you for looking after Elana for me. I heard you did a pretty good job.'

'I'm walking Elana back to her house,' said Moneva. 'Everyone has agreed that someone will be with her at all times. Haven't they, dear?' she asked the priestess.

Elana rolled her eyes. 'I'm sure I'll be perfectly fine now.'

'I'll come with you,' said Belwynn.

'WHAT WAS THAT ABOUT?' Moneva asked her as the three women were ushered through the gates of the royal castle and walked down to the town. 'With your brother?'

'I told Soren I'm not going with you.'

'Thought so.'

'It's not because of me, I hope,' said Elana. 'I am perfectly happy to carry on by myself, Belwynn. I feel that my current duty is to build this community. But getting the weapons is of the utmost importance, of course.'

'It's not just because of you, Elana,' said Moneva. 'She needs to stay with Theron, too, don't you, Belwynn?' she asked with a knowing look.

'Of course, how silly of me,' said Elana, unable to suppress a little smile from hovering about her face.

'Yes, the Knights need me,' said Belwynn archly. She was damned if she was going to let these two embarrass her over Theron.

Moneva made a face and puffed air out of her cheeks in mock outrage at this remark, but let the topic slide.

'So, who is raising an army against us?' asked Belwynn.

'The head priests of the temples, who want Elana dead,' said Moneva. 'They've formed an alliance with Straton, who wants rid of the Knights. His friend, the Count of Ampelios, escaped with Straton last week. Straton has authority as heir to the throne, Ampelios apparently has money, making them a dangerous pair.'

'Sebastian's enemies within the Order are also rumoured to be involved,' added Elana. 'Do you remember a knight called Euthymius, Belwynn?'

'A little.'

She remembered him from The High Tower, as the most vocal supporter of Galenos, the former Grand Master of the Knights whom Sebastian had displaced.

'He is supposed to be gathering knights who are loyal to Galenos, even though Galenos himself is still imprisoned in the Tower. Sebastian is worried about it. He fears not only the force that Euthymius might raise but also the affect it could have on the rest of the Order. Many knights may choose not to get involved on either side for fear of having to fight their own brethren. And that could give an advantage to Straton.'

They had reached Elana's house. They had told Belwynn enough to make her realise that the threat was serious. But while she acknowledged it, she felt too tired to worry about it until tomorrow.

They said brief farewells to Elana, before Belwynn and Moneva retraced their steps back to the castle, where the guards saw them coming and had the gates open for them.

Saying goodnight to Moneva, Belwynn made her way to the tower where her room was. She quietly opened the door and peered in. Soren lay asleep in one bed, and Lyssa in the other. The thought of an uncomfortable night squeezed in next to Lyssa didn't appeal. She let the door shut, then padded back down the tower stairs.

Without really thinking about it, Belwynn found herself outside Theron's room. She raised her hand to knock on the door. Maybe she *should* think about this. She knew if she did, she would leave, so she knocked on the door before she could talk herself out of it.

The door cracked open and Theron peered out. He opened it fully when he realised who it was.

She had got him out of bed. He was half dressed.

'Belwynn, is everything alright?' he asked.

'Everything's fine,' she reassured him. 'I've just lost my bed, that's all. So I came here.'

'Come in,' he said.

She entered his room, and he shut the door behind her. Her stomach was swimming with butterflies. What did she think she was doing here?

She turned to face him. He was looking at her and she looked back at him, feeling her heartbeat race, her breathing getting shallow. *We both want this so much,* she told herself.

'Can I sleep with you tonight?' she made herself ask him.

'What are you saying—' he began.

'You know what I'm asking,' she told him.

He moved in close. 'Belwynn,' he murmured, his voice sounding husky. 'You know I have my vows.'

'I don't care about them,' she said.

He put his arms around her, pulled her into him. She looked up at him, parting her lips, putting one hand around his neck, and then his lips were on hers, his hands on her body, and she knew his vows were broken.

* * *

NINETEEN OF THEM had made it through the winter. Nineteen had come down from their camp in the Dardelles mountains, and the irony was, that was when they had come closest to death. Hordes of Drobax were crossing the mountain range into Haskany, and they had nearly got trapped. They had hidden in a cave and had to wait out an entire day before it was safe to move.

The original plan to cross into Persala was dead. Each time they made an attempt, they had encountered armies, or scouting parties: if not Drobax, then Haskans or Isharites. So they had hugged the mountains, gradually heading south-west, getting hungrier and weaker every day.

Nineteen emerged onto the Plains of Kalinth. Eight Barbarians; six Persaleians; two men of Rotelegen; two Dog-men; and a Magnian.

Clarin, worn down by the burdens of leadership, prayed to Toric, Madria, and every other god he had ever heard of. If the Drobax hadn't crossed into Kalinth, they had a chance.

They had left the mountains behind them, but Kalinth remained a rugged landscape, and their progress was painfully slow. They walked at the pace of the slowest, which was the pace of Jurgen, the Rotelegen. He had a permanent limp, the result of a spear wound he sustained in the fighting at Samir Durg. He used a stick to help him balance. The Dog-men carried his possessions. His cousin, Rudy, was always by his side, usually by the end of the day with Jurgen's arm around his shoulder, taking his weight, encouraging him. Even so, Jurgen was the slowest.

At the worst times, when he was tired and fed up, Clarin had thought about killing him. Just thoughts, crossing his mind when there was nothing else to think about except putting one foot in front of the other. He'd sometimes see the same thoughts in other people's faces, but no-one had talked of it. Clarin hadn't seriously considered doing it. If they killed Jurgen, would they then turn on the second slowest? What if Clarin himself got injured? Would they finish him off? No, they had survived this far by sticking together. As unlikely a group as you would find in the whole of Dalriya, but they all shared the experience of slavery in the mines, had fought their way out of Samir Durg together, and they weren't going to turn on each other now.

Kalinth was a sparsely populated land. There were few villages like they had in Magnia. Mainly isolated farms and hamlets, with more sheep than humans. They avoided contact. Clarin was certain that the local population, tough border people, would see them as a threat, and he didn't fancy getting stuck with an arrow by an anxious farmer. They didn't—couldn't—avoid the sheep, however. On an evening they got a fire going and ate roasted lamb; Clarin genuinely believed he had never tasted anything so good.

It was only a matter of time before they were challenged. When the Kalinthians arrived, there were only ten of them. They looked good, though. Fine horses, fine clothes, tall lances, armour polished and shining in the mid-morning sun. Clarin had heard all about the Knights of Kalinth, supposedly the best heavy cavalry in Dalriya. He was sure he was looking at them now.

'They're keeping their distance,' observed Cyprian, the Persaleian, as the riders drew up a hundred yards away.

'They're outnumbered two-to-one,' said Clarin. 'And we must look like mean sons of bitches by now. And not just them,' he added, gesturing at the Dog-men, which got some laughs, easing the tension a little. 'I'll go talk to them.'

'I'll come with you,' said Zared.

Zared was a young man, only in his early twenties, yet he was clearly the leader of the Persaleians.

The two approached while the Knights sat astride their horses, waiting for them. They were an intimidating sight, and Clarin couldn't help feeling nervous as he approached.

'Well met,' he began. 'I should explain our presence in your lands. We are men from all over Dalriya—from Persala, the Empire and elsewhere.'

'What are you doing here?' asked one knight, interrupting.

He was a young man, perhaps Zared's age. But he presented himself as the leader and so that was who Clarin addressed.

'We have escaped from the prisons at Samir Durg. We have been on the run since last summer. We tried to head through Persala, but it's impossible.'

'Samir Durg?' repeated one of the other knights. 'Leontios,' he continued, talking to the leader, 'isn't that where Lady Belwynn went to rescue her brother?'

'Wait,' said Clarin, looking from one knight to the other, not quite believing what he had just heard. 'You know Belwynn?'

Leontios, to his credit, loaded them up with precious supplies before sending them on their way to Heractus. Perhaps that was his way of ensuring they weren't tempted to butcher any more sheep. He couldn't spare horses, though. Indeed, it turned out that those ten knights were all that remained of the garrison of a town called Korkis. Furthermore, from what Clarin could tell, that garrison was the only one anywhere near the Persaleian border. If—more like when—the Isharites turned their attention here, Kalinth would be in terrible trouble.

The reason, Leontios had explained to him, was a civil war brewing in the country. Even the Knights themselves were divided in their allegiances. It was a strange and confusing situation for Clarin's group to find themselves in. The idea of fighting a civil war, when the Isharites and Drobax were on the march, seemed to Clarin the height of lunacy.

Be that as it may, his group found themselves walking again, albeit with the permanent, exhausting fear of the previous weeks now gone, and enough food in their packs to get them to their destination. It wasn't such a long way in the end, and two and a half days after leaving Korkis, the city of Heractus appeared before them. It was a sizeable settlement, with grey stone walls surrounding the city and a camp to the south. Once they got closer, Clarin could see that it was an army camp, well-made tents set out in organised rows. More evidence of the threat of war, though the camp looked new, and the soldiers cared for.

Another good sign was that they were challenged promptly upon approaching. Clarin handed the wary looking soldiers a letter written by Leontios, which Zared had assured him vouched for who they were and asked that they be taken to one of two men, either a Theron or a Sebastian. Once the soldiers had found someone to read it, they agreed to let them enter the city, on condition that they handed in their weapons.

Clarin's group balked at this demand. These were men who had sworn never to let themselves be taken captive again, and so persuading them to disarm was nigh on impossible. In the end, it was agreed that the group would be found spare tents in the camp and Clarin would go into the city alone.

Heractus had a solid, if unspectacular looking castle, made with the same grey blocks of stone as the city walls and many of the houses. It was to the castle he was taken, and at the gates the letter did the trick once more, a castle guard leading him into the main hall where he was offered a place at the fire and told to wait until someone fetched him.

He took a seat on the floor by the fire, and let the flames warm his tired body. In the mountains, during what seemed to be an unending northern winter, he had thought he would never feel warm again. Now he sat so close that the fire burned him. His face felt red, a trickle of sweat ran down his side, and yet he was loath to move farther away. He felt like he could sleep for a week and had to stop himself from lying down there and then. The trouble was, with all the military activity going on, these two knights whom Leontios had mentioned in his letter probably had a dozen better things to do than meet with him.

'Clarin!' came a voice from the other end of the hall, and he turned to see someone he had thought he would never see again.

Belwynn, smiling, came running over, closely followed by Elana. He got to his feet and opened his arms to grab her. She pushed away too soon, and then he was hugging Elana, though in truth he only had eyes for Belwynn. He had promised himself many things since his capture in Edeleny, and one of them was that if he ever found this girl again, he would never leave her. She looked more beautiful than ever and she looked happy; happier than he remembered her.

'You're a lot thinner,' said Belwynn.

'Yes, well, being starved for eight months will do that. I swear, I never understood what hunger meant.' He looked around. He had hoped there would have been more. 'Soren? Gyrmund? Did they not make it?'

'You've just missed them, by two days,' Belwynn replied. 'They're heading north, to the Jalakh Steppe. I'll explain why later. Moneva is with them, too.' She looked at him. 'I forget, there's so much you don't know. I am so sorry we left you. Herin?'

We left you? Had Belwynn been in Samir Durg? It sounded like there was much he didn't know.

'Herin,' he began, answering her question. 'We held out in one of the towers of Samir Durg. He went missing. I looked for him as best I could, vowed to myself that I would never leave without him. The others helped me, but there was not a single sign. If he was dead, I am sure we would have found a body. But nothing. And there was little time. If we didn't leave when we had the chance, we wouldn't have left at all.'

'Who's we?' Belwynn asked. 'The other prisoners? Gyrmund told us about them. What did he say?' she asked, turning to Elana.

'There were humans,' said the priestess. 'Dog-men. A Bear-man?'

'Yes,' said Clarin, smiling, and told them about his new companions, those who had survived. Then they told him of what had happened in Kalinth, of Dirk's death, of their invasion of Haskany, and finally of Belwynn's time in Samir Durg, teleported in by Pentas the wizard. How Gyrmund and Moneva had somehow rescued Soren. How they had all ended up in the throne room, and how Moneva had used Toric's Dagger to kill Erkindrix.

'That makes sense,' said Clarin. 'The Isharites had all but defeated us. We were ready to make our last stand on the roof of the tower. And then they all left. That must have been when Erkindrix was slain.'

'I am sorry we left you,' said Belwynn. 'I don't know whether it was the right thing to do. I was unconscious—'

'Nonsense,' said Clarin. 'You saved us when you all helped to kill Erkindrix. They had to take you to safety at that point. Anyway, what now?'

'Oh, I completely forgot,' said Belwynn. 'Theron told me to take you to see him.'

Belwynn and Elana led Clarin to a room where the knight, Theron, was sitting at a desk, bits of parchment spread about it. He stood up and welcomed them in. He was young, confident, but looked careworn. Clarin understood. Many were counting on him to win this war the Kalinthians were involved in.

'It's an honour to meet you, Clarin,' said Theron once they were all seated. 'Belwynn and the others have told me so much about you. To have a warrior of your prowess here is a boon, I can tell you. The letter Leontios wrote,' he said, trying to find it amongst the various bits of parchment on the table before giving up, 'mentioned a number of other escaped prisoners?'

'That's right, there are nineteen of us in all. Two of them are Dog-men. I know that may sound strange, but they have been loyal to me and we wouldn't have survived without them.'

'I understand. I'm in no position to discriminate against them, even if I was so inclined. Look Clarin, I will be frank with you. You will have picked up that we are in a dangerous situation right now. I can offer you and all your friends accommodation, food, and even wages. On one condition. You all join the Kalinthian army.' Theron looked at Clarin's expression. 'I'm sorry to have to do it, but I have no choice. We're desperate.'

Clarin looked from Theron to Belwynn and Elana, then back to the knight, but none of them cracked a smile.

They all looked at him with deadly serious expressions. But they had to be joking. They *had* to be fucking joking.

RED SERPENT

VII

They used the Great Road to travel south, before leaving it to travel south-east through Gotbeck. This part of Godfrey's duchy was well-organised and flourishing farming country, and he admitted he rarely needed to visit.

'My early years were taken up with the crusade against the Lizard-men,' he expounded, as Farred and he rode just behind the head of the column, his soldiers positioned at the front and rear, Hajna and her two companions behind them. 'Vicious creatures, who raid our people and don't think twice about killing women and children. I was often frustrated by a witch who dwelt in the marshland. She protected them, altering the paths through the swamps so that my soldiers got lost, or trapped. I had my suspicions,' he added quietly, glancing behind and then leaning over to whisper to Farred, 'that the Sea Caladri were also involved. No firm proof, but—', he nodded sagely at Farred, as if they both understood that a lack of proof was suspicious in itself. 'Then the bitch died, and we got the swamps under control. As soon as that was accomplished, these damn missionaries from the Confederacy began arriving, spreading their dangerous ideas.'

And so to Godfrey's religious persecution. Farred knew it wasn't wise—that he should focus on his mission—but he couldn't help examining the issue.

'What's so dangerous about these priests?' Farred asked. 'If you'll forgive my ignorance on the subject.'

'No need for forgiveness, my son. I am equally ignorant of the issues facing Magnia, I am sure. Or perhaps,' added Godfrey, smiling with satisfaction, 'we should both ask for forgiveness.'

That was the kind of glib comment Farred had got used to hearing from the Archbishop.

'The Empire is a mix of different peoples, and these peoples have many religions: different gods and different beliefs. Our ability to live together in harmony rests on many pillars, but one of the most important is the Brasingian Church. Here, all gods may be worshipped, and all are treated equally. This institution was created by Emperor Ludvig, and is often overlooked or under-appreciated by foreigners, if I may say so. Anyway, to the Confederacy. The religion they are promulgating has it that there is one god only, and all others are false. What does this mean? That those who worship these false gods must be 'stopped' from doing so. Now, I ask you. Do you see how this idea, if allowed to infect the Empire, could cause untold harm? It undermines entirely the principle of our Church, and creates fanatics whose energies are turned to fighting the beliefs of others, instead of respecting them. That is what I am up against here in Gotbeck.'

Farred had been expecting some bigoted defence of Godfrey's persecutions. But he understood. He saw how the Empire was a different polity to Magnia and needed more work to keep it united. He saw how protecting religious freedom was crucial to that. He had, he was forced to admit, somewhat misjudged the Archbishop.

'I see,' he said. 'I thank you for the lesson.'

Godfrey nodded solemnly, and they continued their journey.

GODFREY EXPLAINED that the best place to cross the border into the lands of the Sea Caladri was nearby. The north-west tip of the Caladri lands, next to Cordence, was some distance from the Cousel and the marshland that surrounded it on its final journey into the sea. Here, the land was dry and mostly wooded. Trails took them through the woods, and they could proceed on horseback. As they approached the border, they came across a small fort, now a ruin. The woodland had mostly reclaimed it: trees grew from its roof and moss and ivy covered most of the walls.

'There were others built in a line here,' Godfrey explained, pointing to the east. 'Maybe a dozen in all. I think they were abandoned soon after they were built. Your cousins are not a warlike people,' he said to Queen Hajna.

'They chose this place to escape war,' she said. 'They have had hundreds of years of peace. In that time, they have become expert sailors. And that is why we are here.'

She sounded almost jealous to Farred. If her people had been fighting the Shadow Caladri all this time, without help, maybe jealousy was natural.

'I could have some of my men escort you farther,' said Godfrey. 'But in truth, your passage may be more straightforward without us.'

'I believe you are correct,' said Hajna. 'I am most grateful for your help, and I will tell my cousins of the aid you have given me.'

'You are quite welcome, of course,' said Godfrey. He took Hajna's hand and placed a kiss there. He turned to Farred, and they shook hands.

'It may be that the gods decide our paths will not soon cross again,' said the Archbishop. 'In which case I wish you good luck in your endeavours.'

Farred nodded, then turned to look in the direction they would travel. Apart from the abandoned fort, there was no other sign that the land ahead was claimed by the Caladri. Gentle woodland stretched ahead into the distance and he could see that their trail continued. He wondered whether it was used by Gotbeckers or the Caladri themselves. Some contact, for reasons such as trade, could surely exist here, where it was so easy to cross from one country to another.

He followed the trail, nudging his mount carefully ahead, and Hajna followed, with her companions, Marika and Vida, at the rear. They were quiet, almost subservient to Hajna, who always spoke on their behalf. Vida had a sword strapped to his waist, but whether he was a bodyguard, it was hard to tell. Gyrmund had advised Farred that Hajna was a powerful witch, in which case she hardly needed protection.

The four of them followed the trail through the woods. Hajna was content for Farred to take the lead and choose the route. She seemed unconcerned about the direction they took, but while the Queen seemed relaxed about their journey, Farred felt more anxious the farther they went. He didn't know what kind of reaction the Caladri would have to their unannounced arrival.

He wasn't sure how it happened, but one moment the path ahead was clear, the next it wasn't. A small group of Caladri riders had appeared ahead of them. Farred touched the hilt of his sword and looked around. Behind them, a few yards down the trail, a second group of Caladri had appeared.

He looked from one group to the next, nervous of them, even though they appeared to have no weapons, either in their hands or at their belts.

Hajna took the initiative and approached the group in front of them. 'Well met. I am Queen Hajna of the Blood Caladri.'

'*Queen* Hajna?' responded one of the Caladri. 'Then King Tibor has died?'

'Last summer,' Hajna confirmed. 'In the fighting with the Shadow Ones.'

'I had not heard,' said the Caladri. 'Please accept my condolences. I am Darda. I can take you to see our Council?'

'Yes, thank you. I have with me Farred, a nobleman from South Magnia. He comes with a message from his Prince. I vouch for him.'

'Well met, Farred,' said Darda. 'Since Queen Hajna vouches for you, you are most welcome here. We will take you to our capital, Mizky. It is a long ride, we will need to stay one night on the way.'

'Thank you for your hospitality,' Farred replied.

With no further ceremony, Darda turned her horse around and took the trail south. Hajna followed her, and so Farred did likewise, Marika and Vida just behind him. He looked about him as they rode. There was no physical sign that he had crossed into another realm. But nonetheless, he felt acutely aware that he was possibly the sole human, in an alien land.

Farred was sitting outside his tent, letting the morning sun warm him after breakfast. He was thinking, and that was never good these days, for his thoughts always turned to Burkhard Castle, and the horrors of the siege he had witnessed there. Bodies piled up at the bottom of the crag, countless Drobax forcing their way up the path, day after day. But he always ended up thinking of Ashere, lying in agony as the poison from an Isharite blade dealt him a lingering death.

'It has to be you, Farred,' Ashere had begged him. 'I can't ask anybody else. Please.'

And what else can you do when someone you love begs you for help? Nothing else, but give them what they want.

His memories were interrupted as two figures approached him—Vida and Marika, the two Blood Caladri.

'We are going to visit the harbour,' Marika said to him. 'Would you like to come?'

'Yes,' said Farred, jumping to his feet. He had come to the conclusion that Marika and Vida were in a relationship, and in normal circumstances, he would have avoided getting in their way. But with another empty day ahead of him in Mizky, he was bored.

He wondered what Gyrmund would say, his great explorer of a friend, if he was to learn that Farred was in one of the few places in Dalriya that Gyrmund had never been, and couldn't wait to leave. He smiled to himself. He wouldn't be impressed.

They left the field of tents, which was their temporary home, heading downhill to the harbour area of the city, where most of the citizens worked. Vida and Marika walked either side of him and linked their arms through his. Gyrmund had warned him back in Coldeberg of the over-familiarity of the Caladri, and Farred was glad he had, because it took some getting used to. It was in stark contrast to the Sea Caladri, many of whom openly stared at him as they walked down one of the main streets that led to the sea. They were not hostile, exactly, but he had certainly found them to be unwelcoming, and he was glad to have had the company of Vida and Marika over the last few days.

He had only made one very brief appearance in front of the Caladri Council. Hajna had already met with them beforehand to explain why they had come. Farred's role, therefore, was simply to provide a formal offer of safe harbour in the ports of South Magnia. From there, their fleet could help to re-open the sea lanes across the Lantinen Sea, which had been closed by the Kharovian navy. Hajna's companion, Szabolcs, had told them that one of the magic weapons they were searching for, the Giants' Spear, was somewhere in Halvia. Re-opening the Lantinen was a necessary first step to finding it.

The Sea Caladri had been polite enough, thanking Edgar for his offer and all the usual pleasantries, but they were clearly not involving Farred in their decision making. So instead, while they deliberated, he was left to his own devices in Mizky.

They reached the sea front. Here, a natural spit of rock that knifed into the sea had been extended by the Caladri to make a large, sheltered harbour, and whenever Farred came down to the sea front, the area was a hive of activity. The three of them sat on a wall to watch what was going on, the sea breeze tugging at their clothes, as passers-by stopped to stare at Farred, the stranger in their midst, before walking on.

A shipyard took up the near side of the harbour. Here, many Caladri men and women were working on a large vessel. The carcass was already complete: wooden planks overlapped to create an unusually deep and wide hull. Farred knew enough to identify it as a trading ship, the large hull constructed to carry goods long distances across the ocean. The shipwrights were working on the frame, the internal ribs of the vessel. It was an impressive sight. They worked hard, and each of them seemed to know exactly what their job was, with little direction needed from the master shipwright.

The central part of the harbour was for fishing vessels, which regularly came and went, depositing barrels teaming with fish and crustaceans. The locals bought them freshly caught on the sea-front for their evening meal; the remainder were carted off to the nearby factory to be salted. On the far side of the harbour were Caladri warships, moored onto wooden piers. On his first visit, there had been half a dozen; now, there were twice that number. It may have been coincidence, but it suggested that the Caladri Council were gathering a fleet, should a decision be made to sail for the west.

A Caladri man approached them, brawnier than average, with the weather-beaten look of a sailor. 'You're Magnian?' he asked Farred directly, apparently not as shocked by his presence as his compatriots.

'That I am,' Farred replied. 'Why do you ask?'

'I've been told to consult my charts on the routes to Magnia, so it seemed likely that is where you are from. You don't look Magnian, though.'

'My family is Middian in origin,' Farred explained.

'Ah. Not sailors then, I wager?'

Farred chuckled. He had a funny way about him, this Caladri sailor. 'No, I am afraid not. I can't even swim.'

'Well, I know plenty of sailors who can't swim. They're fine so long as they don't fall off the ship. What do you know of this Kharovian fleet then, my lord? Do their ships sail as far south as Magnia now?'

'Not that I know of, not South Magnia certainly. Our fishing boats still go out with no trouble. I doubt that their patrols regularly get farther south than the Guivergnais coast.'

'That's what I would have guessed.'

'Are you the captain of one of those warships?' Farred asked.

'That I am. She's the best of the lot, too. Red Serpent.'

'I don't doubt it. Have you been told to sail to Magnia?'

'Not as such. I've been told I might be asked to sail there. So have a lot of other captains. Since few of us have sailed all that way ourselves, I have been consulting charts, drawn up by earlier sailors.'

'How long does it take?'

'It's not an easy voyage, my lord. You must sail all the way around the Avakaba Coast, a long way south, where the waters are treacherous, before sailing back up into the Lantinen Sea. The length of the voyage depends on the winds, but it has been done in four days in the past.'

'The Avakaba Coast?'

'You know them as the Lippers.'

'Well, thank you for the information. I am Farred, by the way,' he said, offering a hand.

The Caladri took it. 'Captain Sebo,' he said, then gave a twitch of a smile. 'Maybe we will make this voyage together.'

'Maybe so,' said Farred with a smile.

'If so, I recommend my ship,' said Sebo. 'It would be an honour to have you as a guest with us.'

'It would be an honour to sail with you,' replied Farred, now feeling somewhat better about Caladri hospitality.

It would be two more days before the final decision was taken; though as the harbour in Mizky continued to fill with warships, it was plain to see which way it was going. The Sea Caladri would sail a fleet to the Lantinen Sea. Their goals, Hajna explained to him, were somewhat limited: to open up transport across the Lantinen. If that meant conflict with Kharovia they were prepared for it, but they would not be seeking out Kharovian ships, declaring war, or anything of that sort.

Once Hajna had passed on a summary of what was happening, she explained that she would be sailing back to her homeland that very day. She had been away for some time, and she was concerned that her husband, the new king, needed her support.

Farred walked with the Blood Caladri down to the harbour, for Marika and Vida would of course be returning with their mistress. Theirs was a small, sleek ship, which could skim atop the waves and take them swiftly north along the Itainen coast. He said his farewells, receiving a hug from Marika and Vida, then left them to it.

Now you really are alone, he told himself.

On a whim, and with nothing better to do, he walked along the seafront to look at the warships. He wondered whether he could spot Captain Sebo's ship, that he had named Red Serpent. It was busy here, as sailors readied the vessels for the voyage, bringing aboard supplies to keep the big oarsmen fed, weapons should they be needed, and goods for trade. The ships came in different sizes, but the largest were far longer than any he had seen elsewhere. They were also more high-sided than the typical construction in Magnia; altogether, they were an impressive sight. Farred walked along one pier then the next, until he saw a ship painted scarlet red, with the body and head of a great snake on the prow of the vessel.

'So, destination Magnia!' came a voice, and there was Captain Sebo, peering down at him from the deck of the ship.

'She's a beauty!' said Farred. It wasn't the biggest of the ships, but it certainly looked fine, and praising a captain's ship is like praising a mother's child: an obvious compliment, but one that always works nonetheless.

'Come aboard!' the captain shouted, indicating the gangplank that was resting on the wooden pier.

Farred made his way up the plank carefully, wary of slipping. Once he reached the top he saw that it was a significant drop down to the deck.

'There,' said Sebo, indicating a raised platform that had been built along the side of the ship.

Farred stepped from the plank onto the platform, then onto the deck. He looked at the platform.

'For fighting?'

'Yes, it gives us quite a height advantage over most other ships. Fill that platform with archers and you can win most encounters without risking life or limb. Come Farred, let me show you around.'

Sebo showed Farred the deck, which had two masts, with sails that would be unfurled when the captain wanted to catch the wind. There were many other features of the ship he showed Farred, who only half followed what he was being told.

Sebo then showed him below deck. This was where the oarsmen were located, in rows of seats with one oar each, which exited through a hole on either the port or starboard side. The conditions looked cramped even without the seats filled. At the fore of the ship Sebo had a small cabin and at the rear was storage, mainly for food and drink. This was a fighting ship and there was no room to carry large quantities of goods: that required a ship of a different design.

They returned to the deck.

'Will you be travelling with us, then?' Sebo asked.

It was the only offer Farred had, so he was pleased to accept it.

'We are sailing first thing on the morrow, I believe?' said Sebo.

'I'm not sure,' Farred admitted. 'I haven't really been kept informed.'

'Ah well,' said Sebo, looking a little embarrassed. 'You will have to forgive my countrymen. Most of them lead a secluded life here. They don't come into contact with foreigners. Being a sailing man of course means my life is rather different. Anyhow, I will see you first thing tomorrow. We sail for the Avakaba Coast, against the wind, so we will need an early start.'

'I look forward to it,' said Farred, looking about the ship. 'I think I will enjoy the voyage.'

FARRED HATED IT.

The roll of the ship as it crested a wave and then dipped down, up and down, up and down, made him violently sick. His body seemed unable to adjust. He couldn't stay on his feet, and any lurch of the ship made him ill. So he stood on the starboard fighting platform, hands gripping the side, head stuck over the edge in case he had anything left to throw up. He watched the south coast of Dalriya, the lands of the Sea Caladri and the Cordentines, gradually slide away as they got farther out to sea, and regretted ever having set foot on the Red Serpent. Once there was no land left to look at, he watched the other Caladri ships. They bobbed on the waves alongside Red Serpent, banks of oars pounding into the sea to keep them moving. Most were warships like Sebo's, but they were also accompanied by the wider shaped trading vessels. Although their design made them less sleek, they sat much lower in the water, and they could hold their own with the warships in these conditions.

Captain Sebo approached him, his face a mix of pity and humour. 'Middians make poor sailors, I fear.'

'Why didn't you make that clear before we set sail?'

'I just wanted it confirming.'

'Turn your fucking ship around,' said Farred, 'and take me to the south coast of Magnia. I'll get off there and you can carry on.'

Sebo scrunched up his face. 'Can't do that, I'm afraid. It would take far too long. We'd lose contact with the rest of the fleet. Seriously, Farred, I do have a suggestion. Why don't you try pulling an oar for a while?'

Farred looked at him, wondering if it was a jest. But no, the captain was serious.

'What if I puke up down there? That's not going to make me very popular.'

'I doubt you've got anything left. You might find it better down there. The motion of the ship isn't so severe.'

'Alright. I'll give it a try.'

Sebo led him down, then looked at his oarsmen, giving the matter a little thought, before picking one of them to give up a seat for Farred.

Farred clambered clumsily into position, before grabbing hold of the oar in front of him, two handed.

'Just follow the rhythm of the others,' advised Sebo. 'Concentrate on that and you'll get the hang of it soon enough.'

It took him a while. He copied the other oarsmen, whose range of movement was small, their hands always in front of their chests. Several times he got into a rhythm and then his timing went wrong, the blade of his oar dipping too early, or in the wrong position, slapping into the water rather than pulling it. But each time he started again, and began to eradicate the errors, until he found a settled rhythm. Sebo was right. Perhaps it was because the rowing gave him something to focus on, but he felt a lot better below deck. His shoulders and back muscles ached, but he wasn't going to show himself up amongst the Caladri, and he pushed through the pain, his body adjusting to the demands of the motion.

It was hard to tell time below deck. Sometimes it felt like it dragged, each pull of the oar a burden. Then his mind would drift off, thinking of other things, until it was drawn back to the ship and the oar and he wondered how long he had been down there.

Eventually, a group of sailors came down to replace some of the oarsmen, including Farred, and he made his way back up to the deck. He stretched out his back, enjoying the sensation after sitting for so long. He looked out to sea. He could see the other Caladri ships; some ahead, some behind. It was comforting to know that they weren't alone in the ocean. But there was no land to be seen in any direction now. He didn't like the feeling of being surrounded by nothing but waves, not knowing where the nearest shore was.

Sebo was right. He wasn't a sailor.

The captain approached him. 'You did well, I hear?'

'Well, I certainly feel better for it. How are we doing?'

'Well enough. I expect us to make landfall in daylight. We are having to row hard against the wind on the way south. If we have any luck, and the wind stays, our journey will get much easier when we reach the Lantinen Sea.'

Sure enough, it was early evening when they approached a Lipper settlement. Sebo identified it as Chobo. It was perfectly positioned in a wide bay. There was limited docking space, and so the warships waited out at sea while the traders went in first, turning their ships around, then securing their vessels and unloading the goods they had brought to offer to the Lippers. For the rest, there was a long shallow beach which had enough space for all the ships to find a berth.

As they got into the shallows, Sebo ordered his men off, and Farred jumped off the side and landed in the waves, his shoes plunging into the sandy seabed. Ropes were thrown overboard. Farred found a space on one rope, and when all the sailors had a grip, they pulled and heaved, dragging Red Serpent onto the shore. Farred slipped over and fell onto his arse, hands grabbing at him to haul him back up. He wasn't the only one to fall, though obviously the Caladri had experience on their side, not to mention their clawed feet that sank into the sand and found purchase better than his leather shoes.

Once they were out of the shallows and the ship was on firmer ground, it suddenly became much easier, and Farred found himself running backwards, the rope taught, and Red Serpent slid smoothly along the wet sand until it was secure above the high tide mark. Farred had a huge grin on his face despite his wet shoes and trousers, and decided that a life on the seas wasn't quite as hellish as he had found it to be initially, though his favourite part was getting back onto dry land.

The Lippers were already coming out to meet them at the beach, and Farred wandered over, fascinated. They were tall and broad shouldered, with dark skin just like his own. But if they resembled Middians in appearance, they sounded nothing like them. Farred could hear their strange voices talking to the Caladri traders. It was a series of meaningless noises to him—he couldn't make out a single word.

He was surprised that the Caladri traders could talk back in the same language. They laid samples of their goods out on the beach for the Lippers to inspect: worked timber, wool, and iron implements.

Sebo walked over and stood next to him. Farred looked over to the ship and saw the captain's men were busy putting up tents for the night.

'What do the Lippers offer in return?' Farred asked him.

'They have gold, cotton, spices—many things. I am hopeful they will feed us, too. Otherwise it's salted fish for dinner.'

'You have learned their language?'

'Me personally? I know a few words that come in handy. The traders know their language. The people back home do not.'

'What did you say they call themselves?'

'Avakaba. It means The Ones Who Left.'

'Left where?'

Sebo shrugged. 'That I don't know.'

'In Magnia, we know nothing of these people. They are our neighbours, but as far as I know, we don't trade or communicate with them at all. Looking at this, that seems very foolish.'

'It is very foolish,' Sebo agreed. 'And long may it continue. For the Sea Caladri take goods from the Avakaba, sail north as far as Haskany, even the Jalakh Steppe, and trade with the northerners. It makes us very rich.'

Farred nodded. He could see how.

'You say you sometimes sail as far north as the Steppe?'

'Sometimes.'

'I have a friend who needs to travel there. It is connected with this mission your fleet has been given.'

'Then he would have been far better coming with you and taking a ship there. It is very dangerous to reach the Steppe by any other route.'

'Yes,' agreed Farred. The overland route involved marching through Haskany, under the noses of the Drobax and the Isharites. 'Although if I had to trust anyone to do it, I would trust Gyrmund.'

MANOEUVRES

VIII

The Drobax was standing a good ten feet lower down the slope from the ledge Gyrmund occupied. He adjusted his body line to the angle of the shot, pulled back the string to his ear, held for a second, then released. The arrow struck, and the beast went down.

He turned behind him and waved Moneva and Soren on.

They didn't have much time.

The Drobax were crawling all over the Dardelles mountain range, sent south by their masters in ominously large numbers. Gyrmund spared a brief thought for whoever this army was being sent against. But he had no time for more, because they had been spotted. If they didn't find a secure place to hide, they were finished.

He jumped down the rocks, risking injury in exchange for speed. When he reached the Drobax corpse, he breathed a sigh of relief. He was right; the monster had been standing outside a cave. This was their best chance of escape.

He pulled the arrow from the head of the Drobax, fitted it to his bow and peered into the dark cave. He could feel Moneva's presence behind him and he walked forward carefully. He was wary of marching straight in when his eyes had not adjusted to the darkness, yet fearful of taking too long and being seen entering by the Drobax.

He was right to be careful. As he inched forward, a figure ran at him out of the darkness. He released his string on pure instinct and it took down what he could now see was a Drobax. But a second monster followed close behind and Gyrmund had no time to nock a second arrow or draw his sword, instead holding his bow as a staff.

Moneva was a blur that came past him. The Drobax adjusted the swing of its weapon from Gyrmund to Moneva, but it was a clumsy move. Moneva avoided the swinging club and stepped in, burying her sword through its neck, then shoved it to the ground before finishing it.

Dropping his bow, Gyrmund drew his sword and stabbed down at the first Drobax, making sure it was dead. Once done, he turned back to the entrance of the cave.

Soren had entered behind them, and, with Onella's Staff aloft, was concentrating on the cave entrance. The wizard turned to look at Gyrmund.

'I am making the entrance appear like a solid wall of rock. If one of them studies it closely, or leans against it or some such, the illusion will break. That would be unlucky.'

Gyrmund looked around the cave. That would be the end of them. It was a large space, but there was no other exit. They would be trapped inside.

He spied something on one of the walls and walked over to investigate.

'What is it?' asked Moneva, joining him.

There was a slash mark on the cave's wall.

Gyrmund smiled. 'I'm just wondering. Something very sharp made this mark. And recently, too. Soren, could you have a look?' he asked, before looking around the floor of the cave as best he could in the dim light.

There had been a large group in here. He approached the far end of the cave. The stink was oppressive, for it had been used as a latrine. He could see what looked like dog hairs on the ground. He turned back to see Soren looking at the mark.

'Clarin?' asked the wizard.

'That's what I thought,' said Gyrmund. 'It looks just like one I saw him use when we were heading to the Wilderness.'

'Yes, it does,' agreed Soren.

It was only yesterday that Belwynn had contacted Soren to tell them of Clarin's miraculous re-appearance in Heractus. Many of Gyrmund's fellow prisoners had escaped with him, including his friend Cyprian. Herin, however, had not been with them.

'Clarin was here?' Moneva said, incredulous.

'It's a sign that Clarin left for his brother,' Soren said. 'To tell him he was here.'

Moneva looked at Gyrmund.

'It's good,' he said, allowing himself a smile.

Clarin had made it out of Samir Durg. And if the big man thought there was a chance Herin had too, then Gyrmund had to share the same hope.

* * *

CLARIN FOUND it hard to lift the spirits of his men. It was only natural that each one of them had kept close to themselves a dream, private and intimate, of what they were escaping to.

A reunion with tearful loved ones who had thought them dead? Or at the very least, a bar full of captivated listeners to their heroic stories, while the tankards of frothy beer kept on coming long into the night. But to escape and be immediately impressed into an army in the middle of a civil war? That fell a long way short of the dream.

It wasn't as if he could fully explain to them why they should care about this war. The enemy was a complicated, nebulous list of names and groups to them.

The side they were on wasn't convincing, either. Sebastian, Theron and their Knights had captured the king of Kalinth, and the king's son was trying to free him. It was hardly a heroic cause—indeed, half the Knights of Kalinth clearly didn't support Sebastian's seizure of power, taking the side of the prince. They had also bungled their revolution. Theron had apparently sent the enemy army and royal guard home last summer, only for them to reappear as combatants this year.

It was hard for Clarin to understand Belwynn's total investment in this conflict. She had stayed in Kalinth for this? While Soren and the others left to continue the quest without her? Something didn't add up.

The army left Heractus for the south-west of the country. The Knights had ridden ahead on their expensive horses, each of them bringing at least one spare, while the infantry had to walk behind, eating their dust. It was a ragbag infantry force Theron had collected, and to give him some credit, at least he knew it.

Clarin had been put in charge of a division of a hundred soldiers. Apart from his group from Samir Durg, the rest were Madrians, half of them women—followers of Elana whom the priestess had persuaded to fight for the cause. She had gone up in the world, the leader of a powerful Church now. And he had witnessed her using that power. She had insisted to Sebastian that her religion should now be the only recognised creed in the land. That was her price for recruiting so many men and women into the army. And while the priestess had made her demands, Belwynn had smiled peacefully, as if it was the most wonderful outcome in the world.

They camped outside the first night, in a rocky landscape that was the southern end of the Dardelles mountains they had traversed on their way through Haskany. It wasn't a bad spot, with views across the countryside that would afford them early warning of enemy activity.

Theron also went up in his estimation a little that night. By the time his force trudged into camp, the tents had been put up for them and hot food was being cooked. The Knights also took on lookout duty, leaving the infantry to rest after the march. Clarin did a quick round of his troops, trying to take his new officer role seriously, though his heart wasn't in it. Eventually he settled down at a fire with Rudy, Jurgen and the two Dog-men, happy to be left alone with his thoughts.

His thoughts, inevitably, turned to Belwynn. They nagged at him, not letting him relax. Because Clarin was the one who had got his dream. His dream, during the days in the mine, the nights in the pit, was to see Belwynn again. And he had. But it wasn't how he had imagined it. She was pleased to see him, but she hadn't thrown her arms around him and kissed him. He hadn't had a chance to speak to her in private, to tell her how much she meant to him. She was always busy with Elana; or Sebastian; or Theron.

Theron. The man behind this madness. It was Theron who Belwynn spent her time with. It was Theron who she looked at, the way Clarin wanted her to look at him.

He looked across the fire at Rudy and lame Jurgen, forced to walk all day again so soon after their escape, in the opposite direction of their homes. They hadn't got their dreams yet. Clarin had got his, and it had already turned sour. Which of them was the worse off?

* * *

SEBASTIAN, Theron and Belwynn walked up a gravelled pathway to the home of Diodorus, Count of Korenandi. His house was fortified, much the same as Sebastian's home of Sernea; strong enough to withstand minor attempts at entry rather than entire armies.

Theron lifted a hand to knock on the front door, but before he got the chance, it had swung open, and a servant gestured that they should come in.

In the hall of his house stood Diodorus, with what Belwynn presumed were his wife and two sons. It was an oddly formal way to greet them, but she supposed this was the traditional way to welcome guests. Once the introductions and pleasantries were over, the family departed. The Count led them into a side room, where he sat them down in comfortable chairs next to a blazing fire. He offered them a drink called arak, perhaps again what tradition demanded. But they weren't really here for a pleasant fireside chat, and they all declined the offer.

Diodorus poured himself a drink and took a seat. 'Straton is raising an army against you,' he said.

'He has asked you to join him?' said Theron.

'Of course.'

'And?'

'I declined. I am not so popular with the royal family after I surrendered their army to you. There is no reason for me to risk my life to see Straton rise to power.'

'You have also declined our summons,' said Sebastian sternly.

'I see no reason to risk my life or those of my people for you, either,' countered the Count.

He spoke slowly, with little emotion, but Belwynn detected the undertone of melancholia in his voice and face that she had noticed when they had spoken with him last summer. Then, he had made a wise decision not to fight them. She hoped he would do the same again now.

'These are not easy times,' Sebastian admitted. 'You may think otherwise, but the last thing I wanted to do was stand against my king. But the future and the honour of Kalinth was at stake. It still is. Standing on the sidelines isn't an option, Diodorus.'

Diodorus took a sip of his drink. 'My father left this county to me and I would leave it to my sons. I would not see it destroyed. If I side with you, there will be reprisals from your enemies. It is not what you want to hear, but I intend to stay out of this conflict.'

'You can't,' said Theron. 'We are desperate for infantry. One hundred extra men, well-armed, could make all the difference when we fight Straton. We need you to give us a hundred men. If you refuse, we will bring our army onto your lands, take this house, and force you to give us a hundred men. That's the choice you have. A hundred men now or a hundred men later. Staying out of this isn't a choice available to you.'

Diodorus looked at them all in turn, his eyes blinking owlishly. They stopped at Belwynn. There was something about her he didn't like. She could sense it, but couldn't put a finger on it. Something more subtle than hatred or fear. He didn't want her here in his house. She shouldn't have come.

'Is this what the Knights of Kalinth are now?' he asked.

'We have no choice either, man!' said Sebastian, losing his temper. 'You know we fought with the Isharites last summer! They will be back. They want to see Kalinth burned to the ground, our people enslaved. I can't afford division, internal conflict. I can't afford men with the title of count who sit back and do nothing. Give us the men and we'll let you be. We'll return them to you once Straton is defeated. I give you my word.'

'You give me no choice,' retorted Diodorus.

'Now you understand,' said Theron.

Diodorus looked in his drink, as if he would find an answer there. 'I'll give you your men. I'll lead them myself, and when your war is over, I'll lead them back home. And if you break your word to me, you will have made another enemy. How many more can you make, before you lose your grip on this country?'

Neither Sebastian nor Theron answered that, though Belwynn was sure they both knew the answer. Their grip on Kalinth was already slipping, and it would take very little for them to lose it completely.

* * *

THEY LEFT Chobo and shadowed the Lipper coast, using the oars to row farther south. After two days, they rounded the southernmost tip of Dalriya, a rocky land where strange animals roamed the shoreline. Great fat creatures that Sebo called suliks lounged on the rocks, then suddenly dived into the sea. Farred saw that underwater they became agile and powerful, and worried that they might attack the ships, before Sebo laughed off his concerns.

Once Red Serpent turned to the north, Sebo unfurled the sails. Until now, the crew deck had had little to do, but now their experience was needed to steer the ship and adjust the sails. Sebo was in his element at the centre of things, shouting out orders. At times, orders were relayed to the rowers to row hard to get the ship moving again. At others they could rest, as the sails caught the wind and Red Serpent effortlessly cut through the waves.

In the afternoon, Sebo gave himself a break, relinquishing the helm to his second in command.

'It's easy to make a mistake when you are tired,' said Sebo, by way of explanation to Farred.

'We seem to be making good time,' Farred observed. Indeed, while he could see ships to the rear of Red Serpent, there appeared to be none ahead of them.

'Aye, the wind is on our side now. There are few hazards, save not to stray out too far to sea.'

'Why is that?'

'My charts tell me to stay clear of the Asrai, who dwell out in the Lantinen.'

'The Asrai?' repeated Farred. This was the name given to a people by the Caladri wise man, Szabolcs, who had said that they took a weapon to the fight with the Isharites. But no-one in that meeting seemed to know who or where they were.

'Before you ask,' said Sebo, 'I've never seen 'em, nor has anyone I know who isn't a drunk or a liar. I just know them from stories and what's on my charts, drawn up by explorers.'

Despite Sebo's words of caution, Farred grew excited at the possibility that he had stumbled onto something. 'Could you show me these charts?' he asked Sebo.

The captain gave him a look. 'This to do with those weapons?' he asked.

'Yes. It could be.'

Sebo reluctantly set off to grab his charts, coming straight back with them. The parchments he brought back looked new.

'I had them copied,' said Sebo, as if reading his mind. 'With the best will in the world, everything gets wet on a sea voyage. I never bring originals with me. Anyhow, I have two maps which reference the area. Here,' he said, passing Farred the first and pointing to the location.

The word Asrai was written in an area of sea out to the west of Dalriya and south of Halvia. Next to the text, a hand had been drawn, apparently reaching out from the ocean.

'And here,' he added, passing a second map.

This time, the text spelt 'Ashray' rather than Asrai. It was written in a similar location, next to what looked like a collection of small islands.

'And why avoid this area?' Farred asked.

'All Caladri seamen are told to avoid it because it belongs to the Asrai. Various stories say that the Asrai will pull a ship under the water and drown everyone aboard. Or capture the crew and make them work as slaves, never to return home. Or some other variation. With no reason to sail in that direction, no modern mariner that I know of has taken the risk.'

'And what if there is a reason to go?' asked Farred.

'Then still, neither I nor anyone I know would do it.'

With that, Sebo took back his charts.

. . .

The Caladri ships harboured on a beach that Sebo said was in the far north-west of the Lipper peninsula. There was no history of trade here and the local inhabitants, if they knew of their presence at all, stayed away.

The crews could fill their skins from a nearby stream, but food was getting scarce and when the sun rose, everyone seemed keen to move on. Minor repairs were held off until later, and one by one the crews dragged the ships into the shallows.

The winds continued to be favourable, carrying them on the last leg of their journey to Magnia. It wasn't long before Farred began to recognise landmarks he knew, though they looked different from the new perspective afforded by Red Serpent.

It was still morning when they approached Fripport, located in a sheltered bay near the border with North Magnia. It was the largest harbour in the country and the only place capable of holding such a large fleet. Farred could see Magnian ships moored in one corner—what amounted to Edgar's fleet, but it was insignificant compared to the wave of Caladri warships that were about to join them.

Red Serpent was the first to dock on the wooden piers. Farred almost felt like he would miss her when he found himself walking down the plank and returning to Magnia for the first time in two weeks.

The local officials were already at the dock, waiting to deal with the logistics of mooring the Caladri fleet and accommodating the sailors. Farred spied Aescmar, the leading magnate of the area, directing his men as more and more Caladri ships approached his port.

'You've brought the Caladri with you,' Aescmar said, as Farred approached. 'Edgar will be pleased. I've already sent a rider to tell him the news.'

'You're well organised here,' said Farred, impressed.

'We did get some warning of your approach. Which is just as well, because if we don't see a fleet of this size coming, the whole of South Magnia will be in trouble. Is it right that they have trading ships with them as well?'

'Yes, stocked up with goods from the Sea Caladri and from the Lippers. You would do well to open negotiations with them. I will tell the captain of the ship I travelled on if you like.'

'I am much obliged. Trade has totally dried up since the Kharovians took the Lantinen, and there are many here whose livelihoods have suffered. This could be a boon to them.'

. . .

AESCMAR WAS good enough to put Farred and Sebo up in the house he owned in Fripport. The rest of the Caladri were allocated to various patches of land inside and outside the port. Soon, a forest of Caladri tents had sprouted up, doubling the population of the town. They were polite guests, however, and there was no trouble. They paid for their food and the traders amongst them wasted no time in bringing their goods to shore, so that an impromptu market appeared. Caladri and Magnians bartered with each other good-naturedly, and in the end there were few locals who failed to turn some profit from the arrival of the fleet.

By the evening of the next day, Edgar arrived. Aescmar accommodated him and his three companions at his house. With him came Elfled, sister of Cerdda of North Magnia. Farred had first gained her acquaintance last year, when he had visited the North Magnians on Edgar's behalf.

In addition, Edgar now had two bodyguards. Brictwin had come, and Farred was pleased that Edgar had followed his recommendation and appointed Morlin as a second bodyguard. The man had served with distinction under Farred in the Empire last summer, and had the ideal temperament for the job. Edgar had been reluctant to replace Leofwin, Brictwin's uncle, who had died while preventing an assassination attempt on the prince. But Morlin was intelligent and easy-going enough to fit in.

They ate a late supper in Aescmar's dining room. Edgar was keen to hear about Farred's adventures since they had left Coldeberg, which he duly recounted, with Captain Sebo adding in details of a nautical nature that he felt Farred had overlooked.

'I must know for sure, though,' said Farred, 'about your own news since leaving Coldeberg. Elfled's presence by your side is a good sign,' he added.

Edgar grinned, and Elfled smiled too, touching the prince's hand.

'I visited with Elfled's family in North Magnia after leaving Coldeberg,' said Edgar. 'Then Elfled and I visited with my mother. Having received our family's approval, Elfled and I can announce our engagement.'

He took Elfled's hand and held it up so that they could see her engagement ring. A deep red garnet was set in rose gold, on a finely worked silver band.

'Congratulations,' said Farred, his words echoed by the others at the table. 'And did you ask Elfled amidst all that approval?' he asked.

'Don't worry about that, Farred,' Elfled said. 'I've already made it quite clear that this is going to be a partnership.'

Edgar rolled his eyes, and Elfled gave him a slap. Aescmar asked them about their wedding plans and Farred watched the two of them talking. It was good to see Edgar so happy. His expedition to the Empire had left him looking exhausted, but Elfled was obviously good for him.

'How have you celebrated your engagement?' Sebo asked the couple.

They looked at each other. 'Coming here, I guess,' replied Edgar. 'We haven't had the time for anything else yet.'

Sebo frowned. 'Not good enough. It would be an honour for my crew and I to take you out on a pleasure ride on my ship, Red Serpent. I promise to make it special enough to suit such a joyous occasion.'

Edgar and Elfled looked at one another.

'It would be something we would always remember,' she suggested carefully.

'Why not?' agreed Edgar. 'Can we find the time tomorrow?'

'Tomorrow?' Sebo said. 'Why not now? You two are young enough to stay up a while longer, surely?'

'In the dark?' questioned Farred, peering outside.

'There is nothing so special as a moonlight boat ride,' said Sebo, turning to Edgar and Elfled. 'Just don't bring him along. He will just spend his time throwing up Aescmar's delicious food.'

They smiled, agreeing to the idea, and Sebo set off to round up those of his crew who were in a fit enough state to man the ship. The rest of them spoke for a while longer, before leaving Aescmar's house to head down to the harbour.

Aescmar walked ahead with Elfled, while Farred fell in with Edgar. The two bodyguards walked on either side. Farred realised that they now had two people to protect. That fact must have convinced Edgar to take the step of recruiting Morlin.

'This is another great service you have done for me, Farred.'

'You are welcome, Your Highness.'

'I must find a way to repay you properly. I have been thinking about it a little. It is perhaps time you settled down too. Neither of us are getting any younger, after all.'

Farred nodded, trying to be noncommittal. Edgar was straying into awkward territory.

'The easiest way for me to reward you would be to find you a wife who comes with a nice estate. I would like to see you become a bigger landowner here in Magnia. It would help me as well as rewarding you. What do you say?'

What should he say? *Edgar, I like men?* Maybe Edgar wouldn't care if he did. *Edgar, I fell in love with your fiancée's brother and now my heart is broken?*

'It's something I should think about,' he said instead.

'Yes, we'll talk more. Oh my.'

They all stopped walking to look.

Sebo had Red Serpent ready. He had placed candles all over the deck and it looked beautiful—ethereal—in the moonlight. Farred wasn't sure that candles and wooden ships were a good combination, but no doubt he was the only one worried about that.

The captain held out a hand to help Elfled up the plank, and Edgar and his bodyguards followed. Farred and Aescmar stood at the shore while Red Serpent slowly, majestically, manoeuvred into the dark expanse of the ocean. As she left the harbour, it felt like Farred was watching a heavenly vessel leaving this world and sailing to paradise.

'That is some sight,' murmured Aescmar, seemingly to himself as much as to Farred.

It was, and it prompted in Farred a realisation of sorts. In Magnia, his future, as Edgar had laid out, was as landholder, nobleman, husband. But too much of that was a lie.

At that moment, Red Serpent, a vessel of light bobbing up and down on a black sea, represented an escape from that future. It was an escape that Farred hadn't even realised he wanted until now.

THE GRASS SEA

IX

Clarin looked up and down the line of knights, queueing up for their turn. They lounged about, bandying insults back and forth, as all soldiers do before a battle. But as they neared the end of the line they quietened, grew serious. When it was their turn, they approached Belwynn solemnly, drawing their blades and kneeling in front of her. She put her hands on theirs, said a few words, and they left, a look of serenity on their faces.

Clarin had never seen anything like it. He couldn't tear himself away from the spectacle, all the more curious because it was Belwynn who was carrying out the blessing. Belwynn, a regular girl from Magnia a year ago, now the Lady of the Knights.

'Come on,' said Diodorus, interrupting his thoughts. 'You can get your sword blessed later.'

Clarin followed the count into Sebastian's tent. They had been invited to attend the discussion of tactics before the battle. Theron stood at a table with quill and parchment, as officious as ever. Sebastian and Tycho were also there, along with a knight he had not met yet. Sebastian noticed.

'Clarin, this is Remi, my closest friend. He has been tracking Straton's forces for us.'

Clarin and Remi shook hands. Remi gestured to the parchment, where Theron had drawn a diagram of what they believed to be the enemy's disposition.

'Euthymius has largely failed to turn the Knights against us. He leads a small number, probably less than one hundred. The rest of the cavalry are noblemen Straton has recruited. I would expect Count Ampelios to lead this group into battle.'

The knights under Euthymius and the mounted noblemen under Ampelios were positioned on the flanks. Clarin understood that these would be the better fighters, using the power and mobility of their horses to dominate the battlefield.

'The infantry are largely made up of men-at-arms raised by the nobility, or members of the temples who have allied with Straton. They have greater numbers than us, but not greater quality.'

Here, Theron had predicted three divisions of infantry positioned in the centre. Behind them, Theron had scrawled more words, which Clarin assumed would be the reserve, where Straton himself would command.

'Our problem is matching their infantry,' explained Sebastian. 'I propose we dismount some of our knights, fifty say, and position them in the centre division to strengthen it. Anyone else who can fight will go there, giving the impression of further strength. That includes squires. The knights will have to do without them.'

'Sending squires in to fight?' Clarin said. 'They're little more than children.'

'I'm not happy with it,' said Sebastian. 'But we're desperate. They'll be at the back. Clarin, your unit will be to the left, and Diodorus, you will command the right. Watch out for them trying to get around you. I'll let you decide how to organise things. You know what you're doing. I will put myself in the centre with the dismounted knights. I think my presence will reassure them.'

Theron frowned. 'I understand the thinking, uncle, but I'm not sure it should be you.'

There followed a debate between the knights about who should be placed where. There were four of them and four positions to allocate: two on the wings with the cavalry; one with the reserves; one with the infantry. Theron wrote in and scratched out names until they were settled. Sebastian was persuaded to take the reserves. Tycho would fight with the infantry, leaving Theron and Remi to lead each wedge of knights.

Clarin had no problems with the plan. The truth was you could talk for hours before a fight—when it came to it, it was chaos and desperate hacking every time.

. . .

Clarin put himself in the centre of the front line. To his left, Tamir led the Barbarians. He was still a tall and formidable figure, though he now fought left-handed after losing three fingers in the fighting in Samir Durg. To his right were the two Dog-men, then Zared and the Persaleians. Theron had given them whatever armour and weapons they had requested. Clarin already knew they could fight like monsters, so he had no worries about his front line.

He had told Rudy and Jurgen to lead the Madrians, who stood in four rows behind him. They would have to react once the battle started, supporting Clarin's front line or moving out to prevent any attempts at flanking their position. Clarin could not predict for sure how these men and women would react. For most, it was their first time in combat. They had behaved with discipline to this point, borrowing Elana's icily cool demeanour. But hand-to-hand fighting was something different altogether. He knew that some of them would be able to do it, and some would not.

He could see the enemy infantry ahead. They, too, had settled into their units and were waiting for the order to go.

The terrain was uneven, with grass and flowering gorse covering the area between the two armies, some of it waist height. He had told his men to tread carefully. There was a slope, too, the high point on the right of their position, where Theron's cavalry was located. The dip had more or less flattened out by the time it reached Clarin's position on the left, and gave no particular advantage to either side.

Clarin was relieved to hear the blare of trumpets from behind him. The waiting was over. He picked up his spear and shield.

'March!' he shouted.

They walked steadily, keeping to the same pace as Tycho's central division.

Clarin worried. It wasn't like him to do so. But he felt different to previous engagements he had been involved in. On those other occasions he was full of emotions. But today he felt empty. It was hard to summon up hatred for the enemy he was about to fight. He didn't know them.

The sound of drums and shouts filled the air. Looking up, he saw the ranks of infantry facing them begin to move. The tension and noise on the battlefield ratcheted up as the two sides moved towards each other. The gap between them closed more quickly. Clarin could see that the enemy was more numerous. The danger of them outflanking his hundred soldiers was all too real. He could now pick out individual fighters coming to meet him. They presented a wall of shields, with spears, maces and other weapons ready to carve into his own forces.

Then it happened. Clarin felt the danger and the fear. The rage came next, and as the two infantry lines closed, he was ready. Rather than waiting for the Kalinthians to come to his line, he sprang forwards, relying on the Dog-men and the Barbarians to support him.

He shoved his spear forwards. It was turned by a shield. He reached forwards and grabbed at a shield, using his strength to pull the soldier out of the line, where he was quickly skewered by a spear. The Dog-man to his right rushed into the gap, teeth snapping and clawed hands swiping. Clarin risked another lurch forward, slamming his spear over the top of a shield and into the shoulder of a Kalinthian. He released his grip and drew the sword he had named Cutter. The pink crystal blade of the Isharite weapon flashed dangerously.

His front line had supported his move and the Kalinthians who opposed them hadn't coped with it. Defending against his men had left their line of shields ragged, and a gap yawned in front of him. Readying himself, putting his body behind his shield, his face down, his sword arm trailing behind, Clarin grimaced and charged. He buffeted the enemy, using his strength to strike out and barge at those around him with his shield. He had to trust that his soldiers came with him, harrying the rest of the Kalinthian line.

Clarin twisted at the waist and used his hips and thighs to impart power into another barge. He felt the man in front give way, and he staggered forwards, walking on top of the man who had gone down. Now he swung his sword over his shoulder. It connected with the man in front, and he found he could push further forward. Suddenly, he had space around him. He had broken through.

He allowed himself a brief backwards glance. His front line had followed him, carving a hole through the enemy. Now he could take advantage, but he had to be quick. Opening up his body, he slashed his sword at the disorganised enemy around him. He launched himself at one soldier, chopping down so viciously he heard the arm bone crack. He located the next nearest soldier, hurrying toward him. This one defended Clarin's blow with his shield, and then moved backwards when Clarin slammed his shield at his face. Clarin feinted to strike, and the soldier retreated again. Behind him, Tamir launched a two-handed downward strike, his giant steel blade connecting with the man's shoulder. The blow knocked him to the ground, and it was then easy for Clarin to deal the death blow.

Clarin now led his men against the exposed end of the enemy line. Men who moments before had been ready to come around Clarin's soldiers and envelope them now found themselves fighting for their lives.

Clarin looked up when he heard the thud of cavalry.

Sebastian, quick to understand what was happening, had led his reserves to join in. The remaining enemy infantry, separated from the rest of their forces, ran or died, as Sebastian's cavalry tore into them, lances thrusting down, huge warhorses kicking and buffeting. The Knights knew what they were doing. As Clarin turned his men to face the rest of the enemy infantry, Sebastian was free to take his cavalry in behind them. Straton's infantry was now in a vice, under attack from three directions as Tycho's dismounted knights, Clarin's force and Sebastian's reserves, all targeted them.

Victory seemed inevitable, so long as the enemy units were kept isolated. Clarin looked across the rest of the battlefield. He could see Remi's cavalry engaged with the Kalinthian Knights led by Euthymius. Theron's cavalry wasn't in sight. With any luck, that meant they had the upper hand.

Another stretch of fighting ensued, but it must have been clear to Straton's infantry that they were on their own. They began throwing down their weapons, and instead of slaughter, Clarin's force turned to capturing and disarming the enemy infantry. Sebastian left him to it, taking his knights off to join with Remi.

Clarin bumped into Tycho.

'I will put guards on them,' the knight said, gesturing at their prisoners, who had been made to sit on the ground in small groups. 'Can you organise the wounded?'

Clarin nodded. 'You think we've won?'

'Almost certainly. Theron drove Ampelios off the field. I think they will be chasing down those that fled. If I know Theron, he will try to capture Straton.'

Clarin ordered his unit to separate from Tycho's, in an effort to bring some order to things. He assessed the damage. One of Zared's Persaleians was dead, bringing the number who had escaped from Samir Durg down to eighteen. They had suffered another half a dozen fatalities from amongst the Madrians, as well as various wounded. As he began trying to work out who needed help, Elana and Belwynn appeared. Belwynn seemed used to such a job and began to organise those that needed to see Elana urgently. Other Madrians helped, and Clarin left them to it.

He walked away, keen to know how the Knights had fared. Two knights were riding over in his direction. He walked over to meet them, as did Tycho and Diodorus. It was Sebastian and Remi.

'Well?' asked Tycho.

'Euthymius is dead,' said Remi. 'It was tough fighting—I lost a few, as did they. We have captured the rest.'

'Any news from Theron?'

'Not yet,' said Sebastian. 'We will have to wait a while longer. Well done, everyone. Whatever news Theron returns with, we've scored a major victory and kept the loss of life to a minimum.'

Clarin sat and waited, relief and exhaustion kicking in. The knights saw to their horses first and eventually squires were sent round with food and drink for the soldiers. Elana worked her healing magic on those who needed it. Sebastian gave the order to strip the corpses. Unclaimed bodies would be burned together, he said, since they were all Kalinthians.

Eventually, Theron's force returned. They led a large number of prisoners, who walked along in a group, surrounded by mounted knights. Theron steered his horse over. He was pale with exhaustion, but looked satisfied enough.

'Straton tried to escape,' he croaked, climbing off his horse stiffly.

Tycho handed him a cup, and he drank deeply before continuing. 'It took a long time to track him down, but we got him. We also captured Ampelios in the first fighting. What news of Euthymius?'

'Dead,' said Remi.

Theron looked about, trying to take in what he saw, but his eyes glazed over. Clarin could see the strain he had been under, not just today, but during the campaign as a whole. Defeat would have seen the end of the regime he and Sebastian had established, and a return to the policies of King Jonas. Kalinth would have become subservient to Ishari once again.

On that count, Clarin grudgingly conceded, maybe it had been worth it.

* * *

The mountains took their toll on Soren's body. Day by day, the recovery he had made under Elana disappeared; day by day he reverted to the state he had been found in at Samir Durg. He lacked the stamina he once had, and too much climbing and walking put such a strain on his back that he had to stop and rest before the day was done. Gyrmund, uncomplaining, would have to find food and make camp without his help. He became too exhausted to do the exercises Elana had insisted on, crawling under his blankets as soon as he had eaten supper.

The nights were bitter at such a height. Gyrmund and Moneva slept on either side of him. There was a tension between them, and they were avoiding lying next to one another. At first, it made him feel awkward to be stuck between them. But after a while, he was simply grateful for the warmth.

When he woke on a morning, his back had always seized up and he was virtually blind. He would reach out for the staff, panicking if it didn't come to hand immediately, until his fingers grasped the smooth wood. The feel of it as he gripped it in both hands would calm him and his back would loosen. The staff allowed his mind to feed information to his eyes, rebuilding a version of the world around him he could see and understand.

Then one morning, the staff didn't work so well. He could see, but his back and limbs remained stiff. A chill had entered his body, and neither breakfast nor the morning walk removed it. He didn't mention it at first, concentrating all his energy on moving without falling, using the staff to support himself.

The irony was they were leaving the mountains, descending to the grassy plain of the Jalakh Steppe. They would get the occasional glimpse of it now and then, when they ascended to the top of a peak. The grasslands stretched out forever, flat like a green ocean. At those moments it seemed deceptively close, and Soren would redouble his efforts, the end in sight. Then hours would pass without a sight of it, just bare rock and stunted trees all around them, and he would come close to despair.

As the sun fell on another day, Soren got warmer and warmer, trickles of sweat running down his body. He put his hand to his forehead. It was hot and clammy. A fever. He had to tell them. Gyrmund walked them on a bit farther until he found a suitable place to stop. He built a fire and made Soren a hot soup with the herbs and medicines he had to hand. Soren forced himself to drink it before giving in to sleep.

The next morning, he had to be woken up and lifted to his feet. His head pounded so much he felt sick. He leaned on his staff, drawing as much strength from it as he could. He knew they had to get down off the mountains.

That day and the next were lost days of delirium, half-remembered fragments, of Moneva helping him to walk, following a path that led them out of the high ground, of collapsing into the grass of the Jalakh Steppe. Gyrmund and Moneva talking to each other in hushed voices. They needed to find help, Moneva said. But there was no-one around, not a settlement, not a field or a wall or a single cow or sheep to show that anyone lived here. His fever needs to take its course, Gyrmund said. Soren let himself lean back into the grass. It supported his weight, just like he was floating on water. He let the grass carry him away, his broken body floating along to wherever the wind blew him.

The next memory he had was waking with a canvas roof above him instead of the sky. It felt like he was still floating, but how could he be with a roof above him? Then he realised that the movement was different. It was the slow, bumpy movement of a wheeled wagon. And Belwynn was there. How had she got there so fast?

Soren, can you hear me? She was saying. *Soren, where are you?*

He tried to reply, but all that came out was a croak. It was too difficult to talk, far easier to just close his eyes and let the wagon wheel him along.

He woke up, the memories playing in his head. He tried to clutch at them, tried to make sense of them, but they refused to be caught.

He scrabbled from one side to the next, desperately searching for his staff. There. He gripped it and his sight returned. He pushed himself up to a sitting position. He was alone in a circular felt tent. A round hole in the roof let in sunlight. It was a yurt. A Jalakh yurt. He looked down. His part of the yurt was covered in rugs and blankets and cushions.

He was weak, but it felt like his fever had broken. Gyrmund and Moneva had somehow found help. That was the second time they had saved his life.

Belwynn? he called, remembering hearing her voice, though whether he had only dreamt it he didn't know.

Soren? she replied immediately, her voice full of concern.

I'm safe, he said. *I fell ill. But I'm alright now. We've made it. We're with the Jalakhs.*

IN SHADOW

X

When Bolormaa had explained that all of the Jalakhs were travelling to Tosongat, Gyrmund had assumed that she was exaggerating. It appeared not.

The Oligud tribe who had picked them up and taken the feverish Soren in their wagon had merged with other tribes heading east, becoming a horde on the move. And when they had arrived, Gyrmund could see that other hordes had arrived from every direction on the Steppe. No longer a tribe or a single horde, a nation had come together in this one place.

Surely, this was the most likely location for the Jalakh Bow. But he had to be careful about revealing their intentions.

'Moneva and I would like to look around Tosongat,' he said to Bolormaa.

She looked at him appraisingly. She was wily, still handsome and strong, even though she was now a grandmother. She knew they were up to something, and yet she was the one who had taken them with the tribe, a decision that had probably saved Soren's life. Gyrmund couldn't help thinking that she was up to something, too.

'Now I see,' she said, 'you are here to witness the Great Contest.'

Gyrmund raised an eyebrow.

'We come here at this time every year that the Jalakhs need a new khan. The Great Contest decides which man will be khan.'

'The greatest fighter becomes khan?' he asked.

Bolormaa pursed her lips. 'That is the idea. The Contest began this morning. You and Moneva should watch it. But if you want to watch, you will need to dress appropriately. I will also send Gansukh with you.'

Bolormaa had Gyrmund and Moneva dressed in the traditional deels of her tribe. She advised them that each tribe had a distinctive cut or pattern of deel, so that the other Jalakhs could see which tribe Gyrmund and Moneva belonged with, affording them some protection.

Bolormaa's eldest son, Gansukh, led them through the camps of the various tribes, a maze of yurts that they would have got lost in themselves. Roaming freely about the place, in greater numbers than the Jalakhs themselves, were their horses. A totally different beast to the great warhorses bred by the Kalinthians, the Jalakh horse wasn't much larger than a pony, with shaggy hair. They were allowed to graze wherever they wished, but Gyrmund saw that when their owners whistled they came back, like obedient hounds.

Unlike his mother, Gansukh said little, grunting at them if he wanted their attention. He walked with a young man's swagger, letting all who looked his way know how highly he thought of himself. Gyrmund wondered whether Gansukh considered himself a candidate for the Great Contest.

Gansukh grunted and drew their attention to a large roped off area of short grass, around which many Jalakhs sat or stood. 'This is our Contest,' he said. 'You can watch with me.'

Gansukh led them to a space where they could see. The space inside the ropes was empty, but before long, a section of rope was untied. First one rider entered the area, then a second. They were introduced one at a time, their name and tribe called out, after which their supporters, who had gathered to watch, cheered and banged kettle drums. Both men wore scale armour and helmets, and were armed with scimitars, curved swords made for slashing.

Moneva turned to Gansukh. 'It's a fight to the death?' she asked.

He nodded. 'Yes.'

'But that's so wasteful.'

'Only those who truly believe they can win will fight. Otherwise, any man could enter the ropes and the Contest would never end.'

The two adversaries moved to either end of the ropes. There was a shout, and the fight began. Both men hurtled forward at incredible speed, their mounts strong and agile. Once they got within distance of each other, their horses sidestepped and they leant in, trying to land a strike while defending themselves and their mounts. The speed of their blade-work was impressive, doubly so when one considered they were using one hand to hold the reins, while constantly nudging their horses back and forth or to the sides, trying to manoeuvre an advantage for themselves, or lead their opponent into making a mistake.

The ring of steel on steel filled the air. Both men landed blows, but they hit the armour of their opponent, skidding off the scales to no apparent harm. They broke apart briefly, then moved back in, their swords a blur of frenetic slashes and blocks. Then one man scored a hit. He slashed at his opponent's hand and lower arm and his blade came back with a spurt of blood, the blow somehow penetrating armour. The fight continued, the injured man not done yet, even though Gyrmund could see a steady trickle of blood coming from his hand. Depending where the wound was exactly, it could make his grip more slippery.

Perhaps it was the injury driving him to take more risks, but the warrior drove in close, aiming a blow at his opponent's head. The second warrior's horse skipped aside at the last second, and he then found the space to land a strike on his opponent's mount. The poor creature collapsed, sending its rider skidding to the ground. Ruthlessly, the mounted warrior wasted no time. He rode in close, leaned over and cut down, twice, then three times, until the floored man was dead.

Staying on his mount, he raised his arm in the air, receiving the adulation of his tribe, who made a cacophonous noise. He left the roped area, before the members of the other tribe moved in to recover the body of their fallen champion.

'Both were good fighters,' commented Gansukh. 'But their riding was not so good.'

'What happens next?' Gyrmund asked.

'Next, a champion from another tribe will challenge the winner.'

'Would that be you?' Gyrmund asked with a smile.

'I will enter the ropes,' said Gansukh proudly. 'But Bolormaa will tell me when.'

'When does it end?' asked Moneva.

'It ends when there are no more challengers.'

Gyrmund and Moneva shared a brief look. No doubt this was a tradition that went back many generations, and had its uses, in binding the tribes together. Nonetheless, Gyrmund thought it a flawed system for choosing a leader.

'Is there anything else to see in Tosongat?' Moneva asked Gansukh. 'Except more yurts?'

Gansukh frowned, as if wishing to see anything further was greedy. 'Just our temple.'

'Temple?' asked Gyrmund.

'It is only for priests and royalty to visit.'

'Can we see where it is?'

Gansukh shrugged. 'Follow.'

He took them away from the ropes and away from the yurts. Here, in an area which the tribes had left empty, was the only permanent structure Gyrmund had seen. A large rectangular area was surrounded by wooden walls, only reaching the height of a man. Peering over, Gyrmund could see that inside was mostly open to the elements. On his side of the wall was a ceremonial garden, with developed trees, plants and a pond. He could see walkways had been constructed around the garden. Elsewhere within the walls, he could see one storey wooden buildings. He could hear rather than see animals: sheep, probably goats, were kept somewhere behind the walls. At the far end, it's protruding eaves visible in between the branches of the trees, was a pagoda. It was elaborately designed, with five small towers emerging at the top of the building.

Moneva peered over the wall, too. 'It's beautiful,' she said.

'Only priests and royalty are allowed in there,' Gansukh repeated.

Gyrmund and Moneva shared another look. Surely this was where the Jalakhs would choose to keep their Bow.

* * *

THEY FOUND SOREN, awake and alert, sitting up in the yurt belonging to Bolormaa. He listened, leaning back on his cushions and sipping at the drink he called kumis. Moneva remembered giving him the same drink in Samir Durg, when they had rescued him from the Tower of Diis. It had revived him then, and it looked to be doing so again—his face less pale, his eyes sharp and inquisitive.

'The question, then,' said the sorcerer, having digested their description of the Tosongat Temple, 'is whether we explain our need for the Bow, and ask the Jalakhs to give it to us. Or try to take it without their knowledge. Both approaches have their dangers.'

'Take it,' said Moneva instinctively. 'They're not going to hand over a precious relic to a group of outsiders. The Temple is barely defended. I can find the bow, take it without them realising it has gone.'

'I'm not so sure,' said Gyrmund. 'I would favour talking to Bolormaa. She may be able to help us.'

'Why would she?' countered Moneva.

They both looked at Soren, who seemed to have the deciding vote.

'If the Jalakhs had a leader, a khan with the authority to grant us the Bow, then I would take that option,' Soren said. 'But they don't. Who would we ask for it? Bolormaa is an impressive woman, but even if she helped us, how would she persuade all the other tribes to agree? I think, if we can take it undetected and leave, that is the better option. I could come and help, I'm feeling much better.'

'There's no need,' said Moneva, pleased at his decision. 'I just need Gyrmund to help me over the wall. There's no benefit to more than one of us moving about in there. It just raises the chances of getting caught.'

'Alright,' said Gyrmund, conceding defeat. 'When do we go?'

'Tonight,' said Moneva.

MONEVA AND GYRMUND crept through the fields of yurts, matching each other in the silence of their movements. The Jalakhs slept on, and if there were any still awake who heard a movement, they would put it down to a grazing horse, since each tribe had hundreds if not thousands of the animals moving freely in the area around their camp.

It was the first time they had been completely alone together in a long time. Her mind should have been completely focused on the job at hand, but once they moved out of earshot of the last group of yurts, Moneva stopped.

'Gyrmund,' she whispered.

He stopped immediately, looking about in case she had spotted trouble.

'I need to talk to you. About Samir Durg.' She took in a breath. She had to make herself keep going or she would never get it out. 'I had to sleep with Arioc. I'm sorry.' *Why was she apologising? That wasn't what she meant to say.* 'I mean, it affected me afterwards. When we got back to Heractus. I didn't deal with it very well.'

She paused. She had been thinking about what exactly to say to Gyrmund for several days now, and it had all come out a jumbled mess, anyway. She looked at him, but it was too dark to read his expression.

'I understand,' he said quietly. 'Moneva, I can never repay you for what you did in Samir Durg. You got all of us out of there, when we all thought we were dead. You're an amazing woman. Truly amazing. I'm sorry if I didn't support you properly.'

She heard his voice catch, and a lump came to her throat. Part of her said this conversation was stupid. But another part knew that it was important, and that they should have had it a long time ago.

'No,' she said. 'I didn't want to let anyone in. I wanted to deal with it myself. That's just what I'm used to.'

Gods, how pathetic, she told herself. Since her father had died—no, probably since her mother had died before that, she had been alone. She had learned to deal with things herself. It was better, safer, to be like that. But now, when she heard herself speak, she sounded like a bloody mess.

'I had a lot of time to think in Samir Durg,' Gyrmund said. 'I lost all my family when I was young. An illness—I was the only one who survived. I lived with Farred's family after that. I never spoke about it, no-one ever asked me about it. I got on with things, but I couldn't wait to leave. As soon as I was old enough, I went wandering around Dalriya, telling myself how free I was, what an exciting life of adventure I had. But part of that, a big part, was me running away from what happened. Being by myself, not having to care about anyone else, moving on before I put down roots anywhere, before I got close to anyone. In the mines, I realised that was wrong. I do want to be with someone, and that someone is you, Moneva. I promised myself I wouldn't give up, wouldn't take the easy option and walk away any more. So I'm always going to be here if you want me.'

Moneva moved into him, put her arms around him, and he did the same. She felt a tear rolling down her cheek. A simple hug—it felt so good, made her feel so much better. She needed to allow herself this. Be kinder to herself. If she had done this six months ago, she would have felt a lot better a lot sooner.

There, she was doing it again, telling herself off. Gyrmund said she was an amazing woman. Maybe it was about time she believed that and let someone else care about her.

They stood that way for a while before, reluctantly, she pulled away. 'That's enough of that nonsense,' she said. 'We've got a job to do.'

They made their way to the Temple, peering over the outer wall. There wasn't much to see—no lights, no sounds of activity, either.

'Alright,' she whispered.

Gyrmund bent at the knees and linked his hands together, forming a step. Moneva put one foot in. He stood up, and she pushed up with her foot, placing one hand on his shoulder to steady herself. She touched the top of the wooden wall. It was rough and sharp, so she removed a blanket she had tied around her waist and placed it on top of the wall. She placed her hands on the blanket. Fine. She looked over the top of the wall to the ground directly beneath it. Just grass. Confident, she took all her weight on her arms and vaulted over, landing securely inside the Temple.

If the Bow was stored here, it was almost certainly in the pagoda, on the other side of the complex. She walked through the garden, using the paths and being careful where she placed her feet. It was quiet. The only sound she could detect was animals moving about in the wooden sheds that lined the walls to her left and right. She found herself in the centre of the garden. All the paths seemed to meet here, though they clearly took their own individual meandering routes. Here, one gigantic tree stood, dominating the other vegetation in height. The larger branches that radiated out were themselves the size of trees. Moneva had the sense that it was ancient, probably predating the Temple itself, but beyond that she could discern nothing more, not even the species.

Moneva walked through to the end of the garden, approaching the pagoda. Here, it became clear that few, if any, people actually resided in the Temple. Outside the pagoda there were some small cells, nothing more than wooden shacks, so thin and tiny, each with a little individual door, that they could only fit in a bed for one person, with no room to stand. They didn't seem to be permanent living quarters, more like places to sleep while on a vigil of some kind. Jalakhs who were visiting for other reasons, Moneva considered, would almost always bring a yurt with them and have no need for accommodation.

She crept up to some of the cells, listening intently. She could detect breathing in at least two, but the idea that someone was sleeping in one of them next to the Jalakh Bow was a ridiculous one, so she moved on to the last and best option. The pagoda.

It was a pretty little building, full of fanciful curves where each tier of the building met the one above.

Moneva circled around the pagoda, checking for entry points. On the other side of the one she started from was a grand opening. Four pillars supported a roof, and this structure faced a gate in the outer wall, the main entrance into the complex. Moneva walked up a small set of steps and passed between the two middle pillars, moving under the roof. Two double doors faced her, the wood heavily decorated in geometric patterns. She approached the doors and, ever so carefully, pushed at one of them. The door gave, barely making a noise, and she slipped inside.

She hesitated briefly, but decided in the end to leave the door open. It was riskier, but allowed some moonlight into the ground floor of the pagoda. Even with this light it was still dark, and Moneva allowed her eyes to adjust for a little while. Around the wall were stairs with a railing, circling all the way to the top. A central pillar reached up. She could just make out thin planks of wood radiating out from the pillar above her, with lattice style flooring on top, making a second floor. She walked a full circle around the pillar, returning to where she entered. Four statues had been placed around the pillar. Looking closer, she could see they were identical representations of the same man. Flowers, presumably cut from the garden, had been placed next to each statue. It was hard to understand what she was looking at. She went down on her knees, touching the statue, feeling to the sides. But there were no other offerings but the flowers, and no sign of a bow or a place where a weapon might be kept or displayed.

Deciding not to waste any more time, Moneva took the stairs. She walked up to the next level. Tentatively, she placed a foot on the latticed wooden floor. It held her weight no problem. She moved over to the central pillar. Nothing, and the cobwebs she found told her all she needed to know. No-one ever came up here, except perhaps when the structure needed maintenance work on it.

Knowing she was wasting her time, but just to eliminate the chance, she explored all the way to the top of the pagoda. It was the same story. She had found nothing of any use, and if she stayed any longer, she was taking unnecessary risks. She moved quickly now: descending the stairs, then out of the pagoda, closing the door softly behind her. She retraced her steps, back into the garden, and through it to the outer wall she had climbed over. The blanket was still there.

'Gyrmund?' she hissed.

'Still here,' came his voice. 'I've got the blanket.'

Moneva reached up to grab the end of the blanket that hung over her side of the wall. With Gyrmund holding the other end, she used it to pull herself up, feet jammed against the wall until she could reach the top. She clambered over and landed on the other side, pulling the blanket with her.

'Well?' asked Gyrmund.

'Nothing. It's certainly not on display anywhere. There wasn't much to look at, to be honest. I'm fairly sure it's not there.'

'Well, we tried.'

'Still,' said Moneva, 'it wasn't a completely wasted trip.'

'How's that?'

Grinning, she pulled Gyrmund in, and they kissed, the passion of it taking her by surprise. At that moment, she didn't care very much about finding a stupid bow.

* * *

Siavash walked along the dimly lit corridor until he found the cell with the prisoner he wanted.

'This one,' he said.

The guard stepped forward and unlocked the door.

'Leave.'

'Yes, lord.'

Siavash entered the cell. He allowed himself a bitter smile. This was where he had kept Soren imprisoned, who had dared to challenge him, in the Throne Room of all places. He and Soren had unfinished business. But then, he conceded, without the Magnian's insurrection, Erkindrix would still be the Lord of Ishari and he would merely be a member of his Council. That way of looking at it meant that he owed Soren a favour. He would enjoy deciding what to do with him when he was caught and returned here.

He glanced briefly at the Haskan prisoner. He was unharmed, as Diis had commanded. The man, on his knees in chains, looked terrified. As well he might, Siavash allowed, though what exactly was going to happen here he didn't know. It was time to find out.

He called to Diis. Diis, who had chosen him above Arioc, above all the others. He would prove to his lord that He made the right choice.

Diis emerged, His face inside Siavash's face, His body inside his body. It took all of Siavash's strength to keep Him contained there, for he was a God, who should not be constrained to live inside a mortal's body. He would not need to for much longer. It made Siavash wonder about the hundreds of years during which Erkindrix had been a vessel for Diis, and he found he gained a new respect for his predecessor.

Diis looked about the cell, coal-black eyes finding his bearings. The prisoner whimpered and began rehearsing a prayer. But he prayed to some other god and Siavash knew that wouldn't help him.

What news do you have, demanded Diis, speaking inside Siavash's mind, not so very different to when Siavash spoke to Soren in this room.

We have completed the reconquest of Haskany and re-established control over Persala, Siavash informed him. *My reforms to the army are complete and each host is ready to be given their orders.*

He had defeated both Arioc and Pentas to secure complete control over the Isharites, the Drobax, and their dependent states. But he almost felt more pride in his reforms, that gave him greater personal control over the army than Erkindrix had ever had. Betrayals like those of Arioc and Pentas would now be a thing of the past.

But Arioc and Pentas are still at large, Diis bellowed in anger from somewhere inside him.

He whimpered, the prisoner staring at him in horror.

You are right, Siavash admitted. *With all my foolish pride, I have hidden those grave failings from myself.*

For each failing, you owe me a sacrifice, Siavash. You are stronger than Erkindrix was, and you can endure the punishment.

Yes, Siavash agreed. He would willingly make such a sacrifice.

Erkindrix and the Council made a great mistake. They underestimated the Krykkers and the Kalinthians. This allowed my enemy to use her weapons against me. We cannot afford further mistakes. Soon I will help you open a portal to my birth world and together we will bring forth a creature that will help us destroy the Krykkers. When I am in full control of this world, I will have the power to bring many such creatures here. But for now, one will suffice.

Siavash couldn't help but exult at the prospect. The destruction of the Krykker race would remove the last great obstacle to a complete conquest of Dalriya.

Now, I will take your first sacrifice.

Without warning, Siavash felt a horrendous, tearing pain engulf him. It was more than a physical pain. He could feel Diis, his claws sharper than diatine crystal, ripping at his very soul. He tried to withstand the pain, tried to maintain consciousness.

Then he saw something out of the corner of his eye. Something that had been hiding, almost fully obscured in the dark prison cell. He saw his shadow move without him, and with a last agonising tear, Diis completely severed it. Siavash turned in shocked disbelief to see his shadow slide around the wall of the room, free of him, moving of its own volition.

Your shadow, said Diis. *It can now do your bidding, allow you to move around Dalriya while your body stays here, safe from harm.*

Siavash was speechless. This was a thing of nightmares, a void of colour moving about the cell. And yet, when he concentrated on it with only a fraction of his powers, he saw that he could indeed move it. Control it.

But a shadow is useless without a body to inhabit.

Siavash understood. He drew his knife, strode over to the prisoner and grabbed him by the hair, yanking his head up.

Not the neck, said Diis.

Siavash did as commanded, plunging the blade with all his force into the middle of the prisoner's chest. The prisoner's scream was cut off when he withdrew the blade and he sagged down, unconscious. Blood poured from the injury.

It is better to make the injury somewhere it can be hidden, Diis explained.

Siavash began to appreciate the possibilities. If his shadow could control the corpses of his victims, it could pass unnoticed, hidden in plain sight.

He concentrated on his shadow. It approached the prisoner, and he forced it to enter, to reattach itself to a body, but this time a different one.

The prisoner's head jerked up.

'Release me from the chains,' hissed his shadow in a Haskan accent.

Siavash stared in shock. The Haskan soldier had returned to life in front of him, speaking again with his own voice. But he knew it to be nothing more than a reanimated corpse.

You will go to Kalinth, Diis commanded.

HALVIA

XI

Rabigar stood on the wharf, watching the tall ships of the Sea Caladri out on the shimmering turquoise of the ocean. It was a beautiful sight, one he didn't think he would ever see. But then, he hadn't expected to ever be back home amongst the Krykkers, and here he was.

One of the ships had furled its sails and was now heading in their direction. As it came nearer, he could see the oars on both sides moving up and down, propelling it towards them. Red eyes painted onto the sides of the ship glared at them, as if she was a sea serpent come to lay havoc to the coastline.

They waited as the ship was manoeuvred into position. With Rabigar were two chieftains: Maragin of clan Grendal, and Hakonin of clan Swarten. They were going to cross the Lantinen Sea to visit with their cousins, the Krykkers of Halvia. There had been no contact with them for a year, not since the Kharovians had defeated the Vismarian fleet and established an iron grip on the Lantinen. The pirates of Kharovia would not be pleased to see Caladri warships in what they had declared to be their waters.

But they were going to Halvia for a specific purpose, too. Szabolcs, the wise man of the Shadow Caladri, had identified Halvia as the location of the Giants' Spear, one of the missing weapons of Madria. The Giants, everyone seemed to agree, were long gone. The Krykkers of Halvia, therefore, were the first step in tracing the Spear's resting place.

If Maragin and Hakonin were going as representatives of the clans of Dalriya, then Rabigar was going as the holder of another of Madria's weapons, Bolivar's Sword. He touched the hilt of the weapon, scabbarded at his side. His ownership of the sword wasn't a popular choice amongst the Krykkers. No, it was downright unpopular. But he enjoyed a rather unique position amongst the Krykkers now—he was clan-less, exiled from the Grendals for killing Maragin's father, and never formally brought into a new one. Should any other Krykker claim the blade, they would be opposed by all the other clans, demanding to know why it wasn't going to them. No alternative claimant had come forward, and the longer it went on, the more secure Rabigar was. He had made it perfectly plain that he would not give up Bolivar's Sword. Not to anyone. And it would be a brave Krykker who dared take him on.

The Caladri ship was tied off, and the plank came down. Rabigar put one foot onto the wooden board. It flexed worryingly. He hated water and ships, didn't know many Krykkers who didn't. But it wasn't going to stop him. He took a breath and marched purposely up the plank. He grabbed an offered hand when he reached the top and stepped onto the deck.

He was surprised to see a familiar face amongst the crew. 'Farred?'

It was Gyrmund's friend—he had met him in Coldeberg. Quite what a Magnian was doing on a Caladri ship he didn't know.

'Hello Rabigar, good to see you again. This is the captain of the Red Serpent, Sebo.'

Rabigar and Sebo shook hands. He then introduced Maragin and Hakonin, who had made their way on board.

'Welcome aboard, all of you. It is an honour to have three Krykker lords sailing on my pride and joy, Red Serpent. Any questions or requests, please don't hesitate to ask. If you'll excuse me for a few minutes, I need to get her going, then I will come and speak with you some more.'

There followed an unpleasant lurching sensation as the ship cast off and the oars pulled it away from the wharf.

'Well, I wasn't expecting to see you here, Farred,' Rabigar said. He pointed at the Krykker countryside they were leaving. 'Don't know the last time a human was allowed to see this view. Clan Swarten's lands are something of a secret, eh Hakonin?'

'That's right,' said Hakonin. 'It suits us for others to think of all the Krykker lands as impregnable mountains. But my people's lands are the exception. Flat, and good for crops. We're called the breadbasket of the Krykkers. We used to trade with the Halvian Krykkers when the Vismarians controlled the sea. Now you know our secret, I'll have to kill you,' he smiled.

Farred laughed. 'Well, maybe you'll spare me if I exchange a secret?'

'Go on,' said Maragin. 'You have us intrigued now.'

'Well,' said Farred, looking more serious. 'I sailed with Sebo all the way from Mizky. He showed me the charts he used. Two of them have the same people marked at the same place, in the South Lantinen. The Asrai.'

Rabigar looked at Maragin and Hakonin. The two most obscure weapons mentioned by Szabolcs, the Spear and the Cloak. They were closer to finding them both.

Red Serpent joined up with the full Caladri fleet and they made a course for Halvia. The Sea Caladri weren't taking any risks, and they were right not to. Captain Sebo pointed out to the starboard side and Rabigar could just make out dark smudges on the horizon, in the direction of the island of Alta.

'They've seen us,' said Sebo calmly. 'They're following, at a safe distance.'

'Will you try to intercept them?' Rabigar asked.

'No. Our orders are clear on that. We have authority to defend ourselves, but we are not to seek out conflict. If they are merely watching, we will let them.'

'And what if the Kharovians are bringing all their ships to destroy you?'

'Then we will be ready for them.'

The Caladri ships cut through the waters of the Lantinen, pulled along by the powerful oars. The oarsmen worked in shifts, allowing small groups to rest and regain their strength. Farred took a turn on the oars, leaving the Krykkers to watch the coastline of Dalriya gradually disappear, before Sebo called their attention to the bow, where the Halvian coast was coming into view.

Hakonin joined Sebo, using the maps in his clan's possession to help find a port for the fleet. The coastline was rocky, as Krykker lands should be. But it meant that it was dangerous for such large ships to get close to shore, which they had to in order to identify the landmarks that would take them in the right direction.

Eventually, and with a minimum of fuss, Red Serpent led the Caladri fleet to an inlet. They sailed down the channel, steep cliffs on either side, before it opened into a wide bay. Here the waters were still, and while there were jagged rocks they needed to avoid, a large section of the bay was salt marsh that was safe enough to beach the fleet.

It took a while for all the ships to execute the manoeuvre, by which time a group of armed Krykkers had arrived, forming up on higher land that overlooked the marsh. What they made of a Caladri war fleet appearing in their bay, no-one could know for sure. Rabigar and his two companions walked off to meet them, keen to explain their appearance before the Halvian Krykkers decided they were hostile.

As they approached, they saw that a good two hundred Krykkers were arrayed in battle formation, fully armed. It was a relief, then, when Hakonin declared that he recognised the leader of the force as a clan chief.

'Crombec!' he shouted. 'I am Hakonin of clan Swarten, come from Dalriya. You knew my father well and you know me.'

One of the Halvians took a step forward from the front line. He ripped off his helmet, releasing a bush of grey hair, and squinted down at them.

'This is Maragin and Rabigar of clan Grendal,' Hakonin added into the silence.

'That's all very well,' Crombec shouted back at them, before gesturing down to the shoreline. 'But who the fuck are they?'

WITH A BIT OF WORK, Crombec was persuaded to stand down his troops, and instead lead the three Krykkers up into the mountains of his homeland. The Sea Caladri decided they could not stay in the bay, explaining that it left them too vulnerable to a Kharovian attack, who could seal the inlet and trap them inside. They would sail back to Hakonin's lands in Dalriya and return to Halvia in five days' time.

As they walked with the Halvian Krykkers, Rabigar and Maragin relayed to Crombec the recent events in Dalriya, and the significance of finding the seven weapons of Madria. When he learned that Rabigar was carrying Bolivar's Sword, he insisted on handling the weapon, eyes sparkling with joy as he gripped the hilt and squinted at the magnificence of the blade. Rabigar felt a flush of anger, a desperate desire to take the sword back, but he controlled himself, and Crombec reluctantly returned it to his keeping.

Not so very high up, they came to Crombec's hall. It was well positioned to get a view of the sea and Rabigar deciphered that coastal defence was the key role of his clan, the Pecinegs.

'I will call a Great Moot of the clans,' he told the three Krykkers. 'That is most likely to unearth any knowledge we may have of the whereabouts of the Giants' Spear. Our legends say that the Giants lived in the far west of Halvia. But that is too vague a starting point for an expedition, if that is your intention. It will also give us the chance to tell you what has been happening in Halvia in the past year. You may not be surprised to learn that we are facing problems of our own.'

. . .

RABIGAR, Maragin and Hakonin travelled with the Pecinegs to the site of the Halvian Great Moot. Unlike the Great Meeting Chamber of the Dalriyan Krykkers, an underground cavern carved into the mountain Kerejus, Crombec led them to an open-air building. It was circular, surrounded by high stone walls. The walls contained three arched entrances, one for each of the Halvian clans.

Clan Chief Crombec led the Pecinegs through their entrance. Steps led them up to a seating area that belonged to their clan. Crombec sat Rabigar and the others on the front row with him, while the rest of his Krykkers took their places on the tiered rows behind. In front of them was a platform, raised above ground level, where a speaker could address all the clans at once.

As the Pecinegs took their seats, a second clan filtered into the building. Crombec identified them as the Vamorins. He explained they manned the Western Walls, a series of towers that marked the Krykker border with the untamed western half of Halvia.

They waited until the third and final clan arrived. Finally, the thud of boots on steps could be heard, and the Binideqs appeared. Rabigar stared at this third group. There was something wrong.

'Humans!' Maragin hissed.

Mingling with the Binideq clan were human men and women. They took up a good third of the seats, between the Binideqs and the Vamorins.

'They are Vismarians,' Crombec explained. 'Refugees. Some of them have lived in our lands for two years now. We have given them a voice at the Moot.'

Rabigar shared a glance with Maragin and Hakonin. Such a thing would be unthinkable in Dalriya. It was a reminder that they were not in Dalriya anymore, and that the Halvian Krykkers, for all their shared ancestry, had led different lives since they had been separated by the Lantinen Sea.

Once everyone was ready, Crombec took the floor. He explained to the Moot why he had called it, introducing Rabigar and the others. Rabigar went next, explaining in more detail the events in Dalriya so that the Halvian Krykkers could understand why the search for the Giants' Spear was so important. He proudly held aloft Bolivar's Sword, letting the Halvian Krykkers see the weapon they had only heard stories about. He gave way to Wracken, chief of the Binideqs.

'Our guests have brought us news from Dalriya, which we were ignorant of, and for that, we give them thanks. Now they must know about events here in Halvia before we can proceed. They should know that the Drobax have become a mighty force on this continent, ferried across the Lantinen in huge numbers by the Kharovians. The Drobax have run amok in the north of Halvia, relentlessly attacking Vismarian settlements. This has been a war of destruction, with the massacring of whole communities. While the Krykkers have fought with our allies, it has not been enough to stop it. Most Vismarians now live here in our lands, contributing to our society with their skills. Those that remain beyond the River Drang are those that have found shelter in the most remote and hidden locations. The West of Halvia is a wild and unknown land. It is the Vismarians who have explored the western reaches in the past. They are the ones who will know the most about the Giants, if they are willing to share this knowledge with us. I therefore invite Sevald of the Vismarians to speak.'

As Wracken left the stage, this Sevald took his place. He was tall, strong, long-haired like all his people, and if he had any doubts about speaking at a Krykker Moot, they were well hidden.

'I once again take the opportunity to thank all the Krykker clans for their help to us in our time of need. To the Krykkers of Dalriya, my people say this: we understand you arrived here by Caladri ships. Please, the Kharovians outnumbered and overwhelmed our fleet. But we did not give it up. Here, and in other places, our ships are ready. Let us join with the Caladri to defeat the Kharovian menace that threatens both Dalriya and Halvia.'

He looked at them then. It wasn't desperate or pleading, but it was a look that demanded a response. Rabigar found himself nodding in agreement, even though he had no control over what the Sea Caladri did.

'As for this question of the Giants. Our stories say the Giants lived far to the west. Where exactly, and how to get there, none of us here knows. It is a dangerous land, which none of us have ventured very far into. There are Vismarians of an adventurous nature who have journeyed into the west. Nothing good has ever come of such expeditions. In particular...' Sevald paused. He looked reluctant to continue. 'There is a family whose home is in the north west. They claim to be descended from Giants. They are an eccentric group, even by Vismarian standards,' he said, allowing himself a smile. 'No-one has heard of them in months. They may have been killed by Drobax. The probability is that they have. But I am willing to lead a group back into Vismaria to try to locate them. If anyone can offer you a specific location, or route, it is them.'

. . .

THE MOOT CONTINUED until everyone who wished to had their say, but no more progress could be made. They had succeeded in getting the support of the Halvian Krykkers and of their allies, the Vismarians. But the more they had learned, the more the recovery of the Spear sounded like a challenging and problematic task.

It was time to return home. Crombec took them back to the bay where they had arrived for the rendezvous with the Caladri fleet. The ships were already there. The whole fleet had made the passage, testament to their concerns about a Kharovian attack. Bidding Crombec farewell, they spotted Red Serpent and made for Captain Sebo's ship.

They were welcomed aboard. Farred had made the journey again, though he and Sebo both wore grave faces.

'What is it?' asked Rabigar, sensing they had news to tell.

'The Isharites have invaded the lands of the Grand Caladri,' said Farred. 'The Caladri who had resettled their lands were forced to retreat all the way back into the Krykker mountains.'

'We had expected the Isharites to return, possibly to move against us,' said Maragin grimly. 'We must prepare to defend against them.'

'There's something else,' said Sebo. 'The Caladri who escaped say the Isharites had a monster with them.' He exchanged a worried look with Farred. 'They say they had a dragon.'

* * *

STRATON AND AMPELIOS travelled under armed guard in one of the supply wagons as the army made its way back to Heractus. Diodorus and his soldiers left to return to his estates, while the rest of the army began the return journey to Heractus, making a camp in the open a day's march from the capital.

The mood was low. Theron and Sebastian had ensured they remained in control of Kalinth, but it had been an empty victory; an unnecessary loss of life. Theron was drained, physically and emotionally, and went to sleep as soon as he got the chance. So Belwynn sought out Clarin. She had barely spent any time with him since he had returned from Samir Durg.

She found him sitting with the rest of the escaped prisoners of Samir Durg outside their tents. With no need to worry about enemy scouts any more, the soldiers were building their fires high to keep off the night chill, and drinking up the last of the ale and wine in the army's supplies.

Clarin and his friends were no different, but in other ways, they stood out.

They were an intimidating looking group, scarred men with grim, thin faces. Then there were the two Dog-men, former servants of Ishari, who had become Clarin's loyal hounds. With their powerful protruding jaws and their clawed hands, they had a monstrous appearance in the flickering light of the flames. These were Clarin's people now. They had all changed since they had left Magnia nearly a year ago. Belwynn knew that. But she felt Clarin had changed more than most.

He saw her standing a few feet from the fire and hastily got to his feet. He came striding over, his long legs making up the distance in no time.

'Hello Belwynn,' he said. She could smell the alcohol on his breath. 'Would you like a place by the fire?'

'I'm fine. I just wanted to say hello. I feel rude, like I have been ignoring you. But we've all been so busy the last week. I've good news, too. Soren spoke to me from the Jalakh Steppe. He got ill on the journey there, but he says he's recovered now.'

'That's a relief. I'm glad you came, Belwynn. I've been wanting to talk to you. How about we take a walk to keep warm?'

They strolled slowly around the camp, the fires of the soldiers lighting their way in the darkness.

'Sebastian told me you broke through the enemy line. You've really won his respect. He said they needed men like you. You could have a place here in Kalinth if you want. A valued place.'

Clarin gave a nod. He seemed unimpressed with the compliment and the offer. No doubt he had other things on his mind.

'I know how hard it is for you,' she said. 'With Herin. I had the same thing when Soren was captured. It was the not knowing that was the worst part.'

'Yes,' he said. 'It's not easy. That's not what I wanted to talk to you about, though.' He paused, thinking, as if trying to choose his words carefully. 'When I was a prisoner in Samir Durg, I faced the very real possibility that my life would end there. We all did. It makes you think about your life—makes you look at yourself. I asked myself, if I was ever going to get out, what did I want from life? And the answer was you, Belwynn.'

They both stopped walking. Belwynn felt taken by surprise, hadn't seen this coming. She didn't know what to say, just stood there gaping at him.

'I love you,' he continued into the silence. 'I always have, but I was too young and stupid to do anything about it before. But I'm not that man anymore. I want you, Belwynn. I want to make a life with you.'

'Clarin, this is so sudden. I didn't know. It's difficult, I—'

'Theron?' he asked, his mouth forming a sneer when he said the name. 'I've seen how you look at him. But I don't trust him. And he doesn't know you like I do, doesn't love you like I do.'

'Clarin, stop. Stop for a second. I can't think.'

He grabbed her arm in his hand, holding it tight. 'I don't want you to think, Belwynn. Gods, I need you. I need you to say yes.'

He was scaring her now. *How much had he had to drink? How much of this was his emotions from Samir Durg, repressed for so long, now pouring out?*

'Let go of me, Clarin,' she said.

'Sorry,' he said, letting go immediately and looking ashamed.

What do you want from me, she wanted to say, feeling angry. *Why now? When it's too late? If you had said this sooner. If you had arrived in Kalinth even a day earlier, and said all this, I might never have gone to Theron's bedroom. But you didn't, and I did.* But she wouldn't say any of that, because it would only make things worse.

'Clarin, I'm glad that you've told me. But you must understand, I wasn't expecting it. You need to give me some time.'

He nodded, a mournful look on his face. 'Yes. I'm sorry. It didn't come out right.' He sighed. 'I'm a clumsy fool.'

'Come on,' she said. 'Walk me back to my tent.'

WHEN THEY RETURNED TO HERACTUS, Belwynn and Elana made straight for the Temple of Madria. Elana had to speak to her flock, who needed to be told about the outcome of the battle. The Church of Madria was busy, especially so after Elana's deal with Sebastian that it should be the only recognised Church in Kalinth. They had already taken over all the religious buildings in the capital. Now they had plans to expand into the local settlements and to the larger towns.

Belwynn was keen to spend some time with Lyssa, and escape from the business of war and politics. The girl had been looked after at Elana's Temple while Belwynn was on campaign, her time filled with chores, and she was happy enough. Belwynn had begun to teach her some basic reading and writing skills, for she was completely illiterate. It was a struggle. She didn't really show much interest in it. Belwynn wondered what to do with Lyssa. Other children her age were already learning a trade. Was that best for her? Should Lyssa be treated as Belwynn's own daughter? And what kind of life would that lead to? *Because what am I, exactly?* she asked herself. *Apart from the Lady of the Knights?*

Lyssa was a town girl, and Belwynn resolved to teach her something of country life. They spent a pleasant afternoon on a walk, just the two of them. Lyssa was captivated by everything, from a gurgling stream to a patch of wild flowers, from the birds signing in the trees to frogspawn in a pond. She talked nonstop, and they both felt disappointed when it was time to return to Heractus.

It was remarkable how easily and completely she had withdrawn into this little world, and so it was a jolt to find Clarin pacing about outside the Temple upon their return.

'Do you know what he's doing?' demanded the warrior.

'What? Who?'

'Come see.'

'Alright Clarin, but let me see to Lyssa first.'

She entered the Temple and made sure that Lyssa was suitably supervised before returning outside.

He led her into the city centre. A crowd had gathered, and Clarin had to take her closer before she could see why. A man knelt there, hands tied behind him. He shivered, face pale.

'Who is it?' she asked.

'Count Ampelios, the nobleman who surrendered to Theron in the battle. They're killing him anyway.'

Theron approached the crowd.

'No, Theron,' she whispered under her breath. 'Why do you have to carry out every unpopular task?'

'Count Ampelios, you have been convicted by the royal council of treason. Your sentence is death.'

An executioner approached, holding a large two-handed sword. Belwynn didn't recognise him. She was sure he wasn't a knight. If he was an official executioner, it looked a little better than the Knights doing it themselves.

He didn't waste any time, and he did it well. While Ampelios was still kneeling, he launched a massive swing of the blade, which cut the head clean off the shoulders. Belwynn turned away at that point, and many in the crowd screamed and cried out.

She looked up.

Clarin was looking at her. 'Is that justice?' he hissed.

What did he want from her? It was horrible. Did that make it wrong? She wasn't sure what she thought.

'Don't pretend there are easy answers, Clarin,' she said. 'Leniency and gentility allowed Straton and Ampelios to escape and look where that got us. A bloody battle with hundreds of deaths. I don't want that to happen again.'

'Treason?' Clarin said, pursuing the issue. 'He was imprisoned here when the Knights took the capital by force. He escapes and fights for the heir to the throne, and that's called treason? I know treason when I see it, and I'd use that word for someone else.'

Belwynn looked around them. 'Be careful what you say, Clarin, for Madria's sake.'

'Or else I'll have *my* head cut off? I don't understand, Belwynn. What has happened to you that you defend him like this? Why are you here, when Soren and the others are away looking for Madria's weapons?'

'Is that what this is, Clarin?' she retorted, hearing her voice rise with anger and trying to control it. 'Attack Theron, so that I will fall in love with you instead? It doesn't work like that.'

He looked at her, a stunned expression on his face. 'I think I'll go,' he muttered, sounding defeated. 'If this doesn't open your eyes, nothing will.'

'I think that's best.'

She watched him go for a while, then walked away herself, keen to get as far away from the scene as possible. Before she realised where she was going, she found herself walking up to the gates of Heractus Castle. The guards let her in and she took the familiar route up the tower steps to Theron's room.

She knocked on the door.

There was a rustle, and he opened it. He stared at her, a haunted look in his eyes.

'I saw,' she said simply.

'Oh,' he said quietly. 'I didn't want you to see that.'

He walked over to his bed, wearily taking a seat. 'I'm sorry. You may hate me for it. But if we didn't do that, demonstrate the consequences of rebellion, it would never stop. An endless civil war where we tear ourselves apart, with the Isharites waiting to finish us off.'

Belwynn took a seat next to him. 'I know all about civil wars,' she said.

He looked at her. It was a look of raw gratitude. 'Thank you. For understanding. I never want to do that again.'

He flopped down, putting his head in her lap.

She stroked his hair, looking down at her knight.

You would, though, she said to herself. *If you had to, you would do it again.*

JOINED

XII

High-priest Wulfgar of the Temple of Toric would not have been Edgar's first choice to conduct his wedding. But he was the leading prelate of South Magnia. He wasn't the most spiritual of men either, but there was some benefit to that. He had kept the ceremony mercifully brief and to the point. After exchanging rings, and sharing a kiss, Edgar and Elfled could turn to face the congregation in the Temple as man and wife.

Applause and cheers met them. On one side of the circular central chamber sat the South Magnians. Edgar's best man, Wilchard, grinned over. Leading noblemen such as Otha of Rystham and Aescmar occupied the front rows with their families. Behind them, those less titled such as Oslac, mayor of Halsham, and Ulf the smith had been found room. On the opposite side of the room, the front row was occupied by Elfled's family. Her brother Cerdda, Prince of North Magnia, with his wife Irmgard. Their mother, Mette, had also made the trip. Behind them, foreign dignitaries from as far as the Brasingian Empire had come to witness the union.

For it was a love match, Edgar was sure of that. But it was also, he knew, political. The rival families of Magnia were uniting. And, should Cerdda's marriage remain childless, any children that Elfled gave him might one day lay claim to both parts of Magnia.

He shared a look with his new wife, her dark ringlets of hair spilling over her white dress, and he knew he had never been this happy. But he also took a moment to acknowledge those who were not here. His father, Edric, dead these four years, whose statesmanship had paved the way for this marriage. His mother, too frail in body and mind to make the journey. Ealdnoth, his trusted adviser, and Leofwin, his rock of a bodyguard, both killed in Barissia by the bastard Salvinus. The same man who had dared to invade Edgar's realm and desecrate this very temple. No. He would think no more of him today.

Holding hands, Edgar and Elfled led the congregation out into the large temple complex. Toric had blessed the day with bright spring sunshine. They all gathered outside, everyone keen to have a word with Edgar and Elfled before they were called into Wulfgar's hall for the feast.

First was Coen, Duke of Thesse, not the kind of man to wait politely for his turn. With him was Frayne, the Midder chief who had fought with them against the Barissians. Edgar introduced them both to Elfled.

'Ah!' she said. 'The heroes of Lindhafen! I have to thank you for keeping my husband alive last year! I would love to hear all about the campaign. Edgar never talks about it.'

Both men beamed at the prospect of recounting their war stories. Elfled was very good at all this; much better than he was. Edgar detached himself and located Walter, the new Duke of Barissia, who was standing with Russell, a soldier from Morbaine, who was here on behalf of Duke Bastien.

'Congratulations,' both men said as he approached, before they each shook his hand.

'Your new wife is stunning.'

'Thank you, Lord Russell.'

'You didn't stand a chance,' Walter added.

Edgar laughed, turning to Russell. 'I wonder when the new Duke of Barissia will be caught? Surely the most eligible man in the Empire?'

Walter made a horrified face.

'Ha, you look just like Farred when I mentioned the idea to him.'

'Where is he?' asked Walter. 'I had been hoping to see him here.'

'He's too much of an adventurer to stay here, I'm sorry to say. He travelled with the Sea Caladri fleet north.'

'I see. I hope he finds success. Freeing the Lantinen would be a welcome development.'

'Couldn't agree more,' said Russell. 'The Kharovians are a menace to all of us.'

'How is Duke Bastien?' Edgar asked Russell.

'Bastien sends his apologies. The duchess is very close to her due date, and he wants to be there for her.'

'Of course. Please pass on mine and Elfled's best wishes. And,' he said, turning to Walter, 'I must ask about news from the north.'

'Bad news, I am afraid. We know Siavash has won control over the Isharites. We had let ourselves hope that a civil war might occupy the enemy for some time. Gustav reports that a great battle took place in Haskany. The Haskans were defeated, Queen Shira killed. Arioc's army was defeated there too, though he may have escaped. Siavash has restored Haskany and Persala to his empire. It can only be a matter of time before the Drobax are sent south again. They may be sent to Kalinth, or to the Krykkers. But we must prepare for the monsters to return to Brasingia. As we speak, my men are getting Burkhard Castle ready in case we must defend it again.'

Edgar nodded solemnly. He had to ask, though the answer couldn't help but sour his mood. The silence after Walter had spoken hung around him, urging him to offer his aid in the coming conflict. But he wasn't going to do that. Magnians had shed enough blood in the Empire last year. They had helped to defend Burkhard Castle, and they had helped to defeat Emeric. Baldwin now had a united realm with which to withstand the Isharites. This time, Walter and Coen could lead the Barissians and Thessians north should the need arise. Surely that would be enough to withstand the new Lord of Ishari?

* * *

SIAVASH'S SHADOW, occupying the body of the dead Haskan, had climbed into a wagon, been given a guard of elite mounted Isharite soldiers, and driven south-west towards Kalinth.

The journey gave Siavash a chance to get used to the experience. When he slept, his shadow lay unmoving—but not asleep, for shadows didn't know sleep. If a noise or movement alerted it, Siavash would wake, full of confusion, until he realised what was happening. When awake, he tried to get used to managing his own affairs while controlling the shadow's movements at the same time. Gradually, he became able to control both bodies, so long as neither required too much effort. When a job required his full attention, the shadow was left to slump on the floor of the wagon. After experimenting in such a way, he realised that once the shadow was active in Kalinth, he would be forced to stay in his rooms so that he could properly concentrate on its mission. It was a frustration, but would perhaps be worth it once the shadow got to work.

The wagon reached Masada, the fortress that the Kalinthians and

Krykkers had taken the previous summer. It had been reinforced and was now fully garrisoned by Haskans. A servant of Diis named Harith was also stationed here. He reported to Siavash alone, and his presence helped to ensure the loyalty of the Haskan soldiers. Siavash was delivered to him, with written instructions. The Isharite broke the seal, looking from the words on the parchment to Siavash and back again, until his eyes widened.

'My Lord,' he stuttered, getting to his knees. 'It will be an honour to serve you.'

'Your service will be remembered,' said Siavash, speaking in a stranger's voice, the voice of the dead man he inhabited. 'Now, waste no time.'

None was wasted. Two horses were saddled immediately. They rode south, crossing the border into Kalinth. They had to be careful now, since this area would be patrolled by Kalinthian Knights.

Siavash, his real body all the way in Samir Durg, decided it was best to sleep for the rest of the day and move again at night. His Haskan body was left to lie on the hard ground, eyes open and staring. Before sleep took him, he caught Harith glancing at the living corpse in horror.

THAT NIGHT they moved through the Kalinthian countryside, looking for a victim. Harith argued that the isolated farmsteads were less favourable, since their inhabitants were more alert to danger. The small villages, where many families gathered together, gave them a false sense of security. Siavash accepted this and waited on the outskirts of such a village as Harith approached a house.

Harith climbed onto the roof, where he pulled out an area of thatch before dropping inside. Time passed and Siavash heard nothing, waiting patiently.

Harith emerged from around the corner of the house, obviously having exited from the door. He was walking backwards, dragging a body behind him. When he reached Siavash, he let it drop to the ground. Siavash could see that it was a young man, not yet fully grown into his body. As instructed, the wound was in the chest, and could be easily hidden.

Siavash concentrated, forcing his shadow to leave the body of the Haskan. His shadow resisted. But it had already been detached once before, and this time it left more easily. Willing to find a new home, Siavash was able to insert it into the new body. He stretched, flexed his hands, moved his limbs, before standing up.

Harith was staring at him, jaw wide open in awe.

'You have done well,' said Siavash. 'I will continue alone now. Show me the way.'

Harith nodded, visibly reasserting control over himself. He pointed in the direction to be taken.

Siavash wasted no more time and began walking. It would be wise to leave the vicinity of the village as soon as possible.

He turned at a noise. Harith was riding away, back to Masada, holding the reins of the second horse. Siavash could just make out the dark shadow of the Haskan soldier that had been left on the ground. He turned back and resumed his journey.

SIAVASH WALKED THROUGH THE NIGHT. As the sun began to rise, he found a secluded spot to lay his new body down in so that he could sleep. He awoke at midday and resumed his journey.

He came upon a road, which suggested that he was going in the right direction. Making his shadow follow the road was easy. It needed no food or water or rest. He passed some travellers going the other way. They mostly called out a greeting, to which he responded in kind, never stopping to talk further and risk arousing suspicions.

In the middle of the afternoon, he heard the clip clop sound of a horse and cart from behind. He moved to the side of the road to let it pass. The driver stopped the cart.

'Ayup, young man,' the driver called out. 'Where to?'

'I'm going to Heractus,' Siavash replied. Where else would he be going?

He could see the driver looking him up and down, especially his lower half. What is he looking at? Siavash wondered.

He looked down and saw that his shoes and the bottom half of his trousers were caked in mud. He had to be more careful about his appearance if he wanted to avoid attention.

'I was walking during the night,' he said.

Perhaps that would satisfy the man's curiosity. If not, he would kill him.

The man grinned. 'Hop in the back.'

Siavash looked at him blankly, before turning to look at the cart. It had four big wheels with a wooden box made of rough planks of wood.

'Thank you,' he said to the driver. He placed one foot on a spoke of the rear wheel and then clambered over the side into the box. He moved aside some bags of grain and vegetables to make himself a space and sat down, before banging on the side of the box.

The Kalinthian farmer called out to his horse, and the cart rumbled onwards.

THE FARMER WAS WAVED in through the gates of Heractus. Siavash, ensconced in the back of the cart, wasn't asked a single question. It wasn't just the security that was lax; the walls and defences of the city were ludicrously weak. If the Drobax were sent here, the Kalinthians would be crushed. But Siavash intended to break them without the need to waste an army on the task.

He familiarised himself with the layout of the city first. He knew much about his targets already. He knew that pliable King Jonas had been replaced with a more stiff-spined regime, who had dared to invade Haskany. He knew all about Soren's group, of course: his sister; Madria's priestess; and the others. They had been busy on Madria's behalf, collecting her weapons, engineering the death of Erkindrix, all the while protected by the treacherous Pentas. They were in league with the Kalinthians and Siavash knew they might still be here.

He located the castle, and determined that was where the political leadership governed from. He located Madria's Temple, where her priestess and the rest of her followers worshipped. These were his targets. And in a city where he seemed free to go where he wished, it dawned on him how impossibly easy this was going to be.

When he saw the woman and the girl, a thrill ran through his body. He knew her. She had been in the Throne Room of Samir Durg, with Pentas. He followed them as they walked from the castle down into the city centre. He decided to speed up and walk past them, taking a surreptitious look. He reassured himself that she couldn't recognise him, because he wore the face of an unknown Kalinthian man.

There was no doubting the resemblance. This was Soren's sister, an individual he had wrested from the Magnian's mind during his imprisonment in the Tower of Diis. He remembered Rostam striking her to the floor in the Throne Room. It was the one victory that worthless man had ever enjoyed, may Diis take revenge on his pathetic soul.

She had obviously recovered from that episode. If she was here, then it was more than likely Soren was, too. Siavash exulted at the possibilities. He could take her body and kill Soren with it. And what of the girl, presumably her daughter? A small body such as hers could make a very useful assassin, perhaps. No-one would suspect her.

He stopped walking and then turned, waiting for her to approach. But she had stopped to talk with a man. He was powerfully built, doubtless a warrior, perhaps a leader here. Siavash edged closer to listen.

'It's a strange logic, I admit,' the man was saying. 'But with the Isharites having regained complete control of Persala, Zared believes this is the best time to return to his homeland. Their armies will be moving elsewhere. He thinks if I go with him, I have a good chance of finding it.'

'If you trust him, Clarin.'

'I do.'

'It's just, wouldn't it be better to wait for Soren?'

So, Soren isn't here. Where have you gone, Soren, I wonder?

'Zared thinks that he and the other Persaleians will have contacts there who can help me. The Persaleians might trust me when otherwise they wouldn't. It honestly feels like the best chance to get the Shield now, before it's too late.'

I see, Siavash said to himself as realisation dawned. *They are after the Shield of Persala. A very useful conversation to have stumbled onto. This soldier will find he won't be the only one looking for it.*

'I just wish we were parting on better terms,' said the man she had called Clarin. 'I'm sorry about the way I've acted—'

Suddenly, the man stopped speaking and swung around to look straight at Siavash. 'Can I help you, son?' he said, an angry frown appearing.

'Er, no. Sorry.'

Siavash turned away, flustered. So stupid to have been caught out like that! He walked away towards the centre of town, feeling their eyes on his back as he went.

They know this face now, he berated himself. *I can't let them catch me out a second time. I must get a new one.*

TO THE ROCK

XIII

Gyrmund stood outside the walls of the Jalakh Temple again, this time waiting for both Moneva and Soren to return. The wizard had insisted on looking inside, in case he could interpret what Moneva had seen differently and find some clues, if not the bow itself. If he didn't, they were stuck for ideas.

He heard a whisper from Moneva and moved over to the blanket that hung over the top of the wall. As he did, he saw Soren's head emerging on the other side of the wall. Soren kept on rising, revealing his shoulders, chest and legs, all the while maintaining a perfectly straight face. He floated right over the wall and then down next to Gyrmund. Gyrmund shook his head, grabbing his side of the blanket and telling Moneva to climb over. He had seen Soren do many things he had not thought possible, and he had never got used to it.

'Well?' he asked when Moneva had made her own way over the wall.

'Nothing, really,' said Soren. 'Moneva is perfectly correct. It's not there. Which means it may well not be in Tosongat at all. It could be kept by a particular tribe... We need to think carefully about our next move before we do anything else.'

Next morning Gyrmund awoke early. He left the yurt he shared with Moneva and Soren. He stretched, wondering what to do with himself.

Some of the Oligud warriors had allowed him to join in with their archery training yesterday, and he was pleased to have demonstrated enough skill that they had invited him back today. The composite bows, the weapon the Jalakhs were famous for, were not much different from his own longbow to use. However, he would never possess the skill of the Jalakhs, who were taught to ride and shoot from a young age. Gyrmund was content with staying on his feet.

He spied Bolormaa, sat around a fire with a group of Oligud women. He edged over. He knew that Soren and Moneva were not keen on involving her in the search for the Jalakh Bow. But maybe, if he was careful, he could find something out.

'Come!' she called over to him.

He sat down next to her. On the fire was a pot of Jalakh tea and, without asking him, Bolormaa scooped a cup into it and handed it to Gyrmund. He thanked her, though that was out of politeness. It was very milky, salty rather than sweet, and Gyrmund had not acquired a taste for it. The women were preparing meat, which would be tossed into the tea later on for the midday meal.

'How long until the Great Contest is done?' he asked her, sipping at his drink.

'No-one knows for sure. A champion must last for seven days to become khan. If there is no champion, the Contest finishes at the end of this month. That's in twelve days.'

Gyrmund thought about this. 'So, a champion wins a bout. He is then challenged the next day, and the day after, and so on, for seven days? He will get tired, pick up injuries, while each day he faces a fresh warrior?'

'Just so.'

'Then it is almost impossible to become khan. That is why you have told Gansukh to wait until late on to enter the Contest? That is his best chance.'

'Yes. But many will adopt such a strategy. It is still virtually impossible to last for seven days. Then, as I say, the tribes return to their lands until next year.'

Gyrmund thought some more. 'When was the last time the Jalakhs had a khan?'

'Over sixty years ago.'

Sixty years since the Jalakhs had a ruler? This was a strange people. 'Surely people can't be happy with this system?'

Bolormaa turned towards him. 'I am not very happy, Gyrmund, but some people are. With no khan, the tribal leaders have no authority above themselves. With no khan, there are no wars to fight. Many tribes like things exactly the way they are. And if Gansukh were to win two or three bouts, these tribes will send their best warriors in against him, until one of them cuts him down.'

'Then why is he entering the contest?'

'Because,' she said fiercely, 'Gansukh wishes to be khan!'

Clearly, it wasn't only Gansukh who wished it. His mother did, too. A thought crossed Gyrmund's mind. 'Did Gansukh's father enter the Contest?' he asked.

'He fell on day five.' She said it in a matter-of-fact way, but he could feel the pride and fury that she tried to hide.

Gyrmund sipped on his tea, thinking so hard that he didn't even notice the taste. 'We could help him,' he suggested, quietening his voice so that only she could hear.

Bolormaa's eyes locked on to his with an intense look. 'And what,' she asked slowly, 'would you want in return?'

Here it was. Their opportunity to get help, or the moment the Jalakhs turned on them. Gyrmund looked back to the yurt, but Soren and Moneva were still asleep. It was his call.

'We want the Jalakh Bow.'

She cackled then, a sound of surprise and genuine mirth. 'You don't want much, then.'

'Is it here? In Tosongat?'

'Is it here?' she repeated his question, a sly look on her face. 'In a manner of speaking, yes.'

'Could you get it for us?'

Bolormaa's humour faded away, replaced by a deadly serious look. 'If you help Gansukh become khan, he will give you the Jalakh Bow. This is the only chance you will have of getting it, I should add. So. Do we have a deal?'

Bolormaa offered her hand. Hesitating only briefly, Gyrmund reached out, and they shook. She broke out into a big smile. 'Wonderful!' she cried. She grabbed his head in both hands, pulling him in. At first Gyrmund thought she was going to land a kiss, but instead she pulled his head down and sniffed the top of it before letting him go.

'You haven't asked me why we want the bow,' he noted.

'The Jalakh Steppe is remote, yes,' Bolormaa said. 'But remember, we are neighbours of the Isharites. I am not ignorant of what they are. The Jalakhs need a khan now, more than ever. And those who oppose Diis need weapons to do so.'

Gyrmund nodded. 'I think I may have underestimated you, Bolormaa.'

She flashed him a smile. 'You are very wise, Gyrmund. One thing. You must never speak to Gansukh of our deal. He is a very proud man.'

Gyrmund nodded. No doubt khans didn't like it said that their mothers helped them get the job. He looked over at his yurt again. There were a couple of people he *should* tell about this deal. He just hoped they would understand.

* * *

SOREN WATCHED Gansukh ride into the roped off arena. The Jalakh approached the area where Soren was seated, surrounded by the members of the Oligud tribe, and raised his sword. The Oligud screamed and cheered, banging drums so loudly the noise reverberated around his skull. It hardly made his mood any better, and he stared balefully at Gyrmund, who was clearly responsible for all of this, while Gyrmund studiously avoided making eye contact.

Gansukh's opponent was already there, eliciting a similar response from his own supporters, the Yahmet tribe. He had already won two bouts and was considered a tough first opponent for Gansukh.

The shout went out and the two warriors went for each other, blades whirling at incredible speeds, horses agile and clever, seeming to understand what their riders wanted them to do.

Soren felt the nudge of power buffeting Gansukh's horse, trying to disrupt his sword arm. Soren pressed back, protecting Gansukh from the attacks. The two warriors continued to fight, trying to find an opening in each other's defences, too focused to be aware of this secondary contest. They were evenly matched. It seemed wrong, somehow, to interfere in this fight. But if this was truly the only way to get the bow, he had to do it.

Soren went on the offensive, weakening the strength of the other warrior's blows, reducing their speed. The Yahmet wizard, whoever they were, reacted violently, pushing back with force. But now a third force entered the fray. It began to work with Soren. If Soren defended the Yahmet attack, they went on the offensive. If Soren tried to impair the Yahmet warrior, this third power focused on defending Gansukh.

Then, suddenly, it was all over. Gansukh launched a flurry of strikes and his opponent was too slow to counter them. The first landed, then a second, then a third rattled through the slit in the helmet, the blade crunching through bone into brain, killing the Yahmet warrior instantly.

Gansukh celebrated his victory, and the Oliguds cheered wildly for their hero.

Soren looked about. Somewhere among this group, the Oligud had a magic user of their own.

Bolormaa approached him, a sly smile on her face.

And then it clicked.

'Oh, I see,' he said, as she sat next to him.

'Well done, Soren,' she replied. 'I knew your life was worth saving. Now, all we need to do is keep my son alive for seven days.'

* * *

It was a strained journey across the Lantinen Sea. They all wanted to get back as quickly as possible, and fears about what was happening in Dalriya made people anxious and short-tempered. Maragin and Hakonin perhaps felt it the most, since they were absent when their clans needed their leadership.

Kharovian ships could be seen to the north, tracking their movements, still not making a move of their own. Their presence added to the tension on board, and Rabigar let out a sigh of relief when he saw the Krykker coast come into view.

When they had docked, they immediately went their separate ways. Farred left for the south, travelling to the lands of men to warn them of the new threat. Hakonin remained, to guard the coast from the Kharovian threat. Maragin and Rabigar took half of Hakonin's Swarten soldiers and headed east, to the border threatened by the Isharites. They would pick up her soldiers from the Grendal clan on the way. They had to hope that when they got there, the border was still intact.

Before they reached the border, they met a defeated army coming the other way. The first few soldiers could be seen emerging from the tree-line ahead of them, and the two forces came together in a rock-strewn mountain clearing. The retreat seemed orderly enough, but Rabigar could see the panic in Krykker eyes and the relief at seeing Maragin with her Grendals.

'I need to speak with the leaders. Gather them here!' she shouted.

The troops under Maragin's command were ordered to help carry the supplies, and the wounded. Keeping the Krykkers moving was essential, because it wasn't clear how far behind the enemy were.

It was a sorry looking group that appeared to speak with Maragin. Jodivig, the new chief of the Dramsens, looked fraught and out of his depth. Kelemen, the Grand Caladri governor, was also there, leading the remnants of his people.

'Where's Guremar?' Maragin demanded.

Guremar's clan, the Plengas, controlled this area.

'He stayed behind with a group of our soldiers,' said a Krykker Rabigar didn't recognise. 'He said he would hold them off while we escaped, otherwise it would turn into a massacre. I—I don't think there will be any survivors.'

'Shit,' Rabigar muttered under his breath. There was no love lost between himself and Guremar, but he was one of the strongest clan leaders. If he was gone, that put even more responsibility onto Maragin's shoulders.

'What happened?' asked Maragin.

'A huge Drobax army entered our forest,' explained Kelemen. 'There was no stopping them. We were forced to retreat west into Plengas lands. Guremar raised an army and led it to the border. He prepared well enough, using the high ground. I thought the Drobax would give up, our position seemed impregnable. But then the dragon came—' He stopped, as if unable to continue. But no-one else stepped in. 'It flew above our position. We fired some missiles, but we didn't have many. Nothing stopped it. It flew over and blasted fire, again and again. We had no protection. It killed scores each time it passed. That's when Guremar ordered the retreat.'

Drobax and a dragon. What could the Krykkers do against such monsters? Rabigar looked at Maragin as she looked at him. They both knew the answer.

'I need to see,' he said. 'I need to see them before I leave.'

'I'll come too,' said Maragin.

It went quiet. Clearly, not a popular request.

'I'll take you,' said a voice.

Rabigar turned. Standing behind Jodivig, so that Rabigar hadn't even seen him, was Stenk, the young Dramsen Krykker he had befriended. Stenk, after some persuasion, had arrested Rabigar upon his return to his homeland last year. They had fought side by side against the Isharites in Haskany. Rabigar was happy to see him alive.

'You're the perfect man for the job,' he said to Stenk. 'Now, you just need to take us close enough so that we can see them, then you turn around and come back to join this army, understand?'

'Keep moving,' Maragin said to the rest. 'We'll catch up.'

RABIGAR PUSHED his face through the rock, looking carefully about. There were no Drobax. They were using the path twenty feet away to climb the mountain. It was high up here, high enough to burn the lungs of Krykker folk, never mind creatures such as Drobax, whose bodies weren't used to it. There was no reason for them to come this way anymore.

He pushed through, emerging fully from the rock while glancing at the sky above. By the time Stenk had shown them this location, the dragon was gone. It had perhaps found somewhere to rest. Rabigar knew nothing about dragons, but he imagined that flying around at this altitude, casting fire, was exhausting.

Maragin pushed through the same section of rock. Wordlessly, they began to look about. The ground was covered in a grey soot. Charred bodies littered the area where Guremar had made his stand. The place still stank of burned meat, and something about that upset Rabigar's insides. He tried not to think about the suffering too much. But soldiers clad in metal armour, exposed to fire of these temperatures, would have died in agony. They had come to bear witness, and to check for survivors, however unlikely. Clearly, there were none here. If Guremar had Rock Walkers with him, they may have been able to escape. But there was nothing else they could do now.

'We'd better head back,' he said to Maragin. 'What will you do?'

'We have no choice,' she said, and he already knew that. 'We must order the tunnels closed and we must evacuate.'

The underground tunnels and caverns were the last line of defence for the Krykkers. They could explode the tunnel entrances, creating an underground lair that was virtually impregnable. Certainly not a place a dragon could do any harm. But only a few Krykkers could live in those conditions for long. All the rest would have to leave their homeland.

'I will lead the group who stays,' he said to Maragin. 'You will be needed elsewhere.'

She smiled at him. He had thought he would never see that sight again. He stopped talking, so that her smile stayed on her face for as long as possible.

'We both know that's not going to happen. The Rock Walkers will follow me; not you. You are the one who claimed Bolivar's Sword. You must see that through. You need to go back to Halvia to find the Spear.'

'I don't know that,' he argued. 'You can do all that instead of me. Here,' he said, unbuckling the sword. 'Take it.'

The last thing Rabigar wanted was to see Maragin buried alive in the mountain caverns. That wasn't the last image of her he wanted in his head.

She snorted disdainfully. 'Please, no romantic gestures at your age. It's sad. I am the best person to lead the defence here; you must find the Spear;

Hakonin must lead our people in Halvia. We both know those will be our roles, so stop wasting your breath.'

Rabigar felt he had never loved, never respected her more than in that moment, when the chances of seeing her again suddenly dropped to virtually nil. Not that he had the right to feel sorry for himself. He had killed his chieftain. He had killed Maragin's father. That act still—would always—stand between them. So Rabigar stopped wasting his breath, and they both returned to the rock.

CONSUMMATUM EST

XIV

Lyssa skipped along the street, pleased to have escaped the Temple.

It wasn't that she hated it there, exactly. The people were sort of kind. But they were always making her do things. She didn't mind it so much when Belwynn made her read, because she liked spending time with her. But she hated it when the women kept making her learn to sew. In Korkis, she was used to doing what she wanted, when she wanted. She didn't want to go back to that life. No way. It was just that, now and then, she needed some time to herself.

Coronos was on guard duty at the castle.

'Welcome back, Your Highness,' he said to her, bowing deeply, before allowing her to pass through.

Lyssa giggled at him. Walking into the castle did kind of make her feel like she was a princess, though.

She went to the Tower where she shared a room with Belwynn, but halfway there decided that she wasn't in the mood to sit around. She'd much rather go exploring around the castle.

She walked up and down the corridors. As she walked along, she saw Queen Irina leaving the castle library and closing the door behind her. Irina turned to walk in her direction, and it was too late for Lyssa to change course, so she kept on walking towards her. When they passed, Irina gave her the look of displeasure she always gave her, while Lyssa kept her eyes on her shoes.

She kept on walking and stopped outside the library. She looked back down the corridor, waiting for Irina to disappear. The Queen was one of the few people who ever used the library, so there was a good chance it was empty now. Nervously, she turned the handle and peeked in.

Yes! It was empty!

Lyssa slipped inside. She liked the smell of the room. There were several shelves of books and comfy chairs to sit on. She didn't like the room because of the books, though. She liked it because of the secret door she had found.

She went straight there now, pulling at the door that was painted to look like it contained shelves of books.

No-one had exactly told Lyssa she wasn't allowed to go into the secret passage. She knew that Belwynn hadn't lived in the castle very long, and might not even know about the secret door to tell her not to go in. Queen Irina had lived here a long time. She might know about it. Maybe that was why she was here before? Anyway, whoever knew or didn't know about it, to Lyssa it felt like a forbidden part of the castle.

She walked in and pulled the secret door shut. The passage was very narrow and not very high, but they weren't problems for Lyssa. It was almost completely dark, which she didn't like so much, but she crawled along on her hands and knees and that helped her to avoid bumping into the walls.

She stopped when she heard voices. This was where Sebastian's rooms were, and she recognised his voice first. Second, Theron. They were always talking about boring things up here. Nevertheless, she peered into the room.

There were four of them altogether. Tycho was there. He always wanted to arm wrestle with her, even though she always beat him. Remi was there, too. He always winked at her when he saw her, but didn't talk much.

She listened in. They were kind of arguing with each other about what to do with Count Ampelios's lands. The Knights seemed to think they were on the good side, but they had just killed Ampelios and now they were taking his family's lands. Theron wanted his friend Tycho to have them. Sebastian said Remi should have them. If they really were good, maybe they should give his lands to people who didn't have any of their own? Maybe they shouldn't have killed him in the first place. Then there wouldn't be anything to argue about.

Theron and Tycho left Sebastian's room.

'I'm sure we can find a compromise,' Sebastian said to Remi.

Remi shrugged. 'I don't care. I have more important concerns.'

Sebastian frowned at him. 'Oh? Like what?'

'This.'

Suddenly, Remi drew a dagger, leaned over to where Sebastian was seated, and plunged it into Sebastian's chest.

Lyssa had to grab her mouth to stop herself from crying out. She didn't want to look, but she couldn't make herself stop watching.

Sebastian tried to stop Remi, but the other knight pushed him back with one hand, while pushing the dagger deeper in with the other.

'You thought you could stop us?' Remi hissed. 'You thought you could invade our lands with no consequences? You fool!'

Lyssa turned away. She wished she hadn't opened the secret door now.

Moving slowly to avoid making a sound, she began to crawl back down the passage.

* * *

BELWYNN HALF-WALKED, half-ran through the garden at the Temple of Madria. She had to stop suddenly to avoid crashing into Elana and Prince Dorian, coming the other way.

'Sorry,' she said breathlessly.

'Is something the matter?' Elana asked.

'Have you seen Lyssa anywhere?' Belwynn asked, slightly embarrassed. 'She seems to have run off without telling anyone.'

Dorian smiled kindly. 'I'm heading back home,' he said. 'If I see her on the way, I'll be sure to bring her back.'

'Thank you.'

'I'll help you look,' said Elana.

'It's alright, I don't want to waste your time.'

'I'll help,' Elana insisted.

They said farewell to Dorian and began to search the grounds of the Temple, where an unruly child might have decided to have an adventure.

'I'm not sure what to do with her anymore,' Belwynn confessed. 'I feel like she needs her time structured properly, learning something useful.'

'Don't fret,' said Elana. 'It's perfectly normal for children to go off exploring. It's good for them. I'm sure she'll turn up.'

'Yes,' said Belwynn absently. Lyssa wasn't in the garden. She had gone into the city, she knew it.

'Belwynn, I haven't told anyone this, not even Dirk.'

This sounded serious. Belwynn gave Elana her full attention.

'Before all this started, back in Magnia, I had a family. A husband and two children. Girls.'

Belwynn's mouth dropped open. 'What happened to them?'

Elana smiled. 'Nothing, I hope. I hope very much that I will be able to go back when this is over.'

'You mean, they're back home now? In your village, what was it, Kirtsea?'

Elana nodded.

'How could you do that?' Belwynn blurted out. 'Do they know what you're doing, that you're alive?'

Elana pursed her lips and Belwynn could see tears threatening to spill.

'Sorry, I didn't mean—'

'I didn't choose this, Belwynn, remember? Madria chose *me*. Sometimes I wonder why. But I have to see it through. And what would I tell them, so that they could understand why I left? How could I explain that I still love them, but can't be with them?'

'I'm sorry, Elana. Truly. Soren will get the weapons. We'll win, and you will get to go back home.'

Elana smiled wanly. It didn't seem like she believed that. 'Where do you think we should look next?'

'Eh?'

'For Lyssa?'

'I think she went into the city. Hopefully just back to the castle. I'll head there now.'

'I'll come with you.'

They made their way out of the Temple grounds and onto the street outside. They hadn't walked very far when they saw her, walking towards them alongside Dorian. He had one arm around her shoulder protectively, as if shielding her from something.

'Found her heading this way,' he said. 'Couldn't get out of her where she's been. She seems a bit shaken up.'

Belwynn looked at Lyssa, who stared ahead listlessly. She seemed withdrawn, removed from their immediate conversation.

'Are you alright, girl?' Belwynn asked her.

Lyssa turned to her. There was something in her eyes, something like fear, but she didn't say anything.

Belwynn and Elana shared a look. What was up with her? Had something happened?

Before she had time to question her further, Dorian had turned to look back up the street. 'It's Sebastian!' he said.

Sebastian was walking towards them. Belwynn watched him approach. He seemed stiff; older somehow. Perhaps recent events were weighing on him more than she had realised.

'Well met, Grand Master,' said the prince.

Belwynn wondered at Dorian. Sebastian had defeated his older brother in battle but a week ago. Theron had ensured that Straton was now locked up, unable to leave the capital again. What did the younger brother really think about these developments?

Sebastian nodded at them all. 'I have come to talk with Elana.'

He sounded grave.

'We'll go back to the Temple,' said Elana, and she and Sebastian left in that direction.

'Well, I really should be getting home,' said Dorian.

'Thank you for finding her,' said Belwynn, glancing down at Lyssa.

She was startled when she looked at the girl. She looked stricken, staring at the departing Elana and Sebastian in terror.

'What is it?' Belwynn asked her.

'I-I saw Sebastian killed. By Remi.'

Belwynn frowned at her, but getting those words out seemed to open a floodgate in Lyssa. 'I was hiding in the secret passage behind the library. I know I shouldn't have been. Theron and Sebastian were arguing about who should get the lands of Count Ampelios. Theron and Tycho left the room. Then Remi killed Sebastian. Just like that. For no reason. Then—' she stopped, pointing after Sebastian and Elana, who had now gone into the Temple.

'Then you saw Sebastian alive?' Belwynn asked.

Lyssa nodded, looking up at her like a little mouse, expecting Belwynn to solve the problem for her. Belwynn looked at Dorian.

'Maybe you fell asleep, Lyssa?' he suggested. 'Had a nightmare?'

Lyssa looked from Dorian to Belwynn. Belwynn could sense her desperate need to be believed. And maybe most people would have dismissed her wild story as a dream. But Belwynn had grown up with Soren. She had no reason to doubt the existence of the mysterious—of dark powers. And what she had witnessed in the last year had only confirmed that.

'I think we should check on them, just in case,' she said.

Dorian nodded. 'And there *is* a secret passage at the back of the library,' he added.

She looked at him. It was no joke he was making. If Lyssa had witnessed Sebastian's murder, who or what exactly had walked off with Elana?

'Come on!' she said, suddenly feeling the need to act quickly. 'Stay here!' she said to Lyssa.

Belwynn and Dorian ran together into the Temple. 'Elana?' Belwynn shouted at the startled followers of the priestess.

One of them pointed down a corridor to Elana's private room, an obvious place to take Sebastian. Private, but dangerous, for there would be no witnesses.

Belwynn ran in that direction, her lungs burning from the effort, Dorian still by her side. He got to the door first, shoving it open.

Despite Lyssa's warning and her own mounting dread, Belwynn still couldn't process the scene before her. Elana lay on the floor, a pool of dark blood visibly growing around her. Sebastian, knife in hand, turned to them, a repulsive snarl on his face. Lyssa had to be right. Sebastian wouldn't have done this.

Dorian charged him, avoided a knife swing, and then tried to wrestle the weapon from Sebastian.

Belwynn barely cared. Her eyes fixed on Elana. The priestess's eyes were open, and she was looking back. She mouthed 'Belwynn'. In a daze, as if she was in her own nightmare now, Belwynn walked to her, kneeling in the blood. She located the wound in Elana's side, putting her hand to it to stop any more from leaking out.

'Can't you heal yourself?' she asked desperately.

There was a crash behind her. Dorian had been thrown to one side, the knife clattering across the floor, and Sebastian, with a final look at Belwynn and Elana, ran from the room.

Dorian got to his feet. 'I'll get him,' he said and gave chase.

It was deathly quiet in the room.

'Belwynn,' came Elana's voice, weak and breathy. 'There isn't much time. I need you to hold my hands.'

Belwynn grabbed one of Elana's hands and put it to the injured side of the priestess. 'Here. You are on the wound. Heal yourself.'

Elana smiled. It was gentle and full of sadness. 'I can't, Belwynn. Hold my hands. Please.'

Belwynn shook her head. No. This wasn't happening. Elana wasn't going to die.

She took Elana's hand back, sticky with blood. She held Elana's other hand. Elana closed her eyes. A shudder ran through her, and she winced in pain.

Belwynn felt something. It felt like a tiny spark in her mind. Some sensation, not quite an itch, or a pain, in the back of her head. A presence.

Then the sensation started to grow and swell, filling her mind, her head, her heart, her body, then her soul. It blazed throughout her like a fire, and it burned like one, blinding her. She cried out in pain, overcome by the force that had entered her. She thought she could hear Soren's voice calling to her, but she couldn't focus on anything, her senses overwhelmed. She knew she was going to lose consciousness. She tried to pull her hands free of Elana, but it was too late.

* * *

STRATON SLUMPED ON HIS BED, a snot-filled handkerchief by his side, a half-finished meal on the floor. His cold had stolen his appetite, and he had no energy for anything. So he sat on his bed, staring about his room, brooding.

Since the defeat, he had lurched from impotent rage to a lethargic despair and back again, and this torment, coupled with his confinement, had made him ill. It was a gilded cage he had been given, under guard in his own rooms, treated with the utmost respect, nothing but the very best from the kitchens delivered every day. He would rather have been given a prison cell in the dungeons for everyone to see the truth. But Theron was too clever for that. He had imprisoned the royal family here in their own castle, and yet no doubt the citizens were falling over themselves to praise him for his magnanimity.

The door opened, and a knight stepped into the room.

'Excuse me, Your Highness. You have a visitor.'

Straton looked up in a disinterested way.

Dorian. The one member of the family not kept under lock and key, strolling around Heractus without a care in the world. He looked full of purpose, staring at the knight until the door was shut and they were left alone.

'What do you want?' Straton demanded.

Dorian looked about the room, his eyes coming to rest on the plate of food, the handkerchief, and finally on Straton.

'I've come to get you out of here.'

Straton laughed. There was something absurdly funny about that. 'You've come to rescue me? Where were you when I was fighting for our family against the Knights? When your help might have actually made a difference?'

Dorian showed no remorse. Instead, he walked over to the bed. He grabbed Straton by the front of his shirt.

'Quit whining,' he said, a look of utter contempt on his face.

Straton didn't know how to react.

'You've allowed the Knights to walk all over you and ruined every opportunity you had to regain control.'

This was so unlike Dorian, so unexpected, that all Straton could do was stare into the seething anger of his brother's twisted features.

'I'm going to make you king, so get out of your pit and do what I tell you.'

BETRAYAL

XV

It was a sombre gathering in Maragin's hall, in the highlands of the Grendal clan. Rabigar could take no pleasure from his return to the place where he was raised, despite the flood of memories that assailed him as he once more entered rooms, strode past buildings, looked out on the stark mountain views, that had then been the daily sights of his youth. For, despite their victory in Haskany some eight months ago, the Krykkers had effectively been defeated in a matter of days. The dead littered the mountain slopes of his homeland: butchered by Drobax, burned by dragon fire.

'There is only one location open to us,' Maragin argued. 'The Isharites may fall on Kalinth at any time. The Empire and Guivergne will also fall to a sustained attack, and we cannot be sure that our people will be welcome there for a long spell. We must evacuate to our cousins in Halvia.'

Most reluctantly agreed, having come to the same conclusion. If that decision was easy enough, the logistics of it certainly weren't. It would involve the Krykker people travelling across the Lantinen Sea, with the risk of being targeted by the Kharovian fleet. If it went wrong, it could be catastrophic.

'What of my people?' asked Kelemen.

Rabigar studied him. He had that fierce look that comes when you have gone past exhaustion and you are living off your last reserves. His people had already come close to being wiped out by the Isharites. There were even less of them left now.

'Would they give us sanctuary?' he asked.

'I would say so,' said Rabigar. 'They have given such sanctuary to the Vismarians, and that people could hold the key for us. When we visited, they told us they still had ships. If the warships of the Sea Caladri can keep the Kharovians away, the Vismarians could help to transport our people across the Lantinen.'

'What say you, Captain Sebo?' Kelemen asked the Sea Caladri captain.

'We were given orders to only engage the Kharovians if necessary,' Sebo said. 'But at that time, our Council had no way of knowing that the fate of our cousins, not to mention the Krykker people, would be at stake in such a way. We are ready to do whatever it takes. I suggest a crossing of the Lantinen now. I will need to speak with the Vismarian captains and agree a strategy. What we are suggesting is a very complicated manoeuvre.'

'Are you suggesting your entire fleet sails again?' asked Maragin.

'No. That would be too risky, and may alert the Kharovians to our plans. I will take Red Serpent across on a night-time voyage, to avoid being seen.'

'I'll go with you,' said Rabigar. 'The people there know me now. I'll persuade the Vismarians to help us.'

'So be it,' said Maragin. 'Meanwhile, we continue the evacuation. The Grendals will hold the mountain passes for as long as possible. Our people are to be gathered in the lands of clan Swarten, ready for the crossing. We need those ships, Rabigar, or it will be a massacre.'

* * *

MONEVA STOOD NEXT TO GYRMUND, looking on as the fighters entered the roped area for the Contest.

Gansukh's fourth day, and the opponents were appearing thick and fast now, the best of the best arguing over who should be the one to kill him. Bolormaa had warned them of this. If Gansukh lasted seven days, he was khan. Those who did not wish to bend the knee to a superior would risk their lives between the ropes, to end the threat to their independence.

Qadan was the man who had won the right to defeat Gansukh today. He was huge, towering at least six inches taller than his opponent, with broad shoulders and huge limbs. His mount was the largest Jalakh horse Moneva had seen—it had to be to carry that weight and still be able to move fast enough to compete in the Contest.

A roar erupted as he was introduced, and not just from his own tribe. The area was heaving with Jalakhs from all tribes, many keen to see Gansukh defeated, others wondering whether they were witnessing history being made, with the making of a new khan.

Bolormaa and Soren sat next to each other, ready to use their powers to help Gansukh to another victory. They would be opposed by any sorcerers from Qadan's tribe, and, Bolormaa had warned, others who wanted Gansukh to lose.

The shout went out and the two combatants charged forwards to meet in the centre, horses circling, curved swords swirling. Qadan was faster than Moneva thought possible for his size, his blade sizzling forwards to attack and moving across to parry with what looked like relaxed ease. He was not, perhaps, quite as agile as Gansukh. But his blows were stronger, forcing Gansukh to move back or to the side. They allowed Qadan to go on the offensive more often than not, dictating the pattern of the fight.

She looked across to Soren, recognising the signs of strain that showed he was using his powers to blunt Qadan's attacking prowess. Then, a new expression appeared on his face, one of shock.

Moneva nudged at Gyrmund, telling him to look at Soren.

Then, suddenly, the sorcerer shuddered, and shouted out loud. 'Belwynn?' He looked about him desperately, blindly, as if she might be here.

Moneva and Gyrmund rushed over to him, as the members of the Oligud tribe he was sat with stared at him.

'What is it?' Gyrmund asked Soren, kneeling next to him.

'Belwynn!' he shouted out loud again, then slumped over.

Moneva caught him and laid him down on the ground. She placed Onella's Staff back into his hands, hoping that the weapon might revive him, but it seemed to have no effect.

'I don't understand,' she said to Gyrmund. 'Why shout out Belwynn's name?'

He shrugged, no wiser than she was.

Next to Soren, Bolormaa was visibly sweating as she concentrated on her son's fight, lacking the support that Soren had been providing.

Moneva turned to the fight. She wasn't surprised to see Qadan gaining the upper hand now, driving Gansukh back, his defence getting more desperate. Then, a brutal blow landed on Gansukh's shoulder, smashing through his scale armour and cutting into flesh. A gasp emerged from the crowd. Gansukh reeled backwards but somehow stayed on his horse, weaving away from Qadan's follow up attacks. Excited talk babbled across the crowd as they discussed the wound that Qadan had inflicted. Even if Gansukh didn't die right now, his quest to become khan seemed over. Moneva knew it wasn't the gash itself, so much as the damage to Gansukh's movement that was the issue. If he couldn't move his shoulder and arm properly, he would have no chance of defending against further attacks. The situation was critical.

Gyrmund knelt down to Soren, talking in his ear, even giving him a slap on the face in an effort to wake him.

Moneva could see tears in Bolormaa's eyes, but she maintained her focus. Her face was red with effort.

Qadan and Gansukh clashed again. Gansukh made no attempt to attack, his energies directed at moving, guiding his horse this way and that, unbalancing Qadan so that he failed to land a clear blow. It was an impressive display of horsemanship, but it was surely only a matter of time before Qadan landed a second blow. And that might be it.

Soren stirred, mumbling incoherently.

Desperate, Moneva and Gyrmund lifted him into a sitting position.

'Belwynn?' he asked drowsily.

'Soren,' said Moneva. 'We need you to focus on the fight right now. Gansukh is injured.'

Soren frowned. She saw his knuckles turn white as he squeezed his staff, perhaps drawing on its energy to revive himself. He opened his eyes and stared at the fight ahead of him.

Gansukh parried Qadan's blows, but he was getting weaker. He couldn't lift his arm properly. Qadan was growing frustrated, trying to batter his way through Gansukh's flimsy looking defence, his chest heaving with the exertion, his horse's sides lathered in sweat.

Then, Gansukh turned it around. He went to parry a blow, dodged it instead, then flicked his blade at Qadan's wrist. Qadan managed to hold on to his sword, but Gansukh was on to him, lightning fast, sending blows to the left, then the right, at his face, then his sword arm. Qadan never completely recovered, desperately trying to get back to neutral. Gansukh faked a high blow, circling around instead, then plunging his sword into the horse's neck before withdrawing it in a fountain of blood.

As the horse fell, Qadan somehow landed on his feet, charging at Gansukh in a last bid for victory. Gansukh's horse didn't need to be told what to do, skipping out of the way, and as Qadan's blow fell way too short, Gansukh chopped his scimitar down, the razor-sharp edge cutting through bone and detaching his enemy's sword-hand from his arm.

Qadan stood there briefly, gazing at his raised stump, in apparent disbelief that the fight had ended in such a way, before Gansukh finished the job.

The Oliguds cheered, rushing to the ropes to guide their champion back to the embrace of his tribe.

Bolormaa, shaky on her feet, immediately ordered that Gansukh be sat down and his wound inspected. Her son had won, but she wore the face of defeat.

She tutted at the injury as Gansukh was cut out of his armour. He needed rest for it to heal, but if he was to become khan, he had to fight again tomorrow. And his opponent would know exactly where to target.

'It's over,' Bolormaa muttered, but Gansukh raged at her, saying he would never withdraw.

'Her husband died on the fifth day,' Gyrmund said quietly for only Moneva to hear.

They turned away from the scene and went to check on Soren.

He was still sitting on the ground, his staff resting on his knees, a dazed expression on his face.

'You called out Belwynn's name?' Moneva asked him.

'Something's happened to her,' he said dully. 'Something—' he paused, looking up at them, as if trying to find the right words, and then giving up. 'Something I don't understand. She's not replying to me.'

'Did she say anything?' Moneva asked. She felt a sense of dread. They shouldn't have left Belwynn and Elana alone for this long. It had been a bad mistake. She knew, as much as anyone perhaps, what the Isharites could do. Heractus wasn't safe.

'No. I felt her pain, a sense of loss. And I felt something else. It reminded me of Samir Durg,' he said, his face ashen, 'when Siavash was inside my head.'

A sense of helplessness came over Moneva then, a feeling she had sworn she would never tolerate again. All this time wasted, and they were still no closer to getting their hands on the Jalakh Bow, their one chance fading away in front of their eyes.

She walked over to Bolormaa. The woman looked exhausted, observing her son's wound being cleaned before they would sew it up.

'I need to talk with you,' said Moneva.

Bolormaa looked up at her. She seemed ready to tell Moneva to get lost, before relenting, and the two of them walked away from the crowd gathered about Gansukh.

'We need to try something else,' Moneva said. She didn't have to explain why. Gansukh had barely come through that fight, and no-one expected him to win tomorrow. 'Show me the main challengers to Gansukh; the men who are likely to enter the Contest tomorrow.'

'Why?' asked Bolormaa. 'What will that achieve?'

'I'll make sure they never make it to the ropes.'

Bolormaa stopped walking, instead looking Moneva in the eye. Moneva didn't look away. What was the woman's problem? Had her suggestion gone too far, challenged some sacred rule that Bolormaa wasn't prepared to break?

'Very well,' said Bolormaa at last. 'I will show you.'

* * *

EIGHTEEN OF THEM crossed from Kalinth into Persala. Eight Barbarians; five Persaleians; two men of Rotelegen; two Dog-men; and a Magnian. Clarin decided they'd go no farther this day. It seemed a decent place to stop for the night.

A cluster of buildings on the Persaleian side marked the border. Here, the authorities used to regulate traffic passing between the two countries, but they were now abandoned. Trade was dead, and the Persaleian government destroyed when the Haskans had invaded and taken the capital, Baserno. They could only speculate about who was in charge now. A Drobax army had been seen crossing from Persala into the lands of the Grand Caladri days ago. That suggested that both Haskany and Persala were now firmly back under the control of the Isharites.

Either the people who lived here hadn't left in a hurry, or someone else had come since and cleaned the place out, because there was nothing much to show for it after they carried out a sweep of the buildings. Still, the inn was cosy, with a good roof. Spring was different this far north compared to Magnia. The days were pleasant enough, but the nights were cold. Cyprian got a fire going in the hearth and they all made their beds in the main hall. Clarin organised two lookouts at a time, in short shifts, and everyone enjoyed a comfortable first night.

When the sun appeared, they continued east, using a road that Zared confirmed would take them to Baserno. As they walked along, Clarin quizzed him about his country. Cyprian, Clarin knew, came from the east of Persala, the port city of Lumberco, whereas Zared had told him he had lived in the capital. He would know the area better than anyone else.

'How long will it take us to get to Baserno?'

'At this pace, with no interruptions, three days.'

'What have you heard of the Persaleian Shield?'

'Nothing. This long-ago war against the Isharites you speak of—alliances with Krykkers and Caladri, magic weapons—it's not a story that Persaleians know. Our history begins with Avilius, founder of Persala. We then conquered the north: alone, not with allies; by force of arms, not with magic. Two centuries after Avilius, our armies drove the Drobax away at the Battle of the Tarn. If this war fought with magic weapons did happen, it was before our empire was born.'

Clarin didn't really know his history, not like people such as Soren. Although Belwynn had told him what the Caladri wise man, Szabolcs, had said in Coldeberg, he was more than vague on the when of the story.

'If it did exist,' he persisted, 'forgotten somewhere, where would it have been kept?'

'Baserno. There are two obvious locations: the Imperial Palace, or the Temple of Ludovis. The Temple has a depository where the wealthy can store their money and possessions. It's known to contain many ancient artefacts.'

'Have you been?'

'I've been to the Temple plenty of times. But my family never had anything worth putting into the depository, nor do I know where exactly the items are kept. That's a secret kept by the priests, because the riches held there would be a target for thieves.'

Clarin knew he wasn't the smartest. He'd always been content to leave the thinking to people like Herin and Soren. But he had worked out there was more to Zared than the young man let on. He said his family had modest wealth, that his father was a shopkeeper. But at some point, he had been trained to fight properly. Then, there was the fact that the rest of the Persaleians deferred to him, despite his young age. There was something he wasn't telling Clarin. No doubt he had his reasons. And as long as he helped Clarin to find the Shield, which he'd promised he would, did it really matter?

THEY FOLLOWED the road to Baserno. This part of Persala was sparsely settled, heath and gorse stretching out in every direction. A good morning's walk saw them approaching a settlement. Zared named it Bineto, a town that straddled the road to Baserno. He described it as a focal point for the local area, as well as a market for Kalinthian traders in years past.

Clarin deliberated over their tactics one last time. His instincts told him to skirt around the town, but Zared and the Persaleians argued against this.

'From now on,' Zared said, 'there will be town after town, then cities. There is no countryside we can hide in: this is Persala. Either we pass through these places or we give up.'

Zared's plan was simply to walk boldly into Bineto. Once there, they would get a feel for the situation. If challenged, they would pose as soldiers serving Ishari. Clarin knew they had a chance of getting away with such a ruse. The Isharites had humans in their armies. But the two Dog-men were key. It was known that their kind served Ishari, so their presence made such a claim more convincing. Zared would do the talking if his countrymen asked questions. But if it didn't work, they would be in serious trouble, seriously fast.

And it wasn't just that. The farther they got into Persala, the more Zared was gaining control over what they did, and the more Clarin was fading into the background. Had he made a mistake coming here in the first place?

Clarin sighed, shaking himself out of his introspection. They were here now, and Zared's plan was the only one they had. It was pointless to think about it anymore. They walked for Bineto.

BINETO HAD KNOWN BETTER TIMES, that was for sure. The streets were filthy, uncared for. Many of the houses were run down, if not empty, and when they got into the town centre, many of the shops were boarded up. The townsfolk had a sullen, fearful look about them. They made for the market area, where a few stalls huddled together in one corner of the square, the rest of it empty.

Zared and Cyprian moved over to the stallholders with purpose, hailing them in loud, confident voices, as if they were meant to be here. The following conversations were quieter, and Clarin, stood with the rest of the group out of earshot, looked about them and tried to think.

There were no soldiers here. That said something. The Isharites had sent an army south—they were set on conquest. They wouldn't want to waste men occupying the towns of Persala if they didn't have to. From what Zared said, there were many settlements bigger than Bineto. It suggested that they would likely be unoccupied, too. The population were cowed, serving their new masters. Should a rebellion stir, troops would be sent in to put it down, from the larger centres such as Baserno. Clarin nodded to himself, feeling like he was gaining a sense of the state of the country. A large population, defeated and leaderless, no doubt many pressed into the Isharite armies. Relatively few occupying troops—just enough to keep them submissive. It was possible, in such a place, for them to pass through unchallenged. To somehow make their way into Baserno. And once there? They had to find a shield that no-one knew existed.

The three Persaleians returned, arms full of loaves of bread and rounds of cheese that they had purchased from their compatriots.

'Well?' asked Clarin.

'Not very talkative—suspicious, as you might expect,' said Zared. 'Siavash is in charge in Samir Durg, his opponents dead or fled. Haskany has no king or queen any more, the country is said to be as reduced as Persala is. The people here pay heavy taxes, mostly in foodstuffs and other items for the armies. Many of the younger men have been recruited to fight, making life harder for those who remain. Other than that, so long as they do what they are told, they are left alone.'

'The other towns are likely to be the same?' Clarin asked.

'Yes.'

'Good. Then let's get moving. The sooner we leave, the sooner these people forget we were ever here.'

THEY CONTINUED EAST, stopping at places much like Bineto. Each town had the same layout, central plazas surrounded by parallel roads. Some were larger, some smaller, but in its essentials, their experience was the same at each one. Communities that were suffering, but somehow surviving, under Isharite rule. Zared spoke with the people: sometimes it was traders, at other times mayors or other dignitaries, even passers-by on the street going about their own business. They were cautious, wary of strangers. When pressed, each said the next town along was the same as them. In one town, a place called Pontecchio, they spent the night in a row of empty houses, their occupants either taken away by Isharite soldiers, or had left of their own accord, trying to make a better living elsewhere.

The next morning, Zared announced a change of plan.

'There's news of soldiers in the next city,' he explained. 'It would be better for us to detour around it, just in case. It only involves going down some less travelled roads to other settlements, and then cutting back to the main road, bypassing the city. It will not add much to our travel time.'

They set off. A minor road, better described as a track, took them north of Pontecchio, where they passed the well-tended fields of the Persaleian countryside. It seemed to Clarin that in the rural areas, life carried on not so differently than it had before.

There was something about the outdoors that made Clarin feel better about things. His mind wandered to Belwynn, how he had made a right mess of things in Heractus. He had genuinely thought that he would declare his love, she would return it, and they would settle down on a farm somewhere to live out their days. In hindsight, he had been stupid. She was with Theron now. And maybe he just had to admit to himself that she was better off that way. That didn't mean it didn't hurt, though. He had already lost Herin. Those were the two people in the world who really meant anything to him.

'We'll head up here,' Zared said from the front, speaking in a voice loud enough to carry to everyone. He was pointing towards a steep slope that led up to a mound. 'We can get a decent view of the area from up there. Check we're going the right way.'

Wordlessly, the group followed Zared and the Persaleians up to the top of the mound. It was tough going, Clarin's thigh muscles protesting by the time they got to the top. The group shrugged packs off shoulders and looked around.

There were, indeed, good views of the surrounding countryside. A pile of stones, some very large, had been placed in the middle of the mound. Clarin walked over to inspect it, making his legs stretch out a little after the climb. They had definitely been carried up, he decided. Maybe they were atop a burial chamber. It reminded him of the vossi mound in the Wilderness, where they had been surrounded by the creatures, close to defeat, before Soren had cast a spell to scare them off. Maybe once, many years ago, vossi had lived here. Or some other group of humans. Or Caladri, or Lippers. Maybe this mound was the most important place in the world to them. Now, no-one even knew what it was.

'Clarin!' came a shout, urgent sounding.

He turned to see Jurgen gesturing at him. He and Rudy were at one end of the mound, looking down the slope.

Clarin ran over, one hand on the hilt of his sword. Men in armour, holding spears, were making their way slowly up the mound, looking up at them. They were spread out all along the base of the mound.

The Dog-men barked a warning. Turning, Clarin looked at their position a few feet away. He didn't need to go over to confirm that there were men there, too. They were surrounded.

At the far end of the mound, where Zared and the Persaleians had positioned themselves, armed men had already made it to the top of the slope. Zared and his men were helping them up.

Clarin took a few paces towards them. Zared gave him an apologetic look.

A spearman stood next to Zared, as big and strong looking as Clarin, with a huge shield. He pointed his spear in Clarin's direction, then at the other members of the group, as more soldiers crested the mound behind him.

'We're going to need you to drop your weapons.'

EXODUS

XVI

The Caladri warships had already put to sea. Their role was to offer protection to the armada that would transport the Krykker people—plus the Grand Caladri refugees—across the Lantinen. This armada consisted of the Caladri trading vessels, and the Vismarian fleet, which had crossed the Lantinen with Red Serpent. Rabigar had asked for their help, and they had given it. Their leader, Sevald, the same man who had spoken at the Krykker moot, hadn't wasted time debating it, or demanded anything in return; they had gathered their ships and sailors and set off immediately. Rabigar would always be grateful to them for that.

Rabigar stood with Maragin, looking down on the long, patient line of Krykkers, waiting their turn to embark on foreign ships. It was natural to think that they had somehow failed their people. But even now, a wave of Drobax, unstoppable in number, roamed over their lands. And wherever the Grendals had manned mountain passes to fight this plague, the dragon had arrived. Destroying their forces, burning Krykker and Drobax alike until the passes were cleared, it left only grey ash as a sign of its passing.

Maragin had put an end to using her soldiers in such a way. She had blocked all the entrances and tunnels that led underground, except for the one they now stood by. She had conceded all her clan's territory above ground to the invaders. Halls, houses, fields; all lost. Whatever could be saved they'd taken underground. Enough food to feed a small army. Underground wells provided an endless supply of water. The Krykker resistance would continue. They would never give up their homeland.

It was time to close the last entrance, before the Drobax reached them. Maragin ordered her soldiers to set fire to the wooden props they had put in place underground. Once they gave way, the walls would collapse, and a tonne of stone come crashing down where they now stood.

Maragin had chosen a thousand Krykkers who would stay behind. Many of them were rock walkers, capable of forcing their bodies through Krykker rock. Rabigar allowed himself a grim smile at the thought of them emerging, with night as cover, to slaughter the Drobax above ground, before disappearing again. He wished he could be with them. But as Maragin had said, he had other responsibilities.

He paced backwards, taking a last look at Maragin, before she disappeared into the darkness of the tunnel behind her.

He kept moving back. He felt the ground shake, and saw small stones and debris sift down the wall of rock above the tunnel entrance as the ground underneath it weakened. Then, without further warning, the rock gave way. Huge chunks of it cascaded down towards him, and he skipped backwards faster to avoid the cloud of dust that came behind. He knew that the same thing had happened inside the tunnel.

He waited a while, allowing the dust to settle. The wall and the entrance had disappeared, replaced by an untidy jumble of cracked rock. The Drobax wouldn't even know that an entrance had once stood there, never mind be able to clear a way inside. There was nothing else for Rabigar to see here. He turned around and made his way down to the harbour.

Here Hakonin, leader of the Swarten clan, was organising the evacuation of a whole people. The pier was full of Vismarian ships and Caladri traders getting loaded. Once full, they would cast off and sail out to sea, while the next vessel would steer its way in to replace it.

'Get on the next ship,' Rabigar said to Hakonin. 'We need to make sure you get across. You're in charge now.'

'Is it done?' Hakonin asked, looking up at the rocky scree where the tunnel had stood a few moments before.

'It's done. It worked. They won't get in that way.'

Hakonin nodded. He signalled to his household troops, who stood in a group along with family members, and they made their way down to the harbour, identifying a Caladri trader that looked large enough to hold them all.

That was the last of the stragglers. Everyone else was already in the line, waiting their turn for the next ship. They had nearly done it. Only the crossing itself to go, and they would have pulled off a remarkable logistical feat.

Then he heard the noise. Turning, he looked back towards the rocks. He saw nothing, but he knew what he had heard. Drobax.

'They're coming,' he whispered to himself.

Rabigar placed a hand on the hilt of Bolivar's Sword. He would make a stand here if necessary.

The noise came again, the shouts of thousands of Drobax, echoing down to the shore from the mountains. Rabigar still couldn't see anything, but with only one eye he knew that didn't mean they weren't visible to others.

The Krykkers in the line for the ships had heard it this time, and panicked voices reached him, urging those ahead to go faster. He turned to look.

'Calm yourselves!' he barked. The last thing they needed after all this was a last-minute stampede for the boats. They were Krykkers. They were better than that.

Some of the Krykkers left the line to stand with him, ready to fight if need be.

'Can you see anything?' he asked one of them, a man half his own age.

'They're on the high ridge, some already past it. They've seen us.'

Rabigar nodded. 'Then they may get here before all the ships have left. We must keep them away.'

'I'll fight with you, Rabigar Din,' the man said.

Rabigar grunted.

They waited, a thin line of Krykkers, Rabigar straining his eye to see, until he saw movement high up. The Drobax were moving fast, keen to get to them before all the ships were cast off. But they were in a disorganised mess, not moving in regiments, but in ones and twos. Rabigar was sure they could hold them off for a while. He looked anxiously into the sky. So long as the dragon didn't make an appearance.

'Look!' someone shouted, pointing.

Rabigar turned to see. Those Drobax who were nearest were under attack. Emerging from the rocks, groups of Krykkers intercepted them. The Drobax behind screamed in anger, their attention diverted to the new threat.

Maragin's rock walkers. Their intervention was already working.

Rabigar smiled. 'We'll be fine. Come on, let's go.'

They returned to their positions in the line. They all cast the odd look behind them now and again. The rock walkers had disappeared, but they had done their job.

The line was diminishing, and soon Rabigar boarded the last ship, a Vismarian vessel. It was big enough to take on the remaining Krykkers, though to Rabigar it didn't have the same feeling of stability he had experienced on Red Serpent. Still, if it got them across the Lantinen, he would not complain.

Taking a place on deck, Rabigar made himself look back towards his homeland. So recently he had gained the right to return, after half a lifetime as an exile. And now he had been forced out again.

The first of the Drobax had descended from the rocky scree to the shoreline, looking out at their escaped quarry. Forced out of his home by those creatures. He made himself look, holding on to the image, so that when he needed to, he could recall it and use his anger to do whatever he had to. Because whatever it took, he would return his people to their homeland. That was his vow.

SUNLIGHT REFLECTED off the deep blue of the ocean. The sound of oars hitting water filled Rabigar's ears as the Vismarian ship followed the rest of the armada west across the Lantinen Sea. Dalriya receded from view and the world of the Krykkers contracted to a few tiny ships bobbing up and down on the waves.

It may be that my people have never been so vulnerable, Rabigar told himself. Krykkers were used to having the safety of rock underneath their feet, if not all around them. Here they were in an alien, dangerous environment, and they wouldn't be safe until they made landfall in Halvia.

Somewhere to the north, not visible from Rabigar's ship, the Sea Caladri warships patrolled, protecting them from a Kharovian attack.

The sun gradually withdrew, making the horizon turn orange and the sea purple. But it was still light enough for the Vismarian sailor to spot the smoke to the north.

He raised the alarm and Rabigar, like many others, rushed to the starboard side to look out. He saw one, then two, then half a dozen: great palls of black smoke could be seen rising into the sky.

'What is that?' asked a young woman.

Everyone else shared a look. They all knew.

'The Sea Caladri are out there,' someone answered her. 'The Kharovians have come.'

There was nothing they could do except tell the crewmen to row harder. Those on deck looked anxiously to the bow, for signs of the Halvian coast, then back to starboard, for signs of the sleek Kharovian warships. Neither came into view. The smoke continued to darken the sky to the north until the disappearance of the sun made it invisible. Then, they could see fire where the smoke had been. The two great navies of Dalriya were clashing out there, and it was impossible to know which way the battle was going.

At last, they could see lights on the Halvian shore. It was close. Many of their ships must have already landed, and were lighting the way for those that remained. Rabigar could feel the relief flow through the vessel after hours of anxiety.

But the relief was premature.

A sailor called out a second warning, and this time he pointed into the sky.

Rabigar knew it was the dragon before he saw it. Doubtless, the creature was responsible for much of the fire and smoke they had seen to the north. It had now flown south, looking to wreak more destruction.

What Rabigar wasn't prepared for was the fear that seemed to roll off the creature down onto the ship. The people on the deck moaned, no longer able to speak. It wasn't possible to say what, exactly, caused it. The shape of the thing, perhaps—the long tail and neck at each end, the outstretched wings. The size of it, unlike any creature they had seen before. That it was airborne, making it faster as well as more powerful than they were. The fact, of course, that they were stuck on a drifting pile of wood, exposed, with no rocks to hide under.

Rabigar succumbed to the fear, just like everyone else. But his hand brushed against the hilt of Bolivar's Sword and the weapon gave him the courage to react. It was just in time.

Its wings furled back and a great roar erupted from its long throat. The sound of death. The dragon dived through the air towards them, a green devil hurtling through a grey sky.

'Into the sea!' Rabigar shouted. 'Get overboard!' He drew his sword, facing the oncoming beast.

Some reacted quickly enough, running to the sides of the ship. He heard the shouts and splashes as they hurled themselves into the Lantinen, but he didn't see, for his eyes were now trained on the dragon. It was coming right for him, his defiance provoking its wrath.

The dragon opened its maw and flames erupted down onto him. The sudden heat engulfed him, as if he had fallen into a fire. He held Bolivar's Sword in front of him. Somehow, the weapon protected him from the flames, deflecting them to the sides. Wherever they went, the ship caught fire, ablaze in a matter of seconds. Even though the flames didn't touch him, the heat became too much for Rabigar and he wilted, collapsing to the deck, only just able to keep his sword aloft.

The dragon passed overhead with a screech of fury.

Rabigar was surrounded by flames and now he panicked, unable to see anything but fire and smoke. It got in his eyes, his nose, his lungs. Desperate, he pulled his cloak over his face and began walking. He resisted the urge to run, knowing he could trip, bang his head, and that would be it. He could feel his skin crackling and burning. A rope, still taut, blocked his passage, and he moved around it before resuming in the same direction. He was rewarded when he bumped into the side of the ship. Still holding Bolivar's Sword, he swung one leg over the side, before half jumping, half falling out of the burning ship.

He plunged into freezing water. He held his breath, trying not to flail about as held onto his weapon for all he was worth, kicking with his legs, until somehow he emerged into cold air, gasping for breath.

Rabigar knew enough that he should tread water at first, letting his body adjust to the freezing temperature of the sea. The flames of the ship blinded him, so that he could see nothing else. Fearful, he scanned the sky for the return of the dragon.

He decided he had to move. Krykkers weren't built for water. His heavy torso, encased in its natural armour, pulled him down, and the blade in his hand prevented him from using the smooth, controlled strokes that would have seen him cut through the water. He turned to face the Halvian shoreline and tried to pull himself in that direction, splashing about and not getting very far. Waves crashed into him, preventing him from gaining any kind of rhythm.

He would not let go of Bolivar's Sword. He would not be the Krykker to lose the greatest treasure of his race, the weapon of their greatest hero. He would rather drown with it than wash up on the shore without it.

He looked about him. Ahead was another Vismarian ship, also set alight. To his right and slightly behind him were the burning remains of the ship he had escaped from. He couldn't see anyone else in the rolling black waves.

Wait, Rabigar thought to himself. *Why is the ship so far to the right?*

The sea. The sea is pushing me in that direction. He looked ahead again. He wasn't getting any closer to the Halvian shore, where the rest of his people had set lights to guide the last of the armada. He was being drawn away by the tide.

Rabigar had to fight down the panic that gripped at his insides, that clamped his throat.

He had to swim hard for the shore now, while he still had enough energy. If he left it any longer, he would be dragged farther out to sea.

Rabigar put his head down and pumped with his arms, kicked with his legs. He threw his head to the side, gulping a breath of air, before pushing ahead again. He didn't waste energy looking about him, checking how far he had got. He just pushed and kicked, his arms burning with the effort, his lungs ready to burst.

He stopped, looked up. He could see the shoreline, but he was still too far away. He put his feet down. Maybe he was close enough to stand? No.

He started swimming again, but he had given everything he had now. He was too tired, unable to move his limbs properly. He felt dizzy. If he lost consciousness now, he would drown. But if he stopped moving, he was dead anyway.

Drop the sword. Part of his mind was telling him to leave the weapon behind, to save himself. *No. Never.*

He gave it one last push, trying to drag his heavy body to shore. He began to sink under. He held his breath. He could see Bolivar's Sword in his right hand ahead of him, sinking down with him. At least he hadn't let go of the sword, he told himself idly, as the oxygen left his brain. At least they would drown together. That was some comfort.

It was time to give up now. He'd done his best.

Then Rabigar was pulled up, his head breaking through the water, and he took a choking mouthful of air.

Strong hands clamped onto him and picked him up, his whole body leaving the sea.

He looked about, head lolling, feeling impossibly high, as he was carried towards the shore. He heard the slosh of legs walking through shallow water, saw the sandy beach, and suddenly he was flying straight toward it as whoever carried him threw him onto the sand.

Rabigar lay there for a while, unable to move, like a fish out of water.

His hand twitched. He was still holding the sword. He was alive, and he still had Bolivar's Sword. It gave him a last spark of energy.

He pushed himself up onto his hands and knees. Half a mile down the beach, dancing light caught his eye. When he looked, he saw the shoreline was aflame. The dragon had torched the armada. The Vismarian fleet, saved from the Kharovians, was now destroyed. Just like the ships of the Sea Caladri.

He heard a wheezing sound and turned to look in the other direction.

Rabigar got such a shock he let go of his sword. Stood in the flickering shadows cast by the bonfire behind him, bent over, hands on knees as it got its breath back, was the largest human he had ever seen. At least eight feet tall, it was large in every respect, seawater dripping down from its hair and clothes like a sea monster that had emerged from the depths.

And, for some reason the most shocking of all, it was a woman. This woman had literally picked him up and carried him to the shore. She was still bent double, chest heaving from the exertion. Despite everything that had happened, Rabigar couldn't help but look at her chest heaving up and down, for like everything else about her, it was unfathomably large.

She turned her head, standing up to tower over him, before putting her hands on her hips.

'Well, I've found a right one here, haven't I?' she asked him. 'Bloody dragon come and burned us all to bits, and all you can do is stare at me tits!'

COMEBACK KINGS

XVII

Time is a strange enemy, Farred mused, as the Kellish countryside slipped by on either side.

Everyone agreed that the fastest way to get to Essenberg from Guivergne was by river barge, but it didn't feel like it when you were sat on the deck, impatiently waiting to reach your destination. Their pace was determined by the flow of the Cousel, and there was little that could be done to alter it. If he had taken the roads on horseback, at least he would have felt like he was getting there faster.

Farred was satisfied that he had given the Guivergnais good warning of the threat they faced to the north. The Drobax had overwhelmed the lands of the Grand Caladri and had now turned on the Krykkers. They were unlikely to stop there. Moreover, the Isharites had sent a flying monster that the Grand Caladri had identified as a dragon. They had told Farred in no uncertain terms that the beast was unstoppable.

The Duke of Martras, whose province bordered the Lantinen Sea, was quick to understand the stakes. He had accompanied Farred to the capital, Valennes, to speak with the king, Nicolas. Farred had found Nicolas to be withdrawn and suspicious. He had looked sceptical at Farred's talk of dragons. Well, so be it. Farred had done his part. It was now up to the Guivergnais to defend themselves as best they could.

Eventually, the walls of mighty Essenberg came into view. Baldwin's Bridge towered above them, spanning the Cousel. Two catapults were trained on the river, ready to sink any craft deemed hostile. Emperor Baldwin had built the defences when Guivergne was considered to be Brasingia's greatest threat. To Farred, such petty rivalries now belonged to an age long gone. But a mere two years ago, everyone here would have agreed that the Guivergnais were the national enemy. Time was playing tricks on them all.

The bargemen shouted up to the soldiers, who waved them under the bridge and allowed them to dock inside the city walls. Passengers were allowed off first, and soon Farred was standing on the harbour of the Market Quarter, saying his farewells. He wasted no time in joining the Valennes Road, passing the market stalls stacked with greens and other vegetables. The food purveyors were roasting lamb with mint, and his mouth drooled at the smell of it. He forced himself to walk on, taking the Albert Bridge, the main thoroughfare across the Cousel.

From the north bank, he could see the whitewashed, square towers of Essenberg Castle. He made straight for it, walking down streets lined with the opulent town houses of the merchant and noble classes. The central square opened up before him, and his gaze was drawn to the fluttering flag of the Empire atop the castle. A stag, with seven antler tips, each representing a duchy of the Empire. Only four of those duchies had fought for the Empire at Burkhard Castle last summer. But the sickness at the heart of the Empire had been cut out, thanks to the intervention of Farred's prince, Edgar. Emeric was dead and his duchy of Barissia was now in the hands of the Emperor's brother, Walter.

One of the more welcome things that had come from Farred's role in the defence of Burkhard Castle was that he was on close terms with many of the most powerful men in the Empire. So that when he presented himself at the castle, it didn't take long for the chain of command to respond to his arrival.

Rainer, Baldwin's chamberlain, came to meet him personally. He was a reassuring figure: tall, intelligent, with a firm grasp on facts and figures. He wasn't entirely surprised to hear Farred's news.

'We know Siavash has won control over Ishari. Gustav has warned us of great armies marching south. He is travelling back and forth to the northern realms, so that we have some warning of an invasion. We are expecting it soon. Duke Walter has already based himself at Burkhard, readying its defences.'

Farred remembered watching the Drobax leave Burkhard Castle. He had known then that they would return, but the thought of having to go back there so soon, and face it all over again, made him feel sick.

Rainer read his expression. 'It's not an easy path we have. To my shame, part of me feels glad that the Drobax have hit our allies first, because it buys us a bit more time. The Emperor—he carries the biggest burden of all of us. It is no surprise that he has been suffering with the responsibility. I think it will do him good to hear your news from you, Farred, rather than listening to the same old voices. He has begun to blank us out, rather.'

Farred wasn't sure what Rainer meant by that.

'Would you be willing to wait here while I fetch him?' the chamberlain asked.

Farred agreed, somewhat unsettled by the exchange.

Some time passed before Rainer returned alone.

'The Emperor has asked that you come to his rooms,' said Rainer, looking uneasy.

Farred gave his consent and followed the chamberlain along corridors and up stairs, keeping pace with the lanky official, who no doubt made such journeys several times a day.

Arriving in a quiet corridor, Rainer rapped on a wooden door. A murmur came from behind the door, and the chamberlain opened it, gesturing Farred inside.

'His Imperial Majesty, Emperor Baldwin,' Rainer said, looking red-faced. 'Lord Farred is here.'

As Farred stepped into the room, he saw that the emperor was lounging on a bed, wearing shorts and with a bare torso. A fire was going on one wall, making the room unusually hot and smoky. Sharing the bed was Inge, the young apprentice to Gustav. She wore a silk dress, and they each held a wine glass, a bottle and nibbles in front of them on a wooden tray.

He recalled a similar scene last summer in Burkhard Castle, where they had shared a room. Baldwin had been asleep, and Inge had seemed to enjoy intimating to Farred that they were sleeping together. But that had been at Burkhard Castle, during a siege when Baldwin had every reason to believe he had days to live. This was in the royal castle, when presumably his wife and children were in the same building.

'Farred!' exclaimed Inge, 'it's so good to see you again!' Her mocking tone put him on edge, but Baldwin didn't seem to hear it.

'Indeed!' Baldwin agreed. 'I will never forget the debt I owe you, Lord Farred. Rainer barely had to twist my arm at all to persuade me to see you. Even though I understand your news is sure to sour my mood.'

'I am afraid so, Your Majesty,' said Farred, bowing slightly.

Baldwin waved a hand at his chamberlain. 'You are dismissed, Rainer.'

Rainer exited the room, gently closing the door behind him.

Farred proceeded to tell Baldwin of his journey with the fleet of the Sea Caladri, of Rabigar's expedition to Halvia. He finished with the invasion of the Grand Caladri and Krykker lands by the Drobax, and a fire-breathing dragon.

As he did so, Inge crunched on a handful of nuts from the tray, washing them down with her wine, before refilling her own glass and Baldwin's.

'What adventures you have had!' she said when he was done.

Farred would have liked nothing better than to give the girl a slap. But he realised she was dangerous. He was certainly no match for her.

'It's not all bad news,' said Baldwin thickly.

Toric only knows how much wine he has consumed, thought Farred.

'The Krykkers are no pushovers, and then the Drobax will have to get through Guivergne before they reach our borders. It's about time they got a taste of what we've had, anyway.'

That didn't sound like the Baldwin Farred knew. Inge gave Farred a little shrug. What did that gesture mean?

There was a knock at the door.

'Yes?' said Baldwin in exasperation, as if tired of constant interruptions.

It was Rainer. 'Your Majesty, your queen is asking after you. She is in the hall. I thought it prudent to come and warn you.'

'Shit,' muttered Baldwin.

'Oh, what does that bitch want now?' sighed Inge.

Baldwin looked torn. He looked from Rainer, to Inge, to Farred, as if unsure what to do.

'It would be a great honour to meet the queen,' Farred said into the silence.

'Of course,' said Baldwin. 'What, you've never met Hannelore? Come, come, Farred, let's see what she wants.'

He leaned over to Inge and they kissed, tongues probing each other's mouths, until Baldwin pulled away, got off the bed, and got dressed. It was uncomfortable and odd, Farred not wishing to share a look with anyone else in the room.

He was relieved when the three men left the room, Inge remaining sprawled on the bed.

Rainer led them in the direction of the hall.

'Farred, you were in Coldeberg,' Baldwin said. 'You saw Hannelore then, no?'

'I saw her, but we were never formally introduced, Your Majesty. It was a busy couple of days.'

'Ah well, we shall correct that.'

'I admired from afar, however. She is a handsome woman.'

'Mmm? Yes. Big chested, if you like that kind of thing.'

The tone Baldwin used made it clear that he didn't. But it was the words themselves that Farred found so odd; so out of character. Had the strain on the Emperor caused some kind of nervous breakdown? If so, how would that affect the Empire's ability to defend itself?

They crossed a courtyard to the hall. When they got inside, it was empty.

'Where is she?' Baldwin demanded.

'Oh, forgive me, Your Majesty. Perhaps she gave up and returned to her rooms, or went looking for you herself. I will track her down, don't worry.'

Rainer gave Farred a look as he left. Had the chamberlain made it all up to get Baldwin out of the room? If so, that was a dangerous game to be playing.

Baldwin sighed. 'A dragon, you said?' he asked Farred.

Farred nodded. 'I heard reports of it. It turned its victims to ash.'

'Farred, think for a second what such a beast could do to Burkhard Castle. I wonder if you are willing to help me, Farred. I'm asking you because I trust you, and you're the best informed. Walter is at Burkhard now, fixing the defences. Could you ride north and tell him? He's a clever man, my brother. Perhaps, given some time, he could find a way to mitigate this threat. Even if there's not much he can do, I think he needs to be told. As soon as possible. Rainer will arrange everything, supplies and expenses, for your time and efforts.'

Suddenly, it was like Baldwin was back—like he had sobered up. And, given what he had witnessed here, Farred didn't think that saying no to the Emperor was an option.

* * *

CLARIN SAT cross-legged with the rest of his group at one end of the mound. Armed Persaleians had been set to watch over them. Zared and the rest of his men were nowhere to be seen.

So, Zared had played him for a fool. No doubt he had made contact with these allies in one of the many towns they had passed through, arranging to meet at this very spot so that they could take Clarin and the others captive.

Why he had done it, well—that was less clear. Would he give Clarin and the others up to the Isharites for some advantage? Maybe. After all they had been through together, Clarin hoped not. He couldn't even find much to reproach himself over. He had trusted Zared to get him to Baserno. Had that been the wrong move? Or the best option, that had turned to shit nonetheless? He couldn't decide.

The big man with the spear and shield came over, looking Clarin over. Clarin stared back. He levelled the spear at Clarin.

'Come. We need to talk.'

Slowly, Clarin got to his feet. He shared a glance with Rudy and Jurgen; with the Barbarians; even the two Dog-men. They gave him steady stares. None was panicking yet. They had all survived Samir Durg, after all.

The two of them walked to the edge of the mound and made their way down, taking care since the slope was steep and it would have been easy to slip and twist an ankle. At the bottom, two men were sitting on the ground, looking up at them. Zared and another, a man Clarin hadn't seen before.

Clarin and the spearman walked over, the spearman gesturing that Clarin should sit. Once he did so, the man sat down with them, making it a foursome. Clarin looked at the other two. The man next to Zared was significantly older, with a weathered, soldierly face. But there was a similarity in features that must have been more than coincidence, even down to the loss of hair on top.

The older man offered his hand.

'Clarin, welcome,' he said, his voice dry, tired sounding. 'Zared has just told me much about you and I am honoured to make your acquaintance. I am King Mark of Persala.'

Initially, Clarin was shocked, even dubious, looking at the three faces in front of him. Then it all clicked, and he laughed at his own slowness as much as anything else.

'And this is your son,' he said, indicating Zared.

Both men smiled then, pleased with Clarin's reaction.

'I'm sorry for the deception, truly,' Zared said. 'I was captured soon after the invasion of Persala and sent to the mines. The Isharites didn't know who I was, but the other Persaleians in the mines did. Not one of them gave me away. They kept my secret, many to their graves. If I had told you the truth, and it had gone wrong, then those men's bravery would have been for nothing. I hope you can understand.'

Clarin shrugged. 'If you did what you thought was right, I'll not judge you. So, what of the rest of us now? Prisoners?'

'Certainly not,' said Mark. 'I needed to see and speak to my son first, to learn exactly what the situation was. How he managed to get back home. He has told me the story, including your mission here. The Shield of Persala, eh?'

'From what I've been told,' said Clarin, 'by people far cleverer than myself, we need it to defeat the Isharites. Have you heard of it?'

'Of course,' Mark said, sounding insulted. 'I was once king in more than name, you know. Privy to all the secrets of the Persaleian Empire. I know it was kept in the Temple of Ludovis, a relic forgotten by most, though not by the priests—they forget nothing.' He looked at Clarin, a reckless smile coming to his face. 'I'm minded to help you get it, too. But know this. I barely escaped the invasion alive. I've been hunted throughout my country ever since. The Isharites would love to display my head on the walls of the capital, to make it clear to my people that they are in charge. That there is no hope. Like my son,' he said, slapping Zared's thigh affectionately, 'I owe my life to others who have risked theirs for me, some paying the ultimate price. In the last year I've hidden up trees; under floorboards; in a hole in the ground no bigger than the size of a coffin. If I'm going to risk my life, and the lives of those who have stuck by me, I need to know that the price is worth paying.'

Clarin nodded. Mark had a fair few soldiers with him. But if this was all that was left of the once great Persaleian army, that had conquered most of Dalriya once upon a time, it wasn't so many.

Mark seemed to be thinking, finalising his plan. Hopefully, committing to the mission. 'Alright. First, we need to ascertain whether the priests of Ludovis still have the Shield. Second, will they hand it over to us? If they do and they won't, we must be prepared to take it.'

'So, what now?' Zared asked his father.

'Now we all pack up and move out. We're going to Baserno.'

* * *

BELWYNN WASN'T sure she could get through this. Sebastian's funeral yesterday had been bad enough. But Elana...

She was in the Temple of Madria, sitting on a pew, gripping Theron's hand as tightly as she could, as if that would hold back the tears. It didn't.

Bemus was at the front, tall and gangly, his glum voice echoing throughout the building as he recounted stories of how Elana had healed and treated the people of Heractus. How he did it without breaking down, when the room was full of people crying, some even wailing, she couldn't comprehend. The stories went on and on, but they were stories people knew, had witnessed, and that made them all the more powerful. They emphasised, too, just what a loss Elana was. Bemus addressed this too in his service, forcefully arguing that her mission should be continued, would live on. But how could it, Belwynn wanted to ask. Lives that had been saved would now be lost.

The image of Elana dying on the floor returned to her mind again, unasked for but irresistible. She had saved so many, and when she needed help, there had been no-one. Just Belwynn, kneeling in the blood; useless. She couldn't shake the thought that it was on her. If she had acted more quickly to stop the thing that had possessed Sebastian, Elana would still be alive. She was Elana's second disciple, and when Elana had really needed her, when she could have made a difference, she had failed her.

As she lay dying, Elana had clutched her hands. Belwynn wasn't sure what she had wanted, but a strange force had overcome her and she had collapsed, unconscious. When she came around, it was too late. Elana was already dead.

She wanted to leave the temple, to run away. But the least she could do—the very least—was to sit and listen.

OUTSIDE, Elana's body was carefully lowered into the ground. Belwynn stayed awhile, to speak with the community, before Theron led her away from the Temple and up to the castle. They held hands as they went, both of them instinctively needing each other's company after the losses they had suffered.

It was hard, but they didn't have the time to grieve properly.

Sebastian's body had been found not long after Elana's death. Dorian, who had chased him from Elana's rooms, had left Heractus with his older brother Straton.

Not everyone wanted to believe it. But Belwynn was sure, and she had made Theron understand too. Some creature, some nightmare sent by the Isharites, had killed Remi and taken his body. Despite a thorough search, his body was still missing. As Remi, the monster had killed Sebastian. They only knew this because little Lyssa had been playing in a secret tunnel and witnessed the murder. As Sebastian, it had killed Elana, and almost certainly Dorian. As Dorian, it had killed two more knights, before leaving the city with Straton in tow. The Isharites had taken their revenge for the Kalinthian invasion of Haskany and for the death of Erkindrix. They had killed Madria's priestess. And the creature was still out there.

More was to come.

Belwynn had come close to despair at Elana's death, had assumed that all hope was lost. But she had talked with Soren, and he had turned her around. They still had three of Madria's seven weapons. He believed he was close to getting a fourth. Clarin had gone to Persala to find the fifth. They had to continue.

Belwynn and Theron took the familiar route through the gates of the castle and up to his rooms. Tycho was already there waiting, no doubt with a list of tasks for Theron to tackle.

The Order of the Knights of Kalinth had lost their Grand Master. It wasn't official yet, but everyone knew Theron would replace his uncle. His first task would be to hunt down and kill the creature that had torn their world apart. Belwynn hadn't even dared to voice her fears on the subject. What if it couldn't be killed?

Only the weapons can kill it.

A voice in her head. But not like Soren's. Not words, even. More like thoughts, or ideas. Belwynn clasped the sides of her head, sinking to her knees.

Theron and Tycho both stood at once, turning to her with concern.

'What is it Belwynn?' Theron asked.

'A voice! I don't know—'

Since Elana's death, she felt different. Something had changed. Was she going mad?

You know who I am, Belwynn.

* * *

THEY TRAVELLED MOSTLY IN SILENCE, Dorian hunched over the reins, staring ahead as if in a trance, the two horses clip-clopping their way along the road south from Heractus. Straton had tried to make conversation, but his younger brother wasn't interested, seemed to be locked away in his own private world. The back of the cart was empty, save for an item, the same size and shape as a body, wrapped up in canvas.

'Just ignore it,' Dorian had told him when he had spotted Straton looking at it.

So Straton didn't look at the item in the back of the cart, ignoring the smell of rancid meat. He didn't interact with his brother. He sat there and thought. He'd never been much of one for thinking—he'd never pretended otherwise. He was a doer, and that was how he liked it. But in the last few months he'd been forced, with no company but his own, to think. A lot of the time he thought about Theron, of the various punishments he could inflict on him when he was defeated. But instead, he knew he had to think more clearly about *how* to defeat him. He had thought he had done it, escaping with Ampelios, raising an army together, allying with Euthymius. But Theron had beaten them. That had hurt.

Defeating Theron was his greatest desire. But Euthymius and Ampelios were dead. How was he going to raise an army again, with no support but from his brother, who seemed to be suffering from some kind of brain-sickness?

THE CART STOPPED and Straton's eyes flew open. He'd drifted off to sleep, lulled by the movement of the cart and the lack of conversation.

'We're here,' Dorian said.

Where was here? Straton looked about, still befuddled by sleep. Then he saw the elegant spires of the High Tower, seat of the Knights of the Kalinth. What was Dorian doing, leaving Heractus just to go to the headquarters of their enemies?

'Get down,' Dorian added.

Nervous of his brother, Straton got down and followed him round to the back of the cart. Oh no. He had hoped he would be able to forget about the contents of the canvas sacking, but Dorian reached over and grabbed an edge, sliding it along the cart towards them.

'Help me with this.'

Straton took the weight on one end, holding what was unmistakably the legs of some victim his mad brother had slaughtered.

They carried the body about a hundred feet into the woods by the side of the road. Straton stood panting with the exertion. His brother seemed unaffected. In fact—

'Go back to the cart and wait for me. I won't be long.'

This was now getting too odd to just go along with. 'Dorian, let's get out of here. We'll raise an army together, fight the Knights.'

'Yes,' his brother replied. 'We'll do all that. I just have one thing to do here first. Wait in the cart for me.'

THIS WAS RIDICULOUS. He had a good mind to drive off and leave Dorian here. If it was anyone else but his own flesh and blood, he would already have done so by now. As it was, he would give him one last part of the hour to get back. Then that was that, brother or no.

A rustling sound from the trees made him turn. At last, Dorian had returned, and he had brought someone.

Straton recognised Galenos, Grand Master of the Knights, or at least that had been his title before he was replaced by Sebastian and imprisoned in the High Tower. Dorian guided the man over to their cart. Straton had met him enough times over the years to know it was Galenos, but he looked different. Thinner and frailer than the man who had enjoyed his position as the second most powerful individual in Kalinth. Well, no doubt Straton had looked better before his captivity.

Dorian indicated Galenos should get into the back of the cart. The old Grand Master looked anxiously from Dorian to Straton.

Straton thrust a thumb towards the back of the cart. 'Get in,' he said. If Galenos thought he was going to give up his seat in the front, he was sorely mistaken. Straton was just pleased that Dorian had left the dead body in the woods.

They climbed into the cart.

'Galenos has agreed to help you become king,' said Dorian.

Straton turned to Galenos, who gave an anxious nod.

'Many thanks, Grand Master. In return, I shall ensure that you are fully returned to your rightful position, and that the traitors, Counts Sebastian and Theron, are hunted down and executed.'

He smiled magnanimously, frowning when Galenos didn't respond.

'Thank you, Your Majesty,' the old man managed at last.

Straton held back a shake of the dead. It seemed like the old man had lost it. Still, not such a bad thing for him to have an enfeebled Grand Master when he took the throne.

'This will help us bring many knights to our cause,' said Dorian. 'But we will need more soldiers.'

'Yes, well, I've been thinking about that,' said Straton proudly. 'With Ampelios dead, the biggest landholder in Kalinth is Count Diodorus. He fought against me last time, but maybe he can be persuaded to switch sides.'

'I'm sure he can be.'

THE JALAKH BOW

XVIII

Zared was given the leadership of those who would enter Baserno. With him went Clarin and the rest of their group, plus ten of Mark's soldiers, led by the big spearman, Duilio. It was a big enough number for a fight if it came to that. Mark would wait for them outside Baserno with the rest of his force. If their attempt to get the Shield led to disaster, he would still be around to continue the resistance to the Isharites.

Thick, curved walls greeted them as they approached the capital, interrupted by squat round towers. It looked impregnable, and yet the rumour was that Arioc and Shira of Haskany had taken the city in a day. Clarin would have liked to witness such a feat.

They passed through the West Gate, lodged between two of the round towers, in one large group. Zared claimed they were a unit of the Isharite army ordered to the capital. They were waved through with little fuss. Clarin didn't know whether the guards at the gate believed them, or were in on the deception. Recent events had made it clear that he had little control over what happened in Persala. He had to go with it, hoping that they somehow got their hands on the Shield.

A wide road took them in a straight line from the gate towards Baserno's Central Square. Clarin gawped at the great city. They passed statues of Persaleian gods and heroes at regular intervals along the route. The buildings they passed were constructed of white marble, with gloriously tall pillars everywhere.

Carved creatures appeared on the pillars and walls, leering down at them as they passed. And huge windows, everywhere. Clarin had never seen so many all in one place—indeed, was convinced that nowhere else in Dalriya could rival it.

It was odd. There was no obvious sign that it was a city under occupation. The buildings and statues had not been despoiled. No foreign soldiers patrolled the streets. There was no symbol of Isharite power that Clarin could see. He thought of the walls of Samir Durg, sparkling with diatine crystals, and of the huge towers they had fought through on the walls of the Isharite fortress. The Isharites had made no effort to turn Baserno into an Isharite city. It seemed that once the Persaleians had capitulated, the Isharites had largely ignored them.

Then he realised what the difference was. Baserno was quiet, the streets half empty. He compared it to Essenberg, the great city of the Empire. In Essenberg, there was constant noise, movement, bustle, at any time of day and long into the night. Baserno was sedate; polite. Where had its people gone? Some into the army, some sent to the mines in Samir Durg, others Toric only knew where. Nowhere nice. Visually, Baserno had been left virtually untouched, but the people who actually made it a city had been scattered. They were walking through a diminished version of Baserno—a museum—not the real city at all.

When they arrived at the Central Square, Clarin's jaw dropped a second time. He could see Rudy and Jurgen, and the Barbarians, sharing awed expressions. He had been expecting to see the Imperial Palace, the Temple of Ludovis, and that would be it. Instead, he found himself looking at a vast square filled with buildings that would each be the centre of attention in virtually any other city. There were a dozen temples altogether. Then there were monuments, obelisks, giant statues, theatres, fountains, bathhouses and a large circus with a race track. It made Clarin wonder why one city would need all this for itself. And it made him realise that all the other cities of Persala he had seen were attempts to copy Baserno. Inferior versions of this city had been spawned for miles in every direction, aping the design and layout, unable to come close to matching the grandiosity.

The population of Baserno was reduced, that much was plain, but thousands of citizens were still crammed into the Square. This was where people met to socialise and do business. Vendors hawked their wares, many selling from within the temple precincts which were hubs of noisy activity. Their group of twenty-eight was not so many that it made a difference to the atmosphere. Those that paid attention to their arrival were the street peddlers who approached them with their goods or shouted out their offers as they walked past.

They stopped when they reached the huge, rectangular site that was the Temple of Ludovis. Tall pillars stretched to the sky, holding up a substantial peaked roof. Through the gaps between the pillars, Clarin could see a walled building.

'Some of us need to go in,' Zared said quietly to those around him, 'ascertain the situation. The rest be ready to move in if they don't hear anything. No more than an hour afterwards.'

'I'll lead the second group,' offered Duilio, one hand clutching his huge spear. 'Me and my men are more the fighting type than the talking type.'

Clarin thought he may have found a kindred spirit, but nonetheless, he offered to go in with Zared. He wanted to play a full part in finding the Shield.

So it was that Zared, Clarin and Cyprian took the steps up to the Temple, while Duilio and the rest waited for them outside.

Up the steps and past the pillars was an area set aside for stallholders, positioned either side of the route into the main building. It was busy, and they squeezed through a throng of shoppers before they got to the open doors of the main temple building. Zared didn't pause, marching straight inside and accosting one of the priests.

Clarin looked around the interior of the building. Smaller pillars ran up the length of the building, with decorative arches between them. They supported a gallery above, from where people looked down over the main space. The floor was made from coloured mosaics, natural scenes with animals and plants decorated the edges of the floor, while in the centre were scenes featuring Persaleian men and women, or perhaps their gods. An altar to Ludovis stood in an open space at the far end of the building. Statues lined the walls, each one given its own alcove with a pair of pillars and a peaked roof. The altar and the statues drew worshippers, but all about the space Baserno citizens mixed with the orange robed priests of Ludovis.

Zared caught Clarin's eye and gestured that he should follow. The priest led them towards the far corner of the temple. They approached a second priest, talking quietly with two visitors. He was short, broad-shouldered, with hair turning grey. He glanced their way, continuing his conversation. They waited patiently before he extricated himself from his conversation. The first priest whispered in his ear before leaving them to it.

'Prince Zared,' he said, tilting his head in a small bow.

'Flamen Aulus,' Zared replied. 'Thank you for seeing us.'

'Of course. Any news of your father?'

'He is well. I am representing him today.'

'I see. I am pleased to hear of your father's health. These are truly difficult times. I understand that you have come looking for the Persaleian Shield?'

'Correct. These are my friends, Cyprian and Clarin. We escaped from Samir Durg last year.'

Aulus raised his eyebrows at the news.

'We have contacted other groups outside Persala. There is an alliance to defeat Ishari. To do so, we need the Shield.'

'The Persaleian Shield has been in the hands of Ludovis since time immemorial. During that time some have sought to claim it, but it has never been given up.'

'Now is the time to do so,' Clarin said.

'So you say,' Aulus responded frostily. 'Only a select few even know of its existence. What has prompted the interest?'

'Other weapons have already been collected,' Clarin said. 'The Dagger of the Lippers, the Sword of the Krykkers, the Staff of the Caladri. It is time for the humans to make their contribution.'

Aulus looked at them, his expression giving nothing away. 'I will give you a chance to claim it,' he said at last. 'If what you say is true, and it is the will of Ludovis, it will be yours to wield. Come,' he said, starting off.

'Where to?' asked Zared.

'The treasures of the Temple are not kept *in* the Temple. That would be very foolish. We are not fools, Prince Zared.'

When they exited the Temple, Aulus was quick to spot the rest of their force lounging about outside.

'I hope there are no plans to take our treasure by force,' he said sternly. 'That would not work. The Shield is in a secret location. I don't know where it is. You could pull all the nails from my hands and feet, pull out all of my teeth, and I wouldn't tell you, because I don't know.'

'Please, Flamen Aulus,' said Zared, visibly taken aback by his words. 'We are not here to take it by force, I assure you. Those men are here for our protection. This is dangerous work we are about.'

'Very well. Then you will ensure that we are not followed.'

'Of course.'

Zared's eyes shifted in his head at the predicament. 'Cyprian, stay with the others. Impress on them the need to stay exactly where they are.'

Cyprian nodded and headed over to speak with Duilio and the others.

Oh shit, Clarin said to himself. *We're on our own.*

Aulus led them north out of the Central Square, up what must be the Great Road. The road stretched from Haskany in the north to Cordence in the south, one of the great legacies of the Empire the Persaleians had created. It made Clarin wonder who else had passed this way, which great emperors and armies had set off from Baserno to conquer the other peoples of Dalriya.

Soon, though, Aulus took them off the Great Road. Right, then left, then right again. The streets of Baserno all ran parallel to one another, so while Clarin didn't feel completely lost, it became hard to spot recognisable features, as one street looked much like the next. They were walking through a residential area. The houses were still built from the same beautiful marble as the rest of the city, but it was eerily quiet, as if most of them were empty.

Finally, Aulus led them to an unexceptional looking house half way down the street. Clarin had to admit, it was a better place for the priests to hide a treasure than in the temple itself.

Aulus approached the wooden door and knocked slowly, five times. They waited. Clarin wanted to ask who lived here, but that would be revealed soon enough. Patience was needed.

Eventually, they heard the noise of several locks sliding open and the door was opened. An old man appeared before them. He had unkempt hair and a long, straggly beard. His clothes looked like they hadn't had a wash since last spring.

'Aulus,' he said in a croaky voice, as if not used to speaking.

'I bring visitors who would speak with you, Ennius. This is Prince Zared, son of King Mark.'

Ennius stared suspiciously at Zared, then gave a harrumph. 'Mark was a usurper, traitor to the imperial line. He brought this catastrophe on us!'

Zared stared wide-eyed at the old man before recovering somewhat. 'I am not here to discuss politics,' he said.

'And who is this lump?' Ennius asked.

'I am Clarin.'

'Clarin who? Clarin from where?'

'I am from Magnia.'

'A Magnian, by Ludovis!' Ennius declared, bushy grey eyebrows rising up and down. 'The only people in all of Dalriya to resist the Persaleian Empire! If they were all as big as you, I can begin to understand why. Come in, then,' he said, turning around and disappearing inside his house.

They followed Ennius into his front room. A small fire in the grate gave out smoke and not much heat. There were enough chairs for all to take a seat. Ennius didn't offer food or drink, instead he sat waiting for someone to start.

'Zared and Clarin have requested the Shield of Persala,' Aulus explained.

'Very well,' said Ennius, apparently unimpressed by the news. 'That's simple enough. Just give me a name. Tell me who wants it and it's yours.'

Clarin thought about it. Was it some kind of riddle? Who wanted it? Well, *he* did. He had come all this way for the Shield. And what was more, he fancied wielding it, too. Soren had the staff. Moneva, the dagger. Why shouldn't he have the shield?

'Clarin,' he said.

Ennius turned to Aulus. 'He comes all the way from Magnia, dares to ask for our Shield, and then gives me his own name? Why have you brought these fools here?'

Oh, Clarin said to himself. *That's clearly not what he was looking for.*

'King Mark,' said Zared.

Ennius gave another harrumph and turned away from them all, staring into the fire.

Zared looked at Clarin in mute desperation.

Think, Clarin, he told himself. *Who wanted the Shield? Who wanted the weapons?*

'Madria,' he said.

'You'll have to do better than that,' Ennius said, still staring furiously into the fire.

Have to do better than that, Clarin reflected. But he hadn't sounded quite so cross. Was he getting closer? If not Madria, then who?

'Elana?' he offered.

Ennius stopped staring at the fire and turned to look at Clarin. Deep brown eyes stared at him, suddenly magnetic in their intensity.

'Not quite correct, unfortunately,' Ennius murmured, his voice quite different now—hushed, expectant.

Clarin felt angry with frustration. What kind of test was this? If Madria was close, and Elana closer, then who?

Elana was the priestess of Madria. Belwynn was her disciple. But why would Belwynn be correct if Elana wasn't? He almost said her name, then stopped. *Don't be stupid, Clarin,* he told himself. His infatuation with her was muddling his thinking.

'Go on,' said Ennius, in the same voice.

I don't have a name, old man! He wanted to shout. *Oh, sod it.* 'Belwynn.'

'Yes,' Ennius said simply.

'What?' blurted out Aulus and Zared in unison.

'That is the correct answer,' Ennius said simply. 'The Shield must be passed into this man's keeping.'

'How do you know Belwynn?' Clarin demanded.

'I don't, you great Magnian muttonhead! Aulus, will you fetch it?'

'I don't know where the Shield is kept, remember Ennius?'

'Oh yes. I forget myself. It's just next door.'

'What?' asked Zared.

'It's kept in the house next door,' Ennius repeated. 'It's easier that way.'

The Persaleian Shield was circular, covered in leather that had been painted red, black and yellow. In the middle, the head of a bearded man had been painted, with two horns emerging from his forehead.

'Ludovis,' Ennius explained when he saw Clarin looking at it.

The sight of the shield had a profound impact on Clarin, while the touch of it caused a shiver to run through the tips of his fingers to the rest of his body. This was much more than an ordinary shield, yet if he had been asked to explain why, he couldn't have put the feeling into words.

They all knew there wasn't time to waste. Reluctantly, Clarin wrapped the shield in sackcloth and strapped it to his back.

'Farewell Ennius,' he said, still without understanding what had happened in the old man's house.

'Use it well.'

Aulus led them back to the Temple, where the group was still waiting for them.

Zared nodded curtly at Duilio and the rest of his men. Their eyes widened, but they controlled their reactions. They all knew that their mission was only half complete until they had safely left the city with the weapon.

'Thank you, Aulus,' said Zared, shaking the flamen's hand.

'I pray that what we did today takes you a step closer to liberating our country,' Aulus said. 'Good luck.'

With that, they left the Temple of Ludovis behind. Clarin gave the Central Square of Baserno one last look. The Shield of Persala had been resting here long enough. It was time to use it.

* * *

Elana's death had wounded them all. It had never been spoken out loud, but Gyrmund was sure they had all shared a sense that they were doing this for her, collecting the weapons for Madria's champion. Now she was dead, struck down by some hellish creature that had taken Sebastian's form. Gyrmund found it hard to take. He had seen a touch of innocence to Elana. A gentle goodness that had been unique to her.

But if Gyrmund was struggling with his grief, the reaction of the other two was more severe. At least Soren knew Belwynn was alive and safe. But this didn't seem to soften him. He wore a hard face now. It reminded Gyrmund of the Soren who had appeared in Edeleny, grabbing the Grand Caladri elder Agoston, taking his magic in order to restore his own powers, before discarding his husk of a body. And Moneva, who had only just come out of her shell, only just started smiling again, was even worse. She barely spoke to anyone, a look of murderous intent fixed on her face.

The morning after Gansukh's fourth fight, three Jalakh warriors were found dead. Their throats had been slit in the night. Angry recriminations followed, the Oligud tribe accused.

But Gyrmund knew it was Moneva.

A challenger still appeared on the fifth day to fight Gansukh. It had been a close contest for a while, Gansukh having to fight with an injured arm. But after five minutes, one of the Jalakhs in the crowd started screaming, before a sudden haemorrhage left him sprawled on the ground, blood shooting out from his nose and mouth as if his head had exploded. Soren, face grim, had bent the rules, targeting a Jalakh wizard rather than the fighter in the ropes. The chaos completely distracted the other tribes, while Soren and Bolormaa turned all their power on the fight. Gansukh's opponent could barely move, held in a web of magic, before Gansukh slew him with a strike to the head.

The Oligud warrior was livid, railing at his mother and Soren, demanding that she send the three foreigners away. But that was the last thing Bolormaa was going to do.

The sixth day began with two more murdered warriors. Gansukh entered the ropes, but there were no challengers.

On the seventh and last day, the Day of Destiny, Gansukh again entered the ropes unchallenged. A sea of Jalakh people, sullen faced, cowed, all bended the knee.

They had a new khan.

. . .

'They can't come in,' said Gansukh, gesturing angrily at Gyrmund, Moneva and Soren.

The new khan was already asserting his authority. But his mother wasn't so easily put off.

'They got you here,' she whispered to him fiercely. 'When they've gone, you can forget that. Take all the credit for yourself. All the Jalakhs will forget it. But while they're here, no-one will forget. So I suggest you give them what they want soon, then let them go.'

Gansukh's face curled into a snarl. He looked at Gyrmund and the others, but what he saw was Soren, the implacable wizard who had given him his victories in the ropes, and Moneva, a killer who worked in the shadows, and he seemed to think better of resisting them. He screwed his face up, thinking.

'Just him,' he said, pointing at Gyrmund.

Gyrmund looked at Moneva and Soren, raising his eyebrows.

They shrugged their acceptance and Gyrmund stepped forwards.

Gansukh, content that he had been obeyed, turned around and walked through the gate in the outer wall of the Temple.

A small group followed behind. As well as Bolormaa and Gyrmund, there were a few other notables of the Oligud tribe, and a few of Gansukh's friends, men who would now perhaps become his generals.

A trio of priests met Gansukh as he entered the Temple grounds. He bowed his head, and they each placed a wreath of flowers around his neck before leading him on.

Ahead was the entrance to the pagoda, which Moneva had described to Gyrmund, though this was the first time he saw it for himself. A small set of steps led up to the entrance, while four pillars supported a roof that extended out towards them.

Bolormaa saw him looking at the pagoda and fell in with him. 'Gansukh will spend the night in there,' she explained, as the three priests led them past the entrance. 'Our rituals say he will enter as an Oligud and awake tomorrow as a member of all the tribes—as a khan.'

She spoke with pride and reverence.

'Your husband would be proud,' said Gyrmund.

'He is.'

The group left the pagoda behind and joined a path that wound its way into the sacred garden. The priests stopped when they faced a giant tree that stood in the centre of the garden. They all stood facing the tree in a semi-circle before one of the priests produced a saw and handed it to Gansukh. He approached the tree, studying it for a while.

'This one?' he said, pointing at a huge branch that grew out toward the Jalakh tents beyond the temple.

Gyrmund smiled as he saw that it pointed directly at the location where Moneva had climbed over the outside wall, in a failed attempt to find the bow.

'A wise choice, great khan,' said the priest.

Gansukh set to work, making a notch cut first, then cutting into the branch slightly further along, pushing back and forth with his saw. It was as thick as some trees, and it took him a while to cut through, while the rest of them just stood and watched. He grew red-faced and sweaty, and had to stop to rest more than once. But he cut through the last section cleanly, the branch dropping to the ground.

The three priests gathered around the fallen branch.

'See!' one proclaimed. 'The Tree of Destiny has provided us with the Jalakh Bow!'

'What?' said Gyrmund, turning to Bolormaa in shock.

'The priests will now use this branch to make the Jalakh Bow. Gansukh will hunt antelope, and the horn and sinew of the beast he kills will be used in the construction.'

Gyrmund found this difficult to process. 'So, wait? The Jalakh Bow doesn't exist? You said it was here, in Tosongat,' he said accusingly.

'I said it was here in a manner of speaking. The Jalakh Bow is made by order of the khan. Legends say that the Tree of Destiny grew when the original bow was planted into the ground. Or maybe the original bow was also made from this very tree. Come, Gyrmund,' she tutted, that sly smile of hers reappearing. 'You didn't think the *original* Jalakh bow, made from wood hundreds and hundreds of years ago, would still be in existence?'

Gyrmund didn't know what to say.

'But don't think we are giving you an ordinary bow. The Jalakh Bow is made from the Tree of Destiny, using methods preserved by our shamen. It will be the finest weapon in all of Dalriya.'

'How long does it take them to make it?' he asked.

'Not long. But it must be allowed to dry properly. You will be able to use it in days.'

Gansukh approached him, along with his councillors and friends from the Oligud tribe. 'You will take care of our bow?' he asked Gyrmund.

'Of course, Your Majesty. It is an honour to receive it.'

Gansukh nodded. 'My first act as khan is to give away our most precious weapon. But my mother insists that we share the same enemies, so it will still be used for the Jalakh people.'

'I will use it wisely and I promise to return it to you when it is no longer needed.'

'So be it,' said Gansukh, waving a hand in the air as if to be rid of the whole business.

Gansukh, his mother and the rest of the Oliguds left the way they had come.

It took all three priests to carry the branch away. They were presumably going to start work on it immediately.

Gyrmund was left alone in the garden. He looked up at the tree, at the cut where the giant branch had been. He approached, placing one hand on the trunk.

'Thank you,' he said.

BEYOND THE DRANG

XIX

It had taken time to gather their wits after the dragon attack. Rabigar was relieved to learn that the Krykker losses had been a few hundred. He had feared they were much worse.

The dragon had fired the Vismarian fleet, and the Caladri trading vessels, but most people had already made it onto shore. They had run into the swamps and hills of the Pecineg clan. The dragon had not pursued them, flying away over the ocean.

The Sea Caladri had not been so fortunate. Only four Caladri warships limped back to the shore of the Halvian Krykkers. They spoke of a sea battle where they had gained the upper hand over the Kharovians, until the dragon had turned the outcome of the battle, destroying ship after ship, until the Caladri that remained broke away in an effort to escape. They confirmed what Rabigar had already suspected. Captain Sebo's Red Serpent had been in the thick of the fighting and had gone down. They held out little hope that many more than a few other ships had escaped the destruction. The Sea Caladri fleet, the greatest in Dalriya, was no more.

They hadn't dallied. Rabigar couldn't blame them. Picking up those of their race who had crossed the Lantinen, they departed south to deliver their devastating news to their countrymen. The Krykkers were now stranded, the ships of the Sea Caladri and the Vismarians all lost in one day. More than one Krykker could be heard lamenting over their chances of ever returning home.

But Rabigar had other priorities. He was here to find the Giants' Spear, and that was his only concern right now.

His hopes, it seemed, lay in the form of Gunnhild, the Vismarian woman who had saved his life. She had lifted his sinking body from the seabed and deposited it onto the sand.

The Vismarian leader, Sevald, explained that he had led a small party north hoping to find a family who had knowledge of the paths into the wild lands of western Halvia. He had returned with Gunnhild. She had agreed to take Rabigar into the west. But there was a catch. The area they needed to reach was swarming with Drobax.

So it was that Rabigar left the land of the Pecinegs with an army. It contained about two thousand souls altogether. Chief Wracken of the Binideqs led his soldiers, who would guide them through their clan-lands to the River Drang, that marked the northern border of the Krykkers. Jodivig, chief of the Dramsens, had recruited a force of Dalriyan Krykkers that matched the numbers under Wracken. Sevald came with his Vismarians, men and women who knew the lands north of the Drang. Finally, Ignac of the Grand Caladri led a small group of his exiles. Some of them, like him, were mediums. Their magic might prove useful once they entered the dangerous lands to the north.

As they followed Wracken's force north, Rabigar fell in with Sevald and Gunnhild. The woman's stride was huge, meaning she had to walk in an odd sort of dawdle to travel at the same pace as Rabigar.

'Where did your family live?' he asked her.

'We hunted in the far north, where the cold turns your snot to ice and freezes your eyes shut in the night. Our size allowed us to survive up there, where tiny men like this would shiver and cry,' she said, giving Sevald an almighty slap on the back. He smiled good naturedly at the ribbing.

'We would hunt all manner of beasts, living off elk and bringing back bear and wolf pelts to trade with the lowlanders. What a life it was.'

'What happened?'

'The Drobax came. So we started hunting those bastards instead. But we must have upset someone, because they came for us. And I don't mean like Drobax usually do, running around aimlessly like squirrels looking for their acorns. This was an ambush—well planned. I saw my father go down. My brothers escaped to the north, but I got cut off from them. I pray they got away, that they're hiding in the icy wastes, somewhere too cold for the Drobax to follow. Anyway, I was chased miles to the south. That's where Sevald found me, talking some nonsense about giants and spears.'

'What do you know about the Giants?' Rabigar asked.

'Oh, plenty of stories about the Giants in my family. Stories that we're descended from a giant. The truth is they left for the west. A long, long time ago.'

'How do we find them? Or find where they went?'

'Farther west of where the Vismarians and Krykkers live, there are miles and miles of ice fields. Not much lives out there. If you tried walking that way, you would fall through the ice, sooner or later. Even if you're a lucky bastard, and all the odds are in your favour, it will still only take a few days before the ice gets you. The only way to travel west is down the Nasvarl. The source of the Nasvarl is in the northern wastes. But they say it flows west, all the way to the edge of the world. If we head northwest from here, we will reach a good spot in the river that thaws early. From there we can head downriver.'

RABIGAR HEARD the Drang before he saw it. Chief Wracken had chosen to reach the river at sundown, when their activity was less likely to be noticed by any Drobax in the area. Rabigar looked out from the southern bank and saw the Drang was wide and full, bringing huge quantities of meltwater from the highlands of Halvia to the Lantinen Sea. A strange looking apparatus sat in the river.

Chief Wracken sent twenty of his soldiers towards it and then, noticing Rabigar's interest, approached him to explain.

'We've destroyed all the other bridges across the river. So far, it's kept the Drobax from crossing in significant numbers. This is now the only way for us to go beyond the Drang.'

As Rabigar watched, the Krykkers on the bank lowered a drawbridge-like contraption onto a small, artificial looking island that lay about a quarter of the way into the river. Once lowered, they crossed the drawbridge onto the island, where a second drawbridge was lowered onto a larger, natural island that lay in the middle of the river. It was big enough to hold a few wooden buildings. Rabigar could see that two further drawbridges would complete the route and allow them to reach the north side.

'Ingenious,' he said, enthused. 'It allows you to cross but denies passage to the Drobax.'

'Yes. I will leave a few men on the south bank and on the middle island for when we return, just in case we need to make a quick crossing.'

Wracken ordered his soldiers to cross first, securing a bridgehead, before the rest of the army followed behind.

Despite the late hour, they had attracted the attention of a small number of Drobax. By the time Rabigar got across, the brief encounter was over, a pile of Drobax bodies casually dumped next to where the latrines had been marked out. But it didn't bode well.

They were quick to make a camp. Each of them carried a sharpened wooden stake that were used to build a defensive perimeter around the camp. Wracken insisted the Binideqs would handle the night watch, and so Rabigar settled down to eat his rations with the Dalriyan Krykkers. He was surprised to see a familiar figure come over to join him.

'Stenk? I had no idea you were here!'

'Jodivig asked me to come,' Stenk said proudly.

The truth was, Rabigar was surprised to see the young Dramsen Krykker. Stenk had fought in his very first battle with Rabigar last summer, against the Isharite army in Haskany. But, Rabigar supposed, that now made him a veteran. When you factored in the many losses suffered by the Krykkers, and accounted for the fact that Maragin had kept many of the best warriors with her in the underground tunnels of the Krykker mountains, that made Stenk one of the more experienced fighters they had left to call on.

'We're going to find a spear?' Stenk asked, his brow creasing in confusion.

How many of these soldiers really understood what they were doing, Rabigar wondered. Events had moved too fast to explain things fully.

Rabigar drew Bolivar's Sword. 'When Bolivar defeated the dread lord of Ishari at the Battle of Alta, he had six other champions with him.'

He turned to see that other Krykkers were looking at him, listening intently to what he said.

'There was a Lipper, with a dagger. A Caladri medium, with a staff. A human with a shield. A Jalakh archer. And there was a Giant, who wielded a great spear. We need to find this spear here in Halvia, far to the west. When these weapons are assembled, we can use them to defeat the Isharites.'

'How?' pressed Stenk. 'How will these weapons rid the Drobax from these lands? From our lands back in Dalriya?'

Rabigar felt all too aware of the eyes on him. They were hungry for answers—certainties—when there were none.

'Remember,' Rabigar answered, making sure his voice carried. 'My friends stole into the very heart of Ishari, the fortress of Samir Durg. Who did they kill there?'

'Erkindrix,' someone offered.

'Yes, the dread lord himself. And who knows what weapons they had with them? Not our sword, for no Krykker went with them.'

'The dagger and the staff,' said Stenk.

'Correct. With just two of these weapons, they entered the dread lord's own lair and killed him. And at that very time, the forces of the Emperor of Brasingia were defending Burkhard Castle, that great fortress that our ancestors built. When Erkindrix was slain, the horde of Drobax, the Haskans and the Isharites, all turned around and fled. So, imagine what will happen when we have all seven weapons together.'

Rabigar's people nodded, satisfied. None of them was so foolish as to believe that they were saved. But they believed they had a fighting chance, and that was all a Krykker should ever ask for.

Wracken woke them while it was still dark. He wanted them to move out without being seen.

Bedrolls were packed, stakes collected, and breakfast taken on the march. But they weren't free of the Drobax. When sunrise came, they could be spotted: small, grey figures, coming in and out of sight. Rabigar saw one looking at them from the top of a hill. Later, someone pointed out a small group, walking through the trees to their right, before the woodland hid them from view again. The Drobax were following them, on each flank, but keeping their distance.

Sevald and the Vismarians now led the army, choosing which route to take through their lands. They avoided the deeply forested areas, in case the Drobax were waiting for them there. But Vismar was wild terrain: heavily wooded, no roads, and full of rocky outcrops, streams and other obstacles. Each time they had to slow down to cross a stream, or their vision was obscured by knoll and hummock, or they descended into a valley, there was a threat of ambush. Scouts had to be sent out, and the constant state of vigilance began to drain energy and fray tempers.

It happened when they were climbing out of a valley. Screams behind them signalled the Drobax were finally attacking. Wracken's Krykkers at the rear turned to face them. Meanwhile, streaming down the valley slopes on either side of their position, more Krykkers came.

'Up!' Sevald shouted. 'We need to take the high ground.'

The Vismarians moved forward at pace, aiming to climb out of the depression. Jodivig, leading the Dalriyan Krykkers, followed the Vismarians. Rabigar went with them, slipping and sliding on the muddy path as he tried to get purchase. They rounded a corner where they stopped, running into each other. Ahead, the Vismarians had come up against a force of Drobax who had been waiting for them. Logs across the path blocked their progress. Drobax hurled stones and rocks down on the Vismarians, who backed away from the trap.

They were surrounded. But what sent a chill down Rabigar's spine were the voices. He saw them. These Drobax were taller and broader than any he had seen before. They were shouting out instructions to the rest of their kind.

'Hold!' some of them shouted, keeping the Drobax behind the logs where they held an advantage.

There was something so unnatural about seeing Drobax opening their mouths and speaking that Rabigar stood rooted to the spot, unable to react.

Meanwhile, the Vismarians turned and retreated, Sevald leading his warriors back down the path. Rabigar could see Gunnhild at the back, her giant frame a target for Drobax rocks, battering them away with her shield.

Jodivig ordered the Dalriyan Krykkers to move back down again, to make room for the descending Vismarians.

The Drobax on the flanks now reached them. Rabigar grabbed his shield from his back, drew Bolivar's Sword and met them. He slashed at one, too quick for it defend with its club, his blade crunching into its shoulder and sending it sprawling to the ground. A second he smashed into with his shield, shoving it backwards, then thrusting his sword forward so that it slid into the chest cavity of the creature. Yanking it out, he saw that a group of Krykkers had come with him.

'Pull back!' came a voice above them.

Rabigar looked up to see one of the larger, new breed of Drobax some distance up the slope, shouting out commands. It looked straight at him, and its sharp face made a vicious grin. It knew the Drobax had the advantage so long as they kept Rabigar's force surrounded. All it had to do was contain and wait for reinforcements.

Rabigar turned to see that Sevald had arrived and was talking with Jodivig. The Krykker chieftain's eyes were wide, close to panic. Rabigar joined them.

'Rabigar,' said Sevald. 'They're too entrenched up there. We need to break out the way we came in.'

Rabigar looked down to where the Binideqs were engaged with the Drobax who had come at them from behind. More Drobax were descending the sides of the valley.

'Alright,' Rabigar said.

It seemed the only option, but it would cost lives. And once they moved, the Drobax at the head of the valley would leave their enclosure and come at them from behind, squeezing the door shut in their trap.

'Rabigar!' came a shout.

It was Ignac. Together with a group of his Caladri, he was trying to get to Rabigar, but the path was too congested.

'We can protect your backs while you break out!'

'Agreed!' Rabigar shouted back.

He held Bolivar's Sword aloft, trying to get the attention of those around him, before pointing it back down the valley to his target. Waiting no longer, he moved, Krykkers and Vismarians following him down the path.

Rabigar led his force off the path and up the side of the valley to his left. Here, they could present their shields, held in the left hand, to the Drobax descending to meet them. The first Drobax swung down at him, using all its strength. He braced himself, taking the blow that rattled up and down his arm, before swinging out with his sword, chopping away the legs of the creature. It came to earth with a crash and as it sprawled there, Rabigar was free to pick his spot, pushing the tip of his blade under the chin and into its head.

He kept moving, circling around the rows of Binideq Krykkers who stood on the path, before coming at the Drobax on their flank. Two of them moved out of position to meet him and he charged them, flinging all his weight behind his shield at the first, knocking it to the ground and barely staying on his feet. He whirled around, sword and shield in front of him in the hopes they would take the expected attack from the second Drobax. The strike came, a short spear glancing off his shield and striking him on the chest, leaving nothing more than a scratch on his tough, armour-like skin.

Jodivig, following in his wake, smashed a battle axe into the back of the creature's neck, completely severing the head, which sailed into the air, eyes still staring out in a look of surprise.

More Krykkers followed them, short weapons for close work at the ready, and Rabigar led them into the Drobax. The battle mist came over him then, the unthinking part of his brain taking over, reacting to threats by raising his shield arm, lusting for blood with his sword arm. Bolivar's Sword hummed like a death machine, dripping red with Drobax blood.

The stink of battle rose as the body count grew, the ground treacherous with piss and shit and gore. The Drobax had brought the numbers, but the Krykkers were better armed and better trained. Finally, the Drobax gave ground under the onslaught.

The Krykkers punched through, retracing their steps down into the valley, aiming to come back out the other side. But although the Drobax had fallen back, they had not retreated. Their leaders, the large ones who spoke, ordered them to harry, as they marched along the path that led through the valley.

Rabigar stayed at the front, leading the army forwards. He began to ascend back up to the other side. The battle fury was leaving him now, and he felt aches and pains. His legs felt heavy, his lungs burned. Behind him, his comrades were struggling with exhaustion, some walking wounded, others supporting those too injured to walk by themselves. He looked back across to the other side of the valley and saw half a dozen tiny figures—the Caladri mediums—holding back a force of Drobax, ready to descend the valley towards them.

Up they marched, desperate to escape the trap the Drobax had laid for them. Rabigar allowed his mind to consider this. Until now, the Drobax had been a mindless enemy, reliant on orders and firm control from their Ishari masters. But this new breed of Drobax seemed to change that. They could communicate, give orders, prepare an ambush and ensure it was carried out. All of which made the threat from the Drobax even more grave.

The creatures continued to hound their movement, while staying clear of Krykker steel. But eventually Rabigar crested the top of the valley. The front ranks dragged themselves onto the flat terrain above, just as the Drobax at the other end of the valley were released and threw themselves down, howling for blood.

Rabigar looked about him, wondering where the most defensible location in these parts would be. He found Jodivig and Wracken. The Binideq leader had taken a blow to the side of his head, his hair matted with blood. Sevald joined them, too. Below, Rabigar could see Gunnhild bringing up the rear of their forces as the Drobax closed in on three sides, her shield deflecting blows, her giant hammer forcing the creatures to keep their distance or else risk being flattened.

'Can we get to a fort or defensive structure?' Rabigar asked Sevald.

Sevald raised an eyebrow. 'There's too many of them,' he said simply. 'We could struggle to a hill or some such, but all that would do is prolong the slaughter.'

'We need to fight our way back to the Drang,' Wracken added. 'That's our only hope of survival.' He spat a mix of saliva and blood onto the ground. 'And that's a faint hope.'

Rabigar shook his head. 'I need to get the Spear.'

'Are you mad?' Wracken demanded angrily. 'Look where that nonsense has got us!'

Rabigar pointed down at the horde of Drobax coming towards them. 'Look what will happen if we don't. You think the Drang is going to keep them out forever? This is a taste of what awaits.'

Ignac appeared. 'We can transport a small number away a short distance. I don't know the area, but perhaps past the valley,' he said, pointing vaguely to the north-west, beyond the Drobax enclosure.

Sevald shrugged. 'It may work, if there are no Drobax waiting for you there. The terrain is gentle enough.'

'Then that's what we do,' said Rabigar. 'Myself and Gunnhild are the two who need to go. If Ignac can send more, whoever else that wants to and could be of use.'

'I'll die with my men,' stated Wracken flatly.

Sevald and Jodivig echoed his sentiments.

'Could you come with us?' Rabigar asked Ignac. 'A medium may be useful to us.'

Ignac nodded. 'Coming with you would make the teleportation easier. That leaves three of our enchanters left who can stay with the army.'

Rabigar saw Stenk waiting a few feet away. He wanted his young friend to live. But were his odds better with the army, retreating to the Drang, or heading west through the treacherous lands of Halvia with him? It was impossible to know.

'Do I have permission to take Stenk if he will come?' Rabigar asked Jodivig.

'Of course. Good luck.'

They all shook hands there and then, for there was no more time to waste. As soon as Gunnhild arrived, she was guided over to the waiting group. Without argument, she took Rabigar's hand in one massive palm and Stenk's in the other. The Caladri mediums made their magic and Rabigar felt himself moving, just like he had done before when Ignac had found Rabigar and his friends wandering lost in the forests of the Grand Caladri. Most of his senses were taken from him, leaving the sensation of movement. It stopped almost as soon as it had begun, leaving a sick feeling in his stomach.

He opened his eye and focused on his surroundings.

They stood in a meadow, a few feet from a stream in one direction and a wood of birch in the other. It would have been possible to believe that they were miles away from the bloody confrontation they had just been a part of, if it wasn't for the sound of howling Drobax carried to them on the air.

Rabigar looked at his companions: young Stenk, giant Gunnhild, and the Caladri magic user, Ignac. All that was left of the army that was supposed to march to the Nasvarl. They had fatally underestimated the strength of the Drobax.

'It was as if they were waiting for us right from the beginning,' he said.

'It was the same with my family,' said Gunnhild. 'They have leaders now.'

'Will the others get back home?' Stenk asked.

'No problem,' said Rabigar quickly.

Maybe Stenk believed him. He could see from the expressions of the other two that they didn't.

'Thanks for bringing me,' Stenk said quietly.

'Glad you're here,' said Gunnhild. 'You can keep an eye on that one,' she said, pointing at Rabigar. 'I swear, all he does is stare at me tits!'

Stenk's eyes bulged as his gaze was drawn, irresistibly, to the chest area of the giant Vismarian.

Gunnhild slapped her thigh and gave a rambunctious, uninhibited laugh, loud enough to alert every Drobax in the region to their precise location.

THE GIFT

XX

FARRED LEFT ESSENBERG BEHIND, taking the Great Road to the north.

It wasn't long before he began to pass groups of people coming the other way. These weren't merchants laden with supplies for the capital. These were family groups, taking with them all the possessions they could carry.

When he asked why, he got the same answer. An army of Drobax was heading for the Empire.

The people were mainly from Rotelegen; some from Grienna. They had learned from what had happened last year. Rotelegen wasn't safe. The imperial army wouldn't defend it. The best option was to abandon the duchy, find refuge in Essenberg, and hope that the Drobax would leave again. Hope that Burkhard Castle could hold against the enemy a second time.

Farred rode on, apprehensive about what he would find when he reached the fortress.

He never made it.

Riders appeared on the road ahead. Scouts of the imperial army. One of them recognised Farred and stopped to speak with him. Walter, Marshall of the Empire and Duke of Barissia, was returning to Essenberg with urgent news.

Farred waited. Soon, Walter's small force of riders appeared. Walter was at the front and next to him was Gustav, Archmage of the Empire. The duke hailed Farred with a smile and asked him to ride with them. He didn't have time to stop.

'I wasn't expecting to find you on this road, Farred,' Walter said. 'Last I heard, from Prince Edgar, you were sailing north with the Caladri fleet.'

Farred briefly explained to the duke, and to the archmage who listened in, that the invasion of the Krykker lands had led him to warn the human realms of the threat. Walter and Gustav shared a dark look at the mention of the dragon.

'How are we supposed to defend against that?' demanded Walter wearily.

Gustav shook his head, seemingly bereft of answers. He looked at Farred. They had developed a close relationship of sorts in Burkhard Castle. Walter had persuaded Farred to support Gustav when he made his transformations into a hawk. It had been an experience Farred had never really got used to, and didn't talk about. 'The Isharite sorcerers have been more active recently. Defending their borders, preventing me from crossing into Persala. The appearance of their army wasn't a total surprise, therefore—though I only saw it once it had crossed into Trevenza. In most respects, it is the same as the force that came at us last year. Thousands upon thousands of Drobax. Isharites, Haskans and other forces in support.'

'Jeremias and Adalheid are evacuating Rotelegen,' Walter added. 'We defend Burkhard, just like last time.' He gave Farred a grave look. 'You and I knew they would return.'

Farred nodded. This was all well and good, but he had a concern he couldn't shake off. He resolved to tell them both. 'You may have a problem,' he began. 'Baldwin and Inge. It began last summer, at Burkhard. Maybe I should have told you then. But when I was in Essenberg, they were in bed together. Baldwin didn't seem himself—' He stopped, not knowing what else to say.

Walter and Gustav shared another look.

'We know,' said Walter quietly, clearly finding the topic awkward. 'My brother has a lot of pressure. Everyone, inside and outside the Empire, looks to him to deal with the Isharite threat. But we all learned something last year. He *can't* deal with it. *We* can't. That's a difficult position to be in. Deep down, he knew this day would come again. So, this affair, it has been a diversion for him. A distraction for his mind until the time comes to fight again. And, after all, emperors and kings with mistresses aren't exactly uncommon.'

'I understand that,' said Farred, unconvinced. 'But Inge isn't a simple mistress,' he said, glancing briefly at Gustav. 'She has powers. I fear she has some control over him.'

Gustav twitched his mouth. It was now his turn to look uncomfortable.

'Inge has power, yes. Is she using her magic on Baldwin? Perhaps,' he admitted. 'But women have ever sought to beguile men, whether they are magic users or not. And men—' the archmage paused, struggling for the right words. 'Sometimes they want to be beguiled. That is what I believe is happening between Baldwin and Inge.'

'If your concerns remain,' said Walter, studying Farred's reaction, 'know two things. I have already sent messengers out to all the dukes of Brasingia, warning them they will soon receive imperial orders to raise an army and take it to Burkhard Castle. And now, Gustav and I ride straight for Essenberg, where we intend to persuade Baldwin to send out such an order. Have faith in my brother. He has always done what is right.'

* * *

BELWYNN AND LYSSA left their room for the other side of the castle, where the chapel was located.

You have it? she asked Soren, desperate for some good news.

Sort of, he replied. *The Jalakh priests have made it. They need to finish it before we're allowed to take it.*

Alright. Come as quick as you can. We need you here.

We will.

Right. Now it was time for her news.

Soren, there's something else.

Yes?

I can sort of speak like this to someone else now. Since Elana died. I can speak with Madria.

Silence. Soren probably thought she had lost her mind. Had she?

You're speaking telepathically to Madria?

Yes. It's more feelings and ideas than words. Maybe this was what Elana experienced, why she thought she knew what to do, but was vague on the details.

Are you sure? What I mean to say is, are you sure it is her and not someone else in your mind? Remember, in Samir Durg, Siavash was able to enter my mind and talk to me.

Yes, it's her. I'm positive. Well—I'm pretty sure it's her.

Belwynn, just be careful. Don't do anything hasty. I'm going to come back as fast as I can.

Alright Soren. Bye.

See you soon, Belwynn.

Don't be hasty. That was easier said than done. A monster was on the loose in Kalinth. It had already killed the two most important people in Heractus. Now Prince Straton and Galenos, the former Grand Master of the Knights, were busy raising an army for it. Doing nothing just wasn't an option.

They walked into the chapel, usually reserved for the royal family. Today it was needed by the Knights, for a ceremony that would normally have been conducted at the High Tower. It was meant to be a celebration, though Belwynn had mixed feelings about it.

Pages guided them to their seats near the stage. Belwynn found herself next to Philon, the young sandy haired knight who had first approached her for a blessing last summer. He had risen up the ranks quickly since that day.

'My lady,' he said politely. The nervous knight from last summer had been replaced by a man of quiet confidence, Belwynn noticed. It had been less than a year, but they had all changed since then.

Belwynn peered to the front, where a group of six young men—children, some of them—were kneeling on the floor.

'There he is, Lyssa,' she said, pointing out Evander, his broad back and neck length dark hair allowing her to identify him.

Lyssa stood up and looked over. She sucked in a breath.

'We don't call out to him, remember,' Belwynn said quickly, causing the girl to sit back down with a grumpy expression.

'Theron says these squires owe much to your efforts on the training ground,' Belwynn said to Philon.

'Some,' he agreed modestly, 'though it varies. Certainly, young Evander has been well trained by Grand Master Theron himself. I could add very little to what Evander already knew.'

Grand Master Theron was a title Belwynn struggled to get used to, for many reasons. It was a title she thought she would always associate with Sebastian, and it sounded strange attached to anyone else—even Theron, who surely deserved it. Then, of course, it represented the end of their brief affair. The Grand Master devoted himself to the Order. Like all knights, he could have no wife. Belwynn's little dream, that Theron would leave the Order for her, was over.

As she was thinking of him, Theron appeared on the stage with King Jonas. The king looked older than when she had first met him—face puffy, muscled torso now partly turned to fat. She wondered what Jonas thought of recent events. His two sons escaped from the capital, raising an army against his captors. Had he heard the rumours that his youngest, Dorian, was no longer Dorian at all? That he was a monster? She felt a pang of grief for

Dorian, almost forgotten amidst her deeper pain at the loss of Elana. He had seemed a gentle, benign soul. He hadn't deserved such a fate.

The chapel quietened, and Theron spoke a few words of introduction to the knighting ceremony. The congregation hung on his every word. There had been no dissent whatsoever to Theron's elevation to the head of the Order from the men who had worked and fought with him over the last few months. He was the obvious choice—in truth, he had been the driving force behind their achievements, albeit too willing to take on the unpopular tasks to spare his uncle from them. But out in the country, opinion was more divided. He wasn't as universally respected as Sebastian had been. And he had a formidable rival in the former Grand Master, Galenos. That made the choice of whom to give loyalty to more difficult. It made the option of avoiding making a choice at all, the easiest course to follow.

This ceremony was all about addressing that problem. With the loyalty of some in the Order in doubt, Theron was making new knights. Belwynn didn't like it. Evander was far too young and inexperienced to be knighted, to go into battle with Theron and Tycho. But she knew that Theron was desperate, that he needed all the manpower he could get.

And so, Evander and five other youths well short of the usual age, were called up one at a time to the stage, where they knelt in front of their grand master and their king. First, Theron delivered the blow, a cuff on the side of the head landing from ear to neck. Then, Jonas lifted his sword and tapped the flat of the blade once on each shoulder. The Order had lost six squires and gained six knights.

After the ceremony, Belwynn and Lyssa joined a circle of people congratulating Evander and the other boys. Theron and Tycho were there, beaming with pride; Tycho punching each boy on the arm several times in pleasure.

Bemus approached her, his long face as serious as ever. 'We are ready when you are,' he said, as if passing down a death sentence.

Theron grabbed her elbow. 'Good luck.'

'Evander says he will look after me,' said Lyssa, in a blatant attempt to avoid being taken down to the temple, where she would doubtless be made to do chores.

Belwynn was about to tell her no when she caught Theron's stern gaze. She stopped herself. Evander was a knight now: it would be disrespectful to imply that he wasn't capable of protecting Lyssa.

'Of course,' she said. She made her excuses and followed Bemus out of the room.

. . .

Belwynn steeled herself to enter the main chamber of the temple, which just two days before had held the funeral service for Elana.

I'm not sure I can do this, she said to Madria, the new voice in her head.

You have a unique gift, Belwynn, Madria replied, the thought appearing in Belwynn's mind rather than the words themselves. *It is time you used it to its full potential.*

The heads of Elana's congregation turned to look at her as she followed Bemus up the central aisle. Some smiled supportively; some didn't. She was known to most as Elana's second disciple, the organiser who used to decide which patient had priority. To others, she was the Lady of the Knights, the woman who lived up at the castle. These people had idolised Elana, followed her every word. Belwynn wasn't sure what they thought of her. Or how they would react when she tried to claim leadership of the movement.

Bemus said a few words, his voice a comforting drone. The man already thought of himself as the new leader, she knew. Not that he saw her as an enemy—just less equipped to lead than he was.

Bemus retired to a seat on the front pew. All eyes turned to Belwynn.

She thought of her gift as she prepared herself to use it once more. Her telepathy. She had been able to speak with Soren like that since they were very young—neither could recall exactly how or when it had started. Belwynn had always assumed it was because Soren could do magic. That it was because of *him.* Then she thought of her singing, how she could use it to connect with and touch an audience, sending them into a collective stupor. What if the telepathy and the singing were, in fact, the same thing? What if her ability to speak to Soren's mind was down to *her,* not him?

She looked out at Elana's flock and a feeling of serenity descended on her. 'I bring a message from Madria,' she said, projecting her voice to the very back of the chamber.

She was met with a range of expressions. Surprise. Doubt. Scorn.

She concentrated. It's just the same as singing, Belwynn, she told herself.

I bring a message from Madria, she said.

Gasps of fear and shock filled the chamber. People looked at one another, desperate to know whether they had shared the same experience.

Belwynn's voice in their head.

Bemus slipped from his pew to his knees, his long body crumpling. 'Tell us her message!' he pleaded.

REVENGE

XXI

Theron says we need to fight them now, Belwynn said to Soren.

Despite trying to explain to him how much the situation in Kalinth had changed, Soren didn't seem to fully understand. He counselled her against hasty decisions, asking her to stay where she was.

We have the bow now, he said again. *We'll be there in a matter of days.*

Get here as soon as you can, she asked him. *We're leaving today. We can't afford to wait and let them grow any stronger.*

Alright, said Soren, sounding disappointed that he hadn't dissuaded her, anxious about her claims that she was in communication with Madria. *We'll get there as soon as we can. Look after yourself.*

Barely a soul remained in Heractus as the army assembled in the fields outside the city walls. Belwynn had emptied the city, recruiting its people to her cause using her gift of telepathy, magnified by Madria's power. Already believers, thanks to Elana's work, they now submitted themselves to Belwynn's instructions, who told them that this was a battle that simply had to be won.

The Temple of Madria was left in the hands of those too aged or too young to join the army. Much to the girl's disappointment, Lyssa was amongst them. She had tried to persuade Belwynn how useful she would be to the army, but Belwynn had put her foot down. She couldn't afford to worry about the girl's whereabouts on top of everything else. Men, women, and those not old enough to be called either, were now ready to fight and die for this cause.

Madria told Belwynn that it was necessary, that there was no guilt; no sin involved. Belwynn wanted to believe that.

Theron was grateful, for she had solved his ever-present problem, the lack of an infantry force. He led the cavalry part of the army, the Order of the Knights of Kalinth—or at least those knights who had chosen him over Galenos.

More soldiers had come in from the countryside to swell their force. Theron's estates in Erisina had been stripped of men of fighting age; likewise, Sebastian's estate of Melion, which Theron had now inherited from his uncle. Theron's friend Tycho, the new owner of the estate of the traitor, Count Ampelios, had arrived back only yesterday after raising a force from his new lands. Finally, Leontios, the young knight who had been tasked with defending the eastern border out of Korkis, was recalled with his forces.

It was desperate times; the country left completely undefended. If the Kharovians or Drobax should descend from the north, they would find no-one to halt their passage to Heractus. Belwynn had asked Theron whether it would have been better to wait behind the walls of Heractus and see whether Straton's army materialised, but Theron had ruled that out. His knights needed to fight out in the open. He had described a scenario where they were stuck in the city, the rest of Kalinth taken by their enemies, starving and forced to eat their horses for food. The image had done its job of persuading her that they needed a battle.

So they marched for the south-west of the country. Philon returned to the army to pass on the information that his scouts had collected. Reports said the enemy army was led by the princes, Straton and Dorian. They could only assume that Dorian was the creature that had killed Elana and Sebastian. Many noblemen had flocked to the banner of the two young men, responding to their claims to leadership of Kalinth, their accusations against Theron, and the opportunity for advancement if they were successful. Galenos, formerly a prisoner at the High Tower, had allied with them, and many knights had chosen to fight with him. Diodorus, the Count of Korenandi, had added his soldiers as well, despite having fought with Theron only three weeks past. The enemy was growing in size, and this only reinforced Theron's view that they needed to deal with them immediately. Hanging over their heads was the fear that they may soon face an even greater threat. The Isharites could turn their attention to Kalinth. If they were to stand any chance, they had to avoid further civil war.

They marched hard all day, not stopping until they had crossed the Pineos. This part of the country was controlled by their enemies, and Belwynn could sense tensions rising as Theron gave orders to make camp, ensuring that sufficient knights were put on watch to give them warning of an attack.

Without realising what she was doing, Belwynn found herself walking off the path, until she came to a flat piece of rock by the river. She placed a palm on its surface as tears came to her eyes.

She had come upon this rock once before, when another army of knights had marched from the High Tower to Heractus. She had sat here in the sunshine with Elana and Dirk, as the priestess had healed her first disciple. A group of young knights, led by Philon and Leontios, had approached and asked her to bless their swords. Elana and Dirk were both gone now. She would have to sit here alone.

When she sat down, she saw a figure making its way from the camp to her location.

'I thought I might find you here.'

Theron took a seat next to her and they sat together in silence for a while.

'What are you thinking?' she said at last.

'Lots of things. Maybe I've made a terrible mistake. Would Kalinth be better off if I hadn't started all this?'

'No. We freed Soren. Moneva killed Erkindrix. They've got the Jalakh Bow. The Isharites will be defeated. Thanks to you.'

Theron smiled. 'Thank you. I needed to hear that.' He tapped his scabbard. 'I seem to remember the Lady of the Knights giving out blessings here. Maybe she could bless this poor knight's sword? I think I will need to use it tomorrow.'

'Of course. But you think we will fight them tomorrow?'

'Yes. Neither of us will give ground. There's an inevitability to it now.'

'You need to tell me what you want Madria's soldiers to do. And there's something else.'

Theron looked at her, one eyebrow rising inquisitively.

Belwynn stared into his eyes. *Can you hear me?* She asked him.

Theron's eyes widened. He frowned, concentrating. *Yes,* he replied.

Belwynn smiled with pleasure. Although she could now communicate telepathically with Madria's servants, none of them could talk back to her. But somehow, she had known that Theron would be able to.

'Good,' she said out loud. 'When the battle starts tomorrow, you can tell me what to do.'

Soren! Belwynn tried one last time.

Where the hell was he? Surely he wasn't still asleep at this hour! Had something happened to him?

She couldn't know, and she had to put it out of her mind. Because the enemy had been sighted, and it was time to fight.

From her location behind the army, Belwynn ordered Madria's followers to their position. They marched, the flags showing the Winged Horse of Kalinth rippling in the breeze. They were to be the centre of the army, and they must not break. She communicated with them, reassuring them that whatever happened today, they had Madria's grace.

On either side came the rest of those who would fight on foot, men drawn from the estates owned by Theron and Tycho. Some were trained—some were even former knights. But most had never fought before.

The elite fighters were the knights, who were all on horseback. Theron led the right flank, Tycho the left. Leontios had been given another rapid promotion, leading the small force of reserves. Evander, one of the newest knights, would fight at Theron's side.

Move them forward fifty paces, Theron said to Belwynn from his position on the battlefield.

Their ability to communicate gave Theron an advantage in managing all these disparate forces.

Forwards, Belwynn relayed to her followers, and the Madrians walked in a disciplined line, gripping their spears, matching each other's stride, until Belwynn called a halt. The leaders of the other infantry units had orders to follow the Madrians, and they now marched, stopping once they had drawn level.

Those with the best eyes pointed ahead. They could see the enemy army. Belwynn peered ahead, just about making out shapes moving on the horizon—the enemy units getting into formation.

How many? She asked Theron.

Less than we have.

It was what they had hoped. The Madrians gave them an advantage in numbers. And in the end, more knights had sided with Theron than with Galenos.

Theron ordered them to advance another fifty paces, then he declared himself satisfied, waiting to see what the enemy would do. What they did came as a surprise. A small group on horseback detached themselves from the army, carrying the white flag of parley.

What is there to talk about? Theron asked her suspiciously.

The group stopped at the midway point between the two armies and waited.

Well? Belwynn asked Theron.

Well I suppose I will speak to them.

Me too, she demanded.

Alright, he said, in a resigned way.

Belwynn asked Leontios for a horse, while she told the Madrians to rest and meditate. She climbed into the saddle and rode ahead, passing between the units of infantry.

Theron and Evander appeared from the right flank of the army, Tycho from the left. They trotted their horses towards the middle of the field.

Waiting for them were five figures. The soldier holding the flag she didn't recognise, but she knew the others. Diodorus, puffy-eyed and sad looking, sat his horse a few yards away from the others, as if he didn't want to be there. And so he should, thought Belwynn. Galenos and Belwynn had never exactly met, but they had once shared a look in the Great Hall of the Knights, at the High Tower, as she roused his Order against him. He grinned at them now, seemingly confident about the revenge he would get for what they did to him that day. Finally, the two brothers, Straton and Dorian. Except they weren't brothers, for surely Dorian was dead, his body inhabited by the same monster that had killed Elana.

'You've got a bigger army than you did last time,' Straton said to Theron conversationally when they drew up. 'Where are they all from? There can't be many soldiers there.'

'They're loyal Kalinthians,' said Theron, 'prepared to fight our enemies even if you have chosen to fight alongside them.'

Diodorus had the grace to look to the ground at that comment, but the others didn't. Straton gave a light smile, looking away, somewhere into the distance.

'Loyalty?' retorted Galenos, his voice high-pitched and hysterical sounding. 'You have the gall to sit there and lecture us on loyalty? Oh, I will enjoy your humiliation today. Very much.'

'Have you asked us here to trade worthless insults?' Tycho said angrily. 'What does your leader say?' he added, gesturing at Dorian. 'The monster that inhabits the bodies of its victims! What kind of creature do you take your orders from?'

'It is time I introduced myself to you,' said Dorian. At least, it spoke with Dorian's voice, but it was clear to Belwynn that it wasn't really him. 'I am Siavash, Lord of the Ishari. I have come at the bidding of Diis, my master.

When I visited in Heractus, I killed the leader of the Knights and I killed Madria's champion. My armies have conquered the Krykkers of Dalriya. The fleet of the Sea Caladri is destroyed. As I speak, our armies descend on the Brasingian Empire, on our remaining enemies in Halvia. The war is over. I have brought you here to make it clear to you that your continued resistance is pointless. If your people lay down their arms, they are free to return to their homes. Kalinth will be incorporated into the Isharite Empire. Straton will rule as king. I will not seek vengeance or pursue vendettas. If you choose to fight, all you will achieve is the slaughter of Kalinthians.'

Siavash? The man who had replaced Erkindrix? Belwynn wondered at it. She wondered why he would risk coming to Kalinth alone, albeit he had succeeded so far.

Tycho was one step ahead of her. He urged his mount forwards, drawing his sword as he did, before shoving the sharp end of the blade into Dorian's chest.

Siavash cackled. He grabbed the blade, pulling it out. No blood came with it. 'You cannot kill what is already dead,' he explained simply.

'You strike under a white flag?' Galenos demanded, looking outraged.

'I strike a demon!' Tycho retorted.

'Enough,' said Theron. 'We did not come here to surrender. Your revelations change nothing, except to make us more determined to defeat you today,' he said, pulling at his horse's reins, turning away from them.

'I will let you live,' said Straton quietly. 'I will rule justly. Theron, we have no real choice in this. Don't kill our people without reason.'

Theron ignored him, moving off. Belwynn glanced surreptitiously at Siavash before following him. The Lord of Ishari had killed Elana, Madria's champion. Did he suspect that Madria had chosen a new one? It didn't seem so.

They rode back to their lines.

'It changes nothing,' Theron insisted.

None of them disagreed. But now they knew it was Siavash who somehow resided in Dorian's body. And that he couldn't be killed.

Soren! Belwynn called with desperation.

But Soren didn't answer.

I'M NOT WAITING any longer, Theron declared.

Trumpets blared across the battlefield. The Knights on each side of the army moved forward. They were the best fighters, the ones who could win the battle for them. Straton's army, inferior, held their position on higher ground, waiting for them to come.

Belwynn knew enough about battles, mainly from listening to Clarin's stories, to know that Straton's army would have dug in, prepared unpleasant traps and other surprises for the horses. They would defend, and somewhere the knights under Galenos would be waiting, ready to counter-attack.

The Knights picked up speed, streaming away from their lines. There was a nervous energy amongst those left behind, who had to wait for their turn to fight.

Like so many others, Belwynn peered ahead, fruitlessly trying to make out what was happening, to see whether the two sides had engaged yet. Theron had told her, in no uncertain terms, that she must stay with the reserves and give out her orders from there. The Knights had constructed a small tower, giving Belwynn and Leontios something of a view over the battlefield. It was enough for Belwynn to oversee her unit of Madrians. For Leontios, it would help him decide when and where his small force should intervene.

We've engaged, Theron finally told her. *They've dug in. It's hard to get to them.*

Belwynn passed the message on to Leontios. The young man nodded coolly enough, but Belwynn had some idea how difficult it was for him to wait it out while his brothers were fighting.

Belwynn! It came as a shout, Belwynn shocked by Theron's voice echoing around her head. *We're in retreat! Tell Leontios! You need to move the infantry forwards to cover us!*

'Leontios, they're retreating here, I think he wants you to help, I—' Belwynn paused, as Theron passed on more information. She went cold, her mouth opening and closing in mute shock.

'What is it?' Leontios demanded, his face full of concern at her reaction.

'Theron says it's the Drobax. The Drobax are here.'

March! Belwynn ordered the Madrians. *There are Drobax coming! Be prepared!*

What kind of affect her words had on them, she could only guess. But they did as she ordered, moving forward in close formation. The other infantry units followed. Belwynn couldn't warn them. She tried to reach out with her mind to them, but there was no connection that she could use. They were unknowingly walking into a Drobax horde coming for them, and she doubted whether they would hold out for long.

Leontios took his mounted reserves to the left, swinging around the infantry units, whereupon he would lead them into the Drobax coming their way, trying to give the rest of the Knights time to retreat and regroup. He had insisted on leaving someone behind with Belwynn, and so Philon stayed with her on the tower, watching his friend ride away into battle.

The meeting before the battle made more sense to Belwynn now. Siavash's offer of an end to the conflict. The confident grin of Galenos. Straton's diffidence. Diodorus's shame. They had all known about the Drobax. Known that if it came to a fight, they were going to win.

Then she could see and hear the Knights. They made a noise like thunder, Theron's and Tycho's forces both returning to their original positions on either side of the infantry.

Halt! she ordered her soldiers, keeping them in place while the Knights arranged themselves. They seemed to be spreading out much more thinly than before, leaving larger gaps between each other. She could hear shouts but couldn't make out the words. She could hear the neighs of horses as their riders frantically turned them around, trying to get them into position. Somewhere out there, too far away for Belwynn to see, Leontios would be harassing the enemy, buying them precious time.

Belwynn! Every message Theron sent now came as a shout. *Get them ready. When the Drobax come, they need to advance to meet them.*

Belwynn relayed the instructions to her soldiers, and it was just in time, because the Drobax now came into view. They howled when they saw the Kalinthians, picking up speed from a fast march to a jog. There was little real order to their march, each creature travelling at its own pace. Belwynn could see their weapons, mostly crude wooden things, in their hands. Few wore armour. But it felt like none of that mattered, because more and more kept coming. The horizon darkened with Drobax, and yet there seemed to be no end to the numbers.

Belwynn told the Madrians to ready themselves: lock their shields in place, point their spears ahead. The Madrians let out a roar of their own as they did so, finding strength in the shields of the men and women who stood to either side of them.

Now! said Belwynn. The Madrians moved as one, shoving shields forwards to stop the Drobax, striking out with their spears at unprotected flesh. They had a few seconds of freedom, targeting the exposed Drobax who had arrived without the safety of a shield wall. But that was all they got, because then the Drobax coming behind hurtled towards them. The Madrians locked shields together, presenting a wall of death. The Drobax crashed into it, pushed forwards by the weight of numbers behind them.

From Belwynn's position it resembled a wave crashing against rocks, her

Madrians arriving first, then behind them the rest of the Kalinthian infantry, following their advance. Finally, the Knights on each side moved ahead, using their height and long lances to skewer the Drobax before they got too close.

It was a strange sensation, then, as Belwynn ignored all else and focused on her Madrians. They punched ahead with their left arms in unison, smashing teeth and noses with their shields, then lunged forward with their right arm, a forest of steel coming at the Drobax all at once, impossible to escape. It was like Belwynn was the queen bee, and the Madrians her workers, following her orders without thinking for themselves. No fear; no sense of self-preservation. When one of them fell, they were replaced. This sense of unity, of harmony, was enough to withstand the greater numbers of Drobax.

Belwynn couldn't say how long this lasted, before she was pulled out of her reverie by Philon.

'My lady,' he warned her, pointing ahead.

Belwynn's Madrians had withstood the Drobax attack, but the infantry forces to their left and right could hold no longer. Men were turning and running from the monsters, and once a few of them left, more and more followed, in an effort to save their lives. Staying to fight suddenly became futile, and the units collapsed, turning to flee and outrun the Drobax while they still had a chance.

They ran toward Belwynn and Philon, some dropping weapons in their haste to escape. The Drobax gave chase, though surely it was only a matter of time before some of the monsters moved around Belwynn's Madrians and surrounded them.

Philon gestured behind them. 'They're running to their deaths,' he said, bitterness filling his words. 'They'll never cross the river.'

Belwynn turned around to look. The fast-flowing Pineos waited for those who made it that far. Some might gain the bridge in time, but most would face the choice of turning to face their pursuers or taking their chances in the water.

'I need to get you out of here,' he added.

The fleeing Kalinthians were drawing the Drobax toward their position, but where could they escape to?

Belwynn pointed towards the Madrians ahead of them. 'Take me there,' she said.

Philon looked around, his expression full of indecision. There was the bridge across the Pineos, perhaps still the safest option. He looked across the battlefield to where Theron fought. He could get her on a horse and ride to safety from there, but they would have to get through the rampaging Drobax to reach Theron's knights. The Madrians ahead of them were closer, but how long would they hold out?

'I need to be with the Madrians,' Belwynn insisted.

'Alright,' Philon reluctantly agreed. 'Come, we must be swift.'

Descending the tower steps, Belwynn ran after Philon towards the battle, while not much more than a hundred feet away, Kalinthians were running past them in the opposite direction. They began to attract the attention of the Drobax following the Kalinthians, some of whom broke away in their direction. However, the thought of running hard back the way they had come seemed to dissuade them, and they reverted to their original quarry.

As they got closer, Belwynn could see her fears becoming realised. The rear of the Madrian unit was being attacked by the Drobax, who had all but encircled them.

'Come,' said Philon, urging her on, though her breath was getting ragged now.

Three Drobax came to meet them. Philon, sword already drawn, approached them, but he couldn't stop one of them moving for Belwynn. She drew her short sword.

'It's alright, Philon,' she assured him, sensing his anxiousness. 'I can hold it off.'

She focused now on the creature, holding a wicked looking club. She had been taught enough of sword fighting not to panic. It came for her, but she used her footwork, moving to the side as it approached. It made a vicious swing in her direction anyway, but the club sailed harmlessly past. Belwynn knew that a proper soldier like Clarin would have attacked at that point, but she simply backed away, not willing to risk getting into trouble. The creature grinned at her, but she wasn't intimidated by that. She feinted at it with her sword, making it think twice about charging at her. It moved towards her, twirling the club, perhaps ready to be a bit more patient this time.

But it didn't have time. Philon appeared behind it, chopping down with his sword on its skull. It dropped to the ground, where he made sure it was dead. He had already dispatched the other two Drobax.

However, the fight had drawn more Drobax in their direction. It didn't look like they could get past them.

Help me, Belwynn ordered the Madrians, not really thinking, just acting.

They came at once, swiftly moving from defence to attack. The Drobax were forced to turn and meet the threat.

Philon ran at the Drobax, using his sword to punish them for turning their back on him. Between the advancing Madrians and the knight, the Drobax were either killed or forced to retreat.

Belwynn slipped in amongst the Madrians, safe for now. *Hold! Fight for Madria!* she ordered them.

But they were being pressed from all sides, and Belwynn could tell that they wouldn't be able to hold for much longer. When their defences were breached, there would be no chance of an escape to the river. They would be surrounded and slaughtered.

REAPPEARANCE

XXII

THEY LEFT BASERNO BEHIND THEM, Clarin carrying the Persaleian Shield on his back. He enjoyed the weight of it; enjoyed being close to it.

Would Zared and his father allow him to keep it? Allow their people's shield to leave Persala? He couldn't be sure. If they didn't intend to let him have it, why take him to Baserno with them in the first place? Unless they had somehow known that he was the one who could claim it from the old flamen, Ennius. Ennius had only given up the shield when Clarin had said Belwynn's name. The strangeness of that stayed with him. Why Belwynn?

Zared and his father's champion, Duilio, focused on leading their group to the rendezvous location with King Mark. Maybe then Clarin would get some answers.

They soon left the Persaleian roads to cut across country, heading for one of the old places of Persala, away from the towns and prying eyes. By a track that continued on to a collection of farm buildings stood a giant oak tree, that had perhaps served as a meeting point when the Persaleian Empire was at its height. Here they threw off packs and sat down for a bite to eat.

Zared paced up and down, waiting for Mark and his force to arrive.

Clarin sat with Rudy and Jurgen, watching the Rotelegen massage his leg. Jurgen had taken a spear to the calf muscle in Samir Durg and had been lame ever since.

'You two must be tempted to head south from here, to your homeland,' Clarin commented.

The two cousins looked at each other. 'We've discussed it,' Rudy admitted. 'Don't know what we'll find there if we do, with Isharite armies heading every which way. And from what you say, finding yon shield could do more good for our people than anything else. But home does call to me. We have family who would feint in surprise to see us alive, that's for sure,' he said, grinning at the thought.

'I appreciate your help and loyalty,' said Clarin, 'and I'd be honoured if you stayed. But I'd understand if you didn't.'

Jurgen nodded. 'I can't go on walking like this for much longer. My body needs rest. But like Rudy says, two of us marching south, into only the gods know what kind of mess? You've kept us alive this far, Clarin. Against the odds. I'm not keen on doing something hasty and throwing our lives away after what we've lived through.'

Shouts disturbed their talk. Clarin jumped to his feet, Rudy pulled Jurgen up to his.

'Soldiers!' came the warnings.

Presumably they weren't Mark's.

Duilio's men pointed to the east, from the direction of Baserno. Tamir and the Barbarians pointed to the fields that stretched to the north. Disciplined ranks of spearmen marched towards them from both directions, supported by cavalry. They numbered in the hundreds, too much of a match for their group of twenty-eight.

Cyprian ran back to their camp from the direction of the farm. 'Soldiers coming!' he declared, then looked at their faces. 'What?'

'There're soldiers coming from every direction,' Zared said, a sad smile on his face.

They stood together, weapons drawn. No-one asked Clarin what they should do. They knew there was no answer.

Clarin pulled the sackcloth off the Shield of Persala, inspecting its decorated leather surface, before putting the strap around his shoulder. If it came to a fight, at least he would get to use the shield once—get to see exactly what it could do.

The three forces closed in on them in a perfectly executed trap.

'They must have known we were coming here,' murmured Tamir, the tall Barbarian chief hefting a long spear.

The Barbarians were ready to go down. So too were Rudy and Jurgen; the

Dog-men; and Zared's Persaleians. Men who had suffered and not scared of death if it was coming. Duilio's ten men looked more nervous, but held their weapons at the ready, nonetheless.

The first two divisions stopped some fifty yards away, but the third, from the farm, kept coming closer, until they too came to a halt.

Four figures detached themselves from the front line and strode farther towards them. They were strange companions, but all Clarin could really focus on was one man in the middle of the group.

Because it was his brother. It was Herin.

Shock slammed into Clarin. Herin caught his eye, smiling sardonically at him. But Clarin pushed the shock away. Maybe it was because he was holding his sword, Cutter, and his new shield, ready for battle, that he was able to do so. Some of the others: Rudy, and Cyprian, called out to Herin in greeting. But Clarin knew better. He knew Herin too well to mistake the look on his face; to mistake what this was.

'Hello brother,' Herin said.

'I looked for you. For weeks. We all did,' Clarin said, waving his sword at his friends.

'I knew you would,' said Herin. 'I'm sorry. But I knew you would leave me in the end. And you did.'

'Why did you do it?'

'Because while I was stuck in the mines with all of you, I realised a truth. The Isharites are going to win this war. And, so the old saying goes, if you can't beat them, join them. I knew none of you would willingly follow where I had to go. You would have tried to stop me, Clarin. You would have come with me and tried to change my mind. It was better this way.'

Clarin shrugged his shoulders. 'Maybe I would have. I'm glad you're alive, by the way. But you're wrong. Very wrong. We've already killed Erkindrix. We're going to destroy the Isharites. And that means we'll destroy you, too.'

'With that shield?' Herin asked, a smug look on his face.

He turned to the creature next to him and nodded. The creature was Drobax-like, but larger. It reached into a bag it was carrying and dragged out a bloody mass, holding it by the hair. It took Clarin a moment to process what he was looking at, before the creature presented it to them, holding it out for them all to see. It was a decapitated head—Mark's head.

Zared let out a bellow of rage, but his men acted quickly, grabbing him, pulling him to the ground before he could run at Herin.

'Someone's upset,' said the creature.

Gasps of horror met this statement. Clarin couldn't help but stare in revulsion, bile rising in his throat. A Drobax that could speak?

'What kind of abomination is that?' Duilio demanded.

'That's not very nice,' said the creature, casually dropping the head onto the ground.

'This is Kull,' said Herin. 'Did you ever wonder why there were just men in the mines in Samir Durg? Well, now you know why. Your womenfolk were busy breeding with the Drobax to produce a superior stock. Something Ardashir had been working on apparently—Diis protect his soul. Drobax with the strength of humans, who can talk, and think. The new officer class of the Drobax army.'

Now it was the turn of the Barbarians to curse and rage, moving forward threateningly. It must have been their tribes who Ardashir had used in such a hideous way.

Herin held a hand up. 'Please. Gods, I'm not saying I approve. No offence to you, Kull, but the whole thing disgusts me.'

Kull put on a hurt face, his expression and mannerisms oddly human.

'But it takes me back to my original point,' Herin continued. 'The Isharites are going to win. It doesn't matter what I think about it. They've already destroyed the Krykkers, destroyed the fleet of the Sea Caladri. Kalinth is about to fall. There's really no-one left to stop them. I'm not going to die trying. Neither should you.'

'They should all die,' said another voice.

Clarin turned his attention to the other two men standing with Herin. Next to him was a flame haired human. At the end of the line was an Isharite, who stared at them with hatred under the hood of his black cloak. He was the one who had spoken. Neither man wore mail. Both, Clarin suspected, were wizards. Herin had not just brought an army with him, but magic users, too.

'What do you want?' Clarin asked reluctantly.

'Mark and his men are dead. No-one is coming to help you. All I want is the shield. You can all walk free. Now, I know you're not going to agree to that. I can see it in your eyes, all of you. This is what will happen. I will send my Haskan soldiers and Drobax against you. Rimmon and Peroz here will use some pretty terrifying magic, too. You'll fight well. Clarin, we'll all get to see what that shield does. No doubt it will turn you into an even mightier killing machine than you already are. But you'll die in the end. And between you, you'll kill—let's be generous—a hundred of my soldiers. But I don't care about them. I don't even know their names. No-one will miss them. I'll be more upset about your deaths, to be honest.'

Clarin glanced at his men, back to Herin and his lieutenants. Nothing Herin had said was untrue. Where was he going with this?

'So, here's my offer. I swear on our father's life that it is a faithful one. No-one dies here but you or I. We fight one another for the shield. You don't get to use it in the fight, of course,' Herin said with a smile. 'That would be unfair. The winner gets the shield. The losing army walks away. If I lose, my forces leave and let all of you go free to fight another day. If I win, I let your men leave Persala in peace.'

'Ridiculous,' said Peroz, spitting with fury. 'I order you to kill them all now. Siavash will have you flayed for this.'

'See,' said Herin, turning to the Isharite, 'I don't think so. If I win, I'm giving Siavash the Shield of Persala and the head of King Mark. I don't think he's going to care about my methods. If I lose, all he'll have to punish is a corpse.'

'Don't do it, Clarin!' Zared, surrounded by his men, was crouching on the ground, his face raw with anger and grief. He'd only been reunited with his father three days ago. Herin had taken Mark from him. 'We're ready to die.'

'How did you know we were here?' Clarin asked his brother.

'Siavash knew as soon as you left Heractus.'

All this time? Clarin said to himself. They'd let them get the shield from Baserno, just waiting to take it from them.

'Like I said, Kalinth is about to fall, if it hasn't already.'

Clarin looked at Herin, fear and anger boiling inside him. 'Belwynn is in Heractus,' he hissed.

At least Herin had the grace to look apologetic. 'I'm sorry about that. Then you may still have a chance to save her. Throwing away your life now gets you nothing, save a sense of false heroism.'

'Alright, brother,' Clarin said, unable to avoid putting heavy sarcasm into the second word. 'I'll fight you.'

'No!' said Zared, storming over, pushing away those who tried to stop him. 'You think we can trust these bastards!?'

'We've agreed to it,' said the red-haired Haskan, speaking up for the first time. 'We've sworn to respect the outcome of the fight.'

Clarin held up a hand as Zared reached him. 'Listen,' he said quietly, just for the young man to hear. 'If you're right, if it's all a trick, then we all die anyway. The outcome's exactly the same. If it isn't, you and your men escape this. Persala gets a new king-in-exile. Your father's fight carries on. You must take that chance, Zared.'

Zared looked at him, pain visible in his features. He said nothing, but he turned and walked away, rejoining his men.

Clarin pulled the strap over his head and laid the Shield on the ground.

Herin drew his own sword, built from dark blue coloured diatine crystal, and walked over to meet him. He saw Clarin looking at his weapon and smiled. 'So, we both fight with these things now,' he said.

'I'm stronger than you, brother,' Clarin warned him. 'You know I'll beat you.'

Herin's smile disappeared. 'We'll see, Clarin.'

They backed away from each other, preparing to begin. When Clarin looked over at Herin, he couldn't help but step back in time. As a child he had idolised Herin, desperate to learn sword-craft from his father just like him. When he grew big enough, he had two teachers, his father and his older brother, and he had loved every minute. Loved travelling around Dalriya and working with Herin, content to let his brother make all the decisions for them because he was so happy they were together.

Well, times had changed. He had to forget the past. Herin had made a decision that he could never follow, and now he had to kill him.

They closed in on each other, both holding their swords two-handed. Herin was more aggressive than Clarin had expected, trying to land a blow from the outset, and Clarin had to defend and keep moving, before he was able to counter-attack, using his strength to push Herin away.

Men from both sides shouted encouragement, advice and insults, but the noise soon faded into the background. It became just Herin and Clarin. They had sparred together countless times, knew each other's strengths and weaknesses intimately. Clarin could never have guessed that he would ever have to use that knowledge to kill his brother.

Herin came at him fast again, feinting high and then spinning his blade low. Clarin's attempted block didn't go low enough and Herin's blade landed, rasping his ankles. Herin had left himself open, though, and Clarin gave him an elbow in the face before he leapt away. Now Herin let Clarin come on to him, moving left to right, forward to back. This was more Herin's way, using his speed and agility to entice Clarin into making a mistake, or if none came, slowly tiring out his bigger opponent. Clarin gave him nothing. He stuck to his form, not doing anything rash, not wasting energy. But his blows were that bit heavier, that bit more dangerous than Herin's, and he only needed one to get through.

Herin advanced again, plunging his sword with incredible accuracy into the gap above Clarin's right greave. A sharp, burning pain erupted where the crystal blade struck. But again, Herin's aggression gave Clarin the chance to land a blow of his own. Herin pulled his sword up to block his head and the top of his body, but Clarin put all his weight into a mighty blow that crunched onto Herin's thigh, twisting the armour. Herin pulled away, but it satisfied Clarin to see that he was now limping. His brother's movement was compromised, and Clarin had the advantage.

Maybe that realisation prompted Herin to launch another reckless attack. He moved inside Clarin's swing, thrusting his blade up, piercing through chain mail and into Clarin's armpit. Clarin lurched to the side, delivering a massive two-handed swing that connected square on with Herin's bicep. Herin pulled away. He still held his sword, but it dangled limply. He could no longer move his arm.

This was it. His brother could no longer move properly, or swing his sword. Herin transferred the weapon into his left hand, not looking like he was ready to give in. But he couldn't win from here.

Clarin was sweating profusely from the fight. He felt his face burning up. He edged towards Herin, who backed off now, wary of getting involved in another exchange after coming off worse each time. Clarin darted forwards to close the gap, but Herin anticipated it, scurrying away.

Clarin felt dizzy now. He had to stop to get his breath back.

Herin waited, watching him closely, not making a move of his own.

Clarin hefted his sword up, readying himself for a final effort. He tried to wipe away the sweat that was dripping into his eyes. His sword suddenly weighed a ton. Then it slowly dawned on him, his mind so foggy that his thoughts travelled at a snail's pace. This wasn't normal. Herin had only scratched him three times.

Poison.

His brother must have put poison on his blade. That was why he had attacked so much, why he had taken Clarin's blows. Because each cut Herin had made had put more poison into Clarin's bloodstream.

Clarin turned to face his friends. They won't have realised. He had to warn them. But his throat had constricted and he couldn't get any words out.

Now Herin came for him, slowly, stalking like a cat with a baby bird. Clarin could barely focus on Herin's approach, his eyes watery, his gaze hazy.

Herin skipped towards him. Clarin tried to swing out, but his legs were jelly and he tottered forwards, dropping to his hands and knees, his sword sliding from his grasp.

This was unfair. If he was going to be killed by his own brother, at least let it be from a fair fight. Not this way.

Not like this.

He looked up, trying to make his eyes focus.

A blurry black shape came towards him.

The last thing Clarin saw was the sole of Herin's boot.

RESCUE

XXIII

B*elwynn! Where are you?* came a shout. It took her a moment to process it. Part of her mind told her it must be Theron, but it didn't sound like him.

Soren!?

We're here. Where are you? he repeated.

I'm with the Madrians. The— she panicked, desperate to get her words out, struggling to describe her situation so that he would understand. *The infantry on the battlefield. The ones who are still fighting.*

Right. We're coming.

Hold on! she directed her soldiers. *Reinforcements are coming.*

Theron? she shouted. *Soren is here!*

Seconds passed without a reply, and she feared he was dead, but then she heard his voice.

Good, he said, no doubt struggling to talk to her while fighting. *Stay alive, Belwynn.*

Belwynn was now forced to fight as the Drobax surrounded the Madrians and, one by one, pulled them down and killed them. Philon fought by her side, more than once stopping a blow that would likely have killed her. She tried to keep the rhythmic work of the Madrians going—left arm shield, right arm spear—but they were tiring now, and the reality was few of them were soldiers.

It was hardly noticeable at first, but the pressure on them began to ease.

Belwynn noticed the Drobax on the left had reduced in number. The last of them turned and ran. Belwynn looked over in that direction and saw three figures walking towards their position. Three figures she knew very well.

Soren held aloft Onella's Staff, and around him was a large, invisible shield of magic, which the Drobax couldn't penetrate. It was just the same as the spell he had used in the Wilderness to defend against the vossi, rebuffing all attempts by the Drobax to penetrate it.

Next to him was Gyrmund, the two men leaning on each other for support as they slowly approached. Gyrmund was sending arrow after arrow at the Drobax. Each time he released the string, a thrum echoed across the battlefield. It was a sound that Belwynn realised she had been hearing in the background for some time. Each arrow sped from the bow at a frightening velocity, and each seemed to find its mark, puncturing through flesh and armour alike, embedding in Drobax chests and skulls.

Ahead of them, Moneva led the way, her two short swords drawn. Whenever a Drobax got too close and Soren's magic repulsed it, she was there to strike it down, moving the corpses out of the way so that they didn't trip the other two.

They continued to advance, clearing a path through to Belwynn and the Madrians. The ground was littered with Drobax pierced by arrows from Gyrmund's bow, and yet he still had more to fire.

'The Jalakh Bow,' Belwynn whispered to herself as she watched them approach.

The remaining Drobax had taken enough. No longer willing to stand and wait for their turn to be killed, they ran. It turned into a wider rout. On both sides of the battlefield, Belwynn could see the Drobax detaching from the knights and running back the way they had come.

She walked over to her brother, each collapsing with exhaustion into each other. No need for words. Pulling herself away, she embraced first Moneva, then Gyrmund.

'You got the bow, then?' she asked.

Gyrmund smiled ruefully. 'Not a moment too soon.'

'Your fingers!' said Belwynn, staring at where the skin was rubbed off and red raw.

'Hmm, don't think I've ever fired that many arrows at once,' he said, keeping his smile.

'I'm sorry about Elana, Belwynn,' said Moneva. 'The creature is here?'

Belwynn nodded, pointing to the other side of the battlefield, where the enemy was located. Still not defeated. 'The creature is Siavash,' she told them.

Soren's face twisted up, full of hatred. 'Then let's waste no more time.'

'It isn't Siavash himself,' Belwynn tried to explain. 'He has somehow occupied the body of Prince Dorian. Tycho struck him with a sword before the battle. It did nothing. I think, because the body is already dead.'

She watched their faces register this: repulsed, fearful, hate-fuelled. They all knew they had to kill the creature.

'How did you get here?' she asked them.

They turned around, looking towards the left flank of the army. Two figures were heading in their direction. One was Tycho, hobbling as he walked and grimacing in pain as he leaned on the second man.

Pentas.

'How—' began Belwynn, astonished to see the wizard here.

Soren shrugged, allowing himself a grim smile. 'The Isharites failed to kill him. He found us on the Jalakh Steppe. Got us here.'

Pentas gently lowered Tycho to the ground.

'Philon!' the big knight called over, his lungs apparently unharmed, even if he carried a bad leg injury.

Philon came over, and they clasped hands.

'I'm done,' Tycho admitted. 'Can't walk or ride. Will you take my place? We've taken a battering, but some of them can still fight. We need to take the bastards out while we still have the chance.'

THERON JOINED THEM, tired looking but uninjured. He assured Belwynn that Evander still lived. Leontios arrived soon after, his small band of knights somehow escaping their encounter with the Drobax horde, relatively unharmed.

With screams coming from the direction of the River Pineos, the Knights reluctantly agreed that they had to deal with the Drobax to the north first. They couldn't just allow a slaughter of Kalinthians to take place, nor leave an enemy force at their back.

Theron, Leontios and Philon led those Knights free of injuries to the river. The injured knights and the Madrians remained, casting anxious looks to the south where Siavash, Straton and the other leaders were presumably dealing with the repercussions of the Drobax retreat.

It was difficult for Belwynn to bear. Injured men and women looked at her, mute pleas for help on their faces. Elana would have been busy healing them by now. But Belwynn didn't have such powers. She could talk to them, instruct them to fight and kill, but couldn't save their lives when they were dying. She was a poor replacement for Elana, and she wished the priestess was here.

Instead, she walked amongst them, praising their efforts, reassuring them that Madria was still with them. A small group was fussing over a body. Bemus. Elana's disciple had fallen amongst her flock, his body mutilated from half a dozen wounds.

'On your feet, those who can,' came the rich voice of Pentas the wizard, full of authority. 'They are coming for us.'

He pointed ahead. Rows of infantry were coming into view, a slow, methodical approach compared to the Drobax. In between these units, and on the flanks, were mounted soldiers, the Knights of Kalinth loyal to Galenos.

Theron, Belwynn said, *they are coming for us. Come back as soon as you can.*

Will do, Belwynn, he replied. *Try to hold them off.*

Belwynn ordered the Madrians to form ranks. They did so without complaint, but they were heavily outnumbered by fresher troops.

If Siavash attacked now, it would be over in minutes. But his infantry moved slowly, and his cavalry went at the same pace.

Belwynn glanced behind her. She imagined she would see Theron and his Knights riding to the rescue, but they weren't in sight.

'Soren!' Pentas shouted.

It looked like Galenos's knights were done with sticking to the pace of the infantry. Perhaps the Grand Master only now realised just how vulnerable his enemies were, with the knights off the field. For he had ordered a charge. They left the infantry units behind, riding for Belwynn's Madrians. Each carried a lance under an arm, which they would soon level and aim at the front rank. The flag of the Kalinthian Knights, detailing Stephen defeating the Dragon, came with them. Belwynn suspected that Galenos himself rode there, keen to take his revenge on his enemies.

The Madrians had to hold against them. If they turned and ran, it would be a massacre.

Pentas and Soren walked towards the approaching cavalry, past Belwynn and the Madrians, then stood waiting. Some knights looked confused, unsure whether they should target the two wizards or ignore them.

Then, acting together, they unleashed. Fiery bolts leapt from Pentas's outstretched hands and from Onella's Staff.

Bright flames burned across the intervening space and struck mounts and riders alike. Horses crashed to the ground, turned and sped away in fear, ignoring their rider's commands. Soldiers fell from their mounts, pulled on reins in a panic, crashing into one another as they did so.

Pentas and Soren walked forwards now, sending more fiery arcs at individual riders foolish enough to stay too close.

Gyrmund then joined in, releasing the string of the Jalakh Bow, the thrumming sound echoing around. His arrows could travel farther than the wizard's flames, targeting those knights who thought they had gained a safe distance. The Knights wore full armour, but the arrows more often than not found a way through anyway—puncturing chest mail, finding unprotected faces. If in doubt, he targeted the horses. Although armoured, there were bigger gaps in the beast's defences, and Gyrmund's accuracy with the bow allowed him to find them.

The charge was over almost before it had begun. The flag lay smouldering on the ground: maybe Galenos with it. Pentas and Soren had devastated the enemy with their power. And for the first time since the Drobax had appeared, Belwynn believed they would win the battle, because they now had two wizards with them, and the enemy had none.

With the outcome of the battle poised on a knife edge, the enemy continued their march. Shouts rang out as they tried to speed up the march of the infantry. Belwynn understood that Straton's best chance was to drive her Madrians from the field before Theron returned. Pentas and Soren still stood against them, but how much more did they have to expend after seeing off the knights?

The enemy infantry came faster, save for the unit on the right, which fell behind.

Hold firm, Belwynn instructed the Madrians. *The Knights will return soon.*

The enemy drew closer and now Belwynn could see the front rank. Leading the soldiers was Siavash, still in the body of poor Prince Dorian. His men marched with him, fooled into thinking they fought to return their royal family to the throne.

I can see you, came Theron's voice. *We will be there soon.*

Relief flooded Belwynn.

The enemy now came faster. Soren and Pentas unleashed their magic again.

The soldiers on either side of Siavash were caught in the flames. Clothes set alight, as warriors desperately covered faces with arms, or rolled on the ground to put out the flames.

The fire didn't stop Siavash, however. His clothes burned away, his skin melted, but the body of Prince Dorian kept on coming. An arrow whistled into his chest, but he still came on, pulling his spear back. It plunged into

Pentas. The wizard grabbed the shaft, trying to stop Siavash from pushing it further into his body.

Soren raised Onella's Staff, but Siavash reacted quickly. Pulling the spear from Pentas's grasp, he cracked the blunt end of the weapon into Soren, once, then twice, the second blow knocking him over.

Belwynn ran towards them, leaving the Madrians behind, desperate to stop Siavash. She watched as he turned back to Pentas, raising his spear to finish the wizard off.

Pentas shot an arm out, sending a blast of magic that sent Siavash flying into the air, landing in a heap several feet away.

Pentas dropped to the ground.

Soren slowly pushed himself up with his staff.

Siavash got to his feet, Dorian's body smouldering from the flames. But nothing could stop him.

The Kalinthian soldiers had stopped. They now looked at their prince, clothes and skin burned away, but still standing. Only now would they ask themselves what manner of creature they served.

Belwynn still ran. To her left, she saw that Gyrmund and Moneva came too.

Gyrmund stopped, fitting another arrow to his bow. He fired true, a second missile slamming into Siavash. The creature took a couple of steps backwards from the impact, but otherwise, the weapon didn't harm it. If neither Soren nor Gyrmund could kill the thing, what could do they do?

You must destroy it, Madria told Belwynn.

But how?

Belwynn and Moneva arrived together, Siavash studying them, a grin on his face.

He made a feint towards them before moving at astonishing speed towards Soren, whipping his spear in a long arc. It connected with Onella's Staff, knocking it from Soren's hands and sending it spinning away.

Belwynn knew what that meant for Soren—the loss of sight and movement. Did Siavash know, she wondered.

He cackled. 'I knew we would meet again, Soren,' said Siavash, though he sounded like Dorian. 'We have unfinished business, you and I. Killing you would be a disappointment. Pentas, on the other hand,' he continued, gesturing at the prone wizard, 'took much longer to destroy than I would have liked.'

Moneva came for him then, swinging with her short swords, but she could not get close. Siavash sent a straight jab with the spear at her chest, before swinging low and taking away her legs. He looked at Belwynn but dismissed her as a threat, before turning back to Moneva with a smile.

'Another chance for revenge,' he cooed at Moneva, 'on the one who dared to kill Erkindrix. Diis will be pleased with today's work.'

'Moneva!' Belwynn shouted at her. 'Give me the dagger!'

Lightning fast, without hesitation, Moneva grabbed Toric's Dagger from her belt and threw it to Belwynn.

Without time to doubt herself, Belwynn caught the weapon, grabbing the hilt in her right hand, and advanced on Siavash.

'Now Belwynn!' shouted Pentas.

He had risen to a sitting position and now tugged at Siavash's spear with his magic. Siavash pulled back, loathe to lose his weapon.

Belwynn launched herself at him, raising her right hand high and bringing the blade down on top of his skull.

'Die!' she screamed, and as the words left her lips, she felt a channelling sensation. The forces that had entered her upon Elana's death now awoke, streaming from her body, down the length of the weapon, and into the head. Her arm jolted, and there was a loud bang.

Then Dorian's body suddenly went limp. It fell to the ground, and Toric's Dagger came free as it did.

Siavash was gone.

THERON and his Knights arrived soon afterwards. They stopped short of engaging with the enemy. Those who had attacked with Siavash remained on the battlefield, apparently leaderless. Some had witnessed Dorian's death; some had seen enough to question whether it had been Dorian at all—but many still saw Theron as the enemy, and the situation remained delicate. Over on the right flank, the second unit still kept its distance.

Belwynn, Soren, Gyrmund and Moneva gathered around Pentas. He was deathly pale, but still conscious.

'A shadow,' he said, trying to explain what Siavash had done. 'Diis must have separated Siavash's shadow from his body, allowing him to occupy the bodies of those he killed. That's how he did this.'

'And he's now dead?' Moneva asked.

'We destroyed the shadow. Siavash is unharmed. He and Diis must still be defeated.'

He coughed, desperately trying to find his breath. Soren gripped his hand. After a moment, Pentas calmed his breathing enough to talk again.

'I am sorry about Elana. Mostly, of course, because if she were here, she could have saved me.' He smiled wanly at this, though Belwynn struggled to see the humour in it. 'Siavash succeeded in killing Madria's two servants. He thought he had won.' He turned to look at Belwynn, grimacing in pain. 'Now he knows that you are Madria's new champion, Belwynn.'

The others looked at her after that statement, questions in their eyes.

'He will come to kill you,' Pentas continued. 'But you can kill him. You can kill Diis,' he wheezed, struggling to speak. 'As ever, it's the weapons. You must find the remaining weapons before it's too late.'

Belwynn nodded. 'We will,' she said. A promise to a dying man she had no idea how to make happen.

Nonetheless, Pentas seemed satisfied that she understood.

Events on the battlefield grabbed their attention. The second unit of enemy infantry, seemingly reluctant to move until now, had marched towards them. Above the front line, they held a white flag.

'Go,' said Soren to the others, still gripping Pentas's hand. 'I will stay with him.'

Theron was dismounting, as Belwynn, Gyrmund and Moneva made their way over to join him. The four of them walked the short distance to a location between the two armies. The second unit halted, and two men left the front rank, one of them the flag bearer.

'Diodorus,' Theron said in disgust, recognising the count who walked beside the flag. 'The traitor has come to wriggle out of this mess.'

Diodorus signalled to the soldiers who had fought with Siavash until two men detached themselves from their ranks and came to join the parley.

The two groups of four eyed each other warily, one of the soldiers staring fearfully at the Jalakh Bow that Gyrmund carried.

'Dorian is dead?' Diodorus asked.

'Yes,' Belwynn said. 'Though it wasn't Dorian.'

Diodorus nodded in his sad way. 'I realised that much,' he said.

'I recognise you,' Theron said to one of the other soldiers. 'You are Proteus, a Knight of Kalinth. You fought for Galenos?'

'Yes,' the man said defiantly.

'Does he live?'

'He died, engulfed in the flames sent by your warlocks,' Proteus replied bitterly.

Theron nodded, unmoved by the man's hostility. 'Well?' he said, turning to Diodorus.

'I am here to submit to you as victor. We will lay down our arms if you spare the men's lives.'

'We will do no such thing!' objected Proteus. 'We have the numbers still!'

Diodorus swivelled his large head to look at the knight. 'If you try to fight on, I will order my men into battle against you. It's over.'

'Treacherous swine!' Proteus declared.

'Just state your decision, Proteus,' Theron interjected, face implacable.

Proteus looked from one to the other before giving up. 'I have no choice, do I? I will order a surrender.'

Theron nodded. 'I accept. Though don't think you can escape this with your life, Diodorus,' he warned the count. 'The punishment for treachery must always be death.'

Diodorus nodded. 'I know that,' he said. 'Though I would ask a favour. Dorian—or whoever he was—'

'Siavash of Ishari,' said Moneva.

Diodorus raised an eyebrow at that, and Proteus frowned, unable to comprehend the statement.

'He took my two sons from me. Kept them as hostages to ensure I fought with them. They are back at the camp. He told Straton to—to kill them should I waver.'

His eyes went down to the ground, wrestling with his emotions, before he looked up again. 'I would appreciate your help in finding them. I would like to know whether or not they live. They are young boys, innocent in all this.'

'Very well,' said Theron. 'I will accompany you.'

They returned to their soldiers, the battle done at last.

It is over, Belwynn said to the Madrians. *Rest now.*

They returned to Soren.

'He is gone,' he said to them as they approached.

Pentas's eyes were closed now. Without those red eyes, he looked like a normal, unremarkable man. Of course, that couldn't have been further from the truth.

'Where would we be now without him?' Belwynn asked out loud.

'Do you remember when we first met him, waiting for us on the road to Coldeberg?' Gyrmund asked. 'That was the first time he saved our lives.'

'He got us out of Samir Durg,' Moneva said quietly.

'He had been holding back the Isharites for a long time before that,' added Soren. 'I don't know how we will manage without him.'

No-one had an answer to that. Pentas had said that she must do it, but why had the burden suddenly fallen on her?

'I'm going with Theron,' she said, keen to escape the question.

Belwynn and Theron rode with Count Diodorus to the enemy camp. Wagons full of supplies, soldiers' tents, and the other accoutrements of war lay all around, though few soldiers remained.

'Where did the Drobax go?' Belwynn asked.

'Back where they came from,' Diodorus replied.

Belwynn remembered Siavash boasting that he had conquered the Krykker lands. She spared a thought for Rabigar, hoping he had somehow survived.

'It was hastily done,' Diodorus added. 'The Drobax had marched all the way here. They were tired, leaderless. But there are many of them. I fear they will be back.'

Theron shrugged. 'If the Krykkers truly are defeated, the Drobax will not only be sent here, but all over Dalriya. Nowhere is safe. That's why we must stand against the Isharites.'

Belwynn put a hand on his arm. He sounded tired; empty. He had been arguing for the Kalinthians to stand up to Ishari for years. And he had ended up fighting his own people instead. She understood his despondency.

'There,' said Diodorus, pointing at a covered wagon. 'They kept my boys inside.'

They trotted their mounts over, dismounting when they reached the wagon. Belwynn felt an unpleasant ache in the pit of her stomach. She didn't want to find two dead boys here.

They walked to the back of the wagon. A man leaned against it. It was Prince Straton.

'When the Drobax ran past,' said the prince, with no preamble, 'I thought then we might lose after all.' He shook his head wryly. 'Seems like I'll always lose to you, Theron.'

The prince looked at Diodorus's expression. 'Oh! Your sons!' he said. 'You know I would never have done anything to them, don't you?'

Straton turned around, pulling aside the canvas. 'Come out, boys!' he said. 'Your father's come for you, just like I said.'

Two boys, neither as old as ten, came to the back of the wagon. Diodorus walked over, lifted them both out, one in each arm, and deposited them onto the ground. He knelt there, hugging them and saying nothing. Belwynn, Theron and Straton walked away a few paces, giving them some room.

Straton looked over at the family. 'I'm not a monster, you know,' he said defensively.

'You've been serving one,' said Theron accusingly.

'Dorian?'

'You know it wasn't Dorian,' said Belwynn, her anger at the prince bursting out.

Straton nodded. 'He said he'd make me king,' he said simply, as if that explained it all.

Theron shook his head.

'It would have been better if he had,' Straton said to Theron. 'Now the Isharites will destroy Kalinth.'

Theron looked at him, teeth gritted. 'There's no longer any need for you to worry about that,' he declared, before launching himself at Straton. He knocked the prince to the ground, diving on to him and drawing a knife from his belt.

'Theron!' Belwynn shouted.

But he didn't stop, pushing the knife into Straton's neck, holding it there until the prince stopped struggling.

Belwynn didn't intervene.

Theron rose to his feet. Straton's blood covered his face, neck and chest. Turning to Diodorus, his fingers gripped the hilt of his sword.

'Theron,' said Belwynn, 'don't you think we've shed too much blood now?'

He turned to face her. 'Too much? Maybe my mistake has been in not shedding enough.'

'What, then? You'll kill him in front of his children? He could still be an ally.'

Theron drew his sword and approached. Diodorus looked up at him, saw Straton's body sprawled on the ground, then gently moved his children to one side.

'You are pardoned, Diodorus, if you swear to serve me faithfully from now on. Not to serve the kingdom, or some other oath you can wriggle out of. Me.'

Diodorus got to his knees. 'I swear it, on the lives of my boys. I am yours to command.'

* * *

Clouds scudded across the sky and a breeze kept them cool, as soldiers, servants and other hangers-on took the Great Road north.

Farred didn't fully understand how his decisions had led him to return to

Burkhard Castle. He had certainly never wanted to go back there, let alone go through the misery of another siege. Edgar had offered him a wife and lands just three weeks past. He had turned the offer down. Some men might call themselves stupid. But Farred was starting to believe that it was fate that was bringing them all back to Burkhard. And fate cannot be denied.

If his thoughts on their destination were bleak, Farred was at least relieved at the manner of their departure. Archmage Gustav had spoken privately with Inge, and Duke Walter had done the same with Baldwin. Whatever they had said worked, for the Emperor wasted no time in sending out his orders and preparing to lead his army to the fortress in person. Baldwin had given all the signs of being back to his old self, and that was surely what the Brasingians needed.

It had been an affecting scene when he departed. Queen Hannelore visibly upset as she bid her husband goodbye. The two daughters wept for their father too, though the young boy didn't seem to understand. There was surely only a slight chance they would see him again.

Farred saw a figure on the road up ahead and called out a warning. The soldiers stopped their horses and checked their weapons, just in case.

'It's Gustav,' said Inge, her eyes the sharpest, or else she knew by some other means.

Baldwin and Walter nudged their horses forwards. Farred, intrigued, joined them.

Gustav stood on the road, no mount in sight. Farred knew full well how he had got there. He still had that healthy appearance about him that Farred didn't associate with his kind, but he looked tired. There was something else too, a troubled look on his face.

'You have news?' Baldwin asked his wizard.

'Yes, Your Majesty. The Isharite army approaches the border of the Empire. The Rotelegen are making good progress with the evacuation, and Duke Jeremias should arrive at Burkhard not long after you do.'

'I sense there is something else, too,' said Walter.

'Indeed, you are perceptive as ever, Your Grace.' Gustav seemed to consider his words for a moment. 'There is no other way to say it,' he decided. 'The Isharite army has a dragon with it.'

ABOUT

Four weapons claimed, three still to go.
The Weapon Takers return in Book Four, The Giants' Spear.

Many thanks to everyone who has supported me.
Special thanks to Marcus Nilsson & Phyllis Simpson for beta reading.

Thank you for taking the time to read The Weapon Takers Saga Books 1-3. If you enjoyed it, please consider telling your friends or posting a short review.

Word of mouth is an author's best friend and much appreciated. Thank you, again. Jamie

Sign up to Jamie's newsletter and get a free digital copy of his short story collection, Mercs & Magi
subscribe.jamieedmundson.com

facebook.com/JamieEdmundsonWriter
twitter.com/jamie_edmundson
bookbub.com/authors/jamie-edmundson
goodreads.com/Jamie_Edmundson
amazon.com/Jamie-Edmundson/e/B06ZY1WDPH

Turn over for a preview of Book 4 of The Weapon Takers Saga...

The Giants' Spear

PROLOGUE

Siavash sat on the throne where Erkindrix had once sat. His arms rested on the carved red crystal. It was his now, and he had got more than used to that idea. Golden light shone down from the dome high in the vaulted ceiling, bathing him in warm colours. He would have felt like a god if he didn't already have one living inside him.

Diis was with him: an oppressive presence, impatient for the victory over Madria that still eluded them.

His mind repeated the moment when that bitch, Soren's sister, had struck the corpse of Prince Dorian with the dagger. There had been a blinding flash, a bang, and Siavash's shadow shattered, evaporating away into nothingness. Lost to him forever—and lost cheaply, because he had not even succeeded in defeating the Kalinthians.

The doors opened and the Magnian, Herin, strode in, walking towards the throne in a self-assured way. Siavash could feel Diis focus his malevolence on the human, and he saw the human's spirit quail, though he maintained an admirable show of bravado.

'I am honoured to present you with these gifts, Lord Siavash,' he said, bending down on one knee in front of him. From a sack, he pulled a decapitated head.

'King Mark evaded us long enough, but he has met his end now,' Herin said, holding the face towards Siavash so that he could see the former King of Persala's features.

Siavash had never met the man, but his informants had already confirmed that this was indeed the head of the king-in-exile.

'My force also successfully recovered the Shield of Persala, as you ordered,' said Herin.

Dropping the head unceremoniously to the floor, he now held up the shield, the leather exterior decorated in the gaudy colours of the Persaleians.

Siavash felt Diis stir, a mix of hatred for the object brought before him, and elation—that at last one of the weapons of Madria was in their hands.

'You have served us well,' Siavash admitted, 'and will be rewarded. I need generals with the ability to carry out orders. You will have your own host to command.'

Herin lowered his head, acknowledging the scale of the reward. 'I am honoured,' he said, raising his eyes to look at Siavash once more. 'What orders will this host have?'

'The same as three others. All four hosts will leave for Kalinth immediately.'

'Four?' Herin asked. 'All for Kalinth?'

'The Kalinthians must be crushed!' Siavash shouted at him, letting loose the anger and loathing he had carried since his defeat. 'Everywhere in Dalriya, and even in distant Halvia, our enemies are subdued or on the verge of defeat. And yet that pathetic kingdom still holds out. Almighty Diis demands its destruction!'

A shadow passed over Herin's face, but he bent his head in obeisance yet again.

'Leave your gifts here and go,' said Siavash, tired of the man's presence.

He waited for the Magnian to exit the doors at the end of the throne room before calling out to the shadows behind him, where he had his private rooms. 'Well?' he shouted irritably. 'Come, then.'

Out came Peroz, servant of Diis. Siavash had reformed the Isharite military, so that every unit had at least one servant attached to it, reporting back directly to him. It imposed discipline and loyalty, reducing the chances of another such as Pentas from betraying them.

Siavash allowed himself a smile at the thought of the red-eyed wizard. He recalled the sensation as the spear, wielded by his shadow in the body of Dorian, penetrated deeply into his enemy. It hadn't quite all been for nothing in Kalinth, he reminded himself.

'What of him?' Siavash asked Peroz.

'He can't be trusted, my lord.'

'I don't trust him. That's why you have this task. But he's able.'

'He fought and killed his brother for the shield. But then he let the rest of our enemies leave, no doubt to return to Kalinth.'

'There's something I've learned about humans,' Siavash explained to his servant. 'Despite all the evidence of what Diis will do to this world, they still think they will be saved. If they show loyalty, or are useful in some way, they think we will spare them, their family, their friends. It is the way their minds work. This Herin will do as I order him because he thinks it will save him.'

Siavash studied Peroz, looking to see whether the lesson had been taken.

'And if he doesn't,' Siavash added, 'you know what to do.'

Printed in Great Britain
by Amazon

42183513R00453